JACQUELINE BRISKIN
The Onyx

A TOWERING SAGA OF LOVE, AMBITION, A DREAM, AND A DYNASTY

"Has the feel of a winner. . . . The automobile and sex make a heady mixture. The combination works well in this vigorous novel depicting an industry, a family, and an enormous fortune. . . . The author has painted the story in broad strokes of her own. . . . The historical research is thorough and integrated, giving the story substance."

—*Publishers Weekly*

"Fast-moving. . . . Jacqueline Briskin has created a powerful protagonist (often bearing a striking likeness to Henry Ford) and other memorable characters within the scenario of America's perhaps most glamorous industry."

—*Bestsellers*

"Another blockbuster . . . a sprawling family saga."

—*Book World*

"There is never a dull moment in this swiftly paced tale. . . . Briskin fills her tale with romance and very complicated relationships. . . . Perfect for summer reading."

—*The Chattanooga Times*

By Jacqueline Briskin

CALIFORNIA GENERATION
AFTERLOVE
RICH FRIENDS
PALOVERDE
THE ONYX

THE ONYX

Jacqueline Briskin

A DELL BOOK

Published by
Dell Publishing Co., Inc.
1 Dag Hammarskjold Plaza
New York, New York 10017

Dell ® TM 681510, Dell Publishing Co., Inc.

ISBN: 0-440-16667-5

Reprinted by arrangement with Delacorte Press
Printed in the United States of America
First Dell printing—May 1983

For Bert

PROLOGUE

This was not a funeral.

The funeral, like all rites of the Bridger family, had been private. Now crowds lined the street, and the indelible flash of news cameras captured the slow procession of Swallow limousines followed by Onyxes that became smaller and more snubnosed, a model from each year backward in time. The afternoon of March 12, 1947, held respectfully still: sparse snowflakes halted in the beam of headlights, the smoke from Onyx Main's eight monolithic power-plant stacks neither drifted nor faded but coiled immobile above the Detroit River, the flags of sixteen nations hung soddenly at half-mast in front of the Onyx World Headquarters Building. Here the crowd was thickest, pressing on the sidewalks, jamming the overpass. Everyone wore a black armband.

The first limousine, empty, adorned with black satin rosettes, slid by. Men removed their hats or caps. "The wrong Bridger's gone," a drill-press operator said. "Nah," responded his neighbor. "We'd soon be out of a job if it was the old man. A bastard, that's what keeps things moving; Onyx needs a genuine bastard like the old man."

Wind gusted briefly, swirling snow, dipping the smoke into a hundred tattered gray lace veils, hurling the wisps toward a staff sergeant. The taut-faced young man gave a smile, and the salute he snapped toward the empty limousine was a parody of respect for the dead.

Sergeant Ben Hutchinson had spent his eighth year in Detroit, and certain incidents clung to the corners of his mind, not wholly remembered, never completely forgotten, now inextricably mingled with the horrors he had witnessed at the liberation of Buchenwald.

People were craning to see the flagged official cars that bore President Harry Truman, Governor Kim Sigler, the mayor, Senator Arthur Vandenberg, but Ben turned, shoving his way to Archibald Avenue, which was empty. As he tramped in the direction of the river his thick GI boots cut through freshly fallen snow to reveal the ugly brown slush below. From time to time he halted, gazing through wire mesh at gigantic glass-walled machine shops linked by conveyors, a triple-decker flatcar laden with new sedans, conical mountains of coal and limestone and silica rising along the wharves, the enormous rolling shed and foundry. This was the world's largest industrial complex, the incomparable mother of mass production whose womb spewed forth a car every two minutes.

After perhaps an hour and a half Ben started back toward Jefferson Avenue. The parade was over, traffic back to normal, the crowd dispersed. Late for his appointment, he trotted the mile of empty sidewalk in front of the administrative offices, jogging up the red brick steps of a handsome new colonial building with "Onyx Museum" carved into the gray-blue marble above the fanlight. A wooden sign, CLOSED, barred the doors. He pushed both. The left yielded to him. Taking off his cap and overcoat, he flung them, a wet khaki heap, across the admission desk. The thin wintry light seeping through the glassed dome proved the rotunda empty.

It was a moment before Ben glanced toward the dark, cavernous halls.

Here, at the head, in a place of honor, was a single exhibit: an odd little dragonfly of a contraption with four fragile bicycle wheels supporting the mechanical thorax. On its narrow seat a man hunched over the steering tiller. His face was slack with grief, yet even in this bad light the angular length, the thick, glossy white hair, the mouth pulled into a permanent, sardonic slant, were familiar. Ben had seen that face in a thousand newspaper photographs, encyclopedia illustrations, *The March of Time*, scurrilous cartoons. "Sorry I'm late, Mr. Bridger," he said.

"Ben?"

Awe mingled with well-nourished hatred to form a shell of truculence around Ben. "I'm Sergeant Hutchinson, yes."

The briefest smile twitched the sorrowing mouth. "I called your father by his first name."

Ben shrugged. "What's this about?" He pulled a tattered telegram from his uniform pocket. "Why should Caryll Bridger have willed *me* anything? Why should he leave me two hundred and fifty shares of Onyx?"

"Hasn't your father explained?"

"He said since you'd asked me to come here, it was your nickel—Dad said you'd tell me."

"Justin. . . . Yes, Justin would do that. He's a fair and decent man, your father, always so decent . . ." The long fingers trembled on the pale wood of the tiller, a feeble tattoo of sorrow, age, bewilderment.

"I'm sorry about your son, Mr. Bridger, but there's no reason he should leave me anything. Bridger is to Hutchinson what snake is to mongoose. Natural enemies. Besides, he never met me."

The older man dismounted stiffly. "I'll take you through the museum. Maybe it will help you understand."

"I saw enough obsolete cars in the parade."

"You asked a question, Sergeant Hutchinson. If it's answers you want, then you'll have to bear with me."

"First Dad. Now you. I don't get it. Why all the mystery?"

Tom Bridger sighed. He pressed a switch, lighting row upon drab gray row of sturdy little vehicles. "The answer to that one," he said, "is the long, regrettable story of my life."

BOOK ONE
The Quadricycle

If a future historian were to examine the major causes of changes in human life on this planet during the twentieth century, he would have to first fix his attention on the automobile.

The Automotive Age: A Biography of Thomas Bridger by Michael E. Knes

CHAPTER 1

The year was 1894. The cool silver light of the early morning sun dissolved distances and extended the sweeping autumnal panorama of the central United States: the immensity was seldom marked by the glint of a rail or the hairline trace of a road. Distance was an enemy to be painfully vanquished.

On the Great Plains, so recently settled, it was a losing battle. There, the sod huts and treeless gray farmhouses were islands of defeat, too remote for their inhabitants to go to church or to Grange socials, too far for a neighbor woman to help another through the terrors of confinement or to reach a doctor to ease death's pain, too lacking in the companionship that might take the edge off a drought-stunted crop of Fife wheat. The loneliness had broken Coraline Bridger and many another.

Southern Michigan, however, had been long settled. The gummy coal haze of industry clamped down on crowded cities. For as farmers were exiles in rural isolation, so city dwellers were imprisoned by their need to live close to work. In Detroit the meaner streets near the river were filled with men, women, and children trudging to factories. On the outskirts, however, in the rich residential area around Woodward Avenue, great oaks, sycamores, and maples guarded substantial houses whose owners were not yet about.

II

Beyond ironwork gateposts Tom Bridger held open his watch, but in reality he was examining Major Stuart's place. A fat dove rustled upward to perch on one of the tall, glittering weather vanes. With its symmetrical gray limestone corner towers, steep gray slate roof, bewildering array of long windows, the fleurs-de-lys etched fancifully above its deep hem of porticoes, the architecture was vaguely sixteenth-century French—Detroiters in respectful redundance called the imposing heap a "chateau castle." Tom's stomach gnawed with anxiety, but the sole clue to this was a shrug.

At two minutes to seven he snapped shut the steel case and went into the garden. Beds of well-watered zinnias had survived the recent hot spell, and their sharp scent mingled with the memory of burned leaves.

Climbing the front steps, Tom removed his worn cap. His hair, thick as plush, like the heavy bands of his brows, was black-brown, accentuating the pale, clear gray of his eyes. His long, pleasant face had a faintly sarcastic expression: at nineteen, Tom was an expert at hiding sensitivity. He was tall, lean, and wore a cheap, ill-fitting sack suit. Oil ingrained the lines of his palms. His fingers, long and almost femininely narrow, were scarred with burns, and the nails were black-rimmed shells.

In the deep shade of the portico he halted for a calming breath. The door jerked open. A squat woman whose ferociously starched white pinafore and cook's hat made her appear troll-like stood glaring up at him.

"Major Stuart's expecting me," Tom said. "I'm Thomas K. Bridger. From the Stuart Furniture."

Somewhere in the tenebrous depths of the oak-paneled hall, a clock began chiming the hour.

"You're late," she snapped. And her skirts hissed around the pillars of the reception hall. Tom, assuming she was rushing to summon the Major, waited politely. She turned. "Put down roots, have you?"

Reddening, Tom bolted after her.

The Major sat at the far end of a thick-legged Jacobean table—it had been made by his top cabinetmaker. He presided over china bowls, crystal compotes, rotund silver pitchers and covered dishes.

"Ahh, here you are, my boy, right on the dot." He shook out a large napkin, adjusting a corner between the two top buttons of his vest. "Come on in and sit down."

Tom clutched his cap. Having spoken to his employer only twice, he had never anticipated the ordeal of breakfasting here. Besides, he wanted what might appear a favor. Tom's intractable pride made any request seem like begging to him. The Major, however, was indicating a place set to his right, with the genial smile of one accustomed to having his own way. Tom shoved his cap into his pocket and sat down.

The woman left, the green baize door swinging back and forth in her wake. "A sour woman, Ida," the Major said. "I keep her on because she's the sweetest cook in Detroit." He ladled generous dollops of oatmeal into two ironstone soup bowls. "Taste this, my boy. She lets it simmer all night."

Tom salted his. The Major shook on brown spoonfuls of Demerara sugar that oozed downward, liquid bronze on lashings of yellow cream. The ugly cook carried in a silver platter mounded with pink fried ham slabs and fried steaks while an elderly, rawboned servant limped after her with golden scrambled eggs and beaten biscuits. Next came fluffy croquettes of Lake Michigan sturgeon. Delicate pancakes—crepes, the Major called them—nestled around crimson stewed cherries. A tray of cream cheeses surrounded by homemade crackers. Tom, a spare eater by both necessity and inclination, took little of the enormous breakfast. He tasted nothing. The Major enjoyed second helpings.

The Major wore his graying beard trimmed in the style made popular by the Prince of Wales, to whom he bore a marked resemblance—flesh-sunken eyes, pink lips, benignly self-indulgent expression; a similar stoutness.

This resemblance went beyond the physical. Like the aging heir to the British throne, the Major was a roué, and his gray slate roof sheltered a succession of lushly constructed young women directed here, or so it was said at Stuart Furniture, by the infamous Mrs. Corbett in New York. Tom himself had seen brightly dressed young women preening at the Major's side as his matched black pair trotted around the Grand Circus Park or across the Belle Isle Bridge. After several months' residence each guest would depart from the Union Station amid a volcano of new hat boxes, brass-bound steamer trunks, gladstones, dressing cases, jewel cases.

The Major's imperturbability to gossip, his unimpeachable social position—both sides of his family were old Boston—his youthfully distinguished military record with the Grand Army of the Republic, the three-story frame structure of the Stuart Furniture Factory along the Detroit River, enabled people to overlook the trollops revolving through his front door, and though no lady would enter this house, the Major was welcomed in the city's best homes, many of which clustered around this recent extension of Woodward Avenue.

The Major set down his coffee cup. "Not much of an eater are you, my boy?"

"A minnow compared to you, sir."

"So you have a tongue, and a witty one." The Major chuckled. "How long have you worked at Stuart Furniture?"

"Eight months."

"Trelinack tells me you have a vocation. 'What a mechanic the boy is, what a born mechanic!' " The Major mimicked Trelinack's Cornish lilt. "He told me when the Beck steam engine broke down the other day you merely touched it and—presto! It worked. He called you a regular Merlin."

"No wand, sir. A couple of bolts had worked loose, that's all."

"Trelinack's a good foreman; he doesn't exaggerate. Besides, I know the table shop had to close down five hours while the other mechanics tinkered with the engine, Bridge."

"It's Bridger, sir. With an *r* on the end."

"Bridger, then. Where did you get your mechanical training?"

Tom looked down at the black lines tattooing his palms. As long as he could remember he'd had the touch, and even when he was only seven or eight his father had let him fix the threshing machine, the pump. At the forge he'd experienced a mysterious easy joy unconnected to the drudgery of farm work. "I worked at Hallam Arms Works for two years."

"Mmm, yes. Hallam uses precision machinery on their rifles. Why did you and Hallam come to a parting of the ways?"

Tom had had qualms that he was manufacturing death. But he simply said, "I quit."

"Don't talk much about yourself, do you?"

"Sir, you're the one with the gift of gab."

"That I am," the Major said. "Well, my boy, what is it you wished to talk to me about?"

Tom drew a breath. "The small building in the yard, the one near the street entry—"

"My show room."

"Yes. It's empty and I have a use for it—I'd pay you rent, sir, of course."

The Major's chair groaned as he leaned back. "Well, well, well. Bridge—"

"Bridger."

"You'd be surprised at how unique an occasion this is. When a man at the factory wants something from me, it's invariably a raise in salary. So I've evolved a little trick. I make him come here to ask for it. This house overwhelms him, as does dour Ida's excellent table. Besides, there's my august presence. Few get out their request, Bridger—I got it correct this time, didn't I? You're the first to come here requesting to pay *me*."

"Then I can rent the building?"

"What do you want it for?"

"A shop. Trelinack generally asks me to stay overtime on call. This way I could keep busy in between repairs."

"So you tinker in your free time, too, ehh? What miraculous contraption are you building?"

Tom's upper lip raised as he smiled, making him appear vulnerable. His teeth were uneven and very white. "Sir, do you know anything about horseless road vehicles?"

The Major had been selecting a cigar from his tortoiseshell humidor. He shot Tom a sharp look, and then with a secret smile busied himself lighting the Havana. "I've heard the usual idle talk about a mechanical replacement for the horse," he said finally.

"It's more than idle talk. There have been articles in *American Machinist*. I'm working on an engine right now, and so is a friend of mine, Henry Ford."

"Ford? Is he here in Detroit?"

"Yes. Chief engineer at the Edison Illuminating Company. There's work going on all around the country. So far, though, the successful vehicles are in France and Germany, made by Daimler, Benz, Panhard, the Peugeot brothers."

"And you're tossing your cap into the American horseless carriage ring, I take it."

"Yes."

"Won't you need cash for your experiments, a good deal of cash?" The Major's questioning tone was sincere, his bearded face sober; however, he was a stout cat relishing his game.

Tom, clenching scarred, oil-grimed hands on the table, did not recognize he was a mouse. "You pay me well."

"Yes, but you're young. Why play Faust? Why waste youth on foolish inventions?"

"A machine faster than a horse, more reliable, never needing to be rested or watered, never bolting—is that foolish? Sir, with this vehicle farmers wouldn't be nailed down to their farms, people could move around, life would be better for factory workers."

"So your machine will be cheap enough for everyone?"

"Eventually, yes. Most families will own one."

The Major hid his smile by clamping down on his cigar. "Mmm, I see. What sort of power plant will your carriage run on? A steam engine?"

Tom shook his head. "Some people are thinking about steam, but as far as I'm concerned, the furnace and boiler are far too heavy. The internal-combustion engine's light. It runs on gasoline—that's a by-product of crude petroleum."

"Last month, when I was in Paris . . ." The Major blew a ring of smoke before pulling out his plum. "Last month in Paris I saw one of these petrol wagons. It was built in the Panhard and Levassor shop."

Redness blotched Tom's neck. "Then I've just made a horse's ass of myself, explaining the machines. You already knew . . ."

"Ancient as I'm sure I seem to you, Bridger, I'm no dinosaur. I keep up on modern invention, I keep up. Naturally I was curious to see this new idiocy."

Two white marks showed in Tom's flushed jaw. Yet neither anger nor embarrassment could stay his excitement. "How far did you go? How fast?"

"Great God, Bridger! Petroleum's highly volatile. The machine might have exploded at any minute. Naturally I didn't entrust myself to it."

"But you saw it run?"

The Major wrinkled his nose in disgust. "Run? It rattled at a snail's pace down Avenue d'Ivry leaving a trail of foul odors and shying horses. Then it shuddered violently. And stopped. The driver jumped out and began tinkering with the engine. As far as I know, he's still tinkering."

"I wish I could have been there!"

20

"Bridger, I realize you're an enthusiast, but if you had heard the devilish rattling and jarring, got a whiff of the stink, seen that driver drenched in black oil from his hat to his boots, you'd accept that only a certifiable lunatic would travel in such a machine."

"The engine must have been faulty."

"Believe me, not even a sorcerer like you could keep one of those things in running order. The whole idea's preposterous. If this were a sound commercial venture, why, the carriage manufacturers and bankers would be fighting like cocks to get a toehold. But none of this matters. I can't let you have the building."

"What, sir?"

"We need storage for the overstock of adjustable bedside tables. They aren't selling."

Tom's pride would not allow him to show disappointment. "Then I guess I'll have to find some other millionaire to pay rent to."

The caustic remark relieved the Major. He had given himself over to the delights of ragging the boy, yet an innate softness shrank from viewing the pain he had inflicted. He rose. His gray-striped morning suit adroitly concealed an enormous belly. "I'm not going right to work, but I'll give you a lift down Woodward—in a horse-powered vehicle, of course."

Tom hesitated. He was off today because tonight he would overhaul the three-drum traveling belt sander. He lived a few blocks from the factory, though, and having correctly read a command into the Major's good-natured offer, he said, "Thank you, sir."

III

As they emerged into the hall a girl was descending the staircase, moving swiftly through the varicolored light of the Tiffany glass window, one hand skimming down the thick banister, her navy skirt catching on each step for an infinitesimal fraction of time to reveal a white foam of petticoats.

When she reached the bottom the Major said, "Antonia, my dear, you're up with the birds. Come here and let me introduce one of my most valued men. May I present Mr. Bridger. Bridger, this is my niece, Miss Dalzell."

The previous March, Tom, along with all Stuart employees and members of Detroit's best families, had stood in the driving sleet by the open grave of the Major's father, Isaac Stuart. The Major was the only relative at Woodmere Cemetery. Tom, therefore, knew *niece* was a euphemism. For mistress. Factory gossip had it that the Major always referred to his mistresses as "niece," or "my young cousin."

The girl smiled at him.

She's beautiful, he thought. An instant later he was changing his mind. The shiny mass of black hair loosely confined by a bow, the large, thickly lashed eyes, also very dark, were certainly beautiful. So was the luminous skin. But the impetuous thrust of her narrow nose was not. And the eagerly smiling mouth was too full in the sparely fleshed face. Too tall, Tom decided, and entirely too thin. Her white cambric shirtwaist barely hinted at breasts, her shoulders were childishly fragile, her hips narrow. She can't be more than sixteen, he thought.

But the poignancy of her youth dissolved for him when she linked her arm in the Major's meaty one. "How nice to meet you, Mr. Bridger," she said. "You're the first Detroiter I've met."

"My niece arrived the day before yesterday."

"A shame for you, Miss Dalzell. You missed our summer. Heat brings out mosquitoes, and the largest, finest mosquitoes in North America are found in Detroit." Tom attempted a bantering tone. He always did with girls. They flurried him, all of them, including the chippies he paid upstairs in the Golden Age Saloon.

"Ah, well," said Antonia Dalzell. "I'll have to imagine I've been bitten."

"You won't be able to conjure up our mugginess. It's the envy of Turkish baths."

"Alas for me, so deprived."

"Maybe we can manage an Indian summer for you."

She laughed, a musical sound.

The Major frowned. "I hear the carriage. My dear, I'll see you this evening."

"You better be on time," she warned.

Obviously this was a joke between them. The Major chuckled. "I'll be devilishly on time."

Antonia extended a narrow, ringless hand, and her fingers briefly warmed Tom's. "I'll be expecting that Indian summer, Mr. Bridger. It was a pleasure meeting you."

"Likewise, Miss Dalzell," Tom said. She was beautiful, he had decided, breathtakingly beautiful. And when the Major kissed her cheek, Tom was charged with an emotion that he had never experienced before and that he could not comprehend. How could Antonia Dalzell be a "niece" of the Major's?

IV

Woodward Avenue was broad, seventy-five feet wide, and the Major's lacquered victoria joined the smart equipages now rolling toward downtown. Hooves drummed cheerfully on the uneven cedar paving blocks and the bells rang as bicycles swerved around steaming fresh horse apples.

In Cadillac Square the Major reined at the raffishly ornate marble wedding cake that was the Soldiers and Sailors Monument. "I have an appointment with Senator McMillan at the Federal Building," he announced. "I'll let you off here."

Tom plunged into the industrial warren paralleling the Detroit River. The busy waterway was hidden from him by enormous sheds and tall factories with smoke-blackened chimneys. As he neared Union Station the bustle grew furious with hacks, drays, wagons: a team of Percherons crushed him into a line of foreign laborers waiting outside Fulton Iron Works' employment window.

The particles of soot drifting like black snow, the roar clattering from every window were the breathing pulse of the new age. His age. Burdens were being lifted and incalculable gifts bestowed by machinery, and he was part of it. He forgot the hurt imposed by the Major.

He turned onto an unpaved alley. Three ragged boys stopped their game of floating stick boats in a puddle to watch with respectful eyes as he climbed sagging front steps. The inhabitants were considered aristocracy because the subdivided old house had electricity.

Tom lived upstairs in the back. A pair of crude pine stools were shoved under the marble-topped table that had been Coraline Bridger's prized possession, and there was a sink and wood stove, but otherwise the room was fitted out as a shop. It smelled of oil and fresh-worked metal. Racks of tools lined one wall. The window ledge was crowded with bottles of acid. Tom halted at his bench, turning the flywheel of a little contraption.

"Tom?" a boy's adolescent voice cracked. "That you?"

Tom frowned, opening the door next to the stove.

This long, narrow closet, once part of the corridor, was just large enough for two straw pallets placed head to head. Hugh Bridger lay below the oval window that rinsed his yellow hair in sunlight. He clutched a drawing pad. He was covered with his own and Tom's winter jackets—that disastrous first winter in Detroit they had been forced to sell their mother's hope chest bedding.

"So the high school's declared a national holiday?" Tom asked sourly, in no mood to hear his younger brother's complaints.

"Right after you left I got an attack, a fierce one. I had to breathe in steam so long that my eyeballs ache."

"If the asthma's bothering you how can you draw?"

"It helps me forget how bad I feel."

"You're playing hooky," Tom said, irritated.

"I'm sick!"

"Ballocks! You're embarrassed to wheeze in class."

Stung by this truth about his vanity, Hugh slammed down his drawing pad. "A fat lot you know! You've never had iron bands strangling you!"

At thirteen Hugh Bridger resembled one of the angels that hover in medieval paintings, blond hair waving about a curved forehead, round pink cheeks, eyes of bright Saxony blue. His mouth, though, did not suggest angelic smiles or pouts. Even in this petulant moment it was a firm, calculating mouth. He lay back, rasping out each breath with a shudder.

After a minute Tom asked gruffly, "Need me to boil the kettle?"

"Later, please," Hugh assented.

Tom's being six years older, strong and dominant, was bad enough: his weekly pay envelope weighted the fraternal relationship unbearably. It was no wonder that Hugh used hypochondria to tilt his side of the scales and to the younger boy's credit, he cared as much for Tom as Tom cared for him. The affection between the two ran deeper than either comprehended.

They did not speak as Tom took off his good suit, hanging it inside the slit of a bedroom, and unbuttoned the celluloid shirt collar, but sensing bad news, Hugh asked, "Didn't Major Stuart let you rent the shed?"

Tom shook his head. "No. But he played me along, pretending he would. He made me explain about horseless carriages. Hugh, he's seen one! In Paris. Oh, he made me into a fine monkey before he turned me down."

"The fat old bastard," Hugh sympathized. "Tom, what was the house like?" Hugh often strolled up Woodward Avenue at dusk in the passionate hope that the electricity or gaslights would go on before curtains were drawn so he could spy on the servant-pampered, exotic life within. "Is it like Ma's family had in Massachusetts?"

"You know we never saw that house, Hugh."

"Ma described everything often enough. The fanlights, the rose-wood furniture like our table, the silver engraved with the Neville crest."

"There's no Neville crest on us," Tom said uneasily.

"There is! We *are* descended from them. Through the Neville that was known as Warwick the Kingmaker back in the fifteenth century. We're related to English royalty. Ma explained it all!"

The coin of Coraline Bridger's despairing mendacity had grown thin-edged from passing between the brothers, yet Hugh's belief in its counterfeit shine remained painful to Tom. "The Major's house. Well, the front hall's enormous. There's a huge stained-glass window on the landing—you can see it to the right of the porte cochere. The dining room bulges because it's part of one of the towers. We had breakfast in there."

"We?" Hugh cried. "You ate with the Major, Tom? What did you have?"

As Tom described the ugly servants and excellent food the gnawing hunger he felt in his gut had little to do with the neglected meal. He longed to say something, anything, about Antonia Dalzell. "He's got a new somebody out there."

"You met his mistress?" Hugh sat up, his thin arms hugged across the chest of his torn union suit.

"As we were leaving a girl came down. He introduced her as his niece."

"Maybe she is," Hugh said, disappointed.

"He doesn't have any relatives. It's just a smoke screen."

"Is she all rouge and golden tossing curls? Does she have enormous bazzoms like the redhead we saw him with outside White's Grand

Theater? Does she smell of French perfume? Was she in a satin and lace negligee, the new whore?''

Tom had been grinning at his brother's spurious guesses. Antonia had the look of innocence. Yet at the word *whore* he saw, distinctly and clearly, a trimmed gray beard brushing against a luminous cheek. "She's just that," he said coldly. "The Major's new whore."

He kicked the door shut.

V

He stood at his bench, his breath rapid, his hands clenched at his sides. His fury bewildered him. Oh, he had a quick and foul temper, he admitted that—but why this trembling rage that a black-haired young girl earned her living at the oldest profession? He had seen her for three minutes at most, so what did he care if she slept in the Major's bed?

He frowned down at his engine.

Few people would have recognized it as that. Tom's rudimentary engine, rather than being heavy or cumbersome, was deceptively delicate. The cylinder, reamed from one-inch gas pipe, resembled the barrel of an ancient handgun and was connected to a few gears and a lathe flywheel. A few months earlier Tom had seen the diagram of an elaborate internal-combustion engine in *American Machinist*. He had no technical training—indeed, he had never been to any kind of school—and he possessed no die-cutting tools. A five-dollar credit line limited him at Gundel's Hardware, so of necessity his mechanism differed from the diagram.

Tom's eyes hardened to a steel gray, and he bent over the engine, checking the clasps that fastened it to the board. Lugging it to the sink, he attached the grounding wire to the faucet. Then he climbed on a stool to unscrew the light bulb over the sink. Working carefully, he attached the filaments to the socket. He needed electricity for the ignition. Taking a tiny screwdriver, he adjusted the two brass clock valves. His angular face grew intent, his miseries forgotten.

"Hugh."

The younger boy pushed open the door. Kneeling on the end of his mattress, he looked apprehensively at the engine covering the sink.

Tom said, "I need you a minute. She's ready."

"You're going to try here? Tom, that's crazy! You'll blow up the whole building. Trelinack said so."

"He is a cabinetmaker, not a mechanic. I know what I'm doing."

"Can't it wait?"

"What for? I didn't get my shop, did I?"

"You'll find one."

"Like hell. How many places in Detroit are wired for electric? Get on over. You'll splash in the oil."

"Me?" Hugh wheezed violently. "I'll strangle from the fumes."

"Hugh!"

"Gasoline explodes, it burns, it—"

"Marine engines run on it, and so do Silent Otto motors," Tom snapped. "I'd feed the oil myself but I need both hands."

Hugh inched reluctantly across cracked linoleum.

Tom handed him an oiling can. "See this." He pointed to a hollow tube. "When I tell you, drip into it."

Tom adjusted a screw under the oil cup and at the same moment gave the flywheel a vigorous spin. The cylinder pipe sucked in air and petroleum, the light flickered as if a thunderstorm raged. A hard mechanical cough pulsed through the flat. The engine worked with a four-stroke method. On the first stroke the piston drew gasoline into the cylinder, the second stroke compressed the fuel until at deadpoint the spark caused an explosion, which drove the piston back down, its third stroke. The fourth stroke discharged the burned gas, leaving the cylinder ready for another intake of gasoline.

The steel piston rod began to move, its flash reflecting in Tom's eyes. Light sweat shone on his forehead. "She works, Hugh," he whispered. "She works. . . ."

Hugh, shifting as far as possible from the tiny yellow flames that licked from the exhaust, extended his arm to feed the engine. After what seemed to him an interminable minute, he asked, "Is that enough?"

"Yes."

Hugh, slamming shut the door, threw himself on the pallet. Tom continued to gaze at the engine long after it had coughed into immobility.

VI

When Obediah Bridger delivered Tom, his first child, Coraline Neville Bridger's mind already had been affected by the treeless monotony, the crude sod cabin, the choking summer and bonebleak winter, the awesome loneliness of the Dakota Territory. She and her husband had come west a year before, she a bride accustomed to the niceties of a Massachusetts township, he a farmer lured by the promise of cheap land.

Obediah's blue eyes were deep set, the shadow of the occipital bone intensifying the color. What Tom would remember most about his father were those deep-set blue eyes.

Coraline's natural loquacity bubbled around Tom. It was she who drilled the boy in his lessons, for the school house, fifteen miles away, may as well have been on another planet. His father needed him for chores, though, and before the child was nine his schooling had dwindled to an occasional winter lesson. Hugh was six years younger, and by the time he came along, Coraline was embroidering her incessant chatter with fantasies of wealth and a chivalric Neville ancestry.

With her curling yellow hair and dimples she had been considered a pretty girl, so maybe it was inevitable that her fantasies should take a sexual turn. She began visualizing a dragoon captain riding to abduct her, his helmet's magnificent horsehair plume bobbing above the tall Fife wheat. One hot night in September, after Obediah was asleep, she ratted her fading hair into a pompadour, pinched color into her cheeks, and crossed the moonlit yard to the barn.

The next morning Tom found her. Dried blood from her wrists stiffened her nightgown. Her body fluids had already sunk, pressing her into the straw so that with her mouth open in a *rictus sardonicus*, the smile of death, she looked as if she were amorously engaging a lover.

The following June, Obediah screamed away his life in the agony of a burst appendix.

Tom, who was fourteen, dug his father's grave with savage strokes. The same enemy had killed both his parents. Distance. The lonely deprivation of distance. He loathed the tepid green, infinitely remote prairie. He sold the farm to a Swede for the price of two railroad tickets to Detroit. (Hugh was only eight, but Tom never considered leaving his brother in the orphanage at Fargo.) That first year in Detroit, Tom worked in a foundry, dangerous labor far too hard for his adolescent strength. He did not earn enough to feed the two of them properly, much less rent them a place of their own. He repaired watches evenings and Sundays. That year his face took on the black-shadowed, pared look of a runner beyond the limit of endurance.

This brutal boyhood compressed his capacity for love.

VII

Major Stuart visited with Senator McMillan, his old friend, until after ten. By then Fort Street was less congested and he held the reins laxly while his mind wandered back to the mechanic. Unusual boy, the Major thought. But why? What set young Bridger apart from other employees summoned to the house? His offer to pay rent? His self-possession? No, it was more than that. When he had talked about the horseless carriages, he had seemed stronger, larger, his cheeks were taut, his gaze intently fixed—something compelling about those gray eyes. *Damn me*, the Major thought. *That's the way I must look when I ache to bed a pretty woman.*

"Passion," he said aloud, slapping his stout thigh. "The boy has passion."

Othello was switching his glossy tail, Iago arching his neck. Magnificent animals. No wonder since time immemorial man had thrilled to horseflesh. But that evil-smelling vehicle lurching down the Avenue d'Ivry—who could become passionate about *that*? A mechanic, the Major thought, laughing. Only a mechanic!

He was still chuckling as he came to a block-long frame structure. Above the flat roof rose ironwork letters:

STUART FURNITURE COMPANY

In the precise center, below the NIT, an arched entry led to the yard, and this tunnel had an amplifying effect on the cacophony within, shooting it out like a cannonball. The Major had already taken out his silver-handled whip, using it smartly on his pair.

On the steps of his office he squinted through the resinous haze at the building Bridger hungered after. A thick coat of beige dust obscured the windows, streaks weathered the double doors. The Major's red lips drew into a hard line. Normally he avoided looking in this direction. Priding himself on his business acumen, he disliked looking upon his failures. Five years earlier he had started a line of inlaid marquetry dining room furniture, erecting this cottage to display a sample suite: in overestimating the public's demand for top-notch cabinetry, he had lost a good deal of money. And now there was the overstock of those miserable bedside tables to be stored here. Another failure. He turned and opened the door.

The narrow-shouldered man at a typewriting machine looked up, touching his green eyeshade in an obsequious little salute. "Good morning, Major, sir. Fine day isn't it, sir?"

The Major, abstracted, nodded to his secretary. "Heldenstern, we have a mechanic called Bridger. Find him, will you, and send him in to me."

A few minutes later Trelinack, the head foreman, was admitted. "Sir, Mr. Heldenstern tells me you want Bridger directly. But Tom's set to repair the three-drum sander tonight, so he's off now."

John Trelinack was a sturdily compact Englishman with wide, sloping shoulders, a Cousin Jack—one of the Cornish tin miners who had fled the sweet-stinking starvation of the potato blight. In the United States, Trelinack had abandoned his ancestral labor for carpentry and had risen to foreman at Stuart. He owned an unencumbered frame house and considered himself a huge success, rarely grieving that his wife had given him no sons but only three girls christened Maud, Melisande, and Yseult.

The Major snapped, "Does Bridger always demand a day's rest in exchange for a little nightwork?"

"He's our best mechanic, that boy, a regular Merlin, but he needs a clear head with the sander, and steady fingers. The time off was my idea."

"You're partial toward Bridger?"

"He's a proud sort, he doesn't ask anything from anyone. I wish I had a son like him, sir."

"Then you're as keen as he is about these horseless carriages?"

Trelinack's eyes rounded in honest shock. "How do you know about that madness, sir? Well, you mustn't hold it against Tom. I've told him time and again to settle down and keep his mind on his work. But he's young and the young have mad ideas. Life teaches them better."

30

The Major's swivel chair creaked as he settled back. "These carriages without horses have been raced from Paris to Belfont."

"That's the French for you. A peculiar tribe, sir, eating snails and the like."

"The French take pleasure in every possible way," said the Major with a benign wink, and then added, "I'll send for Bridger at home."

VIII

As Tom entered the outer office he lifted his cap, wiping a hand across his sweating hairline. The Major's note in his pocket stated only he should come immediately, but Tom read bad news into any summons from a superior.

The Major indicated a stool near the unlit coal stove, and Tom sat.

"That matter we discussed this morning, the showroom cottage," the Major said. "I've given orders that the drummers get rid of the bedside tables at a low price. You can have the place. How does two dollars a week sound to you?"

It sounded high; however, Tom made a good salary—the top in Detroit for a skilled mechanic—sixty a month. "I can manage that," he said.

"Due on the first of the month." The Major inspected the red tip of his cigar. "And I'm in with you for twenty-five percent."

"As my partner? But I'm paying rent!"

"It's a common practice in a business venture for the landlord to get a share."

"You don't believe in the vehicles. As far as you're concerned there'll be no demand. So why do you want a quarter of my profits?"

"Profits?" The Major's brown eyes twinkled. "Who said anything about profit? I have a passion for any type of race. Doubtless you heard of that run from Paris to Belfont?"

"Yes, last July. Fifteen horseless carriages completed the course. In a couple of months there's supposed to be a race like that around Chicago."

"Well, if you succeed in building your machine, I'd like to be your sponsor in Chicago."

"Racing's not my interest, sir. What we need is easier, cheaper transportation."

The Major did not attempt to repress his smile. "I saw a vehicle in action, Bridger. Take it from me, there's only one use for this thing. To wager on. Which will crawl across the finish line first—if any do. They're a fad, a joke."

Tom's eyes went dark and he was unable to repress his angry glare.

The Major laughed without rancor. "A true visionary, aren't you? Complete with conviction." He puffed his cigar. "The showroom's yours, Bridger. Two dollars a week, and no strings. Forget the twenty-five percent. And I'll throw in the electricity."

"Thank you for that, Major," Tom said. Awkward sincerity overlaid his anger. "I do appreciate everything."

"God knows why I'm doing this," the Major said. "Maybe the place depresses me, maybe I'm just hoping for some unexpected diversion. Damned if I know." He held out a large brass key. "Here. Just don't use my premises to lift petticoats."

Tom paced off the twenty by twenty-five-foot cottage, leaving proprietary footprints in the thick dust. His first shop. The first shop of the horseless road vehicle magnate, T.K. Bridger. Standing in the center of the sawdust-powdered room, Tom said aloud, "This calls for a celebration."

At the Golden Age Saloon he blew foam from his lager, glancing around. At the far end of the bar three men laughed with a full-figured redhead. "Belle!" Tom called, waving to her. Belle was the most accomplished of the three whores who worked the Golden Age. She sauntered over.

"Well, Tom, aren't you the early one."

"Out catching the worm," he said.

Winking, she leaned closer, engulfing him in cheap lilac water. "So you're in the mood for a little fun."

Noon sunlight poured through the saloon window, and he could see the white powder caked in the lines around her eyes, the grime on her yellow taffeta bodice. Belle looked precisely what she was. A whore who charged fifty cents to take you upstairs to a cubbyhole that stank of sulfur. All at once Tom remembered the Major's "niece," that vibrant, black-haired girl.

Belle was stroking his sleeve.

"Another time," he said.

"A strong young fellow like you, Tom? Why not now and later, both?"

"I'm on my way home. Have some very big news for my brother." Tossing down a nickel for his beer, he left the Golden Age.

CHAPTER 2

The first road carriage powered by an engine was invented by a German Jew named Siegfried Marcus in 1864 and roused interest only in the police, who barred the noisy little contraption from the streets. The idea languished. In the 1880s two other Germans, Gottfried Daimler and Karl Benz, working independently of each other, managed to harness an internal combustion engine to wheels. This time the wagon proved somewhat more successful, particularly on the smooth gray roads of France. By the mid-1890s there were several hundred machines and an automotive vocabulary rich with French words like garage, carburetor, chauffeur.

In the United States, with vast plains and mountains and remote horizons waiting to be gathered together, the innovation should have impressed bankers and manufacturers. But smart money stayed away. It was left to obscure young Americans to attempt the vehicles, lean young men with holy visions of the future. They weren't eminent men, so their doings went unrecorded. They knew nothing of one another's work unless they chanced to live in the same city.

In Detroit, Henry Ford, Charles King, the redheaded Dodge brothers, Ransom Olds, and Tom Bridger sometimes met at the Golden Age. The planning and prophecies ignited Tom, yet he felt like an outsider. He lived most fully when he was alone in his shop.

The two dollars' rent he paid the Major left him strapped for money. And the hours he worked left him strapped for time. Never enough time, never enough money. But his dream was taking tangible form.

One cloudy afternoon in November the red-cheeked Stuart messenger boy brought him a folded note. "The Major expects an answer," said the boy, peering around. Everyone in the factory knew Tom Bridger was inventing a devil wagon—the older Polish cabinetmakers crossed themselves when they neared the shop. The boy, though, saw nothing mysterious, only the usual lathes, a workbench, a forge, some bicycle parts. He didn't recognize the gasoline engine on its trestle.

Tom shook out the note: *One of the clocks at my home has stopped. Do you think you can repair it? A. S. Stuart.*

Tom was confident with any timepiece, yet he hesitated. The Major lived three miles away. Tom would have to walk because he didn't have carfare, and that would kill the afternoon. He glanced up at one of the dangling light bulbs. The Major didn't charge him for the electric. And there was always the possibility he'd catch a glimpse of Miss Dalzell.

II

The squat cook, Ida, answered the door. Showing no recognition, she stared pointedly at the worn leather satchel holding Tom's precision tools. "Well?" she snapped.

"Major Stuart asked me to mend a clock."

Her stubby finger jerked toward a fork in the gravel drive where a sparrow perched on an arrow-shaped sign. "Didn't you see that? Can't you read? The tradesman's entry is to the back."

Tom had rejected the sign. "The Major asked me as a favor, and—"

He was interrupted by a light rush of feet. "Who is it, Ida?" Antonia stood behind the cook. "Oh, Mr. Bridger. Good afternoon."

"The Major has a clock that needs repairing."

"Yes, he telephoned. We're expecting you."

"He'll track muck into the hall," warned the cook.

The girl was smiling at him. "You'll freeze out there. Do come in."

He stepped across the threshold, warmth tingling on his ears.

She was dressed as before, in a plain white shirtwaist and no jewelry, yet about her clung the look of what Hugh, fancifully, would call a lady born. Tom was relieved he had taken the time to go home and change to his good suit. Still, what did he care how he looked to her? They were both paid by the Major, she for considerably the less honorable purpose.

The cook stalked across the hall, slamming a distant door.

"Barks but seldom bites," Antonia murmured, leading him to the first door on the left.

The study was far less intimidating than the hall or dining room. It was a cozy room, with Persian rugs softened by age to rose tints and an antique book case containing stacks of old periodicals. Above the sagging horsehair sofa hung the Major's faded Civil War sash and his gold-handled saber. The clock on the mantel was probably a hundred years old. A pair of massive bronze lions raised their paws to support a bronze face over which spread the wings of a gilt eagle. The hands had stopped at five past eleven.

"There it is, the horror," Antonia said.

"Can heirlooms be horrors?" Tom asked.

"Horrible heirlooms are the commonest kind." She walked over to the fire, holding out her hands. "Mr. Bridger, I'd hoped you'd be visiting us before now."

"Why?" asked Tom, taken aback.

"Oh," she replied, "I'd just hoped."

Flustered, and not knowing how to respond, Tom mumbled, "Miss Dalzell, could I have some newspaper? I don't want to get oil on the desk leather."

While she was gone, Tom lifted down the clock. He had the case open before she returned. She carried the *Free Press* and a black lacquer tray with a spouted pot and some pastry.

"On a day like this you deserve something hot," she said.

He watched her pour foaming chocolate. "It's very thoughtful of you."

"That's not what you're thinking."

"It is."

"Then why're you staring at my wrists?"

He had been considering them, wondering if her ankles were as slim and had the same sharp, delicate knobs, yet the pleasure she took in the exchange was infectious and he wasn't embarrassed.

She handed him the cup and the pastry. "Ida's strudel, baked this morning. I tried to help, but the dough has to be stretched until it's fine as a handkerchief linen. I tore some, then gave up."

"Is that what you do in the daytime, cook?"

"Sometimes," she said, resting her elbows on the desk to peer into the clock. "The inside's handsomer than the outside. Once you take it apart, how will you know where the pieces belong?"

"I'm a genius," he said.

She laughed.

After she left he munched rich apple pastry. What sort of life was it for her, shut up in this gloomy mansion, her days policed by ugly, disagreeable servants, her nights pinned down by the Major's stout body? She's a better paid version of Belle, that's all, he told himself, and whores know what they let themselves in for. He opened his satchel.

A tooth had broken. He hoped he could replace the pinion. Darkness already lapped at the windows, though, and by the time he could get downtown the jewelry shops would be closed.

He went to the door. "Hallo," he shouted, hoping Antonia would be the one to answer.

Instead a large woman in a blue-striped nurse's uniform descended the stairs. *"Je ne parle pas anglais,"* she said, her frilled cap bobbing.

Tom knew a little French from dealing with Canuck cabinetmakers. He managed to explain that he would leave the clock as it was, and put it together when he returned with the necessary part the following morning.

III

A cold drizzle started falling as he went from shop to shop: by the time he reached the Major's, rain was driving down. Sheltered by the portico he stamped, trying to get the water out of the pulpy cardboard that lined his soles. The front door opened.

"Mr. Bridger," Antonia cried. "You're drenched."

"Sorry I'm late. I had a time getting the right size pinion."

As he hung his things to drip noisily into the tin-lined inset of the coatrack, she ran off. He was at the study fire, standing one-legged to warm the other numbed foot, when she maneuvered through the door with a tray that held a substantial platter of triangular sandwiches, a silver coffeepot, and a brick-shaped yellow cake as well as dishes and silverware for two.

"Ideal weather for a picnic," she said.

That they were to share a meal delighted him and at the same time

37

jabbed him with the identical guilt he would have experienced had he borrowed the Major's gold-handled saber without permission. He remained standing as he ate roast beef sandwiches.

She handed him a slice of cake. The dough was gummy and tasted of baking soda. Before he could swallow she shook her head. "Don't say a word, not a word! Your expression says it all. My only excuse is it's my first cake."

He downed the mess with coffee. "You're a late starter."

"Father loved to travel and I grew up in inns and hotels across Europe. When I was little I truly believed food emerged whole-cooked from dumbwaiters. And note," she added triumphantly, "it didn't fall."

On the high throat of her shirtwaist, where most women wore a broach, she had pinned a yellow hothouse rose. Tom could smell its sweetness.

"You should leave here," he heard himself say.

She looked up. The rain was the only sound in the warm study. "But why?" she asked. "I'm happy." The softening of her full underlip told Tom that she lied.

"This is wrong for you, all wrong."

"Detroit?"

"With all your traveling, you must speak a lot of languages. You could be a teacher."

One delicate black brow arched questioningly.

"Your father's dead, isn't he?"

She hesitated. "Ill."

"Then why not find another way to support yourself, and him?"

She continued to look at him in perplexity. All at once she reddened to the hairline. The petals shook at her throat. "Ida's hinted about Uncle, but she's never come right out with the truth. So he *did* have them here."

For a moment, utterly confused, Tom saw only the rosy blur that was her blushing face.

"You really are his niece?"

The pinkness had receded, leaving her cheeks vivid. Tilting her head coquettishly, she fluttered her lashes.

"You are, aren't you?"

"Ahh, and I imagined it discreet when he set me up as a kinswoman. But you've found me out. Well, nothing remains but to confess and seek your advice. You know Major Stuart. You've seen how he's been with his other, uhh, nieces. Tell me, Mr. Bridger, what can I expect in the way of jewelry?'' She touched the rose and both earlobes. ''Diamonds and emeralds? Or does he give on a more modest scale? Turquoise and garnets? I won't accept paste. No. Definitely paste won't do.''

''Miss Dalzell, how shall I apologize? What can I say?'' He spoke stiffly, attempting to hide his mortification, then burst out, '' I'm a prime fool, aren't I?''

''Perceptive. All Europe knows me as *La Grande Horizontale*.''

A log fell in the fireplace, and at the sharp crack they both jerked. When their eyes met again, she touched the rose, this time a shy gesture as though she regretted the raciness of her last remark.

''Father and Uncle are half brothers,'' she said. ''Father's here too.''

''He is?'' Tom gulped. ''My only excuse is you and your father weren't at old Mr. Stuart's funeral. I have no excuse except—''

''Enough, enough,'' she interrupted, smiling. ''Mr. Bridger, Uncle tells me you're building a wonderful no-horse-shay. What will you do when you're finished?''

''Sell it. I need the money to build more.''

''How many?''

''A million or so eventually.'' He atoned for his disastrous stupidity by exposing the full extent of his dream, not even voiced to Hugh. ''Just think. People will travel long distances, and fast, twenty-five miles an hour, without any worry about watering or feeding or resting a horse.''

''Like on a train?''

''Yes, but not tied to the track.''

She clasped her hands around her knees. ''I've always admired people who have their futures charted out.''

''You will too. Later.''

She shook her head. ''I'm one of those rowboats that drift along a canal on sunny days, pausing occasionally to enjoy some pleasant shade.''

Footsteps moved across the colonnaded hall. Antonia jumped up, the napkin falling unnoticed from her lap.

''Mademoiselle?'' said the French nurse.

"Excusez-moi. Je ne savais pas qu'il était si tard." She turned to Tom. "Mr. Bridger, please excuse me."

He watched her run upstairs to be engulfed by the gloom of the landing. A door opened and closed quietly. Tom retrieved her napkin, his eyes somber. He knew that whatever Antonia Dalzell found behind the door was as oppressive to her as his mother's high, racing voice had been to him.

IV

Given the belief that certain characteristics show like dye stain through a family, it would be easy to infer that Mr. Dalzell and Major Stuart inherited their self-indulgence from their mother. It was their sole shared trait. The Major, younger by five years, was a large, exuberant man who enjoyed his business successes as well as sensual pleasures. Mr. Dalzell, narrow and drawn into himself, fed his virtues on a lack of energy. He had no ambition beyond an urge to view cathedrals and sites of classical antiquity. At eighteen, coming into a small inheritance, he sailed for Europe, where a favorable rate of exchange cushioned his wanderings. In his forty-first year he married the spinster daughter of an impoverished Florentine house. Ill health plagued her and she died before Antonia was three. Had Mr. Dalzell found the child less winning, he would have deposited her in some convent school, but her liveliness diverted him, so wherever they halted he engaged a chambermaid to tend her physical needs. Her education he handled in a scattershot method, buying a wide variety of books that she read herself. He tried to curb her enthusiasm. "You mustn't devour your ice that way," he would tell her. Or, "It's not necessary to clap so loudly at every joke Punch makes." Or, "If you hug the scullery maid like that, Antonia, you'll lose her respect." In the end, though, his daughter's joyous nature proved too strong for Mr. Dalzell, who adored her completely. She continued to squeeze her small delights to herself as she did the kittens he took forcibly from her each time they moved on.

Mr. Dalzell was the one fixed point in Antonia's life. She loved him utterly.

They chanced to be in Paris on her sixteenth birthday, and to celebrate he took her to hear Madame Galli-Marié in his favorite opera, *Alceste*. During the intrada he was taken with a chill. By the time they reached their hotel a fever shuddered through his narrow frame.

Antonia, terrified, cabled the uncle she had never met. The half brothers had not exchanged a letter in more than ten years, yet the Major set out immediately for Paris, a gesture that bound Antonia to him in grateful love. Eventually the Major brought them to Detroit.

V

Antonia closed the door quietly. "Good afternoon, Father," she said.

Mr. Dalzell sat in an armchair by the fire, a bed pillow propping his head, his hands resting laxly on knees, slippered feet parallel. His maroon dressing gown moved perceptibly with each breath. Strands of hair were neatly combed across his bald skull, his jaw was faintly rosy from recent shaving. The petulant lines around his mouth had relaxed so his narrow lips were serene.

"I'm sorry I'm late, Father," she said. "I was talking to Mr. Bridger, he's mending Uncle Andrew's clock—he's the best engineer at the factory. Father, it's just as well you didn't meet him." She tilted her head. "Do you want to know why?"

Rain dashed against the windows.

When Mr. Dalzell blinked, Antonia answered her question. "You love the past, and for him it's all the future. He's inventing a machine that'll take the place of a carriage. He's positive it'll change the world. He's very unusual."

Firelight glowed on her enthusiasm. She believed, as she believed in God, that her father retained his critical mind, and she wanted him to like Tom. Accordingly, she described Tom's ability to restore an eighteenth-century clock.

After a few minutes she selected a bonbon from a large beribboned box, nibbling the milk chocolate coating from the nougat below, sitting on the chaise near him, her knees drawn up luxuriously, opening a book to its leather marker. " 'Natasha had not a free moment all day,' " she read, " 'and not once had time to think what lay before her. In the damp chill air, in the closeness and half dark of the swaying carriage, she pictured to herself for the first time what was in store for her at the ball, in the brightly lighted hall—music, flowers, dancing, and the tzar, all the brilliant young people of Petersburg. The prospect before her was so splendid. . . .' "

Antonia's voice grew dreamy as it always did when she read the scenes about willful, wonderful Natasha who embraced love. Mr. Dalzell's eyes closed, his chin dropped, and Nurse Girardin, having returned, covered him with a crocheted afghan.

"Father listened longer today," Antonia said, shutting her leather-bound *War and Peace*.

"*Oui.*"

"He's getting better. Definitely improving. Don't you agree?"

Nurse Girardin lifted Mr. Dalzell's feet to the ottoman. She had never heard of a recovery in a case like Mr. Dalzell's. Antonia was gazing at her hopefully, though, and the nurse had become very fond of the girl. "*Certainement,*" she said.

Antonia flushed and left the sickroom. She leaned against the black walnut paneling, her eyes squeezed shut, her nails clenched so tightly into her palms that the knuckles shone, holding in her terrible grief, which she could not express. The Major had made it very clear that one never discussed disturbances of the mental process either inside or outside the house. After a minute she straightened up and went slowly to her room.

VI

"Antonia, I want to talk to you," said the Major. They were in the study awaiting dinner. The Major stamped to the fireplace. "Ida tells me that you lunched with Bridger."

"We had sandwiches in here, yes." She looked at the clock. "He has it keeping perfect time."

"Bridger worked for a watchmaker," the Major replied. "That's why I chose him."

"That is a very old clock," Antonia said. "An antique."

"I'm aware of that."

"He couldn't have seen another one like it."

"The principle of the mechanism is the same." The Major banged at a smoldering log.

"Uncle," Antonia said demurely. "I do believe you're telling me I shouldn't find anything admirable in Mr. Bridger's mending your monstrosity."

"On the contrary. I'm informing myself that when a pretty, vivacious girl lives in a house only a blundering idiot sends a mechanic to call."

"In America isn't everyone equal?"

"It's the same here as Europe. People of certain social level don't mix with tradesmen." The Major dropped the poker. "I'm not blaming you, my dear. I'm blaming myself. You're a vivacious, charming girl, and I'm an old bachelor. I should have recognized that you aren't the type to be shut up like this, with no friends your own age."

"I've never had friends, Uncle," she said, summoning a wraith of a smile. "When Father's better I'll be dancing all the time."

The Major touched her hand gently. "Antonia, you're like me. You like fun. You need good company. I'll arrange a party for the young crowd, and by Christmas, you'll see, you'll be in the swing."

The Major's entertaining had been limited to an occasional evening of poker and bourbon with his cronies. He had, however, a circle of married friends, some of whom were parents of children about Antonia's age. At his instructions Heldenstern wrote eighteen invitations to a "Dessert Social" and Flaherty, the Major's Irish coachman, delivered the creamy linen envelopes.

The following morning's mail brought half a dozen regrets. That left a good many acceptances to dribble in.

At seven thirty the evening of the party Antonia came downstairs. The hem of her white tulle dress showed a faint circle where it had been lengthened but otherwise was fresh and charming with its large puffed sleeves. High around her slender throat she wore a strand of seed pearls that had belonged to her mother. Her mass of dark hair was caught up in a Grecian knot from which wayward black tendrils escaped. She looked nervous, excited, radiantly eager.

The Major waited at the foot of the staircase. Bowing, he said, "Exquisite."

"You're being gallant, Uncle," she said. Her voice shook with uncertainty and hope.

"Take my word, the boys'll be at your feet." He offered his arm.

They went into the drawing room. The potted hydrangeas Antonia had brought in could not hide the faint musty odor emanating from the huge Spanish tapestry. The telephone rang three times in rapid succession. Ida, her face angrier than usual, came in to tell them that three of the guests had come down with cases of grippe.

Antonia's gloved hands were so tightly clasped that the tulle of her bouffant sleeves quivered.

By eight thirty the last of the guests' parents had telephoned. Antonia sat pale and stern, her enormous dark eyes glistening as though she, too, suffered from grippe. The Major could not look at her. He cursed himself for a fool. Of course none of his friends would permit their tender adolescents under his roof when their ladies refused to venture past his gateposts. Breathing hard, he stamped from the room, returning with a freshly opened bottle of Lafite-Rothschild and two delicate tulip-shaped glasses that he filled.

"Here, my dear," he said gruffly.

Antonia's fingers convulsed on the narrow stem. There was a loud snap. Both parts of the goblet fell, shattering on parquet.

"Your beautiful Baccarat!" she cried. "Oh, Uncle, the set's ruined. I'm sorry. I'm so clumsy. I ruin everything!"

She ran upstairs.

Her childishly brave attempt to disguise the true cause of her misery touched the Major, and he stood longing to follow her but knowing she did not wish it. In the few months Antonia had been in his house he had come to care for her in a way he had never cared for anyone before. For the first time in his life he felt something difficult, responsible, binding. "The child needs a proper father," he muttered to himself.

VII

The rest of that year and the following January were mild, but at the beginning of March a freezing blizzard clamped over the Midwest.

One morning, as Antonia helped the Major on with his coat, he inquired, "Can you skate?"

"Adore to!"

"Good. Then this afternoon we'll go to the Belle Isle pavilion," he said. "I need something to cheer me. This morning I have a most unpleasant meeting with a debtor. Lewis Emporium, they're in Cleveland, has gone under, and they owe me a great deal of money. A nasty mess."

Antonia handed him his homburg, her face solemn. "If I help more with Father, Nurse will have time for other work. We won't have to keep the extra laundress." Mr. Dalzell required great piles of fresh linen daily.

The Major's eyes narrowed. He had come to resent every minute she spent with the invalid. "You know my feelings. I want you in the sickroom less, not more. It's painful for you—" He raised a silencing palm. "No, Antonia, don't argue. I've seen you leave pale and shaken. And it's so futile." Again the broad palm went up. "Let me finish. Poor Oswald's not himself anymore, not at all." The Major's tone went throaty with fraternal benevolence. "If he were merely paralyzed, you know I'd be delighted to spend my free evenings with him, it would be my dearest pleasure." He glanced around to make certain they were alone, adding quietly, "Both specialists agree that the fever has destroyed his rational processes."

"Dr. McKenzie says he'll recover."

"McKenzie's not a specialist. He's a family doctor. And besides, he said it was only a remote possibility."

Passionate, obstinate denial showed on Antonia's face. She said nothing.

"There's a delightful little café in the pavilion," the Major coaxed consolingly. "Would you like to have a pastry there?"

Antonia did not reply.

She gets over her moods quickly, the Major articulated to himself, pulling his sable collar around his ears. "Flaherty'll bring you around at two," he said.

VIII

Antonia had never been in this or any other factory. As the carriage jolted from the passageway into the yard, she pushed down both windows. Noise rushed at her with physical force. Involuntarily she hunched her shoulders, smiling. The roar and bustle were as exotic to her as Count Tolstoy's historical Russia.

Men in shirt sleeves packed crates, edging muslin-covered furniture into enormous raw-lumber boxes, wadding in the straw. Hammers glinted swiftly in the sun.

Antonia spied a freestanding cottage with a peaked roof. *That must be Mr. Bridger's shop*, she thought. The carriage brakes jarred and they came to a halt. They were in front of the offices, and Mr. Heldenstern was flying hatless down the steps to help her down. "Good afternoon, Miss Dalzell," he shouted, his sour breath clouding the cold air. "The Major will be with you in a few minutes. He has several more telephone calls."

"Oh, then, Mr. Heldenstern, you can give me a tour."

"The Major asked me to bring you inside."

Just then the cottage double doors opened and Tom emerged, stretching his arms.

"Mr. Bridger!" Antonia knew he could not hear her so she waved to attract his attention.

Heldenstern moistened his lips. "The Major gave instructions you were to wait in my office, Miss Dalzell."

But Antonia was already skimming across the snow-cleared yard.

Before he saw her, Tom was bracing himself with deep, invigorating breaths of fresh air. For the past two days he had not gone home; Hugh had brought him food that he had heated on the forge and wolfed down. He had not slept, and though he had worked his normal twelve-hour shift, he was not weary. Exaltation raced through his blood, stronger than any drug. He took out his watch. *At 2:05 on the cold sunlit afternoon of March 12, 1895, T.K. Bridger completed his first horseless road vehicle,* he thought, grinning.

Then he saw Antonia, her narrow black boots twinkling toward him. He had not seen her since that excruciating day he'd blurted out that absurdity about her being the Major's whore. So his elation turned into embarrassment, which in no way interfered with his pleasure in seeing her.

"Good afternoon, Mr. Bridger," she said breathlessly.

"Miss Dalzell," he said. "So you're willing to talk to me."

"La Grande Horizontale is always gracious."

Tom reddened. "I . . . must have been crazy," he managed.

"Ahh. So you don't believe men shower me with jewels?"

"I'd never met a real lady, like you."

"I should hope not!"

"Tell me how to apologize?"

"Mention I'm worthy of my title, then let it go," she said, smiling. "How are you doing with the horseless wagon?"

"She's ready."

"You mean you've built one *already*?"

"Finished her a couple of minutes ago."

"Where's the champagne?"

"We're pouring tonight—if she runs."

"May I see?"

He opened the door wider, expecting her to peek. Instead she walked into the shadows, circling a peculiar machine that resembled nothing so much as an enormous wheeled dragonfly.

"Definitely not a buggy or a carriage," she said. The racket was muted in here, and she did not have to raise her voice.

"I call her a quadricycle."

Its relationship to a bicycle showed everywhere in the spare little body. The suspension wheels, propped on wood blocks eighteen inches above the floor, had nickel spokes and pneumatic rubber tires. A brown leather bicycle saddle rested between the rear wheels. The drive chains came from a Pope Bicycle. There was a bicycle bell affixed to the steering tiller.

But the uncovered engine was something never seen before: a labyrinth of tubes, oil cups, polished brass cylinder casings, valves, nuts, bolts, gears, flywheel. There was a circular steel carburetor and a battery in a varnished cherrywood box.

"You built everything?"

Tom was choked with pride. "Some of the parts were made in machine shops to my specifications. I had to modify them all. I'm rotten at planning on paper. A trial-and-error man. A couple of fellows helped me put her together. Charlie Bixby. Trelinack."

"Mr. Trelinack . . . isn't he Uncle's head foreman?"

"Yes. That's him out here, checking the shipment."

"The foreman worked for *you*?"

"That's my one talent, getting people to lend me a hand around machinery," Tom said. "Well, what's the verdict?"

"I expected some sort of locomotive in front."

Tom heard too many arguments favoring steam over gasoline for Antonia's remark not to strike him as criticism, and he said hastily, "Steam engines are heavy. A free-moving road vehicle has to be light, the one thing that counts is lightness. She weighs less than five hundred pounds, and the motor has the power of four horses."

"But what will you use to pull it?"

Tom's smile gleamed in the dimness as he pointed to the engine. "This."

"I'm not very bright, am I?" She circled the machine again. "I don't understand how the motor pulls."

"Want a demonstration?"

"Could you?"

Tom bowed smartly. "At your service, Miss Dalzell."

He grasped the lever set at the side of the vehicle, cranking it around. A metallic grating. His torso twisted and pivoted as he threw his strength into each revolution: the result, a series of impotent, grating coughs. *She started ten minutes ago,* he thought, cursing the faithless machine. His shoulder muscles bulged, sweat beaded his forehead. Suddenly smoke exploded with a bang. Antonia jumped. The engine sang putt-a-pop, putt-a-pop—a tune that would become the anthem of the unborn century. Tom listened, his eyes intent, his mouth dreamy. The quadricycle shivered on its blocks, increasing its resemblance to a hovering dragonfly.

He swung his leg over the bicycle seat and the machine shook him in its embrace as he pointed to the gears that would transmit power to the chain drive. Antonia, her hands clasped under a white fox muff, gazed at him in rapt concentration. Sharing this moment of creation, they were closer than a man and woman joined in a sweet, damp sexual embrace.

He turned off the machine. It continued to clank and putt as he turned wordlessly to her.

She let the muff dangle by its cord as she opened her arms wide, in a gesture of wonderment. She did not lower her lashes but gazed steadily at him. Tom, dizzy from exhaust-fumes, thought without concern about falling into huge dark eyes, drowning.

Above the roar of the factory and the fading sounds of the quadricycle, came the imperious bass of a carriage horn. Antonia blinked. Without saying good-bye, she ran across the yard to where the Major, a bearded, square figure in a sable-collared coat, stamped impatiently around his matched trotting pair.

IX

Later there was a good deal of cloudiness about which pioneer leaped into his machine and putted along in the first American-made automobile. Each man had tunneled like a mole toward his dream, each was buffeted by the laughter of doubters, each labored mightily before he gripped the steering tiller and *moved*. So what does primacy matter? They earned their triumphs: Frank Duryea of Springfield, Elwood Haynes in Kokomo, Ransom Olds in Lansing, Hiram Percy Maxim, whose father had invented the Maxim gun, Alexander Winton, Charles King, Henry Ford, Tom Bridger.

At ten thirty that night Hugh peddled into the yard, heavily bundled, a scowl on his angelic face. Tom had borrowed this Pope so that Hugh could ride ahead ringing the bell to warn anybody who might still be about. *I could be killed, as if that matters to him,* Hugh thought. A cloud obscured the full moon: Tom's shop, with its doors wide open, formed a cavern of light.

"Tom?" Hugh called.

"All set." Tom had his cap on, and the wheels off the blocks. "Let's go."

The engine refused to cooperate. Tom cranked until the shop resounded with his panted-out gasps. The brothers, each coiled in separate anxieties, stared at one another.

"Why not put it off until tomorrow night?" Hugh said, hoping to postpone this insanity.

"Like hell," Tom said, redoubling his efforts. When, finally, the quadricycle putt-popped, he jumped into the seat, gripping the tiller. Pneumatic tires turned, wheels inched forward. The quadricycle jolted down the shallow step onto the cobbles.

Tom was preoccupied in the unfamiliar, unknowable task of coaxing and guiding his invention. But Hugh, who had lived—uncooperatively—through the machine's creation, understood that for Tom this was the culmination of three years of sleepless nights, the pettiest economies and denials, of painful burns, of trial and seemingly limitless error. As his brother jounced down the step, he shouted, "Hooray! Tom, hooray! You've done it."

One of the night watchmen emerged, his lantern casting wavery shadows. It was old O'Reardon. "Holy Mother of God," he cried. "Save me!"

Hugh peddled well ahead of the machine through the passage and onto Fort Street. This being the week of the full moon, Detroit's towered arc lights were not on, and the Pope's small nickel-plated acetylene lamp could not dispel the darkness. The road, not properly cleared from the storm, was mounded with snow and slick with frozen puddles. Hugh, ringing the bell for dear life, was afraid to go too fast and even more afraid to go slower. The horrendous machine snapped and barked at him. He hated his brother for giving him this terrifying task, but his anger and fear were overwhelmed by a fierce fraternal pride. *Tom's done it,* he thought, *Tom's done it!* Soon he was thinking, *We've done it.*

They had prearranged a circular route of six blocks. A knot of excited people were being held outside the passage by three night watchmen.

A couple of Stuart mechanics waited in the yard.

"Hey, Tom. Why waste all your time and money on something a horse can do a thousand percent better?"

Hugh shouted, "Let's see you build one!"

And at the same time Tom laughed. "I don't enjoy looking at horses' asses, that's why."

The others helped them push the still clattering machine into the shop. Alone, the brothers embraced.

"Jesus," Tom said excitedly. "I never dreamed she'd run that smooth."

"I'm going to help, Tom."

"You? When? Here?"

"I'm not much around machines, but my penmanship's the best in class. I can write the letters. Keep the accounts, too. And with my drawing, I'll learn draftsmanship easy."

"What about Central High? You've got to finish." Tom, who had no schooling, spoke adamantly.

"I'll work part time." Hugh's sincerity was marred by a whine. It was difficult, surrendering those spacious dreams of Hugh Bridger, significant, powerful, wealthy—and out from under his older brother.

Tom's face was gaunt with fatigue. Selecting a small screwdriver, he said, "The motor stopped as she came into the yard. I'll check out why, then we'll head home."

Hugh blinked, rebuffed at Tom's seeming indifference to his offer, telling himself it was the icy wind blowing on the ride that caused the tears in his eyes.

X

The following morning around ten the Major sent for Tom. A coal heater warmed the crowded office that smelled of cigar smoke. The stuffiness was more unpleasant to Tom than the penetrating chill of his shop.

"Sit down," said the Major, indicating a rungback chair facing his kneehole desk. "Everybody in the plant is jabbering about your machine."

"I ran her last night."

"You sound less than overjoyed."

"I was plenty proud last night. But I need a braking device; the transmission chains make a terrible racket. The spring of a sparker broke and we had to push her into the shop. . . . A million things wrong."

The Major leaned back. "There is something I want to say to you, Bridger. It concerns my niece. She was raised in Europe. She has no female relatives, no intimate older woman friend to advise her. She is quite unprepared. A complete innocent. One mustn't take her natural enthusiasm as proof of friendship."

Tom, confused by the sudden change in the conversation, felt as if his blood were frozen: *Antonia*, he thought. *Antonia?*

The Major was watching him closely. "Her mother came from a titled Italian family, an old and noble family. Mr. Dalzell's father, like my own, was a gentleman. And her paternal grandmother, my mother, was a Cabot."

"What does Miss Dalzell's ancestry have to do with my vehicle?"

"You're no fool, Bridger, so don't try to act one. Before we enter into a business arrangement, I want it clear that it is just that. Business." He paused for a moment, and then added, "I'm willing to back you."

"And in return you want a vow of abstinence?"

"Bridger, what a sarcastic boy you are!" snapped the Major, then drew a calming breath. "Yes, I want you to stay away from my niece. I can see why she feels a curiosity about you, but I assure you curiosity is all that it is. And I certainly understand any interest you may have in her. But surely you must see that nothing can come of such a mismatched friendship. What do you know of her world—of books, music, servants, fine clothes? You're a mechanic. You live and belong in a workingman's world."

Tom, smarting from the Major's insults, remained silent.

"I was wrong about the machines. *Harper's* reports that the Prince of Wales is ordering one from Mr. Daimler. A certain group will take them up now. The custom trade. As an entrepreneur I'm forward-thinking. We'll build them and patent your ideas."

"I don't believe in patents."

"That's nonsense. And you need a backer. I've presented myself." The Major extended a handwritten sheet. "I'll have Heldenstern draw up a proper legal agreement later."

Tom did not take the paper. The Major dropped it in front of him on the desk.

> In return for 25% (twenty-five percent) of any profits from the shop of T.K. Bridger, Major A. S. Stuart agrees to back his credit.

"It's the same magnificent offer you made when I rented the shop," Tom said. "I work my balls off and you get twenty-five percent of them to put in your pocket."

"You have as much to learn about manners as business. How much is your credit at any store? Five dollars?" the Major asked. "With my backing you'll be able to get the metal work done, a proper carriage. Nobody will buy a heap of wood and scrap metal— that's your own account of the machine."

Tom wasn't listening. As he stared down at the fine linen paper, he felt a hard anger and at the same time an infinite melancholy. He was a poor nobody and he knew only too well that poverty kills. Antonia Dalzell had a titled mother and a millionaire uncle. The Major was right. It was an unthinkable wrong to try to bring her into his world. Any thoughts he had about her might as well be scotched here and now. That Antonia might have had thoughts of him did not occur to Tom at all.

The Major unscrewed a gold fountain pen. Watching Tom sign, he leaned back in relief. "Well, Bridger, I hope this is the beginning of a long and fruitful business relationship." He spoke perfunctorily and stood to indicate the interview had ended.

CHAPTER 3

One bright afternoon in May of 1899 the Major sat in his office brooding over a large black-bound ledger. Next to his chair stood a well-worn, gold-cornered pigskin attaché case.

In the four years since Tom had created that first quadricycle, the Major had altered considerably. He had put on flesh—his excellently tailored frock coat could not disguise his enormous paunch—yet his face had grown thin. Above the trimmed beard his cheeks were no longer round, and the sagging whorls of wrinkles had the crazed effect one sees on old china. Despite this aging and his worried concentration, he remained a prosperous, worldly figure.

He tapped a manicured fingernail on numbers written in red ink, his self-indulgent mouth drawing into a downward curve. He dreaded his upcoming trip to New York. His only purpose was to ask J. P. Morgan, his banker and friend, for a loan. A loan had become stark necessity.

The depression had flooded like a tidal wave across the decade, drowning innumerable businesses while others, like the Stuart Furniture Company, frantically struggled to stay afloat.

The Major gazed at the quiet, sunlit yard. A dray of lumber was being unloaded by a single laborer wearing outlandishly wide trousers: where there had been three hundred employees were now eighty, most of them recently arrived foreigners willing to accept a pittance.

His glance veered to Tom's shop. Pale new shingles and brighter paint showed where last year's addition had doubled its size. By the

53

open doors stood one of the machines. The Major's gloomy expression altered to one of disdain. Why, he thought, can't Bridger build something substantial and rich-looking like the Daimler 12 motor that the Prince of Wales was photographed driving in? The Curved-Dash Bridger indeed! To the Major's eyes the vehicle resembled a child's sled perched atop a wheeled coffin. True, it could attain an amazing twenty-five miles an hour, but on his single ride, jouncing along at Bridger's side, the Major had been positive his all too substantial flesh would be shaken from his bones, so what price speed? During that drive the Curved-Dash Bridger had halted twice, refusing even to bleat until its inventor had crawled underneath to tinker.

Given the dismal economy, who would believe they had sold forty-two?

Bridger had resisted each sale. About his machines he was as willful and vigorous as a salmon swimming upriver to spawn. He wants perfection, the Major thought irritably. As if this impossible toy could ever be reliable! The thing is to cash in before the fad ends. They cleared a profit on each machine, but Bridger insisted on wasting the money to develop the parts.

The chair creaked as the Major swiveled back to face his desk. Taking a small key from his vest pocket, he unlocked a drawer, removing two rolls of blueprints, slapping one thoughtfully against his palm before packing both into his pigskin briefcase. He locked the case with a small gold key affixed to the same chain as the drawer key.

With an unhappy glance at the ledger he reached for the brass bell.

Heldenstern poked in his head. "Yes, Major?"

The Major tapped the ledger. "Excellent work here," he said.

"Thank you, sir," Heldenstern gratefully said.

"Come in, Heldenstern. That's right, close the door. Sit down." The Major leaned across the desk, saying in a low, confidential voice, "While I'm in New York there will be meetings with financiers. I always say, what's the point of cluttering minds with unnecessary figures."

Heldenstern's wrinkled eyelids descended uneasily. The Major knew the obsequious little secretary was thinking about his crippled wife, his two plain spinster daughters, the mortgaged brick house on

Bagley Street, the scarcity of jobs in Detroit, his fifty-seven years. After the briefest hesitation Heldenstern replied, "Perhaps I better clarify the . . . details, as I did for your last trip East."

"I'm taking the 10:08 tomorrow morning."

"Then I'll return here after supper. It's easier for me to work, sir, when the factory is quiet."

"Much more efficient to be alone when there's accounting," the Major agreed. "Bring the two ledgers to me at the station."

II

To see him off, Antonia wore her new fawn spring outfit with the matching high-collared pelisse trimmed in crimson braid.

"That red sets off your cheeks and black hair," said the Major, leaning back in the carriage pillows to survey her fondly.

For long stretches of time he forgot Antonia was not his child. He doted on her, he suffered with her, he was irritated by her trivial faults. She made him forget his problems, of which she hadn't a clue. Life in the chateau did not reflect his financial difficulties. The Major himself could still obliterate his worries during a lusty cavort, and the one bright spot of his trip to New York was his arrangements for rooms in Mrs. Corbett's luxurious brownstone bordello on Madison Avenue. Yet it was Antonia alone who somehow managed to make his money problems less calamitous.

"You must promise me one thing, Antonia."

"A final request? Uncle, you make it sound as if you're going to New York to face a firing squad."

The Major winced. "I want you to spend more time with young Hutchinson."

"More? He drops by so often."

"I know, I know," said the Major sympathetically.

"Oh, why does he have to be so very nice? It would be much easier if he were just a stodge."

"I admit he's no brilliant wit, and he has those buck teeth. Still, he's the one eligible bachelor in Detroit who isn't embarrassed to come to our house. He keeps you out of the sickroom."

A bright morning, the carriage top was down and the horses had their yellow fly-nets over them: the ear cutouts were ornamented with gold-braid tassels. Antonia, holding her parasol straighter, watched the tassels bounce. "Uncle, you know how ill Father has been. Doctor McKenzie believes the grippe might go into his lungs if he doesn't move about. I need to walk him.''

"That's Nurse's job," snapped the Major. "For the life of me I cannot understand why a pretty young girl would rather immerse herself in sickroom details than enjoy a young man's company.''

"It's not fair to encourage him.''

"Use him to practice your wiles, then. A teething ring of sorts.''

"You're wicked." She attempted a stern look, then collapsed back in laughter.

Claude Hutchinson's large, handsome face was marred by protruding upper teeth. Nearly thirty, a lawyer with an income of his own, he had met Antonia with the Major at the Belle Isle skating pavilion two years earlier, and since then had visited at least once a week, stolidly ignoring both Antonia's lack of interest and the invisible pentagram that Detroit society had drawn around the girl. Though behind Claude Hutchinson's back the Major mimicked him, he thought him a steady young man and made him welcome. An eligible suitor bearing flowers and satin-tied boxes of Antonia's favorite chocolates relieved the Major's guilt about her nonexistent social life.

"My affairs might keep me awhile in New York, and after that there's some business in Washington. It's probable I'll be gone several weeks. Invite him to lunch or tea; it won't hurt you and I'll be happier knowing you have company.''

The train gave three long, piercing shrieks. Flaherty had already seen to the Major's steamer trunk and put his gladstone in his compartment. The Major held only his briefcase. He peered along the crowded platform looking for Heldenstern, who was nowhere in sight. But outside the elaborately carved Pullman Palace Car stood Bridger.

The Major had dealt in a way he calculated would insure no further meetings between the two young people, and his instincts had proved sound. Bridger, though obsessed about his machines and caustic of tongue, was honest. Bridger understood they had struck a bargain. Or did he? The Major examined Tom. The twill serge, though obviously inexpensive ready-to-wear, fit his lean body well: with his lightly tanned skin and air of vitality he could have been a

56

rising young doctor. The Major never underestimated the power of physical attraction.

"Antonia, my dear, this is far enough," he said decisively. "Go on back to the carriage. Flaherty's waiting for you."

But Bridger was raising his straw boater, hurrying around a family group toward them.

"Miss Dalzell, it's a pleasure," he said courteously, then turned to the Major. "I met Heldenstern leaving the office with these." He held out two larger black ledgers.

The Major's cheeks quivered. "You have no right to interfere with my secretary's duties," he snapped.

"I was bringing you this and I thought I'd save him a trip." Tom also held a photographer's thick cardboard envelope. "When I heard you were going to New York, I figured you could show our Curved-Dash to people."

"I'm not taking this trip to be your drummer," barked the Major. Antonia was staring at him oddly. "Well, it's a thought," he said. "Yes, Bridger, not a bad idea at all to show photographs to my sporting friends. Antonia, my dear, take this case. I can't manage everything."

She held the handle with both hands. "It's been far too long, Mr. Bridger," she said. "Several years!"

Tom's very white teeth showed in a smile.

"New York. All aboard for New York and points en route."

"I'll miss my train," said the Major. Clasping the ledgers and the envelope to his rounded chest, he hurried her along the platform, handing her up the high, narrow steps.

In his compartment he raised the window, peering around the coal-smoky depot. Bridger was nowhere in sight. Wiping his forehead with relief, the Major commenced his adieux.

III

Tom, near the barrier, stared at Antonia, as she stood on tiptoe by the open window, then ran alongside the train. The wheels began to turn amid the smoke. She was left behind, waving. Tom wound through the crowd, his gaze fixed on the tall, slender figure in creamy beige. She did not see him until he greeted her.

She was panting a little. "You're still here," she said.

"Waiting for you."

"Oh?" Her eyes were shining. "Is that what Uncle was afraid of?"

"He wasn't his usual subtle self, was he?"

"He's really such an old dear. He worries about me, that's all." She cocked her head. "You look different."

"Responsible and successful?"

"Exactly!"

They were emerging from the station into the surrounding crush of carriages, wagons, drays with their prancing, shying horses. "Miss Dalzell—"

"*Mister* Bridger, will you stop being so formal? You do know my name is Antonia."

"Antonia then. Have you seen the view from the top of City Hall?"

She shook her head.

"Would you like to?"

She hesitated. "I promised my father I would be back for early lunch."

"It's only a little past ten. There's time to spare."

"Then I would adore to." They were emerging from the depot into the surrounding crush. "I'll go tell Flaherty," she said, and dodged lightly through the melee of horsedrawn traffic toward the Major's carriage.

The land around the city is flat, so from the 180-foot tower of the City Hall they had a panorama that faded into the distant lavender haze of timberland. Farms wore their bright spring skirts of blossoming fruit trees and new green crops. Nearer in, church spires poked through freshly leafed branches. Ferries, tugs, barges, deep-water vessels, sailed over the sunstruck Detroit River. From here one could see the entire town of Windsor, as well as Belle Isle, which, as Antonia pointed out, was shaped like an arrowhead. Directly below them throbbed the business heart of the city with its traffic-clogged arteries.

Antonia circled the tower eagerly, and because of her effervescent delight Tom, too, saw the varied beauties of the landscape. On the walk here she had asked about the shop. He had told her that Trelinack, his brother Hugh, and five mechanics worked with him.

"Tell me about your family?" he asked.

"Family?"

"I only know the Major."

"Father . . ." Sighing, she watched a lavender pigeon separate itself from the flock to sit alone on the parapet. "Father's a brilliant scholar, a historian. He knows everything there is to know about Gothic architecture."

"And your mother?"

"Mama died when I was two. All I can remember about her is that she had warm, soft arms. She came from Florence. I never met her family. Father doesn't like them."

"Why?"

"He's never really said, but I think it's because they argue a lot with one another—and everybody else. About once or so a year we get a letter from Italy, asking for money."

It didn't sound an impressive connection. Before Tom could question further, he noticed a man carrying a small boy on his shoulders step onto the deck.

"Henry!" Tom exclaimed.

"Tom Bridger," the man replied, his greeting smile pulled out of shape by the child's hands. Setting him down, he took off his curl-brim bowler to Antonia. Wiry, of medium height, with a brown mustache and wavy brown hair parted neatly near the center, his one compelling feature was his eyes, a sharp, intense blue. "So this is what you do all day."

"I never thought I'd meet *you* here during working hours, Henry."

"I've been promising Edsel a treat for months."

"Hello, Edsel," Tom said. "Miss Dalzell, I'd like you to meet a good friend of mine. Edsel Ford. That old gentleman is his father."

The boy took off his cap, gravely extending his hand. Antonia knelt to shake it before she took the father's hand. Tom was lifting the round-faced child to see over the parapet. "Look at that jam-up down there, Edsel. See? At Library and Farmer a horse swerved and his wagon got stuck. For twenty minutes nothing's moved."

"One day there'll be no traffic problems," said Henry Ford.

"The roads'll be safer—and cleaner," Tom said. "We won't have runaways or—"

"Dad," interrupted Edsel, his round face worried. "Not a single horse?"

"Well, maybe a few," his father replied.

"None," Tom said firmly. He turned to Antonia. "In case you haven't guessed it, Henry and I are in the same line."

"Tom and me, Miss Dalzell, we intend putting the people of this country in motor carriages."

"Automobiles," Tom said, letting the French word roll in his mouth. "Ford and Bridger automobiles will be what you see down there."

He glanced over Edsel's head, meeting Henry Ford's blue gaze. The May sunlight was too real for their dream, the obstacles and impossibilities glittered like fool's gold in their eyes. They both blinked. After a few moments Tom and Antonia said good-bye to the Fords and started down.

As they descended the first flight Tom said carefully, "The Major's serious about us not seeing each other."

"Tom, I wish . . ."

"What?"

"Oh, it's so stupid."

"Stupid? You're his niece, and I'm his mechanic." Reaching the landing, they halted. They stood close enough for him to feel—or imagine he felt—the warmth emanating from her slight body. "But he's not the point. Your father's the one who counts. I'd like to meet him."

"You can't. He's ill," she said sharply. Outside the tall window, pigeons circled, casting odd shadows in the dust-streaked sunlight. "But I've told him all about you. When you came to fix the study clock I told him. Since then he's been interested in motorcars. He marks his journals and magazines to read me the news about them." She spoke rapidly.

She's lying, Tom thought. Hurt, angry, he tasted the bitterness of rejection. Clearly, her father wouldn't approve of him, any more than her uncle had. *She's a rotten liar.* The small muscles below her cheeks worked as she fought back tears, and to his rush of other emotions was added an infuriating urge to take her in his arms and comfort her.

"In that case," he said coldly, "he and I will have something to talk about."

"The doctors don't allow him visitors."

"None?"

"Not yet."

"I see."

She drew a deep breath. "Thursdays I shop at J. L. Hudson's. Would you believe it? At two thirty I am invariably in the dry goods department."

Sneaking, Tom thought. Do I want to sneak?

She gripped her parasol handle. "Thursday," she said.

"Thursday?"

She nodded, smiling. It was a timidly hopeful little smile.

"By coincidence that's the exact time I do my own ribbon shopping," he teased. He took her arm, leading her swiftly down the stone steps. Laughing breathlessly, they emerged from City Hall.

IV

That Sunday afternoon Antonia led Claude Hutchinson to the high-ceilinged drawing room that, inevitably, reminded her of that unhappy Dessert Social. Setting the box of Duval's divinity fudge that Claude had handed her on the round table, she turned to him. Her face was very white.

"Claude, you mustn't visit unless it's to see Uncle."

"But you have a sweet tooth, Antonia, and I promised him to feed it in his absence."

"No," she said, fiddling with the bric-a-brac on the whatnot. A Meissen angel nearly toppled: with a gasp she rescued it. "You aren't to call on *me*, Claude."

Claude sat on a love seat, hunching his shoulders. He was not overweight, yet his obvious distress gave an obese ungainliness to his movements. "I'm sorry," she murmured.

"You never gave me any reason to hope," he said. "Everything I do is because I . . . care for you, Antonia."

"Claude, you're so kind . . ." She had not realized how profoundly he'd cared for her, and she struggled against tears.

"I assumed it was because of your age." He stared down at his knees. "That's why I never declared myself."

"There's somebody else. We've known one another a long time."

"How long?"

"Since the first week I came to Detroit."

"Well, well, what a discovery," he said, attempting to disguise his misery with a jocular comment.

There was a long silence. He did not raise his head.

"Claude, you're too nice. . . . I feel terrible about this." Her voice shook. "I never should have permitted Uncle to keep inviting you. It's all my fault."

"So that's an end to that," he said in the same heavy, jesting note, and pushed to his feet. His shoulders bent, he walked cumbersomely from the room. She followed.

After the front door closed behind him, she sank into a straight-backed, comfortless hall chair, burying her face in her hands. It was not in Antonia to witness Claude's hurt and humiliation without feeling the pangs as keenly as he.

V

Belle Isle, the city's largest park, boasted not only the ice-skating pavilion but also a shingled building that housed the Detroit Boat Club (the country's oldest river boat club), tennis courts, a baseball diamond, a deer park. However, this sunlit Thursday afternoon Tom and Antonia avoided these attractions, meandering along a seldom used path where the marsh had been dredged. Oaks and maples dappled the sunshine as they walked around a little pond. Halting at a bench, Tom used his handkerchief to dust off a place for Antonia. Water lilies floated, and there was an occasional splash of an unseen frog.

"It's so lovely," she murmured.

"Peaceful," he agreed, twining his fingers with hers in a fugitive, trembling clasp.

They watched a squirrel, tail raised in a question mark, scamper across the path, and at the same instant turned to face each other. Tom felt the green world, the tranquil water, rush at him then recede. His heart pounded. Leaning toward her, he touched her mouth with a tender, light kiss. "I've thought of you every day since I first saw you. It was nearly impossible, staying away," he whispered against her ear.

"Tom . . ."

"I promised your uncle I wouldn't come around until I had some prospects."

"Tom . . ."

Putting his arm over her shoulder, he said, "You're beautiful, wonderful, far, far above me." He touched the soft warmth of her earlobe.

"No. . . . I'm not. . . ."

"Antonia." With his forefinger he traced the satin smoothness of her lip. Again the drooping branches and bobbling water lilies rushed toward him and withdrew, leaving him scarcely able to breathe.

A boy rolled a hoop along the path. They moved apart, rising.

They said very little, but their hands were clasped, and the afternoon melted as if touched by a watercolor brush.

VI

The Major's timing was terrible.

Andrew Carnegie had begun the process of gathering the steel industry into his arms, and the Major's financial kingpin, J. P. Morgan, was the steel magnate's banker. The very day of the Major's arrival in New York, Morgan was called to Pittsburgh. In his absence the Major sounded out other bankers regarding a loan on the largest furniture factory in Michigan, situated on prime Detroit River frontage, insured with Lloyd's of London for $250,000. He never got a chance to display Heldenstern's meticulously doctored books. Some bankers were courteous, others blunt, all informed him that no loans were being made on such collateral as a furniture factory.

The Major felt himself falling into an abyss. Continually he reminded himself that he and Pierpont were good friends, they had shared raffish good times aboard the financier's yacht, the *Corsair III*, Pierpont would not let him down. To escape the stifling claustrophobia of his doubts the Major attached himself to one of Mrs. Corbett's protégées, a tall, slender, black-haired Southern girl of undepletable sexual talent and most extravagant taste.

The Monday of the second week of Morgan's absence, the Major boarded a crowded early train to Washington to visit his patent attorney, Mitchell Polhemus.

In the well-polished office the Major unlocked his pigskin case, taking out the two rolls of blueprints.

"More?" inquired Mitchell Polhemus. A hunchback, he wore his frock coat in the generously cut style of thirty years earlier. "Are these also connected to the horseless carriage?"

"Yes. Improvements of the carburetor and cooling system."

"Major Stuart, do you honestly believe this machine has a chance of becoming popular?'' Mitchell Polhemus was an honest lawyer. Never casual about his profession, he played devil's advocate with his clients before a blueprint crossed the cherrywood desk.

"Popular? Never, Mr. Polhemus, never. But quite a substantial number are being built in Europe, and this year in America maybe a thousand were sold."

"That many? I never would have believed it."

"The figure came from *Horseless Age*, so doubtless it is exaggerated. Still, think of Newport. Mrs. Belmont has motorcar tournaments on the lawn of Belcourt—her friends decorate their vehicles with flowers. The Vanderbilts, Stuyvesant Fish, the Whitneys."

"The toys of a few won't bring you royalties enough to pay my fees."

"Other wealthy people around the country will copy them," said the Major.

Mitchell Polhemus nodded gravely. He had done his duty. It was time to get down to business. "Would you like your previous applications to be acted upon? As we discussed before, from the date of issuance a patent has a life of seventeen years."

The Major stroked his beard thoughtfully. "Is it more profitable to wait and see if there's a larger demand? Or by the year 1916 will this novelty be long forgotten?" He frowned down at the desk. "More shops open each month."

"I'll do as you wish."

"Put off filing," the Major decided.

Mitchell Polhemus's long hunchback's fingers took the rolls of crisp paper. "And these are to be filed like the others? In your name?"

"Yes, in my name alone," answered the Major without hesitation. "As I told you previously, the inventor, my young mechanic, is a wizard at this type of thing. But he has no concept of orderly business dealings. He's against patents."

"No!"

"Imagine this, he believes that the patent office has the express goal of stifling ideas. I must go behind his back to protect both of us."

"He's lucky to have you as a mentor," said the attorney, rising to put the rolled blueprints in a deep cabinet. "The young can be dangerous to themselves."

"Foolishly, idealistically dangerous," agreed the Major.

The two men shook hands.

The office was on Pennsylvania Avenue. On the bustling thoroughfare, the Major, untypically, did not eye the pretty women in their soft, light summer frocks, nor did he notice the self-important governmental officials, the glossy horses and lacquered carriages. His business was accomplished, and he had fallen blindfolded and muffled back into his nightmare. His fears that Pierpont might not come through sent chills through his enormous belly. He ached to return to the glowing warmth of Antonia in Detroit, yet his financial needs forced him to ignore his personal comfort.

Sighing, he raised his arm to attract a cabbie's attention. He traveled in a daze to the depot and took the first train back to New York.

CHAPTER 4

Tom bit down on the hard-boiled egg, his eyes taking in the five automobiles in various stages from the bare angle-iron chassis to the completed, bright yellow job. His expression showed both pride and irritation. They might be Curved-Dashes, but they certainly weren't Bridgers. Not having enough capital for machine tools meant he must rely on engines from Leland, wooden bodies from B. F. Everitt, and so on. Each part had to be tested and modified—and even then he could never be certain of quality. Swallowing the egg, he thought, *What I'd give for proper control!*

He was having lunch with Hugh and Trelinack. Through open shop windows drifted lazy voices of his mechanics eating in the shade outside.

Trelinack downed his schooner of beer. Running a thumb and forefinger down his waxed mustaches, he said, "Thursday's come again." He winked broadly at Hugh.

Hugh lounged backward, lifting the front legs of his drafting stool. "Yes, Thursday."

"In an hour or so our Tom'll be deserting us," said Trelinack.

"Off on his mysterious Thursday errand," said Hugh.

"All barbered this way, he puts me in mind of my courting days back home."

Tom's neck flushed dangerously. "The hell with that!"

"Oh, so you do hear us," said Trelinack. "I was wondering if you'd lost your hearing the same as you acquire a cloak of invisibility—or is that only when you're with a certain black-haired bit?"

Hugh looked at his brother. The sly teasing was fine, but he did not like the angry set of Tom's jaw.

At seventeen Hugh surpassed Tom by a full inch; however, his was the rapier slender height of a dancing master. His pearl-gray alpaca suit fit him like a stocking—he dressed the dandy on work days, his excuse being the efficacy of a smart appearance when inveigling prospective buyers. Though his face had lengthened into manhood, it retained an appearance of ingenuousness. His angelic good looks camouflaged a financial shrewdness, while Tom, who was far more straightforward, appeared a tougher business opponent. (Another comparison between the brothers was equally deceptive. Concupiscence persistently jolted Tom, yet he had a nice gentle streak, a decency, that prevented him from approaching a virgin— any woman he did not pay. Hugh's sexual needs were sluggish, but his vanity had prodded him to succeed with the two prettiest girls at Central High. He was renowned as a hot trotter.)

Tom said coldly, "You know the lady's name."

"Last Thursday my Maud was buying some ribbon for her seam-stress work. She saw you and Miss Dalzell leaving Hudson's together."

"What of it."

"What if Major Stuart knocks your block off when he gets back to Detroit?"

Tom's face still burned. "It's her father's concern."

"So she has one, then? Have you met the man? No, I thought not. Maybe he's a wondrously concocted tale?" Trelinack had never adjusted to his mechanic becoming his boss. He still spoke to Tom as he did everyone who worked under him, in bluff tones. "And as far as this not being the Major's concern, I hear that his interest goes in quite deep, if you get my drift."

"No, Trelinack, I don't get your drift, Trelinack. Explain your drift to me."

"The missus and the girls are forever mentioning it. Why, they ask me, why don't they see her name in the social columns alongside the Major's? I don't know what to answer. They're my wife and daughters. How do I explain to them why she isn't invited to decent homes? I can't say to them that for the Major the local whores aren't good enough. He has to bring in fancy bits and call them relatives."

"She *is* his niece!" Hugh cried. "Tom told—"

"Come outside," Tom interrupted his brother.

Trelinack remained straddling his chair. His rolled-up shirt sleeves exposed massive forearms covered with curly copper hairs. He was an expert boxer.

"No, Tom, I'm not coming to blows with you over this. I don't want to hurt you. You're a friend. I just wanted to set you straight about her."

"Come on out, you shit-mouthed cocksucker."

Trelinack, growling deep in his chest, rushed into the yard.

The shop men, along with the Stuart workers, also on their lunch break, formed a circle about the pair. Sun beat down fiercely. Foreheads were mopped. Money was held out and bets made in a variety of languages. The combatants approached each other.

Trelinack outweighed Tom by thirty pounds of brawn. He crouched, his boots shifting delicately, his arms curved as if grasping a large balloon. He feinted with his right hand, gauging the distance, then with a perfectly timed movement his left fist shot out against Tom's nose.

Tom heard the crunch, his eyes filled with involuntary tears, but the fury that surged through him anesthetized the pain. Trelinack wrapped both arms around him, hugging him close. A clinch. Tom, panting, broke away. With squared fists he pounded at Trelinack's large, firm belly, his full strength behind the blows. The skin of a knuckle split.

Trelinack's legs sagged. He skidded in a puddle of oil and fell slowly onto his back, resting on his elbows. Tom stood gasping over him.

Hugh pulled at his brother's arm. "That's enough! Tom, what's the point? No more. Please. I can feel an attack coming on."

"Fight, fight, fight."

Trelinack looked up, dazed. "Who would of believed it?" he mumbled. "You have me on the ground with hardly a blow. It must of been that last beer."

"Fight!"

Tom pinched the bridge of his nose. His fury had evaporated. That he had downed Trelinack, his friend, filled him with self-loathing. He extended his hand. "Here."

The crowd groaned with disappointment.

"I shouldn't drink beer on the job, heat or no heat," said Trelinack, draping a heavy arm over Tom's shoulder as they went back into the shop. "So she really is a niece, this Miss Dalzell?"

Tom balled his handkerchief against his nose to stanch the blood.

It was Hugh, closing the doors, who explained. "The Major's half brother lives out at the chateau. Apparently he's ill a lot. An invalid. She's his daughter."

Trelinack said gruffly, "Well, anyway, Tom, you can tell one and all that you knocked down John Trelinack. I'm sorry for my mouth."

Tom wanted to return the apology, but the words would not come, so he pressed the handkerchief harder, wincing.

Again Hugh spoke for him. "You know Tom and his temper."

"Yes, his own worst enemy." Trelinack folded back newspaper from plump, golden-crusted Cornish pasties redolent of potatoes and lamb, handing one to each brother. "I shouldn't of repeated lying gossip. But sneaking around alleys with the young lady won't help her reputation, either."

II

"Antonia, there's an automobile ready for the final test. Want to take a ride this afternoon?" They were leaving Hudson's dry goods department. "Like me to chauffeur you?" *Chauffeur* was the French word for driving or for anyone in the driver's seat.

"Tom, I'd love to!"

"When Major Stuart gets back, he'll hear about it. Your father'll hear about it."

"Tonight. From me," she said. Her brightness seemed forced.

On Gratiot, outside the red-brick and brownstone department store, an excited group was clustered around the yellow Curved-Dash Bridger, more people gathering as Tom draped the long scarf over Antonia's straw sailor. Men threw him the usual half-admiring, half-jeering questions as he checked the gearbox and grease cups. When they pulled away, small boys tossed pebbles after them.

Tom headed in the direction of Grosse Pointe, where the Major's friends summered in chalets and cottages bordering Lake St. Clair. At this time of day the streets were quiet, but Tom slowed whenever a horse approached—there was always danger of shying and accidents. Antonia clasped her small needlepoint reticule very tightly, saying nothing. Despite his involvement in the task of chauffeuring,

Tom was acutely aware of her silence. It dropped between them like a chasm.

As city became country they jounced along a narrow, deep-rutted lane. The previous night a soft drizzle had fallen, not enough to impede them with mud but sufficient to dampen the earth so there were no dust clouds. Trees draped with ivy, berry bushes, and wild lilac spread lushly on both sides of the road. *It would be perfect*, Tom thought, *if only Antonia were not so silent*.

"It's so strange, moving this fast, and without a horse," she said finally. "The scent of the trees and bushes and flowers comes at you."

"All I smell is gasoline," he said. Easing his foot from the pedal, he shifted back the clutch stick, tugging with all his strength on the brake. Gears ground shatteringly. With a series of jerks the automobile halted in a patch of wild wheat. "I have to check the carburetor anyway, so we might as well take a look around. There ought to be a view of the river beyond those trees."

"Along the little path?"

"It's going in the right direction," he said. His mouth was dry.

She kept on the duster, for the narrow track took them Indian file through a blackberry thicket. The path widened into a clearing as they came to a stand of ancient sycamore whose branches intertwined far above their heads. The dense foliage had kept out much of the rain, and the warm air was humid and still as a greenhouse.

Tom said, "There's no state law we have to meet on Thursday afternoon."

She turned to him. "Don't you want to, Tom? I thought you did, but maybe that's because . . . ." Her voice faded.

"Because what?"

"Why are you angry?"

"Me? What about you?" His voice rang loud. "You've been a million miles away."

Antonia turned away, toward a mossy tree trunk, and burst into body-wracking sobs. Feeling helpless and tender, he touched her shoulder.

"I'm sorry, Antonia. Please don't. I never meant to bark at you. I've been crazy, that's all. You mean so much to me."

Drawing in gulping breaths, she controlled herself, and blew her nose. "It's Father," she said.

"He's found out about us?"

"He's known all along."

"So he's ordered you to stay home?" Tom's hand lingered on her shoulder.

"No."

"What does he say about us?"

"Nothing."

"What's wrong, then?"

"He's had a cold."

"Cold?" Tom asked. "That's all? A cold?"

"He's had it for nearly two months, and in his condition . . ."

"It's turned into something worse?"

"Dr. McKenzie says it's just a cold."

"Nobody gets this upset about a cold. It can't be only a cold. Tell me what he said about us."

She looked up at him. The delicate, irregular nose was red, her eyes full. She said in a low, rapid voice, "On my sixteenth birthday, we were in Paris, he became ill. A very high fever. Since then he doesn't speak."

"The fever caused that? Does he write everything down?"

Her fingertips pressed together as if in prayer. "He doesn't react properly," she whispered. "He'll recover."

"You mean his mind has gone?"

"There's nothing wrong with his mind," she said firmly. "His mind functions, but he cannot communicate with us. That'll come back when he recovers." She straightened her shoulders. "For the time being he can't look after himself. That's why it's so important for me to take care of him. This cold—what if it goes into his lungs?"

"It won't," he soothed. So this was the secret that kept her so silent. He ached with loving pity, yet at the same time he knew that such a revelation meant she loved him. "Antonia, he's getting the best care."

"This morning Nurse Girardin said it would be best if . . . if he did get pneumonia. Dr. McKenzie didn't answer her, but he thinks the same. I'm the only one who sees him as a man, the way he really is, not a medical case. The others think of him as a burden."

Tom kissed her damp forehead and with great tenderness said, "I'm glad you told me."

A flock of sparrows blundered into the clearing, chirping their way upward to the high branches before swerving in the direction of the river. Wild birdsounds faded into the soughing of the old trees.

Tom put his arms around her. Her body melted into his, her breath shivering moist on his neck. The softness of her breasts against his chest, the scent of her heavy, satiny hair—a fragrance like roses—excited him unbearably, yet the moment went far beyond the physical, reaching into the recesses of his being, releasing an ungovernable mass of feelings, joy, pride, wonder, relief, a sweet yet inscrutable sadness. Her fingers trembled on the tendons of his neck. He moved to kiss her, and with both hands he slipped the duster from her shoulders and the heavy canvas rustled onto the mulch at their feet. She was caressing his neck, his throat. In this timeless place where trees grew forever, he accepted that she was no princess in a limestone castle, she was Antonia, Antonia whose tender, wandering caresses were for him. He spread the duster and they fell embracing onto it. Kissing the shirtwaist over her racing heart, he undid the pelisse's crimson frog, fumbling with the gold bar pin at her throat. Soon they were surrounded by her white embroidered underwear and his own clothes. He stared at her, awed. The delicate curves glowed white. "You're so beautiful," he whispered.

"Ahh, Tom . . ."

"I'll love you always," he said, his mouth open on hers. When he reached the barrier, she flinched, her nails digging into his shoulders. With a frantic jab he found his home. She gave a small cry, and then her arms circled his waist, pulling him closer. He heard his own rasping breath and hers, an echo. Kissing her face, her neck, her ear, he began moving faster, deeper, and at the ultimate moment, called her name.

When they had quieted, he raised on his elbow. She smiled, then gazed up at laced branches whose greenery was reflected dark in her eyes.

"Mine?" he said, tugging a strand of her loosened hair.

"I love you."

"Always?"

"Forever."

"I want to marry you now, but I can't support you yet. Not with your father, too. This year, though, we sold twice as many automobiles as we have in the whole time since the shop opened. Soon—six months at most—I'll be able to.'' To speak of money, which had never meant a damn to him, when his emotions were molten fire and should stream out in song or poetry! ''We'll be married then.''

''Yes.''

''Some things about me aren't so wonderful. Antonia, I needed you to belong to me, so I took advantage of your unhappiness.''

Taking his hand, she held it between her breasts. ''I wanted you, too, Tom,'' she said, and kissed his chin.

On the drive back to Detroit, he told her about his father's screaming death, about his mother's madness and suicide.

III

A buggy with a rubber top waited under the porte cochere.

''Dr. McKenzie's here!'' Antonia cried. Before Tom could help her, she climbed out, missing the oval footstand, losing her balance and falling to her knees, pushing rapidly to her feet, skimming over the gravel, lifting her skirts to take the porch steps two at a time, slamming the knocker of the side door, a wild bird beating against the cage.

Almost immediately the door was opened by a short, spare man carrying a leather bag.

''Dr. McKenzie! What's happened to Father?''

''Nothing, nothing at all. This morning you were so worried that I decided to drop by on the way home. The chest's clear as a bell.''

Antonia was taking off the duster and goggles and scarf. She handed them to Tom. ''Thank you for the demonstration, Mr. Bridger,'' she said, her voice joyous. She ran inside.

The doctor extended his hand: the weathered skin, like that of his face, was covered with freckles. ''I'm Dr. McKenzie.''

''I'm Tom Bridger.''

As they shook hands the sharp hazel eyes fixed professionally on Tom.

''What happened to your nose?''

Tom had forgotten the fight this noon, and Dr. McKenzie's reminder made him aware of the pain. ''It's nothing. I bumped into a machine in the shop.''

''It could be broken. Let me take a look.''

''I'm fine, thank you, sir.''

"As you say." The doctor walked up to the automobile. "So you've been taking Miss Dalzell out in a horseless carriage."

"A Curved-Dash Bridger." Tom folded the duster and scarf with the goggles into the wicker basket.

"Now I remember. That's where I heard your name. So you're the Major's young partner." He circled the machine. "In Chicago I rode in an electric brougham. But this runs on gasoline. I can smell it. What keeps your contraption from blowing up?"

It was a doctor's trick. While Tom explained the internal-combustion machine, McKenzie watched him intently.

The doctor glanced up at the house. "Not much of a life, not the way for a lively, pretty girl to live, cooped up with elderly servants and an invalid. And it's not even her own choice."

"But she thinks she's the only one who can look after Mr. Dalzell," Tom said, then paused. "The Major, does he insist?"

"Andrew? He dotes on the child. He uses every means short of force to keep her out of the sickroom."

"But you said—"

"Her nature traps her, her own nature. Bridger, I've been in this profession nearly thirty years, so I've had ample opportunity to observe humanity at its best and worst. And there's still matters beyond my comprehension. Why are a few people so defenseless against their emotions? Most of us learn early on to chloroform ourselves against feeling the extremes of pain or pleasure. Most of us are dulled to real joy or real agony—it's for the best, of course. But then there's the few. The sensitives, I call them. They love more deeply, they have greater happiness. And their misery is correspondingly more terrible. I fear for her. Mr. Dalzell's present condition has improved, but he's gravely ill." The doctor avoided the knowing glance that would have been professional betrayal. "To be honest, I worry less about my patient than his daughter. She's so exceedingly vulnerable. Have I made it clear what I meant, no choice?"

Tom held himself immobile in the late afternoon sunlight. "She's a wonderful girl," he said.

"With the Major in New York, she's very lonely."

"I'm her friend."

"Why do you think I've been unburdening myself to you? Here, bend down. I'm going to look at your nose."

As light fingers moved on his face tears came into Tom's eyes.

"Not broken," the doctor pronounced. "I'll put on a proper plaster."

"Thank you, sir."

When Dr. McKenzie closed his bag, he said, "My prescription for Miss Dalzell is that you take her riding." He climbed into his buggy, clicking the reins. His brown gelding circled wide around the Curved-Dash Bridger as though sensing they were inimical.

IV

"A racer?" Hugh asked.

"Two cylinders, not one like the Curved-Dash. Light, though. Powerful and light."

It was not yet six, and they were on the way to work. The bronze sun glared. It was already a scorcher.

"You've lost me." Hugh pushed back his straw hat. "You must have said a thousand times that racing doesn't interest you."

Tom was grinning. "And you must have told me a thousand times it's the way for people to hear about the Curved-Dash."

The devious streak in Hugh's nature prodded him toward a new profession called public relations, the art of getting your name before the public without paying. The Major had been right about competition. There was a lure about automobile racing, a crude, raw excitement that came from speed, and the newspapers catered to their readers: each rally meant columns about the winning machines. Free advertising.

Hugh said thoughtfully, "There's a race being promoted right here. Tom, think of the play Detroit papers would give a Detroit chauffeur. We'd be deluged."

"First I have to build her."

"I have every faith," Hugh said.

Tom always had been propelled by forces he could not fully comprehend. Now, though, he understood what drove him. Thursday afternoons weren't enough. He wanted to wake mornings with her, he wanted to have constant access to that smile, he wanted to possess her gifts of joy and happiness.

Through that hot June and July he blazed like a spinning comet. He hammered up a board partition, cutting off a few square yards of the shop. Here he worked on the racer whenever he could. Mostly at night. Hugh crouched yawning over the drafting desk, trying to sketch parts visible only in his brother's teeming brain. Oh, those plans were rough going. Tom was a cut-and-try man, Hugh no skilled draftsman, so they bickered constantly, their arguments often reaching the cursing stage, yet being brothers they continued to work where outsiders would have walked away.

By August the racer had taken form.

If the quadricycle had been a dragonfly, this was a grasshopper, a long, narrow skeleton of angle iron, steel, and reinforced wood waiting to spring forward on pneumatic tires specially ordered from the Goodyear Tire and Rubber Company in Akron.

V

When the Major's train pulled into the Detroit depot, he was counting and recounting his belongings—ledger, valise, hat, coat, umbrella, briefcase—with an old man's morbid lack of self-confidence.

For the Major the past few days had been the emotional equivalent of a crippling stroke. On August 6, J. P. Morgan had returned to New York and the Major had immediately hurried to the triangular, six-story marble banking house on Wall Street. There, in his friend's glass-encased office, he had requested a loan. At first the banker had been warm, advising him to pull in his horns and ride out this damnable depression. The Major explained that the loan was imperative. Morgan repeated his advice, this time a cold financier. *Ride it out*, he said. *Be thankful you have other assets.* The Major, having dipped deeply into capital for his personal expenses, was too ashamed to admit its depletion. "I have excellent collateral," he said, placing the carefully worked-over ledger on Morgan's desk. The banker waved it away. "I'm sorry, Stuart, but I cannot in good conscience float a loan on any furniture factory, even yours." The Major, bracing himself in his chair, had breathed heavily a full minute before he told the banker, "Make arrangements to find me a buyer." As he had spoken a sharp pain had torn at his throat. Selling the factory that his grandfather had founded, that he and his father had built, was like selling an arm, a leg, his eyes.

The wheels stopped and the Major jerked back into the plush seat. "But what choice do I have?" he mumbled. His outside income came to around a thousand a year, barely enough to stint along with a couple of raw Irish servant girls in the house. No cook, no carriage, no horses, no rowdy entertainments, no London tailoring, no pretty women. The Major feared the loss of his physical comforts as keenly as he feared the humiliation of poverty. "I can't let an asset insured for a quarter of a million stand idle, can I?" He pushed open the door to the narrow corridor.

Antonia had boarded the train. Brushing hastily by the passengers that crowded the corridor, she flung herself at the Major, hugging him with a child's unfettered, rough embrace. "Uncle, Uncle. It's been so long!"

He kissed her cheek, then drew her into the compartment, holding both her hands to look into that glowing, utterly unique face. "My dearest girl, my dear, I missed you so. . . ." His sigh degenerated into a sob. Then he pulled himself together. "How delightful you look. Young Hutchinson must have been bringing you the right kind of bonbons."

A subtle pink clouded her face. "I asked Claude not to call," she said.

"What's that?"

"I told Claude he mustn't visit me."

"You never mentioned this in your letters. Is it that foolishness of yours? Guilt? I've told you over and over not to feel guilty because you're capable of turning a head or two."

She laughed. "It's dreadful to be such a delightfully clever girl, and so charming, with such a pretty voice." Wordlessly she sang two bars of Papagena's music.

The Major gave an unanticipated snort of laughter. God, she cheered him!

She looked down. "Tom's been chauffeuring me out to the country."

"Tom?"

"Mr. Bridger. Your partner in the Bridger Automobile Company."

The Major sank down into the seat, resting his head on the starched lace antimacassar. He was experiencing that same tearing pain in his throat as when his friend had refused him a loan. Betrayals, everywhere betrayals.

Antonia sat next to him. "Uncle, what is it?" she asked in a frightened voice.

"I'd like to get home," he said thickly. "My business didn't go well."

"That's awful. You look so pale. Tired. How could I not have noticed?" She took his pigskin briefcase. "I'll find a porter. You go out to the carriage."

By the time the brougham was moving under the shady trees of Woodward Avenue, the Major's color had returned.

Antonia said, "Part of your business has been doing wonderfully well. Last week Tom sold two automobiles in a single day." Though she was smiling, there was that determined tone in her voice the Major had come to recognize. "He's entering a race in October. *That* should draw buyers like flies."

"So far no profit's come out of his shop, nothing, not a single dollar."

"He's been expanding, buying machinery, lathes and things."

"The time has come when all my resources must pay." The Major paused. He wanted to tell her about his terrible problems, but instead he said, "I can no longer indulge myself by subsidizing his shop."

The shadow of her parasol fringe wavered on her forehead. "Uncle, you can't take this out on Tom."

"There's no connection, none. But I'm glad you've brought up the matter." The fear that he was losing Antonia, child of his heart if not his loins, made his face go stony. He might have hated her as he said cuttingly, "A decently bred man would have asked permission."

"He's coming tonight, Uncle."

"Then you told him about your father?"

"He's coming to see you," she murmured.

It's worse by far than I imagined, thought the Major, closing his eyes on the bright August afternoon.

VI

Antonia sat in the dark gazebo. Honeysuckle vines were trained to drape over the scrolled ironwork, the domed cupola rose to a fantastic spire, the rustic bark furniture had been built by a top Stuart cabinetmaker. This was Antonia's favorite hot weather retreat. Here she would bring her sheet music to practice a new song, or dreamily pull stamens from bugle-shaped honeysuckle blossoms for the drop of nectar as she read, or simply luxuriate in the outdoors. To-night, however, she took no pleasure in the velvety warmth, the rich night scents, the moonless, star-peppered sky. She was concentrating on the yellow light streaming through the curtains of the study windows. Her uncle had ushered Tom in fifteen minutes earlier, banging the door closed after them with the firmness of a jailor.

The Major's vehemence against Tom should have infuriated Antonia. Each time her anger rose, however, she remembered the Gare du Nord and the stout, cigar-odored presence who had come to Europe for the one purpose of helping her father.

A shape moved, ghostly and insubstantial behind the curtain. It was impossible to tell whether it was Tom or the Major. The second shadow moved close in an implied hostility that made her shudder, then moved out of sight swiftly. She knew it was Tom.

Tom . . .

Even now, in her anxiety, thinking his name weakened her thighs and made her grow moist. Lately she had become alarmed at the ruthless physical dimension her love had taken on. With her odd, isolated upbringing Antonia knew even less than most well-bred girls of her time about the mysteries of sex—that is, the so-called facts of life. The act itself had become an essential part of her being. Everything to do with Tom drew her toward it. She would watch him talk and be reminded of his kisses; his odors, masculine and tinged ever so faintly with gasoline, recalled to her that violent, convulsive bliss when acrid sweat drenched them both; even her admiration for his incorruptible vision dissolved into a sensual yearning for him. Her nature was ardent, her love innocently passionate.

The front door opened. Tom came out.

Antonia was on her feet. "Tom, wait," she called softly, hurrying along the narrow summerhouse path to the driveway. His footsteps crunched on the gravel, not slowing. She caught up. Ahead of them shone the gate torchères, and by this thin light his face had the bleached look of skulls she had seen in the Roman catacombs. "What happened, Tom? What did Uncle say?"

"Can't you guess?"

"Was it very bad?" she asked.

"It seems that when he agreed to back my credit, I was meant to realize that you were off bounds. Permanently."

"What?"

Tom shrugged. "He thinks I welshed on him. All I wanted was

not to hurt you. How could he have thought I'd sell being with you?''

In the darkness she lost her balance, stumbling, not feeling the gravel against her ankle as her stocking tore. Regaining her equilibrium, she ran after him.

"When's your birthday?" he asked.

"April eighteenth."

"You'll be twenty-one, and can resume your contact with me—should you so desire."

"Tom, please don't be sarcastic."

"You asked what your uncle said. I'm telling you. You are his obligation now, he says, and he makes all your decisions. After your twenty-first birthday you can resume contact with me, should you so desire."

She sighed. "He hasn't been well."

"I'll mail him a sympathy note." They had reached the gates, and the torchères shone on Tom's deathly pallor. "And then there's the little matter of the shop. By the first of October we're to be clear of his premises—and I'm to have paid him off for his share in the machinery and unsold automobiles."

She put her hand on his arm. "He needs to do something more profitable at the factory. He told me that business has been bad, very bad."

"You've just heard that?"

"You knew?"

"So does everybody else in Detroit. There's a giant slump here. People are hurting."

"He never said a word to me. I remember wanting to take up the slack for Nurse so we wouldn't need Minnie, she's the second laundress, and Uncle was angry. He's never stinted on us."

"You're his princess. And I'm not keen on playing swineherd—even if I do have the right dirty fingernails." Tom spoke loudly. Gnawing at him was his bitterness that the Major, whom he occasionally grudgingly admired, believed him capable of relinquishing Antonia—for a credit line!

"Tom, he's so sad. He looks ten years older than when he left. Did you notice? His color's bad, and his beard's turned all white."

"I gather then that you're siding with the old bastard?"

Though Tom could be obscene, this was the first time he had been in Antonia's presence. Stepping back, she said, "He's been wonderfully generous to Father and me." A sigh tempered her coolness. "You'll find another backer, another shop."

"Didn't you hear, Antonia? He won't let us see each other."

"We have to, we must. So we'll manage as we were doing before."

"Hudson's on Thursdays? Sneak like burglars? Wonderful!"

A thrush sang. Startled, they turned in the direction of the liquid sound to peer into the darkness.

Abruptly Tom's bitterness drained, leaving dregs of hopelessness. He was being thrown out of his shop, he must pay the Major off for his share of the machinery, the racer was not finished. A life with Antonia seemed the sick fantasy of an overzealous imagination. "That income of your father's," he mumbled. "How large is it?"

Antonia understood what he was asking. Could they marry now? "Nurse Girardin is expensive. She trained at Hôtel-Dieu to handle Father's sort of case. She massages him, exercises him, she knows the right foods—everything. There's medicines. Laundry—bales of laundry. The specialist, Dr. Abler, comes once a month from Chicago, and sometimes he brings Dr. Roussel. Dr. McKenzie has his bills. I don't know what it adds up to, but Father's income can't cover a fifth of it."

Tom's mouth twisted miserably. "I see."

Prudence warned her to keep silent, yet she continued. "It doesn't matter what the income is. I couldn't leave. Not now, not at this time. I don't know what happened to Uncle in New York, but it must have been murderous."

The hissing gas torches illuminated her expression of determination. Momentarily Tom wanted to slap it away, but when he noticed her hands hanging at her sides, the fingers jabbing into the palms in nervous little twitches, he touched her gently. In order not to destroy her he must accept that she loved and was loyal to her uncle, his enemy.

"Hudson's?" he asked. The name seemed dishonorable retreat.

"Tom, thank you," she said, clasping his shoulders, pressing kisses on his jaw, his chin, the fine bones of his Adam's apple. At first he stood unresponsive, bitter, then a wordless rumble sounded deep in his throat, and he pulled her to him, kissing her mouth, a kiss that was all teeth, tongue, and desperation. They clung together as one being, one feeling, the blood hammering through them as from the same heart. "The summerhouse," she murmured shakily.

"I won't set foot on his property."

"The Hammond place?"

Across the broad street from the Major, Hammond, a lumber baron, had built himself a wooden stronghold, bulbous leaded windows, fanciful spoolwork, Gothic towers, then hidden his grotesquerie behind double rows of boxwood. Tom drew Antonia into the black shadows, spreading his jacket on prickly grass. They blindly fumbled with each other's clothing, and without undressing in the warm summer night, they obliterated their differences.

CHAPTER 5

On the afternoon of September 15, a Western Union boy bicycled into the Stuart yard. The Major hurried out, tossing the child a coin. He carried the telegram back to his office unopened, and stood weighing the yellow envelope in his trembling palm.

In the weeks since he had left, no word had come from New York. The Major had written four letters of inquiry to J. P. Morgan, letters that on rereading to his eyes seemed anxious, needy. He could not bring himself to mail them. Instead he had formulated a plan. The weather had been unendurably hot even for late summer, and through the nights he lay sweating into monogrammed sheets, refining his plan. His most profound hope was that Morgan would deliver him from using it.

Letting out a sigh, he used his ivory-handled paper knife, reading:

> HAVE RECEIVED OFFER OF FIFTY THOUSAND DOLLARS STOP PLEASE
> ADVISE FURTHER ACTION MORGAN

All color drained from the bearded face. Crushing the yellow paper in his fist, he shuffled to the sawdust-coated window, looking down into the yard. *What is it,* he thought. *A factory. A big, slowed-down factory. No more. No less. Why should I feel it is as much a part of me as my blood, my bones, my heart?*

His eyes dampened with tears.

Blinking fiercely, he pulled back his shoulders in a travesty of his old military posture, and again surveyed the yard with its pale barricade of well-seasoned white fir planks, its squadron of dark, uneven secondhand lumber that he had picked up last week for a song, good enough, as he informed everyone, to be hidden below the veneer of cheap export cabinets. Then he returned to his desk. He found a telegraph form, writing, *Seventy-five thousand least will accept. Negotiate. Stuart.*

He rang for Heldenstern.

Holding out the form, he said, "Here. Take this to the telegraph office."

"Immediately, sir."

"Just a moment, Heldenstern. Is anyone out there with you?"

"No, Major. I'm alone, sir."

"Good. Before you go, I need to talk to you."

Heldenstern removed his green eyeshade, nervously smoothing his sparse gray strands over his pate.

"First lock the outer door," said the Major in a commanding tone. His face was sternly set.

II

Two nights later, at eight twenty, Tom stood over the sink rubbing gritty mechanic's soap on his arms up to his elbows. At nine he was to meet Trelinack and a rental agent. The shop he had found on Anthon Street had scarcely room to assemble three automobiles, a miser-windowed, dark little place, but the best he could afford—and at that, the landlord, distrustful of "these damn horselesses," demanded Trelinack's signature too.

Hugh sauntered in from his drafting table behind the partition, leaving the door ajar, peering at a fresh newspaper clipping that he had tacked below the time sheet.

> The big automobile race to be held sometime this October at the new Grosse Pointe track bordering the Detroit River will be the most important in the history of the sport. The turns have been banked for a breathtaking mile-a-minute pace.
>
> Four events are planned, including a mile dash for electric vehicles and a five-mile race for steam mobiles. The major sweepstake of twenty-five miles is for gasoline-powered vehicles. The entry list is prestigious, including Winston (Cleveland), Apperson (Kokomo), Bridger (Detroit), and W. K.

Vanderbilt, whose famed French machine, "Red Devil," is reputed to have cost $15,000 plus $7,000 duty. Detroit's smart set as well as the city's automobile-minded citizens are expected to be on hand for the races.

Hugh read the final paragraph aloud with smug pleasure. " 'Of special interest is the Detroit chauffeur, Thomas K. Bridger, manufacturer of the "Curved-Dash" Bridger. His racing machine has been tested on the boulevards. Without effort it covers a half mile in thirty-six seconds, according to Hugh Bridger, the chauffeur's brother.' "

Tom dug his fingers into the jar for more soap. "How often do I have to hear that damn thing?" To his teasing clung grizzles of respect.

Working on the racer had changed the relationship between the brothers. Until then Tom had protected Hugh, supported him, worked far beyond his strength for him, so it was natural that he felt no respect for him. The race, a promotion, held up a magnifying glass to the fine print of Hugh's abilities. Tom was amazed at Hugh's smooth, wily repartee with reporters, his shrewd ploys with the race manager. And Hugh, in this new equality, found himself able to deposit into the fraternal bank the same unalloyed affection that Tom always had deposited.

"I got the name Bridger mentioned four times in the *Detroit Evening News*, didn't I?"

"And what was that about her being tested?"

"*You* said she'd go fifty an hour." Hugh's altered status did not preclude fraternal sparring.

"I said I *hoped* she would," Tom retorted. "Ahh, why nitpick? The article will help do the trick." He glanced at the partially assembled automobiles: quick sales were imperative, they were desperate for cash to pay the Major his twenty-five percent share of the tools and machinery. "She better go that fast, otherwise it's *requiescat in pace* Bridger Automobile Company."

"Latin from you?" Hugh asked.

Tom held his arms under the spigot to let water bubble away the soap. "Isn't that the translation for 'if we don't win the race we're up shit creek'?"

III

After Tom left, Hugh returned to the other side of the partition and his drafting stool. The *Evening News* reporter had requested a sketch of the machine for the paper, and the dangling light bulb cast a benedictory glow over Hugh's blond head as he drew an illusion of speed, elongating the racer's body, penciling the driver's hair straight back as if windblown. He had a natural aptitude, or so the rotund art teacher at high school had told him, and with training he could make his mark as a commercial artist. She had not tempted Hugh a moment. He had cast his lot with Tom, and his future would be rich, elegant, swank. Perhaps it was inevitable that Tom, possessed by creativity, had no interest in wealth while Hugh anticipated his rewards in concrete form. As he flattened his pencil to draw marks under the tires, he was thinking of a mansion with ivy-covered gables on Woodward Avenue, a butler opening the front door, himself in a swallowtail, a satin-gowned, extravagantly beautiful woman adorning his arm as he graciously received guests for one of those soirees he read about in the rotogravures. His breathing grew labored. Absorbed in his dreams and his sketching, he did not realize that the smell of smoke was irritating his bronchi.

Hissing crackles made him glance toward the window.

A blackish pink sheen, redder to the far left, illuminated the panes.

He ran to the other room for a better view. The stacked fir planks blazed with masses of small flames that glowed like orange fish scales. Clouds billowed. Sparks exploded, floating upward, luminous spores carrying fire. It had not rained for weeks. The pile of used lumber was burning in several places and the drying kiln, too, had caught, the flames reaching ominously toward the entry passage.

O'Reardon, the ancient Irishman, the only night watchman still on the Major's payroll, scuttled across the gaudily lit yard. "Fire! Fire!" His yells faded into the roar of flames as he scurried into the tunnel.

Hugh's impulse was to flee shrieking after him.

But he paused in the fire's brilliant illumination, looking around at the fragile sled-shaped automobiles, the two drill presses, the chain shaver, the grinding wheel, the new forge, all the tools that Tom had struggled to buy.

Beyond the partition stood the racer.

"I must drive her out," Hugh muttered.

The decision cut against every grain of his character, yet it was not born of panic. His mind had leaped to a shrewd calculation. Everything they had would go. The racer had cost a vast amount, and even if Tom could remember its every change and modification, they could not possibly afford to build another. With it Tom would win prize money. With it they would find a new backer. With it they could start over.

He opened the doors wide, recoiling from the yard's heat. His eyes streamed, he breathed with raspy, shallow coughs.

Turning the ignition, he pushed in the battery, and in his haste forgot to retard the spark. When he grabbed the crank, it spun. He fell back as if kicked by a mule. His thumb bent outward at a peculiar angle, yet he felt no real pain. He gripped the side of the racer, using his damaged right hand to aid the left. His long, slender body bent forward. As is often the case, terror endowed him with super-normal strength. Sobbing, gasping, he shoved. The outsize wheels turned.

IV

A system of alarm boxes was connected to the City Hall bell so that it pealed whenever there was a fire. Tom and Trelinack were in the shop on Anthon Street waiting for the rental agent when the wildly discordant ringing started.

"Another fire," Trelinack said, and went over to the narrow window. His voice clotted. "My God, Tom. It's over near the Stuart!"

Tom ran outside, staring at the red glow, then he was pounding down Anthon Street. "Wait!" Trelinack shouted behind him. Tom did not slow.

Outside the factory a crowd was growing, stimulated as crowds are by a conflagration, getting in the way of a horse-drawn hose wagon that clanged up Fort Street, pressing around the hook and ladder. Police struggled to hold back thrill seekers.

The ten-foot iron letters, STUART FURNITURE FACTORY, glowed a dull crimson. Below, the windows of the stockrooms had exploded and smoke was pouring out. Sharp little teeth of fire showed in the roof of the entry passage.

"Tom!" O'Reardon clutched at his arm. "Praise God. Ye're safe."

"Where's Hugh?"

"Hugh?"

"He was working in the shop."

"Sweet Jesus! He was? I ain't seen him."

Tom shrugged off the arthritic old hand, fighting his way through the crowd until he was pushing against a policeman's shoulder.

Deep in the passage he saw a glint and, peering, he recognized the racer's brass cooling jacket. It inched uncertainly along beneath the flames.

"Hugh!" he screamed. "Leave the fucker! Get the hell out!"

His voice was swallowed by the thermal roar. The racer continued nosing through smoke.

He elbowed by the policeman. A fireman turned on him, flinging out both arms to bar his way. "Get back, you damn fool! That front wall's about to go!"

Unhesitatingly Tom aimed a blow at the red, sweaty face and ran forward into heat so intense that it felt icy against his skin.

The racer's engine was afire.

"Saving . . . her . . ." In Hugh's blackened face the mouth was a moving open wound. "Saving . . ."

"Let go!" Tom tried to pull the burned hands from the chassis. Like the dark, obstinate claws of a bird of prey, they gripped and clutched. With the same unhesitating force that he had hit the fireman, Tom aimed at his brother's chin. As the boy fell he grabbed for him, lurching back to the street.

Ninety seconds later the front wall shivered. Molten letters swayed. Flames briefly receded into smoke. With a torrent of sound the two upper stories of stockrooms gave way, crashing into the tunnel, burying the blazing racer.

V

A few minutes before this the Major had been stamping up and down his study's Shirvan rug. In the hall the telephone gave its signal. He went to his desk, sitting there, waiting, his eyes fixed on the door. A knock.

"Yes?" he said.

Ida's troll face mingled sympathy with the satisfaction that comes from being first to report bad news. "Major, there's a Paddy O'Reardon on the line—"

"My night watchman. What does he want?"

"I'm afraid it's bad news. A fire at the factory, a big one."

The Major was on his feet, leaning on his desk. "Has he called the fire brigade?"

"He said so."

"Tell him I'll be there directly." The Major spoke in a strangled voice. "And get Flaherty to hitch up."

By the time the Major arrived, the barrels of resin in the store-room had exploded and every building was aflame. There was no way to save any of the bone-dry wooden structures, so the firemen were wetting down the surrounding factories and giving thanks for a windless night.

The crowd parted for the Major's carriage, gazing in respectful awe.

The chief himself came over. "I'm Chief Beldon," he said, raising his leather helmet to wipe his forehead. "We did all we could, but the blaze was too far along before we got here. I'm sorry."

The Major's eyes dully refracted the glare. "My grandfather opened his cabinet shop before I was born . . ."

"A terrible personal loss," said the chief. "On the bright side, there was only one man inside."

"O'Reardon, my night watchman."

"The old Mick was out in plenty of time. No, somebody was trying to rescue one of those damn horselesses. I shouldn't be surprised if the gasoline didn't have something to do with this fire—gasoline's highly volatile, you know."

The Major gripped his cane. "Bridger was in there?"

"I think that was the name. Yes, the older brother said so. They took him over to Providence."

"So it's the young boy. He's in the hospital, you say?"

"With a fire this size," the chief soothed, "one fatality's nothing."

The Major's hands shook more violently. His cane fell, rolling across the carriage floor. "The boy's dead?" he whispered.

"He won't last through the night. I've seen enough like him. Oh, excuse me, Major Stuart." A fireman had come over to consult with him.

There was a maddened roar as the shingled roof of Tom's shop collapsed. Enormous sparks showered into the street, and the crowd jostled back. Long after Flaherty had calmed the bucking horses, the Major's thighs shuddered, twitching as if both legs had been amputated.

He sat through the night in his Jacobean dining room, as he had when each of his parents had died. He did not drink the whiskey or the cups of tea that Antonia brought him, but he asked her to stay with him. In the little room off the hall the telephone sounded constantly. Ida brought messages: he found himself unable to speak even to his oldest friends, and only after newsmen persisted in an unpleasantly threatening manner did he agree to meet with the press at ten in the morning.

When the mantel clock, the antique that Tom had repaired, struck the hour, he went into the study, leaning heavily on his cane. Antonia followed, sitting quietly next to him, a fact that every reporter jotted down. Most of the questions, unsubtle to the point of crudity, pointed toward how the losses would affect him financially. The Major explained that he had been in the process of retiring from business life and his banker, the famed international financier, J.P. Morgan, had procured him an excellent offer: he had forfeited a large sum, but his loss went far deeper than money. "My grandfather opened his cabinet shop before I was born. . . . This means the end of the Stuart name."

"What about the serious injury at Providence Hospital?" asked the man from the *Detroit Tribune.*

"When the fire broke out, the brother of my partner in an automobile venture was at work." He heard Antonia's small groan and went on more rapidly, "I'm certain that the young man is on the road to recovery."

After Ida ushered out the group, the Major slumped back in his chair. "They were like a pack of wolves, waiting for me to falter." An accurate enough summation. In Detroit's eyes, Major Andrew Stuart had too long existed rich, carefree, publicly flouting the moral laws that everybody else had the decency to break behind drawn curtains. The reporters knew that his comeuppance would sell out the special editions.

Antonia sighed. "How can they think only of money? Why

couldn't they understand how terrible this is for you?" She went to the tantalus, pouring him a drink. "Uncle, you need this."

He took the snifter with both hands, not to warm the brandy but because he trembled so much that he could not have held the glass otherwise. "I never could have faced them without you, my dear. Having you with me made all the difference in the world."

"They're gone, Uncle. It's over."

"Thank God."

Touching his shoulder lightly, she asked, "Can Flaherty drive me to the Providence Hospital?"

A few drops of brandy trickled from the side of the Major's mouth, and he, normally fastidious, did not wipe his beard. "What?" he asked. "Why?"

"The reporter said Hugh's there."

"That boy's nothing to you, nothing."

"I've been seeing Tom," she said evenly. "I've kept on meeting him. When I shop downtown. Sometimes when I walk in the evenings. If I can't have the carriage, I'll find the way on the trolley."

"I don't want to argue with you, I can't." The Major forced himself to sit more erectly. "But there's no point for you to visit, no point at all. Providence is a Catholic hospital, very strict. You won't get through the doors. Only close relatives of ward patients are permitted inside the building, only the nearest family." He was not positive of this, but he would get McKenzie to back him up.

Antonia was passing the cut-crystal decanter stopper from hand to hand, an unconscious habit of hers, he had noted, playing with some small object when she was distraught.

"The reporter said he was seriously injured."

"He did?"

She nodded.

"I didn't hear that. Well, this *is* worrying news. Don't cry, my dear, please don't, I can't bear it. Antonia, don't. I'll tell you what we'll do. I'll ask McKenzie to go over and find out about the boy's condition. No, better yet, I'll ask him to take the case. McKenzie's the best doctor in Detroit. He'll keep us informed."

CHAPTER 6

When Hugh arrived at Providence Hospital, it was not discussed whether he could survive the lung damage or the third-degree burns sweeping over the upper half of his body. He was in shock. A few hours in deep shock is irreversible. A stomach tube was jammed into his raw nostril and he was fed glucose water, his blackened clothing was scissored from him, he was bundled in quilts, surrounded by heated bricks.

In the dispensary a nursing Sister of Charity smeared carron oil on Tom's burns: his palms and fingerpads were painfully blistered, so she bandaged his hands before leading him to the high-ceilinged, dimly lit corridor where a few scattered figures sat clasping their rosaries in the gloom.

"Wait here," she said.

"But what about my brother? How is he?"

"You'll be told if there's any news."

Tom sat on the hard bench, his body leaden. *Will he die?* he wondered, at the same time reproaching himself bitterly for letting Hugh work late. Was he so besotted with building the racer, with marrying Antonia, that he ignored all other human obligations? How could he have left his younger brother alone in a deserted factory piled with seasoned wood? Tom forgot his own far younger, more rabidly dangerous struggles to survive—and support his brother into the bargain. *Will he die?*

The few times a nurse or orderly moved along the dim corridor, he jerked erect as if expecting the worst, holding his breath until the figure passed him. He left the bench only once, to relieve his bladder.

Somehow first light was touching the clerestory windows. Dawn brought a bustle of attendants.

At two in the afternoon visitors began straggling in, and at three a tall, enormously stout nursing nun opened the ward door.

Tom rose, moving his numb legs from the stiffened hip joints like a wooden soldier.

Hugh's bed, in the far corner, was set off and heavily shadowed by a tall screen. Slow, wheezing breaths emerged from the figure of a mummy. The card attached to the foot of the iron cot told Tom nothing of his brother's condition. The ward sister said there was no change, an ambiguous comment that she either would not or could not clarify.

At the close of visiting hour Tom searched the maze of hallways until he found an intern.

"Doctor, tell me about Hugh Bridger's condition."

"We have a hundred beds here, so—"

"B-R-I-D-G-E-R. In the accident ward."

"Wait a second, I did hear something. Bridger—isn't that the burn case?"

"Yes."

"McKenzie's patient."

"McKenzie?" Tom stared. *"McKenzie?"*

"How did you get a member of the gracious staff at Harper, a high-toned society doctor like him, to come to our humble hospital?"

Tom's eyes went momentarily flat. Who had sent McKenzie? Antonia? The Major? What difference did it make? *Will he live?* "What about my brother? He seems in bad shape."

"Didn't McKenzie explain to you? He's on the critical list. That means it could go either way."

The second afternoon the ominous screen still remained, shadowing Hugh's bed. He was muttering, "Racer . . . racer, must save it. . . ."

"She's fine, Hugh. Just a little sooty."

"Heavy . . . push . . ."

"You got her out." Tom bent over the swathed head. "Hugh, you sure saved our bacon."

"Tommy?"

"Me, yes."

"Help push," Hugh whimpered in a shrill, childlike voice. "Tommy, hurts so bad . . ."

Tom ran the length of the ward to the duty desk by the door, returning with his bandaged hand clamped on the ward sister's full round arm.

The next afternoon a water tumbler of crimson roses spread their perfume behind the screen, banishing the odors of mortally ailing bodies and the acrid aroma of lime-and-water. Warnings posted in the corridors forbade flowers in the wards.

"Doctor brought . . . from Miss Dalzell . . ."

Tom rubbed at the veins of his wrist, his breath coming more easily as he made an irrational connection between Antonia's roses and Hugh's lucidity. "Just a minute, Hugh," he said, and went back between the high beds—each with their visitor—to the duty desk.

"My brother seems better," he said to the nurse. "Is he off the critical list?"

"How did you know he's on it?" she asked, then gave him a close-lipped, girlish smile. "No. But he took some gruel this morning."

For three days and nights a dam of anguish had held back Tom's need for food and sleep, but now weariness trickled down his neck and between his shoulder blades, and he sat on the bed stool, Antonia's red roses blurring out of focus.

II

"Tom."

He jerked awake. Trelinack stood at the bedside.

Next to him was a young woman encased in a brown faille costume whose collar climbed on stays to cup her firm round chin. This was Maud, the oldest of the three Trelinack daughters. Her velvet-trimmed hat, also brown, sat squarely atop thick, glossy brown hair. Her hazel eyes were frank, her coloring high, and though large-boned like her father—sturdy wrists and ankles—she had a trim waist and firm apple breasts. All in all, Maud Trelinack was well favored, and women gossiped why, at twenty-three, she remained a spinster. Trelinack was forever boasting of the pocket money she earned as a seamstress to the upper crust, and the general opinion was that this financial independence plus her unfeminine candor frightened off suitors.

"Good afternoon, Tom." Maud had inherited Trelinack's wide, pleasant smile.

"Hello there, Maud," Tom said.

The visitors bent over Hugh's bandaged form, greeting him with cheerful whispers pitched loud, as if to penetrate his bandages.

"How did you get past the dragon?" Tom asked. "It's relatives only."

Trelinack pulled at his mustache. "We're your Cousin Jacks, aren't we?"

"What about those roses?" asked Maud. "Aren't flowers against the rules too?"

"Miss Dalzell sent . . . through . . . doctor . . ." Hugh whispered. It was obviously painful for him to move his mouth.

"Doesn't she have to go by the regulations?" Maud asked.

"Lass, lass," said Trelinack. "I wouldn't of brought you along if I'd known you were going to argue with our patient."

"Every time I ask a sensible question, Pa, you tell me I'm arguing—or talking like a man," Maud retorted.

Trelinack winked fondly—she was his pet. "Boys, take my advice. When you start a family, never sire daughters. Tom, what about coming back to tea with us?"

Just then a Sister bustled around the screen. "I made a mistake. This patient's allowed one visitor only. Will you please leave the ward." And leveling stern glances at Trelinack and Maud, she returned to her station.

"We best be leaving, lass. Well, Tom?"

"Thank you, Trelinack, but I can't," Tom said. "Visiting hour just started."

"Go . . ." Hugh muttered.

"You feel better when I'm here," Tom said.

Between gauze strips Hugh's lashless eyes closed. The cheerful voices reverberated against his swathed ears. "Ready to sleep . . ."

"I'll wait until you doze off, Hugh," Tom said gently.

"So you'll come?" Trelinack asked.

"If the offer still holds."

"I'll go along directly to alert the missus," Trelinack said. He clamped his bowler on his head. He and Maud whispered loud good-byes.

When Tom emerged he found Maud waiting in the high-ceilinged corridor.

"Pa left me to make sure you show up," she said.

"Think you can handle the assignment?" Tom asked, managing a smile at the short, rounded young woman.

Trelinack aimed numerous invitations at Tom and Hugh, so they were well acquainted with the three Trelinack girls. Tom felt closest to Maud. She was sensible, she earned her own way, she was as honest as a plumb line, she had an endearing way of drawing her brows together to squint nearsightedly up at him. Hugh said with her skills as a seamstress she should look less frumpy; he called her earthbound. Tom thought of her as having her feet on the ground. Maud had no sense of humor, but accepted his good-naturedly.

Outside the massive stone hospital she slipped her arm through his.

"Stopping the prisoner from escaping?" he asked.

She did not release his arm. "Tom," she reproved with her wide pleasant smile.

"What if I try to make a break for it?"

"Why must you always tease so?"

"That's me," he said, and for a minute they walked silently along Grand Boulevard.

"Hugh seems to be on the mend," Maud said, looking into Tom's face, which was slack with fatigue.

"What makes you say that?"

"He wasn't in a coma or delirious."

"You're a funny girl."

"Me? Funny? Why?"

"Isn't the normal comment, 'He looks very strong'?"

"You know I never lie, Tom," she said. "What have they told you?"

"Nothing."

"Nothing?"

He felt tears prickle. "Maud, I'm worried sick."

She pressed her arm tightly to his. "Of course you are. Hugh's your whole family rolled into one."

Tom said fiercely, "He's going to pull through."

"He will."

"You just said he didn't look too wonderful."

"He's going to get well," she said staunchly.

"You're true blue, Maud." His tone held no hint of jest. It was a statement. "A real friend."

Tom's head buzzed and felt hollow. He did not notice a tremor of something like sadness or resignation cross Maud's handsome, high-colored face. "We're alike, Tom, you and me," she said. "When we make up our minds to it, things happen."

III

At the Trelinacks' tight-shouldered, neat frame cottage on East Alexandrine Avenue, tea meant supper. Soft-boiled eggs in china cups, a long platter overlapping with slices of cold ham and beef, pickled onions that were sharp on the tongue, Stilton cheese, a home-baked cottage loaf whose thick slices were spread with butter-thick clotted cream and raspberry jam. Tom had believed himself too weary to eat, but he had not sat down to a proper meal since the fire and he found himself devouring whatever was set in front of him. The conversation was mainly about Trelinack's new job that would start next week. "A top-notch foreman position, at Fenning Cabinets they know a good man," said Trelinack, beaming. The meal ended with great earthenware cups of tea. The women rose to clear off the table.

"Tom," Trelinack said. "You look dead on your feet."

"I am."

"Come on, then." Trelinack led the way to the narrow front porch, closing the door behind them. "Before you go there's something you're bound to hear. That's why I lied my way into Providence, so you could get it from me, straight." He tamped tobacco into his pipe. "This morning I went to the Stuart to see if there was any salvageable metal around our shop—there wasn't, but that's another story. A young dandy in spats was poking around too. A tight-mouthed young fellow—until I told him I used to be foreman.

Then you should have seen him open up. He's the local representative of Lloyd's of London. . . . ''

"Go on," Tom ordered.

"This week he's bringing in a couple of Pinkertons to sift the yard."

"Detectives?"

"There's a fortune involved here. Two hundred and fifty thousand dollars."

"Two hundred and fifty thousand!"

"The Stuart was the biggest furniture factory hereabouts. He told me there's always an investigation in a fire this size. There. Now you won't be hearing a garbling of it. Go on home to bed."

Tom did not move.

"There's murder on your face, Tom. And there's no proof, none."

"Lloyd's doesn't agree with you."

"He said an investigation was a matter of course. Besides, it don't matter what the Pinkertons find, does it? The fire's over. It's happened."

The door opened.

Maud held out a basket covered with a red-checked napkin. "Tom, am I glad I caught you. I've wrapped some of the ham and the rest of Ma's bread for you."

As soon as Tom stretched out on his pallet he fell into a heavy slumber. He had no idea how long he had slept; it may have been several hours or it may have been a few minutes when he jerked awake, his eyes focused up at the dark window. His fists were clenched, his jaw set, his mind clear.

A quarter of a million, he was thinking. *The miserable, whore-sucking old bastard had the factory insured for a quarter of a million dollars!*

And at the same time he could see Hugh, smoke-blackened, his hands pitiable black claws on the racer.

The thought and the image twined together like strands of a steel hawser, strong and indivisible, until he could not separate his certainty of arson from his brother's injuries.

IV

Around six that evening a pair of orderlies had come to change Hugh's dressings. It was considered prophylactic to pick away the charred skin, and Hugh threshed to evade the tweezers, his enfeebled screams rustling through the ward. Sister came running to help hold him down. When petroleum salve and fresh bandages covered his burns, he retreated into a cavern where devils pranced around him with their smoldering pitchforks.

He emerged at a light touch on his shoulder.

"Hush," the low feminine voice murmured. "It's all right. You were having a nightmare."

He swam unwillingly into consciousness. The gas was turned low, and one of the feeble rings of light picked out an unusual profile, a large, glowing eye. Hugh had met Antonia once, on a Sunday when Tom had brought her to see the unfinished racer. "Miss Dal-zell?" he whispered, trying to form the words without moving his raw flesh.

"Antonia," she said, nodding.

"How . . . ?"

"Dr. McKenzie arranged it. It hurts you to talk, doesn't it? We don't have to."

"You . . . please . . . ?"

Antonia appreciated Hugh's need—how often had she attempted to verbally pierce the wall between herself and her father. "What about, Hugh?"

"Your . . . house . . ."

Unpinning her hat, she sat on the stool. "Uncle built it on three acres that he inherited from his great-aunt." She spoke softly, her head close to his, the rosewater scents of her hair banishing the harsh hospital odors. "Uncle meant it to be impressive, and it is. Tom says when he goes inside he feels the house is ready to spit him out. In the hall there's an enormous Waterford crystal chandelier, and every three months Flaherty spends a week polishing the drops. The stained-glass window, Louis Comfort Tiffany made it, is centered with a knight bearing Uncle's crest on his shield. There's a set of fifteenth-century tapestries in the living room, they came from a castle in Andalusia, biblical scenes, they've turned brown with age." She paused.

Hugh's bandaged hand moved, a weak gesture that she continue.

Tom had told her about Hugh's romanticizing of the rich, so she detailed bits of extravagances that might please him.

"Ida, the cook, has a big marble table in the kitchen just to roll her pastry. Every Friday at breakfast Uncle puts gold pieces on the sideboard for her to buy whatever food we need for the week. The oysters come from Chesapeake. And . . ."

Hugh's weakness kept him from comprehending all she was telling him, but her voice held a cool, gentle quality, like falling snow, easing his pain and fear, and as he listened he fell into a dreamless sleep.

V

Two blocks from the Trelinacks on East Alexandrine Avenue, the Henry Fords had rented a flaked-roof bungalow. One evening Tom climbed the six front steps. His knock was answered by Henry Ford, trim in freshly ironed gray overalls.

"Tom. I've been trying to catch you. How's Hugh?"

"On the road, thank you."

"Good, good. Clara and me have been worried."

Ford's air of energy and purpose depressed Tom utterly, for these qualities had drained from him. "Henry, what are the chances of an engineering job over at the Edison?"

"You? Aren't you going back into automobiles?"

"Finished with that."

"Because of the fire?"

"It's more complicated," Tom said.

Henry Ford tugged at his mustache. "I see. Well, I'm going into it full time. My job's open."

"They wouldn't start me as head engineer."

"After me, who's the best in Detroit?" Ford's blue eyes twinkled. "I'll put in a word for you, Tom. Two words. Three. Don't worry about a thing."

VI

Two weeks after Hugh arrived at Providence Hospital, the big, stout sister instructed Tom to return the following morning at eight sharp, with outer clothing and transportation. He came in a hired hack, telling the driver to wait.

At the foot of each bed stood enamel ewers and bowls: two nuns, their habits covered by voluminous white aprons, were bathing the patients.

Dr. McKenzie sat at the duty desk studying a sheaf of papers. Tom had not seen the doctor since they had introduced themselves under the Major's porte cochere. He held out his hand: McKenzie shook it, then inspected the new pink skin on palm and fingerpad. "You're healing nicely. Any pain?"

"None," Tom said. "I've been wanting to thank you, sir, for taking my brother's case."

"I've been going over his charts. Keep him in bed until I tell you. Asthma and smoke are a bad combination."

"You mean he'll be an invalid?"

"Not at all. He won't be up to heavy physical labor, that's all."

"Never Hugh's preference." Tom smiled. "What about the bandages?"

"They'll come off, eventually. For the time being, though, bring him to the clinic twice a week to have them changed."

"He dreads that tweezering. Is it necessary?"

The doctor scratched at his freckled cheek, leaving red marks. His irritation was not directed at Tom, for whom he felt a natural affinity, but at any lay questioning. "Sound medical procedure," he said. "The left side of the face appears to be a third-degree burn. That might mean scarring."

Gazing through the shafts of dusty sunlight that fell from clerestory windows, Tom watched an orderly lift Hugh, help him into the topcoat. "Major Stuart asked you to look after Hugh, didn't he?"

"Yes."

"I'd like the bills sent to me."

"The Major has always taken care of accidents at the factory."

"But this is *my* brother."

The doctor cleared his throat. "I know that your horseless carriages were all destroyed in the fire, and—"

"I'm through with that," Tom interrupted. "I have a proper job now. Chief engineer at the Edison Illuminating Company. I can afford to pay you, sir."

"Bridger, you know you're refusing because of the insurance investigation. Well, let me tell you, that's a fine bit of idiocy. Men sifting through the ashes for a week—what a waste of time! They found nothing. Of course they found nothing. There's nothing to find. Lloyd's is satisfied to pay the claim.'' The tall, stout nun rustled up to the desk. McKenzie ignored her and the patients who were watching from nearby beds. ''Losing the factory is the worst kind of blow to Andrew Stuart. I've known him all my life, and I've never seen him like this, not even when he was wounded at Gettysburg. The man's in utter despair.''

''Send me my brother's bills.''

''All right, all right, you're being foolish, but I understand.''

''Thank you, sir. You'll get the money fast.''

''The fees don't worry me. My concern is the left side of my patient's face.'' The doctor consulted a stiff sheet of paper, then looked at the nun. ''What do you think, Sister?''

She sighed. ''In my opinion, there's permanent damage.''

''I concur.'' He turned to Tom. ''Don't mention this to your brother. We don't want him to brood until he's regained some of his strength. We're lucky he pulled through, very lucky. Now. Take him home.''

VII

A windy, cold morning, drafts prowled the horse-drawn cab, and as soon as they reached the flat Tom heaped the covers from both pallets on Hugh, heating milk and sugar, adding whiskey, a toddy. Hugh drowsed. Tom sat with his hands on the round table, his new pink fingertips curled loosely. Before the fire he had always brought home a spring to fix, a pin to file, a sketchpad to figure a more efficient order for assembly. Now his free minutes disappeared as meaninglessly as pebbles tossed into a murky pond.

There was a light rap at the door. Intuitively he knew it was Antonia.

Though he had not seen her since before the fire, she was forever in his mind. Antonia, Antonia. He had nursed a profound resentment of her guardian before the fire, but now his feelings extended beyond loathing. He could not bear the thought of Antonia living in the gray mansion with the Major. They must be married right away. And the mystery of his decision was how it hurdled every single practical consideration: his lack of money, Hugh's condition, the mound of unpaid medical bills, Mr. Dalzell's expenses, Antonia's own wishes. For Tom there was only this obsessive truth. She could not continue to live with his enemy.

Another rap sounded. Steeling himself to explain his intractably adamant heart, he went to the door.

Antonia's arms were laden. "I brought some things for Hugh," she said, adding in a rush, "Tom, I had to see you, I had to. It's been so long." Delicate shadows underlined her eyes.

"Are you all right?" he asked.

"I've been so worried," she said, setting down the packages: a tissue-wrapped oblong that was probably a book, four hothouse peaches nestling in a basket, a jar of tawny jelled broth. "How is he?"

"Asleep. I just brought him from the hospital."

"Dr. McKenzie told me."

"Have you been ill?"

She shook her head. "No. Very worried."

Antonia looked so pale that Tom did not know how to put his demand. Instead he said, "Thank you for the letters." Each day one or more notes had come from her. "I'm not much at writing, but hearing from you sure helped."

"Tom . . ." Hesitating, she fingered the basket. "There's my seed pearls from my mother, and my gold bar pin. You could get something for them to help start the new racer."

"There's not going to be another."

"But you said entering sweepstakes would attract buyers."

"I'm finished with that," he said firmly. "No more automobiles."

"You've had a setback, a horrible one, but—"

"It brought me to my senses."

"You sold all you built."

"To rich people. Luxurious toys wasn't what I had in mind."

"Tom, please don't be like this. You're such a shining, shining man."

"I've thrown away my silver armor," he said. "How do you like it?"

Her brows raised in perplexity. "What?"

"The flat."

She glanced at the curtainless window, the sink piled with dishes, the cheap, squat stove, then said ruefully, "Anybody would know that bachelors live here."

Of course she would not see it in the light of poverty. Antonia's eyes never pigeonholed the gradations between rich and poor. "Henry Ford's quit. He put in a word with his supervisor at the Edison, and I have his old job. Chief engineer. It pays well." In a louder tone that sounded wretchedly forced to him, he said, "We can be married."

A joyous smile animated her drawn face. "Tom, I think about that all the time."

"Tomorrow morning we'll go across to Windsor and find a justice of the peace."

"*Tomorrow?* Canada?"

"You aren't of age, and here they ask for a birth certificate. Over there they don't."

"Father's been coughing all week, and—"

"Antonia, your father's never going to be himself again," Tom said with as much gentleness as he could. "I need you so much now."

"And I need you," she whispered.

"I figure it'll take me four months to pay off Hugh's bills, then we'll be able to rent a house, hire a foreign woman, bring your father to live with us. He won't even realize you're gone."

"Tom, Father's not a lump of wood. He knows, he understands." She looked down at the basket. "Uncle's ill. Losing the factory's a terrible blow to him. He's broken."

"Doctor McKenzie told me that Hugh'll be scarred."

"Oh, Tom." Her eyes glazed with tears.

"The left side of his face. God knows what he'll look like. *That's* your poor, broken uncle's work."

"You've heard about that stupid investigation." She was on her feet. "It's as if he's lost a child, Tom."

"He didn't lose that child, he sold it for a quarter of a million dollars."

"He was home when the fire started."

"Did I say he lit the match? He owned an unprofitable factory and he needed money, so Hugh was squashed like an ant at a picnic!" Rage quivered through Tom, and to regain his control he bit down on his lip, hard.

"Tom," she said, reaching toward him. "Why are we arguing?"

"*I* was talking about us, about our being married." Tom was torn by the strongest desire to hold her, to bury himself in her slim, ardent body, to reassure himself that she, indeed, loved him, yet in his craze of anger and doubts it seemed perfectly reasonable that he not permit himself to take her outstretched hand. He rapped his knuckles on marble. "The question is, are you coming to Windsor with me tomorrow?"

The fragile jaw raised in that gallant, obstinate determination to hold tight to all that was dear to her. "Tom, I love you more than anything in the world. But Uncle, when I needed him, he came to me, all the way to Paris. He brought Father and me here, he's been so generous—even though it's turned out he really couldn't afford it. He's truly shattered. For a little while I must stay with him. This is the very first time I can help him."

"Then you aren't coming?"

"Uncle—"

"A straight yes or no!"

"He just sits around all day, and Father's—"

"One syllable! Is that so difficult?"

"Tom, please, you're everything to me—"

"Damn you, are you coming with me?"

"Until things have settled down, I can't." Her sigh quivered. "No . . ."

The breath was knocked from him. He heard his own gasp before his lunatic jealousy raged forth. "So you're staying with that degenerate who corrupted you?"

"Tom!" She sank back into the chair. "At the start, you thought that. Such a silly mistake."

"Was it a mistake?"

She looked out the window at the mean, unpainted shacks straggling across what was once the garden. "You of all people should know," she whispered through appallingly white lips.

He needed to annihilate her as completely as her rejection had annihilated him. "All the proof I've had puts it the other way," he said with a dissonant laugh. "Oh, I admit that the first time you put on a fine act of innocence—but after that! Oh, Antonia, after that! I've never been able to afford your class of woman. I've never been sucked and kissed by such a skilled whore." As he spoke memory assailed him, and he actually saw her luminous whiteness in the green shadows, saw her face ablaze with love, felt the exalting joy she communicated with her tender, wandering kisses. *Oh, God, God,* he thought, and wanted to grovel and beg her forgiveness. Yet he also accepted that she was staying with his worst enemy. Her choice was, for him, irreconcilable. "You'll go far. The most sought-after commodity in the world is a whore who doesn't look it, yet practices every kind of whore trick!"

She had been passing her small needlepoint purse from hand to hand, but now she clasped it tight. "The way I acted . . . that was part of love, part of loving you. . . ." Her whisper held a plea. "Tom, wasn't it the same for you?"

She was crying, and he was close to tears himself. "I had one hell of a good time!"

She moved toward the door. He grabbed the soup jar, attempting to force it into her hands. "Here. We don't take charity." The glass fell, shattering loudly, and beef-odored jelly drabbled down her skirt, staining it darker beige. He moved back.

"You sicken me," he said thickly.

A cloud was covering the sun, and in the shadows her huge wet eyes shone darkly; those fathomless eyes seemed to mourn all the inexplicable cruelties and sorrows of time and the world.

She turned away, letting herself out the door.

Tom leaned against unvarnished pine, listening to her light footsteps. He could scarcely breathe.

"Tom?"

At Hugh's call he went slowly to the sink, dashing cold water onto his face before going to the slit of a bedroom. Lashless blue eyes looked from between bandages. "I never thought you were the type to pull wings from hummingbirds."

"So you've been eavesdropping."

"Your shouting woke me up. He must have forced her, the Major."

"Like hell. She was an innocent, a total innocent. She didn't even understand what we were doing."

"Then how could you have said those things to her?"

"I enjoy pulling wings off hummingbirds," Tom snarled, and

dropped onto his own pallet, burying his face in the gray-striped ticking, his shoulders heaving with rusty gasps.

Hugh could not remember his brother weeping, not even when they had buried their mother then their father in that desolate prairie yard. The awful sound grated against his gauze-covered ears, and he longed to comfort Tom, but he was seventeen, embarrassed by this outpouring of grief, weak from the morning's exertion, and besides, he was accustomed to Tom caring for *him*.

CHAPTER 7

The day that Dr. McKenzie removed Hugh's bandages, October 15, an unprecedented early snow fell: the doctor, worried about getting through the streets, started immediately on his house calls.

While he examined Mr. Dalzell, Antonia waited outside. "Your father's a little improved today," he said when he emerged from the sickroom.

"That's wonderful," she said. The gloom of the hall hid her expression. "Doctor, how is Hugh Bridger?"

"The left side of his face is badly scarred."

She put her hand on the dark wainscoting.

"Are you all right, child?"

"A bit dizzy, that's all."

"You're looking peaked and have lost weight. You seem under the weather. Come, let me take a look at you."

She protested, but he led her into the blue-wallpapered room with the curve of windows that overlooked the snowy back garden. After she undressed down to her prettily embroidered chemise, he examined her, asking questions that became more and more clinical. It was not long before he came to a conclusion and confronted her with his diagnosis.

In his experience girls caught this way tearfully denied it or blamed the man. Antonia lay back in the pillows, her enormous dark eyes fixed on him.

Closing his satchel, he asked, "Didn't you guess?"

She shook her head.

108

Grasping the worked-brass footrail of her bed, he said in a stern voice, "You mustn't stay in the sickroom so much. The air is unhealthy. Take proper meals. You're far too thin. Nap after lunch. And—" He was about so say *no monkey business*, meaning no crochet hooks, knitting needles, no salts, packing with pepper, or seeking out kitchen-based midwives, but those huge bruised eyes stopped him short. "I suppose my first prescription should be for you to marry your young man."

She turned away. "Will you explain to Uncle?" she asked.

"If that's what you wish."

The Major sat huddled in front of the study fire, a shawl warming his shoulders, his chin resting on the handle of his cane. He appeared shrunken into his clothes, and it was difficult to believe he was not yet sixty. As the doctor spoke, though, years seemed to drop from him. Pushing the shawl impatiently into the wing chair, he stood.

"Impossible!"

"She denied nothing."

"That's because she knows nothing!"

"I'd say she's three months gone."

"By God, the girl will tell me this herself," boomed the Major, hurling his cane toward the fire screen. The stairs shivered under his step.

Antonia, wearing a loose white peignoir, stood at the bay window, drawn yet not at all overcome with the shame that the Major had anticipated. As he closed the door she threw her head back, her hands hanging at her sides, the pose she assumed when she sang to his piano accompaniment. "Did Dr. McKenzie tell you?" she asked in a rapid voice.

The Major had been despising her for smearing herself, thus ruining the one pure thing in his life. In her presence he was overcome by a loving pity that banished lesser emotions. "Yes, he told me," he muttered awkwardly.

"So then you understand that we need to go away, Father and I."

"Nonsense. You'll marry Bridger."

"That's over." She stood rigid, and the white batiste folds of her robe seemed carved from marble. "We'll go to Newport."

Whatever caused her to select Newport? "Bridger's very fond of you—he begged to court you. And you're fond of him. You've made that too clear." Worrying that this might sound accusatory, the Major stepped closer to her. "My dear, under these circumstances, naturally my objections are withdrawn."

She turned to the window.

"He's bitter that I forbade him to see you, is that it?" asked the Major. McKenzie had told him of Tom's insistence about the fees, so he guessed the younger man blamed him for the brother's injuries; however, he could never bring himself to mention the fire. "You have had some sort of quarrel about my playing the zealous guardian?"

"It wasn't about you. It was . . . about . . . me." She buried her face in her hands, making a soft moan.

Torn more than ever with love, tenderness, pity, the Major helped her to the brass bed. When she was lying down, he said, "I'm going downstairs to write to him."

"No!"

"Nonsense. There's no spat as important as *this*, no lover's bickering. He has every right to know. My dear, the boy's gone on you. He can be a bit brusque and sometimes he's difficult to understand, but it's quite clear he's wild for you."

She was holding back her tears.

He patted her thin hand. "Don't worry about a thing. You'll see. As soon as he gets my letter he'll come running."

II

The Major, though neither cruel nor callous, was a flatly selfish man. In his life he had never put another's needs above his own. Now that he was about to do so, he made a ceremony of it. First he sent for Flaherty. "Are the streets passable?" he asked somberly.

"That they are, sir."

"Good. There's a letter I'll want delivered before luncheon."

Alone, the Major moved his chair several times to center it precisely, lined up his stationery on the blotter, staring gravely at the crested paper before writing the time and date with large, circular motions of his arm.

My Dear Bridger,
  This is the most difficult letter I have ever been called upon to compose. First, let me apologize for treating you badly in regard to my niece. My sole extenuation is that with Antonia's

*arrival a bright and lovely happiness came into my life and I
wished to keep it as long as possible. She is precious to me,
certainly, but she must be doubly dear to you.*

*And now her predicament is such that you are the one she
needs.*

*It is understandable that you might retain bitterness toward
me. No man cares to be thought unworthy of the girl he loves.
You need never see me, you may forbid her to see me. I accept
in advance any terms that you set.*

*Antonia is not penniless. Several years ago I settled twenty-
five thousand dollars on her.* [This was not yet done; however,
the Major realized that Tom would reject any currently settled
dowry.] *She refuses to part from my brother, so I trust you will
permit me to continue my financial obligations toward him.*

Coming to the bottom of the page, he blotted it carefully. As he
read it over his mouth twisted with the pain of relinquishment—and
of abasing himself. He took a fresh sheet, this time writing with
swift jabs that scattered tiny dots of ink.

*Bridger, she had no idea what was wrong with her. None.
She is utterly bewildered. Frankly, her appearance terrifies me.
Please come as soon as possible. She needs you desperately. I
am begging you—come the minute you receive this.*
> *Humbly,*
> *Andrew Stuart*
> *(Major, Michigan Cavalry)*

He folded the letter into an envelope, lighting a round taper to
melt the wax. He was pressing down his signet ring as Flaherty
knocked.

III

Antonia lay on the bed, her eyes open. Since the argument with
Tom she had been unable to sleep more than an hour or two a night,
and this lack both sharpened and dulled her thought processes. The
idea of a baby she could not grasp. To her the tiny pod that Dr.
McKenzie somehow discerned was beyond comprehension.

As usual she was going over the argument. A healthy brain in recollection simultaneously grapples myriad impressions. Antonia's mind was not in a normal state. Her memory of the scene was pinned as if by a thrown dagger to that moment when he had said, *You sicken me. . . .*

She grimaced. She could hear her heart beating and dragging a little in the beat.

Tom, in his own misery, had found Antonia's most vulnerable spot.

Already she had worried about the physical dimension of her love. From her reading she had learned the prevalent attitude that only low, debased women enjoyed love's carnal aspects (a bride's surrender of virginity was novelistically euphemized as the "great white sacrifice"), and now with cringing self-loathing she would count the ways that she had touched him and let him touch her, kissed and been kissed in secret parts of the body, and had involuntarily cried his name as ecstasy shook her. Worse yet, these humiliating reminiscences still caused faint twinges of desire in her pelvis.

No wonder I sicken him, she thought. Suddenly she jerked up on her elbow as though awakening from a nightmare. *The letter*, she thought. *If he comes when he gets Uncle's letter, it means he loves me enough to overlook how I am. If he comes, it means he's not utterly repulsed.* In her precarious mental state the logic was irrefutable.

Energy pulsed through her. She began dressing. She had difficulty drawing on her white silk stockings, and did not notice her camisole was inside out. She forgot her underpetticoat. Her hands shook as she put up her hair, the comb dropped, hairpins showered. She let the glossy black mass hang over her shoulders.

If he comes, she thought, *if he comes*.

She ran downstairs, her eyes glittering with the fevered excitement of a gambler placing his last chip on the roulette table.

IV

Tom struck the match, the little blue head flared, and he passed the flame inside the stove to touch crumpled paper and kindling. Hugh watched, blinking rapidly until Tom closed the black iron door on the fire.

The right side of Hugh's face was a clear pink, smooth as a baby's bottom and as hairless. This morning after the bandaging had been hurtfully peeled off, Dr. McKenzie had reassured him that the discoloration would fade, the lashes and brows would grow in, as would the incipient beard.

The left side, however, was shades darker. A hard shell of discoloration spreading from below his jawbone to his hairline and from his ear (which was now a knob) to his well-chiseled nose. The scar tissue was ropy, drawing up the mouth. This damage was permanent.

Tom asked, "Hungry?"

"Not very," Hugh said.

"Want me to heat Mrs. Trelinack's stew for lunch?"

"Eggs are enough."

"Ham?" Tom asked.

"No thanks."

A knock sounded. Hugh stared around, terrified.

Tom was opening the window to take the food from the screened box on the ledge. "Get that, Hugh, will you." But Hugh was scuttling into the narrow bedroom, closing the door after him.

Tom answered.

Flaherty held out an envelope. Tom snatched it. He was hoping—praying would be a more correct terminology—that Antonia had written to him.

He lived in constant horror at the lying obscenities he had shouted at her. Several times he had boarded the Woodward Avenue trolley, only to jump off at the next stop. After her rejection he could not be first to break the silence. Despairing and hopeful at the same time, he waited for her to give some sign, however infinitesimal, so that he could apologize.

Recognizing the Major's bold writing, his eyes narrowed.

"The Major wants yer reply," Flaherty said. "Shall I be waiting here?"

"Downstairs." Tom slammed the door. His clippers were on the table, and using one blade, he cut the envelope, jerking out the triple-folded paper.

"Gone?" Hugh called.

"Yes."

Hugh opened the door. "Who was it?"

"Stuart's coachman, with this. The Major wants an answer."

"Then he'll be back? The coachman?"

Tom saw the anxiety on the right side of his brother's face, the warped grimace on the left. "It's all right, Hugh. He's outside."

Hugh came back into the room. "Aren't you going to read it?"

"Why? There's only one answer for the old bastard."

Using his clippers, he cut the unfolded linen paper in half.

Hugh laughed sharply. "Right," he said.

Tom cut again, shoving the unread pieces inside the envelope.

"That should give him the general gist," Tom said.

Two children watched awed from a window as their neighbor left tracks in the fresh snow to thrust something at the liveried coachman in the lacquered carriage.

V

Antonia pushed the courses of her lunch around various plates, talking animatedly. When they returned to the study, she continued the same meaningless conversation. Hooves and pneumatic tires crunched over the snow and she fell silent, bending her head so that the mass of straight, shining black hair shadowed her haggard face.

Flaherty knocked.

The Major, seeing his own envelope, said hastily, "Thank you, Flaherty. That'll be all." Closing the door, he said to Antonia, "Another bit of that wearisome insurance business. What a relief it'll be when that's behind me." He slipped the envelope in a desk pigeonhole.

Antonia retrieved it. He moved to take it from her, but the glitter in her eyes made him hesitate.

"You wrote Tom's name," she said, pulling out a scrap.

"Oh, my God," said the Major. "My dear, let me throw that away."

She stared at him. Afraid to touch her, he watched her nervous fingers piece together the sheet. As she bent over, reading, her hands arched up. A long ago memory came to the Major: Wounded at Gettysburg, he had been carried to a crowded hospital tent, and the young lieutenant next to him had arched his hands this same way, clawing the earth in his death agonies.

Antonia looked up, a frown etching her forehead.

"Uncle, when we were talking about Father and me leaving, did I say Rheims or Canterbury?" she asked in a rapid, high-pitched voice.

"Newport," he said.

"Newport?" She circled the desk and paced up and back on the Shirvan rug. "How odd. How very odd. There's no cathedral in Newport. That's his interest. Gothic cathedrals. Uncle, here he has nothing to occupy his mind. Now if we were in Europe . . . He was so enthusiastic about the choir screen at Chartres—he spent two full days examining the carving. Once he's involved again, it's only a matter of time until he's fully recovered. He planned a visit to Turkey—or was it Russia? What's today?"

"Wednesday."

"We'll take the train Friday morning. That gives me this afternoon and tomorrow to pack and book steamship tickets. Uncle, can Nurse Girardin stay in her room until she finds another position? I'm sure it won't take her long. She's very qualified. You've been so wonderful to us that I hate to keep imposing, but you don't mind, do you? We'll go to Chartres first. The trunks can follow us. I'll be able to handle everything until Father recovers."

"Antonia, my dear, do stop walking around. Sit here, on the couch," he said, his voice breaking.

"Not to Paris, though. That would remind him of his illness."

"Your condition—"

"Condition? Dr. McKenzie said something about a baby, didn't he? But he was mistaken. That man's an incompetent! I'm sorry, Uncle. I know he's your friend. But it's true. Look at how he's bungled Father's case. Altering his habits, keeping him housebound. No wonder Father's not himself! What do you think?"

"Well . . ."

"And don't you agree that my taking him to Europe is best?"

"We'll discuss it with Dr. McKen—"

"That quack!"

"So that he can consult with Dr. Abler in Chicago," soothed the Major, turning, hoping she would not notice the tears in his eyes. "I'll telephone him right away."

By three fifteen, when McKenzie arrived, Antonia's voice was hoarse from planning itineraries. The doctor maneuvered her upstairs. Her overwrought, overtired brain fought his laudanum, and he ended up giving her a far larger dose than he considered safe for anyone, much less a pregnant woman. When, finally, she slept, the two men discussed the feasibility of travel.

"For your brother, poor devil, it doesn't matter. But that bewildered child can't stay in Detroit."

"By God, I'd like Bridger's hide!"

"And to think that I *encouraged* him. Of course, I had no idea you didn't want it, Andrew. She was lonely, and he was your partner. He *seemed* decent. Usually I'm a fair judge of character."

"I begged him to come to her—begged." The Major's voice shook, and to control himself he looked out at the sparse snowflakes drifting in the early dusk.

"The boy's a monster! How he pulled the wool over my eyes."

The Major sighed. "What was all that agitation about dragging poor Oswald around Europe?"

"It's a mental trick that we all use to a lesser degree. Throw ourselves into something else in order to avoid the unbearable." The doctor took out his small notebook, scribbling. "I'll arrange for an orderly to travel with your brother. Girardin will have her hands full with Antonia."

"This, uhh, disturbance, it's temporary, isn't it?"

"In my opinion, yes. But the other—she's far too thin and rundown. She needs the best of care. I'll give Girardin instructions. Where do you plan to take her?"

"London seems the easiest."

The doctor tore out a page, writing carefully. "Here's the name of a top man on Harley Street."

That same evening the Major sent for his attorney, three property brokers, and an auctioneer, arranging to divest himself of the factory property, this house, a tract of timberland he owned near Pontiac. He never ceased seeing those thin, arching hands, yet his very real anguish for Antonia did not prevent him from conferring briskly, quite himself again. In his heart he admitted that leaving Detroit suited him to a tee. That insurance investigation had roused a malicious hive of gossip among his friends.

CHAPTER 8

SOCIAL NOTE

Major A. Stuart departed today for an extended tour of the
continent of Europe. Sympathizers hope that the journey will
help him to recover from the tragic loss by fire of the Stuart
Furniture Company, long a Detroit landmark. He was accompanied by his brother, Mr. O. Dalzell, and by his niece, Miss
Dalzell. Major Stuart will be greatly missed by his numerous
friends and old comrades at arms from the Michigan Cavalry.
He—

A knock interrupted Hugh as he dawdled over a late breakfast of
bread and strawberry jam. He knew it was either Mrs. Trelinack or
one of the three girls—they took turns dropping in—yet his voice
cracked anxiously as he called, "Who is it?"

"Me, Maud."

"I'm resting," Hugh said, unfastening the latch, diving toward
his pallet, angling his good profile toward the other room.

"This is on the way to the Newberrys'—today's my day there. I
thought I'd pop in," she said, putting down her basket and taking
off her coat. The bib of her black dressmaker's apron glinted with
threaded needles, and around her neat waist was a belt with a red
pincushion. She peered nearsightedly at the *Detroit Journal* as she
folded it. "So you saw that about Major Stuart?" she asked, piling
dishes to carry to the sink.

"Yes."

"One time I saw Tom leaving Hudson's with the niece. He knew her quite well, didn't he?" Maud's somewhat loud voice was pitched too high.

Hugh's head tilted. Maud was overly blunt, so why this oblique question about Tom and Antonia? It came to him with a little jolt that Maud was setting her cap for his brother. Maud? With her heavy step and appalling candor? That frugal *peasant*? "We never discussed Miss Dalzell," he said.

Nothing could deter Maud. "I did some alterations for her once. She's too tall for such a tiny waist and those narrow hips. What a lively one! It was during the war in Cuba, and she took my specs and pretended to be Colonel Roosevelt charging up San Juan Hill." Maud's brief chuckle was honest. "I never understood why the Woodward Avenue crowd were so down on her—the things they said about the Major and her! Did you hear any of that?"

"Why should I?"

"They said she was his mistress."

"She's his half brother's daughter."

"A lot of them knew that, but they still said she was."

"Nice ladies you sew for," Hugh said, his teeth gritting in a spasm. Antonia was everything Maud was not, light, joyous, well-born, tender, and he resented Maud's repeating old gossip.

"It *was* hard to believe. They're a bunch of drones, society women," Maud said. "Anyway, I liked her." There was the clink of a dish being set on marble. "I brought you a fresh-baked honey loaf. Want me to heat the coffee to go with it?"

"I'll fix fresh later."

"Hugh, there must be a half pot left!"

"Mmm," said Hugh.

"I put in two kinds of raisins."

What a shame that Mrs. Trelinack, with her light hand and lavish ways with butter, had not done the baking. "Maud, you're very good to us," Hugh said, stifling a faint sarcasm.

"Save a slice for Tom."

As soon as she left he poured the contents of the tall percolator down the sink. He felt sorry for Maud. Poor girl, with a crush on Tom. Surely all her common sense should tell her that any man involved with the scintillating, graceful girl Antonia, could never feel anything more than friendship for *her*. Yet Maud was kind. He cut a sliver of the honey loaf, and nibbling, tasted the lard.

II

After supper Tom glanced through the paper. When he came to Social Notes, beads of sweat broke out on his face and his lips moved convulsively. The item had the casual, bloodless finality of a death certificate. She was gone, gone with no word to him, not even a brief note, gone as companion to his enemy. Never, never would he receive permission to kneel and beg her forgiveness.

He thrust the newspaper in the stove, watching it curl and bubble into cinders. He flung open the cupboard, reaching for the nearly full fifth of rye.

He drank until he was sodden. Hugh led him to his mattress, placing a folded towel under his head in case he vomited, taking off his boots, covering him with the quilt, services he had performed quite a few nights these past weeks.

III

One particularly bleak Sunday toward the end of November, Trelinack came by. "The womenfolk are in church," he announced, setting down a bucket of beer, rubbing his hands to warm them. "Tom, if you don't mind my saying so, you look like hell."

"It's tough being on twenty-four-hour call," Tom lied. Having already learned the personalities of the Rice dynamo, the Armington and Sims generator, the angry, crouching Beck steam engine, he had so little to do that boredom bloated his misery. Unhooking the three mugs, he called, "Hugh, Trelinack's brought us some lager."

Hugh disdained beer as a plebeian drink. "None for me, but thanks, Trelinack," he said through the crack of the barely open door.

Trelinack poured himself a mugful. "Tom, a man asked me to put a proposition to you. He's of a mind to invest in an automobile shop."

"Did you tell him I'm through?"

"That I did. He said back that he never figured you for a quitter. And I said to him that you were badly stung by the fire."

"The fire, hell! Only an asshole wouldn't know that the automobile fad's over. Finished. Dead."

"Tom," Trelinack said quietly. "She's left Detroit."

Tom's fist slammed down. Beer sloshed on marble.

"Hit *me*," Trelinack said. "If it'll make you feel better, hit me. But that won't alter the facts. Blood sticks to blood, and she's left with her own people. So you might as well settle down to picking up the pieces of your life."

"You should have gone with the others. Church is the place for sermons."

"I'm a man of my word," said Trelinack, fishing in his vest pocket.

"How many times do I have to say it? No fucking more toys for rich men!"

"It's a good thing we're friends, Tom, or I could take offense at your mouth." Trelinack set down a folded sheet of yellow paper.

Hugh listened to them, the angelic side of his face, the right, broodingly intent. The skin was normal, freshly shaved, the lashes and brows growing in. He was healthy enough, strong enough, to get the white-collar job that his high school diploma entitled him to. Accordingly, a week before that he had set out with a clipped advertisement for an opening with the Soames Importing Company in the Hammond Building. That fifteen-minute walk was Hugh's Gethsemane. People had either stared at him or looked away. After years of pleasure at unearned admiration, he had been stunned by the pain of equally unearned revulsion. At each passerby's examination his body quivered, and this sensation was as horrible as the remembered anguish of his burns. He never had reached the Hammond Building. After seven blocks he had raced back to the flat. *I can't bear the stares*, he had thought, knowing that this cowardice had imprisoned him. He was in for life. And as long as Tom remained in a mechanic's job, he'd be stuck in drab living quarters.

When Trelinack closed the front door, Hugh pushed slowly to his feet. *Go carefully*, he told himself. *You'll probably never have another chance*. He entered the other room.

"Aren't you going to take a look?" he asked, picking up the yellow paper.

A check fell from its folds.

"Tom. Look!" Hugh's surprise was unfeigned. "A thousand dollars made out to you! Signed John Trelinack."

Without a word Tom snatched the check, folding it into his pocket, yanking his heavy jacket from its hook behind the door.

"Where are you going?" Hugh asked.

"The sooner this gets back to Trelinack, the better."

"It *is* a lot of money," Hugh said, judiciously pruning his tone of everything except warm friendship for Trelinack. "He must have mortgaged his house. Can you imagine that kind of trust?"

Tom halted at the door. "What does his note say?"

Hugh opened the letter. " 'John Trelinack backs Thomas K. Bridger to the amount of one thousand dollars in exchange for ten percent of any profits in the Bridger Automobile Company.' Tom, the Major didn't put up any cash, and *he* took a quarter."

Tom shook his head, his expression mingling affection and dismay. He cleared his throat. "I was pretty rough to him."

"You can't just throw this back in his teeth."

"I'll wait a couple of days."

"Pretend you're considering it." Hugh reached for the check, hastily burying it amid aromatic beans in the coffee jar. "It'll be safe here."

IV

That evening Tom slicked down his hair and used his razor. Hugh guessed he was going to the Golden Age for a whore, the first time since Antonia's reign. As he slammed out the door he looked as though he were going to be punished rather than to seek enjoyment in a woman's arms. Hugh waited for five minutes before he took out his sketchbook.

"It's goddamn late," Tom said. His face red, he emanated odors of whiskey, cheap musk perfume, and sex. "What're you drawing in the middle of the night?"

Hugh turned over the pad. "Big brother, I'm old enough to draw whatever and whenever I choose."

Tom flipped over the pad. "The racer," he accused.

"What of it?"

"So long as you don't figure on talking me into anything," Tom said belligerently.

"Who do you think got burned?"

Tom sighed, shaking his head. "I didn't mean to sound off. I'm tired, that's all."

"And drunk?"

"Yeah, some. Ahh, as if boozing does any good." Tom sat at the table, burying his face in his arms. "Nothing helps, Hugh, nothing. The more I try not to think about her, the more she's on my mind." His voice was muffled.

"Would talking help?" Hugh asked with heartfelt sympathy, momentarily deflected from his course.

"I can't. Everything's so locked up and painful."

"I know what you mean." Hugh wet his lips. "That's why I was drawing the racer. To see if I could face up to things."

Tom raised his head, pointing with a dark-rimmed nail. "You got the cylinders too short."

"I did? This is what I remember."

Tom reached for the pencil, drawing. "There," he said.

A cold wind off the Detroit River rattled the windowpanes as they ate breakfast. Hugh finished his oatmeal. "Tom . . ." He hesitated. "Would the Edison hire a bookkeeper who doesn't work on the premises?"

"There's no need, Hugh," Tom said gruffly.

"What about my medical bills?"

"They're getting paid."

"It's like being a ghost! Sitting here, staring at the walls, never pulling my weight!"

Around five that afternoon the generator broke down at the Edison. It was after ten when Tom got home. Hugh slept, a magazine's triangular corner peeking out from under his mattress. Careful not to awaken his brother, Tom extricated it. An old *Horseless Age* from 1898.

Tom pinched his earlobe until it was bloodless, glancing from the magazine to his brother. He bent, poking Hugh's shoulder.

"Wha . . . Oh, Tom. You're home."

"We need to talk."

Hugh looked at the magazine and scowled. "Can't I have any privacy?"

"Trelinack's thousand, it's more cash than I've seen at one time, but even if I kept it, it wouldn't be enough." Tom's words rushed out. "Without credit backing I'm nowhere."

"Tom, just because I was reading an old magazine—"

"We both know you've been working on me since Trelinack came over yesterday," Tom said.

"I'm truly sorry, Tom, that I'm not able to be more subtle about getting you to do what you've already decided on. But at least I had the brains to figure we would start with a Curved-Dash. There's enough of them around to copy. A racer? You'll never remember how you built it. Each part was modified three times then modified again. And it cost a fortune."

"Those cylinders, I've been thinking about those cylinders. There should be four, not two." Tom's cheeks glowed from walking in frozen night air and from the ideas and visions clamoring within him. "How do I manage that financing?"

Hugh swallowed his resentment. Wasn't Tom coming around precisely as he wanted? "We could cut down."

"There's still the medical bills. And we don't exactly lie in luxury's lap."

"What if we found a shop with a room upstairs or in the back?"

"The end of double rents." Tom laughed excitedly. "Come on, Hugh, more ideas."

"Our old suppliers might trust us without a credit line. Horace and John know you pretty well." The rowdy, hot-tempered, red-headed Dodge brothers were friends of Tom's. "And how about going to the men who own Curved-Dashes and seeing if they'll buy shares?"

"You *have* been thinking. Hugh, come on, let's hammer out that agreement with Trelinack."

Hugh pulled on his overcoat and the two sat at the table, their breath showing in the chill as they argued. Tom wanted Trelinack to have twenty-five percent, while Hugh, never having intended the Cousin Jack foreman to get more than the ten he had asked for, demurred. To offer that much, he said, would be to insult a friend.

"Hugh, it's twenty-five," Tom said abruptly. "Go ahead and write it up while I fix myself some supper."

Hugh sat at the table, composing the agreement, reading the few sentences he had written aloud. " '. . . 25% (twenty-five percent) to John Trelinack. . . .' "

"It has a fine legal ring," Tom said. Then Hugh unscrewed the ink bottle to make the final draft. Though he was displeased at the amount they were giving away, he felt a peculiar lightness. It was a relief to know he could only sway Tom where Tom wished to be swayed: a boundary marker put an end to the more worrisome degrees of fraternal duplicity.

V

The next Sunday sleet hammered noisily on the rooftop and window. Just before one o'clock Trelinack lugged in a huge wicker hamper; his bundled wife and daughters followed, each carrying a basket.

The four women, uttering cries about the weather, took off their drenched outer garments. Mrs. Trelinack, a short, stocky woman with thick, wavy gray hair, had a fine fresh complexion and an air of being perpetually newly bathed. She unpacked the hamper swiftly, deprecating the golden Cornish pasties, the fat roast chicken, the fruit pies oozing richly aromatic juices, the trifle, the nuts preserved in honey. Each delicacy, made by her plump white hands, expressed her generosity.

The girls helped her. Maud. Skinny Melisande, who wore her sandy hair in elaborate thrusts copied from those girls drawn by Charles Dana Gibson. And the baby, Yseult, called Yssy (pronounced Yes-*see*), who at sixteen had attained a shelved bosom and her full height of four ten.

To avoid the feminine hubbub Tom and Trelinack retired to the hallway, which was lit by a single small window.

"I'll put in my free hours in the shop," Trelinack promised.

"All help will be appreciated."

Maud came out to stand with them. "Pa. If Yssy and Melisande would help me with the basting and pressing, we could put in more cash."

"Miss Maud Trelinack, Miss Bossy Maud Trelinack," boomed her father.

"The more money the shop has, the better," she pointed out.

"The day I take help from my womenfolk, that's the day I lie down and die."

"Trelinack. Maud," called Mrs. Trelinack. "What is it now?"

"This lass of yours," said Trelinack, hugging his favorite child's trim waist.

Mrs. Trelinack called, "Stop your bickering and come open the brandy."

Trelinack went into the flat. Tom was about to follow, but Maud said, "Tom?"

"What ho?"

"I have a hundred and twenty-three dollars saved on my own. I'd like to invest with you."

Touched, Tom swallowed a lump in his throat. "Why, thank you, honey. But I can't let you do that." His mind switched to another time, Antonia offering him her pearls, her bar pin.

Maud watched his lips part and his expression soften, then grow bleak. She sighed. Her absolute candor left no room for ambiguities, and since she could not know what Tom was thinking, why should she have this attack of sadness? Why this increased consciousness of being an also-ran? *He calls me honey, doesn't he?*

"You're taking in others," she said.

"Maud, you worked very hard for that money."

"I'm a believer."

Tom felt his cheeks grow hot.

Mrs. Trelinack called, "We're ready."

"I don't have any doubts, Tom. Not a one."

After a long pause he shook her short, wide hand. "Partners," he said.

She smiled her frank, open smile, and they joined the others at the laden table.

Trelinack poured his wife's homemade peach brandy into the Bridgers' assortment of chipped tumblers, mugs, and a mason jar. Raising the jar, he said, "To the Bridger Automobile Company."

"No," Tom said sharply.

"What?" Trelinack asked.

"An unlucky name," Tom said.

"I have my drink raised, Tom, and that's one thing you cannot do to a Cousin Jack, stop him in the middle of a toast. Pick another name."

"Onyx," Hugh said from the bedroom doorway.

"What was that?" Tom asked.

"Onyx," Hugh repeated.

He had thought much about the new car's name, and had decided that Curved-Dash Bridger sounded lumbering and heavy. He had looked up the word *onyx* in his dictionary. It was an agate, a variety of quartz. People thought of it as a jewel, yet it was not too precious or rarified. *Onyx* was a strong word, *Onyx* was an interesting word that would look well affixed to a brass radiator.

"Onyx . . ." Tom said. "Yes, it has a ring."

"Then I give you the Onyx Automobile Company," boomed Trelinack.

The others echoed, "The Onyx Automobile Company." The sound reverberated around the shabby room. "To the Onyx Automobile Company."

BOOK TWO
The Fiver

The Fiver was an instant success. Years ahead of its time and priced at the bottom of the low-price field, it had innovations galore.

The Model Five Onyx, A Look at the Changes in an Unchanging Car by Bruce McCalley

CHAPTER 9

At the turn of the century the automotive industry was an explosive burst, atoms whirling in a vacuum without a solar system. Onyx was only one of the hundreds of small shops in various parts of the country, manufacturers that for the most part trickled out a machine or two, then folded.

On April 4, 1900, Tom climbed from his four-cylinder racer, oil blackening him from the top rim of his goggles to the soles of his boots, recognizable only by his uneven white grin. His time on the one-mile track was 5:28 for five laps, less than 1:06 per mile, the new American record.

Two days later he and Maud stood up together, a double wedding with plump little Yssy Trelinack and Rogers Sinclair, who was a salesman for Eclipse bicycles. Few Americans had seen an automobile, and at the beginning it was only because of Tom's racing fame that Rogers could convince the bicycle dealers in his territory to take on his brother-in-law's machines. The first four models of Onyx were the most reliable automobiles on the market, and among the cheapest, from $650 to $870. Onyx, like Marmon, Cadillac, Buick, Franklin, Wayne, Packard, Maxwell, Ford, Olds, was a still-nebulous star in the automotive void.

Then, in 1907, Tom unveiled his Onyx 5 at the Detroit Auto Show.

The Fiver . . .

An odd, high-bodied little terrier with a brass radiator that gleamed like a healthy nose, big round acetylene eyes, a gamely sturdy engine that snapped and barked up the steepest mountains. The Fiver had her peculiarities and you better learn them: She kicked out when you cranked her on cold mornings, and to learn when she thirsted for oil you had to crawl underneath and fiddle with two pet cocks. Once you were her master, though, she repaid you with endless loyalty. She bounced over the worst roads—and American roads *were* the worst. In emergencies, or so owners swore, she grumbled along without gasoline. She came with a year's guarantee, unprecedented in the dubious business, and her parts were interchangeable (a revolutionary idea of Tom's) and easy to replace. The breed had no vanity. Roadsters, touring cars, runabouts, and delivery wagons alike had the same chassis and wore the same dull, very dark gray. Onyx gray.

Her chief virtue was her humbleness.

That first model cost $465.

That spring of 1907 farmers, doctors, shopkeepers—ordinary people who never dreamed they could afford the luxury of an automobile—lined up in windstorms and torrential rains to buy a Fiver. The success was unbelievable, even to Tom. Orders continued flooding in, and he hired Albert Kahn, the industrial architect, to plan a factory with sawtooth glass roofs, and here he synchronized thousands of employees with a fortune in machine tooling.

Over this airy expanse, as over the still operating earlier plant, hung a sword of Damocles, poised to destroy.

The Selden patent case.

II

In 1879, George B. Selden, a Rochester, New York, attorney, had filed a patent application for a gasoline-powered road vehicle, delaying its issuance by filing additions and changes. Not until 1895 did he obtain a patent for his carriage. He claimed that every automobile manufactured or sold during the seventeen-year life of his patent must be licensed by him. At first the men laughed in their automobile shops. Who was this Selden? Why, the man never had even built a machine! But then Selden sued Alexander Winton of Cleveland for infringement. The judge, who knew little of patents and—understandably—nothing of automobiles, declared Selden's patent valid. As is often the case when men are shocked into fear, the herd instinct took over, and like sheep they rushed to join Selden's

Association of Licensed Automobile Manufacturers. ALAM. Once securely penned, they saw the advantages. ALAM could set production limits, could fix prices. ALAM was a monopoly. A trust. Hooray!

In early 1902 a delegation arrived at Tom's new plant on Rock Avenue to explain the association's advantages. Tom told them, "I'm in this to bring prices down so everyone can buy."

"That's insane. If we put an end to destructive competition, if the industry regulates itself, every shop in ALAM will survive."

"I don't believe in patents or monopolies."

"You're going to have to join, Bridger. And in the long run you'll see, Selden's patent is the best thing for all of us."

Tom lost his temper. "You can take that damn patent and shove it!" he shouted, and ordered them off his property.

ALAM told Henry Ford that any application for his shaky new company would be looked upon unfavorably.

On October 22, 1903, Selden, through ALAM, filed suit against Onyx and the Ford Motor Company. To lose meant that the two then-struggling little companies would have to ante up ruinous penalties on each car they had already built. It meant bankruptcy. Going broke did not frighten Tom—he had been there before. But not to make cars? Never to attain his dream, the universal transportation?

The legal battle moved with glacial slowness.

In September 1909 the blow fell.

Judge Charles M. Hough of the federal court for southern New York State upheld the Selden patent.

Tom Bridger and Henry Ford had remained outwardly cordial to each other, yet the inevitable comparisons of the Model T to the Fiver had sapped the old friendship. The two were photographed, grim and stiff together, as they promised to battle ALAM—the automotive trust, they called it. They hired a fresh battalion of lawyers to appeal the decision.

III

Hugh had never recovered from his horror of himself.

When Onyx had begun to prosper and the two brothers had for the first time in their lives money, a lot of it, Hugh had built a Tudor manor house on an isolated tract bordering Lake St. Clair beyond Grosse Pointe Shores. Surrounding his estate was a ten-foot brick wall topped with iron spikes. And he had left the original stands of timber to further hide his domain. He kept to his acreage, seen by nobody but his servants, his two secretaries, and the family. Yet in March 1910, when Mitchell Polhemus telephoned for an appointment, Hugh unhesitatingly invited him to the house. Mitchell Polhemus was chief counsel for Selden and ALAM.

Hugh received the lawyer in his office, a long oak-paneled room with clerestory windows designed so that sunlight never hit the Elizabethan table he used as a desk. In front of him were three telephones, the means through which he ruled Onyx's accounting, public relations, and advertising departments.

The fact that Mitchell Polhemus was a hunchback made Hugh feel more comfortable than he might have, yet he remained in the shadows and spoke stiffly.

"Mr. Polhemus, you take me by surprise. Hearing from the enemy camp! Dare I hope you're bearing an olive branch?"

"I'm here on behalf of another client," replied Mitchell Polhemus. "Mr. Bridger, let me get right to the point. My client has blueprints for automotive inventions that predate Selden's patent—"

"*What?*"

"—and they are to be offered to you."

In his shocked surprise Hugh found himself mouthing irrelevancies. "Isn't this a conflict of interest for you?"

"My clients accept that I have a large and catholic legal practice."

Hugh clasped his fingers, trying to sound judicious. "How much must we pay?"

"There are two conditions. Neither has to do with money."

"Mr. Polhemus, everything has to do with money."

The lawyer's pale, wrinkled face contorted into a smile. "Not for this client," he said warmly.

"Tell me the conditions, then."

"First, you must never for any reason contact my client."

"At the risk of sounding moronic, I don't understand."

"It's quite simple. My client doesn't wish to be involved."

"Agreed. No contact." Hugh shook his head. "We've had teams of attorneys here and in Europe. How could such important patents have been missed?"

"They were missed because they were never filed. I was given orders not to file."

Hugh nodded. "Who was the inventor?"

Polhemus did not answer the question. "The plans, never having been filed, have no legal validity. They cannot supersede the Selden patent."

"I understand that. But I'm sure *you* understand just how important this evidence could be to our appeal," Hugh said, and repeated, "Who was the inventor?"

"They were to be filed in the name of Andrew Stuart."

-The words sank as if into a nest of cotton. A thick, smothering silence that made breathing difficult. The left telephone rang, and the lawyer glanced expectantly at it then at Hugh. There was no further ring: the house had been installed with elaborate wiring that enabled the secretaries in their office to answer any ring. Hugh finally spoke. "He gave them to you?"

"He came to Washington with various drawings in the years between 1895 and 1899. After that he never communicated with me. And now he never will."

Hugh interrupted. "The Major's dead?"

"A year ago last August."

The scar tissue appeared to darken as the right side of Hugh's face paled. A shock rushed through him, catching at his lungs, a paroxysm that strained his chest muscles, drawing raspy coughs. To hide his distress he pushed to his feet, moving to the filing cabinets that were built into the wall and skillfully veneered with the same antique oak as the paneling. The dark old wood blurred in front of his eyes. *No*, he thought, *no. He can't be dead. I won't have him dead. It's not fair*. Hugh had spent countless hours planning methods of revenge, bankrupting the Major, paying one of the servants to administer tormenting drugs of slow-acting poison, not the usual puffed-hot fantasies but carefully worked-out means. He had held back not out of moral nicety but out of fear he wasn't yet powerful enough. A grieving fury chilled him, and he coughed into his handkerchief.

"Mr. Bridger, can I help you?"

"Asthma," Hugh gasped. When he was able to speak, he asked, "Who is your client, then?"

"Major Stuart's niece, his heiress."

Antonia? Hugh ricocheted through a decade into that cold morning when, in pain but not yet aware of his full torment, he had awoken to hear Tom's fury gusting like the wind and Antonia's soft replies. Tom never mentioned her name, but Tom had become Hugh's life, and he was fully aware that though his brother cared warmly for Maud, his capacity for romantic love was locked with Antonia in the dungeon of the past. Tom's calumnies must have stabbed her as deeply as he had pierced himself. Ten years of silence, and then this help? What did it mean? Hugh took a deep, wheezing breath. "Isn't she aware what she has? I'd pay, and so would the Selden people. A fortune, conservatively."

"I advised her of the value." Again Mitchell Polhemus made that rusty smile of warmth. "A most unusual lady. She's convinced that the plans belonged neither to her uncle nor herself."

Hugh sat down again. "Mr. Polhemus, you said there was a second condition."

"That Thomas Bridger never learn the plans came through her."

So Tom was no careless memory to her. "The Major steals Tom's brainchildren, the niece returns them. How am I meant to hide that?"

"Your reputation, Mr. Bridger, your reputation. I've heard that you're singularly brilliant at unearthing information."

The remark was intended as a compliment, and normally Hugh would have accepted it as that. But in the throes of his peculiar subverted grief for the Major, beset by old questions, attempting to fight off an asthma attack, he asked himself how it was that he who had spent his years advancing Tom, he who was desirous only of his brother's good, had earned a reputation as Tom's dark angel, a snoop. "I won't tell him."

"I have your word?"

"I'll obey both of the lady's conditions."

"There's a crate filled with the papers. My chief clerk himself will bring them to Detroit."

Hugh saw his visitor to the front door, then rushed up to his rooms. His black valet, medically trained, administered a soothing hypodermic.

IV

He was completely recovered by seven thirty. The family was invited to dinner, and Hugh—tall, slim, elegant in his evening clothes, his new diamond studs glinting—awaited them in the drawing room. The high, interlaced wood ceiling had been inspired by

Knole in England, plushy red velvet curtains covered numerous leaded windows, the paintings were softly wrinkled with age, the bowls of chrysanthemums aromatic, the needlepoint sofas many. All in all the setting for large, convivial groups. Hugh recalled his youthful dreams of lavish entertaining. *My social life turned out simple, thanks to the deceased Major,* he thought, his hand shaking a little as he inserted a black Sobranie into an amber holder, then the favorable comparison of the size and aristocratic harmony of this house to the chateau on Woodward restored his satisfaction.

Rain hushed the purr of the Trelinacks' Daimler, and the first Hugh knew of their arrival was the sound of the butler opening the front door.

Trelinack's powerful muscles had slackened to fat, and his cheerful face blossomed an alarming purple over his tight wing collar. When he had suffered his heart attack two years earlier, he had begged Tom to buy him out. Tom had paid him four times what he asked, and now the Cousin Jack was an unlikely millionaire. Mrs. Trelinack's thick hair was completely white, her royal-blue satin bosom adorned by a sapphire and diamond necklace, yet despite these changes she retained that fresh look of recently having bathed herself in a farmhouse copper tub.

Greeting anyone, even these kindly, simple old people, made Hugh a trifle uneasy, and he gulped down the sherry his English butler offered. Rogers and Yssy Sinclair arrived next. They had four sons and Yssy was pregnant again. Rogers towered over his plump little wife, a beefy man with the broad smile of a successful salesman. Melisande and Olaf Baardson swept up in their Pierce-Arrow. Olaf, Norwegian born, a handsome six four, had been Tom's first pattern-maker, though whenever this was mentioned, Melisande changed the subject. They had one child, and Melisande insisted that it was for this quiet, pale little girl's future rather than her own social aspirations that she endured the rigors of summering in Newport.

Rogers was in charge of sales, Olaf superintendent of the Rock Avenue plant, and the two began talking Onyx. Mrs. Trelinack, Yssy, and Melisande discussed the doings of the children while Trelinack, confused by his retired status, bumbled between the men and women like a big bee lost from its hive. Hugh, as was his habit, watched from the depths of his wing chair, aware of the glancing around, the air of incompletion, as though the evening were not yet begun.

It was nearly eight, the inviolable dinner hour, when into the sound of rain came the putt-pop barking of a Fiver. The women patted their fur-trimmed dinner gowns, Rogers and Olaf straightened, on the ready to rise, and Trelinack, already on his feet, was all but standing at attention. The involuntary respect made Hugh smile. Yet he himself was hurrying to the door to meet the latecomers.

Tom's brown hair had a premature sprinkle of white, and the lines of his mordant smile were deep cut around his eyes and mouth. Maud was still handsome, but her frank chestnut-brown eyes were permanently magnified by the gold-rimmed spectacles that she now needed full time. The decade, however, had pressed more lightly on their appearances than those of the others. *They don't need to change,* Hugh had once decided, *the world recognizes their invisible crowns.* Recently, however, he had modified this opinion. Tom and Maud Bridger were formed of incorruptible elements that neither money nor power nor time could corrode.

Clinging to Tom's hand was Caryll.

Amid the adults the child looked very small, younger than his age, which was six. His starched collar extended over the lapels of his Norfolk jacket, his black stockings were pulled neatly under his short trousers, a lovingly turned-out child who resembled both parents. Tom's gray eyes shone in Maud's round face.

"Well, Caryll," Hugh said.

Hesitatingly, the child came to him, giving him a peck on the right cheek, a timid kiss. His uncle would have empathized with the boy's shyness—had it not extended to himself. Hugh's shrewdness about human motives had one dangerous blind spot. He attributed every reaction he aroused to his maroon disfigurement. *Why do they have to drag the child everywhere?* he thought irritably, and without realizing it, grimaced.

Caryll pulled away. "Uncle Hugh," he mumbled. "I made you something."

"That was good of you, Caryll."

"I put it with Mother's present," Caryll said, retreating to Tom, who took him on his lap.

V

Hugh had seated Maud to his right, and over the bluepoints, he said, "Caryll mentioned making me a present."

"He found a photograph of five camels and a Fiver on the Sahara Desert, and it tickled him. He cut it out of the magazine and glued it on cardboard. I left it on the hall table with some books I've finished."

"That's very kind of you both," he said. *With all her money,* he thought, *she could buy me new ones. She's as tight as ever.* Yet he was also recognizing that he would enjoy her used books: Maud read voraciously and passed on to him what most pleased her.

Hugh tried, unsuccessfully, to rouse some lively talk as the family ate their way through the oysters, rich and dark terrapin soup, lobster basket, saddle of lamb with chestnut puree and asparagus that were delicate white because Hugh's gardeners had piled earth around their growing spears, a salad of grapefruit and oranges shipped by train from a special grove near Riverside in California, blue raspberries, a snowy mountain of vanilla mousse. The two parlor maids served the food while Larkin poured Château Latour, Moët & Chandon brut, Clos de Vougeot.

The women returned to the drawing room, Caryll drowsing in his grandmother's arms where he had been since the lamb.

Hugh, host extraordinaire, pressed cigars and brandy on the men before saying to his brother, "Could you come into my office for a minute. There's something I want to show you."

The two crossed the hall, and Tom dropped into the chair opposite the Elizabethan table. "What a day," he sighed. Even in weariness there was a tension, a vitality to the lean body. "At four this morning I got a call from the Hamtramck"—he was completing a vast new factory complex in this township, an enclave of Polish labor surrounded by Detroit—"that the new radiator conveyor belt had broken down. Christ! I want it to be right before I go to England."

"I had a visitor this afternoon."

"You?"

"Mitchell Polhemus came to see me."

Tom jerked straight. *"Polhemus?* He came all the way to Detroit? What did he want? To tell us to lie down and die?"

"As a matter of fact he's on to something that should help us."

"Come off it, Hugh. I'm too tired for your games."

"During most of the '90s a client sent him automotive blueprints. None were filed, but they'd be an enormous boost to our side."

"How do we get them?"

"Polhemus says they belong to you."

"Me?" The gray eyes narrowed, the jaw clenched shut in a piercing expression that caused Onyx executives to shiver. "You're telling me that the Major stole my inventions?"

"A kinder word is borrowed," Hugh said sourly.

"He knew I despised patents! So he filed them himself, the lying, thieving, arsonist old prick!"

"We can have the blueprints on one condition."

"Well?"

"We must never contact Polhemus's client."

"*That*," Tom snorted, "he has my word on."

Hugh felt the warmth of a well-maneuvered victory. "So at last we have something to impress the Appeals Circuit. Now go on home and get some sleep."

VI

The house, like the others lining Chandler Avenue, was red brick with a square patch of lawn. A green tile roof peaked above the second floor with its three bedrooms and the one bathroom that the three Bridgers shared with the French-Canadian hired girl. The rest of the family, embarrassed that their new homes were far more opulent, grumbled out of Tom and Maud's earshot that the couple owed it to Onyx not to live so humbly. Maud, though, had gotten a bargain in this sturdy house, and Tom had turned the stable into a satisfactory garage. Neither considered moving.

Tom went to put away the Fiver. After he had pushed the garage doors shut, he stared up at the sky. The rain had stopped an hour ago, and the half-moon rode between filmy, silvery clouds, a cold, sharply romantic night when the opaque shadows were haunting mysteries. Tom's brief spurt of rage at the Major's perfidy had evaporated, and he was left, inevitably, with Antonia. His mind hazed, for how can one remember ecstasy or pain? He could no longer swear whether she had been lovely or too thin with odd features, for with the years she had become less of a person than textures, a swiftly eager movement, the silken feel of inner thigh, the sound of irrepressible laughter, the shiver of joy on his skin.

Wet lilacs spread their perfume, so sweet that tears came into his eyes. *Antonia . . .* Was there any regret like the regret for a lost world?

"Tom?" his wife called from an upstairs window.

"Here, honey."

"Caryll's waiting."

The little boy was in bed, his washed face raised expectantly. This was their ritual. Whenever Tom was home at Caryll's bedtime—and he always tried to be—he shared his day's happenings. Tonight he talked about the foul-up with the conveyor that he'd designed to carry finished radiators from the second-floor shop where they were built down to the enormous hall where Fivers were assembled.

"Father," Caryll said. "I've been thinking. Can't you make some red?"

"The radiators?"

"No, the cars."

"Why?"

"Red looks pretty with dark colors like Onyx gray."

"We have to make them alike, Caryll, so they can be cheap enough for everyone to own one."

"It was just an idea," said the child quickly, placatingly.

"I want your ideas," Tom said, hugging his son's thin, supple body, cupping the curve of skull, abode of numberless questions and thoughts. Again the intensity of his emotions brought him near to tears. "Tell you what," he said into the soft brown hair. "Saturday we'll go to Hamtramck together. Those radiators dangling along overhead are quite a sight."

Caryll lay back in his pillow, smiling into eyes that were the clear gray of his own. Tom kissed him good night.

Maud's glossy braids hung over her blue flannel robe as she sat at her desk entering numbers into the book where she kept track of her smallest expenditure. She stopped writing as Tom closed the bedroom door. "What was that with Hugh?" she asked.

"He discovered some plans of mine tucked away." Tom sat to unlace his shoes. Close as he felt toward Maud, he could tell her no more. Those purloined plans were entwined with Antonia.

"Will they help the appeal?"

"I'll say!"

"Isn't that the end?" Maud took off the robe. Her silk and wool nightgown showed womanly curves, the frank pressure of large, round nipples. "Onyx spends a fortune on lawyers but Hugh digs up the important evidence." She climbed into the sturdy walnut bed, setting her glasses on the table. "Good night, dear."

Tom slept naked, and after he undressed and turned out the light, he curled against her warm back, kissing her shoulder, tracing her firm, ample breasts through the soft fabric. Her nightgown and the linen smelled faintly of sachet, the scent of their marital nights.

"Oh, Tom," she sighed. "I thought you were tired."

"It's been a long time. . . ." His hand moved downward. Gentle, encouraging, a supplicant.

She shifted. "All right, if you want."

"Don't you ever want, honey?"

"It's different for a woman," she said.

For once Tom wished his wife had compromised her honesty. His mind flashed to that summer when emotions had poured from her like liquid gold. Ashamed that his erection was for a different time, another woman, he rolled onto his other side.

"Tom, you're always a romantic about it. Turn around. It doesn't bother me."

"Bother?"

"Melisande and Yssy both hate it."

"You mean you discuss our private—"

"No," she said. "*They* do. Women talk, Tom, they talk. Melisande says it's a horrible mess and she always bathes right after. And Yssy says it usually hurts but she puts up with Rogers because she wants more children. A little girl. I hope she gets one this time."

Was it his imagination or had her voice wavered in the dark? When Caryll was born the doctor had stopped a hemorrhage and there would be no other children for them. In a hidden crevice of his mind Tom regretted this bitterly. He reached for Maud's hand. "Honey, I'm sorry."

But Maud was too practical to grieve over never-to-be-born children. "I have everything I ever wanted. You. Caryll. This house." She touched his arm. "Tom . . . ?"

"It's all right, honey."

"Good night, then, dear."

Tomorrow, he decided, *I'll go to lunch at the Pontchartrain.* The automotive men drank at the green marble bar of the Pontchartrain Hotel, they ate in the dining room and drew carburetors, gears, transmissions, on the white damask tablecloths, and afterward some of them would head for a two-story house several blocks away, excursions that did not brush Tom with guilt. The casually bought, unsatisfactory sex had nothing to do with Maud, who was his best friend.

Her breath lengthened.

Sleep eluded Tom. His nights had become insomniac with worrying about the appeal. If they lost, he would be ordered to fork over ruinous royalties, money he did not have. Though he gave huge annual bonuses to executives and generous ones to his workers, he took very little out of the business himself. Hugh was forever nagging at him to put aside massive sums for the contingency of losing. Caution was impossible for Tom. Like a drunk, like a God-possessed saint, he had no control. His goals shimmered eternally ahead of him, and he plowed back his profits.

Pulling on his robe, feeling his way down the stairs to the sitting room, he stretched out on the sofa. How many nights had he lain here brooding about those black-robed judges with their calm, unrelenting faces? What would they decide?

The windows were growing light when he finally slept. He dreamed he was in that clearing, green shadows of the sycamore dappling Antonia's luminous white body as she held out her arms to him, a tenderly erotic invitation. "Ahh, Tom," she murmured. "How I've missed you. . . ." The dream, like all his dreams of her, was colored with an intensity that tied every detail to his soul, and his possession of her was so real that he awoke with a harsh, triumphant cry. The embarrassing thing that happens to adolescent boys had happened to him.

VII

Hugh sat back in his office chair, frowning at the single page that had come from the envelope marked *Personal and Confidential.*

Hugh had gravitated quite naturally to snooping.

Rogers Sinclair was in charge of sales, but Rogers was a salesman, a glad hand with no fine touch, and certain early Onyx dealers had been deadbeats, swindlers, and in one publicized case, a bigamist. Hugh had therefore hired a two-man team of traveling detectives to check out every dealership candidate. The reports, a lifetime of intricate secrets, had proved heady reading for the recluse. From time to time his investigatory probing ran far afield from dealerships, and on these occasions he retained a New York firm.

It was their London correspondent who had compiled the list of Antonia Dalzell's vital statistics from 1899 to the present. Hugh was frowning because a small fire in the registry office had destroyed the two statistics most vital to him.

These were the date of her marriage to Claude Hutchinson, American—the letter informed him that this marriage had occurred sometime in either 1899 or 1900—and the birthday of her oldest child, a son, Justin, in 1900.

The remaining information was precise. Oswald Dalzell, her father, had died of pneumonia on January 27, 1901. Her youngest child, a daughter, Zoe, was born on September 1, 1906. There was a middle child, a son, Arthur; however, he had died of scarlet fever on March 25, 1908. A week later Claude Hutchinson had succumbed to the same disease. The widow had a leasehold on a house in Rutland Gate, London, inherited from her uncle, Major Andrew Stuart, also of that address, who had died of cancer on August 17, 1909.

The boy, Hugh thought. *When was Antonia's boy born?*

He would never have been asking this question had he thought more of Caryll or less of Tom. But as it was, perceiving Caryll as afraid of him, he deplored the fact that this timorous mumbler was his brilliant meteor of a brother's only child. Or was he? Hugh frowned a long time at the paper before he refolded it along its three creases.

Tom whistled. "Quite a hunk!"

The brothers were going over Onyx's profit and loss sheet in Hugh's office. The black number at the bottom was very substantial.

"Tom," Hugh said. "Draw it all out."

"Are you crazy? I need this—and a damn sight more—to build the English plant."

The idea of putting up a factory in England had come to Tom a year earlier when Montgomery Edge, who held Onyx's London franchise, had visited in Detroit. Monty was able, ambitious, and—

most important to Tom—deeply knowledgeable in every idiosyncrasy of the internal-combustion engine.

"This isn't the time to expand," Hugh said. "This isn't the time to build factories."

"You sound like a bookkeeper."

"If the appeal loses, the court'll strip Onyx of everything to pay those royalties. Keep this profit. You'll have a half million to fall back on."

"I'm not about to fall, Hugh, but if I do, I have a cushion."

Hugh was aware how uncomfortably thin this cushion was. The New York detectives had found out for him that Tom had less than ten thousand dollars cash, and that in his wife's name. Hugh marveled that his brother could commit himself so utterly, holding back nothing, though by now he had accepted that this plunging courage as well as Tom's quirky genius were the raw ingredients of his success.

"I'm going to England with you," he said.

Tom had been stretching. His arms dropped. "What?"

"I'll sail with you on the *Oceanic.*"

"Leave your lair?"

"If you're crazy enough to go ahead with this, I must," Hugh said, gazing directly at his brother. "We'll need a good many dealers, and to check the applicants I have to be there."

Tom swallowed the subterfuge. "No sacrifice too great for Onyx?" he said, his voice jaunty with pleasure.

"Right."

"Remember, Hugh? You always talked about traveling in Europe. Maybe we can get a quick boat over to France."

"Strictly business, Tom, though I know you're dying for a social companion."

They both smiled. In the industry Tom was famed for his indifference to the extravagant entertainments of the new automotive royalty—he didn't even own a dinner suit.

The massive carton of fading blueprints was turned over to the attorneys. There was nothing to do but wait. In November the three judges of the Circuit Court of Appeals would hear the oral arguments, ponder the exhibits, read the briefs, then retire to decide the fate of Ford and Onyx.

November . . . and this was April.

On the blustery morning of April 11 Tom and Hugh boarded the Wolverine, the first leg of their journey. As they pulled out of the depot Tom was experiencing the taut nerves that he felt at the start of an endurance race—in a way he was challenging those three judges. Hugh huddled in a corner seat of their compartment, wondering about Antonia's boy. Enmeshed in his schemes, he did not notice the view as the train chugged past the ugly miles of Detroit industry and out onto the windswept farmland.

CHAPTER 10

They had not expected to be greeted at Southampton, but as they emerged from the canvas-covered gangway, Montgomery Edge was waving. When the Englishman had been in Detroit, Hugh had not met him, and during the introduction the recluse gazed stiffly ahead, his face and body remaining rigid as they maneuvered through the bustling, crowded pier sheds. Edge's chauffeur opened the door, and Hugh climbed in hastily. Tom paused to touch the hood of the Rolls-Royce. The mirror finish came from forty coats of paint—each one hand-rubbed—with a final varnishing in a room sheeted so that no dust could penetrate.

"She's a corker," Tom said appreciatively.

"Yes, a decent enough machine, the Silver Ghost," Montgomery Edge agreed. "Their gift to me when I left them."

The limousine glided between horsecarts and lorries. Hugh, his nerves still jumpy, glanced covertly at the Englishman next to him. Montgomery Edge. Of medium height, with fresh pink cheeks and a bristle of mustache that matched his sandy hair, Monty looked born to carry 20-gauge sporting shotguns on long hunting weekends. Hugh, though, had run a superior check on him before giving the go-ahead for the crucial London franchise. Born Alfie Edge, son of a Manchester drayman, he had apprenticed at Henry Royce's electric craneworks long before that alliterative merger with the Honorable Charles S. Rolls. Edge's name had been enhanced, his accent had undergone a metamorphosis, his thrusting brilliance had learned to conceal itself, and he had taken to wife Edwina, glacial daughter of

Nigel Alexander, K.C., a marriage apparently lacking the physical dimension, for Monty had a mistress tucked away in a St. John's Wood flat.

What Hugh could not know was that the Edges had been set for Tom to stay at their home. When Montgomery Edge heard that Tom's peculiar brother was accompanying him, he had brought forth a string of drayman's oaths. He needed time to impress Tom, for he was determined to become commander in chief of the Fiver's conquest of Britain.

Hugh's personal secretary, who had gone up on the train with the baggage, was waiting at the Hyde Park Hotel. Though it was after four, Hugh sent the pallid, efficient Harvard graduate out to make contact with the London detective firm.

The following afternoon Hugh received a photograph of the third form at Eddington College School on Wigmore Street. Justin Hutchinson, the third from the left in the back row, was the tallest of the sixteen boys. Hugh peered at the dark-haired oval, and decided that the chemical imprint had caught a brooding depth of eyes that was familiar. He took the picture to a window. Maybe the child had moved. A slightly blurred enigma.

II

Tom and Hugh slipped back into their old bachelor ways, bickering yet close. At breakfast, sniping about some business matter, both seemed to forget they were in a large, comfortable hotel suite with a view of Hyde Park and acted as if they were impoverished boys back in that drab flat. Tom left early each morning with Monty to search for factory sites, and on the two evenings that they returned home in time, the Edges entertained him. Hugh spent his days and evenings poring over dealer applications, Onyx's local balance sheets, the British advertising. The photograph of the third form was locked in the hotel safe. Craftily Hugh awaited the propitious hour to spring his news: if he spoke too soon, Tom might suspect his sudden willingness to go on this journey.

They had been in London eight days before they dined together. After the dirty dishes were wheeled out, Hugh cracked a pecan, carefully extracting the nutmeat. "I have some news, Tom. Major Stuart is dead." He spoke without emotion, although inverse grief afflicted him as acutely as ever. "He died of cancer more than a year ago."

After a long pause Tom said, "I'm not putting on an armband." His eyes remained on Hugh.

Antonia, they were both thinking. *Antonia*.

"I'm not in mourning, either," Hugh said.

"You haven't finished."

"She lives here."

Tom's face went slack. His pupils expanded. He rose, moving like a sleepwalker to the window, pulling back the heavy drape. A spring shower had broken: streetlamps and the lights of carriages and motorcars were reflected on the shimmering black streets. "You mean London?" he asked finally.

"Yes. Number twenty Rutland Gate. It's close by."

"Why here?"

"I don't know. She married an American. Claude Hutchinson. He's dead too. She's a widow."

"Hutchinson . . . she knew him before . . . in Detroit."

It was Hugh's turn for surprise. "She did?"

"She said he was nice but stodgy, dull. She married him?"

"Yes." Hugh poured two brandies. "That's all I know. That, and she was generous enough to send us the blueprints."

"She?"

"Yes." Hugh went to Tom with a snifter.

Tom ignored the drink. "I thought it was the Major."

"She asked that you not know."

"Then why are you telling me now?" Tom said.

Hugh did not know how to answer. He had sworn not to tell his brother, and yet here he was, in the most calculating way, blurting out this news. "We're brothers, aren't we, Tom? And brothers don't keep secrets from each other." He turned away, quickly, knowing that his duplicity would appear obvious to Tom.

But Tom, with a dazed look, was walking stiffly to his bedroom and didn't even hear Hugh's reply.

III

The next morning—Saturday—was unseasonably warm: the sun shone in a clear-washed blue sky. In Rutland Gate, an early Victorian square off Hyde Park, tall, creamy houses linked shoulders around an iron-fenced private garden where pruned elms rustled their new leaves above the daffodils swaying in crescent-shaped beds. Tom's steps seemed to bounce on the glittery pavement, but his smile was dreamy: Hugh's disclosure quite literally had stunned him, and he was drifting in a moony sea of amorous recollections.

Coming to number twenty, he climbed the steps and halted. The brass nameplate was engraved: *Mrs. Claude Hutchinson.* At this well-polished reality his dreamy smile faded. This was her name. Not Antonia Dalzell, a vibrant girl in her teens, but Mrs. Claude Hutchinson. And he was a married man, contentedly married to the person in this world that he considered his best friend. He and Antonia were not the two people they had been ten years before. He touched the nameplate, recoiling at the thought of their last scene together. *What am I going to say to her? What sort of apologies can I make?* He felt a stabbing pain above his eye. It never occurred to him to go back down the freshly washed steps.

Abruptly he raised the mermaid doorknocker.

The door was opened by a short, pear-shaped manservant in an alpaca jacket.

"Is Mrs. Hutchinson home?"

"What's it in regard to?" the servant replied, looking at Tom without raising his eyelids.

Tom forgot he was undisputed owner of a company capitalized at over twelve million dollars. "I'm a friend of hers," he said, berating himself for not halting at that florist's or—better yet—the elegant confectioner's across from the hotel. "I had business with her late uncle." He extracted a card from his leather cardcase.

T. K. BRIDGER
ONYX AUTOMOBILE COMPANY
DETROIT, MICHIGAN

The man examined it and then said, "Will you come inside, sir."

He led Tom up a flight of stairs, leaving him in double reception rooms that ran from the front of the house to the rear: the partitions were folded back, and Tom, alone, stared around. There were no draperies, only lace curtains that curved out in the breeze. On the shining parquet floors, dark and carpetless, rested random chairs and two low sofas slipcovered in pale linen. A copper tub of massed flowers was placed casually near the window. The room had a spareness that deflected the eye to the numerous paintings, and these were brightly colored vistas, rosy family groups, flower gardens, unposed naked women. Naïve paintings drenched in innocent light, rather than dark—and valuable-looking—hues. The drawing room had the happy, transitory charm of a tented summer pavilion.

Tom could not help recalling that even when they were very poor, Maud had saved for heavy, durable furnishings; her motto: *Good things are cheaper in the long run because they last.* Briefly he wondered about Antonia's finances, then reminded himself that she kept a butler and lived in an exclusive square off the park.

A child's laughter rang through the rear windows.

Tom swung around, bewildered. *A child?* How could he not have taken that possibility into account?

A shriller cry. "No! Justin, no! I want my turn over!"

Children, he amended, going to the long windows.

Below was a small city garden whose walls were hidden by white-blossomed rhododendron bushes. The sunlit part of the lawn was covered by an Oriental rug. And there was Antonia. On her stomach, propped up by her elbows, one leg raised, the pump adangle from her stockinged toes, a pink and white striped skirt falling back to expose a frothy edge of petticoats: from this distance she appeared unchanged by the decade. She faced two children across a gameboard. From his view above and behind the pair, Tom could tell only that the boy had Antonia's shining black hair and was a good deal older than Caryll, while the girl—almost a baby she was—had hair the unusual clear, molten gold of a California poppy. All three laughed as the tiny girl lunged to wrest the dice cup from the boy, who held her off easily.

Tom had the sensation of looking at yet another artlessly happy painting, one into which he would soon be welcomed.

He heard the doors open below. Antonia, pulling her skirt over her ankles—those pretty, delicate ankles—rolled over, sitting. The servant appeared and handed her a card.

A cannon shot might have exploded in the garden.

Even from this distance Tom could see the terror in her eyes as she glanced up at the window—he was positive she could see him through the Brussels lace. Scrambling to her feet, she pulled the boy to his. He came to her shoulder, and something about the boy's height momentarily nagged at Tom. Then Antonia swooped at the baby, who kicked with a small white boot in protest at being lifted. A collie rose from the shade, barking around them as they disappeared.

Tom stood motionless, peering down at the empty garden where the gameboard had spilled onto the lawn. He hadn't been sure what would happen in the way of reconciliation, but the disparity between this cataclysm he had caused and the night's romantically adolescent maunderings made him physically ill. If she hated him this way, why had she returned his blueprints? The manservant's heavy tread echoed up the stairs.

"Mrs. Hutchinson is out, sir."

"But I just saw her in the—"

"I'm sorry. She's not home."

"When will she be back?"

"If you'll follow me."

Tom wiped his forehead. *I've managed fine for years without seeing her,* he thought as he went down the stairs, *so if she still hates me, the hell with her, it doesn't matter, she's nothing to me anymore.* Yet he was remembering the sweet dower of her naked body against his, seeing her pale, drawn face in his dingy apartment. His thoughts came in violent bursts that had nothing to do with indifference. *The hell with her.*

IV

He did not tell Hugh of the debacle, nor did he mention Antonia, but she occupied his mind, center stage, tormenting him like a lecherous succubus in nightmares that were the antithesis of his earlier tenderly erotic dreams. She seduced him with unspeakably loathsome degeneracies, she flagellated him with doubts and self-contempt, she caused his intractably foul humor.

He interviewed the candidates Hugh had selected for the Birmingham dealership, rejecting all three. Monty drove him to building sites endowed with every specification he had outlined: he found fault with each.

At the end of the week Monty said in his most offhand tone, "We're going to the Comstocks' tomorrow night, a ball, and they've asked to meet you."

A *no* was on Tom's tongue, but weary of his own negative despotism, he replied, "Sounds fine to me, Monty."

*   *   *

The door to the bathroom was open, and Hugh watched his brother rinse one of those new Gillette safety razors. "I wonder how many strings Edwina Edge had to pull to get this invitation."

"Why see plots everywhere?" Tom said sourly. "You're a fox, but that doesn't mean everyone is."

"The Comstocks are in Court circles, Monty is a drayman's son, and in this country the twain never meet. The Edges are out to impress you."

"Why would they want to impress me?" asked Tom.

Hugh stared at his brother. It occurred to him, and not for the first time, that Tom, in his way an ascetic man, had never appreciated the silky steel of power. He ignored its enjoyable aspects. He had very little idea that in ruling thousands of lives his whims and moods were catered to and feared. "The way your disposition's been lately, Edge is positive that British Onyx is a dead issue. Or his part in it, anyway. She's proving to you that her husband is worthy."

"Good thing you've explained it. Until now I just figured they were dragging me along to a party I didn't want to go to," Tom said, and began to dress in his new evening clothes: this morning a tailor had been hastily summoned.

V

Oval mirrors on the broad staircase reflected footmen in crimson livery as well as the ascending guests, who spoke to one another in subdued tones. Edwina Edge maintained her pace a step ahead of Tom and her husband. She was two years older than Monty, and in her drab russet lace, her face marked with furrows from nose to mouth, that intractably cold look in her eyes, she might have been ten years older. Yet her air of unflappable assurance convinced her friends that dowdiness and age were the feminine qualities prized by Montgomery Edge—and indeed, Monty was glancing with proud fondness at his wife's angular back. Just as Hugh figured, she had maneuvered this invitation: ambition being the bond between the Edges, they worked more closely than most couples.

Across the rear of the second floor stretched the finely proportioned ballroom with its intermingled resplendencies and shabbiness. Black-insulated wiring cut across the beautifully carved rose garlands of the paneling, gilt eroded from the line of fluted columns, and watermarks stained the magnificent, domed ceiling. By and large the guests were less lavishly turned out than their counterparts would have been at a New York dance: some of the men's clothes were dated, and some of the women's gowns were by no means elaborate, while much of the jewelry was set in the heavier styles of other eras. The mélange of wealth and carelessness could be carried off only by a long-entrenched aristocracy.

Tom, uncomfortable at large social functions, stalked down the three shallow steps to where the host and hostess stood greeting their guests. Lord and Lady Comstock were a stout couple in their fifties, he with a white walrus mustache, she double-chinned, both smiling cheerfully. Edwina presented Tom.

"Ahh, Bridger," said Lord Comstock, pushing back his shock of gray hair. "I saw you race once. A place with some barbaric name. Rippie something."

"Rappahannock."

"Exactly. You drove that slate Onyx like a shot. Are you giving England a chance to see you do your stuff?"

"Sure. It's the way I push the product."

Monty and Edwina stiffened at this gaffe, but Lord and Lady Comstock laughed heartily. "That's right," said the hostess. "You *make* the little monsters."

More at ease, Tom moved into the ballroom. The eddying conversations, the calls and cries of greeting, the footsteps on the waxed floor, made a deafening thrum, and Edwina moved closer to point out the distinguished guests: Prince Louis Battenberg held court in one corner, and in an alcove Princess Louise and her husband, the Duke of Fife, looked slightly bored with their entourage.

A burst of masculine laughter drew Tom's attention to a window embrasure. Five men, three in brilliant uniforms, circled a tall, slender woman in cream silk. She wore no tiara in her China-black hair, her only jewelry a strand of small sapphires around her throat. Tom had caught her in profile. The wall fixture formed a path of light along the delicate contours of her nose, which wiggled as she told what must have been an amusing anecdote.

It took Tom several beats to recognize Antonia, for this was not his solitary love; this Antonia was a creature born to captivate groups, to refract her joie de vivre as a diamond flashes light. She raised her hand, a vivid Highland-fling gesture, and the men roared again.

Edwina noticed the direction of his gaze. "She's a countrywoman of yours, Mr. Bridger."

"Who? Where?" Monty asked. "Ahh. Mrs. Hutchinson. Delightful woman, delightful. Would you like to be introduced?"

"I know her," Tom replied. "I was a mechanic at her uncle's factory."

As Monty turned crimson, a loud waltz burst from the minstrels' gallery. Gentlemen placed hands over shining white waistcoats, bowing to ladies, and couples whirled onto the dance floor: the regular beat of shoes, the jangle of spurs, the rush of skirts, sounded over voices and music. Tom pushed through the crowd to the window embrasure.

"Antonia," he said thickly. "Hello."

She blinked at him, her animation fading. Her hand went to her throat where the pulse beat visibly.

He asked, "May I have this dance?"

"Sorry, old man. The waltz is mine," said a stocky man wearing a crimson evening kilt and a silver-buttoned dress jacket.

"Roderick," Antonia murmured. "This is Mr. Bridger from America. . . ."

Tom, viewing this as acceptance, placed his hand on her narrow, supple waist. At this the man, Roderick, stepped back.

Tom was not a good dancer; he had learned too late and had too little practice. Antonia, however, danced exquisitely. She dipped and swayed gracefully while her feet in their satin slippers moved lightly. But she was silent, holding herself apart from him, her eyes fixed on a point beyond his left ear. Once he managed to catch her glance, and her eyelids trembled, revealing the same fear she had shown that afternoon in her garden. She was afraid of him. But why? True, he had hurled thunderbolts of bitterness at her; still, she had sent him back his blueprints. Ten and a half years, then, must have washed away some of the bitterness. Tom ached to give himself up to the old vertigo of her nearness, but her subdued silence killed his pleasure.

"Your paintings are unusual," he said at last.

Red marks showed on her pale cheeks. "You should never have come to the house."

Hurt, he paid her back. "You didn't have to run away as if Jack the Ripper was calling. I only wanted to say thanks for the plans."

"Mr. Polhemus was never to mention where they came from."

"You've forgotten my brilliance," he said. "Who but your uncle would have stolen my ideas?"

She bent her head. He could not see her expression, but the perfume of her hair—she still used rosewater—reached deep into his memory. "He died the year before last," she said.

"I heard. I also heard that you married your old beau, and he died too." The band, without halting, swung into "The Merry Widow." Appropriate, Tom thought. "Widowhood becomes you," he said.

Under his hand her rib cage expanded and contracted. He slowed his steps. "I've got a mean, hurting sense of humor, Antonia. Remember? I'm sorry." And to bolster his apology, he added, "I saw your boy and girl. They're fine-looking children. I have a boy too. How old is yours?"

Her body tensed. Her feet ceased to move. She stared directly at him. "How dare you!" she whispered.

"What is it? All I did was ask about your children."

"You've become very cruel." Tears were caught on her lower lashes.

"Antonia, I don't understand."

She pulled away from him. "I've turned my ankle," she said. They were at the edge of the floor where older women sat gossiping. She sank onto the nap-worn red velvet upholstery of a vacant chair.

"Does it hurt much?"

She nodded.

"Shall I find a doctor?"

"That's not necessary." She gazed at the energetic waltzers as though they might deliver her from her misery, which Tom knew had nothing to do with torn ligaments in her slim ankle.

Sitting on the gilt chair next to her, he spoke with low intensity. "I don't understand what I've done. Should I apologize for what happened in Detroit . . . ?" The question trailed away. Her eyes glinted with outrage and horror. He changed the subject. "The plans were just what we needed. The lawyers say they're evidence that I developed my automobiles along very different lines from Selden's patent. Crucial to the appeal." He leaned toward her. "Antonia, it's ten years since I was a monster. Isn't there a statute of limitations?"

"Why are you poking and prying about my son?" Her voice shook.

"Your boy? Antonia, I don't understand at all."

"Why did you come to see him?"

"I told you, I wanted to thank you. Is there a reason I mustn't come to your house? Are you engaged . . . or something?"

One of the ladies seated nearby had risen and was approaching them. Diamond tiara aglint in iron-gray hair, she bent her head solicitously. "Antonia, whatever is it? You look ghastly."

"I twisted my ankle quite badly."

"You poor dear. Come into the cloakroom and we'll put ice on it. Can you manage?"

"I'll try, your grace," Antonia said, standing. Tom rose too. Without a glance, she left him.

He watched the two women circle the dance floor. Antonia held the train of her ball gown by its silken loop.

She was not limping.

She had lied to get away from him and didn't care if he knew it! His throat went dry, his hands began shaking. He pushed his way around the crowded dance floor, not seeing the Edges, who had stopped dancing to wave at him, or his host and hostess, who turned from greeting a late arrival to look askance at him. Outside, he gulped at the damp evening air, blindly walking several blocks before hailing a taxi.

"What address, guv'nor?"

"Where there's women," Tom said roughly.

VI

He arrived back at the Hyde Park Hotel around teatime: the guests gathered around the low tables in the lobby glanced politely away from his rumpled dinner clothes.

As he unlocked the door of their suite Hugh jumped up from a desk strewn with papers. "Tom! Where have you been? I've had people out looking for you."

"Oh, shit."

"You've been gone almost a day. Monty said you left the ball early. And it's after four in the afternoon."

"London whores don't punch a time clock!" The taxi driver had wound through the narrow alleys of Soho to a house considerably more luxurious than the one near the Pontchartrain Hotel. He had chosen a bosomy redhead and for the first time in his life been incapable; he had downed Scotch after Scotch, then passed out on the prostitute's useless bed. "Don't spy on *me*, Hugh!"

He slammed into the bathroom. Before he shaved, he peered with bloodshot eyes into the mahogany-framed mirror and scarcely recognized himself.

He emerged shaved, bathed, changed, mumbling an apology. Hugh had ordered tea. Tom, discovering he was hungry, fell on thinly sliced sandwiches and small iced cakes, pouring himself several cups of tea, the strong, dark oolong that his mother-in-law brewed.

Hugh sipped a single cup. "All week you've been a madman, and now this binge. What is it? Worried about the appeal?"

"I saw her."

Hugh feigned ignorance. "Her?"

"Antonia. I went to Rutland Gate last week. She was home, but she refused to see me. And she was at the ball. She pretended she'd hurt her foot to get away. She hates me, Hugh, hates me. And for some reason she's terrified of me."

Hugh set down his cup. "When you went to the house, did you see him?" he asked carefully.

"Then she *does* have a lover. A royal one?"

"The son, I meant."

"The children were in the garden. She hustled them away."

"What does he look like?"

"I saw them for a minute from an upstairs window."

"The boy's ten."

Tom curved his hands around the chair arms, sitting forward to stare at his brother's knowing, divided face. "Ten?"

"I don't know his birthday. I tried to find out, but the records had burned."

A curious emotion, scalding as rage yet not rage, cruised through Tom and he pushed away the tea cart, spilling over the milk jug. He barged out to the anteroom, grabbing his hat.

Hugh ran after him. "Where are you going?"

"To get a few answers."

"Cool down, Tom. Think this through before—"

But Tom had already slammed the door.

VII

The butler lowered his gaze. "I'm afraid, sir, that Madam is not receiving. She is indispo—"

"I'll see her anyway." Tom pushed into the narrow hall.

"Who is it, Drum?" called a boy's upper-class English contralto.

"A gentleman, Master Justin. He insists on seeing Mrs. Hutchinson."

"I'll handle this, Drum." The boy ran lightly down the stairs. Drum retreated to the crepuscular shadows as if to give the youngster rein while protecting him. *From me,* Tom thought. "My mother is resting, Mr.—?"

"Bridger," Tom supplied. The door was open, but it was not the twilight drafts that caused the chills weaving over Tom's body. He was scanning the boy's face: the arched nose already proving its bone structure, the fully modeled mouth, the shining black hair that tousled over his high, arching forehead. On the surface, Antonia. Her child alone. The eyes, however, were not Antonia's. They were wide apart, their deep blue intensified by the shadow of the frontal bone. Looking into those eyes it all rushed back to Tom, his father silently breasting the loneliness of the Great Plains, his father directing him to his chores with a shifting glance, his father staring up after death's monstrous embrace.

Under his scrutiny the child stood more erect. "Mr. Bridger, are you cold?"

"I . . ." Tom drew a deep, visceral breath.

"Maybe we should close the door, sir. You're shivering."

"I'm fine. I was hoping to see your . . . mother."

"Mr. Bridger, did you visit last Saturday?"

"I was here, yes."

The boy's freckles showed the color of a peach against his pink and white skin, and he squared his shoulders under the school blazer. "I hope you don't think this very rude, but Mother has nobody but me. After your last visit she was most frightfully upset. Last night she came home early, ill, but even if she were herself, it seems best if you don't call on her." This final exigency he blurted out, as though he had steeled himself.

"We were friends."

157

"Probably being an American, you remind her of Father," the child offered. "She misses him most dreadfully."

"I don't mean to upset her, son." Tom reddened, swallowing. "What's *your* name?"

"Justin—Justin Hutchinson."

"Justin, I'd appreciate it if you'd give your mother this." He took out a card, penciling on the back: *We have matters to discuss*.

Scrupulously averting his gaze from the message, the boy turned the card. "I say! Onyx!" He had not yet grown into his teeth, and his eager smile revealed him as a ten-year-old rather than knight defender of this narrow early Victorian house and all ladies therein. "You're *that* Mr. Bridger? The racer?"

"Me."

"The paper said you've entered the Ben Nevis run. Is that true?"

"No, I'll be home in Detroit by August."

"Jolly good!"

"Why?"

"I'd rather an English car won."

"Justin!"

At the shrill cry they turned to the staircase. Antonia was skimming down, her loose, silvery houserobe spectral in the dim light, her hair grazing her shoulders.

"Mother, I thought you were in bed."

"Why didn't you let Drum answer?" she demanded.

"I did, Madam." The butler spoke from the shadows. "I explained to the gentleman you weren't receiving." Shooting an indignant glance at Tom, he paced with theatrical steps into the gloom. A door closed.

"It's not Drum's fault, Mother," Justin said, his cheeks red. It was apparent that this virago was an incomprehensible stranger, an unknown incarnation who shocked and wounded him. "I wanted to explain to Mr. Bridger—"

"Go upstairs."

"—that you were ill," Justin finished, resolute, brighter color flooding his face.

"Mrs. Drum has tea ready." Antonia pushed him.

He resisted. "Mr. Bridger, you'll remember what I told you?"

"Yes, I will," Tom said.

"It was a pleasure meeting you, sir." Justin's smile broke. "Wait until I tell them at school you aren't entered in the Ben Nevis!'' He took the stairs two at a time.

Antonia watched him disappear before she turned to Tom. ''Must you keep hounding us?'' she whispered.

''Why didn't you want me to meet him?'' Tom asked.

She glanced around, frightened. ''We can't talk here. Wait. I'll be right back.''

He stepped outside, leaving the front door ajar. The lamplighter was making his rounds, and in a circle of yellow light, Tom brooded.

Having come face to face with a son he had not known existed, he was attempting to sort out his impressions. The boy had been brave to speak like that to a strange adult. Protecting his mother. It had come as a shock that he talked with the precise articulation of the British upper class. Tall for his age. Sturdily built. Over his heart he wore a school crest embroidered with gilt thread and crimson silk. He was thoughtful—or was it the eyes? A trick of pigment and bone structure? He went out of his way to be fair-minded: *Probably being an American, you remind her of Father*.

The boy's image faded, and Tom loosened his tie knot. He was choking with perverse resentment that had nothing to do with Justin— or, rather, everything to do with him. *She never told me*, Tom was thinking. *She left Detroit without a word*. The boy proved with annihilating finality the depth of her loathing.

My son?

Son meant a younger, less forceful boy who looked on him not with veiled hostility but adoration, who did not remind him of his own father's lost battles. Caryll was his son.

VIII

In less than five minutes Antonia came out, hatless, hair tied back, clasping a voluminous black cape around her. In her ungloved hand she held a large iron key. ''We can talk in the gardens,'' she said calmly enough, yet when they crossed over to the gate, she could not insert the key in the lock, and he had to do it for her. Their footsteps crunched along the path to a bench hidden in the shadows of some large, sweet-scented bush.

''He's a handsome boy,'' Tom said, keeping his voice level. ''He's mine.''

She sighed assent.

"I said unforgivable things, but how could you go away and not tell me?"

"Uncle begged you to marry me."

He turned, peering. It was too dark to see her expression. "Never."

"He abased himself. Uncle. He never in his life was humble." Her voice shook. "He told you I was crazy, ill, desperate. He offered you money to marry me, he said he'd continue to pay Father's bills, he said you need never see *him*."

"He gave you a line of bull."

"What is the point of tormenting me?"

"He lied to you."

"Oh, Tom."

"If he'd even whispered you needed me, don't you think I'd have been out there like a shot? My God, I thought the sun rose and set on you."

"Flaherty took it to you."

"Took what?"

"Uncle's pleadings."

Goosebumps prickled on Tom's body. "The letter," he muttered.

"Yes, a letter."

"I never looked at it."

"Tom, stop this, please stop."

"I mean it. I never read it."

"Flaherty brought back your reply." Her murmur was scarcely audible. "I saw your reply. It cut me into pieces of the same size."

"Hugh had just come home from having his bandages taken off, the burn scars were hideous. I didn't want any part of your uncle. . . . I didn't unfold . . . I took the clippers . . . shoved the bits back in the . . . envelope. . . . I never saw . . . never read . . ."

He bent his face into his hands, and the harsh noises coming from his chest were like rocks grating together, not quite human. The wracking physical upheaval was niggling compared to his helpless, hopeless grief. During one fragment of time, one blazing, angry minute, he had cut her life, that black-haired boy's destiny, his own soul, and that temporal chip was buried, not to be resurrected, lost forever. *What might have been* was not a phrase in Tom's vocabulary, yet now each time he heard another say it, he would be haunted by the possibilities, the excruciating desire to relive that moment. He would give all he possessed to relive it. He drew deep breaths, attempting to control himself. Feeling her hand gentle on his shoulder, he clasped the palm to his wet cheek.

"You believe me?" he asked.

"Yes. Hush."

"Oh, God . . . God . . ."

"Now you understand why I was so afraid? Tom, I've been positive you wanted to take him from me."

"Your son?"

"Justin, yes. I was frightened that you would take him—or tell him."

He fished for his handkerchief. "To have done that to *you* . . ."

"Don't, Tom. It's past, it's over."

He blew his nose, and she moved apart on the bench. A cat rustled around the bush, its eyes electrically brilliant in the darkness; a carriage clipped around the square, the sound of hooves fading.

"Justin worshiped Claude," she said quietly. "And Claude loved him more than Arthur or Zoe—I don't know why, but he did. You saw Zoe in the garden when you were here. . . . Arthur . . . Arthur died of scarlet fever just before Claude." She shook her head as though to clear it.

"Anyway," she said, after a long pause. "Claude and Justin were inseparable. In the summer they sailed together. For his fourth birthday Claude gave Justin a Shetland pony and taught him to curry it and they rode together in the park. Claude would take him to cricket matches, motoring. When Claude died, Justin was desolate. He tries to live up to what he considers Claude's expectations. I don't mean he's a prig. He's a boy, Tom, but a very nice one. He hardly ever teases Zoe—and she deserves it. Actually, he'd be just as nice without any good intentions."

"You can be very proud of him," Tom said, and sounded grudging to his own ears.

"Claude's the anchor in his life. If he found out about himself, it would destroy him."

"I don't want to take him from you," Tom said. "I have my own son."

"His name's Caryll." Her smile glinted in the darkness. "You

161

married Maud Trelinack. I knew her. She's beautiful. Nice, too, such a fine, open personality.''

"She helped me get started with her own money, and at the beginning she worked. She's my wife and my friend." Though he was telling Antonia the truth, his tone was vaguely defiant. "So you've kept track of me?"

"It's hard *not* to. You're in the papers so much when you race, and there's been talk of an English Fiver."

"I didn't know a thing about you until Hugh mentioned that you lived in London—he's over here with me."

"Hugh?" That metallic note of alarm. "Does he know about . . . Justin?"

Tom wanted to put the miserable mess behind them. "Of course not."

"You're positive?"

"Nobody knows," Tom said quietly. "He's your husband's son." It was a tarnished sophistry, yet he realized that for him it was true: Antonia's son had nothing to do with him.

"He is," she said. "Claude married me before he was born."

Tom was remembering how she had looked at him at the Comstocks' ball, her beautiful eyes stupid with pain. *My God*, he thought. *No wonder she didn't want me near her*. Sighing, he muttered, "What you must have gone through."

"At first it was terrible. But Claude and I were happy. Very." She paused. "I still care for him, Tom."

"Do you hate me?"

She stood, pulling the cape around her. "I never did," she said. "I couldn't."

IX

Too shaken to go upstairs, she slipped into the room off the front door. Here Claude had met with his clients. His dark law books were interspersed with equally somberly bound Carlyle and Macaulay: his private income combined with the one her uncle had settled on her had made his practice a hobby rather than a necessity, and he had had plenty of time to read the ponderously written history he enjoyed. She did not take off her cape or press the light switch, but felt her way to the desk chair. Tom's grief had been terrible to her, yet at the same time exalting. Those hoarse sobs denied the cruelties, present and historical, that she had never quite been able to attribute to him.

Antonia rubbed her eyes as if she were pushing away the fragments of a nightmare. In the darkness she was again feeling the disjointed panic of those last few days in Detroit. The opiates that Nurse Girardin had needled into her had trapped her in endless visions of Tom berating her for gross sexual uncleanliness. She winced, remembering how she had been tied down in what seemed an eternity of Tom's angry voice counting the ways her caresses and kisses disgusted him. Seasickness had increased her drugged misery, and by the time they had landed she was so weak and delirious that she had to be carried ashore. In London the frightened specialist discontinued the laudanum. Antonia drew a curtain of lethargic melancholy around herself, emerging to read to her father and feign smiles for her uncle. Her nature was too volatile, though, for retreat, and as she grew stronger physically, she began to put out timid feelers. During her sixth month her uncle ran into Claude lunching at the American Club—the younger man confessed he was traveling for the time-honored reason of forgetting love. The early winter dusk fell, and the Major suggested they return to his new home in Rutland Gate. When Antonia came into the drawing room, Claude glanced, startled, at the gentle mound under her loose wrapper. The Major tactfully left them alone. Antonia, ashamed and miserably aware of the last time they had met, in another drawing room, on another continent, went to the fire. Her face colored by the flames, she explained that she still loved the man, but he did not love her enough to marry her.

"He's a fool, then, child, a fool," said Claude—and for once his badinage did not seem out of place. Soon he was again bearing chocolate boxes through snowfalls. He wanted her enough to share her with that mysterious invalid upstairs, the Major, and another man's child—years later he told her he had felt like a condemned prisoner being given a second chance. Between them he and the Major cajoled her into marriage. They were right, of course. She understood that when Claude held the shawled, thrashing infant whose crest of black hair was still moist with mucus and blood, the sign of his arduous voyage through the birth canal. "Our son has a fine head of hair," Claude said, kissing the baby.

Antonia leaned back in the pillows, her exhaustion mildly tinged with embarrassment that Claude should be witness to the postnatal mess—they hadn't yet slept together. Her predominant emotion was humble gratitude for this baby, this husband. "Claude, you've given us everything." She began to cry weakly.

"Stop that, child. You've made me the happiest man alive."

Antonia carried the gift of happiness, and Claude basked in her bounty. She was tender of his solemnity, his too hearty voice with strangers, his awkward embraces, and in this charmingly bright house, warmed by matrimony, Claude no longer believed himself such a dull fellow—and he no longer was. They shared the minor discords, the pleasures, worrisome frets, the prideful smiles common to parents of a growing family.

Antonia curved her arms on her husband's desk, burying her face as she remembered the day when the doctor had pronounced the dread words "scarlet fever," ordering a sheet hung over the front door as a sign of quarantine. Though she could remember her father's and uncle's deaths with sad tranquillity, even after two years the untimely ends of her little son and her husband crushed her with angry, unaccepting grief.

Mrs. Drum's steps rang on the back stairs, signaling that Zoe had been tucked in bed. Antonia went into the hall, hanging up her cape and smoothing her hair in the mirror before she went to kiss her baby girl good night.

She tapped on her son's door.

X

Justin, too, had been sitting in the dark. He sat hunched in front of the unlit fire, one arm around Caesar, his long-legged, predominantly collie dog. As Antonia switched on the light he turned his head from her. Why not? He must be embarrassed by that scene she had made at the front door. They both needed time to compose themselves. She called to Caesar, scratching the flat place between the mongrel's ears.

Justin's room was a large one, and he had arranged his things not too neatly but with what seemed to him a sense of order. His lead guardsmen and hussars, some headless, were lined in squadrons along the shelves in front of his books. One side of the chest of drawers supported his cricket bats—he was considered the best bowler in Eddington's lower forms. Above the fireplace hung a stylized print of a 1909 Lanchester: like many boys his age he was passionate about motorcars and was forever after her to buy one. The ell to the left of the door he had transformed into a shrine to Claude with framed photographs on the wall, an octagonal glass case of relics: Claude's Beta Theta Pi hatband and pin, his heavy turnip-shaped watch, and other gleaming bits of property including the gold cigarette case that she had bought for him at Asprey's.

Antonia sat in the grubby easy chair. "I'm sorry I lost my temper," she said with the same contrite murmur she would have used in apologizing to an adult.

"It's all right, Mother."

"I shouted at you over nothing."

"Mr. Bridger shouldn't have barged in like that," he said forcefully.

She pressed her mouth closed, biting the lower lip, and after a hesitation said, "In Detroit he worked for Uncle."

"He did? You never mentioned it—Mother, you know how keen I am on racing. Uncle Andrew never said a word."

"Uncle rented a building in his factory to Mr. Bridger. They were partners."

"Uncle Andrew owned part of Onyx?"

"In those days it wasn't Onyx, it was the Bridger Automobile Company. In the '90s people threw stones at motorcars and called them devil wagons. Or laughed at them."

"I know that, Mother."

"When Uncle's factory burned down, Mr. Bridger's brother was terribly burned." She spoke breathily. "Mr. Bridger blamed Uncle."

"What a rotter! As if it were Uncle Andrew's fault."

"Lloyd's investigators came to Detroit."

Her son's nostrils flared as he looked questioningly at her.

"The furniture business was doing badly. Uncle was better off with the insurance money than with the factory." She drew a long, sighing breath. "I never knew whether they were right to investigate or not, Justin. It didn't make any difference to what I felt for Uncle. Can you understand?"

Justin went to the window. The curtains weren't drawn, and he stared into the moonless night toward red Mars. Antonia was accustomed to his pauses. Justin assimilated knowledge before affixing right and wrong in his mind: he saw the moral order in black, white, and every shade of gray, an uncomfortable breadth of vision for any age. "In school," he said slowly, "people are beastly to Rosburg, so he's turned into a sneak. I can see that they wouldn't like a sneak. But he's still my friend."

This was the first time he had mentioned Rosburg's misfortunes, but the headmaster had told her that Rosburg, maligned "for his faith," told on his tormentors and Justin, a leader in the scruffy, noisy lower forms, did all he could to protect the Jewish child. Justin's decency made her throat ache with love, yet at the same time she felt a rasp of self-excoriation at her own behavior. What a wall of subterfuges she had built! And was piling yet higher.

"That's exactly it," she said.

"He's a famous racer, Mr. Bridger, but he's not very fair." Justin's anathema.

"Why do you say that?"

"He looked at me as if I were a germ under a microscope. He was against me before I said a word."

"I'm sure you misunderstood," she said, her voice taking on specious adult tones.

"I *admire* him tremendously."

"But you don't like him?" she asked weakly.

"No," Justin said, reddening. "He upset you."

"Justin—"

Her son interrupted hastily, "You don't have to worry, Mother. I tried hard not be cheeky."

"He's not coming here again."

"Mother . . . do you think he felt that way about me because of Uncle Andrew?"

She turned away. "Have you had your tea yet?"

"I wasn't very hungry. Would a famous man like him carry a grudge?"

"Cook is fixing me a tray. Emmy could bring up another plate. Yesterday I bought some new records. 'The Nightingale Song' and Madame Farrar's 'Un Bel Di.' While we're waiting, I'll play them for us."

Justin's eyes were brilliant blue sparks under his brow: one of his greatest delights was listening with her to the trumpet-topped Victor. He was young enough to be seduced by treats. He said, "I'll tell them in the kitchen."

He pounded down the back stairs.

Antonia moved slowly along the dimly lit hall to her room. Though her primal strength was directed at keeping father and son apart, she felt an irrational, obstinate chagrin that Justin had seen Tom in such a bad light and Tom so patently had not fallen for Justin.

CHAPTER 11

"Well, what about Antonia's boy?" Hugh asked when Tom returned to the hotel.

"Sorry to disappoint you. The true-born son of Claude Hutchinson."

"Is that what she told you?"

"His birthday's sometime in late October, Hugh. A conceived-in-matrimony child, and rather a snot." Tom yawned elaborately. "Last night was a real sizzler. After dinner it's bed for me."

Hugh waited in the sitting room for nearly an hour after Tom had retired, then cautiously opened his brother's door. Tom stretched on his back, arms out, breathing in long, deep sighs. Hugh eased the door shut. Though it was after eleven, he telephoned his secretary in his small room on the ground floor, telling him to dress and bring the photographer's envelope from the hotel safe.

Hugh carried the packet into his bedroom, locking the door. He sat in a good light, frowning over the picture posed on the brick steps of Eddington College School.

The following morning he ordered an investigator to be stationed at the Rutland Gate entry of Hyde Park.

II

Justin manipulated the diamond-shaped kite with its red and blue tails, Caesar barking next to him. To catch the vagrant breeze he swerved onto the path. He thudded into the tall man. The man stumbled, regaining his balance, but Justin sprawled, flinging out his hands to protect his face from the gravel.

"I'm ever so sorry, sir," he gasped. "Caesar, down, down." He scrambled to his feet.

"Here's your string," Hugh said.

Justin gave him a brief stare, then said, "Thank you, sir."

"You're hurt. That hand's bleeding."

"It's nothing." Justin pulled out a handkerchief, licking on it before scrubbing away the tiny stones embedded in the graze at the root of his right thumb. "I should have been looking where I was going."

"Difficult when you're trying to get a kite up."

"Do you have them in America—you are American, aren't you, sir?"

"I am. And it's how Benjamin Franklin discovered lightning is electricity."

"Right you are," Justin said, smiling.

Antonia, carrying Zoe, ran toward them. Like all the ladies in the park, she wore black. The second week in May, Edward VII had succumbed to a chill and the country had plunged itself into deep mourning: though Hugh was a fervid anglophile, he had not a grain of sympathy for this mass grief—the late King Edward was a ringer for Major Stuart. As Antonia neared them, her narrow spatted boots slowed.

Eyes widening, she recognized Hugh.

Emotions rushed at her in waves. The initial shock of seeing his scars was immediately swallowed by the pleasure of bumping into an old friend, and this feeling in turn was inundated by the remembrance that Hugh had broken his promise to keep the blueprints secret. Then she was realizing that the man and boy standing on the gravel path were uncle and nephew. *Does Hugh know?* Her grip on Zoe tightened. The child squirmed in protest. Antonia set her down.

"Antonia?" Hugh cried. "Antonia!"

His voice rang with uncomplicated joy. Her doubts fell from her and she ran to him.

Justin, who was using his teeth and left fingers to tie the handkerchief around his wound, looked up to see his mother brushing a kiss at the stranger's misshapen cheek in the way that she greeted her closest friends. Then he was startled to be introduced to someone called Bridger. Lowering his head, he concentrated on his task a moment too long before holding out his crudely bandaged hand. "I'm pleased to meet you, sir," he said guardedly.

"And this is my daughter, Zoe."

Zoe put one buttoned white boot behind her in a curtsy-like dip.

She was a child stepped from a Sargent portrait. Clouds of burnished red-gold hair contrasted with enormous dark brown eyes, and the small features promised lovely regularity. Zoe had stamped her plump foot when confronted with the dark, sensible clothing of little English girls her age, and since Antonia was unconventional enough not to have hired a nurse, Zoe had had her way: in her pink laine frock and its tiny bolero—both mapped with grass stains—she was dressed as if for a pose.

Exquisite, Hugh thought. *Without hyperbole, she is exquisite*. "How do you do, Miss Hutchinson."

"Mummy! He called me Miss!" Zoe cried. "You have a face like a clown."

"Zoe!" Antonia exclaimed.

"A long time ago I was hurt in an accident," Hugh said seriously.

"When *I* get hurt, my scabs fall off, and then there's nothing," Zoe said. "Won't yours fall off?"

"No."

"You're a pretty color, like stewed plums. Can I touch?"

Hugh squatted to take her hand in his, guiding small, damp fingers to the slick, unfeeling flesh. Then he stood, smiling down at Antonia.

"Hugh, how wonderful to meet you like this. You still live in Detroit, don't you?"

"Out beyond Grosse Pointe," he said. "Lake St. Clair runs along one side of my property."

Zoe tugged at her mother's hand, whispering loudly, "Mummy, can we show Mr. Bridger, or will it vanish?"

"I'm sure it won't."

Zoe looked up at Hugh. "We have a secret," she said.

"What kind?"

"Is it time, Mummy?"

Antonia glanced at her enameled lapel watch and nodded.

"We'll take you," Zoe said.

"Then your secret is a place?"

"No. It's magic."

"Magic? What kind?"

"Come and you'll see."

"Do," Antonia interjected warmly.

Hugh said, "If it's all right with Justin."

Justin glanced up from rewinding his kite string. "Please join us, Mr. Bridger," he said, polite, aloof.

They curved along the path in the direction of the Albert Memorial. Hugh's heart pattered and jerked as each passerby inspected him. Zoe grasped his and Antonia's hands, occasionally abdicating her weight to them. Justin either loitered a pace behind or moved ahead with his dog, not joining in the conversation unless Hugh directed a question at him.

Hugh resolutely forced himself not to stare at the boy. When first he had gazed down at the sprawling child, the memory of other wide-apart, deep-sheltered eyes had shimmered remote yet clear in his mind, and an elated stir had twisted in his abdomen, a blood knot tying itself. Had he not been reasonably certain of Antonia's boy's paternity, he never would have ventured forth from the hotel, yet he was unprepared for this atavistic burst of kinship. He had never felt any tribal bond with Caryll, whom he considered a weak excuse of a child. *This boy's one of us,* he thought with a covert glance at Justin.

The boy's reaction when they had bumped into each other had been vital, open, warm. Now the eyes were narrowed under the porched brow. (Antonia thought of this as his Heathcliff look.) *I wonder what drove him into himself,* Hugh thought. *Well, certainly he's not afraid of me.*

Zoe tugged urgently. "This way," she cried, pulling him into the shadowy gap between walls of boxwood.

They were in a miniature grove. Here, on the hidden patch of grass, three tapestry pillows surrounded a cloth set with Limoges demitasse cups, a platter of buttered brown bread, a silver chocolate pot from which steam still curved.

Hugh gasped spontaneously.

"The fairies do it, but only for us," Zoe chortled. "All the time I bring my best friend Janey Smith-Tolliver and her nanny here, but there's never anything. It only happens when Mother, Justin, and me're together. Fairies are like that, you know."

The dog stretched out, its tail thumping, Zoe and Justin sat, and Antonia knelt gracefully to pour the cocoa. "Here, Hugh," she said.

"I'll share with Zoe." She must have arranged every detail of the midmorning picnic with her servants, yet as she looked up at him over the gold-scalloped rim of the miniature cup, her glance held no trace of compliant adult amusement, only the same pleasure that shone in Zoe's eyes.

Hugh sat between the children. "Delicious. Miss Zoe, I'm glad I'm not Janey Smith-Tolliver. I wouldn't have missed this for the world. And you know the most magical part? This is the first time I've left my hotel rooms."

Justin turned. "You haven't seen the Tower?"

"Not even the changing of the guards." Hugh's fingers tensed on the miniature handle, and worried he might break it, he set the cup carefully in its saucer. "The truth is, Justin, I'm a coward, a terrible coward. I cannot bear to have people staring at me."

"But you're such a pretty color," consoled Zoe, her fingers reaching for his face.

Antonia caught her daughter's buttery hand. "Cowards never admit what they are, Hugh," she said softly.

"That's true, Mr. Bridger." Justin's reserve had dissipated, yet there was no trace of pity in his response to Hugh. He turned to Antonia. "Mother, I have an idea. Remember when you hired the motor cab during the Easter hols?"

Antonia and Zoe nodded, and the three turned expectantly to Hugh. They wanted to take him sight-seeing! When the stares of the nannies and other strollers in the park already had carved him into Quasimodo! His starched collar went chokingly tight and his mouth dried.

"Nobody saw us," Justin said, his cheeks reddening. "We stayed in the motor cab and drove by the Tower, the Houses of Parliament. We saw the new front of Buckingham Palace. Everything. We'd seen it all before, walking. But this was different. Motoring, everything glides by like a lantern show."

"I wish I could, but we're leaving tomorrow morning." Three weeks he had waited on a razor's edge, then, as he abandoned hope, this morning's telephone summons.

"There's this afternoon, Mr. Bridger," Justin said firmly.

Hugh looked into a grave face unmolested by age or doubts. *What an eagle of a man he'll be*, Hugh thought. *A leader. Tom's real son.*

I can take a bit more. "It sounds like a perfect way to end my time in London."

Antonia jumped to her feet, brushing off her skirt. "Cook'll pack us a lunch basket while Drum arranges for the motor cab," she said.

The rumpled cloth and strewn French crockery were left in the glade.

III

The afternoon spread untrammeled by time, one shapeless wad of happiness. As they returned to Rutland Gate a brilliantly striped balloon swept overhead, the tiny, distant passengers waving from its gondola: Hugh could swear that Antonia somehow had contrived this dusk-hazed vision as her final delight.

"That was the best afternoon of my life," he said sincerely. "Why did we have to bump into one another at the end of my trip?"

"We're going to write long letters," Antonia said.

"I can print," Zoe told him.

"I'll post that picture." Justin had already promised to forward his new form photo as soon as he could have a copy made.

"Remember to mark the boys you told me about," Hugh said. "Now the ice has been broken, when are the Hutchinsons going to visit me in Detroit?"

Antonia said hastily, "You'll come here and stay with us. You haven't seen a dot of London."

The driver, who had deposited the large wicker basket in Drum's arms, came to stand at attention by the open taxi door. Antonia touched a kiss near Hugh's unscathed cheek, Zoe hugged him. Hugh turned to Justin, and saw the boy's regret at parting. They shook hands.

"Good-bye, Mr. Bridger," the boy said.

"Now that we're going to be pen pals, Justin, make it Hugh."

"Bon voyage, Hugh," Justin said gravely. It was apparent that he treasured calling a grown man by his first name.

They halted on the top step, Antonia holding Zoe, Justin next to them, the three smiling and waving. Hugh's great attribute in carrying out his plans was lack of haste; he could sit with feline patience until events arranged themselves in readiness for his molding, and as the cab pulled away he was thinking: *Tom's true heir, that's a beginning.* He waved back.

The Edges' chauffeur was to drive them down to Southampton. That evening when Hugh telephoned Monty to say good-bye, he said casually, "By the way, I believe we have a mutual friend. Mrs. Hutchinson."

"Yes, I do know her. Charming woman, charming. Tom ran into her at the Comstocks' ball."

"I've known her forever."

Nothing as yet had been settled about British Onyx.

"Want me to keep an eye out for her?" Monty asked with the eagerness of a man hoping to give an unexpectedly small down payment on a large, coveted piece of property.

"Nothing special," Hugh said. "But she is a friend of mine."

IV

On November 22, 1910, three judges met in the old Post Office Building of New York to reconsider the Selden patent case. Though more than forty attorneys crowded the chambers, each side was granted less than five hours to present oral testimony before the judges retired to poke and prod at the accumulated mass of briefs and exhibits. The only new evidence submitted was a carton of coiled, yellowing drafting paper. Blueprints of Thomas K. Bridger's early motor carriages.

Tom's sleep grew yet more migratory, his hours at Hamtramck more frenzied.

His savage fever, however, was only in part for Onyx: his powerful and complex urge to be with Antonia bedeviled him until his entire being strained and struggled against his entrapment on the Western Hemisphere. Only the hours he spent with Caryll brought him surcease.

After six weeks of deliberation, on January 9, 1911, the judges reconvened in the Post Office Building to read the petrified phrases of legal language. The Selden patent, they had decided, was restricted. It covered only one kind of engine. Neither the Ford nor the Onyx automobile infringed on Selden's patent.

That night Onyx and Ford hosted a victory banquet at the Pontchartrain. Behind the red carnations that graced the head table sat Tom, Rogers Sinclair, Olaf Baardson, Henry Ford and Edsel, who was now eighteen, and Ford's partner, James Couzens. Their recent ALAM opponents, men like William Crapo Durant, head of General

Motors, and Ransom Olds, were at the round tables. A boozy conviviality settled old differences. After an enormous meal, a black quartet played "The Ford March & Two-Step" then "Come Drive in My Fiver," and red-faced, newly moneyed men brayed out the lyrics of the two popular songs.

Rogers Sinclair rose to his feet, lifting his beefy arms for silence. "Your hosts thank you for the tribute of those beautifully rendered anthems," he said. He read aloud a few of the congratulatory telegrams, dropping them back with the others in the overflowing laundry basket. "That's as much crowing as you're going to hear from me. But I am a salesman, and accordingly I aim to sell you on the advantages of having one George Selden and his patent out of the way. Now there'll be no more clamps on production. From here on in, all of us can set our minds to turning out the cars that the public is crying for—I prefer they cry for Fivers rather than Model T's, but don't let Henry know it." At this Henry Ford allowed a whimsical smile, everyone else roared. Rogers teetered on his stout legs before signaling again for quiet. "On a serious note, you see at this table the two greatest men of the automotive age. Tom Bridger and Henry Ford. They battled the giant Trust. They won the good fight. Because of them, every man in the country, rich and poor, can have his own transportation. And this, as we all know, is what our grand new industry is about." Vigorous applause stirred the haze of cigar smoke. "I'm going to ask our sturdy warriors to express their feelings on this victorious night. First, my brother-in-law, Tom Bridger. Well, Tom?"

Rogers had gulped far too many bourbons, otherwise he never would have called on Tom, who disliked and distrusted oratory.

Tom half stood, resting his palms on the table. "Free," he said in a dry, sardonic voice. "That's the word I'm going to say. I feel free to go ahead making the best damn cars at a scratch low price." He sat back in his chair.

Soon after, he left. He did not return to his house, where Maud was putting on a dinner for Mrs. Trelinack, Yssy, Melisande, and other Onyx wives deprived of their husbands' company by the banquet. He sped out on Jefferson through the cold moonlight to Hugh's. "I'm going back to England to start that plant," he announced.

"By all means," Hugh said, a little tipsy on Mumm's.

"Immediately."

"Sail on, O Tommy, sail on. Build us a world empire."

V

He arrived in London around eleven in the morning. The Hyde Park Hotel was freezing—the boiler was being repaired, the reception clerk said apologetically, so the central heat was off. Tom kept on his coat, telling the hall porter that he would unpack his own valise. Alone, he examined the telephone with bemused wonder, as if the familiar instrument were a machine from a far-advanced civilization. He picked up the earpiece.

Evidently the hotel dining room was not dependent on the main boiler: a luxurious warmth spread from the radiators along the wine-colored walls. The clothes worn by the lunching women were misty lavenders and grays—half-mourning for the late monarch. The tables hummed with cultivated voices, and from behind a bower of potted palms came the haunting sweetness of violin, harp, and cello.

"What's that they're playing?" asked Tom.

" 'Meditation' from *Thaïs*," Antonia replied.

"Pretty."

She nodded.

"Until you walked into the lobby," he confessed, "I was terrified you wouldn't come."

Smiling, she bent her head, and the soft white feathers of her hat trembled on glossy rolled black hair.

Tom raised his glass. "Thank you for being here."

Waiters gathered, ceremoniously boning and serving the trout, pouring more wine from the bottle chilling in the three-legged silver ice bucket.

Neither ate much.

Antonia's silences were not awkward but in harmony with the silvery tenderness of the rippling music, and Tom sipped pale wine, imagining himself back in their green Belle Isle languor.

After the charlotte russe he said, "I have a present to you from Onyx. A token. Not nearly what you deserve for winning our case. It's upstairs." He did not mean this as a snare, a lure, a deceit, yet the final sentence seemed to hover above the small yellow fringed table lamp. He slashed his signature across the bill. The fragile mood had snapped.

The lift and hallways were wrapped in cathedral chill, the unkind winter dampness penetrated the cold of his suite. "Be right back," he said, hurrying into the other room for his gift, and the bed with its folded green satin eiderdown, an explicit double bed, dispersed the last evanescent trace of his romanticism. He fumbled through his valise for the gold mesh evening purse he had deliberated over at Tiffany's in New York.

In the sitting room she was smoothing wrinkles from her white kid gloves. He remembered her habit of playing with some small object when she was upset.

Putting down the box, he wrapped his arms around her, reaching under the satin lining of her cape, which was made of a long-haired, creamy fur. They clung together, hip to hip, breast to breast, cheek to cheek, not kissing, the breath of each thrusting against the other's eardrum. Her eyes were squeezed shut, his were open and suffused by a pale, intense light. The leverage of their arms shifted to enclose each other more securely. After a minute he pulled back, peering into her eyes. She flushed. The pinkness allotted him courage to go unsteadily to lock the door.

When he awoke, the room was wadded with purple shadows. *It must be after four*, he thought, moving his palms up her spine and across the delicate shoulder blades: her spareness seemed to make the intimacy of their nakedness more eloquent.

"So you're awake," she said.

"Did you sleep too?"

She shook her head.

"Have I told you how lovely you are?"

"Several times."

Though snug under the blankets and satin quilt, he saw that their breath showed. "What would they say if I offered to give them a hand with that boiler?"

"Go back upstairs and dress, guv'nor."

He laughed. "I'm very, very happy. Was it good for you, too?"

"Beautiful."

"Then why the pensive look?"

She sighed. "You never used to ask questions."

"You wanted me, didn't you?"

"So much that I'd made up my mind not to see you. But when you telephoned, the will went out of me, the way the waiter boned our trout."

He touched her lips and she kissed his fingertip. "Happy?" he asked.

"Yes, very. But there are other considerations."

He touched her hair, sighing. Yes, there was guilt. There was no way he could rationalize that making love to Antonia in any way resembled his other marital defections. "I know."

"We're not the same as we were."

"I won't patronize you by saying Maud means nothing to me. I wouldn't hurt her. Ever. We're close in so many ways." He tried to conjure up an explanation of what he felt for his wife, the warmth, concern, friendship, and totally banked passion, without sounding disloyal, all the while knowing in his heart that lying naked with Antonia, whom he loved, was the ultimate disloyalty. "But this part doesn't mean anything to her. You aren't committing any larceny. She doesn't want me like this. . . ." A spasm of misery caught at his throat before he realized this was the oldest line that any man could give his mistress.

She moved a long, slender leg to touch his. Sympathy.

"Antonia, I meant it when I said I adored you. Was it the thrill of the moment when you said you loved me?"

She turned her head away. "I never stopped," she murmured. And he could tell that her confession came from a conscience as festering as his own. *We both married decent, well-meaning people. Jesus, what a mess.*

Yet Antonia's vague melancholy pleased him. "I'll come over often," he said. "We'll drown our guilts together."

"No."

"But I explained about Maud. She's on *my* conscience. And you have nobody to feel guilty toward."

"I'm terrified about Justin."

"Your boy?" Tom blinked with surprise.

"I can't risk this sort of thing, Tom."

Tom put his thumb under her chin, making her look at him. "Is there somebody else?"

"Men take me to the theater, dining, Ascot." The covers moved as she shrugged her shoulders. "Nobody like . . . I have no lover. I never have. It's Justin."

"You aren't making sense."

"Ever since you came to the house I've had this dream. In it, Justin finds out about himself, and his face disintegrates like wax melting."

"A nightmare."

"I know, but . . ." He felt the shudder run through her. "You're the one man I could never allow to become part of my life."

"Antonia—"

"He's sensitive and thoughtful, he'd put two and two together. It would destroy him."

In the dimness her eyes shone with tears. The small hairs at the back of Tom's neck prickled. He realized that however implausible this rationale might sound to him, an interdiction lay in her heart and mind, and Antonia was quite capable of sacrificing their love on the altar of some hallucinatory threat to her son.

Hallucinatory? A chill ran through him. He thought of his wife and how honest she was with him—what would the knowledge do to her? He thought of Caryll, *his* son. He said, "It's just as important to *me* that people not know."

"This was a miracle." Her whisper caught. "A one-time miracle."

"Nobody's going to find out," Tom said, reaching for her hand, pressing her palm against his heart. "Your son will never know Claude Hutchinson isn't his father."

"You can't promise that."

"The owner of Onyx can. I have money, I have power. I swear it to you on my life, Antonia."

"Secrecy can't be bought, Tom."

"You bet it can." He pulled her toward him, the level arrogance of his voice roughening to urgency as he repeated, "I swear to you on my life, Antonia. Do you believe in that?"

Her long, tremulous sigh was one of acquiescence.

"Thank you," he said, touching his mouth to hers, raising the covers over their heads so she would not be chilled as he kissed the small hollows below her neck. Her pulses beat faster, her skin grew hot, and his erection pressed against her thigh. She shifted. As he went into her they both gasped.

"Darling, this time let me," she whispered.

He remained still and she pressed around him, slowly, insistently carrying him farther and farther from himself, and soon he no longer noticed his heart slamming against his ribs or the pressure of her kisses on his shoulder, he knew no physical sensation other than this undulating joy. It was as though a vestigial, prehistoric sense were returned to him, as though this hard core of his being could experience the infinity of tenderness and wonder in the world. All at once the waves surged violently and she cried out. A light burst through his blood. Yet at the ultimate moment he fell prey to the tick of sadness inherent in each human joy: *This could always have been mine*, he thought.

After their breathing quieted, he said, "Antonia, I give you my word. The boy will never know." His voice was a grainy rumble. "Trust me."

"Ahh, Tom, I must, I must." She spoke in such a passion of love and hopelessness that he pulled her face to his chest, consoling her.

VI

Upper Swithin Place, two miles or so from Rutland Gate, was a treeless enclave of apartment blocks where none of her friends would venture, yet too distinctly middle class for her servants to visit. The tall crimson-brick building had a vacancy on the ground floor, and this particular flat opened onto the side path, a narrow cement ribbon visible only to tenants who might be leaning out of the overhead windows. Tom went to great lengths to ensure that the flat not be linked to him or to Antonia. He put gold guineas into a bank for the estate agent who would pay the rent, arrange for furnishings, hire a charwoman to clean two mornings a week. Tom even went so far as to have cards printed *J. Foreman* so he could slip one in the small iron frame above the doorbell.

Those first few afternoons proved typical of their hours in Upper Swithin Place. Being the more prompt, Tom would arrive to draw the chintz curtains, then Antonia would hurry in to press her cold, glowing cheek to his: she always brought something for him—maybe from her gloved fingers would dangle the strings of a pastry box, or in her chinchilla muff would be tucked new sheet music that she would later sing, accompanying herself on the upright piano. First things first, though. She retired immediately to the bathroom, where she inserted something called a pessary that during her marriage she had secured from a Dutch physician, a blessed device that obviated the need for condoms. They made love unhurriedly and to their mutual delight—if they made love a second time it was swift and guileless, an embellishment of their good-bye kisses. They put on dressing gowns and went into the other room for tea. The shaded wall brackets and false-logged gas fire cast a glow. To his surprise Tom found he could talk about Maud, recounting her doings and praising her good common sense without any wrong notes or sense of shame. His own guilts taught him the validity of Antonia's qualms about Justin. He could not once say Caryll's name. Even in some casual reminiscence about a family outing, coming to Caryll's part in it, his tongue grew thick and he lapsed into silence. In fathering a child on this woman whom he adored, had he not betrayed his legitimate son, whom he loved greatly?

VII

The first ten days, drowning in the liquid purity of Antonia's enormous dark eyes, he did not let Monty know he was in London. Then, early one morning when an icy drizzle fell, he telephoned.

"Jolly glad you're here, Tom," Monty said. "Something interesting's come on the market in Southwark."

"I've had breakfast. Pick me up."

The chauffeur drove them along the south side of the Thames, passing chimneyed factories and endless, prison-like blocks of flats. Shawled women dragged pallid children among stalls whose peddlers hawked their mean wares. A queue of thinly dressed unemployed men hunched shivering in the rain outside an ironworks.

"An excellent labor pool," Monty commented.

"You don't have to tell me. I've lived in places like this."

They came to a long brick wall. Monty leaned forward, rapping on the glass, and the Rolls glided to a halt in front of massive iron gates beyond which railroad spurs crisscrossed acres of wetly glistening cobbles. A row of warehouses blocked the view of the river.

Tom crossed his arms, clasping his elbows.

Yes, he thought. *This is the place. Yes.* Long ago he had determined to build the British plant, and now, because of Antonia, he needed an excuse to visit London often. But the excitement tingling through him did not derive from logic or need. It was an intuitive response.

And time had proved over and over to him the validity of such first impressions.

The chauffeur unlocked the gate chain, and they drove inside.

Monty raised his large black umbrella to protect them both, but Tom strode ahead, barely glancing at the warehouses with their great sliding metal doors, jumping muddy puddles to stand on the embankment of the rain-dotted Thames where boats huddled along, each under its cloud of smoke.

Monty caught up. He pointed to blackened stumps of pilings. "The wharves burned, but there's excellent dockage."

"So I see," Tom said. "The place is fine."

Monty's smile struggled between triumph and disbelief. The shoulders of Tom's gray overcoat had darkened, and the Englishman said, "Here, stand under this. You're getting soaked."

"I won't melt."

"Let's inspect the buildings."

"Why? They'll either be torn down or completely renovated."

"You really are going ahead?"

"Full speed. The British Fiver'll sell for seventy-five pounds."

"Seventy-five quid!" Monty's carefully acquired accent dropped. This, then, was what American automotive chaps meant by Tom Bridger's crazed-missionary streak. He peered into the lean, wet face to ascertain Tom was not joking. "There's not a perishing British motorcar at twice that! My God, seventy-five quid! How'll you cover the losses?"

"Get pretty girls to collect in cans for needy automobile manufacturers." Tom's eyes held a cruel, sardonic glint. "Want to be in charge?"

Monty's sandy mustache quivered. What a devil of a pincers. To be offered his fondest hope—but by a lunatic. He said cautiously, "Maybe we could manage at a hundred and ten pounds—if we set our minds to it. Trim expenses. Instead of vanadium, use ordinary steel and—"

"The Fiver's top-notch. She'll be that way on both sides of the Atlantic."

"How in the devil, at *that* price?"

"We'll reduce the man-hours it takes to build her."

"Tom, I'm quite stupid, actually. Explain that to me."

"It's very simple. The cost of anything, whether it's a loaf of bread, an ocean liner, or a car, depends on the number of man-hours needed to transform it from raw material to finished goods.''

"And what about capital? Have you forgotten capital investment?''

"Capital is a word invented by economists. Jargon. Buildings and machines are made by men, designed by men, built from materials produced or mined by man. In other words, accumulated man-hours." Tom paused. "*I'll* worry about the capital. What we have to do, you and me, is figure how to produce a top-notch, cheap British car.''

They continued to walk. Monty's face pared into the shrewdness of his half-starved apprentice days. "Tom, ever broken down a job into its various steps?''

"What do you mean?''

"A line of men each performing one individual step.''

"Give me an example.''

"Take a flywheel magneto. Everybody in the industry uses skilled mechanics to make magnetos. But say one were to break it down into steps, devise a small assembly line.''

"It might be faster.''

"Yes, but you're missing my point. Each task would be simple. A turn of a spanner, an adjustment.''

"What a rotten, unsatisfying way to spend your life, turning one bolt all day long.''

"We'd save a fortune if we figured out how to utilize unskilled labor." Monty glanced eloquently at the rain-hazed mustard-brick warrens. "Them.''

"It's depressing.''

"*You*'re the one who set the bloody seventy-five pounds. How in the devil did you arrive at that number, Tom?''

"While we were over here, Hugh worked on some statistics. I figured it was a good price for a lot of Englishmen.''

"Your average navvy able to afford a motorcar? Never in a million years!" Monty hooted. "Tom, you're a candidate for Bedlam.''

"You're not the first to give me the news," Tom said wryly. They were back at the Rolls. "Let's get started. The sooner we tackle the estate agents, the sooner we'll have the property.''

"You meant it, then? I'm to head up British Onyx?''

"Unless you'd rather keep the London franchise.''

"*I'm* not a lunatic.''

VIII

"Again?" Maud asked. "You were over with Hugh last spring, then most of January and all of February. And you say you're going back again in June? Why?"

"The Southwark factory's big, Maud," Tom said. "Who else can check the plans?"

He was sitting at the kitchen table while she fixed and served him late-night scrambled eggs.

"What about Monty?" she asked.

"Problems, problems, they come up and I'm the only one who can solve them." He attempted to sound offhand, but his wife's response to his upcoming trip had made him tense with guilty apprehension: flat C exposed as a love nest.

"This brings up something I have to discuss." Maud's high coloring was more intense, and despite the practical apron enveloping her dowdy wool dress, she looked handsome. Obviously nervous, too, as she pulled out a chair.

Tom clenched the butter knife, wishing he had a drink under his belt. "Sounds serious. Go ahead. Shoot."

Her frank, bespectacled eyes leveled on him. "I won't beat about the bush," she blurted. "I heard about a place near the Pontchartrain where there's women. Somebody said you go there."

Tom went weak with reprieve. But then, how *could* anyone have guessed about Antonia? He had been excessively careful. *The guilty flee where no man pursueth*, he chided himself. He looked at Maud and smiled. Another wife would have kept silent about a slip as minor and impersonal as a visit to a cathouse. But his Maud always had to have every single card on the table. He shook his head, his irritation streaked with fondness. "Honey, why listen to gossip?"

"Is it true?"

"I haven't been there in forever." He halted abruptly: he was confessing fidelity to Antonia, not her. "How about some coffee?"

At the stove, pouring from the reheated percolator, facing away from him, she asked, "Are there places like that in England?"

"Not that I know about."

"You're there so much."

"Business."

"Don't snap at me, Tom. I just wanted you to know that I

184

understand about that sort of thing. And I won't say it doesn't hurt me, because it does, but I'd much rather know." She turned.

There was the saddest look on her face, and for a moment Tom remembered their wedding night at the Russell House: they had used her money for the hotel room. Maud had stood staunchly by the drawn curtains, telling him in this same way that she understood she was second choice, an involuntary, sorrowful honesty that drew him to her in sympathy and warmth. Now he got up and patted her firm shoulder. "Maud, honey, you're my wife. I care a lot."

"It's all right, Tom," she said. "The main thing is that we must always be honest with each other. That's the one thing I couldn't stand, you lying to me."

IX

The next three years Tom went often to England.

Antonia endured his absences as she would a jail term, but when she was with him, she could shut out the world. Tom, missing her as profoundly, lacked her ability to live in the moment, and in flat C he was always conscious, however marginally, of the ticking of the Biedermeier clock in the small sitting room, time moving inexorably toward another separation.

Inventions and improvements were cross-fertilized on both sides of the Atlantic.

Monty's flywheel magneto was the first example. When Tom had returned to Detroit, he had taken his old toolbox to the Hamtramck plant, stood with the skilled mechanics behind his own little heap of materials, and, like the others, had assembled a magneto on the flywheel in about twenty minutes. The following Saturday he returned with Caryll. Working very slowly, he assembled a magneto, halting at each step to describe to the boy what he had done. Caryll, gray eyes round with importance, wrote down the description, numbering it.

Setting down his wrench, Tom asked, "How many steps is that?"

"Twenty-nine, Dad."

Tom wiped his hands with a rag. "Come on. Let's get over to the machine shop."

As they left the busy mechanics grinned. Everybody in the Hamtramck knew two things about the boss: He spent mighty little time in his large office suite, and his boy earned his allowance here on Saturdays.

Job seekers formed a perpetual line at the employment office on Conant Street. Ten days later Tom hired twenty-nine unskilled applicants, leading them, a bobbling line of caps and knitted hats, to a building where a waist-high gray iron workbench had been constructed. It was exactly wide enough to hold an Onyx flywheel. Close-together bins were heaped with various glinting scraps of metal. Tom showed each man his simple task. He pulled a switch. A drive chain driven by a worm shaft and worm gear clanked, and the flywheel at one end of the bench shivered forward. A man fed another into the vise.

Tom perched on a stool, his arms crossed, in an attitude of peculiar, watchful relaxation that the camera sometimes caught. He had spent hours arranging and rearranging this moving bench so that each man received his task under his hands, never having to shift his feet. Three of his new employees performed their jobs clumsily. He slowed the belt to eighteen inches per minute. After a while he was able to speed it up again.

The flesh below his cheekbones drew in, his upper lip raised to give him an air of vulnerability. Few would suspect his experiment had been a success. The time it took to produce a magneto had shrunk from twenty minutes to twelve. *It'll be less, far less*, Tom thought, *when they get used to a traveling bench*.

Tom stared a long time at the workers, his thoughts bleakly ambivalent. The repetitive movements desolated him, yet this drab monotony was the way to bring the Fiver—transportation—into everyone's reach.

He walked slowly over to Administration to tell Olaf Baardson, who was now in charge of the Hamtramck, about the new mobile workbench. Over his brother-in-law's arguments Tom ordered that the new unskilled assembly workers receive the same clock pay as mechanics. A few weeks later the engineering department swarmed through the factory, reorganizing and reshaping every shop.

Thus it was that Onyx developed the first moving assembly line ever used, anywhere.

CHAPTER 12

The British Onyx factory had its grand opening on June 2, 1914.

Early that morning it rained for an hour or so, but by afternoon the azure sky held only a few whorling, very high clouds, and sun had dried the miles of tricolor bunting—the white was marked with batik-like pink patterns from the red dye, the blue faded to mauve. Police held back a crowd that surged toward every chauffeured limousine entering the gates. Though for nearly two years now the factory had been turning out Fivers that sold for £80, the engine blocks had been shipped from Detroit. Ten weeks earlier the first fully British-produced Onyx had come off the line, so they were having a public celebration. The young Prince of Wales, as keen on automobiles as his late grandfather, Edward VII, had agreed to cut the opening ribbon.

Alongside the main assembly, striped marquees had been erected to shelter top-hatted men, women wearing summer furs over pastel afternoon gowns, and a few older children, all boys. Monty, flushed and laughing, moved about making his aristocratic guests welcome.

Tom, Maud, Caryll, and Trelinack had come over for the festivities. Trelinack, standing by himself, appeared shrunken into his brand new frock coat: since his wife's death the previous winter he had shed weight like a deserted basset hound and clung pathetically to his family. From his vantage point his anxious eyes could make out only the tan crown of Maud's hat; however, he had a fine view of Tom and Caryll, who were showing the body chute to Sir Henry Royce. Like Monty, Tom was flushed with excitement. Both were high, drunk with the accomplishment of completing the best-equipped industrial complex in Europe.

A cream Lanchester rolled up and Drum, pear-shaped in his maroon chauffeur's uniform, alighted to hand out Antonia and her children.

Tom, engrossed with Sir Henry, did not notice the new arrivals until he heard an American voice, *her* voice. Halting in midsentence, he swiveled around, shocked and confused. Though on this trip they had not met at the flat, she had told him often enough that she would not accept an invitation to any event he was likely to attend. *What if one of us shows too much? Or not enough?* She had never relinquished her idée fixe—indeed, her misplaced guilts and lacerating fears about rousing her son's suspicions were stronger than ever. Yet she was here, tall black-haired son at her side, vividly gorgeous little daughter in front of her. Tom's mental anarchy was suffused by waves of pleasure.

There she stands, tall, slender, in a diaphanous, flowing dress, vibrant yet shy as a wood nymph . . . once we lay amid sycamore trees. . . . He must have excused himself coherently because Caryll was at his side as they moved toward her.

"Why, Antonia."

"Tom. It's good to see you again. And at such a proud occasion!" Her purposefully guarded smile wavered, and he knew she too was feeling the wild electric impulses set up by their nearness. "We were so delighted," she continued a trifle breathily, "when Monty and Edwina sent us an invitation."

"I should have thought of it myself."

"You remember my son, Justin?"

"Sure I do. Hello, Justin."

"Congratulations, sir." Justin's voice was changing, but it was his air of thoughtful strength as much as his physical maturity that made him seem older than fourteen. He extended his hand.

As Tom clasped Justin's boyishly hard, bat-calloused palm, he felt an apostate quiver: a sense of wronging Caryll in Caryll's presence. "Thank you," he said.

Antonia was fingering her daughter's silky red-gold hair. "But I don't believe you've met Zoe."

Zoe's crisp white pleats swirled as she kicked a small curtsy. Her grace was as conspicuous as her beauty. "It's thrilling to be here,

Mr. Bridger. I've only seen his royal highness at the trooping of the color.''

"You'll be much closer to the prince today," Tom promised. "Antonia, this is my son, Caryll. Caryll, Mrs. Hutchinson is a Detroiter, at least she lived awhile on Woodward Avenue. And these are Justin and Zoe Hutchinson.''

"P-pleased to meet you," Caryll stammered. His head remained bent, but he continued to dart timid glances at Zoe, whose thick-lashed dark gaze had remained on him. He grabbed for her hand, which was soft and pliant, releasing it only reluctantly when Justin's large, firm grip enfolded his hand. Caryll's mother having impressed on him the necessity of acting the good host, this improbably lovely little girl having captured his imagination, and Justin's blue eyes being warmer than the eyes of the other young English guests, Caryll mumbled, "Would you care for some sandwiches before the tour starts?''

"Delighted," Zoe said grandly.

As they left the adults her eyes glinted with devilment, and she darted like a loosened spring toward the long, linen-swathed buffet. Caryll, infected by her vitality, kept up. Justin, behind them, tried for dignity.

Antonia murmured, "Tom, I—" then broke off.

Maud was descending on them. "Miss Dalzell!" she said with loud pleasure. "Who ever would have dreamed there'd be a familiar face today!''

"It's not Miss Dalzell anymore, Maud," Tom said. "It's Mrs. Hutchinson.''

"And you're Mrs. Bridger," Antonia said. "What a wonderful occasion.''

"Tom's day." Maud beamed. Normally she avoided public displays of affection, but she linked her arm with Tom's. She was feeling the sweet, heady satisfaction of well-turned tables. Years ago she had sewn for Antonia and been jealous of her because of Tom. *And here I am, Tom's wife, hostess of this splash.* To Maud's credit she rarely thought of herself as a multimillionaire—but could any woman alive not relish this triumph? "How wonderful to see you again," she said sincerely. "So you married an Englishman?''

Antonia shook her head. "An American.''

"But those *are* your two with Caryll?''

"Justin and Zoe, yes."

"She'll be a real beauty—she is already. I'll bet you have a real time keeping your husband from spoiling her." Maud glanced around. "Where is he? I'd love to meet him," she said.

"I've been widowed quite a few years."

"Oh, I am sorry." The lowering of Maud's voice paid homage to death, and she held more tightly to her own husband. "It must be quite a chore raising children alone, especially a boy."

"I cannot tell you how well Justin keeps Zoe and me in line." Antonia's scrolled lips were pale, but her tone was *sec*.

Maud gave her loud, cheerful laugh.

"Caryll's a fine boy," Antonia said. "He certainly resembles you."

"That's what everybody says. But he has Tom's eyes, doesn't he, dear?"

Tom nodded. His breath was shallow; he felt as if liquid were being forced down his nostrils. This suffocation had nothing to do with Antonia's unanticipated presence—the joy of her nearness continued to hum along his nerves. No, it was the queer coyness of Maud's pressure against his side that he could not assimilate.

"Tom." Monty had come over. "Can you excuse yourself from this charming company for a minute?"

"Of course he can," Maud said, giving her husband a little push. "Go on, dear. Antonia and I have fifteen years to catch up on."

"Hush." Antonia put a finger to her lips. "You're giving away state secrets."

As Monty drew Tom away Maud was laughing again.

She eyed Antonia, thinking, *She's still far too thin, I'll bet she doesn't weigh one twenty, but that Grecian cut has Poiret all over it. She's as lively as ever. A widow, hmmm.* All at once a thought popped into Maud's mind. *She certainly was cozy with Tom when I came over.* It was never Maud's proclivity to delve into the nuances of moods, but looking into Antonia's face, she saw that the luminous skin was pale and small muscles showed around the smile. Her warmth faded and a little chill penetrated through her new astrakhan cape.

"So you're great friends with Monty and Edwina?" she probed.

"We're at the same parties sometimes."

"Then you must run into Tom."

Antonia's lashes drew down. "I haven't seen him in years. But Hugh was over here, and he and the children write to one another. It's very kind of him—they don't know many Americans."

"But the Edges are forever entertaining Tom, dragging him to parties," Maud persisted. "If you're in *their* set, I don't see how you've avoided him."

"I suppose it is odd."

"He was quite sweet on you."

"That was back in the ice age, Maud, our salad days." Antonia spoke lightly, charmingly, but her eyes remained veiled.

Maud's forlorn jealousies were resurrected. "I used to think of myself as second fiddle," she blurted.

"Antonia, darling!" a high, girlish voice caroled.

"Penelope. It's been ages." Antonia's reply choked. "Maud, I . . . excuse me."

She ran toward a full-bosomed matron to whom Maud had been introduced earlier, the countess of something. Maud touched her handkerchief to her forehead. Her immeasurable suspicions shamed her, yet the brief conversation had clinked with so many false notes that she—far from subtle—could not ignore the possibilities.

A stir was rippling through the alfresco gathering. Adults set down their champagne glasses, children raised on tiptoes to make themselves appear taller. A long black Daimler with two chauffeurs glided along the cobblestones, halting near the marquee, and a short, fair-haired young man emerged smiling from the limousine. Men bowed. Women curtsied, their big tulle-swathed hats touching their knees.

The twenty-year-old who was heir to the British empire shook hands with an American mechanic and his seamstress wife, their gentle little son, and, finally, with Trelinack, who wept openly. He, a Cousin Jack tin miner, meeting the old Queen's great-grandson! If only the missus could be here to share the golden-haired, handsome royal glory of it!

The doors to the main assembly were barred by a heavy blue satin ribbon that the rain had stiffened. The gold presentation scissors were not sharp. The Prince of Wales struggled. "My mother's better at this than I am," he said with the smile that had charmed the world.

II

Down the five-hundred-yard length of the assembly clanked a grease-coated chain that towed an endless line of chassis frames to which axles, springs, mudguards, lamp brackets, wheels, and myriad other parts were bolted or seated or adjusted or tightened or secured, connected, grease-gunned, inspected, tagged.

Visitors, a brilliant swarm of gnats, hovered around laboring ants who wore tiny Union Jacks in their lapels. As the handsome young prince passed each worker briefly halted at his task, raising a hat, bowing: the prince, intent on listening to Tom amid the thunderous clangor, extended his upheld palm in a regal blessing that was surely descended from the ancient time of kingly priesthood. Tom's mouth curved in wry amusement. Even to his cynical mind the royal progress somehow sanctified his heavy, looming machinery.

The male guests clustered around Tom and Monty, listening. Justin, trying not to shove rudely, stayed very close. To him the platforms, engine hoists, overhead conveyors were heroic as well as huge, and he wished, fervently, that this impregnable fortress of adult masculinity were not the fiefdom of a man so mean-spirited as to blame his mother for old wrongs committed by her uncle.

After a half hour Tom and the prince reached the end of the chain, where a driver was about to get into the completed skeleton of a Fiver.

"May I?" shouted the prince.

"Your Highness," Tom shouted back. "As you can see there's only a gasoline tank to sit on—petrol, I mean."

"Don't strike any matches, then," joked the young man, climbing on. Tom, too, jumped up to the cylindrical, sloshing tank, and the prince drove them off the line. Factory workers cheered, a full-throated sound above the metallic roar, as the royal prince steered their handiwork through the high door. A moment to be treasured and embellished for a lifetime. A white line had been painted along the broad alley, and the prince followed it, throttling the motor to an expert halt at the body chute.

Tom said, "You have a job anytime you apply."

The prince laughed. "Your pay, I hear, is excellent."

Guests swirled after them.

A drab, dark gray body emerged from the second story, jouncing down the tobogganway. Under the surveillance of the prince and his entourage, eight red-faced workers, the shortest one perched atop the improvised ladder of a wooden crate, bolted and adjusted the utilitarian body to the chassis. The assemblies continued, but the visitors were moving to a marquee where Monty presented the Prince of Wales with a gold tray engraved with a Fiver, and then everyone sipped and nibbled convivially.

III

Zoe and Caryll were sharing a plate of cucumber sandwiches.

"How old are you?" Zoe asked.

"Ten and a half."

"I'm nine." Zoe added more than a year and took another sandwich. "What form are you in?"

"In America we have grades. Fifth."

"America! Grades, ha! Is Hugh your uncle?"

"Yes."

"We write and he sends us lovely Christmas presents," she said. "Do you always mumble?"

"I wasn't mumbling," Caryll said louder.

Zoe gave a contented smile. "Americans never talk clearly," she said in a kinder tone. "Have you been to a motorcar factory before?"

"Not this one. But I work Saturdays at Hamtramck."

"Ham-tra-mack," she enunciated scornfully. Her eyes danced and darted as if searching out a mischief. Grumbling roars escaped through a propped-open window. "What the dickens is going on in there?"

"They're assembling parts, I can't tell you which."

"*I* don't care. *I* came to see his Royal Highness. Justin's the one who's batty about motorcars, not me." Finishing the sandwich, she licked her pink tongue across her pretty lips. "Show me."

"What?"

"Silly. That." She jerked her head toward the noise.

"We're not meant to leave."

"You're afraid."

"Not at all," he denied.

"Prove it," she said. Her narrow little black leather shoes flashed over the cobbles, and she disappeared around the corner of the shop.

Caryll glanced nervously about. His parents were each with a different group, his grandfather sat on a chair next to Mrs. Edge's mother, an ancient crone whose mallard-feather hat shook constantly. Nobody appeared to be watching. He set the plate on a passing butler's tray and ran full tilt in the direction Zoe had disappeared.

She lay in wait around a corner. "Yaaaa!" she cried, laughing delightedly when he jumped. She was swinging her straw hat by its pink ribbons. Caryll took off his cap. "That's better," she approved. "Your father makes you work. Does he beat you dreadfully?"

"Dad? Never!"

"Then why were you in such a funk about leaving?"

"It's a special day for him. I don't like to ruin it."

"Justin hates him."

"Your brother? He doesn't even know Dad."

"When I was ever so little, your father came to our house and quite upset our mother. He made her ill."

"I don't believe you," Caryll snapped.

"Justin gave him what for, I can tell you. He never came back."

"Liar!" Loyal anger contorted Caryll's round face, and his tone grated. *"Liar!"*

Zoe stepped backward, her lovely features fairly shriveling, her perfectly cleft chin aquiver. Caryll refused to be taken in. Wasn't this misery mere pretense? Another flagrant means of cowing him? But the beautiful dark eyes were filling with real tears.

To the outward eye Zoe trod swiftly through her school days, a goddess in navy tunic and crepe de chine blouse surrounded by a penumbra of self-confidence. In reality her security rested entirely with Antonia and Justin: her family formed the single constant star of her existence. She knew that they loved her. With everyone else red-hot pokers of skepticism burned her. How could she be assured of adoration? She teetered between moods. Either she bullied and teased the girls in her form—sometimes until they wept—to insure fealty, or she bestowed compliments, secrets, and aniseed balls on which she spent her entire pocket money. Her inconsistency, her erratic behavior, crackled with charm. The baffled mistresses spoke of Zoe Hutchinson as being a terror in the same breath that they admired her excessive beauty and vivid affections.

She reached for Caryll. He snatched away his hand.

"Your father must be very clever," she offered. "His factory's so important that the Prince of Wales has come."

"Mmm."

"There're Onyx motorcars all over the world."

Caryll, who had learned the inflection of surrender only too well from his own misfortunes, knew he could have the upper hand. His innate flaw, gentleness, prevented him from claiming supremacy. "I have an album of Fivers photographed all over the world," he said. "Basutoland, the Himalayas, Siberia." They had reached a green-painted door with a glass panel reinforced by wire mesh. "You've got nice hair," he blurted.

Zoe tugged at a strand of her own, then his. Both children whooped delightedly.

Inside, looming Foote-Burt spindle drillers and Ferracute power presses dwarfed and drowned out their guardians, who smelled of stale perspiration and whose canvas aprons sported tiny flags. The nearest workers, hoping to see royalty, looked up from their rapidly moving machines: seeing only two well-dressed children, they shrugged and went back to their tasks.

"I say!" Justin shouted. He stood panting in the doorway behind them. "What, exactly, do you two little nits think you're doing? You'll have everyone looking for you."

Caryll bent his head.

Zoe crossed her arms over her moire sash. "Even his Royal Highness?" she demanded.

"The prince is getting ready to leave."

"Then you don't mean everybody."

"I mean Mother," Justin said, his deep-set blue eyes sparkling dangerously.

Outside, she took her time replacing her straw sailor, smoothing twin pink streamers down the precise center of the nape of her neck before sauntering back to the marquees.

The whistle screamed. A fortune in machinery clanked to a halt, and more than five thousand workers poured from every building, jostling to see, waving caps, shouting "Huzzah!" as the royal Daimler eased along the recently swept paths of the factory and through the gates. In the street, police linked arms to hold back the shabby, madly enthusiastic crowd that refused to disperse until every limousine had swept by. Antonia's Lanchester was the first to go, the Edges' Rolls—Trelinack and Caryll perched on its jump seats—the last.

IV

Tom had agreed to an interview with a man from the *Daily Telegraph*, and Maud had insisted on waiting. Ignoring the caterers as they dismantled the striped marquees, she stood tapping her glasses into her gloved hand, her head hunched a little so her large, practical tan summer hat formed a toadstool top to her black astra-khan cape.

Alas for Maud. Having connected Tom's numerous lengthy trips to England with Antonia's guilty jumpiness, storms were raging within her. Had he been coming here to be with her . . . ? Yet despite that ineradicable jealousy Maud's literal mind formed a thin membrane of doubt that protected her from the worst. *Suspicions aren't truth,* she told herself.

Tom strode toward her. Hatless, his glossy, prematurely gray hair blowing around a face tanned from the sea voyage, his new suit showing off his well-knit body, he was, she realized with a tremor in her throat, a virile, attractive man.

She asked, "How did it go?"

"All right," he said. He no longer appeared buoyed by the day's triumph.

They were silent as he drove. Along these mean streets the occasional dray was hauled by a blinkered, swaybacked plug, but crossing the Thames, the Onyx became part of motorized streams: solid-tire buses with advertisements for soap or cocoa blazoned across their upper decks, lorries, taxicabs, expensive automobiles as well as Onyxes, Morrises, Austins, Fords. In less than fifteen years the horse had been just about supplanted.

Head lamps—oil, gas, and electric—hazed circles through the purplish green twilight. Maud leaned back into the pressed-air cushion, her body heavy with apprehensive determination. She knew it a powerful error to invade the territory of her husband's heart, her breath caught in anguish at the thought of it, yet she had to know, didn't she, if there was anything between him and that scrawny, black-haired bitch? "She's still as full of life as ever."

"Who?"

"Your old flame. Antonia Dalzell. Mrs. Hutchinson."

The tendons of Tom's hands stood out as he gripped the steering wheel more tightly. "Yes," he said, brusquely changing the subject.

"That reporter gave me a bad time. The press here isn't fond of foreigners. Thank God Hugh had the brains to hire a British public relations firm."

"He saw her when he came over."

"Hugh?"

"But you never ran into her?"

An old-fashioned Gabriel horn blared as a brass-lavished open car swept by. "A 1907 Napier," Tom said.

"She's a friend of Monty's, isn't she?"

Tom said nothing.

"He sent her the invitation. You've never seen her at their house?"

"Years ago they dragged me to a dance," Tom said. "She was there."

"Was her husband dead then?"

"Maud, the *Telegraph* man put me through hoops. I've had enough grilling for one day." Tom's upper lip rose; the expression was reminiscent of Caryll's when he ran home to evade the older bullies up the street—an unhappy, cornered, shamed look that should have been confession enough.

But Maud's mind was a dictator, prodding and harrying her until she had whipped away the last ambiguities.

She swallowed. "He must've left her well fixed. I've sewed enough to know Paris when I see it. That dress was Paul Poiret. Who can afford *him*? Maybe in that set, rich men buy their mistresses extravagant clothes." As Maud spoke she considered the identity of the probable benefactor. She shivered, clasping her icy hands together. "Of course, there was the Major," she said. "I'll bet *he* left her everything. He was very fond of her—the Woodward Avenue bunch never stopped talking about the two of them. What they said!"

"All right, Maud, that's enough," Tom growled.

At this point Maud had fully expected to bring her convictions into the open. But fear, a horrible black fear, canceled her natural honesty.

"Monty's mistress was there today," she said. "That giggly little blonde. Lady Chapin. Did you know about it?"

"I don't come to England to gossip," he snapped.

His temper, Maud sensed, was being reined by thin, cutting wires of willpower. Her mouth tasted salty. She longed to remain silent, yet words kept flooding. "Edwina told *me* right out. She's a chip of ice. I can't imagine accepting it. She says it happens as a marriage wears on. But then we're so tangled up together, you and me. There's Caryll, the Farm." Recently they had purchased several hundred rolling, uncleared acres near Bloomfield Hills, and Maud was working on house plans with Albert Kahn, who had designed the Hamtramck plant. "Maybe these things are different here."

Tom braked at the hotel's red baize carpet, and the doorman hurried around to open Maud's door. A bellboy raced down the steps. Tom was the rare chauffeurless guest, and the doorman's assistants always jumped at the chance to take the wheel. The boy's narrow wedge of a chin fell as Tom said, "Not now, thanks. I'm going on."

Maud, one shoe on the running board, stared at her husband, expecting to see resentful fury. The hotel torchères shone on something infinitely more chilling. Tom's long, angular face suffused with pity. For her.

"Go ahead to Monty's party without me," he said.

V

This trip, his family's first to Europe, they had not arranged to meet at the flat, so when he used his key the scent of roses surprised him. Switching on the light, he saw the tall vase on the piano, a chocolate box on the table. He ate a cream while the operator reached her number.

Drum asked, "May I say who is calling?"

"Mr. Foreman."

Antonia promised to be there in a half hour.

He took one of the long-stemmed yellow roses and went outside, pacing up and down, aware of the delicious fresh night coolness on his face, feeling the spring of his thigh muscles.

I'll get a divorce, he thought.

Halting, he peered at the rose, amazed at the simplicity of what seemed to him a snap decision. In reality he had thought often of a divorce but had shrunk from examining the ramifications out of fond loyalty to Maud, out of love for Caryll. The idea had sunk into his mind's subterranean depths, nearly four years of gnawing, worrying, chewing. Maybe the thought would have stayed there below the level of consciousness if it hadn't been for the joy of Antonia's being there at his triumph, or had Maud not hammered questions at him, then so resolutely attacked his love. Tom began to stride again, his footsteps jubilant, impatient in the quiet street.

Divorce . . .

A taxi's side and head lamps pierced Upper Swithin Place. After counting out silver for the cabbie, Tom bowed ceremoniously, handing Antonia the rose.

"Do you often come here alone?"

Her smile was one of high excitement. "Call me a foolish, romantic woman. I miss you."

They had reached the flat, and he closed the door behind them. "Is that why you were at the reception?"

She was suddenly anxious; stricken. "Wasn't that awful of me? Tom, I couldn't help it. Monty sent an invitation and I was writing my excuses when the children came in. They saw the card. It seems Justin's been dying to have a tour of your factory. And Zoe had a tantrum about seeing the Prince of Wales. The two of them never gave me a chance." Her voice shook. "So there I was, the other woman, the interloper."

"Antonia, you were the one person who belonged. Remember the quadricycle?"

Those pleading lines between delicate black brows eased. "That's what I kept thinking. From that funny little machine to this enormous factory!"

"So I impressed you?"

"Bowled me over," she said. "What about the ball at Monty's?"

He bent, striking a match to the gas jets. "It's proceeding without me."

"You can't miss *that*."

"Sit down."

"Is it Maud? Did she suspect? I tried to be casual, but—"

"Sit down," he repeated, waiting until she was on the sofa. "Antonia, hasn't it ever struck you how ridiculous this is? False names, secret telephone messages, pretending we barely know each other, sneaking in here. For God's sake, we're not international spies."

"It's how people have an affair."

"When was this ever just that?"

"A love affair." She was playing with the snap of her purse. "What else could you call it?"

"I'm getting a divorce."

Her hand flew to her mouth. "No!"

"It's the only way."

"Maud helped you get started. And what about Caryll?"

"She's not petty or spiteful, she'll be good about him."

"I saw how you are together. Your face lights up. And he . . . when he looks up at you, Tom, it's as though he's looking into the sun."

Tom folded his arms on the mantel, resting his forehead on his knuckles. The heat of gas flames penetrated his striped trousers. He gave a long, shuddering sigh. "He's what's kept me going. But I want to be at the center of my life. Antonia, you are the center of it."

"Stop it! Tom, you know this is impossible."

"I made you a promise. It'll be kept."

"You don't know Justin."

"He's fourteen already. In a few years he'll be off on his own. And what about us?" Tom broke off abruptly. Into his mind had come an image of a barren room and a young, ill-looking Antonia setting the various weights of love on her personal scales, a scales whose balance was inevitably tilted in favor of the weak, the needy. "I'm not about to make the same mistake twice," he said. "I won't push you. We'll keep meeting like this if you insist, but—"

"Why a divorce, then?" she broke in. "Maud guessed, didn't she? Is this her idea?"

Tom shook his head. "No. And we never said the words linking you and me, but she knows, she knows. She put me through the meat grinder. Christ! It hurt her, it hurt me, and that's all the good it accomplished. I felt so damn sorry for her that I could have cried." He swung around, staring at Antonia with haunted eyes. "I just can't go on anymore."

Her ambivalences showed as nakedly as his. "Darling, you're grayer," she said in a low, hoarse tone that he thought of as her bed voice. "I wasn't with you when you went grayer."

"Since that afternoon at the Hyde Park Hotel I haven't looked at another woman," he said thickly. "I don't think I ever have."

She took a step toward him, and they abandoned argument and

reason. They had not been together in more than four months, he needed to be joined to love and happiness, he needed her. Their fierce kiss smelled of champagne from the British Onyx reception and lasted while they sank onto the sofa, pushing aside their clothes. They made love, reversing their usual pattern, slithering with heedless swiftness the first time, then later in the bed finding tender, inexhaustible languor that was oblivious to the past or the future. Antonia gave no promises; however, she did not insist, as she normally did, on leaving before midnight, and this, Tom decided, augured well.

VI

Daily Telegraph, Wednesday, June 3, 1914.

FACTORY OPENING

Yesterday afternoon the Prince of Wales cut the opening ribbon at the British Onyx factory in Southwark. Among those present were:

Prince and Princess Louis Battenberg, the Marquis of Whitfield, the Dowager Countess of Milton, Lord and Lady Allingham, Lord and Lady Comstock, Lord Considine, Sir John and Lady Fielding, Sir Henry Royce.

Anyone who has seen the British Onyx factory appreciates it is the most advanced in the world, a matter of national pride. Nothing has been left undone to produce motorcars and lorries in the swiftest, most efficient manner with the use of endless conveyor belts, traveling cranes and a vast array of especially designed machines. The factory's goal, praiseworthy in the extreme, is to meet the travel requirements of the average man at a price many Englishmen can well afford. Mr Edge and Mr Bridger are to be congratulated on their enterprise.

Maud stood reading the paper in the window alcove of the suite's sitting room. She wore a brown-checked traveling ensemble with a loose-waisted jacket that turned her ample curves into a block. Her wide cheeks had lost their color, and she looked weary. She had not slept. Last night she had telephoned Monty, telling him without giving any excuse that she would not be at the party, nor would Tom. Though the Bridgers were his guests of honor, Monty, accustomed to Maud's bluntness and Tom's eccentric social behavior, asked no questions. Then Maud had gone to bed without dinner. She saw Tom's absence as a declaration of war against her. And whether it is a country or a person that enters into a combat, she knew, the old rules of easeful comfort cannot apply. Spartan strengths, extraordinary resources must be mobilized. Thus Maud assuaged her welling grief by formulating a battle plan. She had observed that Edwina, Yssy, and Melisande had kept their respective spouses by overlooking husbandly excursions from the straight and narrow matrimonial bed.

The way to hold onto Tom, she thought, *is to act as though that harlot doesn't exist. How will I manage that? I must.* She buried her face in the pillow so that her son and her father in their adjacent rooms would not hear her deep sobs.

At five thirty, when Tom had tiptoed from the dressing room into the other bed, she had feigned sleep.

"Mother."

She looked up from the newspaper. "Yes?"

Caryll sat at a table strewn with newspapers that he was clipping, his raglan overcoat folded over the back of his chair. "Don't you think we ought to wake Dad?"

"You've asked that a dozen times," Maud said.

"But we planned to leave at nine and it's after ten and he never sleeps late."

"He's entitled to after excitement like yesterday." She set the *Daily Telegraph* in front of him. "Here's another one for your scrapbook."

The bedroom door opened. Tom came in stretching. His too short bathrobe bared strong, brown-haired calves. "I guess I overslept," he said, yawning.

Caryll was on his feet. "We've been ready for hours. Grandpa's waiting downstairs already."

"Something's come up, Caryll. I can't leave today," Tom muttered. They would not be returning to London, and he could not sail without seeing Antonia one more time.

Caryll's round cheeks trembled with dismay. "You mean the trip's off?"

"Are you kidding?" He rumpled the boy's hair. "We'll go in a couple of days."

"But that'll mess up our stops. We planned our stops to buy gasoline so carefully." Caryll picked up a map of England strewn with little yellow flags to indicate where two-gallon cans of BP petrol were available. "Look, Dad, I found another outlet in Cornwall, near St. Just."

"Caryll," Maud said. "It's not like you to pester your father. And there's no problem. You, me, and Grandpa will start today."

Tom looked at her warily, baffled by this unexpected aid when she must surely know the reason behind his delay: she refused to meet his gaze. "That's right," he said. "I'll catch up."

"Grandpa can't even fix a flat," Caryll said dejectedly.

"Chauffeurs aren't expensive here," Maud said. "The hotel can arrange for one."

"Why can't Mr. Edge take care of it, Dad?"

"Caryll, what is the matter with you?" Maud reproved.

Tom turned away from his son's disappointed gray eyes. "I'll meet you in Truro."

VII

When Tom arrived at the Truro Inn, he found Caryll had one of his feverish stomach upsets. Maud had ordered an extra bed in his room, remaining with the child constantly.

Tom paid the chauffeur, who started on the long train journey back to London. Both Trelinacks had been born in nearby villages, and Tom drove his father-in-law to cottages where ancients with faces as red and round and wrinkled as last year's apples reminisced about the old days. In soft drizzle he sat on a dais next to Trelinack, who wept tears as gentle as the misting rain while the cornerstone for the Margaret Trelinack Memorial Hospital was laid.

Caryll recovered. The four of them leisurely explored beaches, pirate coves, quaint stone villages, and the cliff-guarded ruins of Tintagel Castle. "I'm Arthur Pendragon," Caryll shouted into the wind.

Tom never had a chance to talk alone to Maud. Each night, wherever they were, she would retire early to share their son's room. "You can't be too careful with these stomach problems," she said. Tom had no weapon against her refusal to let him broach the topic of divorce. He felt inadequate and cruel, he was dismayed to have caused the subversion of her natural frankness. At times he hated her, other times he quelled a yen to take her in his arms, his sturdy, tenacious little wife, his friend, and cosset her—yet forever he was aware that he and Antonia were flesh of one flesh, born to share the same soul, he was incomplete without her, and he could not remain married to another woman.

On June 22 they boarded the *George Washington* to discover their staterooms jammed with floral tributes and baskets of fruit from satraps of British Onyx as well as those grateful few on whom Hugh had bestowed dealerships.

Tom, his pulses ripping swiftly, locked the door.

"Why on earth are you doing that?" Maud asked.

"I've been trying to talk to you ever since I came down from London."

"Tom, we do appreciate the vacation," she said with her pleasant smile. "You've been wonderful to Pa. And just look at Caryll. Brown as a berry—I've never seen him so happy." A pressed dinner gown had been laid across her bed, and she picked it up.

Tom took the caramel-colored satin from her, dropping it back on the spread. "Honey," he said, wanting to sound kind, yet aware of the grating note in his voice, "I'm not blaming you. It's nobody's fault. But the truth is we haven't been close in years."

"You're my best friend," she retorted. "If it's bed you want, Tom, I've always been willing."

The engines throbbed, a foghorn sounded its lonesome wail. "I'll still be your friend after the divorce," Tom said.

"Divorce?" Her arm, jerking involuntarily, caught the wicker handle of a four-foot-tall fruit basket. With a cry she stopped the beribboned arrangement from falling. "What a waste!" she cried. "Who needs more food on shipboard! You pay for far more than you can ever eat!"

"We just don't have much in common anymore." Tom stumbled into silence as he thought of Caryll, whom they both adored, dressing for dinner in the stateroom across from this. "I don't mean to hurt you," he said gently. "But I know that you realize there's somebody else."

"It doesn't matter how often you shove it into that black-haired bitch, I'm not giving you up!" Maud cried in a high, thin voice.

With a horrified look she clasped her hand to her throat. Her strategy—never admit, never question—had been betrayed not only by her honesty but also by a welter of jealousy, love, and other baffling intangibles. She ran into the bathroom.

The foghorns wailed. Tom gazed at the dark wisps licking at the portholes, inconsolable, convinced that he had altered his wife in ways as dreadful and immutable as if he had drowned her in this shrouded sea.

After about five minutes she returned, her face splotchy, watermarks on her dark blouse. "There won't be any divorce," she said. "We're a family, you, me, Caryll. We're staying a family."

"For Christ's sake, Maud."

She adjusted her glasses more firmly on the bridge of her nose. "Onyx is worth a fortune, and it's getting more valuable every day. Do you think I'd let that go?"

Tom realized that she loved him, and only extreme misery had wrung this from her. But his stomach quivered and his throat filled, a nauseated revulsion that she felt impelled to reduce their unhappiness, her own and his, to monetary terms. "You can have all you want. Can't we manage this so we don't end up hating each other?"

She gathered up the dinner gown, halting at the door of the long, narrow dressing room. "I've given you no grounds, you've given me none. None."

"I'm in love with her."

"Love?" Maud repeated the word as though it were an incomprehensible archaic term. "In Michigan a marriage can be ended because of adultery, desertion, felony, habitual drunkenness. And, at the discretion of the court, for cruelty or neglecting to provide."

"You've been doing your research," Tom said bitterly.

"If you roll on my bed with that whore it won't be adultery, if you parade naked with her, it won't be cruelty, if you run off to England to be with her, it won't be desertion. I'll never claim it to be."

"The state of Michigan doesn't cover the globe. There are other places, other laws."

"Then go someplace else. But I'm your wife, I have my rights. Settling finances like ours could take twenty years."

"How much do you want?"

"I'm keeping it all. And you, too," Maud said, her voice high and thin again. She slammed the dressing-room door.

VIII

Two days before the *George Washington* docked in New York, on June 28, the First Class purser tacked up a black-edged special bulletin. Archduke Franz Ferdinand, heir to the Austrian throne, had been assassinated with his duchess in Sarajevo by a Serbian schoolboy, Gavrilo Princip.

Those shots fired into the archducal limousine echoed and resounded through a Europe trapped in peace, mired in stale, peaceful decades with no events to measure the pulse of the years. The double murders set men in top hats and men in feathered helmets weaving between ministries, making demands, calling on alliances, threatening, negotiating, issuing ultimatums. One by one the fragmented patchwork of countries entered the excitement.

On August 4, 1914, when England declared war, her army possessed not a motorized vehicle—not a staff car, not a motorbike, not an ambulance or a supply lorry. In the country only the British Onyx factory had the capacity to mass-produce an entire car. Soon khaki-painted Fivers were spewing into the Thames-side yard where soldiers hastily trained as drivers awaited them. The vehicles with their replacable, interchangeable parts were more valuable to generals than the frangible men who drove them. A generation was learning that warfare no longer swooped in brilliant cavalry charges but huddled in the earth, dependent on dun-colored motorized transport.

War had never made sense to Tom, and this bloodletting chilled him. He looked out of his personal conflict and was aghast to realize that the Southwark factory, planned so cunningly to conquer his implacable enemy—distance—had become an arsenal.

CHAPTER 13

Foam slithered on top of gray water as Antonia rinsed the razor in the chipped enamel basin.

"Thank yer, ma'am," said Private Mayberry, who needed shaving only once a week.

"There's some good news." With a cautious glance at the opposite cot where a sharp-featured Sister was changing a dressing, Antonia murmured, "Prince Regent placed in the money."

Private Mayberry's haggard child's face brightened. "What'd he pay?"

"Five to one." Surreptitiously she fished in the pocket of her blue-striped Volunteer's apron, coming up with a sixpence and two worn shillings.

"I'd like to send some chocolates to me mam in Leeds. If it wouldn't be too much bother to go to a sweetshop?"

"With my sweet tooth I'm in and out," Antonia smiled. "I have a tip on Blue Charley. Interested in going in with me?" She let the money slip back.

The faint clink of coins drew the Sister's attention, and she peered at them, her face a red hatchet between her goffered white headdress and her high white collar. Last week she had jumped on Antonia for placing a bet for Private Mayberry: a hospital regulation prohibited gambling. Antonia bent, combing sandy hair as she whispered.

When she left the ward, her animation faded and she looked drawn, and the beaky, delicate nose seemed pinched.

"Mrs. Hutchinson," the Sister called, hurrying after her along the icy, dimly lit corridor.

Antonia sighed. "Yes?"

"I've already warned you about the double amputee. I heard the two of you whispering about dog racing."

"I'm *meant* to be cheering his morale."

"This is a military hospital. Staff and volunteers must abide by the regulations."

"I know, but . . . Sister, remember how it was when Private Mayberry first got here? He lay staring at the wall, willing himself to die. And you know better than I that the men usually succeed." Her voice was growing animated. "This is such a tiny pleasure, just to keep him moving toward the future. Until he's stronger, let him have something to look forward to."

"I don't make the regulations."

"But he's seventeen! He's lost his right arm and right leg."

"I know my patients, Mrs. Hutchinson." The nurse's voice was flatly impersonal. "This particular ward is my responsibility. I cannot permit infractions. I'm putting in a request that Matron transfer you." She turned, rustling away.

Antonia, close to tears, glared at the starched back and stuck out her tongue.

II

She got off the number fourteen bus at the row of shops near Upper Swithin Place. It was already dark and blinds were pulled over every window. A blackout. Since early this month, January 1915, German zeppelins had been dropping bombs on London.

First she slipped into A&H Bookmakers to place Private Mayberry's wager—forget that ward Sister *sans merci!*—then she browsed in Jenkin's Confectionary, emerging with the five-pound box of chocolates that had occupied the place of honor on the counter and had been ticketed at nineteen and eleven. She hastened around the dark corner and along the narrow path.

Inside the flat she knelt by the post slot, feeling for a letter. There was none. Kicking off her low-heeled shoes, she pinned the black felt curtains closed before turning on the light. While she waited for the kettle to boil, she sat by the gas fire rereading one of Tom's old letters—she knew them all by heart.

When Tom had hired Irving Elliot, a senior partner in a firm specializing in divorce, she had experienced an immeasurable relief: the matter was out of her hands, so be it, she could neither obstruct nor alter the course of events, her life was surging toward the boundless possibilities of marriage. But now she stood on a figurative poopdeck to hold a questioning spyglass on the future. Sanctified by holy vows, would this reckless confluence of passions and obsessions that was her relationship with Tom become deep, safe love? She hoped so. Often she felt as if her torso were being torn in half below the rib cage by the unrestrainable tidal force of all that she felt for him. Her eyes focused on the letter. *Come back to America. What's indiscreet about us being on the same continent? It will be safer for you and your children here.* The uneven scrawl jumped with his impatience and command, and her mouth softened in tenderness, as though he had touched her.

The kettle whistled. Tucking the letter back in the tin box, she made tea, carrying the tray to the wicker telephone table. She put in her call.

"Hallo, Mother," Justin answered. His voice sounded deeper on the wire, almost a man's voice. "It's a bit late."

"I know. We've been rushed—this morning a new group of wounded came in."

"The war'll be over before I'm old enough to go."

Please heaven, she thought, grasping the receiver more tightly. Justin was a scant three years younger than Private Mayberry. "Would Father have wanted you champing the bit to get your German?" she asked. *Bless you, Claude, for your pacifism*, she thought.

"He wouldn't even hunt, would he," Justin reminisced, his voice cracking.

"How's Zoe?"

"Having tea at Janey Smith-Tolliver's. Mother, remember last spring when Rosburg's cousins came over from Berlin? I've thought a lot about them. They were very decent chaps. But, well, we're at war . . . what if I had to shoot one of them?"

"Had your tea?"

"Not yet."

"Then why don't we discuss it at dinner?"

"Rather!" When he dined alone with her, he savored his small glass of wine, the candlelight, being grown-up. "I'll tell Mrs. Drum." Cook now ran the canteen of the munitions works where the three former housemaids fitted shells: the Drums with one elderly laundress managed the house—and Drum, at sixty-two, talked everlastingly about driving an ambulance at the Front.

Antonia hung up. Taking her cup to the sofa, she considered her son. How he puzzled and worried every moral issue! In a land suddenly rife with pat chauvinism, he maintained his flawless criteria for justice. *But he had his unruly streak,* Antonia thought, smiling. A few weeks ago during the Christmas holidays he and some classmates had been caught when police shut down one of those music halls where girls kicked up plump, black-stockinged thighs, and already this term a master had caned him for smoking cigarettes. Antonia, to be honest, found these crimes endearing. Important to her was that Justin never tormented a weaker boy, managed a fraternal benevolence toward the incorrigible Zoe, and let Caesar, wheezing and incontinent with age, sleep in his room until the mongrel died. *He'll be a very nice man,* she thought, smiling again. *I'll loathe his girls on sight.*

The sofa jolted.

Antonia cried out as hot tea spilled on her lap. The Biedermeier clock had plummeted from the mantel, its case shattering resoundingly on the tiles.

The flat had shaken as though London had twitched its skin.

Antonia tottered on rubber legs to the window, which was still rattling. "The light," she muttered, careening to switch off the lamp.

A lesser explosion vibrated under her stockinged feet.

In the darkness she stumbled against the telephone table. Her tea tray crashed onto the rug. She jumped across broken crockery to unpin the blackout curtains.

In the next building people stood at lit windows. There were confused shouts. "Zeppelin raid!"

At the end of the narrow path an anemic glow brightened alarmingly under her horrified gaze. Shoving open the window, she craned out. Overhead a searchlight beam moved eastward, and in this mobile rivulet of light two zeppelins—sleek sharks—were swimming toward Hyde Park. Toward Rutland Gate! Zoe was with Janey Smith-Tolliver on Harley Street. But Justin was home!

"Justin," she cried, and the tensing of her esophagus twisted the name into *Juzzi*.

She stamped into her shoes, dragging her thick wool cape around her. She forgot her hat, yet remembered the chocolate box. Slamming the front door, she pounded along the narrow cement path.

III

Up the street a four-story building was on fire. Smoke and flames poured from the lower windows. People raced about, a patternless mob, some barging back toward the blazing flats and shops, others scurrying away from the fire. A wild, insistent tintinnabulation. She retreated to the edge of the path as a horse-drawn fire engine erupted past, brass-helmeted firemen clinging to the sides. She began to run in the direction of her home. Ahead of her the sky sucked at brown-tinted smoke. Other fires. She galloped at breakneck, careless speed, not pacing herself for the more than two miles. There were fewer people in the street. Suddenly a white light burst. A frozen moment that affirmed the heaviest coils of smoke lay in the direction of Rutland Gate. *Oh, you German pigs,* she thought. *You dirty pigs!* Gasping, clutching the heavy, awkward box to her overtaxed heart, she began to pray mindlessly. *Please, God, let Justin be all right, let Justin be safe. Please, God, let Justin . . .*

She swerved onto a cobbled lane that led to the Brompton Road. The fire's mottled brown shadows silhouetted ancient cottages. From this viewpoint wasn't the smoke less ominously centered? It no longer seemed to be quite over Rutland Gate. *Please, God.* But how could she be positive?

Holding her skirts above her calves, she raced pell-mell over uneven stones. Sweat poured down her forehead, half blinding her. Her hairpins had loosened, and moist strands flailed at her cheeks, catching on her bared teeth. Blood thundered in her ears.

She did not hear the motor.

The driver of course had on no lights. The first she knew of the car was a sudden blow hitting above the small of her back.

Her mouth opened in a gasp of surprise. The box wrenched itself from her hold, chocolates scattering about her as she slammed against a wall. The force with which she hit the bricks caromed her away.

She fell full weight, as if from a high window.

Ancient cobblestones slammed at her head. The universe cracked with an endless implosion. Nebulae burst and danced behind her eyes.

The driver had braked. Headlights shone.

It's not an Onyx, she thought, and entered into darkness.

IV

She knew she was in a hospital from the familiar chlorine odors, but her other senses were hazed, as if a mucilage protected the outer world from the pain that shrieked inside her head.

Formless shadows drifted, their hoarse whispers traveling through the small bones of her ears to bang hurtfully against her brain.

"She's coming round."

"Mrs. Hutchinson." An earnest masculine voice. "Mrs. Hutchinson. Can you hear me?"

How could he expect an answer when flames of agony immolated her?

"Mother?"

Justin, she thought. *He's safe*. An elusive coolness briefly eased her.

"Mummy?"

A blow crashed against her jaw. Amplified torment blazed through her, and she heard a whimper.

"Zoe! You mustn't touch her. She needs to know you and Justin are here, that's all. Here, stand next to me."

Antonia attempted to smile reassurance up at the shifting light and dark that were her children, but the effort wearied her perilously.

She closed her eyes.

On a flat, featureless, twilit plain stretching horizonlessly, eternally, stood Claude, Arthur, her uncle, and her father, motionless and isolated from one another by intolerable distances: the peculiar contained radiance that illuminated each made the sense of chilling infinity yet more lonely. Her father's vacant eyes were fixed on her. Uncle, his neatly trimmed beard like a halo slipped around his cancer-wasted features, gazed imploringly at her. Claude, his handsome chin raised, held out an arm, beckoning. And Arthur, small, round, sandy-haired, in his striped flannel nightshirt, gave her that flushed, apologetic glance he had worn when he came to tell her that his bed was wet—Arthur, not self-reliant like Justin or imperious like Zoe, just a sweet, pudgy little boy who wanted to sit in her lap and hear "Greensleeves" and "Shenandoah."

Why are they come here, she wondered inside her ring of fiery pain. *Why don't they comfort one another? Why are they come to me?*

"Mother." Justin's voice sounded above the rustlings. How much time had elapsed? She could not tell. Her head shrilled as excruciatingly, yet now she could answer the shape above her.

"Ju . . ."

"It's me," he replied triumphantly. "See, Dr. Smith-Tolliver, she knows me."

The earnest male voice approved.

Another outline, shorter, formed over her. "Mummy, can you see me? Can you, Mummy? It's Zoe."

"Zzz . . ."

"She knows me, too!"

"Mother, you're awake. That's a jolly good sign. Soon you'll be well." Her son's fingers engulfed her limp hand. How resolute his grip, this son of hers who would soon be a man.

The warm, strong hand somehow convinced her that Tom was in the hospital room. *Darling, I hurt so much,* she thought. *Hold me and stop the hurt.*

She closed her eyes. On that eerie, twilit landscape, her father, uncle, husband, and little boy gazed sorrowfully, pleadingly at her.

"Mother?"

"Mummy?"

She looked up, focusing with grisly effort on the mismatched shadows. *Tom isn't here,* she thought, and winced as her eyelids closed.

The others remained isolate in their mephitic gloom, and she accepted with a kind of holy wonder that she was the fixed point of their mortal joys. She did not, even now, realize it was her rare gift to love the unlovable. Instead she thought: *How dear they are, how fine it is that I can cheer them up, can warm them with a kiss. It'll be a snap to make them smile. How alone they look, how sad and alone in that cold land.*

For the last time on this earth Antonia Dalzell Hutchinson was permitted a choice. Her lips parted, her bandaged rib cage expelled air, and the faint sound hung amid hygienic odors as she moved with that swift, impulsive grace into the twilight to comfort the solitary figures of her dead.

CHAPTER 14

MRS HUTCHINSON KILLED ZEPPELIN RAID LAST NIGHT STOP HAVE
TAKEN CHARGE OF CHILDREN STOP EDGE

Hugh gave not so much as a passing query to Monty's taking charge
of the orphans: the Edges and Antonia were friends, she had no
family, and in such situations men of power and importance like
Monty stepped in. The telegram rustled from Hugh's hand, falling
silent on the office carpet. . . . He was remembering a soft voice
guiding him through his black night. He buried his poor clown's
face in his hands. His tears were not exactly grief but a mournful
farewell, the lachrymose equivalent of a final taps sounding for the
youth and joy he had possessed vicariously through his brother.

Tom . . .

Tom had moved to the Pontchartrain, and though he had never
mentioned divorce (Maud, too, continued her atypical sidestepping of
any discussion on that issue), Hugh was well aware of what was up.
These last months Tom had been seized with that same flush of
creativity as when he'd built the racer for Antonia. It was possible to
catch the crackling vibrations of his impatience and feel the physical
force of his happiness. What about all that love? Where would it go?
Cut off, amputated, would Tom bleed to death, like their mother in
her nest of suicidal straw?

Hugh blew his nose. *It's up to me to tell him.* His reddened eyes
rested on the three telephones. Like that? A mortal blow struck by a
disembodied voice? *I'll have to go over there to the factory,* Hugh

thought. The cantankerous nerves of his chest protested. Reaching in the top desk drawer for his new asthma medicine, he popped the yellow pill in his mouth, swallowing it without water, before he spoke to Tom's secretary, telling him to get the boss to his office.

Hugh sent for his chauffeur, ordering the astonished Canadian to bring around the Packard Twin Six.

They drove through a day dismally suited to his task: near freezing, swollen with purple clouds. The cheerless light showed the yellow grass and bare trees of the new small estates that had replaced the ribbon farms along the Detroit River. The city had sprouted tall buildings. Sunk into his gloomy dread, Hugh paid no attention to the altered landscape. But when they came to the small brick houses and Polish shops of Hamtramck, he drew his breath sharply and leaned toward the window, gazing up at Onyx's five looming power plants. The buildings behind cement walls went on forever. The sheer immensity of the place! Pride overcame Hugh's lugubrious dread, and a tingling sensation spread through his entire body. All this from nothing, in less than fifteen years! Tom's accomplishment. After a minute he changed it to *our* accomplishment. The second shift was going full blast but parts were borne from one shop to another by conveyors and craneways, so few men were to be seen in the broad alleyways.

Today was Saturday: management worked only in the morning. Trotting up the wide, deserted brick steps to the empty lobby of Administration, Hugh blessed Antonia for this final act of kindness: for dying on the right day. He jogged up empty staircases, fumbling along deserted corridors until he came to the glass-topped door painted *T. K. Bridger*.

Hugh studied the small, unpretentious gold lettering until the name blurred before his eyes.

Footsteps rang somewhere in the empty hall. Hugh barged inside.

II

It was Saturday, Caryll's day at the Hamtramck. When Tom received the message that Hugh was coming to his office, the portent of such an act had struck him with a deadly cold. He had dispatched the little boy to examine the scale wooden models of the next year's cars. (Contrary to public belief that the Fiver was changeless, there were numerous improvements each year.)

As Hugh rushed in, the waxen pallor of his handsome side made the scar tissue of the other more a dark red carapace. *It's bad, very,* Tom thought, and totted up the possible catastrophes, unable to keep his eyes from his brother's divided face.

Hugh returned the gaze, removing his hat with what seemed intolerably slowed movements.

"Hugh?"

Sinking into a chair, Hugh said in the coaxing, tender voice used with terminal cases, "Come sit down."

"Why?"

"Please?"

Tom sat on a large brown leather conference chair. "What the hell is going on?"

Hugh opened his mouth, and closed it. There were small beads of sweat on the human side of his forehead. "She's dead. . . ."

"She?" For one blinding, cruel moment Tom prayed that he meant Maud.

Hugh was resting a gentle hand on his shoulder. ". . . Antonia . . ."

Tom shrugged away from the hand, standing. He saw with microscopic clarity each knot of scarred flesh, that vestige of an ear. "No!" he said loudly. "You're lying. You're a fucking liar!"

"I wish to God I were."

"*You* wouldn't have heard."

"Monty cabled. He knows she's a friend of mine. An air raid; it happened during an air raid."

Tom's mind refused to work. *Antonia? Dead?* "You miserable cocksucker!" he shouted, and hit his brother across his good cheek, a crisp slap. Hugh did not flinch. As Tom watched the red mark appear in the handsome flesh, a low, involuntary sound spawned deep within his chest, a prehuman howling that lasted a million million years and acknowledged the ultimate and most irrevocable of truths. *Dead. She's dead.* He began to shudder.

Hugh did what he had been unable to do years earlier, when Tom had lost her the first time. He reached out and put his arms around his brother.

For a few moments they stood, the warmth of living flesh attempting to compensate for the eternal ice. Tom, the dry sobs still heaving through him, pulled away. "Thank you for coming here . . ." he said with reasonable clarity. "Now go. . . ."

"But—"

"Hugh." It was a hoarse command.

Hugh took one last look at his brother, who had gone to lean on the window ledge. The back of a shuddering man was outlined against the bleak sky and an enormous factory.

Caryll was in the outer office, crayoning. Seeing Hugh, his eyes rounded with surprise. "Uncle Hugh . . . W-what are you doing here?"

Hugh was wrapped in his brother's anguish. "I had to talk to your father," he said with a horrible ersatz smile.

Caryll's gray eyes rounded apprehensively, and he shrank back to the chair rungs.

Afraid of me, Hugh thought. *What a miserable excuse of a boy.* "He's going to be busy," Hugh said. "Come along. I'll drop you off."

In the car each slumped in his corner. Caryll, sensitive, knew he had somehow insulted his uncle, but was unable to brook the distance of the handmade needlepoint upholstery between them to make it up. Hugh's mind was skipping among the possibilities of supplanting this nephew with Antonia's boy—their transatlantic correspondence had upheld his original opinion that Justin had strength, guts, moral integrity, and he had hoped that marriage to Antonia would prove these qualities to Tom. *Well, death stymies the best-laid plans*, he thought with a deep, wheezing sigh. He considered the brother who was his life, he thought momentarily of the endless factory—of Tom's empire.

I'll have to go over to England, he decided.

III

Ten days later, ensconced in his rooms at the Hyde Park Hotel, Hugh picked up the telephone on its first ring.

Monty's voice said, "We're downstairs."

"The children?"

"Yes. Edwina's along too."

Hugh had never met Edwina Edge. He poured himself a quick sherry.

Edwina entered first, majestically dowdy in her draped mud-green serge, her nostrils flaring as she examined his face.

Monty introduced his wife. "Welcome back to London, Hugh," he said.

Zoe stood close to her brother as the two offered their subdued greetings. Edwina had outfitted them for their orphaned state in thick black clothing several sensible sizes too large. Sleeves adangle to their knuckles, they were mournful, transitional chrysalid creatures. The softness of Justin's face had receded, and the bones of his cheeks, jaw, and high-bridged Roman nose were groping toward manhood. He had shot up and moved his new length of body a trifle awkwardly. The hideous orphans' weeds failed to douse Zoe's beauty. Indeed, the contrast set off the exquisite rose-petal skin and vivid red hair. Her huge dark eyes gazed at Hugh with melting appeal.

Monty said, "I must say I was surprised you made this journey."

"It was most unnecessary," Edwina said. "We have matters in hand. It's high time these two were away at school."

Zoe darted a glance at Justin, and he rested a comforting arm around her shoulders.

Seeing this, Hugh said, "Monty, Mrs. Edge, if you don't mind, I'd like to talk to the children alone."

"We quite understand," conceded Edwina with her chill smile. "Monty and I will have a coffee in the lounge."

As soon as the door closed, Justin's mouth relaxed and Zoe came to sit on the ottoman near Hugh. "With this beastly war," she said, "it was heroic of you to come."

"Nonsense," said Hugh, though he was in consummate agreement. Not only was he braving Tom's wrath—why was his brother so prone to call any well-meant assistance by the ugly name of meddling?—but also wartime high seas. The *Stephen Decatur* had been packed with returning British supply officers and noisy young Americans on their way to enlist, so Hugh had been forced to share a tiny, interior cabin with his secretary. He never had left it. Every claustrophobic, stormy knot had been stained with his fear that some overzealous German U-boat captain might ignore the American flags painted on both sides of the hull. "This will sound strange coming from somebody my age, I know, but outside of family, you two are my only friends."

"We feel as if you're a relative," Justin said.

"We don't have any real ones," Zoe added.

"I can't tell you how sad I am about your mother." Hugh's commiseration was gruff with sincerity. "A terrible loss."

Justin blinked fiercely and swallowed. "I'm going to Trackenham, that's in Kent, and Zoe's enrolled at Lady's Court in Eastbourne."

"We're not even being sent to the same town," Zoe said in a frail, high voice. "Justin'll be a thousand miles away."

Hugh asked, "Didn't Mr. Edge explain?"

"Yes," Justin replied, "and it's wonderfully good of you to ask us to live with you, but—"

"I have plenty of room."

Justin sighed. "It's all arranged. Mr. Edge has already been down to talk to my headmaster, and tomorrow Mrs. Edge and Zoe'll take the train down to visit Lady's Court. You see, it's just . . ."

"I'll die in Eastbourne," Zoe interrupted. Without a preliminary snuffle she began to weep. Antonia's death had hurled her far from the sun, and the thought of being separated from Justin, her sole other source of warmth, spun her into a yet more remote orbit of ice.

Hugh gave her his handkerchief with a jerky little flourish: unused to children, he did not know how to proceed, but when she lifted her arms, he drew her onto his lap, surprised at her small weight, surprised, too, that he cared for this exquisite, crying waif, albeit without the tribal intensity that marked his emotions for Justin. He stroked soft, bright hair.

"I'd love . . . to come to America," she sobbed. "I've told Justin . . . over and over."

Justin sat on the next chair. Whiteness marked the corners of his mouth. "Why can't you at least try to understand my side, Zoe? It's cowardly for me to leave."

"*She* hates me!"

"She's that way with everyone. And Mr. Edge is a jolly good sort. We'll only see her over the hols."

"If she picked the school, it's beastly! They'll whip me, they'll starve—"

"This isn't *Nicholas Nickleby*," Justin interrupted.

"Mother never sent us to boarding school!"

"Everybody goes. In no time you'll have droves of friends." He bowed his head, his voice cracked as he said, "Zozo, for me to leave now is a bad show."

"So that's it, Justin?" Hugh asked. "You feel that going to Detroit would be running away?"

Justin nodded. "Yes."

"I can't see it like that, not if you're using the time to prepare yourself. We have an excellent military academy. It's run by a West Pointer, Colonel Marshall. They have drills and that sort of thing. My brother's boy goes there. They take day students—"

Zoe, sniffling, interrupted. "Is there a girl's day school in Detroit, Hugh?"

"Several," Hugh replied, his eyes fixed on Justin.

"There's a lot to be done here at home," Justin said. "Some of us in the upper forms have been helping teach the lower forms. That way the younger masters are released to join up. There's the same program at Trackenham." Justin looked down at his knee. "Mother was killed on the way home from the hospital. She was a woman and an American, but she was doing her bit. Think of how much more important it is for me."

"Your father was against violence," Hugh enunciated neutrally. "You've mentioned that in several of your letters. It seems to me he would never have wanted his children—his little girl—to live where there were bombing raids."

"Father wouldn't have liked the first thing about this war, and neither do I," Justin said. "But the fact is we're in it. And until we've won, I belong here. You're right about Zoe, though, Hugh. She should go to America."

Zoe slid from Hugh's lap, clutching at her brother's arm. "Without you?"

"Stop being such a crybaby, Zoe."

"Mummy would want us together!"

"You'll be with Hugh."

"Mummy'd want you to look after me and you know it! We'll come back as soon as you're old enough to enlist. By then I won't mind Mrs. Edge. . . . Don't desert . . . me. . . ." She gasped her words dramatically between heaving sobs.

"Calm down, Zozo," Justin muttered, embarrassed and dismayed.

"If you leave me . . . I'll hate you always. . . . You'll be my enemy forever."

Zoe flung herself to the carpet, kicking her clumsy new black shoes and flailing her clenched fists on large Axminster roses. Hugh, flustered by the outburst, yet collusive, retreated to the bedroom for a fresh handkerchief while Justin, obviously an old hand, knelt gripping her shoulders.

"Stop this, Zoe," he ordered. The more desperately loud the boy's commands became, the louder grew Zoe's sobs and gasps. Her beautiful face and vein-knotted little throat turned crimson. Finally her brother capitulated to the torrent of blackmailing shrieks. "*Pax*," he sighed.

"You mean it?" she gasped.

"We'll go to America."

"Both of us?"

"Until I'm seventeen we'll be together," he promised.

She allowed him to lift her to the couch, where her tantrum quieted with unabashed speed to hiccoughing little sighs.

"Then I'll book your passages," said Hugh, who had already arranged for the three best cabins on the *Stephen Decatur*'s homeward voyage.

Nodding, Justin blew his nose. "Excuse Zoe, will you, Hugh. She's awfully upset about Mother." His throat worked, and he continued in a cracking voice, "It's very decent of you to take us." He turned abruptly, but not before Hugh had seen the grief and unquenchable shame in the deep-set, bloodshot eyes.

The Edges did not question the alteration in the children's fates. Antonia had left no will, and one simply did not go into courts of law unless forced to, so it was up to one or the other of her friends to take over as guardians. The couple were hardly about to argue with Hugh Bridger—Tom's brother—when he decided that he wanted the job.

With a frigid little nod Edwina Edge said she would see about the children's clothes. She returned with brother and sister to Rutland Gate, where the Drums were packing boxes, crates, trunks as they closed the house—Drum was joining the Volunteer Motor Drivers and Mrs. Drum was off to Dorset to help on her brother's farm.

Monty remained in Hugh's suite. "There's a matter of some importance to discuss," he said.

By now Hugh shared Tom's opinion that the Englishman had a touch of genius, was intensely capable and trustworthy: he no longer saw Monty's vaulting ambitions as an irritant but as a leash binding him to Onyx. He sat back in his chair. "What is it, Monty? The army contract?" The army recently had doubled its orders for Fivers.

"They now will need in addition a much larger lorry, one with a hundred-and-thirty-inch wheelbase and a forty-horsepower motor. They're offering us the contract. The prime minister approached me."

"Asquith himself, eh? It must be a very important contract."

"Very. For days I've been cabling Tom. Of course we can't use the Southwark plant, it's going at capacity already. In my opinion we ought to subcontract and find a suitable site to set up an assembly, something along the lines of Ford's Trafford Park. I've cabled all the information to Tom. He's never replied." Monty leaned forward. "He already has a tremendous capital investment here. Is he worried that England might be beaten? I know a lot of you Americans are for Kaiser Bill."

Hugh had sailed as soon as possible after his visit to the Hamtramck. But his staff cabled him daily, so he knew that Tom was sequestered in the Pontchartrain, seeing nobody. "Tom's under the weather, that's all."

"Nothing serious, I hope."

"Overwork." Hugh looked thoughtfully at his fingernails. Having none of Tom's flairing aversion to the manufacture of arms—it was ironic that Tom should share this trait, this germ of pacifism, with Antonia's deceased husband—he realized the fiscal advantages of the new lorry. And besides, he was an anglophile from way back. "We'll ship you the engine blocks from Detroit," he said.

The wary lines on Monty's forehead vanished. "Then you're behind us?"

"All the way." Hugh held up a hand to ward off patriotic gratitude. "The next time I see you, it'll be Lord Edge."

"Not by a long shot."

Hugh poured two sherries. "To Sir Monty, then."

Monty laughed, drinking. "You're a dyed-in-the-wool bachelor. Do you believe you can handle those two?"

"Their parents were my friends."

"Mrs. Hutchinson was a charming and lovely lady." Monty raised his glass in tribute. "Still, children are a handful."

IV

That afternoon Hugh went out.

Leaving the hotel, he trembled. On this damp, windy afternoon, though, not many Londoners glanced toward the tall, slender man with the muffler pulled up to his nose and the deerstalker hat angled over his left eye, and by the time he reached the row of fire-gutted shops in South Kensington, his breathing had calmed and he was able to inspect the ruins.

A shapeless elderly woman halted next to him. "A Hun raid," she said. "Four dead. Swine, that's what the Germans are, swine!" Then she turned toward Hugh, and her eyes bulged.

Hugh fled around the corner.

He searched the dingy tiled hall of Eight Upper Swithin Place, climbing two flights of stairs before realizing he must go outside and along the narrow path, where the wind blew more sharply. He admitted himself to flat C with a key that he had procured at considerable expense.

The charwoman, knowing nothing of her pseudonymous employer's death, had continued to clean, so the place was in order except for the broken gilt clock set neatly on old newspaper, but to Hugh the walls already emanated that dankness of long-unused places. He kept on his coat. Opening the wardrobe, he felt through masculine dressing gowns and silvery drifts of negligees that smelled of light floral perfume. He searched meticulously through cabinets and drawers. He was on the ready to let himself out when he spied a toffee box. The crimson guardsmen on the decal seemed a bit worn. He picked up the tin.

Inside were a strew of letters addressed to *Mrs. J. Foreman* in his brother's hand.

Hugh frowned. Tom always dictated, never exposing his chancy spelling or his untutored scrawl.

The little sitting room seemed colder than ever. Hugh let out a shivery sigh. He had come to flat C not as a voyeur or a spy but to carry out a fraternal obligation. Tom had a largeness about him—call it a grandeur of spirit—that prevented him from realizing the infinite number of grubby little details necessary to the keeping of secrets, so he would not even consider there might be any loose ends after Antonia's death. Besides, Hugh had seen the extent of Tom's desolation. He guessed that Tom, unable to force himself to return, would eventually inform the estate agent that the place was no longer wanted and to dispose of its contents. Therefore, Hugh had taken it upon himself to erase any sign of the trysting occupants.

Piling the letters in the kitchen sink, he struck a match. He held it so long that the flame died. He discarded the matchstick and carried the letters to the scrubbed deal table.

As he read his eyes blurred, and he wiped away tears. People spoke of Tom as an enigma, elusive in his genius, more unpredictable than an earthquake, but Hugh, having spent a lifetime in thrall to this phenomenon, having paid a cool fortune to worm out Tom's private life, had felt he shared each of Tom's mental vistas and secret landscapes, a joint tenancy that helped make up for being a circus sideshow. Yet now, as he folded these yearningly tender, erotic love letters, it was being forced on him that his brother had another persona. Or once had. *With Antonia gone,* Hugh thought bleakly, *the man who wrote these letters is dead.*

I should burn them, he thought; *I should.* Yet with a grave robber's shiver he thrust the packet into the deep pocket of his ulster.

CHAPTER 15

The Detroit Military Academy was conceded to be academically tops; therefore parents ignored the drumroll claptrap that vibrated beyond classrooms, and entrusted their sons as full-time boarders. The handful of day students, among them Justin, were assigned fealty to one of the two austere dormitories that jutted to the right and left of the three-story brick school building. These barracks, A Company and B Company, engaged in a tense rivalry in drill squad and athletics that spilled over into the relatively unimportant areas of schoolwork and blue good-conduct rosettes.

Justin became part of A Company. Though he was not yet fifteen, his tests placed him in the twelfth grade.

Antonia's death clutched the boy obdurately, and he sought to assuage his grief in the royal manner, erecting a fanciful Taj Mahal to honor his dead beloved. For his black-haired and lovely ghost, Justin heaped a mound of honors. Far ahead of his classmates in every subject except American history, he concealed neither his knowledge nor his quick intelligence, garnering a First in studies. On the drill field he swiftly mastered the clumping, wheeling elephantine ballet, and at inspection the drill major found never a spot on his blue uniform nor smudges on his white gloves. The baseball season opened: having bowled for the Eddington cricket eleven, he trained himself as a skillful, steady pitcher. The senior elite in both dormitories admitted here was a jewel in A Company's crown. Nobody mentioned this to Justin. He was respected, disliked, and left alone. Mourning enhanced his natural reserve—it seemed as

226

disrespectful as cutting the black grosgrain bands from his sleeves to form smiles or voice the cheerful Americanisms that would have brought him a measure of acceptance. At recess and during lunch hour he pursued his solitary way around the primeval cedars that had been left to encircle the schoolgrounds.

II

The first morning after Easter vacation Zoe overslept. Hugh's chauffeur delivered both children to their respective schools late. Justin's first class was Latin, and being a familiar traveler to Caesar's Gaul, he decided to take an absent for the period rather than a tardy. He trotted down the empty staircase to the basement lavatory where, amid odors of Lysol and human effluvia, seniors were tacitly permitted to break the rule against smoking. He lounged below the row of clerestory windows (these were on ground level outside) to retrieve his contraband cigarettes from under his left garter.

A trio of sixth-graders burst in. The boys were at the stage when growth can spurt unpredictably outward or upward. The dark blue uniforms of the shorter two (they were fraternal twins) strained around thick bodies, while the third was a tall ectomorph with clever, hooded eyes set into a thin face. Justin had observed this triumvirate bullying less fortunate classmates, the myopic and badly coordinated boys. Not knowing any of the three by name, he thought of them as "those thorough little rotters."

He lit a Sweet Caporal, ignoring their envious glances and their noisy urinating contest. They were buttoning their flies when Caryll Bridger opened the door. Caryll glanced at them apprehensively and seemed on the point of flight. Then he saw Justin.

"Hello, Hutchinson." He warded off the trio's depradations by loudly casting the rune of a senior name.

Justin gave him the casual yet benevolent wave he had bestowed on the tadpoles at home. "Bridger," he said.

Caryll, avoiding the urinal and his classmates, edged toward the row of green-doored cubicles.

"Bridger pees squatting," said one of the twins.

"Sure. How else?" drawled the spindly, clever-looking boy—he was the leader. "That's the way girls *do* piss."

With a sickly smile Caryll pushed open the high-hung door.

"Girl, girl, Bridger's a girl," taunted the twins.

Justin had been a prefect at Eddington. Dropping his cigarette, he stood erect. "All right, you three," he commanded. "Get back to class."

The twins scuffled toward the door.

The tall, skinny one stood his ground. "Who do you think you are? Cla-ahss." His daring parody of Justin's broad *a* drew appreciative snickers from his cohorts. He went on, "In Blightyland you might have been a peer of the realm, but around here you're nobody. Come on, Thatchers. Let's do it for B Company. Prove that Bridger's a girl. Pants him!"

Caryll, his breath coming in shallow gasps, darted toward the door. As he neared it the twins glanced at each other and at the same instant lunged with a credible tackle. Tormenters and tormented crashed to the green-tiled floor.

"Stop that!" Justin shouted.

The thin boy, joining the melee of navy blue uniforms, panted, "Go suck, Limey." He reached for Caryll's buttons.

Justin's hands clamped on skinny shoulders. As he jerked their leader away the twins released Caryll, who jumped to his feet, rushing out into the basement corridor and up the cement staircase.

"We'll get you later," called the thin one. "Oh, boy, Bridger, will you ever pay!"

Justin's body went rigid. His fingers clenched into narrow, sinewy shoulders, and he shook the smaller boy as a terrier shakes a rat.

"Hutchinson!"

Kneeling outside to peer through the open windows, his bushy black eyebrows and gray mustache sprouting from his apoplectic face, was Colonel Marshall.

III

That morning Tom visited Hugh for the first time since Antonia's death.

At first the tragedy had felled Tom. For several weeks, incapable of reason or action, he had holed up in his suite at the Pontchartrain, taking none of his many telephone calls, sleeping little, keeping the curtains closed so that one narrow streak of wintry light penetrated his disordered bedroom—he refused entry to the chambermaids, occasionally admitting the room waiter with a sandwich and a fifth of Scotch. The constant chill he felt was an actual drop in his temperature, as though his body as well as his mind were clasped by Antonia's slender, dead arms. Hugh was away. The rest of the family were too awed by Tom—and too afraid of his temper—to find out what was going on at the hotel. It was Maud who dared visit. Her practical eyes saw none of his mental anguish, only that he was very ill. Invoking their son's name, she coaxed him home. He had pneumonia.

When he recovered, his lassitude was gone; his grief was not. He plunged headlong into the Hamtramck, sorrow whipping him to ever greater frenzies.

Ask any stranger on the street the achievements of Tom Bridger and nine chances out of ten you would hear a Fiver joke. If you protested, you would be told, "There's over a million Fivers on the road, aren't there?" And if you persisted beyond that in demanding another achievement, the hypothetical stranger might reply, "He invented this new-fangled mass production out there at his Hamtramck factory."

But Tom, prisoner of his demonic misery, had a different viewpoint of his enormous, shining, glass-roofed plant. *What an inefficient bitch this is,* he thought. *No wonder I can't get prices down.* And in order to bring forth a cheaper Fiver, he conceived the idea of controlling production from the start—ore, coal, rubber, raw lumber, silicates.

He had felt the need to discuss his thoughts about this much larger, vertically integrated factory, and that was why he was visiting Hugh.

As he drove along the edge of Lake St. Clair he raged inwardly at Hugh's busybody behavior and felt the sick, queasy dismay in the pit of his stomach that he experienced each time he thought of Justin ensconced so nearby. *When my poor darling only wanted to keep us apart!*

Hugh, on his part, had gone weak with relief at Tom's terse phone call that he was on the way over. He had been upset—even unnerved—by his brother's continued absence and silence. Yet were it possible to turn back the clock, he would not move even the second hand. It was no longer simply a matter of his long-range scheme: each day brought a deeper affection for the grave, upright boy, and also there were the pleasures of Zoe's compelling if unstable charm. He looked back on his life before the children's arrival as a grotesquely barren desert.

Hearing Tom's ring at the front door, he hurried from his office, trotting nervously along the Great Hall. Greeting his brother, he took a figurative step backward. Rogers and Olaf had informed him that since the bout with pneumonia Tom was a different man: arbitrary, implacable, foul-mouthed. Still, this did not prepare Hugh for the physical transformation. Tom had lost weight: in his angular face the gray eyes shone with tubercular brilliance. Though he was not yet forty, his hair had turned a thick, glossy white.

Ignoring Hugh's outstretched hand, Tom strode ahead of him into the office. Pacing, he launched into a febrile denunciation of Onyx's inadequacies. Hugh sat at his desk, his hand on his chest, torn between pity and fear of the moment when fraternal vitriol would pour over him.

"The thing is," Tom said, "we need to manufacture our own glass, tires, the cardboard we use in the packing. Everything."

"But . . . Tom, that sort of plant would have to be colossal. There's never been anything half that size. It's out of the question."

Tom jerked his head impatiently. "Take tires, for example," he said.

"What's wrong with what we're doing? Buying them from Seiberling in Akron?"

"We sold two hundred and ninety-odd thousand Fivers last year." This was a third of the American market. "Soon it'll be a million."

Hugh forced a smile. "That's not my projection, Tom."

"Your statisticians don't know their asses from hot rocks. Four million tires a year. Plus replacements. I can make them to last much longer than Seiberling does. And I can produce them more cheaply. A man called Farquar owns some woods on the river between here and town." Tom scowled fiercely. To these woods he had driven with Antonia in a Curved-Dash Bridger. "I'm buying his land."

Hugh blinked, puzzled at this conversational shift. "But Maud's already broken ground for your new house."

"Haven't you listened to one fucking word? I need a big new machine that's capable of building every damn part of a Fiver. A new shop."

Hugh stared at his brother. What was this nonsense? A big new

machine? Manufacture ties? New shop? Hugh had *seen* the Hamtramck. No wonder the world's industrialists made pilgrimages to
visit. It was the best-equipped, most ingenious instrument of mass
production. This whole overheated harangue was a delusion born of
poor Tom's grief. Hugh was busy assembling compassionate rebut-
tals when there was a ring on his private line.

Listening to the voice on the other end, he kept his expression
warily in control, but his fingernails rapped against the Elizabethan
table. "I'll send my chauffeur," he said, pausing. "No. I'm sorry,
but that's entirely out of the question." Another pause. "Yes, of
course I understand the seriousness, but I never leave the house . . .
my health." A longer pause. Hugh paled and looked cornered.
"Wait a moment, Colonel Marshall." He held a palm to the mouthpiece. "Tom, Justin's in some kind of difficulty." Though he spoke
normally, his manicured nails continued to tap anxiously.

At Justin's name Tom winced as though a raw blister had been
probed. He said nothing, but his look was dangerous.

Hugh wet his lips. "The principal insists on explaining in person,
he won't let Justin come home until he has. You know Colonel
Marshall well."

"Not this way I don't. Caryll's never needed bailing out."

Hugh cowered a little, but of his two fears, Tom's anger and
horrified glances, Tom's anger was the lesser. "*I* can't go. You
know that." The wheeze in his voice was an effective emotional
trump, and Hugh knew it.

Tom paced to the opposite end of the long office. "When I've
finished talking to Farquar about the woods," he acquiesced.

"My brother will be there soon," Hugh said into the phone.

IV

Justin sat unslumping on a hard bench in Colonel Marshall's
waiting room, his gaze fixed on the opposite wall. He had examined
every detail of the large watercolor of West Point with the words
Duty, Honor, Country afloat in a fat white cloud, and now his
attention remained riveted to the Seth Thomas clock. The hand
jumped. One forty-three. He had been sitting here since eight fifty-
five, when he had finished his terse explanation that in breaking up a
fight between younger boys he had regrettably lost his temper. To
say more, Justin was aware from his prefectorial stint at Eddington,

meant those three little rotters would see to it that Bridger—a member of that outer fringe that surrounds school life the world over—would be denied even the companionship of his fellow rejects. At home the Head would have understood and let Justin off with a perfunctory caning. Here, who could tell?

The three had spent the better part of an hour telling their sides, which he was certain included no mention of Caryll Bridger. As they had passed through the waiting room the tall, skinny boy had darted a smirk of satisfaction at Justin. Since then nobody had looked at him. When Colonel Marshall had left to preside over officers' mess, he had ordered his sallow, middle-aged secretary to remain. Guard duty. She sat behind her low partition reading a magazine with aggrieved little sniffs. Justin clenched his nails into his palms, informing himself it was his continued dwelling on the lavatory scene that caused this ruthless urge to empty his bladder. He could not bring himself to ask the secretary's permission to relieve himself.

The door opened.

Colonel Marshall ushered in Tom Bridger.

Justin's first confused thought was that he had come on Caryll's account, but this he rejected instantly. He was positive those three would not have implicated Caryll, and there was no other way for Colonel Marshall to learn of the involvement. *He's here for me,* Justin thought, and his cheeks grew hot. He had tried to be scrupulously fair about Hugh's brother—after all, he had seen the man only twice, he admired his accomplishments, and besides at a time when most Americans were dead set against any foreign entanglement, Onyx was backing England with a big new plant. But that first meeting had imprinted itself on him, and his animosity persisted. This was his mother's harassing enemy.

He rose stiffly, clicking his heels. "Colonel, sir." He saluted. "Mr. Bridger, sir." Another smart salute.

The Colonel touched his hat. Tom stared at his black armband and nodded brusquely. They went into the sunlit office and closed the door. Masculine voices rumbled, their meanings obliterated.

After five minutes Tom emerged. "Come on," he snapped without slowing his stride. He marched through the halls ahead of Justin.

Mess over, the yard was shrilly alive with blue-uniformed boys, some kneeling over marble games, others playing pop-up or shooting baskets. As Justin descended the steps a hushed stillness fell on the playground.

Somebody near him made a loud, wet kissing noise. Snickers churned.

Justin climbed into the Fiver, staring ahead. Tom started the car, driving around the muddy parade ground where eight widely separated boys, the sun glinting on their patent leather visors, marched punishment tours.

"It was good of you to pick me up, sir," Justin said. He would rather be dead than permit Tom Bridger to see his corrosive humiliation, and therefore the clipped edges of his voice brought him satisfaction.

"At Colonel Marshall's insistence. You're Hugh's responsibility, so far be it from me to interfere."

"Thank you anyway, sir."

"If I *did* have a vote, it'd be for a heavy thrashing. You can wipe off that smirk. I know about the cigarettes to bribe the lower graders, I know how you bat them around when they refuse to jerk you off."

Justin felt the blood drain from his face. In his hours in the waiting room it had never occurred to him that he might be accused of any crime other than illegal smoking and fighting with a sixth-grader. His entire body trembled. His bladder froze in pain.

Tom drove swiftly. A headache bound him above the eyes. This boy, who so resembled Antonia, whom she had adored, for whose sake she had kept *him* tucked away! How dare he turn out to be a pervert bully?

He braked hard at Hugh's entrance bay. "Get upstairs," he ordered. "I'll give it to Hugh straight."

Justin had arranged his room to be as similar as possible to his quarters in Rutland Gate, with his mementos of Claude, his now useless cricket bats, his squash and tennis rackets, his old desk with its warmly familiar scars. Only the full-length portrait of Antonia had not been in his room but had hung in the rear drawing room. He changed into worn flannels and a tennis sweater that was unraveling a little at the elbows, familiar clothes from England. He sat at his desk, which faced the mullioned windows. Beyond the terrace bricklayers worked on the cottage that was two thirds of normal scale, Zoe's playhouse, and beyond that, half hidden by trees, Lake St.

Clair glittered a barbarously hard blue. He stifled his tears, but he could not repress his dislocating, horrorstruck misery.

After a while Hugh came up, stepping into the room inflexibly, as if he were carrying a full tureen of hot soup. Justin did not put on a good face—Hugh was his friend.

Hugh sat near the desk. "Come on, Justin," he said. He had been thoroughly shaken at the malign twist his schemes had taken, but the boy's unhappiness triggered his heartfelt sympathy. "It's not the end of the world. In a few days you'll be at a better school."

"Have I been sacked?"

"Expelled, yes. Colonel Marshall told my brother."

"Hugh, I'm sorry to cause you so much fuss."

"Boys go through this stage, Justin, they do. It's part of growing up. The only wrong move you made was being caught."

Justin traced an old initial with his shaking finger. It was one thing to have his enemies believe the worst of him, quite another to hear Hugh state it so casually. When Hugh left he made a dive for the big bathroom, heaving over the toilet until only a stringy acid came. He was sweating and wiping his face when he heard the car bring Zoe home.

She tapped on the door, inquiring, "What's going on? Why did you leave school early?" She was radically pruning her voice of English inflections.

"Head off, Zoe," he said. "Leave me alone."

He sat with his chin pressing into his palms. His initial shock over, he was able to perceive a ubiquitous substructure beneath all of his lonely misadventures on this continent. The code of ethics, the reticence, the way of dealing with problems that he had packed aboard the *Stephen Decatur* were not cargo that could survive an Atlantic crossing. He mulled this over, avoiding blame, anger, self-pity. Within him was an unassimilable streak, or maybe it was a black obstinacy, that prevented him from easy adaptation. He could not jettison the past that was filled with his father, his mother (he knuckled away an unmanly tear), he could not grow a chameleon conscience, he could not tailor a new self for himself as Zoe was doing. With his penknife he carved into his old desk: *To thine own self be true*, a futile bravado that showed rawly on the oak and did nothing to numb either his grief or his loneliness.

Hugh, a solitary, respected his right to privacy. At dinnertime Zoe knocked again. Again Justin told her to go away. He had not eaten since breakfast, and he felt he would never more be hungry. At ten he undressed and turned out the lights.

Another knock.

"It's late, you little nit," he called. "Way past your bedtime."

"It's me, Tom Bridger."

Tom came in, switching on the overhead light. He drew a breath at the full-length portrait: with slapdash brushwork and strange lavender skin tones, the artist, a modern, had captured Antonia's lively, impetuous charm. He turned quickly away.

"Caryll explained what happened at school. Those little bastards gang up on everybody, he said. They were after him when you interfered."

Justin felt no vindicatory triumph, only a pitying admiration for a young, shy boy with the grace to admit to the woebegone crime of being a patsy. "Any senior would have," he said tersely and lay back in the pillow, hoping Tom would take the hint.

Instead, he came to the foot of the bed. "Why didn't you tell the story to Colonel Marshall?"

"He heard my side, sir."

"Not all of it, not by a long shot. Otherwise he never would have believed Hoenig and the Thatcher twins. As soon as you realized what they were up to, why didn't you telephone him and clear yourself?"

The answer to this lay in Justin's code. Caryll, a younger, weaker boy, needed his protection as much as ever: to waver under fire would be pusillanimous. Yet mud sticks to a sensitive surface, and Justin felt the shame of the charge as hotly as if it were true. "Sir," he said in a low voice, "I was asleep."

"If you're trying to make me feel even more of a shit, you've succeeded. I'm on my way to school now to put this right."

Justin's head raised urgently from the pillow. "No!"

"What's the point of waiting until tomorrow?"

"I don't want you to go at all. Ever."

"That's insane."

"Sir, leave it as it is." There was a surprising command in his tone.

"What am I supposed to do, let him keep on thinking you're a powder-puff bully?"

"This afternoon you said it was none of your affair." Justin rolled onto his side, facing the wall.

"Listen to me. It's not just the kissing noises and the sneers. You're being expelled, don't you understand? You won't get into college and—" Tom stopped. Justin's breathing came in muffled sighs, and the blankets were shuddering. Tom glanced up at the portrait, as if to beg forgiveness for his doubts and anger. *You had every right to be proud, Antonia, he is very special.* "I'll do it your way," he said quietly. "Good night, Justin."

V

The following morning after Tom dropped off Caryll at school, he continued out beyond Gaukler Point to Hugh's place.

At the first curve in the driveway two setters barked around Justin as he walked along, head bent, hands thrust into the pockets of a too small maroon blazer. Tom drove by. Justin glanced up, nodding. Tom parked on the curve ahead, getting out to lean against a front mudguard. When Justin caught up, he asked, "Ever driven a Fiver?"

"Good morning, sir," Justin said in a subdued voice. "No."

"Any car?"

"My mother's Lanchester. Drum—he was our man; you may remember him—taught me."

"Like to try this?"

"Thanks, but I don't feel much like it this morning."

"Things that bad?"

"Nothing to do with the other," Justin said too hastily. The dogs were running circles on the grass, their tongues lolling to catch dew. He looked at them, not Tom. "It was a mistake coming over here. I don't fit in at all."

"Look, Justin, I don't get much comfort from the way I behaved yesterday—"

"No need to fret over that, sir."

"Let me finish. I understand you didn't stoop to set *me* right. There have been times when I've kept quiet, too, after I was unfairly attacked. But I couldn't figure out why you didn't want Colonel Marshall to know what really happened. This morning it came to me. You think if those little turds are punished, they'll never let Caryll forget it. Am I right?"

Justin reddened. "Haven't we given this enough time, sir?"

"Colonel Marshall's come up against this sort of thing before. He'll know how to handle it."

"About an hour ago he telephoned to say he'd been hasty about sacking me. I can do something called a tour of punishment—they do it at West Point. It's only marching."

"And that's your problem? You can't decide if you can take going back?"

"I told him I'd be there tomorrow morning," Justin said and whistled. The dogs bounded to him, planting muddy forepaws on his blazer while he rubbed their silky red muzzles.

Tom's gaze remained on the boy, then he gave his short laugh. "Dressing up like soldiers, pretending Detroit is West Point, kindergartners saluting old farts—what idiocy! You're right, let's forget it." He opened the car door. "Hop in."

The dogs scrabbled over one another to get into the backseat. Justin started around, but Tom handed him the ignition keys. "Here," he said. And when Justin was in the driver's seat, he pointed. "There's the spark."

Justin retarded it.

"In a Fiver you have to push her clear up. That's better. Now. There's the gas—the petrol."

Justin pushed down on the gas lever, switching to battery. The coil box began to buzz. He jumped out, stooping to use his full force to spin the crank, pulling the choke wire carefully so as not to flood the engine. He gave the crank another spin. The engine caught. He ran to get back in, advancing the spark, retarding the gas, switching to magneto.

The engine putt-popped triumphantly.

The Fiver bounced slowly along the drive, picking up speed as Justin gained confidence.

"Hear that?" Tom asked.

"What?"

"*That*. She's missing. Take her round back."

The Fiver circled the house, coming to a shuddering, dust-clouded halt on the gravel outside the big garage. The doors were open, and the new Packard Twin Six was gone. Tom pulled off his jacket, rolling up his sleeves.

"Lend me a hand, will you," he said, opening up the hood.

Together they checked the carburetor, the commutator, and the spark plugs. The problem lay in the commutator. Tom replaced the rotor spring. They went into the garage to wash up.

"Mr. Bridger." Justin dug his three middle fingers into the gritty mechanic's soap. "People think they're wonderful geniuses if they can repair a motorcar, and you built one before there were any to copy. You invented everything. And you're helping the British war effort. . . ." His freckles stood out. "But—"

"You *do* like things square, don't you?" Tom was grinning. "Yesterday I was a horse's ass, Justin, but that doesn't mean it's a permanent condition. I realize you don't exactly love me."

Justin concentrated on using the nail brush.

Hugh, topcoat slung over his shoulders, stepped inside the garage. "Nothing like a little honest labor," he said. "Justin, it's lunchtime."

"Already?" Justin smiled. Retrieving his blazer, he ran into the brilliant sunlight, swerving, kicking at gravel as though steering a rugby ball, an excess of animal energy.

They watched until the servants' door slammed behind the boy. Hugh said, "This is the first time I've seen him happy since he got here."

"Mind if he keeps this?"

"The Fiver?"

"Yes. Your chauffeur can give me a lift over to the Hamtramck. I'll pick up another this afternoon."

Hugh rubbed his thumb against his coat, a thoughtful gesture. Last night the brothers had sat in the big living room, Hugh denigrating himself for believing the worst of his ward. A couple of brandies made him yet more ashamed of himself, and more admiring of Justin's honorable behavior. His self-chastisement was sincere. "Tom, I was up all night. I can't think of a way to apologize without making it worse."

"He prefers it forgotten," Tom said.

Hugh nodded. "Yes."

"So you don't think he'll take the car?"

"He'll realize you're paying him off," Hugh said. "He's going back to school tomorrow."

"It's going to be rough on him," Tom said.

"What a mess."

"Maybe Caryll could invite him on a tour of the Hamtramck."

"He's very intelligent about machinery." Hugh's voice held a trace of smugness.

"Don't get any ideas," Tom said quietly.

"Whose suggestion was it?"

"I swore to her he'd never find out."

A swift darted into the garage. The brothers ignored the frantic rustling of wings in gasoline-odored gloom. This was Tom's first confession of paternity.

"I'd never suggest a word—it would hurt him too much. He's made an idol of Claude Hutchinson. A crazy idol. All I meant is that you're on the right track. He'll need *something* to help him through this."

Tom held his arms under the faucet, rinsing off the soap. "I'll give him a Saturday job."

"Good," Hugh said softly.

"Listen to me, Hugh. I'm not sure why you brought those two over here, but whatever you have in mind for Antonia's boy, forget it." A regretful sigh mitigated the decisiveness in Tom's voice.

"I don't know what you're talking about."

"Hugh, this is me, Tom. No games, hear. I'm not about to draw him into my life. For one thing it's not fair to Maud. She's gone through a lot, and I'm not putting her through any more."

"Justin's a person too. The most honorable, decent person I've ever met."

"*I'm* proud of him."

"Then you wouldn't say it's asking too much for you to be a little generous to him? It's a difficult period of adjustment for him, and after all he's your own—"

"Hugh," Tom said, a low, flat warning that pierced the shadows.

Hugh glanced at the emptiness beyond the sunbright doors. "Nobody heard," he said.

"You're a dead man if you ever say it." Tom did not raise his voice, so it was inexplicable how the low, normal timbre managed to ring with ominous threat.

Hugh backed toward the Fiver truck that his gardeners used.

Tom dried his hands on the grubby towel. After a minute he said, "She asked only that one thing of me in all the years. It meant everything to her."

"Stop worrying, Tom."

"If I go around playing fond benefactor, people might guess. *Justin* might guess."

"I can't see why. You're very generous to the Sinclair boys, and they're nephews. Justin is my ward."

"Hugh, no wheedling, no maneuvering."

"There'll be no leaks from me," Hugh said. He watched his brother fasten his cufflinks. "Come on. Let's have lunch."

"Nope."

"But I had them set a third place."

"No lunches."

"An appointment?"

"Justin's here."

"You worked on the car with him. What difference will one meal together make?"

"Hugh, get it through your head that I'm afraid. What if some extra note of affection slips out?" He sighed deeply. "The only way this'll work is to keep it strictly automobiles between us."

"If that's how you feel."

"No personal involvements."

While Tom started the Fiver, Hugh watched him with that peculiarly satisfied expression usually described in terms of cats and canaries. Tom was indebted to Justin, was proud of him, admired him, was giving him a Saturday job at the Hamtramck, and if that wasn't personal involvement, it was one sweet beginning.

BOOK THREE
Woodland

Woodland was unique in size and function. Here, by the Detroit River, on a tract more than two miles long and three quarters of a mile wide, Thomas Bridger's vision had conceived one enormous machine to mass-produce automobiles.

The History of the United States by Edwardes and Whitney

CHAPTER 16

"A hamburger sandwich?" Justin asked.

"Ground beef on a bun. It's one of our favorite American del-i-cacies," retorted Elisse Kaplan, the cutting edge of her sarcasm not blunted by the remarkable charm of her smile.

"I know. I'm American," Justin said. He had sworn to uphold the United States government and its laws nine years ago, on April 6, 1917, the day that the country had entered the war, the day he had enlisted over Hugh's protests and his own most profound beliefs. "I doubt if you can get one here."

She glanced around Verona's, an eloquent shrug of her pretty shoulders dismissing the velvety lights, the darting, solicitous waiters, the tables with stiff, floor-length damask encircled by well-dressed, middle-aged diners—and him as well, Justin decided, for the unconscionable stuffiness of patronizing what was considered the top restaurant in Los Angeles.

He barely knew Elisse Kaplan.

They had met once before, in London this past June. She was the cousin of his old school friend, Rosburg, visiting from California. Justin had been passing through on his way to inspect the French Onyx plant in Asnières, and for maybe fifteen minutes he and Elisse had sat on the Rosburgs' lounge window seat, afternoon sun shining gold on her curly brown bob as she alternately irritated and entranced him. Breezy, witty, assured girls, the dishes like Elisse, always threw Justin off-balance. He was disbelieving when Zoe informed him that in Detroit he had a reputation as a ladies' man, for though he escorted debutantes and postdebutantes to the usual parties, he had embarked on only two truncated affairs, both with married women: during the course of these entanglements his affection and even his physical gratification had eroded like sand at the necessary undertow of adulterous sneakiness—he had never outgrown that boyhood rectitude. Arriving in Los Angeles on Onyx business, he had immediately looked up Elisse in the telephone book (her father was a musician, he recalled, and his name was Harris Kaplan: in point of fact he had total recall of their brief conversation), inviting her out to dinner. She had hesitated, a long silence on the line that had wrenched him surprisingly, before saying she would meet him at Columbia Pictures' studio on Gower Street in Hollywood.

She was now staring quizzically across the shaded table lamp.

"If a hamburger sandwich is what you want, we're in the wrong place," he said.

"You've caught on."

The word *bitch* clearly in his mind, he rose to pull out her chair. The gray-haired captain swooped around tables. "Is anything the matter, sir?"

"Nothing, nothing," Justin said, tucking a bill into the waiting palm. "We changed our plans, that's all." He hurried after Elisse, whose white pleats swirled around her good legs.

It was dark outside. September's heat was being vanquished by an advance of fog that held the marshy, saline odors of the sea.

"Now what?" He looked down at her, jolted again by the realization of how small and delicately built she was: Elisse Kaplan's personality reverberated far beyond her physical dimensions. "I'm afraid I don't know Los Angeles. Where shall we go?"

"Philippe's," she retorted, unhesitant.

"Will you be able to get your hamburger sandwich?"

She rolled her wrist in an expansive gesture. "A wide cuisine there."

"What about a table?"

"Any difficulty," she said, "and you can slip a tip."

"Elisse, I have the impression I'm being punished."

"It's more a case of being fired on before you have a chance to shoot."

"Shoot?"

"Make a pass," she explained.

"You have a pretty low opinion of my character."

"Character, too? Isn't it enough to be impeccably tall, dark, handsome, and brilliant?"

He groaned. "So *that*'s it."

She was opening her purse to take out a rolled *Time*, the most recent edition with an ink-sketched Fiver—the twenty millionth—on the cover. Holding the magazine up to the streetlight, she riffled pages.

" 'Though the undisputed heir to Onyx's throne is Caryll Bridger, only child of Thomas K. Bridger,' " she read, " 'Detroiters are watching the meteoric rise of twenty-seven-year-old—' "

"I'm twenty-six," Justin interjected. "So much for accurate reporting."

She continued, " '—London born, tall, dark, handsome, and brilliant Justin Hutchinson who, after the War, spent two years training under Lord (then Sir) Edge at British Onyx. He has worked in managerial positions throughout Europe. Thomas K. Bridger's long-standing policy is to avoid executive titles; however, since Hutchinson's return to Detroit in 1923, his sphere of influence, especially at Woodland, the world's largest industrial complex, has grown steadily, and he belongs to the charmed inner circle of executives. A rumor persists among acute observers in the automotive industry that he is being groomed as second in command for the day that Caryll Bridger takes over.' Hey, fortune's tot, aren't you?,'

"The article never mentions that Hugh Bridger—"

"Mmm, let me see. . . . Here it is. 'The automotive tycoon's shadowy, invalid brother is reputed to be a major force in company decisions.' "

"They really have us down pat, don't they? Hugh was my guardian."

"Well, well, a relative, too."

"Not in any way," Justin said, exasperated. They had reached the Fiver, and he opened the door for her, hoping a change of venue would change the conversation. She did not get in. "Hugh was my parents' friend, that's all. But he's been a Rock of Gibraltar. Kind, generous. When Mother died during the War, he brought us over, me and Zoe, my sister."

"Is advancing a ward also called nepotism?"

"I'm not being advanced. I'm not being groomed."

"Just sitting around being one of the charmed knights of the Onyx round table?" She was referring to the paragraph about the big round table in the executive dining room.

"That's how much of the inner circle *I* am. Tom Bridger's never once invited me to eat there." Justin heard his glottal closure—and so did Elisse.

Her fingers touched his sleeve. "You know the trouble with you, Justin? You're too upper-class and British to ever hit a woman."

"I'd rather try that pass," he blurted. "Sorry."

"What for?"

"I'm not much good at this sort of thing. Banter."

"You're doing fine," she said, climbing into the car.

II

Philippe's was near the train depot, a large, barny cafeteria with sawdust on the floor, linoleum-topped high tables, and a long counter where elderly waitresses swiftly cut French rolls, dipping them softside into gravy before piling on meat.

"What about that hamburger sandwich?" Justin asked.

"Verona's is too rich for my blood, especially when combined with a tall, dark—"

"Isn't it time to lay that to rest?"

"Maybe I wanted to prove my power," she said, grinning. "Look. There's two places. I'll save them—Justin, ask for double dips."

He waited in line to order four double-dipped sandwiches, some violet pickled eggs, and bowls of coleslaw, amazingly tasty food. Elisse, whose hostility had shriveled to acerbic wit, dispatched a French dip with remarkable neatness considering the girth of the roll.

"I can't manage another," she said.

"I'll eat, then, while you do the talking. Did you enjoy England? Elisse, tell me about yourself."

She settled back on the stool, hooking her high heels over the rung. The trip to England, her first, had been a charm from beginning to end. Her parents were English, she divulged, and it was their graduation present to her. "Or"—she raised an eyebrow—"or maybe it was a gesture of their relief that I hadn't joined the Party while at Berkeley." There, she had majored in literature, and was putting her education to use as a reader for Harry Cohn, who owned Columbia, one of the small, shoestring studios on Poverty Row, as Gower Street was called.

Justin asked what a reader was. Exactly what it sounded like, Elisse replied. She scanned novels and plays, typing up synopses for the reputedly illiterate Cohn. "Actually, I give them to Sam Briskin. He's the Columbia executive who can read." She was an only child, her father played viola with the Los Angeles Philharmonic. "Mother and Daddy are complete innocents about everything. No political sense at all." Despite her arch facial comments when she spoke of her parents, her hazel eyes projected a softness he had not seen before.

By now he had finished the third sandwich. "When I asked you out, you nearly refused. You aren't wearing an engagement ring."

She held up her bare left hand. The small buffed nails, he noticed, had deep half-moons. "By George, I'm not," she said.

"Is there anyone?"

"Nobody special. Hasn't another impediment occurred to you?"

"I don't understand."

"You do realize I'm Jewish?"

"Of course. You're Rosburg's cousin."

"I'd just as soon not be reminded—Victor's the weasel of the world," she said. "Do you squire around Jewish girls?"

"I don't have the opportunity to meet too many in Detroit."

"It's a big city with thousands of unattached Jewish females, some even wealthy like you. Only you've never met them. Two different worlds, Justin." She was not being flip anymore.

"That's putting it a bit strongly."

"Not at all. Two contiguous worlds that are never meant to mingle."

"Come on, Elisse." The other Jewish people with whom he came in contact circled around the subject of their Judaism. Their touchiness shaded his response now, and he sensed he was blushing.

"I shouldn't complain. There are no pogroms, no ghettos, no tall hats, but maybe it would be easier if there were. At least then you'd know where you were meant to stay. There are all sorts of boundaries. You bump them very hard when they're invisible." The small muscles around her eyes had tensed, and he understood that this glossily suntanned, facile girl was capable of being hurt. Had been hurt.

"Elisse," he said quietly. "You have me all wrong. I don't seem to belong either here or in England anymore. I'm not part of any circle, any world."

"What? No arguments that I'm dead wrong?"

"I haven't thought about it enough to argue. It just doesn't apply in my case." He set down his fork. "Religion doesn't mean much to me. Is it important to you?"

She blinked then flashed him her prettiest, most irritating smile. "Would I have brought you to one of my favorite spots if I believed in outdated bourgeois trivia?"

He relaxed back on the stool. "I'm still going to take you to a dinner with waiters and tablecloths."

"You're very forceful in that understated way, aren't you?"

They strolled along the nearby alleys. The dimly lit, small Mexican and Chinese shops were veiled in mystery by the fog. Stepping from a curb, he took her arm. She was not using perfume but smelled of clean soap and a very delicate natural bodily odor that attracted him fiercely. He continued to cup her elbow as they sparred about the weather in Los Angeles, whether Charlie Chaplin was a genius—she maintained a movie comedian could be one—and Henry Ford's decision to go on an eight-hour day, five-day week: "Copying Tom Bridger again," Justin asserted, then feared she might blame him for Ford's misbegotten anti-Semitic newspaper, the *Dearborn Independent*. Instead, she inquired if he had read *Swann's Way*. He admitted he had little time for novels, and she glanced at her watch. "Speaking of time, Justin, it's five past ten."

"Is failing to read fiction another bad mark?"

"What else?" she smiled. "And you're out with a working girl."

"I'll take you home."

She lived in Beverly Hills on a street divided by a hedged bridle path. Her house would have been a bungalow save for one square tower room, from whose open windows floated the limpid notes of a Mozart quartet.

As she took out her door key he asked, "Shall I pick you up at work tomorrow?"

"Capitalist types *are* sure of themselves."

"I'm not a capitalist any more than you're a downtrodden factory

248

hand. Why pretend this is a class struggle? I've had a wonderful time and I'd like to take you to dinner again.''

The Mozart halted abruptly, a man's voice rumbled, then the viola sang the theme. Elisse's head tilted up to the strong, jubilant sound.

"If," Justin said, "I promise it won't be Verona's, will that help?''

"I'm sorry. I have a meeting," she said in a tone devoid of cleverness.

"This is Thursday. I'm leaving next Tuesday."

"We could have a bite first, I guess."

"The gate at the same time?''

She was still listening to the music. "Yes." She touched his arm and slipped inside without a good-bye.

III

Justin was staying at the Ambassador Hotel. A telegram had been slipped under the door of his cottage: MEET IN SEATTLE SEPTEMBER THIRTIETH TOM. Reading it, Justin's smile held a trace of bitterness.

To the tee typical. The epitome of Tom Bridger's manner with him. Brusque. Forbiddingly businesslike. The one minor familiarity Tom Bridger conceded to him in all these years was the use of his first name.

We'll be staying at the same hotel, eating our meals together, but Tom will behave as if we're on the dais in front of the entire administrative staff, and every word he utters will be connected to Onyx. Justin stared at the yellow paper, the grim smile still on his lips: after so long he should have adjusted to this undeviating remoteness—but he hadn't.

His old enmity toward Tom had flip-flopped to ardent admiration, loyalty—and, yes, into what he inwardly acknowledged was love, a respectful love that he kept under wraps because his white-haired, caustic liege lord remained at a purposeful distance that he, by nature reserved, could not cross. Justin rubbed at his upper arms; he felt a sudden chill. Painful. No denying it was painful. He had never been invited to the Farm, or included in any of the Bridger family's doings. Tom's attitude increased Justin's sense of being a kithless exile, but at least he was no longer shamed by an infantile envy of Caryll or embarrassed by his barmy hurt at being excluded from the executive round table when the three older Sinclair boys were routinely invited—in the old days he'd waxed pretty maudlin about *that*.

There's something too pointed about the way I've always been excluded, he thought. *It's too unflagging.*

He lit a cigarette and gazed with an absent expression at the telegram, considering the paradox of their relationship. When they were alone, he sensed a genuine warmth emanating from Tom, a deep, mellow affection, though even at these times Tom had a stiffness, an inflexibility to his posture. It was as if he were forcing himself to keep it all business, as if he were preventing himself from reaching out or making some intensely personal revelation.

Justin's fingers closed around the yellow sheet. Warmth, deep affection, personal revelations! Fat chance—sheer wishful thinking! Tom had advanced him rapidly, so Justin obviously had his respect. *And that is that*, Justin told himself. *Respect, nothing more.* He tossed the wadded paper into the wastebasket.

The high cheer he had felt with Elisse had vanished; as he caught his reflection in the mirror he saw that he looked tired, dejected.

With a purposeful gesture he loosened his tie; then he opened his briefcase for the yellow legal pad on which he had jotted notes during his inspection of the Glendale assembly. Whatever questions he nursed about Tom's fellowship toward him, there was no doubt about one thing: when he traveled, his dynamic employer demanded daily reports.

Though *Time* was correct in noting there were no titles at Onyx, Justin's sphere of responsibility was the thirty-one assembly plants. When he had returned to America three years ago, these assemblies were a maddening jumble of irregular shipments and missing freight cars: he had spent months devising an intricate clearing house capable of keeping track of every part shipped from the Hamtramck and Woodland, of synchronizing deliveries with the needs of each ancillary plant. An achievement unique in the industry. Mr. Du Pont had personally sounded him out about coming to General Motors. But he had stayed on at Onyx out of love, loyalty—and that nagging sense (or was it merely a pathetic perennial hope?) that in some unstated way Tom returned his affection.

Justin stopped and tapped his teeth thoughtfully with the end of his fountain pen before he wrote his final paragraph:

· Today I was at a dealer's breakfast in the Wilshire district. It was a sad business. Our sales in southern California, too, have slumped badly. And I was shocked to hear that Kleinschmidt-Loring, our top dealership here, has gone over to Chevrolet. Kleinschmidt was embarrassed, but he told me it was becoming impossible to sell style-conscious Los Angeles on a four-cylinder, too-tall mongrel like ours. Tomorrow I am visiting there to see whether I can mend any fences.

He signed his full name. After dropping his letter, he stood by the lobby mail slot, his head tilted broodingly; then he trotted down the wide, deserted staircase to the parking lot.

The unpaved, oiled breadth of Wilshire Boulevard shone like a river in the beams of his headlights. It was after midnight, and he passed very few cars. He turned on Rodeo Drive, halting across from the Kaplans' small stucco house. A dog barked and then there were only crickets. Some bush or tree gave off a heavily sweet citrus odor that drowned all other scents of the moist, cool night. Justin rested his left arm on the rolled-down window, gazing at the mistily obscured white stucco walls. Softly, yet with surprising fidelity, he whistled a few bars of the Mozart quartet. What had the music said to her? Questions and memories rushed at him, a barrage of sensuous details about the girl and the evening. Given neither to impulsive actions nor to dramatic gestures, his act in coming to her house surprised Justin. He castigated himself for being a romantic lounge lizard, yet he sat in the Fiver dreamily smoking cigarette after cigarette. *I don't feel lonely here*, he thought.

IV

"Your meeting, is it a woman's club?"

"Do I seem the sorority type?"

"Listen, why don't I sit in the background? Then I can drive you home."

"This is the other side of the barricade, Justin."

He frowned, puzzled. "You've got me."

"A union."

"Oh."

"Don't say it like that. They're not against the law. We're trying to organize studio grips."

They were at the Ocotillo, a tiny café that served dishes unlike any he had ever tasted, all corn and beans, hot chili peppers, cheese, fragments of heaven-knew-what-kind-of-meat. In the crowded booth Elisse's arm occasionally brushed his: it seemed to him he had never eaten any food so delicious.

"A union organizer who wears pretty crepe de chine dresses and silk stockings?"

She smiled. "They aren't against the law either."

"You're using cologne tonight."

"*L'Heure Bleue*. You are observant."

"Is it for somebody at the meeting?"

"No, you."

"Then leave it off," he said. He preferred that light, natural scent of hers. "Elisse, what's that address?"

"In your own calm way you're very dominating, aren't you?"

From the open windows of the small, bougainvillaea-shrouded cottage rushed a torrent of voices, so he was set for a crowd, but inside, where the air was heavy with cigarette smoke and the ripe odors of too many people on a warm night, he counted only four pairs of eyes—all staring at him. A handsome woman wearing her gray braids in a coronet, a weak-chinned man lounging on the chenille-covered daybed, a one-armed man who sat militarily erect, a stout woman whose eye twitched as she stared.

The man on the daybed, who wore a black turtleneck sweater, was rising to greet them. Justin had been on too many committees not to recognize him as the group's leader. Thirtyish, he had a short, wide, squashed nose that might well have been broken in the line of work, for the broad face was as alertly wary as a boxer's, and the man was built like a bantamweight: a short, heavily muscled weapon. "I'm Mitch Shapiro," he said, pronouncing the patronym Shap-eye-row.

"This is Justin Hutchinson," Elisse said, taking off her jacket to reveal tanned round arms. "He works for Onyx, so I can vouch he's no studio fink."

Mitch introduced the others by first names only. "Has Elisse explained what we're up to?"

"Organizing the studio," Justin replied.

"Right," Mitch said. "We're planning ways to get grips out to a mass meeting."

"I *told* you," Elisse said. "Promise free love and free beer." She opened a folding chair for herself.

Justin leaned against the doorjamb. The talk made it clear that grips were stagehands. *They're working against the odds*, Justin thought. It was nearly impossible to interest relatively well-paid, unskilled labor in a union, expecially when the boss, in this case Harry Cohn, was a tough customer, who worked hand in glove with the police. The group kept argumentatively reiterating the tactical problems. A physical pleasure, an excitement, wriggled through Justin each time Elisse injected one of her needle-edged comments into the planning.

"Yes, Martha," she snapped at the handsome woman with the coronet of braids. "A loudspeaker truck's a real necessity when you expect a horde of a dozen grips or less."

"In Russia," Martha jabbed back, "we'd have thousands, and the police would be on hand to *protect* the comrades."

"Like hell." Justin spoke involuntarily.

They twisted around to stare at him.

"Of course *you'd* say that!" Martha barked. "I know who you are—I read the capitalist rags."

Mitch asked, "Have you been in the Soviets, then, Mr. Hutchinson?"

"Justin. Yes, I worked there for seven months."

"A fact you never mentioned." Though Elisse spoke crisply, her eyes were chagrined.

"It never came up," he said.

Mitch put in, "There's an Onyx plant in Gorki."

"Near Gorki," Justin said. "I helped set it up."

"None of us has been there, to Russia," Mitch said. "Mind telling us a little?"

Justin ran a hand through his thick black hair, a compulsive habit that somehow unsnarled the mental processes below. Thoughtfully, he sketched the huge, unheated factory, the workers bundled in quilted rags or filthy, matted sheepskins. His large, solid presence and his deeply timbred voice controlled them. Even Martha, who licked at her roughed mouth as though ready with vehement protest, remained silent. He told them about Sergei, his Russian assistant,

Sergei with large and capable chilblained hands, a prerevolutionary engineering degree, few words of English, and a tiny, birdlike wife. Sergei wrote three petitions, requesting stoves in the dormitories. Then one morning Sergei's wife came alone to the bare-earth-floored dining hall, standing hunched into her thick clothes like a roosting sparrow. She tiptoed to a corner table, from which breakfasters departed as rapidly as if she carried plague virus rather than lentil porridge in her wooden bowl. By now Justin was accustomed to these sudden, unexplained disappearances, and with a shiver of sadness accepted that he would never again see the courageous, large-handed Sergei. The workers, he knew, weren't cold-blooded or cruel, simply human. It was folly to loiter sympathetically near the families of dissidents. Justin took his food to Sergei's wife's table. Several times after that he made a point of eating with the tiny, red-eyed, trembling woman, of speaking to her in his broken Russian. Nobody else ventured near. It was less than a month before Tom ordered him back to Detroit. Hugh told him that the request for his removal had come from the Comintern itself.

"Propaganda!" Martha shrilled with a near manic glare, leading the chorus of disbelief.

"Forget that Party jargon!" cried Elisse, on her feet.

"Your new friend's a capitalist!"

"So? That doesn't make him a liar, does it?"

Mitch Shapiro raised his hand, a silencing gesture. "We were talking about my yard for the meeting. Any better suggestions? Pablo? Germaine? Eric? Martha? Elisse?" With functional skill he drew each back into orderly discussion.

At ten thirty, as if summoned by invisible bells, the foursome rose, gathering coats, leaving together.

"Cellmates," Elisse murmured as Justin helped her on with her jacket.

"Can you two stay a bit?" Mitch asked.

Justin glanced down at Elisse, and she nodded. Mitch went into the kitchenette, visible beyond an archway, while she puttered around smoothing the chenille spread, emptying the ashtrays, very much at home. Justin lit a cigarette, following her with his eyes.

She sat at the card table next to him. Twiddling a charred match, she said, "A perfect speech for the occasion."

"It gave me a chance to see you spring to my defense."

"Not that you needed me. Now I understand that meteoric rise, Justin. In the movie game we call it star quality. You're a star. You don't have to say what people want to hear, you're so big, sincere, and dependable they'll listen to you regardless. My God—even Martha's mouth turned to salt!"

Her praise sent quivers of pleasure through him, and he touched the hand that held the match, tracing the thumb and forefinger. Her lips parted slightly and her eyelids lowered. His breath caught, and he felt a stirring in his groin. Flustered, he withdrew his hand.

"Coffee's hot," Mitch called.

They drank from chipped pottery mugs.

"I didn't mean to condemn Russia," Justin said. "It's a large order, dragging people out of serfdom. But why should we copy them? Whatever's wrong here, we start out with more."

"Absolutely," Mitch said. "I agree."

Surprised, Justin asked, "Then you aren't a party member?"

"No. But I work with them," Mitch said. "I grew up in the labor movement. My father was an organizer, he went to jail with Samuel Gompers. We moved around a lot. When I was ten—we were in Youngstown—a mounted trooper billy-clubbed me and I lost partial hearing in my left ear. I've been beaten with a sand-filled sock, a pipe length, you name it. I've lost teeth and I've been locked up more times than I can count. And why? I'll tell you why. I'm willing to fight for what I believe. That every man should have a share in deciding how he spends the days of his life. That nobody should be forced by hunger into unsafe mines or factories. That workers should get a pension if they become crippled, and when they get old." There was a jarring, practiced depth to the rhetoric, yet sincerity shone through on the broad, punished face.

Justin drank the sour, gritty coffee, aware of Elisse's speculative hazel eyes upon him. "I'm on your side," he said. "Onyx isn't paradise—"

"Wondrous fair of you to admit that," she said.

"—but let's face it, Tom Bridger's done more for his workers than any union. He pays well, he's a fanatic about plant cleanliness and safety, good lighting. He runs schools to teach English to foreign workers, he hires people of every race and color, he has a savings program that pays higher interest than a bank."

"Rejoice, rejoice, the Messiah's come," Elisse murmured, adding, "Talk about hero worship."

Mitch said, "At least they don't blacklist union members at Onyx."

"We have an open shop," Justin said. "We have a union."

"I know about it." Mitch said somberly. "A company union."

"Why not look on the bright side, Mitch?" Elisse said. "Onyx workers have a fine social club."

As they drove along Sunset Boulevard, Justin asked, "Where did you meet Mitch? At Columbia?"

"No, he's blacklisted by all the studios," she said. "I met him at Berkeley, hotbed of anarchism and wild-eyed revolutionaries."

"He's a lot older."

"He was my poli sci section leader."

Justin swerved around an ancient Model T: it had a rectangular black and brass tail lamp, making it a 1913 or 1914. "Did you go out with him?"

"What if I did?"

"Do you still?"

"I haven't taken the veil or anything, Justin."

"Do you?"

"In my junior year I worked on a student strike committee with him. We had a few dates. He's completely humorless, but he's a good, moral person. Totally dedicated. I admire that. Any more questions?"

They were at a stop signal, and he jammed down the brake. "You two still seem very snug."

"Oh, Justin, stop the badgering."

"You throw me off-balance," he confessed, sighing. "I've never been this way."

"What's the point of being jealous? Los Angeles is only a short stop-off for you," she said in a subdued voice. "Anyway, he's just a friend."

V

Saturday night Justin ducked a banquet for southern California Onyx dealers, taking Elisse to dinner and then to the Million Dollar Theater to see *The Sheik*. Afterward, over sodas at the Pig'n Whistle, she rolled her sparkling hazel eyes, miming Valentino's smoky glances so accurately that Justin, laughing, snorted chocolate ice cream up his nasal passages.

"Such appreciation should be rewarded," she said. "Tomorrow I'll treat you to a picnic lunch at the San Fernando Mission."

He touched the doorbell. She must have been waiting. His finger was still on the button when she opened the door, stepping out and closing it in one fluid motion. Bowing, she handed over the heavy basket. With her sleeveless white tennis dress belted at the hips, the red bandeau pressing against her curly bangs, her quizzical, happy smile and glowing apricot tan, she took his breath away—sweet baby was the expression in his mind—so that he ached to believe her hasty exit was not a slight. Yet he had never been able to warm himself with self-delusion. *She doesn't want her parents to see me*, he thought. *We've gone out every night and she's never introduced me to them.*

She directed him to a winding road across the Santa Monica mountains and then through the orange groves of the San Fernando Valley. At the mission they picnicked on roast chicken, potato salad, fruit, and Vouvray that she had secured from the studio bootlegger. Antique bronze bells chimed as they explored the tumbledown adobe buildings and tangled gardens, but Justin's happiness was marred by the memory of that swiftly closing door.

On the drive home she pointed to a turnoff. "I'll show you Los Angeles," she said. In gear they jolted up hairpin twists to a weedy ledge with a panoramic view: the tawny flatness was dotted with townlets stretching all the way from the city to the Pacific.

There were no houses here, no other cars. In the late afternoon torpor a pigeon crouped, an insect chittered hypnotically, and Elisse and Justin gazed, somnolent, at the scene below. He rested his head on green-striped upholstery—Fivers now came in forest green, drab blue, or maroon as well as gray. Light scintillated behind his closed eyelids and he saw his mother's slender form, arms at her sides, as she sang in her vibrantly lovely soprano some wordless Puccini theme. The innumerable versions of this recurrent dream (Antonia invariably sang) plucked at him in the same way that a harpist draws long, rippled chords from strings: their strains reverberated through him, rousing nostalgic yearnings for a past when he had been engulfed in love, and had lived without loneliness or self-consciousness. The delicate sheen of perspiration on Antonia's forehead brought her vividly alive. Her singing ceased, and her lips curved in that eager, expectant way, presaging some high happiness about to break. "Justin, who is that with you?" she asked, and the joy of her smile made the delicate tip of her nose wiggle. "She's a most frightfully pretty girl."

His head jerked forward and he awoke.

Elisse was watching him. The palm cupping her head stretched the skin around her eye.

"I dozed off."

"A catnap," she said softly.

"I'm sorry."

"Don't be."

He leaned toward her, and at the same moment they twined their arms around each other, smiling. When they kissed, a kiss that tasted of illegal French wine and California grapes, he felt an inevitability, a sense of having completed a circle and returned to where he belonged, a homecoming unhindered by the troubling restraints Elisse had placed on their relationship. His euphoria expanded to tumescence when her lips parted and his tongue touched hers. His fingers reached under the armhole of her tennis frock to trace the curve of her breast through the silk teddy. With a tremulous sigh she caressed the skin at his open shirt collar, a wandering, gentle touch as though—he thought in his swollen, near painful delight—another Elisse, as soft and tender as a baby chick, were emerging from the shell of clever wisecracks and immaculately groomed good looks.

"Sweet," he whispered against her ear.

"Justin . . . darling . . ."

In their little chamber of glass and steel, the mobile privacy granted unto them by the automotive age, she responded with quivers and sighing murmers as he explored the different textures of her, tasted the satin of her warm, moist skin. A delirium he had not believed possible blossomed when he touched the ultimate wet, slick heat.

"Are you, sweet? Have you ever . . . ?"

"There has to be a first time. Ahh, darling . . ."

In the midst of his heavy-breathed love and his boundless lust, he found himself recalling that speech she had made at Philippe's: *Two different worlds, Justin;* and then, quite clearly, he heard the firm closing of her front door. God knows he ached with a frenzy for their joining, the rigid part of himself asserted *that*, yet there was another dimension to him, and he wanted to enter her with flags and banners and triumph, wanted to be part of her world. He shifted back, and the Fiver's steering wheel jarred against his side as he held her face to examine her—he could smell the musky, infinitely tantalizing genital odor on his fingers.

"Justin? What is it?"

"Sweet, I've never met your parents."

Abruptly she moved away, straightening her rumpled tennis dress, then staring at the sun, a crimson disk burying itself in a rufous sea. "What have they to do with our necking?" she asked in a baiting tone.

"Everything. Why don't you want me to meet them?"

"Immaterial, immaterial. You're leaving on Tuesday."

"Are they very religious?"

"Temple twice a year."

"Then why haven't you introduced me to them?"

"Oh, Justin, you don't understand one darn thing." In this dying light, her lipstick gone, her bobbed hair disheveled, she looked young, defenseless, cornered.

Justin steeled himself to continue. "Do they know about me?"

"What do you think I am, a sneak? I pointed out your name in *Time* magazine, and explained I'd met you in the flesh at Uncle's, and was showing you around for the few days you were in Los Angeles."

"And they forbade it?"

"That's hardly their style. But Mother's been sighing a lot and Daddy's had chest pains. If you're looking for approval, Justin, those aren't the signs."

He felt a choking pressure against his windpipe. He was hurt, ludicrously so, at this sight-unseen rejection by two strangers, and into his consciousness welled all he had ever heard of the clannishness of Jews, of their outlandish diet and clothes and synagogues, of their eerie, alien desire to remain apart, the Chosen People. Yet he immediately rejected these stereotypes as not jibing with the Rosburgs' London house and country place, or with this small, pretty, brown-haired girl whom he irrevocably loved. The only remark he could summon was a bitter, "That's wonderful!"

"They're dears. Blame the world, not them."

"For *their* prejudice?" Justin stepped out of the car, turning from her as he undid his trouser button to straighten his shirt. His anger had faded when he got back in. She had not moved. It was too dark to make out her expression. As he peered at her, a foreboding recollection of that Jewish touchiness washed over him. "I never should have said that," he mumbled. "I'm sorry."

"Best to have it out in the open, Justin," she replied wearily. "I'm not about to apologize for my parents, or for what we are. If you want my honest opinion, we have less prejudice, and turn the other cheek more often than circumstances warrant. I've never heard you like that. Nasty. Clipped. Ugly. What *do* you think of Jews?"

"I haven't known many. Rosburg. Miller in my platoon. We were in the trench together when he lost his leg."

"Is that where you got the scar?"

Shrapnel had wounded him in the shoulder. "Yes. At Belleau Wood."

They both looked down at the clusters of electric light twinkling through the brief California dusk.

"Elisse, what you said shut me out, so I hit back," he spoke with difficulty. "Usually I think things through before I blurt them out. But I'm not myself anymore. I've been lonely ever since Mother died, very lonely. And now—even with the obstacles you've set up—I'm not. It's as if I've been let out of solitary."

"You sit across the street after you take me home."

"How do you know?"

"Who else would leave a pile of Craven-A butts?"

"I'm so crazy about you I don't know if I'm coming or going. I don't sleep, I don't taste my food."

"I know what you mean." Her voice sounded hollow, defeated. "I have the same symptoms."

He turned toward her. "You mean that?"

"Oh, Justin. Do you think I offer my pure white self to all men?"

"I haven't ruined it?"

"Would that you could. This is such a mess." Sighing, she picked up his hand, kissing it. "You're my beau ideal."

Through Justin's mind darted crazed images of himself lifting her aboard a train in her white tennis dress and small, dusty sneakers, a justice of the peace in Yuma, endless hours of nonsectarianly legalized priapic bliss in a locked compartment, followed by uxoriously tender married life in the green land of happiness. Married? Was this Justin Hutchinson who weighed every decision, the man who circled every issue, peering into its stygian heart? *What's happened to my measured calm? Elopement?*

"Put on your lipstick," he said. "We're going to your house, and I'll meet them."

"Daddy has a concert tonight, the Hollywood Bowl."

"Tomorrow, then."

"Justin, you have no idea—"

"Tomorrow," he said firmly.

"Oh, you and your screwy leadership qualities. Come to dinner, then," she said, an indefinable tremor in her voice.

VI

Primed to capture the towered bungalow, he stepped directly into a living room dominated by a grand piano. He had a fleeting impression of stacked magazines and a great many table lamps with domed silk shades, but Elisse had opened the door and that crazed, obsessive delight squirmed inside of him: he could scarcely keep from putting his arm around her as she introduced him to her mother. He presented the long box.

Mrs. Kaplan peered into its cellophane window. "Roses," she said with a smile that had a special quality; it made her look gullible as a child. Time had blurred the flesh around her eyes and jawline, yet it was impossible not to see that she must have once resembled those vapidly pretty, flowerlike girls grouped in an Alma-Tadema painting. "How lovely of you, Mr. Hutchinson," she said in a whispery English voice. "Oh, the sweet darlings, they need to be in water." And she wafted in her gray chiffon dress around the arch to the dining room.

Mr. Kaplan was altogether a juicier, livelier proposition. "Mr. Hutchinson," he said, extending a musician's firm hand. "It's always a pleasure to meet Elisse's friends." His mouth was pink and the eyes magnified by glasses were a warm chestnut brown. Balancing on his heels, teetering forward on his toes and back again, he swayed his small, rotund body. "She tells me this is your first

visit to Los Angeles. How do you find it?'' His English accent was
not quite so *comme il faut* as his wife's. Leeds, Justin decided.

''No wonder everybody wants to come here.''

''Have you taken in our sights? Elisse says you missed the
Hollywood Bowl. Are you only keen on this new syncopation?''

''I'm disappointed we missed you and the *Pastoral* Thursday,''
Justin said. ''And to be very honest, the only popular music I like is
jazz.''

''Gershwin uses that idiom in his *Rhapsody in Blue*.''

Though music critics praised the *Rhapsody*, Justin found the piece
shallow, bombastic, and teeth-grittingly annoying, yet on the other
hand Gershwin was Jewish, so this question could be a land mine.
''In Detroit we have some fine colored jazz bands, and sometimes
King Oliver comes from Chicago,'' he temporized. ''I'm afraid I'm
a lowbrow about my jazz.''

''You hear that, Elisse?'' Mr. Kaplan beamed. ''Gershwin should
stick to his show tunes. Jazz is a way of performing music, not
writing it, and that rules out Gershwin's orchestrations. You have
good taste, Mr. Hutchinson.''

Absurdly pleased with this compliment, Justin leaped up—Mrs.
Kaplan was returning back with his roses in a tall Chinese vase.

She moved the flowers around the room to see where they made
the best display. All families have ritual roles assigned to their
members, and briefly the Kaplans fell into theirs. Elisse, the practical cynic, shifting table lamps and magazines with a raised eyebrow;
Mr. Kaplan, the connoisseur, offering aesthetic advice while Mrs.
Kaplan, the pliant, indecisive female, allowed herself to be coerced
into setting the vase in its obvious place on the piano. The small
charade played itself out with near visible lines of affection, and
Justin, the onlooker, was drenched with memories of another trinity—
Antonia, Claude, and little Justin.

''The red of the roses with the yellow of the Spanish shawl!'' Mr.
Kaplan said, kissing his fingertips.

''Do you like them here?'' Mrs. Kaplan asked Justin.

''Exactly right,'' Justin said, his voice so tight that Elisse glanced
questioningly at him.

Dinner was served by an elderly, stern-jawed colored woman
named Coetta.

"Mr. Hutchinson," said Mrs. Kaplan, her fork wavering over her drumstick. "How do you know my brother?"

"Through your nephew. In school, Ros . . . Victor was my friend."

"I wish you'd stop boasting about that," said Elisse.

"Victor's a lovely boy, dear," said Mrs. Kaplan absently, still looking at Justin. "You *do* live in America?"

"Detroit. But you're from England, Mrs. Kaplan, so you know how it is when you move to another country. You never quite belong in either."

"We all know that feeling," she said.

"Not Elisse." He smiled. "The native."

"I meant the feeling of being an outsider," said Mrs. Kaplan, and though her casual tone and fluttery smile had not changed, Justin, looking across the damask linen cloth at her, decided that she wasn't such a dim bulb after all. "She tells us your stay is over tomorrow."

"Yes. In the evening I'm taking the San Francisco train, and from there I go to Seattle. Mr. Bridger's meeting me there."

"How nice. *The* Mr. Bridger." She rang her silver bell. "Coetta, the chicken was lovely. Will you pass it around again?"

After dessert—rich trifle topped with crystallized violets—Mr. Kaplan said, "How do you feel about breaking the Eighteenth Amendment, Mr. Hutchinson. There's a bottle of schnapps in my studio."

Justin followed Elisse's father up the tiled steps. The tower room, crowded by another grand piano, was furnished with music cabinets, chairs, and metal stands. "Up here I give lessons. I'm very picky whom I take," said Mr. Kaplan, pouring brandy into wine goblets. In this studio, epicenter of his being, he did not sway or teeter.

Justin took his glass. "Thank you, sir."

"Nice being shown around by a pretty flapper, eh?"

"I'll say."

"She's bright, too, our Elisse. Graduated from college at twenty and made Phi Beta Kappa. She's only been at the studio a couple of months and they've promoted her to head reader. Still, she's not a bluestocking. She's . . . peppy, isn't that the word nowadays?"

"There is no word," Justin said. "She's unique."

Mr. Kaplan sat on the piano bench and gulped down his brandy. "I'm not much good at this sort of thing, Mr. Hutchinson. If you want to know, I'm only firm with my viola. My music." He shook his head, drumming a finger on the empty glass. "She used to go to high school dances with a Catholic boy. Mrs. Kaplan and I naturally tried to stop it but she refused to listen. So we told ourselves he was just another of her gentile friends. They both were graduated, class valedictorians, and went on to Southern Cal. That first semester he would pick her up in his jalopy. Toot-toot, and out she'd run, all glowing. Any kind of club that bans people, she's against. She didn't join the Jewish sorority. But he joined one. A fraternity. And as soon as he did—" With a clicking sound, Mr. Kaplan waved his hand in a flat, cutting gesture. "As far as *they* were concerned, he couldn't even give a sixteen-year-old Jewish girl a ride to school. I don't know what, if anything, he said to her. But it was as if candles had been snuffed out. She tried to put on a good face—you must have noticed she's ready with quick remarks—but inside she's soft. Sensitive. She transferred to the university at Berkeley. She didn't get over it for a couple of years—I am not sure she's over it yet." He gave Justin an accusatory glance.

Justin reddened, stand-in for a miserable, callow boy he would take passionate joy in punching.

"Did you know," Mr. Kaplan was asking, "that in Europe for centuries there were laws forbidding Jews to marry gentiles? In many places it was a capital offense. Even where it wasn't, mobs would burn and sack the ghetto when such marriages took place. Today when a man or woman marries outside, we still say the kaddish, the prayer for the dead. And in many ways they are dead. They don't belong with either group."

Justin noted the change of tense. "I don't know much about Jewish history," he said.

"It's a part of us, of Elisse. Next time you're out here, it would be best if you ask another young lady to show you around."

"Are you going to tell that to Elisse, sir?"

"Would I be making a fool of myself now if I hadn't already done so?" Mr. Kaplan sighed. "Last night she told us you were coming to dinner, and the evening was important to her."

"To both of us."

Mr. Kaplan wiped his forehead with his handkerchief. "It's been less than a week."

"Once my mind is made up, I have a hard time changing. Mr. Kaplan, I promise you, I'm not like . . ." His voice trailed away.

Elisse's father was looking at him with helpless misery. "That's what we were afraid of," he said. "She's not a little girl anymore. Mrs. Kaplan and I could never, never accept her getting serious about a gentile."

Justin's fists clenched. What right did Harris Kaplan have to build barricades of ancient wrongs that he, Justin Hutchinson, had never perpetrated? What right to reject him impersonally without regard for his qualities, his love, only his ancestry? Unfair, unfair. "Elisse told me. I didn't believe her," he said in a hard commanding tone, a product of hurt.

"We're surprised that you've taken her out in the first place." Mr. Kaplan was forming *his* words as if around a hot stone. "I apologize for saying this, but Onyx isn't a very liberal company."

"Henry Ford published *The Protocols of the Elders of Zion*," Justin said. "Not Mr. Bridger."

"Then you have Jews at the top?"

"We have Jewish dealers, a great many of them."

"But no executives?"

Justin shook his head. "It's hardly a matter of policy, though." Again he felt awkward, defensive, and obscurely in the wrong. Why weren't there any?

"What about the wives?"

Again Justin shook his head.

"I read in that magazine about the future you have ahead of you."

"My job's not the problem."

"When it comes to this sort of thing, you'd be surprised. If you just left tomorrow and didn't write or come back, it'd be the best thing. For both of you."

"I couldn't promise that, Mr. Kaplan. Elisse wouldn't want me to." He could feel the blood pulsing in his veins, yet his manner remained calm.

Mr. Kaplan's mouth worked anxiously. Justin recognized that in this calamitously awkward scratching match, the stout, ingratiating little musician was fighting beyond his strength. "This life you have in Detroit, it will be impossible for her, for our Elisse."

"It *is* a huge decision," Justin said. "We haven't talked about anything . . . serious."

"But you intend to?"

Justin nodded.

Mr. Kaplan opened the keyboard and sounded middle C. "When you have a child, it's like your nerves are tied to another person. You feel their pain, all of it, but you can't do anything to prevent them from getting hurt."

"Not Elisse, never through me."

"Believe me, Mr. Hutchinson, this . . . this friendship is difficult enough for Mrs. Kaplan and me. But Elisse is the one who will take it on the chin."

"No," Justin said.

Mr. Kaplan sounded the note again. "You're wrong for her, wrong for each other."

Justin stared into his brandy. After a long silence, he said, "I won't push her."

CHAPTER 17

Zoe strolled up and down the long platform of the Detroit depot, awed glances and zephyrs of silence trailing her.

Her beauty struck the eye like a blow.

Her luminous, finely pored skin was subtly tinged with pink, her eyes appeared yet more meltingly dark in contrast to the red-gold waves around the brim of her cloche, her full mouth was set in a beguiling pout. But it was her body that dumbfounded. Zoe's curves and symmetries transcended the imagination and overcame the smartly waistless Nile-green ensemble she wore: the sensuality of her lush body was so great it vaguely disturbed yet ultimately delighted the beholder.

"Zoe. Zoe!"

Caryll Bridger was jogging after her in his slightly duckfooted stride. Although tabloids often grappled with the question of who was the world's wealthiest billionaire, the Nizam of Hyderabad, the Aga Khan, the King of England, or Tom Bridger, Zoe saw Caryll not as the heir to an incalculable fortune but as a round-faced young man whose gentle gray eyes shone as he smiled at her and lifted his homburg, just another of the dozen or so automotive executives mad for her.

"Caryll," she said irritably. This was one of the days when his transparent adoration rubbed her the wrong way. "So you've declared a holiday."

"I'm here to meet them too," he said, matching his steps to hers. Caryll, taking after the Trelinack side, was broad of bone and without height. Barefoot in their swimsuits, the two measured the same, but Zoe, dressed up and wearing her green suede high-heeled pumps, was taller than he. "Is it on for tonight?" he asked.

"Whatever are you talking about?"

"The dance," he said. "I asked you last week, and you said you'd tell me. Remember? It's for Mavis and Ted." A scrubby friend from Detroit Military Academy had blossomed into a handsome swan and was carrying off a lumber heiress amid a great deal of prenuptial fanfare—much to Caryll's jubilation. There were so few functions to which he could invite Zoe. The Bridgers never had joined the Yondotega Club, the Detroit Club, the Bloomfield Country Club, they did not mingle with the automotive ascendancy. Their social life was limited to family functions. To these Justin and Zoe were never invited. Caryll was aware that his parents had influenced and encouraged his aunts in this exclusion, yet Maud never mentioned the ban, and this atypical obliqueness threw him so uneasily off-balance that he never questioned her, never asked his Aunt Melisande if he could invite the girl he loved and the man he considered his best friend to her masterfully coordinated thés dansants or balls, never asked his stout little Aunt Yssy if he could bring them along to her noisy, congenial Open Houses. "Paul Whiteman's in town to play for it."

"In case you've forgotten, this'll be Justin's first night home."

"He can come with us. He's never tired. Zoe, *Paul Whiteman!* There's another band, too."

"Oh, who cares? Hugh's looking forward to seeing Justin."

"You love to dance," Caryll persisted. "They can talk tomorrow."

"What about you? I should think *you'd* want to stay home to butter up your father before you spring the new car on him."

"I want to show Justin the prototype first," Caryll said, regretting he had confided in Zoe, who lacked any regard for secrets. "The design's slick, but I'm worried about mechanical problems. Justin's got the knack of finding them."

"You're afraid of your father."

Caryll's smile had frayed. Though accustomed to Zoe's inexplicably shifting moods and insecurities and aware that if he remained steadfast, soon she would be cajoling him, he was too hopelessly in love to ignore her taunts. "I'm not."

"Everybody is. Except Hugh and Justin."

"Dad's a legend, he's famous. No wonder people are intimidated by him."

"We're talking about *you*."

"Every time I try to argue with him about cars, I remember he just about built the industry and all I've ever done is be his son."

"So you let Justin shield you."

Caryll bit the inside of his lip to keep his failing composure. She had come dangerously close to the truth. Though Tom never voiced respect for Justin, and often was inexplicably curt with him, Caryll knew that for Justin alone would his father compromise. Therefore, when it came to pressing his own ideas, Caryll generally went in tandem with his friend. "I can pick you up at ten or eleven—as late as you want."

"When you beg you sound so wet." The platform had begun to shake. The train roared into the station. Leaving Caryll red with mortification, Zoe flashed around baggage carts, passengers, the colored redcaps, arriving at the last car, Tom's private car, before the steward had let down the steps. Justin jumped down.

The young man's reticence vanished in a bear hug that lifted his sister from the ground. "Zozo!"

She printed his cheek with her bright coral lipstick. "You gorgeous man! How I missed you!"

He laughed. "When did you find time? From your letters I got the impression you've been out dancing until three every single night."

"I'm a wreck when you're not here," she said sincerely, kissing lipstick onto his other cheek.

II

That afternoon she stayed in Hugh's antique-paneled office, her spectacular legs coiled over the arm of a leather easy chair, listening quietly as Justin reported to Hugh on the assembly plant departments that were Hugh's bailiwick: social welfare, advertising, public relations. Zoe did not focus on the dialogue—business bored her silly—but on the resplendently warm, deep-toned affection in the masculine voices. She glanced from one to the other as they spoke, these two in whose presence alone she felt confident of her place in the world's scheme. Justin, she noted approvingly, had one shirt cuff showing. Clothes never stayed neat on his large, comfortably muscled body; he was springy, casual. Hugh, on the other hand, in his double-breasted pinstripe, was lithe and elegant. They pleased her equally.

The discussion continued through dinner. The table was cleared, and the three were left cognac and a magnificent Paul Storr epergne overflowing with nuts and large, perfect peaches.

"Did you ever discover what ruined the piston machine in the Glendale assembly?" Hugh asked. "I heard rumors of labor sabotage."

"Nothing so dramatic. The plant manager pushes too hard, that's all. I've told Tom."

"Have you ever realized, Justin, that nine times out of ten you side with labor?" Hugh was smiling.

"Be that as it may, Hugh." Justin smiled back. "The manager speeded up the line until nobody could keep the pace. A tool fell into the machinery. If a foreman hadn't immediately thrown the switch, we'd have had much more damage."

"You haven't mentioned the dealer banquet out in Los Angeles."

"A fine success. Or so they told me."

"Weren't you there?"

"I missed that one."

"You?" Hugh asked, surprised. "Why?"

A stab of intuition pierced Zoe's heart. *He's found somebody,* she thought. *A girl. The girl. He's going to desert me.*

Hugh was chuckling. "No need to look so hangdog, Justin. You're enough of a stickler to be entitled to a night off now and then." He stood. "You two need a chance to catch up. And I have work to do. Good night, *mes enfants.*"

Justin and Zoe strolled toward Lake St. Clair, moving in and out of pools of bluish light cast by Hugh's ornamental ironwork lamps. Zoe's apprehensions made her throat feel bruised and she pulled up the ermine collar of her cape. When she was certain she could effect an easy modulation, she inquired, "What happened on the night of the banquet? Were you bedding Vilma Banky or Clara Bow?"

"I hate it when you talk like that."

"Scabrously dirty, that's me," she said. "You were with a girl, weren't you?"

Justin's footsteps crunched several paces on the gravel. "Rosburg's cousin," he admitted slowly. "I met her in London, but she's from Los Angeles."

"If she got responsible, disciplined *you* to cut a duty for Onyx, she really must be something."

"She is."

"Oh?"

Justin ran a hand through his hair, and said in a pleased, almost shy tone, "She's a knockout all the way, Zozo. Brains. Sense of humor—she has a crisp, funny way about everything. We went dancing at a speak and she does as terrific a Charleston as you. She's caring, she's kind."

"I fear for you, Justin, I fear. Is she pretty?"

"Is she ever!"

"Tall?"

"No, little." He held out his hand at shoulder level. "She has curly brown hair. Well, it's not exactly brown, it has a lot of blond in front. Her eyes are brown with green glints. Hazel, I guess it's called."

"What about her nose?" There was a faint smirkiness to the question.

"Cut that out, Zoe." Justin spoke thoughtfully rather than angrily. Mr. Kaplan had syringed a certain easy wax from his ears, and now he was prepared to catch the enormous number of condescensions and quips that had not heretofore registered: innuendos, an unfairly patronizing tone of amusement, a cloud of nebulous, not particularly virulent anti-Semitism that distressed him and left him helpless because it emanated from people he liked and trusted.

"One thing's clear. You're carrying a very large torch."

"I hadn't realized what a lost sheep I've been."

"You? Stalwart, purposeful you?"

"Since we came over, I've been a square peg. You've found people. I haven't. Zozo, with her, I feel like . . . oh, I can't explain. Alive."

Zoe moved apart from him on the path. She had always stifled the thought of her brother's eventual marriage—or, as she inwardly termed it, desertion. It had been easy enough to do. Justin's calm had attracted its opposite, the frivolously extroverted dumb Doras, yet his thoughtful depth enabled him to see beyond their twitching bottoms, fluttering lashes, their brightly painted mouths, to their essential shallowness. Zoe's fancy had awarded her brother countless physical conquests, yet because he had never tumbled for any girl, she had assumed his heart would remain forever unscratched and pristine. Hers.

Reaching the artificial hill, they silently ascended the sloping path to the domed summerhouse. From its balustrade Justin looked down at Lake St. Clair, black as oil with one yellow-lit tug oozing along, twinned by its perfect reflection.

Zoe gripped the spooled railing. "Does she know you're gone on her?"

"It's been mentioned, yes. But her parents are dead set against anyone who's not the same religion."

"A secret engagement?"

"I haven't actually asked her yet. She's young, about your age. We haven't known one another long enough. And her parents are right, it won't be easy. It's not fair to push her. I'm giving her time."

"Impeccably just Justin."

"We stayed up all night talking about it." Justin crushed out his cigarette. "I'm not naïve, I know it's more than a religion, being Jewish. She's positive it'll be a handicap for me at Onyx. Isn't that ridiculous?"

"Absolutely," Zoe said, nodding in agreement.

"Still, it's in her mind. Besides, she can't bear hurting her parents."

"What about this cooling-off period? How long?"

"December. Christmas."

"Will you be dating other girls?"

"Oh, don't be a nit, Zoe."

"No, you wouldn't. What about her?"

"She's meant to go out. That's what this is all about," he said, clipping out the words. "It's cold here, Zoe. Let's get on back to the house."

As he opened the side door for her he said, "I didn't mean to spill my heart."

"Sometimes even you, brother mine, need a sympathetic ear."

"That I do. But it's private, all right?"

"Mum's the word," Zoe promised.

III

The year after Justin and Zoe had come to live with him, Hugh had added on to his red-brick Tudor mansion. The new wing included filing rooms and secretarial offices downstairs, and a large suite for himself on the second floor where he stood no chance of bumping into his wards' guests. He was in his private upstairs library, his feet on a hassock, reading a sales chart that Justin had brought from Seattle, when Zoe burst in.

She flung that astounding body into the chair next to his. "He's found somebody!" she cried, tears oozing down her lovely cheeks.

It was natural for her to turn to Hugh in her misery, natural for her to betray Justin's confidences to him.

She was ruinously, obsessively in love with Hugh.

Yet Hugh, skilled at unraveling secrets through detectives' reports, incessantly shrewd about motives, never had a glimmer. In his eyes Zoe's smiles, her clinging interest in his conversation, her trust, were natural extensions of her childhood's uninhibited adoration. In a way he was right. Age eight, aboard the creaking *Stephen Decatur*, Zoe had formulated her personal Pygmalion myth: Hugh, having worshiped her mother from afar, had seen in her, Zoe, a younger Antonia to mold as his own, and for this reason was bringing her (and therefore Justin) to Detroit. As Zoe swam into puberty her emotions swerved onto the shoals of sex. She would awaken breathless, her shapely thighs clenched together, heiress to a legacy of libidinous dreams in which Hugh caressed her budding breasts and her private orifices: those dawns she learned a manipulative technique she called "going up and over," and Hugh's image remained the simulacrum on which these self-seductions balanced. Enamored of Hugh as she was, adoring his wily brain, his long, slender body, his hard and sophisticated mouth, the swanlike silvering of his blond hair, the twenty-three-year age gap, his steel webs of power, his politic wisdom, even his dark red scar tissue, she inevitably viewed her legion of admirers, Caryll among them, as young, ineffectual calves.

Hugh gave her his handkerchief. "I had a suspicion. It was bound to happen sooner or later."

"She's from Los Angeles." Zoe's voice, tending to the higher registers, was shrill.

"It's all right, Zoe," he soothed.

"I can't bear some stranger taking him away from us."

"He'll bring her to Detroit. You'll see, it'll be fine. You're always like this at first with everything that Justin cares for. Remember that bitch pup I gave him? You hated her, then you played with her, and later when she got into your cottage and chewed your dolls, you didn't even make a fuss.''

"This isn't a golden retriever, Hugh,'' Zoe wailed. "It's Rosburg's cousin.''

Hugh's exhalation rasped. "Rosburg?'' He forgot himself enough to turn full face to her. "Rosburg?''

"His California cousin. Justin met her when he was in London this summer.''

"What's her name?''

"He didn't say . . . or did he? Alice or Elaine or something.''

"But she is a Jewess?''

"That's the problem.'' Zoe wiped her eyes, accepting that she had now roused Hugh to her own earlier level of alarm, yet not comprehending why the girl's being Jewish had set him off. "He's giving her until Christmas to decide if this is it. But he's dead serious.''

"It's gone that far?''

"Oh, Hugh, what do you think I'm trying to *tell* you?''

"You're not dramatizing?''

"You saw him.''

"He was only in Los Angeles a week. Justin never rushes into things.''

"He's fallen like a ton of bricks.''

Hugh tapped the fingers of one hand into the palm of the other, his eyes far away as his mind went prowling around this new threat. Zoe relaxed, clasping her hands around the short skirt of her aquamarine silk dinner gown, letting Hugh take over.

At last he said, "I can't believe Justin's gone haywire.''

Zoe murmured encouragingly.

"These quick things often die just as quickly,'' he said. "I'm tired, Zoe, dear.''

Rising, she patted his shoulder. "You'll figure out something. You always do.''

"Sleep well,'' he said automatically.

The staccato clicks of her heels faded down the private hall that led to his rooms. Hugh rested his head back in the tapestry cushion, his stiff boiled shirt front moving up and down with each asthmatic breath. *Justin*, he thought, *Justin and some Jewish girl?*

Hugh's feelings for his unacknowledged nephew were possessive

274

and extended far beyond the terrain of mere philoprogenitive love. His respect and admiration for the younger man were fiercely partisan. At first he had been furious with Tom for not personally guiding Justin around the Hamtramck, for not welcoming him to the Farm, for refusing to acknowledge Justin's achievements and decencies, the boy's ability to lead. Oh, Hugh understood that it took a formidable effort for Tom to maintain his seemingly cold-blooded distance. Justin did not. And though it was against Justin's nature to air his hurts or complain, it was more than apparent to Hugh that some vital part of the boy was numbed by Tom's attitude.

Hugh had finally accepted that Tom's yammerings about that antediluvian promise made to Antonia were for real. Tom would never, never replace Caryll—that milky boy—with his firstborn son, his true heir.

The focus of Hugh's life had shifted from his brother to his nephew.

In the years since he had altered his allegiance, he had planned for Justin a palace far larger than Onyx: it was an automotive monopoly far greater than the one that George Selden long ago had hoped to form with his patent. Every manufacturer—Ford, Onyx, General Motors, Marmon, Hudson, Chrysler, Packard, Studebaker, you name them—under one roof to be governed in harmony, efficiency, and decency by Justin. Hugh had already started to construct. He had quietly bought stock in Sterns and General Motors, had aimed subtle propaganda at directors of smaller outfits, who might be coerced into surrendering their companies for shares in this new entity.

Needless to say, Justin had no inkling of this grandiose plan.

Hugh rose from his chair to gaze out the window at the lights of his estate. *This damn girl,* he thought, *she'll queer everything.*

Hugh, perhaps in keeping with his reclusive style of life, bore no animosity toward any group. His sole prejudice was against those people who looked upon him with abhorrence or fear; however, he was too astute to underestimate the bigotry of others. *This industry'll never get behind a man with a Jewish wife,* he thought. *Never in a million years.*

I must find out what's what in order to figure out how to shake her loose. He went back to his chair and sat, waiting.

By midnight Hugh could hear the little creaks and sighs that breathe through a house when all therein are asleep. He rose, stretching like a cat, then locked the doors to his suite. Moving to the adjacent library, he stood before a large portrait, one of those Renaissance renderings of a dimensionless, whey-faced girl: an art historian had authenticated the subject as Lady Jane Neville, and Hugh had forked over a great deal. Ignoring his presumed ancestress, he touched a curlicue in the center left of the gilt frame, at the same time exerting pressure on the lower left corner. The painting swung open on oiled hinges to reveal a safe. His office staff believed all of his private papers were concealed in the capacious walk-in Mosler safe downstairs, as did Justin and Tom. Only Hugh and a New Orleans cabinetmaker knew of the existence of this hidey-hole. Shuffling through manila envelopes penciled lightly in his own meticulous hand, Hugh extracted one, carrying it to his library table.

The top page was also in his hand:

> *Dickson Keeley*
> *b. January 5, 1892, of Persis (Dickson) and Judge Barnes Keeley, in Elizabeth, N.J.*
> *Sexual proclivities (three photo. incl.)*
> *Information from the private files of Mr. Woodrow Wilson in re dismissal from Princeton, 1912.*
> *Dept. of Army documents in re discharge, 1918.*

Hugh had read the dossier before, but he turned the pages again to reassure himself that Dickson Keeley would remain his creature. Locking the envelope back in the safe, he went into his bedroom to use the telephone.

IV

"You weren't very explicit last night, about what you had in mind, Mr. Bridger, but I figured you'd want an eyeful of these." Dickson Keeley swung his briefcase onto the Elizabethan table, drawing out a roll of drafting paper.

During his abortive college years Dickson Keeley had been on the Princeton crew, and one would guess, by the shoulder and bicep development under his conservative dark suit, that he had continued to row. Detroit was the nation's principal port of entry for illegal liquor, and while the rumor that Dickson Keeley had at one time personally ferried booze in from Canada was not true, he indeed had connections among the city's big-time bootleggers. With his polished manners and dangerous smile he was considered—erroneously—to be a ladies' man. His worst enemies, and he had a great many enemies, conceded his reckless bravery. He was heartily disliked by Colonel Hazelford, his boss in Security, which was an arm of the Social Welfare department: Hugh's terrain. Hugh had personally hired him, so his job was secure.

"Plans of Caryll's pet project?" Hugh asked.

"So he's broadcast the news to the family?"

"On the contrary. But I have my sources." Zoe had told him.

Dickson Keeley extended the papers across the table. "Getting these was no lead-pipe cinch. Over there in the museum they keep the doors and windows shut tighter than a rat's ass." In Keeley's cultured, educated drawl the tough's lingo sounded like a foreign tongue.

Hugh waved negligently. "Leak them over to Ford or General Motors."

"The hell you say!"

"Every part'll be altered once my brother gets his hands on the prototype."

"So he's in on it too?"

"Hardly," Hugh said. "But Chevrolet's eating up the market, and if we don't replace the Fiver soon, we're out of business."

"Your nephew's showing Hutchinson the model this morning, and if he, Hutchinson, gives the green light, the two of them plan to spring it on the boss."

"Keep me informed."

"Yes, they've invited me along to take notes and pictures!"

"Don't get cocky with me," Hugh said. "And speaking of Hutchinson, why haven't you been reporting to me about him?"

Dickson Keeley's squarish jaw dropped in surprise. "Hutchinson? He *lives* here."

"Keeley, you do remember why I give you an extra hundred a week and expenses?"

"To check on the top brass," Dickson Keeley said. "Where's the body buried?"

"There's a girl in Los Angeles."

"Name?" Dickson Keeley asked, looking at him with pale, unblinking eyes.

Hugh fought a wave of nausea. In his effort to save Justin from this girl, save him from the oblivion of a mixed marriage, he was betraying the faith between them. *It can't be helped,* he told himself, but when he picked up his letter opener, he slashed at the sealed envelope before him as if he could cut away his self-disgust. "I don't know anything about her," he said, adding, "yet."

V

Three mornings later, at six thirty, Tom was inching through Gate One, part of the crush that converged on Woodland before the shift change. Headlights shone, although the sky was already paling. To his left he could see the outline of three vessels low-laden with what must be ore, coke, or limestone, as they plowed from the Detroit River into the privately dredged canal. A mile and a half to his right, invisible beyond the steel mills, the glass plant, the rubber shop, the main assembly, enormous arc lights were burning so that inspectors could check over Fivers ready to be loaded onto flatcars. Woodland was a monstrous female in perpetual, noisy heat, spewing from her womb a ceaseless litter of sturdy, ugly little cars. This year they had produced—and sold—over a million and three quarters, down from the previous two years, but still more than any other company.

As the next car, a 1920 sedan, edged through the gate the driver recognized him and rolled down the window. "Good morning, Mr. Bridger, boss," called the man in a respectful Slavic voice, and his three passengers touched their caps. Tom lifted his arm in an awkward wave. *I'll never learn to be comfortable playing king,* he thought. More workers in their cars were turning to him in recognition, and he heaved a sigh of relief when the stream of traffic spilled into one of the endless parking lots. Bouncing over railroad tracks and passing under moving conveyors, he arrived at Administration. Though the executive workday did not begin until eight thirty, he noted with approval that in the long two-story building many windows were already lit. Caryll had left home before he had, so why were his offices dark?

Justin stood under the lights, jotting on one of his long yellow pads. Seeing him, Tom sat up straighter and the margins of a smile crinkled around his gray eyes. He sternly rationed his time alone with Justin, and when he stumbled into additional, unplanned moments like these, he felt like a child being handed an unexpected Hershey bar.

His car was the only one permitted to park by the main entry, and as he braked Justin strode down the steps to meet him. "Tom," he said. "I've been waiting for you." .

"What's the problem?" Tom hid his pleasure under a careful acidity.

"Everything is fine. Caryll has something to show you." As Tom lifted his eyes again to the darkened windows, Justin added quickly, "In the museum. I'm meant to steer you over there."

"Hop in, then," Tom said. As they pulled away Tom asked, "Well, what is it? Why'd he miss breakfast?"

Shrugging his shoulders in a noncommittal way, Justin lit a cigarette. Tom glanced over as the match flared briefly on the familiar profile. *How like her he is,* Tom thought.

He had come to rely on this large, reassuringly decent young man who moved with the relaxed authority of an athlete, rely on him in a way that he did on nobody else: not Hugh, not Caryll, certainly not his brothers-in-law nor the three Sinclair nephews who worked at Onyx. Sometimes he cursed his oath to Antonia, but for the most part he blessed it, for it imposed on him a discretion that might otherwise have been lacking. Damn it, Hugh was dead on target about Justin's abilities! Without that old, still sacred promise how easy it might be to shamelessly demote Caryll, whom he loved with the same fatherly tenderness as ever. Tom did not realize quite the extent of the gruffness and rebuffs he aimed at Justin, but Onyx's top dogs often discussed how dedicated the Boss was, advancing a brilliant underling however much he personally disliked him.

"Aren't you going to tell me what this mystery's all about?" Tom asked.

"It's up to Caryll."

"There aren't many men around Woodland who'd hold out on me," Tom said, curving off the bridge toward the museum. "Damn few." A note of approval had crept into his tone.

"I don't know about that." Justin sounded happy.

Tom stifled an impulse to reach over and touch him.

The red-brick colonial structure that housed models of Onyxes and Bridgers was isolated from the rest of the factory complex.

Caryll paced up and down the white pillared portico. Hurrying to the car, he said, "Thanks for coming, Dad."

The exhibit cars were gone, and much of the space was cut off by a divider wall with built-in blackboards. Waist-high benches displayed a gleaming six-cylinder engine, a braking system, headlights, Houdaille hydraulic shock absorbers, assorted parts.

But what drew the eye was a gleaming maroon two-door coupe built low to the ground. It had the sleek contours of a Bugatti Brescia, the gleaming grill of a Marmon, the streamlined fenders of a Duesenberg, the slanted windshield of an Oakland.

Tom balled his fists in his pockets, circling the shamelessly borrowed gaud. Justin watched from the door, but Caryll trailed him.

"What do you think, Dad?" His slight stammer echoed in the barnlike emptiness.

Tom was unable to reply. Outrage was percolating through him in round bursts. *The two of them have ganged up on me. They have concocted this miserable obscenity. They're telling me the Fiver's old! I'm old.*

Caryll said, "She can be modified in every way."

Tom stalked to the benches. The rational part of his brain told him his hurt was caused by time's erosion of his dream, not by Caryll and Justin. But at the moment of violation who listens to reason? Not Tom Bridger. He burst out. "Are the pair of you breaking out on your own? Starting your own shop? I don't remember ordering anyone to build this damn thing!"

"All the dealers' suggestions are incorporated," Caryll placated.

"Shit!"

"It's what p-people want," Caryll stammered.

Justin came over. "Tom, they've been suffering, the dealers. This year they grossed quiet a bit less than last year—three have filed bankruptcy. Caryll's the one who hears their problems and complaints."

"I know Caryll's job! I damn well gave it to him!"

Justin went on calmly, "They tell him the customers want headlights that don't die when they stop the car, they want a shifting gear transmission, and none of them delight in cleaning the sparks every few hundred miles. They want a smoother ride, less noise. They're switching from the Fiver. They'd rather have a used car than a new Onyx. They want what Caryll's got here. Styling.''

Tom, as always, was unable to sustain an attack on Caryll. In his agony he turned on Justin.

"They, they! Hutchinson, whoever *they* are, they can go fuck themselves! *I'm* not in automobiles to make some jazzed-up gadget that falls apart like cowshit in a rainstorm!" He slammed his fist at a fender. The metal did not yield. The spasm of pain shooting up his arm dizzied him.

"We've gone over this often enough, God knows," Justin said. "Is a car transportation, or luxury goods? I respect your opinion, Tom. It's mine, too. Utility. So long as it gets you from here to there reliably, who cares about the rest? But it's not a philosophical question anymore. On this last trip I realized that. Los Angeles is a pacesetter, and Los Angeles doesn't want Fivers anymore. We no longer have a choice."

"We? You forget yourself. *I'm* selling damn near as many Fivers as *I* did last year. *My* shop is first in sales."

"In 1924 you had fifty-three percent of the market and now, two years later, you have forty-one percent." Justin's voice was quiet, yet it reverberated through the hall. "Give me the sack any time you want, but you can't alter those figures, Tom."

Tom felt a vise clamp down, compressing his anger until it was a poisonous bubble in his chest. He had brought forth a miracle, but that was decades ago, and people were no longer content to span distances, they demanded gilded carriages. In tying the world together he had delivered a new symbol of human worth: *What kind of a car do you drive?*

Tom could not let either of them guess at the alarming rate of his heart. *Jesus Christ. Oh, Jesus. My temper. It hasn't aged well.* He rested both palms on the hood, staring into his distorted reflection. He hated them both for being right, for being young, for not having learned the attritions of time, for not knowing the unconsolable and irreversible process that withers the muscles and dries the juices.

Daylight was streaming through the high windows.

Justin went to switch off the dangling, green-shaded fixtures. Tom moved around the prototype again, and Justin watched him. "It's a beginning, Tom, that's all, a place to start. Take an unbiased look."

The voice with its salvationary calm ultimately worked on Tom, transforming him from a wounded lion at bay to a near rational being. His face expressionless—it was the deep lines that carved sardonic humor into his face—he rounded the model again. This time it seemed less a purloined mockery. *Too much flash and jazz,* he thought; *still, Caryll's got the taste to steal the best.*

He went to the engine and stared down. He tapped a cylinder with his finger. "Not a six," he said, the finger still drumming. "We'll want an eight."

"But Dad, an eight'll put us out of the low-priced field," Caryll said earnestly. "Chevrolet's a six."

"Since when do we imitate General Motors?" Tom asked.

"But—" Caryll started.

Justin's laughter burst out, a rippling, joyous, youthful release that proved how successfully he had been clothing his tension. "Wake up, Caryll. Wake up."

Caryll, too, laughed. "So the model's on the front burner," he said.

"Yes, sir, yes, sir, it's hot," Justin replied.

Justin punched Caryll's bicep, Caryll slapped back, a near embrace. Tom watched the two jubilant young men. *They'll drag me into the future yet,* he thought. *My sons.*

Until now he had never permitted Justin to share this innermost place in his heart with Caryll: he had been unable to prevent himself from viewing Justin as a munificent wealth, a beloved person, yet had managed for the most part to keep paternity out of it. He shook his head, dazed. *My sons.* Because it was a fresh way to think, it was therefore more powerful.

My sons, he thought again, sucking on the phrase as he would a delectable fruit.

VI

That morning Tom summoned his brother-in-law, Olaf Baardson, once his patternmaker, along with the heads of the four engineering departments. Men in broad-shouldered dark suits crowded around the maroon coupe and the parts on the benches, pointing out weaknesses and inadequacies and potential problems.

The museum became a design shop, a workshop, a laboratory. Guarded with a secrecy that would have done credit to the czarist police, enshrouded by rumors, this was GHQ for the onslaught on the new model. Meals were brought in, cots set up. Tom rarely left. His wrenching antipathy for the Seven, as they called the future car, had evaporated. He was cresting on a wave of creativity as strong and infallible and possessive as the surge that had built the quadricycle— it was no coincidence that he often dreamed of the summer girl, the thin young Antonia who had dwelled in Major Stuart's chateau.

Caryll, too, bivouacked in the museum, feeling infinitely more secure than when he himself had been the chief of staff issuing the orders. The prototype had been scrapped. He and the designers sketched new and original ideas for the body and interior on the blackboards—in reality blackboard cloths that could be rolled up and saved. For the first time he was happy at Onyx. He was helping form a beautiful car, he was using his own gift of artistic taste. He rarely stammered, his jaw muscles relaxed, and he was able to do something that took more courage than he previously had possessed.

He invited Zoe and Justin home to dinner.

CHAPTER 18

The rainy Thursday evening that they were to dine at the Farm, Justin arrived home a little before seven. On the salver in his room, amid his other mail, was a thin letter from Elisse. He had less than ten minutes to change, yet he took it to his desk, hunching to study the small, angular writing, the Beverly Hills postmark, even the profile of Washington on the carmine stamp before he slit the envelope. As he smoothed open the single folded sheet, the porches of his brow drew down over his eyes, adding a shadow of dread to his expression.

Since Tom, Olaf Baardson, and Caryll had sequestered themselves in the museum, Justin had taken charge of Woodland and the Hamtramck as well as the assembly plants; his sixteen-hour workdays spent unscrambling foul-ups were his salvation. He had no time to brood about letters like this. The first breezy paragraph described her servitude at Columbia, the second, in the same light vein, told of a meeting at Mitch's place, and she closed with her unvarying: *You'll be hearing again from/Elisse.*

He pressed his hands on either side of his face as though to squeeze from his skull the inexorable chain of questions. Was she stringing him along? Had she already decided against the rigors of intermarriage? Had she found some up-and-coming Jewish liberal? Was his Elisse Kaplan real—or had he himself invented a warm, idealistic girl to place below the sleek California suntan?

I can't take any more of this, he thought. *I'll put in a long-*

distance call. An outright violation of their agreement. His hand hesitated over the telephone.

A rap on his door. "Decent?" Zoe called.

Hastily reversing Elisse's letter on his blotter, he called back, "Come on in."

"You aren't ready," Zoe accused.

She wore her indignation like an accessory to her sumptuous beauty. Her simple dinner dress revealed the upper curves of her breasts, then ran like cream to her knees: the narrow diamond bracelet, inherited from Antonia, that encircled the rounded whiteness of her upper left arm was her sole adornment—that bracelet and her enormous, glittering dark eyes.

"You look like a tiger lily," Justin said.

Zoe did not acknowledge the fraternal compliment. "Justin, you know good and well this is the first time Caryll's gotten up the nerve to invite us. In fear and trembling he told me they *mangez* at eight on the dot. As if I hadn't heard it from everybody already!" Zoe's jitters, rivaling Caryll's, stemmed from her infrequent meetings with the Bridgers at Hugh's ritually formal entertainments, anxieties that she connected not to the couple's unrivaled wealth but to Tom's brief, caustic laugh and Maud's unblinking, bespectacled gaze.

Justin patted her shoulder reassuringly. "We'll be there in plenty of time, Zozo." The dressing room door closed behind him.

Zoe moved edgily around, touching his bookends, running a fingertip around the speaker horn of his new Atwater Kent Compact Radio, turning over his letter. Reading idly at first, she sank into his chair, absently noticing that the warmth of his body lingered in the leather. Refolding the paper, she searched through drawers of his boyhood desk until she found a stack of opened envelopes addressed in the same small, angular hand.

She had read eight of the letters and was extracting a ninth when Justin returned, black hair wetly tousled, feet bare as he stuffed his evening shirt into his satin-striped trousers. From the dressing room he stared at her.

"Clever and funny," Zoe said, holding up the unread sheet.

Against Justin's abrupt pallor, his eyes were a startling blue. Striding across the room, he yanked the linen paper from her fingers. "What an absolute beast you can be!"

"Temper," Zoe murmured.

"When you're in the room, must I lock my things?" He shoved the letters and envelopes into the open drawer. One corner caught as he banged, and he had to slam it with his palm to shut it properly.

"Is she actually organizing a strike?"

"Mind your own business!"

"I'd go to all the dances if I were you, I'd get back in the groove. You don't stand a ghost of a chance with the California pink lady."

Giving her a furious, stricken look, Justin stormed back into the dressing room. One of his photographs of Claude slipped askew, and Zoe, humming, realigned it, briefly looking into the handsome face with the cleft chin and very white skin that she had inherited. Claude had died when she was two, so she had no memory whatsoever of him: the filial honor momentarily in her eyes reflected Justin's canonization of her father rather than any emotions of her own.

Had anyone but her brother just raged at her, she would be pressed against the door, healing the breach with her most fetching wiles. However, this *was* Justin, her only blood kin, so she was no more ruffled by his outburst than by her own parting cruelty. *Wait until I tell Hugh there's not a thing in the world to worry about with this Elisse Kaplan*, she thought, raising both shapely arms over her head, wriggling her fingertips upward.

II

Maud and Tom had continued to buy land in Bloomfield Hills until their place—the Farm—was nearly two thousand acres. Much of this land had been cleared, and the mansion crouched with its back to primeval forest that had seen Ottawa and Wyandot braves. The rugged Marblehead limestone walls, the massive tile roof clumped with chimneys, had been planned with Maud's regard for durability rather than lavishness or grace. Yet for all the dark carving and vault-ceilinged corridors, the Farm exuded the homelike odors of Devoe furniture polish and baked apples.

Once Tom's grief had carbonized to its indestructible, diamond core, he was surprised to find that he could live here contentedly with Maud. Yet why not? She was Caryll's mother, her honesty and loyalty were firmly uncompromising, she was once more his best friend. He was grateful that she never complained about the gorgeous-assed mistresses foisted on him by his unfaithful body—it seemed to him that his lust should have died a decent death with his love.

The couple was seated in the library when the front door chimes rang. Caryll ushered in his guests. Tom stood to welcome them.

Maud found herself unable to rise from her wing chair. Long ago Tom had determined not to dredge up old hurts by involving himself—or her—with the Hutchinsons, but since this ban had never been verbalized to their son, Maud had not objected when Caryll told her he had invited Justin and Zoe. Yet now, a dulled, hopeless resentment weighed her down. It was as though Antonia herself intruded with her tall and beautiful children at the glass door to the entry hall. *In my own house!* Maud thought. No gray showed in her hair, her body—that businesslike organism—had acquired a scant inch at the trim waist, yet the elasticity of youth was gone, and while her face retained its high, handsome color and had not wrinkled, the small twin jowls gave a squareness to her fixed expression. And so she sat in her three-year-old brown velvet dinner dress, grim as the last Manchu dowager empress.

Zoe moved into the room. Still euphoric from the letters, she bubbled, "Oh, Mrs. Bridger, what a magnificent home!"

Maud pulled herself together. "It's much less grand than Hugh's," she retorted, her eyes seeking out Justin. Because he was male, she found him less evocative of her old rival and therefore easier to take. "Would you believe it, the architect called the style British baronial."

"It *does* remind me a bit of Monty's country place," Justin said.

Because Maud had thoroughly enjoyed her week in the ivy-covered eighteenth-century mansion that the Edges had purchased from a Kentish baronet desolated by the death of his two sons in the Ardennes, the comment almost pleased her. "I never thought of it," she grudged. "A good, sensible old house, Monty's."

The rain had stopped. The mantel clock gave eight bellicose chimes.

Maud stood, placing her short, wide hand on Justin's sleeve. "Supper's ready," she said.

Caryll glanced tentatively at Zoe, who smiled and took his arm. Tom followed the two couples across the hall, his gray eyes sardonic. The ironies of his life!

The three young people laughed and chatted over a huge, unseasoned meal. "Those extravagant dishes at Hugh's are bad for the digestion," Maud opined. After the apple pie she said, "Tom, one brandy each, dear. No more. Zoe and I will have our coffee in the parlor.''

As the two women went into the drawing room large drops began again to drum loudly on the slate terraces. "What weather," Maud said, banging a poker vigorously at the logs burning in one of the fireplaces: this room, stretching across the rear of the house, boasted a monstrous black marble chimney piece at either end.

She settled herself behind the coffee tray; her glasses caught two red glints of firelight, giving her a strangely blank expression. "You're tall like your mother," she said. "And you have her eyes, but otherwise it's your brother who takes after her."

Zoe, who had been holding her hands out to the blaze, turned. "Mother?" she asked, a tremor in her voice. Though her friends' grandparents fondly reminisced about Major Stuart, some even recalling his father or Oswald Dalzell, none ever mentioned Antonia. Those few years she had lived in Detroit might have been expunged from the calendar. Zoe had grown to accept this odd silence. "You were Mother's friend?"

"Me?" Maud's laugh was loud and humorless. "I was a seamstress and she lived in a big mansion out on Woodward Avenue—it was very swank in those days. I altered some skirts for her." Maud paused, adding bluntly, "She had no friends in this town."

"Hugh—"

"He was as poor as me. He met her once or twice."

Zoe forced a smile. Her private myths jarred downward, but there was no shattering: one or two meetings obviously had been enough for Hugh to tumble as Dante had for Beatrice. "Maybe being lonely was why she didn't like it here. Justin and I have talked about it. She never voluntarily mentioned Detroit, not even when Uncle Andrew was alive."

"He's the reason they stayed clear of her."

"He?" Bewilderment showing in the lovely, sensual face.

"The Major."

"Uncle Andrew . . . Mrs. Bridger, I don't understand."

Maud gripped the ivory handle of the coffeepot, an odd, relentless clutch. "The gossip about the two of them was fierce."

Her meaning, not in the least cryptic, sank like an anchor into Zoe's consciousness. It was not the weight of incest that horrified the girl, it was something infinitely more vile. Necrophilia. Zoe's memories of the Major were faded and confined, like the odor of his sour medicines, to the big front bedroom where he had served out his sentence of cancer. That yellow-skinned, skeletal cadaver joined to the entrancing glow that was Antonia? Hideous and defiling baloney. A lie! Of course it was! So why were goosebumps rising on her bare white arms?

"Cream?" Maud inquired.

"Please," Zoe said dully. "But she was his niece."

"That was the part the social set relished. I sewed in a lot of big houses, and they'd go over and over it right in front of me."

"My grandfather lived in the house too."

"Nobody ever saw *him*," Maud said. "Before she came, the Major always had a girl, the bad sort, living out there. He'd pass them off as relatives. After she showed up, he had nobody. When he took your mother off to Europe, they cackled like it was the final proof." Maud handed Zoe the demitasse cup. "Help yourself to sugar."

"I don't take any," Zoe whispered. The little cup rattled on the gold-washed saucer, and she carefully set the bone china down.

Suddenly Maud's eyes felt hot and dry. Her candor had been tinged with the need to get back at Antonia through the next generation. Yet seeing this gorgeous young creature collapse like a wet dishrag, Maud was overcome with contrition. As a matter of fact, the dinner had gone pleasantly, and looking down her damask-covered table, seeing Caryll's delight at entertaining his friends, she had found herself smiling and laughing along with her son.

"A useless bunch, society women, nothing better to do than invent scandals," Maud said, laying down her weapons.

"Yes, vicious," Zoe said in a high, hollow voice.

"I just wanted you to know I never believed one word." Thus, with her broad, pleasant smile, Maud put her signature on a belated armistice with her dead rival's two offspring.

"I know you didn't, Mrs. Bridger," Zoe said fervently. Turning, she began to heap praise on an enormous, murky still life above the piano.

Engrossed in conversation, the three men came into the room.

Caryll sat on the love seat next to Zoe. "When you're done with your coffee, I'll give you and Justin the grand tour."

Tom said, "I want to discuss the shutdown with Justin. He can see the place some other time."

He spoke in that peremptory tone Zoe had noticed he used often in connection with Justin. Did Mr. Bridger's coldness toward them have anything to do with their mother's supposed affair with Uncle Andrew? Zoe clasped her shaking hands together.

"It's only nine thirty," Caryll said. "Dad, you'll have plenty of time later."

"I've been thinking about the shutdown too," Justin said. "How do we change over to the Seven with the shortest layoff for the men?"

Tom, Caryll, and Justin glanced at each other, their eyes worried—and guilty: they had a staggering task ahead of them and the workers, they knew, would suffer the most.

Detroit always hung on grimly in the months when automobile factories routinely shut down while machine tools were altered in order to manufacture the new models. Some hands managed to find temporary jobs, but most struggled to survive on savings. The Seven, which still had to be designed and built, was to be entirely new, a fast, smart, smooth-riding, revolutionary car. The problems were immense. Every single one of the five to six thousand parts of the prototype had to be designed to the exacting standard that Tom demanded, then meticulously tested. This accomplished, Woodland's fortune in machinery (specifically made to build the Fiver) would be torn from its foundation pits. Gigantic new machines would have to be devised to build the Seven. There had never been a changeover of such scope in American industry, so there was no certainty how long it would take. Tom had hopes of scheduling production on the Seven within a calendar year, so at best this meant that many of the hundreds of thousands of employees at the Onyx Detroit plants and the assemblies would be thrown out of work for a year.

"Once we start installing the new machinery, we can begin a call-in," Tom sighed. "But it won't be easy on them."

"I've beefed up our credit union, and I'm working on a plan for employment agencies within the various plants to find the men temporary jobs," Justin said. "It's no panacea, but it'll help. I'd like to have things pretty well in hand before I take that vacation in December." This last sentence was uttered with a swift frostiness.

Tom said, "Go along with Zoe, Caryll."

III

Zoe slipped her hand into Caryll's as their footsteps echoed around the swimming pool in its glassed-enclosed wing. She kept it there as they peered into the game room with its two Brunswick-Balke-Collender pool tables. They went into the music room to inspect the organ screen, stepping onto the sunporch, which smelled of rain even though the floor-length glass windows were closed. She said little, but her lush body communicated against his side with soft turns and pressures. Attuned to Zoe's precarious moods, Caryll felt not only the normal shivers of happiness and desire but also foreboding. Clearly she was distraught, and he steeled himself against hurt for he knew hurt was inevitable: Zoe, during her squalls, invariably wounded him.

They climbed the heavily carved oak staircase that Maud checked daily with a white cotton glove to insure that the maids had dusted properly. Her door was ajar.

"Mother's room," Caryll said.

Zoe nodded to the adjacent door, which was closed. "Your father's?" she asked.

"No, the sewing room," Caryll replied stiffly. He had long been aware that his parents avoided each other's bedchambers and that his father hopped with agility into the beds of a succession of floozies. Loving both parents, he never affixed blame, yet the situation disturbed him deeply.

"People that age," Zoe murmured.

"Right," Caryll said. He pushed open the door.

A bedside lamp that turned the furniture into looming shadows spotlit Maud's four-poster.

With a meaningful glance Zoe murmured, "Caryll?"

Harrowingly stirred by her invitation as well as the sweet, musky odalisque perfume she was wearing, he raised her hand, kissing it. "Darling."

She put her arms around him, rubbing her fingers deep into his buttocks, her pelvis wriggling against his. Caryll was shaking, embarrassed by a monumental erection.

"I love you so much," he murmured in her ear.

"Must you get sticky before we do this?"

"It means everything to me. Let's go to my car."

"Now," she said.

"Zoe—"

"Of course, if you don't want to . . ."

"Oh, God, Zoe. My study—"

"Here," she interrupted.

"Zoe, it's wrong."

"And you say you love me." Pulling away, she turned. Though she did not bend her head or make a sound, he knew she was weeping.

He pressed against her back, nuzzling his chin on her velvety shoulder. "What is it, darling?"

"She hates me."

"Mother? She likes you. I was surprised, but she likes both of you. I can tell."

"She said . . ."

Caryll felt the tremor convulse her body. "Hush, it's all right, Zoe, everything is all right."

"Ahh, Caryll, it's such a rotten, rotten world."

Closing the door, he fingered the tears from her eyes, his adoration strengthened by a protective tenderness for these strange, wracking insecurities of hers. She hiked up her skirt to let his fingers work the pearl button at her waist, her lace-edged panties fell, and she stepped out of them, and her satin pumps, to sit on the edge of Maud's dressing stool. Caryll knelt before her. In the dim light the rich white flesh above knotted silk stockings glowed elusively. Pressing her thighs apart, he kissed up to the trimmed and scented golden pubic curls, using both hands to raise the moist epithelium toward himself. Soon she lifted her thighs to his shoulders. Her gasping breaths rustled through Maud's bedroom. When she slumped forward, he kissed her bent neck for minutes before standing. Shakily, he undid the buttons of his fly.

They were both virgins. From the time that Zoe was twelve and he fourteen, this worship of unconsummated flesh had kept him from other girls who were most certainly willing to go all the way. (Caryll was not unaware of the aphrodisiac smell of great wealth). Was he the only one for Zoe? Though he savaged himself with doubts, he was fairly positive he was.

After she had made use of his handkerchief, delicately, he pulled her to her feet and took her in his arms. "Zoe, you don't have to worry about Mother."

"I'm fine now."

"She sees how I feel about you, darling. She thinks you're swell, too."

"It's all right, Caryll."

"You need somebody to look after you, somebody you're absolutely sure of. Let's get married." As he spoke his arms dropped to his sides. He swallowed audibly. His proposal came as a shock even to him. True, he had imagined these words often enough, yet he had never had the trust to apply them to craft what was their unpredictable relationship. "Zoe, marry me."

"You're too real," she said, touching his cheek. "I don't mean to push you around the way I do, Caryll. But sometimes I get so scared inside."

"Let me take my chances."

"You're fine, sensitive," she said, bending for her silken pool of lingerie. "It wouldn't work."

"I'd be so sweet to you."

"There's somebody else."

Blood drummed in Caryll's ears, and woodenly as a deaf person he followed her into his mother's camphor-scented dressing room, reaching to switch on the overhead light. "It must be a married somebody," he said, appalled by the balkiness, the inadequacy of his remark.

She fluffed her vivid hair. "That's how much you know."

"Then why doesn't *he* marry you?"

Opening her beaded purse, she applied lipstick to her upper lip, pressing down to color the lower one.

"Is it Phil Sinclair? Buzzie Thatcher? If he's not married, you can tell me who it is."

"I can't see where it's any special concern of yours," Zoe said, her incomparable eyes fixed on his.

Caryll dropped his gaze. *Don't let her get away with it*, he ordered himself. *Have a showdown, tell her she's a tormenting bitch*. Yet a moment later, glancing in the mirror at the beautiful, desolate face, he had to repress a shameful, weak desire to soothe even this particular misery of hers.

God help me, he thought. *I can't keep on like this.*

IV

On the first Sunday in November, Zoe came down with a feverish sore throat that confined her to her bed. By the following Sunday her temperature had dropped and the rawness of her throat dissolved, leaving her with the juicy residue of a cold. A lowering slate-dark sky promised snow, and she lounged moodily around her room, which was crowded with get-well flowers, mostly camellias and gardenias, her favorites. Her Gramophone was playing Negro spirituals.

The mournful depth of Paul Robeson's voice meshed with Zoe's gloom. Illness had cut her off from debutante luncheons and balls, from crowded teas. Solitude had inevitably brought introspection, and the facts about her mother and her great-uncle had accumulated unbearably. Uncle Andrew had bought the house in Rutland Gate for Mother, had lived with her before, during, and after her marriage, had died in her arms, had settled the income of his estate (now resting in trust in the Bank of England) on her and her children.

The record clicked. Zoe fumbled replacing the arm. *I have to know,* she thought. *However bad it is, I have to know the real truth.* A frantic light shone in her eyes, and she began to dress.

Sunday, Hugh was in his upstairs library listening to a concert on WWJ. As she came in he turned off his radio console. "Zoe. Why on earth are you out of bed?"

"I had to talk to you." She gave a sniffling sob and went to look down at the snow-covered entrance bay.

"What is it? You can't still be carrying on about Justin's little fling." Hugh's tone was one of kindly amusement. His own fears had been laid to rest in part by Zoe's information about the letters, in part by Dickson Keeley's report that the Kaplan girl was seeing a labor organizer four nights a week. "Are you in a pet because Caryll's involved with the Seven and isn't dancing attendance on you?"

"This is serious, Hugh."

"Can I help?"

"It's Mother," she said, the unhappiness betraying itself in her cold-clogged voice. "Tell me about Mother when she lived in Detroit."

The rales rasped within Hugh's chest. Years ago he had concluded that eventually he must unravel his entwined loyalties, must defy his brother to give Justin the straight truth: his plans, though, were not advanced enough, and neither was Zoe the oracle through which he would speak. "I didn't know her that well," he said carefully.

Zoe came to sit near him. "But you were in love with her?"

After a long hesitation Hugh said, "She glowed with happiness; she reflected it. My guess is that every man who came in contact with her was a little bit in love with her."

"Even Uncle Andrew?"

The asthmatic tension eased in Hugh. "Who have you been talking to?" he smiled. "Some professor of ancient history?"

"Mrs. Bridger."

"Maud shouldn't repeat stale, ugly gossip."

"But . . . well, Uncle Andrew lived with us. . . . When he got ill, at the end, I mean, he sobbed all night. Hugh, there were nurses, but he wanted Mother. I can remember her sleeping on the couch in there. With him."

"Of course she did. Can you imagine your mother leaving anyone to die afraid?"

"What did our father feel about Uncle Andrew?"

"Zoe, you know I never met him."

Her hand tensed on the pleats of her skirt. "But he *is* our father?"

At this dangerously close thrust, Hugh rose to his feet, glaring down at her. "This is my house, Zoe. Here, the name of Antonia Hutchinson is respected. I refuse to listen to another word." His voice was etched by the elocutionary precision that over the telephone terrified Onyx executives. "You haven't thrown this at Justin, have you?"

She shook her lovely, red-nosed face from side to side, frightened. "Only you."

"It's vicious garbage."

Zoe's lips trembled into a rueful pout. "What a dreadful little fool I am. Of course Mother was wonderful to Uncle Andrew—she was to everybody. Hugh, don't be mad."

"I'm not." He raised an admonitory finger. "But you're not to mention this ugliness again."

"Never," she promised.

"No repeating it to Justin."

"I wouldn't dream of it. He's too idealistic about her."

"Good girl," Hugh said, again kindly and benevolent.

Zoe blew her nose as if in final punctuation of his anger. Replacing her handkerchief in her sweater sleeve, she said, "This sort of lie would shake him to his roots. It's funny about Justin. He went through the war, he's worked everyplace and with all sorts, but deep down he's innocent. Know what I mean? In his heart he believes we're all as good as he is. I think that's the secret of how he gets people to do what he wants. He appeals to their bit of goodness."

She's right, Hugh thought. *Why didn't I ever see that? She cares for Justin as much as I do.* Camaraderie warming him, Hugh put his feet on the ottoman. There was an agreeable lassitude to being with Zoe in front of the fire on a snowy Sunday afternoon, and he began to reminisce. He rarely spoke of that other Hugh, impoverished, burning to be rich enough to set Society on its ear, rebellious of the brother who provided for him, vain of his own angelic good looks, but that old scurvy about Antonia had clicked open a door to the past, and as twilight died into darkness his memories slipped out. Zoe, stifling her sneezes, gazed intently at him as he talked on, with an uncharacteristic loquaciousness.

V

She returned to bed, pushing the cashmere blanket aside. Her fever, which sometimes returned at night, was back at well over a hundred, yet she did not feel headachy or drained.

Hugh's stories, vivid and bright as tropical parakeets, swooped in and out of her mind. Her guardian was no longer an all-powerful, infallible figure, above the doubts and convulsions of love. He, too, had been buffeted by ambivalences; he, too, had been aware of his seductiveness to the opposite sex.

He took out beautiful girls, she thought.

Her light-headedness turned into resolve. She did not touch her dinner tray. She went into her bathroom. The tall electric heater glowed pink on her as she sponged herself, then lavished perfume on her breasts, her thighs, her fast-tripping pulses. Leaving her nightgown on the tiles, she drew on her new marabou-trimmed peach satin robe.

Hugh sat alone. The dining room candelabra cast light across his sleek, graying blond head. "Haven't you been up long enough for one day?" he asked.

Smiling, she shook her head and reached for the brandy. She downed it quickly and took another.

When she reached for the decanter a third time, Hugh laid his hand on hers. "That's very powerful," he said.

"I better look out, then. If I get blotto you might take advantage of me."

For the first time she was speaking to him in the teasing sexual banter she reserved for her boyfriends.

"You've had enough," he said uneasily.

"Nerving myself up," she said, then blurted: "Hugh, why haven't you ever married?"

Quiet ascended to the Grinling Gibbons–inspired carved ceiling above them; falling snow wrapped them in its hush.

After a minute Hugh replied in a purposefully matter-of-fact voice, "For the obvious reasons."

Zoe's dark eyes swam, lustrous with fever and brandy. "To the right girl it wouldn't mean a thing."

An offer was being made.

They both knew it.

Hugh was keenly tempted. Not by Zoe, though Zoe's magnificent eyes were gazing at him with a profound amorousness. How could so well-boiling an infatuation have escaped him? For the first time in decades he allowed himself to think of . . . children. . . . His own genes moving into the future . . . his own sons to fill the airy palace of his plans . . . kingmaker to his own tribe.

While he floundered in his momentary valley of decision, Zoe blundered. As though fearing she had not made herself clear, she stood to tighten her robe sash. Satin outlined her long, perfect legs, her small waist, the magnificence of her full, out-of-fashion breasts with their raspberry-shaped nipples. Zoe's body seemed to present not only a promise but a sexual mission. Hugh understood this with a rationality that was absolutely lucid. He experienced not a quiver of lust. For years he had lived in a celibacy whose purity would be envied by most priests: he had sublimated the remotest fantasy, the tiniest hint of desire into his work and his machinations for those he loved. Sweat broke out on his forehead. *I can't*, he thought. *I can't anymore.*

"Where on earth am I going to find a dried-up old spinster

content to bury herself with a deformed recluse?'' A trailing laugh ended his question.

The brandy had affected Zoe. She did not catch his panic. "If a girl loves—"

"Zoe!"

"—a man the way I—"

Hugh slammed the table, a sharp retort that flickered candle flames. "What's gotten into you today?" he barked. "First destroying your mother's reputation, then getting vicious with me!"

Zoe's face went slack. Her mouth opened and she sank into a chair.

The front door opened. And miraculously delivered unto Hugh were Justin and Caryll, their voices floating down the hallway. The falling snow had muffled the car's approach.

Hugh ran into the hall. "Boys! We're in here, in the dining room."

Caryll, seeing Zoe, halted below the wood-ribbed entry. "Hello," he muttered, and came no farther.

Justin, cheeks red from outdoors, came to kiss her shimmery hair. "Good. You're up and around."

"Hugh's been giving me his famous cold cure." She turned in her chair to fix her febrile glance on Caryll. "Has your uncle ever tried it on you? Three brandies one right after the other. What a nasty man! Now I'm not talking right."

Hugh recognized the importance of salvaging her pride: in her thwarted humiliation might she not infect Justin with her own doubts regarding their mother's carnal irregularities?

"Brandy does wonders for my asthma. Why not for your cold?" His voice was rich with avuncular benevolence. "Have you two Sunday laborers eaten?"

"I'm starved." Justin sat on Hugh's left.

"Caryll?" Hugh asked, his evening pump resting on the nub where the buzzer rose beneath the carpet. "Something hot?"

"No, thanks. I had dinner at Woodland with Dad."

Zoe smiled. "Then you can keep me company upstairs."

Caryll said coolly, "Justin and I were planning to discuss the shatterproof windshield. That's why I tagged along."

"Talking about the Seven while he's eating'll give him an ulcer," she said. "Upstairs, upstairs."

And she ran past him, the Louis heels of her mules striking the Great Hall parquet sharply, setting up a provocative motion in the naked, delectably round buttocks below the satin.

VI

She leaned against the Queen Anne chest on the landing and waited for him. They climbed to the second-floor gallery without speaking, side by side. He could feel the heat emanating from her body in perfumed waves. She swept through the open door of her little sitting room.

"I've missed you, Caryll," she said in a forlorn voice.

"Have you?" His mouth moved stiffly.

"It's been weeks." She glanced around at the vases of white flowers. "I've been ill."

"Justin mentioned you had a cold."

"It's not like you to be such a stranger."

"We've all been working like mad."

"Oh, you know I can't bear it when people are angry with me," she cried.

"I'm tired of being whipped then having to beg your pardon." He circled the overheated, flower-thick room to stand on the far side of the chaise longue. "It's Hugh, isn't it?"

"What are you talking about?"

"Hugh's the unmarried man, the one you're in love with."

Her laughter was high, a little drunken. "That's not funny, Caryll."

"Who else can it be? You're always admiring him, telling me to follow to his advice."

"Justin admires him and listens to him. Do you think Justin's in love with him? Hugh's been a father to us."

Caryll gazed at her uncertainly, his senses swollen by her opulent, feverish beauty and the clinging negligee, his brain off the track, too disorganized to weigh her veracity. "Who is it, then?"

"You've lost me."

"The man you're in love with."

"Oh, Caryll, you nut." She moved closer to him. "Honey bear, I didn't mean to hurt you or make you jealous. I just needed time to think."

Her perfume tickled the depth of his stomach. "About what?"

"The question you asked me." She raised her hand, caressing his cheek.

He gazed into her moist eyes for several seconds. He buried his face in the soft stork feathers. "Zoe. I've been in hell."

Her body was burning against his. "Don't ever leave me again. It's awful."

"Then you mean it? You'll marry me?"

"Do you really love me?"

"Stop tormenting me. You know I do."

"How much?"

"So much that I'm ashamed."

"Will you ever put anything ahead of me?"

"Never."

"Your mother?"

"No."

"Your father?"

"No."

"Onyx?"

"Nothing, darling."

"What if we have children?"

"Not them, either."

"I couldn't bear it if I didn't come first with you."

"You'll be the only." He sank to his knees, touching his lips to the pointed satin toes of her slippers. Kissing Zoe's feet might have seemed an embarrassing high drama to another, yet neither Caryll nor Zoe considered it that.

"I can't stand this house," she said. "Let's get married right away."

CHAPTER 19

Mr. Justin Hutchinson
Requests the pleasure of your company
At the marriage of his sister,
Zoe Claudine,
To
Mr. Caryll Bridger
At six in the evening,
Thursday, December 23, 1926
At the Farm, Michigan

The sound of hammering awoke Tom.

For a moment he tensed, worrying he had overslept and missed the welding of the Seven's rear end, an innovation of his that might (or might not) replace the traditional bolts, then he stretched his legs luxuriously, recalling that the experiment would proceed without him. Today he would not be at Woodland. His first day off in how many months? Yawning, he went to a window, looking down at the bundled-up workmen erecting rows of green canvas marquees that would protect the guests' cars in what he hoped was an unnecessary precaution. The sky was lit by the opaline pallor that precedes a sunny winter day. *Happy the bride*, Tom thought, grinning.

Though Caryll's timing was rotten—engineers were working double shifts at the Triple E Building to design the Seven while Administration was bracing to handle the shutdown—Tom was delighted by his son's choice: Zoe was gorgeous, high-spirited, beguiling, and

Antonia's daughter. Zoe's marriage to Caryll would draw Justin quite naturally into the family circle.

Tom opened his top bureau drawer, extracting the two sheets of paper that a typist had stayed late the previous night to complete. The long, slender fingers lovingly arranged the papers side by side on the desk.

Pulling on a swimsuit with faded gray and blue stripes, then a robe, he jogged downstairs. Ropes of powerfully scented white roses festooned the carved oak banisters. On the first floor all was confusion. Florists on ladders decorated the pair of bronze chandeliers with more white roses, caterers' assistants in monkey jackets bustled about, two bridesmaids flirted with an usher while Mary, the parlormaid, served them breakfast. "Top of the wedding morning to ye, Mr. Bridger," called Mary in her Cork lilt.

Tom made a mock bow and the approval of young laughter trailed him through the passage to the swimming pool, where he stood warming his back at the rough stone fireplace: somebody had remembered to build a fire even on this day of days. Caryll was already churning along. Watching his son's diligently earnest breaststroke, Tom felt tears form in his eyes. A sweet and very tender part of his life was ended, these dawn swims, the hours he and Caryll had tramped through the woods, worked together in the basement shop, shared late suppers at the square kitchen table.

Caryll, raising up for a breath, saw him. "Good morning, Dad," he panted. "Come on in."

Tom squatted by the edge of the pool. "There's something I have to talk to you about first."

Caryll was in the shallow end. He stood, water coursing from his broad, sloping shoulders down his hairless chest into the vest of his swimsuit. "Advice to the about-to-be-married man?"

"There's a subject I wouldn't tackle," Tom chuckled. "From today on, you own five percent of Onyx."

Caryll's head jerked up in surprise.

Tom chuckled at his son's bemusement. "You're a partner in the shop." He continued to use the term to refer to his enterprises: Woodland, the Hamtramck, the thirty-one assemblies across the country, the shipping line, the three railroad lines, the vast stretches of timberlands that had been leased out since 1920 when wood was

302

no longer used in the Fiver's frame, two banks, the twenty-one factories on foreign soil, the mines in Canada and Africa, the rubber plantations along the Amazon. "Five percent."

Caryll found his power of speech. Pushing wet hair from his astonished gray eyes, he said, "Dad, that's a fortune! You flabbergast me! You've always made such a big point of being sole owner."

"Minds are meant to be changed now and then." Tom grinned. "Therapeutic."

Caryll shook his head, still uncomprehending.

"It's a wedding present, Caryll."

"You already gave us one." The million dollars had made headlines. "A lallapalooza."

Wagging his index finger, Tom mimed severity. "Will you quit arguing with your old man?"

"You've taken my breath away. Thank you, Dad."

The shyly wholehearted smile, Tom decided, made Caryll look younger than twenty-two, far too young for this to be his wedding day: his voice caught a little as he said, "After we've finished our laps, you'll come upstairs and sign."

"What about Zoe?"

"The shares are in your name."

Caryll's smile faded. "I can't take the gift, then, Dad."

"You have to," Tom retorted, his pleasure cracking a little. "How else can I give Justin his?"

"Justin?" Caryll cried, gaping. *"Justin?"*

"He's getting the same amount." Tom walked around the pool to the diving board. He did not want to talk about it, and Caryll usually was hypersensitive to his elliptic silences.

But Caryll followed him, churning through the pool until water was up to his shoulders. "Dad, you have me up a tree. I don't understand one thing about this. Why are you suddenly handing out shares in Onyx?"

"Call it a case of advancing senility," Tom said dryly.

"To *Justin* of all people!"

"He's the best damn administrator we've ever had."

"I'll say. But you've never shown him the least favoritism. I know this isn't true—but people say you don't even like him."

"Right now he's extremely hot under the collar because I asked him to postpone his vacation until you get back from Palm Beach. Hasn't it ever occurred to you he might move over to Ford or General Motors?"

"Often, but—"

"Then what's so wrong with dangling a carrot to keep him with us?" Tom's explanation echoed through the chlorine-odored space. He felt ashamed, resentful, awkward. He balked at discussing this most personal and hidden of his relationships—and with his other son. *People say you don't even like him. Jesus,* Tom thought. *Well, it's better than having them guess the truth.*

Caryll's jaw tensed in that dogged way of his. "He deserves the shares more than anyone. But, Dad, what makes you think he'd leave? You're a hero to him."

Unable to go further in defense of his actions, Tom shed his robe. The strong, spare length of body had aged remarkably little, a slight incurving of the shoulders, a few more muscles below the rib cage, that was all. "The transfers are made out, everything's set." He ran along the board, jackknifing into the pool.

When he surfaced, Caryll was treading water near him, looking determined—and also as heartrendingly timid as when Tom had dropped him off at that military school. "Dad, I can't take any shares."

"What's eating you? Justin's supposed to be your best friend."

"It's nothing to do with Justin. It's me and Zoe. She comes first with me, and if you don't want her as a co-owner, I can't take the shares."

Tom's laughter tasted of chlorine and relief. He dog-paddled. "You *do* need premarital advice, son. Stop worrying. From here on, Caryll, what's yours is hers. And what's hers is hers."

"Don't rib me, Dad. You don't realize how I feel about Zoe."

"I'm not blind," Tom said, wanting to cry as he reached out to hug his son's cold, slippery shoulders. If only one could buy insurance against the griefs and inevitable disillusionments of matrimony, he would shell out what he must to insure his son. "I'll have the wording changed," he said. "When you get home from Florida, the both of you'll sign."

II

Tall baskets of white roses formed an aisle leading from the south fireplace through the drawing room and across the hall to join the roses that decorated the banisters. The organ's wandering music ceased. Portentous chords resounded. To honor the sacrament the one hundred and eighty guests sat erect in their gilt chairs. Walter Chrysler. Henry Ford and his plump littla Clara flanked by Edsel and Eleanor. Alfred Sloan of General Motors. William Durant (formerly of General Motors, now manufacturer of the Durant car) with his very young second wife. Shock-haired Carl Sandburg. Senator Couzens, who sat as far as possible from his enemy and onetime partner, Henry Ford. Mayor John W. Smith. Lord and Lady Edge, she dowdy in ice-gray taffeta, he beaming affably despite a cold caught on the *Berengaria*. And in the place of honor customarily reserved for the bride's parents, freckled President Calvin Coolidge, his narrow mouth firmly shut while Mrs. Coolidge smiled.

The Reverend Mr. Johnson, smoothing his surplice, approached the table. Caryll and Tom, freshly barbered and both wearing cutaways, entered by the side door. There was a rustling of approval over Caryll's choice of his father as best man. All five Sinclair boys were ushers: it was the oldest, Phil, who escorted his aunt down the aisle. Maud's tan lace was the most festive, least sensibly serviceable gown she had ever owned, and her cheeks were bright with happiness. In the past few weeks she had become very fond of Zoe, traveling with her to New York, positioning herself in Hattie Carnegie's large, silk-walled fitting room to insure with her seamstress's eye that the lovely child got value as well as style in her enormous trousseau.

The organ halted briefly. The first triumphant bars of the *Lohengrin* wedding march resounded. Rosamunde Baardson, wearing crimson velvet, solemnly bore her sheaf of white roses down the staircase, followed by nine other bridesmaids.

Justin appeared with Zoe on the landing, one hand under her elbow, the other protectively clasping hers. She carried a shower of white camellias strung on narrow white satin ribbons; her bridal gown displayed the front of her charmingly dimpled knees, then curved into a long court train, and her veil, drifts of snowy Valenciennes lace, flouted tradition by failing to cover her exquisite face. He with his thick black hair, Roman nose, deep-set eyes, she in her dewy, voluptuous beauty, they swept down the staircase like tall, graceful birds in paired flight.

Watching them, Tom thought: *Ahh, love, love, how beautiful they are, your children, comely beyond the race of man. . . .* Choking, he bit back tears.

The ceremony was brief.

Afterward, Guy Lombardo's orchestra played Strauss waltzes and crowds formed around the champagne table in the library, discreetly out of sight of the man who had taken public oath to uphold the laws of the land. Fortunately President Coolidge disliked parties and left immediately after congratulating the newlyweds. The caterers' footmen began to pass drinks.

Lombardo gave way to the Perrault band. A Charleston blared. Zoe looped her train over her arm. Eyes glinting like huge black diamonds, veil bouncing on her red-gold hair, slender, voluptuous body prancing, gorgeous legs encased in sheer white silk stockings, kicking and twisting, she bobbed across the floor with her groom, who though clumsier and slower was charged by her sexual electricity.

"There'll be a hot time in the old town tonight," the ushers agreed, winking enviously.

As guests gathered to watch Zoe cut the six-tiered cake, Tom moved next to Justin. "After they take off, come on upstairs."

"No, Tom," Justin said. "Work can wait until tomorrow."

"No heavy manual labor, Justin. I promise. I need your signature, that's all. It'll only take a minute." Tom tapped a passable imitation of Zoe's Charleston step. "Christmas and weddings you get off, Justin."

III

Justin duty-danced with the female guests, fortifying himself between turns. He was gulping a Scotch and soda when Tom tapped his shoulder, drawing him aside.

"Zoe's locked herself in," Tom said quietly. "Her maid says it's been an hour. Caryll tried to talk her out. Not a peep. He's decided she's not in there, and he's flopping around like a goldfish out of its bowl. Checking the garage, the skating house, the barns—he just took a flashlight out to the cars." Tom's cheeks were sucked in, leaving deep hollows. "I'd hate like hell to humiliate him—them—by turning loose the Security hounds unless I have to."

Justin tried to hide his dismay. He stood staring at Tom. "Let me see what's going on," he said at last.

The roses on the staircase had wilted, their odor stained the air. Justin, more than a little drunk, was fighting the urge to get out of this overscented, overheated, overcrowded house and finish the job. Drown himself in a bottle, find oblivion, avoid this newest crisis with his sister, escape from his unremitting doubts about Elisse.

As soon as he had learned the wedding date he had placed a long distance call, explaining why he could not be out at Christmas, promising to be there by New Year's. Then he had been forced to telephone again with another explanation that he could not leave Detroit until Caryll returned from his honeymoon. Tom had come as close to begging as Justin could recall: *It's a hell of a time,* he'd said, gruffly. *Justin, stick around.* Both connections had been rotten, Elisse's voice had risen and fallen as though traveling through ocean waves, the roaring had swallowed entire sentences. She had asked him to repeat. Constrained by the technical difficulties, he doubted he'd been able to convey that the month's postponement was agony for him.

Her letters continued, terse, witty, impersonal. He no longer saved them. Those letters robbed him of his self-esteem. He could no longer see himself as a fair-minded, sensible adult male intent on protecting a young girl from her own impulsiveness by giving her time to think things through. Instead he had become a demon jumping about in rage, jealousy, doubt, and incurable horniness. At one of Zoe's engagement parties he had gone home with a shapely grass widow, then at her front door had found himself backing away from her deep, tongued kisses. He slept badly and for the first time barked at the men working under him. Only one certainty remained. He wanted to marry Elisse Kaplan and live out his days with her.

Outside Zoe's room three bridesmaids in their crimson dresses circled the middle-aged, voluble Belgian lady's maid, whose fluted cap bobbed toward the closed door as she explained what had transpired. The idea of publicly importuning his sister nauseated Justin. Through the clutch of alcohol came what seemed an intelligent alternative.

Slipping into the nearby sewing room, he opened one of the casement windows, leaning across the deep embrasure into frosty night air. Forty feet below, the empty stone terrace was lit by Christmas bulbs that blurred into fuzzy red and green circles. There was, or so he recalled, a smooth limestone ornamental ridge that ran around the second story.

Kicking off his shoes, he climbed out, supporting his weight by gripping the window frame until his stockinged feet were splayed along the ridge. It was far narrower than he had thought, maybe three or four inches. His fingers sought purchase on rough walls; he inched along. Justin Hutchinson, human fly. He scrambled gratefully across another baronially deep window ledge, willed himself to another vertical surface. One of his feet slipped. He clutched a lead drainpipe, his heart banging askew as he blessed Maud Bridger's insistence on solidity.

He reached Zoe's windows cold stone sober, breathing in loud gasps, sweating with fear that Caryll was right, she wasn't inside and he'd have to go back the same way he had come.

He rapped on a leaded pane. "Zoe," he called urgently. "Zoe!"

A curtain drew aside, and a nimbus of light shone around brilliant hair. Hastily she drew the curtains, opening the adjacent window.

He jumped into the room, brushing dirt from his cutaway.

"Enter Count Dracula," she said, waving a near empty bottle of Mumm's. Her enormous eyes were red from weeping, yet her smile quivered with high-strung vivacity. On the floor lay the crumpled wedding gown for which he had just paid a small fortune, and the froth of veil. Her round, luminous breasts spilled from lace-trimmed crepe de chine teddies embroidered with her name, and her velvet thighs were bare above knotted white silk.

He closed the window. "Get dressed," he snapped.

"Here in Castle Carpathia we're drunken on the blood of white gripes—grapes."

"You're not that sozzled," he said grimly. "Get dressed, Zoe. Your husband's going crazy out there."

"Not *my* husband," she denied, holding the bottle to her lips. "How could *I* be married to a boy who lets people walk over him?"

Justin wrenched the champagne from her grasp. "Put on your clothes."

There was a banging on the door. Zoe flung herself on the bed, weeping anew. Her sobs held an anguish that went beyond willful, drunken tearfulness.

Justin sat on the edge of the mattress. "It's going to be fine, absolutely fine," he soothed. "Caryll's not weak. He's understanding. Gentle."

"I've hashed up my life," she wailed. "Like Mother."

"Brides often get the nerve up, Zozo. He's the right one for you."

"You don't know the first thing, not the first thing. If you did, you wouldn't be mooning after some impossible girl who doesn't even want you." Zoe lifted her head. Strands of perfumed hair veiled her tear-filled eyes. "Brother of mine, we're both idiots about love, you and me. We're incapable of picking the right one. It's in the blood."

"*I* can remember our parents," he said. "They had a wonderful life together. Mother and Father—"

"What makes you so sure Daddy was that?" she interrupted in a shrill voice. "Our Father which art in heaven?"

Justin's eyes narrowed. "You shouldn't drink. It makes you ugly."

"That's what I am. Ugly and blue. I've married the wrong man, just like Mother. My mother-in-law, honest in the extreme . . ." Zoe stumbled over the word. "She told me it should have been Mother and Uncle Andrew."

"Stop this, Zoe," Justin snapped.

"Mother didn't need a husband, she needed a front for Uncle Andrew . . ." With a convulsive sob Zoe buried her face in a pillow.

Justin stared ahead blankly, his hands knotting into fists. The old sick question of his boyhood was upon him, that question bound up with his birthday, his parents' never mentioned, never celebrated anniversary. It had been unbearable to think that his revered dead father had succumbed to this itch in the blood, this phallic heat to play the cad with a haloed creature like Mother. Even now, fully cognizant in his maturity that his parents must have been creatures of flesh, blood, and animal urges, he felt unclean probing their sexual proclivities—and the coupling Zoe had suggested was foul beyond thinking. Like her, he remembered the Major in his decline, a ravaged ancient.

Knocks reverberated on wood, muffled voices chorused, "Zoe, Zoe."

"Get up," he commanded.

Gasping and sniffing, she obeyed. He pressed his hand between her naked shoulders, steering her into the enormous bathroom.

"Throw cold water on your face," he said. "Brush your teeth."

He washed his own face and hands under the bath faucet, watching the filthy water drain away. He pulled Zoe into the dressing room, where an ivory suit and a Russian lynx coat hung in readiness.

Twenty-five minutes later the bride and groom ran through a gaudy shower of streamers, confetti, and rice. Younger guests braved the clear, frosty night, trooping outside, champagne glasses in hand, to shout best wishes as the newlyweds climbed into a brand new, custom-built Onyx. The wedding night would be spent aboard Tom's railroad car, which was being hitched on to the Royal Poinciana en route to the Baardsons' Palm Beach winter palace. With a loud backfire the car disappeared into dark woods. All at once it was no longer a wedding but a gathering of people, many of them bitter rivals.

Justin did not go back inside. Without a thought he abdicated his hostly duties and was scarcely aware of his surroundings as he tramped by the limousines lined under marquees to the garage where his Fiver was parked.

He had utterly forgotten about the paper that Tom had asked him to sign.

IV

When Hugh heard the Fiver, he was ensconced in a sixteenth-century bishop's chair that he had recently acquired for the drawing room, celebrating his ward's nuptials in his usual solitary fashion. Going into the Great Hall to ascertain it was Justin, he called, "Here I am!" returning to pour Dom Pérignon into the second glass.

One look at Justin's drained face and Hugh accepted that something at the wedding had gone monstrously awry. He sat back in Genoese ecclesiastical velvet, waiting.

310

Justin took a sip, then set down the glass.

"Hugh, Zoe had a bit of a crisis. She locked herself in her room. No, it's all right now," he said as Hugh moved to stand. "She left with Caryll." He sighed, then looked directly at Hugh. "It seems she was upset by some old gossip about Mother—it's not the kind of thing I care to repeat. But I've always nursed a few doubts of my own. They have to do with, well, my birthday. A few weeks before Mother was killed, I asked her about it. She said she would explain when I was old enough. I certainly knew the facts of life by then. Anyway, it wasn't like her to put me off on the grounds of age." Justin fingered the rim of the crystal glass. "After she died, I let it pretty much alone. Hugh, I don't even like mentioning it, but what Zoe said was unthinkable."

"That business about Antonia and Major Stuart?"

"So you heard it too."

"Gossip. Spitefully malicious gossip."

"But . . . well. There's me. I was born only a few months after they married."

Hugh pressed his hands together in a steeple, looking over his manicured fingertips at his nephew.

Justin's face was the yellowed white of tallow, yet he gazed steadily back. "Can you remember anything about them when they lived in Detroit? Hugh, I've imagined such terrible things. . . ."

Hugh made no immediate reply. That he reveal the truth was asking too much. Tom's rages were a forest fire that destroyed himself and others blindly and sometimes permanently. Hugh had everything to lose. And what did he have to gain? His plans were far from complete. He had nothing to gain.

Yet the deep-set blue eyes held such despair that Hugh heaved a resonant sigh. What was it like for so decent and fair a young man to strangle on the thought of being the fruit of incest?

A log burned in half, falling noisily. They both turned toward the fireplace, which was swathed in Yule greenery. *Christmas*, Hugh thought, *season of comfort and joy*.

"I have some papers that might shed light on the matter," he said slowly.

"Papers?"

"Letters, actually. Nobody has any idea that they exist, and it would be bad for me, very, if anyone found out."

"I wouldn't betray a confidence."

"Of course not. But these . . . well, there'll be a temptation."

"You have my word."

"I'll count on it, then."

Upstairs, Hugh went directly to the portrait of Lady Jane Neville, swinging it aside to reveal a safe that Justin had not known existed. Working the combination, Hugh selected an envelope whose plumped-out accordion folds were tied with faded red string. He handed it to Justin.

"Mrs. J. Foreman," Justin read aloud. "Mother knew people called Foreman . . . acquaintances of hers. They never came to the house. I haven't thought of that name in years."

"It's very important that you never mention it."

"Right," Justin said. "Hugh, I appreciate what you're doing. It's, well, very decent."

More than decent, Hugh thought. *Foolhardy.* Halfway repenting his holiday season generosity, he said quietly, "I'll leave you alone for a few minutes." He went into his bedroom, leaving the safe open, a sign of immeasurable trust.

Justin sat on the couch, pulling off his shoes. Absently he rubbed at soles that ached from dancing. Both socks were torn from his climb. Weariness and the raw devastation caused by his questions about his mother added to the unreal quality of Hugh's secret cache and this fat, mysterious envelope. Oh, he was aware that Hugh, center of Onyx Security, gathered detective reports, yet loving Hugh as he did, it was inconceivable to Justin that he himself should be caught in the sticky web. He lit a cigarette. Holding it between his lips, he slowly, deliberately unwound the string from the packet.

The sheaf of opened envelopes were caramel with age, all addressed to *Mrs. J. Foreman/ Flat C/ 8 Upper Swithin Place/ London/ Eng.* in Tom's uneducated scrawl. Tom! Who invariably dictated to a typist.

Justin opened one at random:

> *Antonia, Sweetheart,*
> *I miss you so much I could cry, sumtimes I do.*

The clumsily formed, misspelled sentences leaped out at him. Tenderly obscene, passionate, yearning. He read swiftly. One small, coherent edge of his mind was embarrassed to be eavesdropping, another was admiring—why had *he* been so stupidly civilized, why had he never written such words to Elisse? The letter was undated. Justin glanced at the envelope. Postmarked March 26, 1911. A few months after his mother had explained that "Mr. Bridger's" anger was due to Uncle Andrew's possible involvement in an arson. Justin read two more letters, finding several references to a previous love affair between them, and to "your boy." The fourth letter he chose was dated September 11, 1914. His eyes jumped to his own name.

Justin looks so much like you. Nobody could guess I'm his father. As far as I'm conserned, Caryll is my only son. I sware to you, sweetheart, after we are married nobody will find out about your boy.

Justin's dress shirt had gone limp with sweat. He was aware of his own breathing, of a pressure behind his eyes, of well-defined nausea. He felt if he read another scrawled word he would vomit. He piled the letters on the hearth, his hand shaking so that he had difficulty using his new gold lighter—Caryll had given him one of the ushers' gifts—making three fumbling passes before he succeeded in lighting the small blaze that Hugh had not lit more than a decade ago on another continent. When the flames died, he touched the lighter to the remaining scraps. He was kneeling at this final task when Hugh came in.

"A lot of things must be clearer now," Hugh said. "Why I brought you here, why Tom has forced himself to be so cold. Justin, he promised her that you'd never learn that he's your father. Keeping that promise is his number-one priority."

Standing, Justin peered down at the mound of ashes. "If I'm not who I was," he asked dully, "who am I?" The question seemed meaningless. He could not think or feel. It was as though he were stricken with a peculiar form of amnesia that blanks out not the past but the present. "I'm nobody. Nothing."

"Don't be ridiculous. You're the son of the richest man in America. Maybe the world," Hugh soothed. "I've always imagined what would have happened if he *had* married Antonia. I've always wanted to set things to right. Justin, you're the firstborn. You're the one who should inherit Onyx."

Justin's hands opened and closed. "How did you get these?" he asked dully.

"When I went to England to bring you here, I cleaned out their flat."

Justin nodded. "Yes."

"Tom loves you, he wants to acknowledge you—but you understand now why he can't."

Justin bent to stir the still warm ashes with his forefinger. He said nothing.

Hugh made one of his rare misjudgments. "Surely you see that it's impossible, you and that Kaplan girl."

Justin looked up. His furious blue eyes glinted through narrowed lids. "How do you know about Elisse?"

"Zoe." Hugh's mouth went dry as he realized his mistake.

"It was meant to be private."

Hugh sat on the arm of the chair nearest his nephew. "You know our Zoe."

"And after she told you, you had Elisse checked out," Justin said, roughly.

"Now you're being ridiculous."

Justin shot a disgusted glance at the open portrait, and at the safe with its neatly heaped folders and envelopes. *"Haven't you?"*

The raw, hard note of command jolted the truth from Hugh. "What if I have?"

"You snooping son of a bitch, prying into *her* life!"

"There are so many other things for us to talk about," Hugh pleaded.

"What gave you the damn right?"

"You're my nephew, Justin, all I have. Believe me, she's not worthy of you, not in any way. She's a nobody, a little red who's already two-timing you with one of her own kind." Hugh took a deep breath. "Forget her, Justin, forget her."

Sweat streamed on Justin's stark white face. "Just keep your nose out of her concerns. And mine!"

Hugh did not know what he had anticipated, but certainly it hadn't been this furious, dazed wet face, this hostile, accusatory voice. This temper. *He truly is Tom's son,* Hugh thought. *I should have realized that.* Yet how could this be Justin? Always the fair one.

Justin, who must surely understand how much he, Hugh, had done for him. Hugh moved from the arm of the chair, turning his unscarred profile to his nephew. "Why don't you go to bed, Justin? You've had a long, draining day. The wedding, Zoe's nerves, now this. It must come as a tremendous shock. In the morning everything will look different."

"You had no right, none!"

"I've *made* your life."

"We're talking about Elisse. How dare you spin your filthy webs around her?"

He looked a resentful child rather than an honorable young man who had just been told his benefactor was also his uncle.

Hugh said coldly, "We'll talk tomorrow."

"Tomorrow?" Justin said, as if surprised that there would be another day. His anger had vanished with disconcerting swiftness. Blinking, he wiped his forehead, scattering droplets of sweat. With stiff, mechanical steps he left the room.

Alone in the corridor, he reeled. He had no clear memory of his outburst. He felt dizzy. Out of control.

He halted for several minutes at the massive carved door that led to the house proper before continuing slowly along the gallery to his bedroom. He turned on a single floor lamp and slumped on the edge of the bed, his hands dangling between his knees. The portrait of his mother, source of consoling comfort during his worst hours, seemed in this particular light to have a mocking, knowing cast about the mouth. The numerous photographs of his father—no, his stepfather—were a mortifyingly sentimental parody. He buried his head in his hands.

Who am I?

I am not Hutchinson, not Bridger.

"Elisse . . ." As he muttered the name the molten pain above his eyes eased a little.

He got to his feet, stripping off his wedding attire, which was clammy and sour with sweat.

A half hour later he was lugging his suitcase down the stairs.

V

Hugh had gone to bed. An insomniac, he usually read until very late, but tonight he did not even try a book. He lay in the dark, his mind fastened on Justin's hideously unexpected responses. He had made a supremely generous sacrifice. Far from being rewarded by gratitude or warmth, he had been brutally rapped on the knuckles as a meddler, a spy. *Justin's a changed man*, Hugh thought.

A car started up. Hugh listened to the distinctive putt-pop tune of a Fiver moving along the private lane toward Lake Shore Drive. Where was Justin going? To get drunk? To find nirvana between a whore's thighs?

Suddenly Hugh sat up in bed, switching on the lamp. His eyes opened wide, staring.

What if he's gone to tell Tom?

He gave me his word.

But he's no longer the same Justin, no longer the soul of honor. He belongs to her. What if . . . Hugh's mind leaped back to the shadowy garage, Tom rinsing soap from his arms: *You're a dead man if you say it.*

I'll deny everything. If Justin mentions the letters, I'll say he stole them, I'll say whatever I must. Hugh wheezed spasmodically. He switched on the light and inhaled from a medical atomizer that he kept at his bedside, then pulled up the quilt and lay awaiting the worst. The phone call with Tom's furious voice at the other end. But there was no sound. Even his wheezing had subsided.

As he lay there rigid a mounting fury matched his fear and grief. It was too painful any longer to blame his nephew for his untoward reaction. Instead his devastation directed itself against the Jew girl, Elisse Kaplan. It was *her* violated privacy that Justin had ranted about, *she* was the one who had diverted Justin from the path Hugh had ordained he would take.

An hour later, his muscles taut, Hugh poured water from the silver carafe, taking two yellow capsules. The only effect of the double dose of strong soporific was a gradual numbing of the facial muscles.

He got up, pulling on his robe to stand at the windows. Above the leafless winter tree stars glittered from the farthest reaches of infinity. Numberless winking, incandescent dots. Hugh gripped the ledge, gazing at the snow dust of the Milky Way. His fear of his brother, his agony at Justin's outburst—and wasn't that unwarranted rage tantamount to rejection?—fed a hatred cold and remorseless as the stars. *This Elisse Kaplan has turned him against me*, Hugh thought.

With a deep sigh he went to his bookshelf and selected *Meditations*, but for once the calm perspective of Marcus Aurelius could not ward off the onslaught of furies.

CHAPTER 20

Elisse Hutchinson crossed the dim breadth of the room at the Hotel Laguna, yawning as she raised the slat of a Venetian blind to peer out at the Pacific. It was not yet fully light; no color touched the sea. The circling gulls and faraway fishing boats showed as they would on a Japanese print: dimensionless black markings.

Justin emerged directly below her on the beach. He looked up at the window, waving, dropping his towel on the sand, pantomiming cold by clutching at his arms as he ran into the surf to dive under the curl of a breaker. Elisse shivered in her new Viyella robe. *Only an Easterner*, she thought. *What sane Californian swims in winter?*

Six days earlier, on the cloudy morning of the thirtieth of December, the studio gatekeeper had rung to ask if it was okay to admit a Mr. Hutchinson. After those damn fraternal letters and two telephoned cool, veddy British postponements, excruciating joy had thrown her into such a state that she had no memory whatsoever of his explanation for his early arrival, or of any discussion to elope. By some legerdemain of time she found herself crossing the border to Tijuana in a mud-plaited Onyx, Justin clasping her hand against his thigh, a druglike sensual haze surrounding her. No chill of reality touched her until early evening, when they checked into this hotel room and she put in her long distance call. Neither parent wished her well, neither asked to speak to Justin, both cried audibly. She had anticipated this response, but that didn't make it any easier. Barely able to hang up the telephone, tears streaming down her face, she had said to her husband, "They're playing this like the road show of *Abie's Irish Rose*."

That was Elisse all over. Her quickly-prickly personality forever battled her character, and as far as she was concerned, the struggle was her one saving grace. She saw herself as a blob pulled out of shape with every tug of her fatuously soft heart. She admired and envied Justin's code of fairness. No such permanently engraved principles ruled her life. Her sympathies pulled her every which way. She had joined with Mitch Shapiro to organize the grips not because she believed in the Struggle but because tears sprang to her eyes every morning as she passed the Columbia Pictures employment office with its sad, docile queue of day laborers hoping for a little work.

Sighing, she rested her forehead against the pane, watching Justin breast a wave. Though she was crazy in love with him, this past week had been far from the land of bliss. Her anguish reached beyond parental rejection. The problem was her beau ideal himself.

In most respects he was perfect. She had come away without a handkerchief, even, and he had bought her a trousseau, waiting patiently on spindly chairs while she tried on all that was available in a size four in an out-of-season resort town; he laughed at her jokes and occasionally made a good one of his own; he ate quickly and neatly; he strewed his clothes reassuringly. Yet, yet . . . He maintained a mysteriously undefinable chasm between them. Had he before? They had been together so few times, and besides, an admiring awe had colored her perceptions of this paragon—matrimony had mitigated it only slightly—but in her heart she admitted he had been, well, *different* in September. She could not put her finger on this difference. How, she asked herself over and over, was Justin remote from her? Sometimes, or so it seemed to her, his eyes went sad and cold, a shrinking of pupils that was the obverse of seeing, as though he were gazing into some frigidly desolate interior landscape.

Justin had cleared the surfline. The sky was lighter, and she watched the ball of his head between his churning arms until she began to cry. Groping her way back to bed, she hugged the pillow that smelled of him, and fell back to sleep.

II

She jerked awake.

Knocking.

"Room service," called a nasal masculine voice.

"Go 'way," she muttered. " 'S too early." Justin had arranged for breakfast to be brought up exactly at nine each day.

Another rap. "Room service!"

She groped for Justin's gold Bulova.

Three minutes to nine!

And he had left before seven! She careened to the window. The overcast sky reflected elephantine grays on a sea that was empty save for one small fishing boat approaching the pier. No swimmers. Nobody on the beach. An outsize white gull perched on Justin's towel, which was where he had dropped it.

She shoved past the elderly waiter and his cart, zipping barefoot down the corridor, stabbing at the elevator button, not waiting, skimming down red-carpeted stairs to the lobby. Gripping the reception desk, she demanded breathlessly, "Has Mr. Hutchinson come back?"

The clerk's double chin dropped as he gaped at her. "I haven't seen him yet this morning, madam, but if you'll return to your room, I'll have him paged. . . ."

She swerved from the desk and ran to the beach exit. Shouldering one of the doors, she slammed her palms against immobile glass before trying the other, which was unlocked. She skidded down red tilesteps, and fell on the bottom one. Jumping to her feet, she pounded down the slope of cold dry sand to the roiling breakers. Morbid energy blazed through her like current through a light filament.

"Justin!" she screamed. "Justin!"

The surf's roar drowned out the name.

She galloped northward, not caring that foam sucked sand from under her arches and drenched her nightgown to her thighs.

"Justin!" she screamed. "Justin!"

And suddenly she understood the dawn dips.

All week he had been swimming long distances, smiling at her warnings about the strong undertow in the Pacific. She had seen his recklessness as masculine bravery.

How wrong I was! she thought, holding a hand over her wildly banging heart. *Justin's big mistake—marrying me—has made him so miserably unhappy that he doesn't care if he lives or dies.*

She whirled about, galloping full speed back to the Hotel Laguna.

In the lobby she gasped out, "Hurry! Telephone the lifeguards! My husband went swimming hours ago!" The clerk's buttery chins were wobbling as he spoke words she could not hear over her racing voice. "I said call the damn lifeguards!"

"—is here," the clerk finished, and jerked his head toward the revolving door.

Circling through was Justin, wearing a heavy, too loose brown sweater over his bathing suit. He was pale, and as he stared at her he grew yet more bloodless. She realized how she must look, the sand-caked gown clinging to her legs and showing the darknesses of her body, her hair all wild. The madwoman of the waterfront. Momentary embarrassment touched her, but she was too weakened by relief to do anything but swoop across the lobby and clutch at him, her sobbing mouth pressed against rough, salty wool. "You're safe . . . you're okay."

"You were right about the pull of the Pacific's current. I swam out a bit far, that's all. Mr. Sandoz's boat came along and he picked me up."

Elisse noticed a thickset, Mexican-looking man in a yellow slicker and black waterproof boots who was politely looking the other way.

"I'd like to give him something for his troubles," Justin said. "Sweet, come on upstairs."

He returned to the lobby with his wallet.

Elisse took her clothes into the bathroom, hanging them on the door while she showered: she let the sharp jets of water strike her face and her sensitive nipples, let her bobbed hair get wet as she bent to soap the knee that had been grazed in her fall. She was accepting how much she had wanted to be melted, fused, converted into part of Justin. *He needs* me *like he needs leprosy or lockjaw*, she thought, *but being Justin he can't suggest the cure for a bollixed-up mixed marriage.* So what if she were crying? The shower washed away her tears.

She was toweling herself when she heard him return: she stayed in the bathroom, dressing in her powder blue costume, straightening the clocks that ran up the sides of her stockings, carefully adjusting her felt hat. In the outfit Miss Kaplan had worn to work on the thirtieth, she emerged.

Justin, who was dressed in gray flannels and a soft shirt, raised one black eyebrow. "Formal?"

"I'm going back to Los Angeles," she said quietly.

"To make our peace with your parents?"

Would they let her in the door? What did it matter? She could not go back to Rodeo Drive. To return to their house would be treachery to every leap of crazy, unrequited love she bore this large, handsome, composedly smiling gentile, her husband. "*I'm* going back. Alone."

Getting to his feet, he said, "Because I swam a bit long?"

"It's how you would plan it," she said in the same dispirited voice. "Work up a swimming routine so it'd look like a simple drowning accident. Proper. Polite."

"You don't really believe that I . . . ?"

"I'm not stupid, Justin," she sighed. "It's too obvious to quibble about."

"The shock, Elisse. You're overreacting."

"We're an emotional lot," she said. "Especially when our near and dear try self-destruction." She was easing off the wedding band. The Tijuana jeweler had sized the ring, his smallest, too tightly, and she had trouble getting it over the knuckle. As she set down the gold band it made a light clink on the glass top of the vanity. "You don't have to make up excuses. Good-bye and good lock—*adiós*, as they say south of the border."

His eye twitched involuntarily. "You're serious, aren't you?"

"A Mexican judge said a few words over us, another will unsay them. It's no capital crime, an elopement that hasn't worked."

"You think you're my problem?" he asked, surprised.

"What else?"

"You're the only thing in my life that's right."

"But you were trying to . . ."

He sighed, nodding. "I swam out too far every morning, thinking if it happens, then it happens. Today the rip caught me and I couldn't get in. God, I struggled. Elisse, I swam like hell. And kissed Mr. Sandoz for rescuing me."

"Justin, why now? What is so terrible, if it isn't me? Why on our honeymoon?"

"That's a fine thing to do to you, isn't it?" He stood by the window, which was open so that the cold, salt wind rustled Venetian-blind slats at him. "I always assumed I was one kind of person. Not spectacularly decent or fair, but aiming to be. Now I see that fairness and decency are a luxury of a stable life." His face was turned from her so she could not see his expression. "Tom Bridger's my father."

The words made no sense to Elisse, so she interpreted them as symbolism. "Isn't that carrying admiration a bit far?"

"He slept with my mother. He did not marry her."

In her consternation, Elisse sat down. Her confusion spun irrationally around what Justin had told her outside Verona's: Tom Bridger had never even invited him to lunch in the Onyx executive dining room. "A well-kept secret?" she said finally.

"I found out on Zoe's wedding night. I've tried to tell you, tried often. I couldn't. I don't much like being a bastard." He pronounced it *barstard*, English-style.

"Oh, Justin, with *me* you're ashamed?"

"With everybody. At first I was in shock. Well, maybe a more accurate way to put it would be that I wasn't thinking straight. I still can't. Nothing, not one single part about myself, is what I imagined it. I can't get a bead on anything. I'm one solid mass of confusion. A ruddy ogre. I want to dig up her poor bones, Mother's, and scatter them. I hate my fa—Claude Hutchinson. He treated me magnificently, as though I *were* his son. I ache to strangle Hugh and Tom. Hugh's been fantastically generous. Tom's been good. But they lied to me, Elisse, all of them. Every minute of my existence has been a lie."

The white linen of his shirt went taut against his shoulders as he raised his arms to clench the window frame. He needed comfort, kindness. She had none to give.

"*I* never lied to you," she said in a tight voice. "In all this mental *sturm und drang*, Justin, what made you decide to come here and marry me?"

"Instinct, pure and simple. I never questioned it."

"Where would a man be without a loyal little woman at his side while he plays Pacific roulette?"

"Don't—"

"If Mr. Sandoz hadn't come along trolling his nets, you know

323

what I'd've been stuck with the rest of my life? That you'd done yourself in to escape me. How's that for a pleasant memory?''

He made a peculiar grunting noise.

She realized he was weeping.

Her indignation evaporated. It shocked her that Justin, handsome, rich, strong, disciplined, the man with everything, would weep. *Oh, you imbecile*, she told herself, *of course he can cry! He tried to kill himself, for God's sake!* Once again that terror for his safety was melting her bones. She clasped both arms around his waist, curving herself to his quaking back. He turned, burying his wet face in the hollow where her shoulder met her neck.

She was engulfed by a lust so pure that it seemed metaphysical, the desire that a parched, yearning woman experiences when a warrior husband returns from the long wars; it was only by the procreative act that she could assure herself of Justin's survival. She kissed his black hair, which smelled of salt and was still damp, kissed his cheek, then opened her mouth on his. Her hands moved between his buttocks. He was caressing her with the same explicit urgency. Neither of them spoke, there was never a thought of undressing; she pushed off her step-ins while he tore at his trousers, sending a button rolling across the floor. They fell onto the rumpled bed. Her thighs spread, her pelvis arched up. "We're not leaving each other, Elisse, not ever," his voice rumbled as he went into her. "We belong to each other."

Involuntary spasms convulsed her womb, shaking along her thighs, her belly, increasing in violence as if she were being torn apart that an unreasoning, mindlessly ecstatic creature might be born. Her pupils swollen, she looked up at Justin in surprise. "Oh, I love you forever and ever, darling," she gasped, her hands flailing on his shoulders as if urging him to move more swiftly. She rose up and down to meet him, crying incoherently that she loved him, forever. . . . Oh, forever. With a sobbing cry he collapsed on her.

Chill ventilation from the open window cooled their sweat-glossed bodies. Justin pulled one of the blankets over them.

"Nice Justin," she said.

"Nice Elisse."

Shyly, she kissed the arch of his nose.

"The one thing I am sure of is that I belong to you," he said.

She wondered that even in her anxiety she had doubted this.

324

Justin's innate decency would balk at marrying her, any woman, without love.

"Those *things*," she said. "You didn't use one."

"Are you angry?"

"You're the one who always remembered. Was it because you didn't want to leave me with a little one?"

Embarrassment showed on his face, but he said firmly, "That's over. We're going to forget that."

"No more polar bear swims, Justin."

"That's the easiest promise I've ever made," he said. "I don't want to die. Today I proved it to myself."

They were lying side by side. She twined her fingers in his. "Tell a simple young girl from the sticks, are there other ways of, uh, prevention?"

"I think a doctor can prescribe some gadget for the woman. I don't know much about it either." He kissed her cheek. "I never realized until just now that the rubber was ruining things for—"

"Never!" she interrupted. "Everything we do is very fine. But that now . . . it was bliss, sheer bliss." She looked at him in alarm. "Justin, what if I'm having a baby?"

He smiled. "It's a bit late to worry. And what if you are? We're married." He flinched. "Elisse, how could he leave Mother in the lurch? He loved her!" Justin's eyes were desperate.

She pulled his face to the rumpled pale blue wool over her breasts. *Thy people shall be my people, darling,* she thought, *but I cannot for the life of me understand them.*

III

The cloudy weather continued, and many of the hotel guests left. Justin and Elisse walked along the deserted beach for hours, he with his trouser legs rolled up, she bare-legged, their purple-tinged feet marking parallels in the wet sand. This was a new Justin, bewildered, with frown lines between his deep-set blue eyes as he spoke about his past. He desired, she understood, to unfold his life to her, and this opening-up served double duty as a catharsis of his morbid inner pressures. He discussed his relationships from a scrupulously fair distance, he omitted damaging evidence, yet even so there were times when she had to pretend it was blowing sand that caused the water in her eyes. The image that rasped most at her heart was Tom

Bridger showing Caryll some vast, cacophonous new machinery at the Hamtramck while Justin, a tall, doubtless somewhat gangly, adolescent, trailed, too proud to beg for attention yet bereft at being ignored by a man he admired, a lonely shadow attached to the real substance of parental affection. *Justin was recently orphaned,* Elisse thought in belated partisan grief: *even if the boy weren't his own son, didn't Tom Bridger know there's a constitutional restraint on cruel and unusual punishment?*

"About my financial situation," Justin said five days after the watery debacle. "I don't have any savings." He did not mention that Zoe's magnificent trousseau and her wedding had wiped him out. "There's a trust fund from my great uncle. Zoe and I can't touch the principle—our children will be the remaindermen. My share of the interest's no fortune, only about three thousand a year."

"Sounds big to *me.* I toil for a hundred and twenty a month," Elisse said. She had telephoned Columbia, and a disgruntled Mr. Briskin had told her that if she were back in a couple of weeks, she'd still have a job. "We're in clover, Justin. Why not wait a bit before you decide what you'll do?"

"I know what I'm going to do." He halted, squinting at the bleak purple line of the horizon. "Pretty soon we'll go back," he said.

"To Detroit?"

"I had things set up so they could manage the shutdown without me. But the changeover's a far bigger job. It's never been done on this scale. To build the Seven every single piece of machinery will have to be new. In Woodland alone that's thousands of machines, some of them monsters. There'll be new layouts in every assembly plant."

"You're telling me—" Her voice cracked with astonishment. "You mean after all that's happened you're staying at Onyx?"

"If Tom wants me." He skidded a flat stone across a wavelet—the tide was out. "If we can look each other in the eye once things are out in the open. I don't mean publicly, of course, but between him and me."

"You're not an indentured servant. You don't owe him one red bean, Justin."

"It isn't a matter of owing, Elisse. I can't run away from what I am."

She shivered, terrified for Justin, who was returning to the fishbloods who had driven him to within an ace of doing himself in, and she nursed a far lesser anxiety on her own behalf about meeting Justin's sister, who was a gorgeous Society girl who appeared in the newsreels. Yet she did not argue. Justin was responding to that atavistic pull that few, apparently, could resist: he was searching for the ties to his progenitor. She reached her arm to encircle his waist. They sloshed through icy yellow-white spume. "I saw some railroad schedules on the front desk," she said.

IV

Hugh ordered telegrams dispatched to Onyx dealers around the world: JANUARY 12 1927/ MAKE WAY FOR THE SEVEN/ TODAY LAST FIVER ROLLS OFF LINE. Hugh also arranged that the press be at Woodland and that Onyx movie photographers film Tom as he accompanied the last engine block down the main assembly. Tom shook hands with many of the close-standing ranks of his employees, who afterward stared down at their suddenly idle hands as they accepted that they were being laid off in the midst of an exceptionally cold winter. Around two that afternoon the final bolt was tightened on the dark gray car. An eerie silence wadded the endless hall. Almost exactly one half of the cars in the United States were Fivers, and now there would be no more.

Snowflakes drifted from mottled clouds as Tom drove the last Fiver to the Triple E Building. A crowd stood under the canopy that sheltered the replica of the quadricycle. Tom tried to make a connection with the hungry, obsessed twenty-year-old who had driven the original, but peering through the tunnel of the years, he could see only Antonia's enormous, dark glowing eyes. As he halted the executives, engineers, reporters, and guests applauded. A path was made for Maud, bulky in her sable coat, as she came heavily down the shallow steps.

"Surprise, Tom," she said, beaming.

Expecting some form of automotive memorabilia or award, he laughed aloud. Following his wife were Caryll and Zoe, who danced ahead to engulf him in perfume as she pressed her smooth, warm cheek to his. "Congratulations, Father Bridger."

"Why aren't you two sunbathing in Palm Beach?" Tom asked.

"What, and miss this?" retorted Caryll, grasping his father's shoulders, hugging him. They smiled at each other, then quickly stepped apart, embarrassed at their public display of affection.

A mechanic had been cranking the quadricycle. Tom said, "Go ahead, Caryll. Show 'em how an old-timer runs."

"I've never driven her."

"Nothing to it. She's warmed up. Just use the tiller to steer."

So Caryll climbed into the vibrating little mechanism, which jerked and swiveled along the snow-powdered company road as uncertain as a bird with a broken wing. Tom had added a brake. Caryll, unable to find the lever, jolted to a clattering halt against a low brick wall. Reinforced bicycle spokes crumpled. Caryll climbed out, crimson.

Tom walked up, shaking his head. "Got to teach you how to drive," he said, trying to ease the situation with a joke. But Caryll barely smiled.

A few minutes later Tom stood on the carpeted platform of Triple E's main auditorium, fielding questions about the Seven.

"Any advance sketches?" inquired the heavyset man from *Automobile Age*.

"Brynie, you know better than that," Tom called back. "Nobody sees her until we unveil her to the public."

"But the prototype is complete?" boomed the man from *The New York Times*.

"Sure," Tom lied. "And she's a beaut." Though he had never felt comfortable at these press conferences Hugh arranged, he had learned to parry with reporters to Onyx's advantage.

From the last row a voice called out, "Who hired Justin Hutchinson away from you? Ford or General Motors?"

"When Hutchinson gets back from his vacation, come on over and ask him yourself." Tom turned to Caryll, who sat on his right at the speakers' table. "Your turn."

Caryll, still red about the ears from his altercation with the quadricycle, further mortified by the smirky glances that slid from him to his bride in the front row, pushed awkwardly to his feet. Tom sat, one ankle on his knee, his arms akimbo, seemingly alert, yet not listening. He had never compared his sons, he told himself, and he wasn't going to do so now, yet impinging on his brain were two images: Justin, replying to similar damn fool questions with unflappable calm; Justin, an English cigarette between his lips, smoothly handling a test car on the Woodland test track. Tom's conscious mind was fixed on the typed papers in his bureau drawer. *I asked him to sign and he took off.*

The shutdown had been one continuous foul-up in the hands of Phil and Artie Sinclair, making Tom more than ever aware of the extent to which he relied on Justin. But his hurt at the defection, so unlike Justin, went far deeper than impotent dismay at the chaos inflicted on Onyx. Though he had behaved like an employer more than a chummy mentor—*people say you don't even like him*— he had always delighted in Justin's respect and warmed to his obvious if unspoken affection. Thus it was a bitter dose of salts that Justin had never confided in him about a serious romance, had not sent a telegraph or letter informing him of the elopement. He would not have known about Justin's marriage if Hugh hadn't told him. *She's some cheap little Hollywood Jewess, and a labor organizer at that. I don't see how we can trust him anymore, not with a wife like that. She's the one who got him to bolt. He's a changed man, I tell you, Tom, a changed man.* A complete new phonograph record for Hugh. Suddenly he was dead set against Justin, because of the girl.

Tom wouldn't have cared if she were a whirling dervish or Lenin's mother-in-law.

He wanted Justin back.

As soon as he had recovered from his initial hurt and sense of abandonment, he had been filled with remorse. *I handled the whole deal all wrong,* he thought repeatedly. Why hadn't he managed to preserve the necessary ambiguities while at the same time stamping a seal of permanency on their relationship?

Tom's fingers dug into his biceps as he gazed unseeing at the audience of newsmen. *The minute Justin gets back,* he thought, *I'll get those damn shares signed, sealed, and notarized. The one important thing is to keep him tied here with me.*

"Dad?" Caryll was looking questioningly down at him. "Aren't you more qualified to answer that one?"

Tom rose. "Repeat the question slowly, will you?"

CHAPTER 21

The heavy mesh doors of Woodland's Gate One were chained shut.

The taxi's three hoots reverberated in the snowy stillness. After a minute the guardhouse door opened and a thin, boyish figure in a khaki uniform came down the wooden steps. "Sorry, no taxis inside," he said. His small, almost delicate hand rested on the Colt .45 in his holster.

Justin, surprised at the military automatic, rolled down the window. "It's all right. I'm Justin Hutchinson, Mr. Bridger's assistant."

The boy blinked nervously. "It's orders, sir. No cabs."

"Righto. I'll walk." Resigning himself to the mile or so to the Administration Building, Justin paid off the driver. "Damn," he muttered when he discovered the pedestrian gate also locked. Trotting up the guardhouse stoop, he rapped sharply at the counter window. An elderly guard with dewlaps appeared. Justin, explaining who he was, demanded the gate be opened.

"Sorry, sir, but you need identification." The wrinkled finger tapped an unfamiliar blue ticket pinned to his lapel below the German silver Onyx badge.

"What is this rigmarole?" Justin snapped. "I'm Mr. Bridger's assistant."

"We recognized you, Mr. Hutchinson," the man said appeasingly. "But since the shutdown we got new rules. Not even the top brass moves through this gate without an identification ticket."

"Let me speak to whoever's in charge."

The boards of the covered veranda creaked as Justin tramped up

330

and down to keep warm. After a few minutes the window opened again and a round, bald head emerged. "They've told me the story, Mr. Hutchinson, and I'm sorry, but the rule applies to everybody excepting the two Mr. Bridgers. We're protecting the Seven."

"I'll use your telephone," Justin said preemptively.

"Sorry, sir. Can't let anyone in the guardhouse."

"What is everybody shaking about?"

"You, sir," replied the bald man. "You're a big shot, but it's our jobs if anybody gets by that's not wearing a blue badge. Mr. Keeley laid down the law to us."

Keeley? Justin mentally scanned through Security's echelons. Keeley rang no bell. *He must be one of those underling strutters who thrive on fear,* Justin thought, and made a mental note to talk to Colonel Hazelford about firing this Keeley, then recalled that he might no longer be in a prodding position.

"I'll find a pay phone," he said.

The hamburger joints and Coney Islands on Archibald that normally did a brisk business at all hours of day and night were closed, and across one window was whitewashed: *Out to lunch until Woodland reopens.* Justin was well aware of the disastrous ripple effects when any automotive plant closed to retool. And Onyx was the largest. *It's a long, cold winter for everybody in Detroit,* Justin thought, thrusting his gloved hands deep into his pockets.

There was nothing open until he reached the Paloverde Oil station at the corner of Jefferson: he often bought gas here and the manager, grousing about disastrous losses to his company, led him to the wall telephone.

Caryll was out of his office, so Justin asked the raspy-voiced secretary to track down her boss. "Tell him I'll be at this number." Feeling chilled, demoralized, an unwanted outsider, yet more darkly apprehensive about the coming interview with Tom, Justin sat on a stool in the unheated garage to await Caryll's call.

II

It was past six and the secretaries were gone as Tom, rotating his tired shoulders, let himself into his private office. The lamp burning on the desk at the far end of the commodious room did not dispel the darkness. Tom, smelling cigarette smoke, peered around.

A shadow was detaching itself from near the drawn curtains. "Good evening, Tom," Justin said quietly.

Exuberant relief and sheer manic joy socked the breath out of Tom. He gripped the oak doorjamb.

"Justin," he called cheerfully. "You damn near scared the water out of me." He pressed the switch, and brass-armed wall fixtures blazed.

"Sorry. I didn't mean to," Justin said.

"Been here long?"

"An hour or so."

"So why didn't you have Mrs. Collins ring for me?"

"She said you were watching a casting."

"Yes, yes. The engine block. Remember? Olaf and his entire engineering crew swore up and down that it was impossible to cast an eight-cylinder engine in a single block. Well, I figured out a way. And God damn if it didn't work! Two banks of four cylinders at an angle of ninety degrees, a Gothic shape. The Onyx Seven'll be as powerful as the fancy ten-thousand-buck jobs."

As Tom explained the details of the engine, he was examining Justin, the breadth and height, the beloved inheritance of black hair and finely chiseled Roman nose, the slightly rumpled clothing that for some reason he always associated with the young man's absolute integrity. Justin's deep-set blue eyes refused to meet Tom's gaze, a reticence that Tom took as endearing proof of a newlywed's embarrassment. Worrying that he might throw his arms around the returned prodigal, he forced a dryness into his voice. "I guess there was no point interrupting me. After a month, why rush?"

"I've been in California. I'm married, Tom."

"So Hugh tells me."

Justin's eyes flickered oddly. "Hugh?"

"You took the plunge on the thirtieth in Tijuana, right?"

"He certainly keeps tabs," Justin said in a level tone.

"Didn't you wire him?"

Justin carefully ground out his cigarette in an ashtray he had already filled. "Nobody except Zoe. She and Caryll were in Palm Beach, so I doubt if he heard it from her."

"That's how it goes," Tom said. His pulses were trotting with inane, juvenile satisfaction that his sibling had also been ignored. "Try to keep anything from my brother."

"Her name's Elisse."

"Elisse, eh?" Grinning, Tom went to the long table that held a scale model of the 1912 Fiver as well as a silver tray with glasses and a tantalus. "How about a drink?"

"I could use one."

Pointing at the Scotch, Tom raised a questioning gray eyebrow.

"Please," Justin said. "Straight."

Tom poured the drinks and raised his glass. "To Elisse Hutchinson," he said.

Justin tossed down the Scotch with a stiff wrist. Normally he took soda and nursed his booze. *I've never seen him with such a case of jitters,* Tom thought. *Maybe he's worried I'm going to can him.* For a pleasurable moment he visualized himself benevolently handing Justin the paper to sign—Caryll and Zoe had signed theirs last week—while a dark, biblically lovely young woman watched in the background.

"I don't have the foggiest how to put this," Justin said.

"Don't say a word. No apologies necessary. Okay, so you took off at an impossible time, but you're back and that's what counts." Grinning, Tom set down his glass. "I understand, Justin. There comes an hour in every man's life . . ."

"It's not about marrying Elisse. It's about you and Mother." Justin reddened as he looked directly at Tom, yet he spoke in his normal incisive cadence. "I know you're my father."

The lights struck at Tom's eyes with an unearthly glow while blood rushed to his chest, swelling the major arteries with such a stormy, violent cramp that he felt he might pass out.

Your son will never know Claude Hutchinson isn't his father.

You can't promise that.

The owner of Onyx can. I have money, I have power. I swear it to you on my life, Antonia.

Tom's right hand jerked toward his chest, then dropped to his side.

In this one single battering moment he reached a decision.

That promise still stood.

Would stand forever.

In this same instant it became abundantly clear why Hugh had reversed himself against his ward, shrilly denouncing Justin's marriage.

Hugh, Tom thought grimly. *Hugh* told *Justin. That's why Justin ran off to marry this girl—no wonder Hugh's so dead set against her. But there's no proof about me and Justin. It's Hugh's word against mine.*

"Tom, are you all right? It was a mistake blurting it out like that."

Only with the severest control was Tom keeping himself in an upright position. "That's some fairy tale you've come up with there." His voice was louder than he intended, scathing, caustic. "Hugh again, right? You really are a gullible ass sometimes, Justin. I figured you had more brains than to listen to Hugh's cockeyed inventions."

Justin looked stunned, as if he had been hit on the head. His suddenly white lips tensed. "This has nothing to do with Hugh," he said.

"Bullshit! It's him all over. Fits right in with that genealogical chart of his."

"This is you and me, Tom."

"It can't be any secret to you that he doesn't cotton to Caryll. He's elected you as heir to the kingdom."

"Forget Hugh. Let's talk about us."

"What's to say?"

Justin, deathly pale, gave him a long, level look.

"Your sister is married to my son, Justin. Our relationship begins and ends there. Hugh and all his crazy ferreting can't make any more of it than that. Believe me. Take my word—I should know."

"One contingency I never figured," Justin said slowly. "That you'd lie."

"Lie?" Tom threw back his head. His short, jarring laugh echoed in the still room. The exigencies of his bond to Antonia had only this one imperative. Lie. Lie. The cost of this lie, his relationship to the son he loved, he dared not consider. "You come to me after taking off for a month, a month when you were fucking well needed, and give me some wild talk about being my long lost son, and *I'm* lying? Oh, that's good!" He waggled his long, slender forefinger. "If Hugh's not in the middle of this tricky little mess, it must be *her.*"

Justin tensed as if Tom had hit him. "Tom, cut this out. I know. I *know.*"

"I've advanced you, and we're related by marriage, so your new bride's built it into a big deal. She intends to blackmail your way ahead, is that it?''

"All right. You don't want to acknowledge me. You never have before, so why should you now? But leave me some way I can face you.''

"I have to hand it to Hugh, he certainly knows about this girl, he's filled me in and—"

"I didn't come here to discuss my wife, Tom." Justin's interruption wavered briefly as he said the name, then he drew a breath. "Let's forget the whole thing.''

Tom no longer had control over the parameters of this battle. It was as if the blood pumping so painfully into his brain were charged with battery acid, painfully burning away all reason. "Yes, she must be the answer. You sneak off with her, and then you're back, trying to play me for a sucker. Well, she might pretend to be a Bolshie, but she can't fool me. Money's what counts to that tribe!''

The flesh of Justin's face had gone heavy, and the shadows under his disbelieving eyes were opaque.

Tom leaned toward the table as if to embrace this son as he had never permitted himself to, yet the reedy, sarcastic voice seemed to have a will of its own as it burst from his parched throat. "She should have held off awhile. I was set to give you some shares. But not now, buddy, not now. I must say I'm surprised at *you*. How did she drag you into this . . ." Tom's imprecations trailed into a long sigh. He fell heavily into a chair.

"All right, Tom?" Justin's voice seemed to come from a half mile away.

"Ahh shit," Tom groaned.

Justin poured a stiff drink, placing it on the table between Tom and the miniature automobile. Tom reached for the glass. His Adam's apple bobbed as he forced down the liquor.

"You're ill," Justin said quietly. "Shall I call your doctor?''

Tom could feel the pain course through his body, a twisting of nerves that worsened in the area of his heart. He shook his head.

"Somebody better take you home. I don't have a car, but I'll call the Farm or the Triple E Building.''

"I'm all right," Tom muttered.

"You don't look it.''

"I'm not on my deathbed yet," Tom said more loudly.

Justin looked down at his hands. After a minute of silence he asked, "Do you have one of those blue tickets handy?"

"What?"

"A Security tag, they're called. I'll need one tomorrow when I come to clear out my desk."

Tom stared stupidly at him. It had happened too quickly. Justin was removing himself from his life. "You mean . . . you're quitting?"

Justin sighed. "There's no choice."

Apologize, Tom thought in that calamitous, becalmed silence. *Say you're sorry. Unbend. You don't have to say he's your son; tell him you respect him as the one decently fair man you've ever known.*

Yet mightn't apology be construed as admission?

And again that hateful, sour voice (surely a thing apart from him) was assaulting Justin. "I'll have a secretary pack your things. I wouldn't want you torn from—what's her name, Sadie? Tell me, is her cooze something special? Is that how she pushed you into this legacy idea?" As Tom spoke he was once again back in that cold kitchen, his hurt exploding against Antonia with this identical vomit of sexual horrors, the same obscenities. His self-hatred was suffocatingly painful. Surely death could be no worse than this anguish. "Is she on to some special tricks?"

The battle was over.

The dying looked at each other in mutual defeat. Justin's irises were leaden blue, his eyeballs seemed almost flat.

Silently he went to the door, letting himself out, his footsteps echoing.

Tom's fists unclenched, and he tried to relax his vocal cords to call out, but the pain clutched him by the throat, a thud, thud, thud of pain that pulled him downward and caught at his breathing. His physical anguish was heightened by the mental bereavement he had inflicted on himself. *Ahh, Antonia . . . I kept my promise*, he thought as he heard the outer door shut quietly.

III

Outside Tom's suite Justin halted, standing listless for a minute before wandering down the empty corridor. He had no plans, no destination. He halted at his own office door.

J. HUTCHINSON

He peered as though he were nearsighted. What did this name signify? That a decent, red-haired man had loved his mother enough to take him on, endow him with a patronym, warmly carry out the consecrated obligations of fatherhood. That his natural uncle had schemed to procure him a place here.

His mind blinked. *Why did both Hugh and Tom have to attack Elisse? Why am I so surprised? Didn't her father warn me?*

Funny. He had not been nearly so jarred by Hugh's bigotry as by Tom's. Well, why not? He had never revered Hugh as he had Tom.

Sighing, Justin fingered the gold lettering. His face was pulled into lines of intolerable sadness, but his predominant emotion was shame. He felt humiliated. Unable to abandon the love and loyalty he bore the unpredictable genius who had sired him, the man who had denied him on surely the most primal level there is, he shivered, thinking: *I never should have brought up the unsavory subject.*

He doesn't want me as a son.

Justin emerged into the freezing chill. He did not put on his coat or gloves—he had not worn a hat, he seldom did. Despite his mental state he walked with his usual briskness across the well-lit spaces of the deserted industrial complex, banging on the pedestrian entry at Gate One, being let out with a cheery, "So long, Mr. Hutchinson, sir."

He found himself on Jefferson. The biting, noisy wind off the Detroit River charged at him, and he was shivering violently before it occurred to him to put on his overcoat.

He thought of his mother in her hospital bed, head bandaged, face like bruised marble, her hand limp in his as she died.

A trolley clanged behind him.

He had been oblivious to the other trolleys, but for some reason the metallic noise pierced through his near cataleptic state.

Elisse, he thought. *Elisse.*

He held up his watch. After nine! *I told her I'd be back by six thirty.* He was miles from downtown. He sprinted up the broad, icy sidewalk, racing with the streetcar. The streetcar reached the stop before him, lurching onward without slowing. The icy wind stung his gasping lungs. Headlights beamed from a car traveling westward. He jerked his thumb desperately to hitch a ride. The new Dodge didn't stop.

IV

By eight Elisse, mad with worry, was sitting on the rose-colored bedspread in their room at the Book Cadillac riffling through the Detroit telephone directory. Already she had asked the hotel operator to dial Onyx's Woodland plant, which did not answer. Each shift, it seemed, had a different number, but only the day shift was listed. None of the Bridgers were in the book. Without much hope she turned to *H*. She found *Justin Hutchinson*. From Hugh's butler she got the number of the house in Indian Village that Caryll and Zoe were renting.

A woman with a heavy brogue answered.

Elisse asked for Mrs. Bridger. "Tell her it's Mrs. Hutchinson—no. Tell her it's Elisse, her sister-in-law."

"If you'll hold on, ma'am."

Elisse's shoulders hunched as she planned light ways of explaining to Justin's gorgeous sister that he was late, she was worried, and she needed some help in tracking him down. Every remark she came up with rang with either hysteria or paranoid jealousy. Elisse remembered Justin's pallor as he came through the revolving door of the Hotel Laguna. *Oh, who cares how I sound!*

The maid's voice said, "It was a mistake I was making. Mrs. Bridger's not home."

"Will you give me the number at the Farm, please?"

"She's not home!" The line went dead.

Elisse's eyes squeezed shut. After a minute she sprawled on the bed, turning over her magazine, wasting several minutes in an attempt to make sense of the meaningless symbols. *Time for action*, she thought, jumping up. She had no clear plan. But she couldn't stay here, doing *nada*.

As the elevator let her out she inhaled the scent of hothouse flowers from the lobby florist's shop. Bellhops in crimson bustled about. Couples moved purposefully toward the dining room, the women loosening their furs, the men straightening their dark wide-shouldered, double-breasted suits. *The automotive industry executive uniform*, she thought. *Praise God Justin doesn't dress that way*.

The doorman, lifting his red top hat, opened a door for her. She paced restlessly toward the lit, rococo monument in Cadillac Square, peering into taxis and glancing over her shoulder to keep an eye on the green bronze hotel entryway. The night wind slid howling between tall buildings to penetrate her coat. Bought on their one day in Los Angeles, it was California weight—Justin had suggested they try the fur department at Robinson's, but she was against fur coats on principle. She was sneezing vehemently and considering going into the hotel for a fresh handkerchief when a man's voice behind her called, "Hello!"

What a night for a pickup, Elisse thought, not turning, walking faster.

"Don't you speak to your old friends now you're married to a big shot?"

She wheeled around. Mitch Shapiro was grinning at her.

"My buddy," she cried. She had written him a letter about her marriage. It explained her defection from the organizing committee that this autumn had met four nights a week at his house. She had used those meetings to take her mind from Justin's absence. "What are *you* doing here in the Arctic Circle?"

He linked his arm in hers, and she felt the warmth of the thick body below the shabby Windbreaker.

"You're shivering," he said. "There's a drugstore. We can talk while you're getting something hot."

"I'd rather the Book Cadillac coffee shop."

"Too swanky for me."

"We're staying there. I'll sign. Come on, be a schnorrer." Elisse seldom used the sparse Yiddish of her vocabulary, but tonight, in her wretchedness, she repeated, "A schnorrer," savoring a disloyal heart's ease as she tugged Mitch into the hotel.

Insisting on a booth where she could see the lobby, she borrowed Mitch's handkerchief. After the waitress had taken the order for two soups, she sat back.

"Tell me why you're here," she said. "And what's happening at Columbia? Anything? No. I would have read if the grips had struck even a miserable, third-rate studio like Columbia."

"Martha's in charge now," he said. "I've been asked to come here."

"By whom? Harry Cohn?"

The waitress returned with steaming bowls of beef noodle soup. Mitch waited until she had gone. The broad, serious face with the smashed nose was conspiratorial. "I've joined the Party."

Elisse sneezed into his handkerchief. "I'm not surprised," she said—in fact she had often wondered what had kept him from carrying a card.

"They want me in Detroit. With Onyx shut down the unemployment'll be fierce, and they figure it's a big opportunity to organize an industrial union. So far, though, I'd have to say auto's one tough nut to crack."

"The movement'll have to get along without me," she sighed.

"What is it, Elisse?"

"Somehow I don't think I'd further Justin's career by cruising the factory gates to hand out leaflets."

"That's not what I meant. You're jumpy as a cat, you're staring at the lobby. Where is Justin, anyway?"

"Seeing his boss."

Mitch gazed at her from Slavic, almond-shaped eyes. "It's your old teacher here. You can tell me what's wrong."

Picking up her spoon, she said lightly, "These mixed marriages—ahh, what's there to joke about? My parents won't see us—they'd be sitting shiva for me, if they knew how to sit shiva. And an hour ago I called Justin's sister—if you've been reading your society columns, you know she's married to Caryll Bridger. She was home, I'm certain of it, but she refused to get on the line—as if my voice might contaminate her!"

"You poor kid."

"I went into this with open eyes." She tapped the spoon on her glass: she had not touched the soup. "I've had a lifetime to get used to being Jewish, but Justin's bewildered. This morning we drove out to Hugh Bridger's—he's Justin's guardian—and the head secretary told us *he* was out. The guy's a recluse, Mitch. It's like saying a turtle's left its shell. He's *never* out."

"Hugh Bridger's a bloodsucker. Every repressive measure at Onyx can be traced to him."

"Spare me the dialectic, Mitch. This is real people. They cared a lot about one another. And now they're hurting one another."

"I know about caring too, Elisse," he said quietly. "Why do you think I didn't join the Party until after you got married?"

Mitch?

Elisse dropped the spoon. It fell between the booth and stiff white tablecloth, but she did not try to retrieve it. *Mitch?* Elisse's physical presence and lively personality had drawn men, but that lousy high school romance had scared her, and as soon as a boyfriend got serious she backed away, contritely apologetic as if she had lured him on by false advertising. *Mitch?* Once, years ago at Berkeley, he had kissed her under the Campanile, the chimes had sounded, the syringa had been sweet in her nostrils, but her blood had stirred not. *Mitch?* Could he have misinterpreted her faithful attendance at meetings this fall as some crazy sort of crush?

"You wouldn't be taken in by me," she said breathily. "You know me for what I am. The dilettante of the Western world. In the labor movement for all the wrong, sentimental reasons. A job I despise. You're an out-and-out atheist, but you know more about the religion than I do. I run around making like a prize daughter, then marry a man my parents are dead set against. God knows I've messed up life for Justin."

"He's a very lucky guy, and my guess is he knew what he was getting into better than you did." Mitch looked down at the oyster crackers he was crushing into his half-finished soup. "That remark wasn't meant to put you on the spot. You looked blue and it seemed a way to cheer you up."

She stared at him, her eyes questioning.

"I joined for the obvious reason," he said. "I need the Party's backing." He smiled at her.

His teeth were crooked, and though his smile did not enhance his face, Elisse felt it was sincere. Relaxing back in the booth, she said, "It would have been more dramatic the other way, wouldn't it? If Justin stays at Onyx, we'll be on opposite sides of the barricades."

"What do you mean *if* he stays?"

"We're not sure yet what he'll be doing—oh! Here he is. 'Scuse me. Be right back." On small, high-heeled shoes that were stained and wet from slush, she ran from the coffee shop.

The couple formed an island amid the swirl of guests in evening clothes that were converging on the Grand Ballroom. Justin faced away from Mitch, but weariness and defeat showed in the slump of his shoulders: Elisse clutched his arm, and in spite of her expression of absorbed sympathy, an exultant blush colored her cheeks.

Mitch ate lukewarm soup as he watched them: his wide features were screwed tight into an expression of jealous despair.

341

V

Dinner with Mitch precluded conversation. After they returned to their room on the fifth floor, the couple dealt with the injuries inflicted at Woodland in their disparate ways.

Justin attempted to belittle the floundering depth of his desolation, his bewilderment, his crushing sense of unworthiness. Elisse verbally hung Tom Bridger on the barbed wire of her wit, and brought forth the possibility with near seriousness that the letters were forgeries of the devious Hugh Bridger—how could Justin have sprung from so malicious and loony a tribe? In bed all the burdensome tenderness of her heart spilled into their joining.

She did not consider the future: *Let us get through this night,* she thought, tightly clasping Justin's naked waist. Eventually, though, worn out by her earlier frantic dreads, postcoitally relaxed, she fell asleep. Her protective arms fell from Justin.

He rolled onto his back and lay staring into the darkness, sunk in a bottomless sea. Tom, faced with the truth, refused to acknowledge the relationship, even in absolute privacy. This was as far as Justin's articulated thoughts could reach. He could only conclude, with a demoralizing acceptance of inferiority, that he was not worthy to be Tom Bridger's son.

A scalding grief overcame him, and he wept silent, corrosive tears.

Elisse rolled onto her side, and he curved around her warm back, disciplining his flaccid mind into paths of practical responsibility. A man with a wife had to work. What would he do? His anguish told him to flee every reminder of Tom—the entire auto industry—while logic told him he must pin down one of the jobs that in palmier days had been offered to him.

One strategy alone stood out clear. Whatever he did, it could not be in Detroit. They could not live in Detroit.

VI

Elisse woke with a feverish sore throat. Justin ordered tea with honey, he went down to the lobby, returning with aspirin and a florist's milk glass vase containing the most perfect spray of bronze cymbidiums she had ever seen, then he hurried back again for Smith Brothers cough drops, magazines, and Listerine for her to gargle with. When he returned the second time, she lay back in the pillows: *He's using this to take his mind off his own problems,* she thought, and then was ashamed of herself. Sneezing violently, she used a fresh handkerchief. It was, she understood, Justin's gift to act even when his own private world collapsed around him.

He proved this by sitting down at the desk to make a series of telephone calls to possible employers. Marveling at his control, she listened to him, and sneezed.

At nine forty-five he was wondering out loud if he should call a doctor.

"Stop behaving as if it's terminal," she said, her voice high with the sore throat. "A cold, Justin, a cold, and you're about to catch it."

"Haven't had one in years."

"You haven't? How can I know everything about you and nothing?" She sucked on a cough drop. "I don't get sick often, either, but when I do, I'm a bear. Let me hibernate, okay? Visit a friend or something."

He sat on the bed, touching his large knuckles to her warm cheek. "Today I planned on taking you to meet Zoe."

She had not mentioned the abortive telephone call. After a brief pause she kissed his hand. "You run along, Justin. I'll be more charming after a snooze."

VII

The snow had either melted or been cleared from central Detroit, but in residential districts like Indian Village it remained. A long, sepulchral mound covered the strip of grass down the middle of Seminole while lumpy hillocks hid the lawn in front of the new half-timbered house that Caryll had leased before the wedding.

Only the master bedroom was completely furnished: Caryll, despite his overload of work before the wedding, had planned this room as a surprise for Zoe when they returned from their honeymoon, filching time from designing the Seven to sketch ideas that he mailed to Sloane's in New York. An enormous sculptured ivory Chinese rug covered the floor, silver tea paper gleamed with burnished depth on the walls, the stalactites of modern Baccarat chandeliers were echoed by the stalagmites of crystal ornaments, and the enormous divan bed, raised up two shallow steps, was upholstered in white slubbed silk. As Caryll had intended, the room resembled a fairy-tale ice palace, a background for his bride's superbly vivid coloring.

A few minutes after ten she was reclining back into a hill of minuscule white lace pillows, slowly, luxuriously licking the sweet brown topping from a schnecke.

The voluble Belgian lady's maid came into the room, announcing, "Monsieur Hutchinson is downstairs."

"Justin?" Zoe sat upright, jolting the breakfast tray on her lap. The Belleek cup fell, spilling dregs of coffee across the inserted satin initial of the white silk blanket cover that was part of the trousseau linens Justin had paid for. "Alone?"

"*Oui*, madame, he is alone. I told Mary to show him into the library, so—"

"Take this," Zoe interrupted in a high, excited voice, shoving impatiently at the tray, popping the small coffee cake into her mouth.

While the maid drew her bath, Zoe dragged clothes from the dressing room closets, strewing them across the bed and chairs, finally selecting a yellow Vionnet wool.

It was eleven when she descended the curving staircase. At the bottom step she halted, uncertainty flickering in her magnificent dark eyes. What if Justin's wife had told him about last night's unanswered telephone call? Zoe still loved Hugh—probably the more for evading her—and respected him, yet she could not for the life of her comprehend his screwy denunciations of Justin's wife's religion. Her own emotion was primitive. A volcano of hot jealousy. This woman had stolen Justin from her. She had been unable to pick up the extension because the words *Mrs. Justin Hutchinson* were quivering along her nerves like lit gunpowder.

Justin had heard her footsteps and come to the door of the library. He held out his arms.

With a small, wordless cry she ran to him. Hugging him, she said, "The same brother."

He kissed her forehead. "Shouldn't I be?"

"You're married."

"There's a non sequitur if I ever heard one." He took her hands, holding her away. "I was right, wasn't I, Zozo? You've never been more gorgeous. Marriage obviously agrees with you."

Zoe's old, unfettered trust asserted itself, and she replied honestly, "I'm delirious, seeing you."

Justin's shadowed eyes were grave. "What about Caryll?"

"Oh, you know him. He's always been swell to me," she said with a deprecatory shrug. Marriage hadn't changed *that*: though she was extremely fond of Caryll, his tender, domesticated adoration elicited her worst qualities. "I told them to fix all your favorites for lunch. Spinach bisque, mixed grill, roast potatoes—"

"I'll have to take a raincheck," he interrupted. "Elisse isn't well. A rotten cold. That's why she didn't come along." There was not a hint of anger or condemnation in his apology.

Zoe gave a relieved nod. The pout of her lovely, full mouth was sympathetic, yet there was a discernible jerk in her walk as she led him back to the nearly empty library. "I'm dying to meet her."

"She's very eager to meet you, too." Justin bent over to light a cigarette. "Did Caryll mention anything about me?"

"Yesterday I told him you were in Detroit, and he went bananas with relief. He counts on you in the worst way, Justin." She added, "This morning he ran off at the crack of dawn to the Farm. Mr. Bridger"—Zoe still thought of her caustically unpredictable father-in-law this way—"isn't feeling well."

Justin dropped his cigarette. "What's wrong with him?"

"Uncle Olaf brought him home last night with a stomach upset. Mrs. Bridger wanted Caryll to convince him to call Dr. Fairburn."

"You're sure that's all it is? A stomach problem?"

"Caryll wasn't worried in the least. But the poor baby—there's some sort of metal casting, and he's always up a tree when he has to fill in for his father at that sort of thing. It really tears him to pieces. Justin, this afternoon you go in and take over."

Justin bent to retrieve his cigarette, meticulously fingering ash from parquet as he said, "I'm not with Onyx anymore."

"You're *what*?" she cried.

"I've quit."

"But . . . ." The lovely, confused dark eyes were fixed on him. "Did lightning strike or something?"

"In a way."

"Justin, you've never worked anywhere else."

"Tell me another," he sighed.

"I don't understand at all."

"It's pretty complicated," he said. "Anyway, Ford needs a manager at their Shreveport assembly. I have an appointment with Edsel tomorrow."

Zoe's breath was trapped someplace deep inside her. "You mean you're leaving Detroit," she whispered.

"I have to," he said expressionlessly. "It won't work, Elisse and me living here."

"You're the only family I have!"

"The Bridgers all dote on you. Caryll worships you."

"They're not related!"

"Zoe, please, I can't stand a tantrum today."

"You're leaving me!"

"You're not eight anymore, Zozo, we're both grown-ups. Married."

A sob welled from her, one involuntary ululation of grief. Yet what did it matter if he departed physically or not? That woman had snatched him forever. He was irretrievably lost. The one person on this earth with whom Zoe could be her own egocentric, willful, yet delightfully vibrant self had deserted her, and she was forever trapped in a black hole, eternally deprived of the light of her own personality.

Justin drew her to the room's one piece of upholstery, the couch that had been delivered yesterday, and sat patting her shoulder. Eventually she wiped her eyes.

"*Pax?*" he asked as he had when they were children.

"*Pax.*"

"You know that if you need me for anything, no matter how small, you can count on me. I'll be here on the double."

Nodding, she examined him in a new, detached way. "Justin, you look terrible," she said. "As if you haven't slept in weeks."

"This decision doesn't exactly have me dancing." He shook his head. "What a way to start married life."

"Poor Elisse," Zoe said automatically.

"She's about the least pitiable person I know. Very crisp and clean-edged. I get obnoxious about her virtues, so when you meet her you'll find out for yourself. She has no sister, either. I'm positive you'll end up as close as Caryll and me." At this he unaccountably reddened. Taking out a fresh cigarette, he paused to light it. "If you aren't worried about catching cold, let's make our lunch tomorrow. At the hotel. Then I can introduce you two."

Zoe knew she could not force herself into the same building—

much less the same room—with the girl who had stolen her brother, yet she had long ago discovered it easier, as well as kinder, to accept invitations, then beg off at the last minute, so her mouth curved into a smile and she said, "What a fine idea."

"I'll call you first thing in the morning," Justin said, gripping her shoulders, hugging her, kissing her forehead.

Zoe felt an unexpected twinge of shame at how important her fraudulent acceptance seemed to him.

VIII

Justin, though, was the one that canceled.

He had been back at the Book Cadillac maybe an hour when the telephone rang. Elisse picked it up.

"Mother!" she cried. "How did you find us? . . . Yes . . . That was clever. . . . Can't you speak a little louder?"

"Elisse. What is it?" Justin asked.

"I see. . . . Yes, Mother. . . . Yes, but what do the other doctors say?" Tears were streaming down Elisse's cheeks, and she dabbed at them with her wadded handkerchief. "Mother, he'll be fine. . . . Yes, of course we'll be there. . . . Don't be silly. . . . As soon as we can." She held the phone to her bed jacket. "Daddy's had some sort of attack."

Justin reached for the instrument. "Mrs. Kaplan, where is he?"

"The Cedars of Lebanon Hospital," said the girlish, faraway voice. "Dr. Levin won't tell me anything."

"I'll try to get through to him right away, then I'll be back to you."

"Oh, thank you ever so much."

"The express leaves Chicago at nine. We'll be on it. Mrs. Kaplan, do you have Dr. Levin's number handy? And better give me the hospital number." He opened his small morocco notebook.

Elisse was already taking clothes from the closet.

BOOK FOUR
The Amalgamated Automobile Workers

When they tie the can to a union man,
  Sit down! Sit down!
When the speedup comes, just twiddle your thumbs.
  Sit down! Sit down!
When the boss won't talk, don't take a walk.
  Sit down! Sit down!

CHAPTER 22

"When were they booked?" Justin interrupted, a pruned, legal query.

"This morning. They were held overnight," Mitch replied. "The police administered their routine clouting."

Justin's lips shaped the words *sons of bitches*. "And the charges?"

"The usual. Illegal assembly and disturbing the peace."

The telephone rang. Dust flew in the sunlight as Mitch reached across the desk to answer. He held the receiver to his good ear. "AAW headquarters, Shapiro speaking. . . . Of course I know who you are. . . . Yes, Pete Fannin's wife. . . ."

December 10, 1934.

A warm, sunny Monday in Los Angeles, the windows were open in Mitch's one-room bachelor apartment, which doubled as the office of Amalgamated Automobile Workers, one of the numerous small locals that swirled futilely around the Depression-stymied industry. The space was crammed with Mitch's battered desk, two gray metal filing cabinets, a stack of folding chairs, a carton of handbills that gave off the thick odor of mimeograph chemicals. To the doors of the Murphy bed were thumbtacked photographs of Mitch with hulking, beatle-browed John L. Lewis, Mitch with William Z. Foster, Earl Browder, and others in the hierarchies of Labor and the Communist party.

Justin, to give the illusion of not eavesdropping, had turned to look out the window. At thirty-four his hair had turned a premature, glossy gray, a hereditary trait that served him well by endowing him with the appearance of vigorous, dependable maturity so prized in the legal profession.

Two days after Edsel Ford had written offering him the head post at Ford's Shreveport assembly plant, a letter had arrived from Henry Ford countermanding the offer—an everyday humiliation inflicted by the tough old man on his talented, sensitive son. By then, however, the correspondence was irrelevant. Justin could not abandon Mr. Kaplan, pale-lipped from gallbladder surgery, incarcerated behind the bars of his hospital bed, or Mrs. Kaplan, weeping and totally at sea. Elisse was ill with constant nausea—caused by her pregnancy, they were soon to learn. Life conspired to keep him in Los Angeles. To Justin it seemed inevitable that he enroll at USC Law School. He was well into his first year, a father himself, before he accepted the implications of leaving the industry that his biological father had almost single-handedly founded to enter Claude Hutchinson's profession. Subconsciously he had desired to carry on the tradition as well as the name—if, unfortunately, not the genes—of the man whom he posthumously loved, respected, and for most of his life had thought of as "Father."

Though Justin graduated into the teeth of the Depression, he was invited to join the two most prestigious Los Angeles law firms. He and Elisse decided, however, that money and position were not fitting goals in this iniquitous new decade. He turned both down. The small family had continued to manage on the checks that arrived quarterly from London. Justin's fledgling private practice—busy from the very first—consisted mostly of *pro bono* referrals from the American Civil Liberties Union and unpaid cases from Mitch's floundering union. Had Justin been forced to grade his two careers according to personal fulfillment, he would have awarded far lower marks to these years of fighting eviction notices and collecting back pay, yet his face wore a sheen of content. Buoyed by a happy marriage, he shed his vitality and grace in a manner he did not recognize.

Mitch hung up. "Mollie Fannin. Another sad story." He shook his head. "Her husband was a punch-press operator at the Chevrolet assembly. Pete. A couple of months ago he joined AAW, he paid his dues secretly, but still they found out. He was fired. Blacklisted. They're starving. Mollie wanted to know if I'd heard of a job for her, any kind of work, even for a couple of days. Not because they're down to eating fried dough, but because she wants to give her children Christmas. The excuses they make up! As if we aren't all in the same boat."

"Maybe she does want some stocking stuffers."

"Santa Claus? When the system's falling apart?"

Justin smiled. "You'll have to bear with us human beings, Mitch. Most of us think about the weather and our kids, not the Revolution." He took out his worn wallet. "Have her clean up headquarters."

"Donations should go to the AAW relief fund."

"Nevertheless. This is for Mollie Fannin." Justin set four crumpled ones on the desk. "It's all I have on me. Elisse handles the finances."

"And she's even more sentimental about giving," Mitch said, shoving the bills into his pocket. He got up to unfold a banged metal chair. "Here, Justin, sit down. There's something I have to discuss with you." He waited until Justin sat. "A week from Thursday this won't be headquarters."

Justin asked sympathetically, "Been asked to move again?"

"For once the landlord's on our side," Mitch said. "No. I'm driving back to Detroit."

"Not again."

Mitch had already made three attempts to organize a local in the automotive capital: on his last tour of duty he had tackled Woodland. Dickson Keeley, now head of Security, had personally kicked him out of Gate One, breaking several of his ribs.

"I'm wasting time here, Justin. What's the point of attacking the tentacles? You have to go for the heart."

The unsettling bleakness in Justin's eyes was not connected to Mitch's persistent failures. When reminded of Detroit, province of the Bridgers, the humiliation of being the family bastard drenched him while at the same time he was stricken with pangs of loneliness for his blood kin. With difficulty he extracted the last Camel from a crumpled pack: years ago he had given up frivolities like imported cigarettes.

Mitch was saying, ". . . in Wayne County fifty-three percent of the auto workers are unemployed. It's murder there. Workers are worse off than slaves—slaves are guaranteed food. You bring in mass production and men become interchangeable, more dispensable than the cheapest tool."

"Conditions are always worse—"

"Children are scavenging through the garbage cans," Mitch interrupted. "Come with me, Justin."

"*What?*"

"Drive back to Detroit with me."

"Impossible." Justin's lips were tensed. "I have cases on the docket all month."

"A vacation isn't what I had in mind. You were trained in every department at Onyx. You'll have no trouble getting a job in the industry."

The implication of these words sank gradually into Justin's brain. "You want me to become an organizing director for AAW?"

Mitch stared across the cluttered desk. "Get wise to yourself, Justin. It's where you belong."

"And what about my family? What about them?"

"Elisse can bring the kids later, on the train," Mitch said. "I know you're not political, so there's no point arguing on ideological grounds." Mitch's own ideology had never particularly meshed with the party line, and he had nearly quit when Central Committee ordered him to head an unemployment council. He belonged, short, muscular body and tough, blinkered soul, to the labor movement. "It's a moral issue, Justin. You're no moral coward; you don't evade the issues. You're a natural for this. It's getting worse back there, not better. You can't shut your eyes to that. Detroit's one big, festering sore."

"I can't change that."

"It's time we had a top man on our side—don't look so indignant. You know you're a natural leader. You could convince those bitter, frightened men that their one hope is collective bargaining." Mitch paused, adding in a less resonant, more personal tone, "You're close to the Bridgers."

"Onyx? Is that where you're going? You want *me* to try to unionize *Onyx*?"

"Outside of Ford it's the most repressive company there is. Woodland's turned into a prison with Keeley's brigades of plug-uglies." Mitch clasped his bicep to his newly mended ribs. "Take it from me."

Justin sat very still. Any movement and he would be on his feet screaming at this infuriating zealot, his best friend. "If it's some jolly tie-in with the Bridgers you're looking for, that lets me out."

"I know you don't have your hand in the pocket of your brother-in-law's family, but you certainly know them. And every bit of inside information about Tom and Hugh Bridger is an advantage."

Justin's hands were shaking. Putting out his cigarette, he clasped them to his knees. His weakest bastion was unwittingly being stormed. How he missed Tom, Hugh, Caryll! How he longed to see Zoe! She had never replied to his letters. When headlines informed him of the birth of Lynn, the oldest of his three nieces, he had sent a sterling porringer: Caryll had written a thank-you note, signing both names, and now the two men corresponded with occasional, faintly elegiac letters that spoke of the past and seldom mentioned their divergent present lives.

Mitch was watching him.

"I'm not going with you," Justin said decisively.

"Oppressed and oppressor, there's only two sides."

"One more, I'm afraid, Mitch. The lawyer's side." Justin managed a smile at the old saw, and got to his feet. "Los Angeles is our home."

Mitch opened a drawer of the nearest filing cabinet where letters were mounded. He shoved a random handful into a folder. "Take these along and read them," he said. "Then make up your mind."

II

That afternoon Miss Gunther telephoned Elisse to explain that Ben was being kept late and it was necessary for her to pick him up. Having received other high-pitched summonses from Ben's teachers, Elisse, unnerved, left the gingerbread ingredients on the kitchen table to run in and waken Tonia from her nap.

The school was six residential blocks to the east. Elisse pushed the lacquered English pram by stucco bungalows with neat front yards sporting recently transplanted red poinsettias and jolly red Santas. Here and there a dark fir tree was festooned with colored lights, attesting that the householder could afford to waste electricity. *This Depression's not all it's cracked up to be,* Elisse thought.

Outside the second-grade classroom waited Miss Gunther: the teacher's gray hair crinkled in the same shade and rough texture as her eternal gray tweed suit. Elisse rocked the well-sprung perambulator so that Tonia would not cry while the district attorney voice rapped out a report of Ben's latest fight over his theft of another boy's lunch.

Elisse glanced through the glass inset of the door. Alone in the empty schoolroom, Ben surely realized that this muted tirade was about him, yet he sat in a rear desk gazing toward the blackboard with his chin lifted in disdainful calm. He had Elisse's delicate frame and her curly light brown hair, which at the moment was tangled over his wide forehead, further shadowing the deep-set blue eyes. Elisse caught her breath at the miracles of heredity. His peachy skin, dusted with golden freckles, clung to the facial bones, giving an odd, adult intensity to his expression.

He leaned back, regarding a thumb before chewing on the nail: no nail-biter, he must have felt a roughness. His hands were sensitive, and though he seldom cried, a grazed knuckle could cause tears of pain—the hands of a musician said his grandfather, who was teaching him the violin. Ben, sharply, nervously intelligent, had skipped a semester. A loner, he never exchanged visits with his classmates. Elisse loved him fiercely, and did not understand him at all.

"He's never had this kind of problem, stealing," she said.

The gold chain of Miss Gunther's pince-nez shook. "I found the lunch pail in his desk."

"I didn't mean I doubted you," Elisse said, torn between defending her son and not alienating the gray witch who had him in her fell clutch six hours a day. "Did you ask him to explain?"

"That," sniffed Miss Gunther, "is up to the parents."

Witch, Elisse thought again.

As they started home Elisse asked Ben, "Didn't your own sandwich and cupcake please you?"

"There wasn't anything in Jerrold's pail, just a couple of hard heels of bread."

"Oh, my God," Elisse muttered. "He is hungry."

"Maybe he deserves to be."

"Taking food from people is wrong, Ben."

The boy's freckles darkened. "I didn't start it."

"But you did swipe his lunch! As soon as we get home you'll go to your room!" Tears standing in her eyes, she gripped the perambulator handle. She decided she was an inadequate mother, she was furious at herself for losing her temper, she felt sorry for the child,

Jerrold; she was perceiving through the blur that the houses with their cheery seasonal adornments were not places of comfort and joy but caves in which deprivation lurked.

She was setting the table and Tonia was gumming a cracker in the high chair when Justin let himself in the back door. After he had kissed her, Elisse rolled her eyes in the direction of the loud, remarkably assured violin attack on Mozart. "Trouble, trouble."

Justin tickled the baby's stomach, touching his lips to satiny, near white hair. "How's my Tonia?" A chortle and beautiful baby smile exhibiting two bottom teeth and clumps of melted Zweiback was his response. "What sort of trouble?"

"Interrogate the defendant."

"I'm sure he'll be less evasive."

"You males," she said in the mock dismay she used when the two drove off on Saturday mornings to the beach or Griffith Park: she and the baby could have gone along, but she knew exactly how much Justin and Ben cherished their dusty, boisterous hours alone. "It's six twenty-five. Mother and Daddy'll be here at quarter to."

III

As Justin opened the door, Ben put down the violin. While the pressure mark faded from his jaw, he paid rigorous attention to refolding the silk handkerchief.

Justin asked, *"Eine Kleine Nachtmusik?"*

"Yeah," Ben mumbled, not looking up. "Grandpa gave it to me yesterday and I'm surprising him tonight." He was resentful, not of Justin but of his fear of Justin, in much the same way that a fox cub resents it paw rather than the cruel-toothed trap holding it.

Justin sat on the bed watching his son fit the half-size instrument and bow in the worn red plush of the case. "I was in the Georgia Street police station this afternoon."

"How come?"

"Six men were picketing the Chevrolet factory. Last week they were fired and then the company hired six other men to take their jobs at half the money. Their placards told their side. They had a permit, but some toughs came along and pushed them around."

Ben sat next to Justin, whose weight sagged the mattress springs so that their bodies touched. "Did they fight back?"

"It was more of a shoving match. None of the others was arrested, only the pickets."

"So you went down and got them out of jail?"

"Not me, Ben. The law. The law gives us—"

"The right of havas corpus—"

"Habeas corpus, Ben. Very good."

"You told me. They give money, it's called posting bail, to show they'll come back for the trial," Ben said. "It's not fair, only the pickets being punished. That's how it is in school. Miss Gunther, she stinks. Even when it's the other guy's fault, she blames me. And you should see her. She writes one word on the blackboard then spells it over and over. It's so boring!"

Ben's retentive and restless intelligence was no delight to his teachers: he finished every assignment first and then ostentatiously, disruptively, whistled complex classical tunes: Bach or Mozart.

"She has to help the others, Ben."

"Dummies!"

"They aren't," Justin said. "They need more time than you, that's all. You learn very quickly. That's a big responsibility, Ben. If a person is cleverer or stronger or richer, that gives him an obligation to help others."

"Hah!"

"That's something I believe."

"And what about me?" Ben cried. And because he still remained innocently unguarded with his father, he exposed his burns. "Should I let them hit me, take my things? Call me swear words?"

Ben had been skipped this semester. An insolent newcomer to A2, younger and kitten-boned, he was picked on mercilessly. For his part, he was incapable of letting any insult pass.

Justin sighed. "When I first came to America, I had a bad time."

"No joke?"

"No joke certainly. I was in a fight, and after that everyone sided with the others. Have you ever heard the word *coventry*?"

Ben shook his head.

"It means, nobody speaks to you. That's what happened to me. I was very lonely. I hated that school."

"Yeah," Ben sighed. That his father, all-knowing, all-wise, stronger than God, had suffered his own torments spread wan prickles of comfort through him, and he pressed closer to the large, warm body.

358

Justin hugged his son. "This morning I was talking to Uncle Mitch. He wants me to go to Detroit with him and work for the AAW. I said it was impossible to move us all there. But remember what we were talking about a minute ago? People having an obligation to help others who aren't as well-off? That's made me think. You know something, Ben? To me the most wonderful world would be one where nobody *needs* help."

"Umm." The conversation, having drifted away from the personal, no longer interested Ben, and he kicked the metal taps of his heels against the bed frame.

"In Detroit so many people are out of work that they'll do anything to get a job. What beats me is how the big automobile companies take advantage of their weakness."

Ben burst out, "What are you going to do to me?"

Justin looked down at his son. "Tell me what happened."

"Yesterday Jerrold beat me up, took my lunch pail, he ate everything and broke the Thermos. Mom was really mad when she saw it was broken. I didn't tell her Jerrold did it. Now today, he called me a curse word, so I took his pail. Miss Gunther, she found it and blamed everything on me. And all *he* had was cruddy stale bread."

"What did you do with it?" Justin's question, deep and rough, reverberated through Ben's body.

"Dumped it in the trash," Ben whispered, frightened.

"I'm sorry you were bullied by Jerrold. That was wrong of him. But regardless, you're never to take food from anybody. Ever. As long as you live."

"I won't."

"You promise that?"

"On my best honor, Dad."

Justin's clasp tightened. "Good, Ben. Good." He kissed the brown tangle as he had kissed Tonia's hair a few minutes earlier.

Ben scowled against the flooding joy of his relief.

"There. That's settled," Justin said. "We better get washed up. Grandma and Grandpa'll be here any minute."

IV

After Tonia bewitchingly acquiesced to the cuddling and belly prodding of her grandparents and was tucked in her maple crib, Elisse announced dinner. A salad of sliced avocado, which even after eight years in California, Justin still fell on as a delicacy, was followed by stuffed veal breast surrounded by richly glowing vegetables. The adults talked and ate with gusto: Ben dug a trough in his mashed potatoes to bury his string beans and carrots. The gingerbread, swathed in whipped cream and drenched in turn by ladles of thick butterscotch sauce, silenced everyone.

"A gourmet meal," pronounced Mr. Kaplan, wiping his mouth. With a maroon paisley scarf knotted at his plump throat and his shirt collar spread outside the lapels of his navy sport jacket in the prevailing Hollywood style, he looked smartly prosperous. And prosperous he was. With the advent of sound, films relied on music to set mood. Harris Kaplan now bowed his viola in the highly talented, highly paid, studio orchestra. The financial tables had turned. He was far richer than his son-in-law. Justin's annual trust income, $3,110, was the equal of what USC paid its tenured full professors, but in these depressed years Mr. Kaplan's $10,000 glittered like a vein of gold.

Ben mumbled "MayIbeexcused" and bolted from the table, snatching a handful of mint wafers.

Mrs. Kaplan's pretty, crumpled face was wistful. "You really have your hands full, dear. Looking after Ben and Tonia, shopping for food, cooking." Both Kaplans chipped away at Elisse's socialist madness of coping without a live-in maid, which she and Justin could well afford.

Mr. Kaplan was swaying back and forth across the table like a sun-satisfied pigeon as he explained a nuance of a concert to Justin.

Elisse's cheeks were pink. *Who would ever believe*, she thought contentedly, *that these middle-aged children once rejected my husband?*

"Be quiet, everybody. I'm ready!" Ben shouted from the connecting living room. A fine gloss covering his intent, peach-hued face, Buster Brown shoes planted firmly, his thin body skirmishing in all directions, he fingered and bowed brightly luminous chords through the food-scented room. His false notes were remarkably few considering that he had left his music stand in his room.

Promptly at nine Mrs. Kaplan put on her new broadtail coat and Mr. Kaplan got his fedora. The studio orchestra had an early call.

It was an evening—placid, *gemütlich*, cherished—like a hundred others.

V

Elisse emerged from the kitchen rubbing lotion on her hands, smiling at Justin, who sat at the cleared dining table, his briefcase open in front of him. She stretched on the green sofa, head in the glow of the lamp, opening *A Farewell to Arms*. After a minute she rested the buckram-bound library book open on her breasts, surrendering to a delicately spun sense of happiness and well-being. Sated with her own cooking, contentedly weary, she had no work to get back to, no projects to complete, no compulsion even to finish the novel; she simply let herself drift without thought or inhibition, giving no more consideration to time than the crickets did outside. She felt herself part of their sweet, mournful chittering, part of the cool, damp California night, part of the two children sleeping in their wallpapered bedrooms, part of this large, thoughtful man. Stretching languorously, she said, "Nice Justin," and went over to kiss pewter hair that smelled faintly of tobacco smoke. "What're those?"

"Mitch's letters. From men he knows at Woodland."

As she heard the plant name, the joy drained from Elisse's face. One delicate eyebrow shot up. "He shares his mail?"

"You might as well hear the worst. He's going back to Detroit in a week or so. He wants me to drive with him."

"The very season for a pleasure jaunt through the frozen Middle West," she said, sitting at the table, the better to watch him.

"He wants us to move there. He's asked me to work for the AAW as an organizer."

"That's Mitch all over! Oh, damn. Justin, the idea's too ridiculous to discuss."

"Just what I told him."

"Firmly, I trust."

"Yes, firmly."

"There's no need to feel guilty, Justin. Handle his legal work, contribute to all his strike funds, that's enough noblesse oblige for anyone, even you."

"Yes. But something's terribly wrong there," he said, frowning.

"It's called the Depression," she said. "We have it right here in Los Angeles. Did Ben tell you about that fight? He took a boy's lunch and there was only stale bread."

"He explained the whole thing, and promised he'd never take food from anybody again."

"That should end hard times in southern California," she said tartly. Clasping her hands on wood that she had polished this morning, she peered at him. "You can't be taking Mitch seriously, Justin. Aside from giving up your practice, it would mean Detroit. And we both know Detroit's poison for you. Pure poison. Tell me you aren't serious."

Justin picked up a typewritten sheet. "Listen to this, Elisse," he said. " 'The minute you enter Woodland a fear comes over you. Not all Security men wear uniforms, so you can't know who they are. They're all around. Talking on the assembly line is forbidden. Even at the break you're meant to keep quiet. Say something and you might feel a tap on your shoulder. Then off you go to Gate Four.' " Justin glanced up at her. "That's where the Employment Office is, it means you'll get your dismissal slip. 'You're constantly spied on, and you feel the eyes on you even after you've shut your own front door.' "

"Nice style," she said. "Good sense of drama." Her voice was high, tense. "You haven't answered my question."

Justin picked up a piece of brown paper that was crumpled as if it had been cut from a grocery bag. " 'The line is so speeded up you can't imagine. I get home twitchy and jump all over the kids. I don't sleep so good. My bowels isn't right. And I'm not much good to the wife anymore. But we got food on the table and I'm paying off the mortgage, so I'm holding on for dear life.' "

The letter had brought tears to Elisse's eyes, and she turned so Justin would not see. "Unions are Mitch's life, not yours. He wants to use you."

"He didn't write these."

"Let him get somebody from A F of L to go with him."

"Who else knows the industry like me?" Justin pushed the letters into a heap. "It's so brutally unfair, Elisse, to grind down poor devils already desperate."

It was, finally, that very quality she adored in him—his innate and never dormant principle of equity—that touched her off. "No need to go to Detroit, Justin! To play Jesus Christ *you* don't need to go anyplace. You don't need wood and nails! All *you* have to do is stand up and hold out your arms!'' Her words rang. ''I'm going to bed!''

A half hour later he came in. She lay tense, facing the windows, and he must have sensed she was still awake, yet he did not turn on the light as he undressed. As was his habit, he stepped into both children's rooms. The clock, ticking loudly, measured his movements.

In bed he clasped her shoulder, pulling her toward him. For several ticks she held apart, then she turned to press against him, splaying her hands on his spine above and below the waist. The nightgown made a silky, slithered sound as she shucked it, and her hair, longer now, trailed on his belly as she flurried brief, ardent kisses on his erect penis. Then she straddled him. Aphrodisiac scents of their bodily moistures blessing their bed, his fingers weaving patterns on her breasts, she glided up and down. All at once she halted, throwing back her head in a kind of waiting trance, her only movement a violent pulse at the throat. He pulled her roughly onto the mattress and, he above, they thrust toward each other as if to annihilate their individual identities.

VI

Mitch drove East alone.

Justin spent that warm Christmas season pondering the evidence. On one side, the misery endemic in Detroit.

Detroit had been largely ignored by the labor movement. The AFL's primary concern was to protect skilled craftsmen, and auto workers were for the most part unskilled, assembly-line workers. Unhappy about their hours and working conditions, desperate about their lack of job security, they formed minuscule industrial unions that lacked leadership. The automobile companies squashed these chaotic little locals cruelly, firing and blackballing the membership so they could not get another job in auto, often inflicting violence. Justin had searched the newspapers for reports of frays that he knew about. He had never found a word. The omission affected him deeply: he felt obligated to go where he could most help in the silent, unfair struggle.

On the other hand, there was his family. First he would ruminate about Elisse. This was her home, she was very close to her parents. Justin would also find it difficult to leave his pretty-faced, vague mother-in-law and the stout little musician with the good-natured, rattling tongue.

And what about Ben, many-faceted, sullen genius of the family? How would a child so complicated transplant? And Tonia, his sweet baby, would probably have a cold all winter.

Justin's decision would have been easier had Mitch chosen a company other than Onyx. His filial love, hatred, resentment, admiration, passed all telling; these confused emotions clouded every issue, and he asked himself whether he could work effectively against Tom. Tom, whose voice came over the air each Sunday at the end of *The Onyx Family Variety Hour*, his flat, dry tones deriding the governmental agencies and the unions that aimed to tell a man how to "run his own shop." Was he, Justin Hutchinson, strong enough to cut that tangle of love and animus to fight what would be a long, bitter, probably vain battle?

Don't think about Tom, he told himself.

The question is whether to put my family on the line.

Nightly, Elisse watched her husband chain-smoke Camels. Fearing what further devastation Detroit might wreak on him, she was terrified lest he decide, as she already had, that Detroit was where they belonged.

CHAPTER 23

Dickson Keeley's star had begun its swift ascendency on May 25, 1932, two and a half years before.

That fine spring day Zoe and her two little girls, Lynn and Clarice (Petra was not born until a year later), were on the way to a birthday party in Grosse Pointe, where the young family now lived. On that quiet stretch of Ottawa Lane where the box hedge grew high, a black Ford sedan was parked catercorner so it was impossible to get around. Zoe's custom-built Swallow halted. From the backseat of the sedan jumped three men with white silk scarves tied around their faces. They brandished Thompson submachine guns. Zoe's muscular chauffeurs were clouted senseless. The governess, watching through the glass panel, turned pale and slumped fainting in her jump seat.

Zoe had always possessed physical valor. Erect on the ostrich leather upholstery, she enfolded Lynn's and Clarice's tiny gloved hands, saying with a breathy heartiness, "Let's pretend we're in a gangster movie."

The scarved men did not attempt to break the shatterproof glass that separated the limousine's passengers from the driver. Suddenly, inexplicably, they leaped back into the Ford, which squealed away.

It was at this hour, three, that the afternoon mail was routinely delivered to Caryll's office. One of the envelopes was typed *Personal and Urgent*. The letter was a collage of newspaper lettering: *One million in twenties behind the same hedge by four A.M. tomorrow morning or mother and girls will get acid in their faces. No police. No Security. No monkey business. We can get at them whenever we want.* Caryll's wealth inevitably attracted the notice of cranks, hoodlums, grifters. Threats like this he handed over to Police Chief Arden. He dropped the paper, choking with horror . . . His pretty little girls . . . his superlatively beautiful wife. He was buzzing his secretary to get him Chief Arden when his private line rang. Zoe's high, breathless voice was on the other end.

Tom, pale and tense, drove his shaking son downtown to the Michigan Bank of Commerce, a mustard-brick skyscraper whose lower floors were circled with Aztec tiled mosaics—Tom owned it. The president himself went to the dozen or so institutions that the bank controlled, searching out the prescribed denominations. Before midnight the Bridgers had deposited two tin suitcases of cash under the box hedge.

Hugh spoke privately to Dickson Keeley. Keeley held ex officio powwows with certain of his connections.

The following afternoon when Caryll and Tom returned to Ottawa Lane, they found the tin suitcases intact. Later in the week a Ford sedan with the bodies of three unidentified men was fished from Lake Erie: this might have been coincidence—the Oakland Sugar House Gang, the Purple Gang, and Palma and Tocco's men routinely slaughtered one another—but in the glove compartment were tucked three white silk scarves.

At Hugh's suggestion, Tom awarded Dickson Keeley the job of protecting the family. The Bridger homes in Detroit became Keeley's personal beat. In addition, Keeley assigned handpicked crews to the gatehouse of Tom and Maud's restored plantation in Virginia. (Tom Bridger had indeed suffered a coronary the day of Justin's departure. In response to doctors' orders that her husband "get way from it all," Maud had purchased the Virginia estate.) And, finally, Keeley arranged for the guarding of Caryll and Zoe's yacht, *Beaufort*, of their hacienda in Palm Beach and their pied-à-terre at the Sherry-Netherland in New York.

The following winter Colonel Hazelford retired as the Onyx security chief. Tom, bedeviled by the seventy percent shrinkage in car sales and fearful that despite Onyx's decent pay envelopes a union might further deprive him of management power in his beleaguered domain, appointed Dickson Keeley as Colonel Hazelford's successor.

The Onyx executives, including Colonel Hazelford, had moved their offices to the new tall Tower near Gate Five, but when Keeley took over, Security went back to the old Administration Building. In a remote, sprawling warren a Gamewall board blinked red lights at the movements of Security patrols in Woodland, and switchboards lit up constantly with the required daily calls from those three thousand khaki-uniformed men, as well as from the plainclothesmen who in turn spied on them. Here was the accounting office for the slush fund—at Hugh's advice, in every plant in the country one Onyx man in four was paid a few dollars beyond his clock time to report on any union activity, however tentative.

Tom thoroughly mistrusted Keeley, and chafed at the mean-spirited times that made him a necessity. Caryll despised the man for his strutting cockiness and hoodlum friends. Yet since the acid-throwing threat both Bridgers had relied on Keeley to protect their families, and later they saw him as the necessary evil that allowed them to maintain their open-shop policy. Neither clearly discerned the miasma of fear that had spread through their clean, well-lit factories.

II

That second week of January 1935 a blizzard blew down from the Arctic Circle, and although an Onyx snowplow had cleared the miles from the Farm to the city, Tom decided to stay home. The annual financial reports had come. After breakfast he went gloomily to the library, where he sat frowning over the wide sheets. Onyx had lost 6.7 million, and the Swallow Company, small as it was, had dropped an additional million. At Caryll's dogged insistence he had bought Swallow in 1930, when it was about to go into receivership. A luxury car! Who could afford luxury nowadays? They had sold less than a thousand Swallows this year. Both deficits would come out of Tom's personal funds, as had similar sums the previous year. Tom always had been indifferent to cash cold in a vault; anteing up was not what had caused his oppression. It was this damn paralyzing impotency. He had lost control. *Maybe it's time to throw in the towel*, he thought, then visualized the hordes of workers who poured daily through his gates. If he threw in the towel, they'd be tossed in with it.

A vicious gust of wind tore at fir branches, and he did not hear the low buzz that meant he had a call. At the second sounding he lifted the telephone.

Hugh said, "So you didn't go in today."

"Seemed like perfect weather to look over the books," Tom replied. "What's up?"

"Hutchinson's coming to Detroit!"

Tom's hand trembled and the gold pencil fell. The brothers rarely mentioned Justin. At first Tom's coronary had prevented frank discussion, and after his recovery it seemed safer not to talk about the young man's self-exile. Tom was uncertain what, exactly, Hugh had told Justin; Hugh could not know whether Justin had given him away by speaking of the letters. Avoidance and uncertainty, while enabling them to coexist and converse about business matters, had eroded their relationship into jumpy fear on Hugh's part and a straitjacket remoteness on Tom's.

"Tom? Still there?"

"Yes." Tom's eyes were gray embers in smoke-dark smudges.

"He's given up his practice. Rented his house."

"What makes you so damn positive he's headed for Detroit?"

"He's shipped his furniture here. The move has something to do with *her*, you may be sure of that. Jews!"

"You're cracked."

"When it comes to that ingrate, I am. At least Keeley'll keep him away from our plants."

"No," Tom said harshly.

"What's that?"

"I won't let him touch Justin." Tom had no inkling that Dickson Keeley was Hugh's creature.

"And you call *me* cracked!" Hugh cried. For a long moment neither brother spoke. Hugh's voice, dulcet in its persuasiveness, broke the silence. "Tom, Justin used to be a fair man, and a decent one. *She* has changed him. Let someone like that get a toehold through him, and before the year's out, Moscow or Jerusalem will be calling the shots at Onyx. You can't let Hutchinson in, Tom. You know their red friend, Shapiro, is here already. I've told you that."

"Keeley knows how to keep the men from signing union cards. We haven't had any real trouble in our plants."

"Tom, listen to me—"

"Justin will never be shut out of my shop!" Tom slapped down the receiver.

His breath coming in deep sighs, he went to the window to watch the curling snowflakes.

Eight years nearly to the day, he thought. *Eight years.*

Though aware that his guilt and the attendant agony at denying Justin had brought on his heart attack, he knew that given a chance to replay the shameful scene, he would have cut the shrieked filth—and nothing more. He would still honor his pledge to Antonia. He would lie his way to hell to keep that promise. It was no longer something he contemplated in a rational way: it had become a mystical religious commandment. Meanwhile the physical damage had been repaired, he had regained his normal vigor. Yet his spirit was changed. His remorseful grief had curved around itself like an arthritic hand, never permitting the sufferer to forget his painfully crippling disease.

Tom rested his forehead against the glass, looking out at wind-driven snowflakes. His son, whom he loved and had rejected, was returning to fight him. Bitter news. Yet a redemptive flicker informed him that any contact would be better than the lifeless limbo of these past eight years. *How could I have screamed that awful shit about his wife?* Tom thought for the millionth time—he attributed Justin's continuing silence to that outburst. Hugh, equally ravaged by the lack of communication, had given in totally to bigotry, finding it simpler to blame Elisse's Jewishness than Justin himself.

Slowly, as if each movement pained him, Tom took out his wallet. Hidden in a leather pocket were two snapshots that he had lifted from Caryll's study. One print, dog-eared and cut by a vein down the center, showed Justin smiling on an angry-looking newborn infant. *Our grandson,* thought Tom, *our only grandson.* It comforted him that all his grandchildren were Antonia's too—that thus he and she would be joined into the unknowable future. The other snapshot, new and clean, was of a baby smiling on a blanket, sunbonnet ribbons untied, plump arms extended toward the photographer, whose feminine shadow fell across the picture.

Tom stared from one snapshot to the other, then picked up the telephone again. When he had Hugh on the line, he said, "No games, Hugh. Anything happens to him, and it's your head."

III

Whatever the prevailing conditions, a plant as enormous as Woodland inevitably took on men every day. The Employment Office would not open until five thirty the following morning, yet at ten, when Justin arrived at Gate Four, a hundred or so applicants were hunched into their coats, coughing or blowing on their frayed gloves. To brave the night a few had swathed themselves in burlap. Here and there small bonfires cast a glow from the depths of trash cans. Justin took his place, stamping his new boots in the slush, a futile attempt to alleviate the painful prickling of his cold-numbed toes. At that he was lucky. Most of the men had on shabby, thin-soled shoes.

By midnight another five or six hundred huddled in docile misery against the seemingly endless brick wall while mounted police patrolled. After the hoofbeats faded, a tall man ahead of Justin took something glittering from his pocket, hitting the object—it was a mouth organ—against his palm. Chords rose with measured sweetness into the icy dark, some kind of folk ballad out of Appalachia that rollicked then drifted sweetly and mournfully into silence. For a long time nobody spoke.

At five thirty a group of khaki-overcoated Security carrying shotguns appeared behind the wire mesh gate.

"Ten in. Ten away," boomed a megaphoned voice.

Amid confused shouts and jostling the first men in line were admitted through the pedestrian gate while the next were sent away.

The applicants twisted and turned, dismayed, counting. The next time the gate opened, though, it was twelve in, twelve away.

"What's going on?" Justin asked.

"They done it the other times I was here," said the big, rawboned job seeker ahead of him. "Some thinks it's Dickson Keeley's way of throwing us off."

Justin's fifteen was the last group admitted before the NOT HIRING sign was hung between the gates.

A clerk behind the barrier in the antechamber pushed back his green eyeshade, yawning as he examined the applicant ahead of Justin. Black hair contrasted with the man's pale, shrunken cheeks. "Pop," the clerk said. "That dye don't fool me."

"I'm thirty-three," said the man. "It's my teeth that are throwing you. I lost my teeth after I was laid off from the foundry last June."

"Man your age couldn't keep up," said the clerk. "Sorry, Pop. We got nothing for you."

"I need a chance," said the man quietly. "I'm as strong as anyone."

"Guard!" shouted the clerk.

The applicant shrank toward the door with EXIT painted above it.

The clerk assessed Justin. "*You* don't dye your hair," he said. "Name?"

"Arthur Hutchins. H-U-T-C-H-I-N-S."

The clerk consulted four long sheets attached to a clipboard, the blacklist of union men, before pointing Justin around the wooden bar to a foreman. The short, bald man circled Justin, prodding his arms and stomach. Outrage tensed Justin's chilled muscles.

"Ever work in tires?" asked the foreman.

In Gorki he had sweated for weeks alongside the burly Ukrainian tirebuilders. "I was a tirebuilder."

The foreman nodded. "How long?"

"Two years. Los Angeles. Firestone."

"You sound like some professor," said the foreman suspiciously. He drew back to look at Justin. "Well, that's okay by me," he said at last. "Mr. Bridger takes all colors and types. You got the height, the heft. We'll soon see how good you are." He extended a slick blue Security badge with *temporary* stamped above the numbers. "Go to Building 8311." A jerk of his bullet neck indicated the direction. "Hoof it. Shift changes in twenty minutes."

"What's the pay?"

"If I'm satisfied with you, then we'll talk money."

Justin hesitated. Tirebuilding required strength, skill, and the starting pay was good. Unscrupulous foremen skimmed a percentage.

The heavy blue cardboard twirled. The bald head turned pointedly to the hopeful, anxious men lined in front of green-visored clerks. "You don't wanta work, just say the word."

Justin reached for the badge.

On the steps outside, the icy dawn stimulating his lungs, the familiar clatter once again assaulting his eardrums, he paused. This time he was not in Woodland by reason of his tortuously concealed relationships; he had been hired simply because he was a large, strong, healthy male animal. His mouth stiffened into a grimace, mordant and faintly ironic. In that instant his resemblance to Tom was startling.

IV

Woodland Park was one of the neighborhoods that had sprung up in the early 1920s after the plant was built. The Hutchinsons' three-bedroom rental, identical to other houses in the subdivision, was matchbox flimsy with a slanting roof from which narrow upstairs windows peered. The exterior wallboards moulted gray flakes—the salt deposits below Detroit played the devil with cheap paint. Two generations of Inland Steel were doubled up in the house five feet to the right. To their left, Mr. Milacek worked in the body assembly at Chrysler Main. The Milaceks' radio stayed turned to Father Coughlin's station so that barking anti-Semitic remarks mingled perpetually with aromas of poppyseed strudel, cheese pockets, and peppery soup. Yet evidently the message evaporated before it reached Mrs. Milacek's frizzy, graying permanent for, even informed of their Jewish origins, she did not hesitate to gather Elisse and the children to her sagging bosom.

Elisse, though, had little time for neighborly kaffeeklatches. As secretary-treasurer of AAW, she watched over the union funds in the black tin box. When Justin had been taken on at Woodland at a substantial $1.05 an hour—minus ten cents to the foreman—she had suggested they endow the union with his quarterly trust payments. "Get the Brotherhood a headquarters, have a strike fund," she had said, and Justin had concurred.

She typed correspondence on her college Remington, she held meetings of the Ladies' Auxiliary, which had three other members. She composed militant leaflets to join AAW, cranking them out on the secondhand mimeo machine that jammed the dark hole of a dining room, then bundled Tonia in her pram to trudge through the narrow streets to slip them indiscriminately in mails slots—most of Woodland Park worked for Onyx. Fitting in cooking and cleaning as best she could, she worked all day and many evenings, and was darted with pangs of conscience at how much she enjoyed it all. In her self-deprecatory soliloquies she told herself she should be crushed and listless from missing her parents, agonizing over Ben's pugnacious refusal to adjust. (Her Ben, adjust?) Yet here she was after all those becalmed years of domesticity sailing full tilt into the fray. Nervy. Alive. As at Columbia Pictures, she shared little of Mitch's heartfelt allegiance to the labor movement. She was here because she had been touched deeply by those agonized letters from the workers at Woodland. She was working like a loony-woman at Justin's side because every word of those letters about the Bridgers' rotten repressions was true.

By the end of that snowy March the AAW had a grand total of eight members, including Mitch, who, blacklisted from auto, worked part time as a recreation director for the Works Projects Administration. Justin's calm exterior did not show it, but he fluctuated between morbid hopelessness and anger.

The Depression and Dickson Keeley had the AAW stopped cold as a dead mackerel.

At Woodland the rule against talking on the line was strictly enforced, and during the break strolling pairs of Security deterred conversation of any kind. Justin, having bought a used Seven, would offer the men in the tire shop lifts home. As soon as they were clear of the gates he would remind his passengers of their right under the National Recovery Administration to form their own union. The men would huddle, silent, and when the Seven halted outside their homes, would make a dash for it. Spies were everywhere. However inhuman the stretch-out, regardless of the downright viciousness of Security, a job was a job, and to be on the blacklist of union activists meant your family starved on relief—if you qualified for it. Besides, most of the hands were loyal to Tom. You couldn't blame the Boss for these stinking times—and he paid top wages.

The eight AAW Brothers gathered twice a week in the confines of what had once been a shoe store. Coats on against the penetrating night drafts, they sat around the fat stove planning methods of recruiting the terrified men who, vilified and ostracized, desperately needed them.

After one of these sessions Paul Zawitsky stayed late. A bear of a man, a recent widower, Zawitsky had worked at Onyx for twenty-five years, and though recognizing Justin's former incarnation, had never mentioned it in front of the others. Justin had invited him home once for potluck, and Elisse had fallen for him.

When he and Justin were alone, Zawitsky said, "Get rid of Brother Winstead. He's a stoolie."

"How do you know?"

"I take Security's bucks too, Prof." The foreman's nickname had stuck to Justin.

"Then why tell me about Winstead?"

"Because he reports on you. I don't. I guess you'd call me a double agent. I'm all for the AAW."

Justin rattled the secondhand folding chairs into a pile. *Beautiful*, he thought. *A minimum of two spies in a membership of eight!*

"Prof, let me explain my position," said Zawitsky, sucking on his pipe. "I got a boy finishing high school, he's bright and he's been accepted at the university. I'd sell my soul to see him finish. There's a layoff every year for retooling. And every year I worry about being hired again. So I kiss my foreman's ass and keep an eye out for Security just like he tells me. No self-respecting man should have to keep his job that way. But that's what I got to do."

"Thanks for the tip," Justin said quietly. "I appreciate it."

He drove home in funereal thoughtfulness.

As he undressed in the center of the bedroom—the roof slanted sharply in the garret-like upstairs, and he was too tall to stand near the walls—he was frowning abstractedly. He should have been booted from Woodland weeks ago. Mitch had remarked several times on his luck at remaining undetected. Elisse, grateful her husband was safe, would chortle to Mitch that Justin was smarter than he.

Unbuttoning his shirt, Justin accepted that he was neither smart nor lucky.

Someone at Onyx was protecting him.

Who?

It had to be one of the Bridgers.

Which one?

Caryll? On his arrival in Detroit, Justin had telephoned to make a date with Zoe. The high, breathy voice had wafted through the instrument to deliver a charmingly dismayed excuse. The family was leaving this *very* afternoon to sail the *Beaufort* in the Caribbean. A week later he had glimpsed Caryll entering the Tower. Did Caryll even know he was at Woodland? Probably not.

Hugh, however, must. If he did not already know through the usual channels, with his finger on Security's pulse, he would surely wonder at the AAW organizer's name. He knew Arthur was the name of Justin's dead half-brother, and Hutchins, well, was Hutchins. Would Hugh spread sheltering wings over him? It seemed doubtful.

Tom? The few times Justin had seen Tom erect behind the wheel of his silver Seven, he had felt a prod like electricity. Tormenting, elemental, disorienting.

Justin stood in the center of the attic bedroom, brooding over his kinsmen, the enemies whom he loved. A low, choking sound rose from his throat.

On stockinged feet he padded to the next cubicle. Elisse sat cuddling Tonia, who had awakened with a stuffy nose. He knelt in front of the rocker, clutching his arms around the baby and woman, resting his cheek on the fuzzed, worn flannel robe that covered his wife's slender, consoling thigh.

CHAPTER 24

A few days later, Caryll learned that Justin was in Detroit. He and Tom were at their routine Friday lunch at Hugh's.

These weekly conferences had begun in 1933. At that time President Roosevelt, fresh in office, was attempting to sweep the economic disaster from the country with his new broom of alphabet agencies that included the NRA. This new code, an experiment in industrial self-regulation, had been signed amid patriotic hoopla by manufacturers who then proceeded blithely to ignore any of the measure's regulations that hobbled them. Tom had refused to sign. He viewed the NRA as another Selden patent, a clamp on competition, and he felt, rightly, that the brain trusters in Washington knew nothing about making automobiles. Furthermore, Onyx paid exactly double the NRA's specified minimum hourly wage. Caryll privately shared his father's point of view, yet the economy was petering to a gloomy halt, and he believed with all his gentle, moderate heart that they must support the presidential effort to get things moving. The country agreed with Caryll. Dealers mailed him hundreds—no, thousands—of hortatory letters, the common plea being that times were disastrous enough without the staggering handicap of trying to sell Onyx trucks and Sevens without NRA's Blue Eagle sticker affixed to their windshields.

Hugh suggested Tom go on the air to explain his holdout. *The Onyx Family Variety Hour*, Sundays at 8 P.M. on NBC Blue, was the most popular program on all four radio networks, and the following day everybody was gabbling about Tom Bridger's good old-fashioned belief in individual effort and American ingenuity—and by God, what about those fat pay envelopes at Onyx? Sales jumped. Hugh wheedled his brother into continuing the brief, flat-spoken pithy comments at the end of each program.

During their Friday lunches the three Bridgers disputed the thrust of Tom's Sunday speech while Argo MacIlvray, his plump white fingers racing across the page, took notes. On this particular Friday, after the *oeufs à la neige*, Hugh nodded and the speechwriter's ovoid form fairly bowed itself from the dining room.

Hugh sniffed his cognac. "That union situation, Tom," he said. "Satisfied?"

Tom, pushing away from the table, did not reply.

"A membership of eight," Hugh said. "He'll soon give up. Keeley's got him stymied."

Caryll's round face had become less fleshy with the years, and at Dickson Keeley's name he clenched his teeth until his jawbones showed. "A new local, Uncle Hugh?" he asked.

"We're talking about your brother-in-law," Hugh said with a faint sneer. Yet there was a feverish flash of pain in his light blue eyes.

"What, Justin?" Caryll asked, surprised.

Hugh shot a glance at Tom, who had gone to the window. "He's working in the rubber department," Hugh said. "An agitator."

"Justin?" Caryll asked, still baffled. "Working at Woodland?"

"Yes. Comrade Justin." Hugh sipped. "You mean to say he hasn't contacted Zoe?"

Caryll had long since jettisoned his suspicions about Zoe and his uncle. "She has no idea," he said.

"Not taking time to see his own sister certainly proves his dedication."

"There are millions of people, Uncle Hugh, who believe collective bargaining is the fair way to settle labor disputes," Caryll snapped, then found himself adding in that sheepish, placating tone he deplored, "The men say our latest speedup is an endurance race, but Uncle Olaf refuses to listen."

"Olaf knows how pinched we are. The deficits."

Pain stabbed below Caryll's navel. These argumentative lunches with their rich food invariably triggered his indigestion. He extracted a tin of antacid from his pocket.

Hugh watched him down one. "You're too soft, Caryll," he said. "When this eternal whining stops and people put in an honest day's labor, then the country'll overcome its problems. Labor's fallen into the hands of foreign agitators."

"Justin's no foreign agitator."

"His wife is. And her friend is a card-carrying one. Justin's cut his conscience to suit them."

Tom had not spoken. There was a heaviness to the set of his shoulders, as if the spot by the window where he stood had a stronger gravitational pull.

II

At five Caryll's car was waiting for him outside the Tower. A thin, cold drizzle was falling into the twilight, and Hoskins settled the beaver rug about his knees. Normally Caryll luxuriated in the Swallow's teak and pigskin interior, which he had taken a big hand in designing, but today he leaned forward to peer at the throng that hurried to be on time for the shift change.

He could not fully accept that Justin might be one of these shabby, trotting men. Justin? Justin, whom he envisioned with a silvery nimbus, like a storybook illustration of Sir Galahad. Justin, who had rescued him from many of his childhood's dark hours. Justin, who had stood up to his father, Justin his friend—Justin, one of *them*?

The Swallow eased out of Gate Two, turning in the direction of Grosse Pointe. Caryll leaned back considering Justin's immeasurable fall to time-clock worker. Yet wasn't there an inevitability to it? *Justin always was for the underdog,* Caryll thought. *He's putting himself on the line because he believes organizing is the only way for the men.*

All at once Caryll sat up straight, blinking. *Suppose Justin's on the right track for all of us,* he asked himself. *Supposing the union were indeed to provide a forum where the men could air their grievances, where we could explain our side?*

Why are we fighting in this eternal, demeaning warfare to prevent a union?

The question had eluded him until now for the simplest of reasons: he had confused the hateful necessity of protecting his family with the goings-on at the plants.

But what was the point of guarding factories as though they were prison camps? Why hire thousands of Security and sink to spying on your employees just to keep out labor organizers? What was the inherent evil in a closed shop? Caryll's mind began to race. Justin was the most moral and the fairest man he had ever known. He and Justin could thrash out reforms, then side by side confront his father.

Caryll knew it would not be easy. He knew his father would fight long and hard before he let anyone tell *him* how to run his "shop." Yet he also knew that his father viewed Security as a malignant tumor. If he and Justin had once been able to convince him to dump the Fiver, why could they not convince him to at least consider collective bargaining?

In a light sweat of excitement Caryll was unaware of the miles passing. Suddenly he had arrived at Grosse Pointe.

His ivy-veined gatehouse arched over and around the drive. Two uniformed Security—Dickson Keeley's top men; still, they were decent enough fellows—barreled forth to unlock the massive iron-banded oak gates. The drive curved around huge, bare trees, coming suddenly upon the welcoming outthrust honey-colored wings of the house. Caryll, with his unrelenting eye for beauty, had worked with the architects for three years, and this unpretentious loveliness was an original amid Detroit's blatantly crude imitations of Hampton Court and Versailles.

Rooms opened one into the other, log fires crackled, and masses of cut flowers from the greenhouse spread their scent. Two Irish setters bounded into the hall to have their ears tickled, and Clarice and Petra flew out from the playroom to hug him. Lynn, they informed him in their sweet trebles, was still having her piano lesson.

Kneeling, he lifted a tiny girl in each arm. Petra, the baby, resembled her Grandma Maud, with bright cheeks and brown hair, while Clarice, the quiet one, his own girl, had gray eyes and wispy hair. He buried his face in their necks, inhaling the clean butter fragrance. They squealed joyously, quieting as they proceeded into the cardroom, where Zoe sat at the bridge table with Berenice Rocheville and Agnes and Joan Sinclair. The guests, in dark afternoon frocks, each with a large diamond pin on her left shoulder, greeted him warmly. Zoe tipped her gleaming, vivid head for his sideways kiss, continuing to play out the hand. As hostess, she wore a tea gown, a rich blue, immaculately seamed garment made for this one hour of the day.

Caryll went to the long silver cocktail tray, pouring the little girls ginger ale highballs, fixing himself a weak Scotch and soda. As he listened to the children's prattle his eyes strayed to his wife.

Zoe's beauty had ripened spectacularly. Rotogravures and fashion magazines in their hyperbole dubbed her the world's most beautiful woman, and even those observers not from the fourth estate admitted she was among the most exquisite women alive. Thick lashes shadowing her cheeks, she bit her full, delicately scrolled lower lip in concentration. With a cry of triumph she leaned over the table, her breasts swaying lightly against the silk jersey as she gathered in the final tricks. That gorgeous and disquieting carnal vulnerability showed yet more in the current, fitted styles.

Agnes and Joan counted out bills with jolly cousinly derision of Zoe's luck, while Berenice, a friend from school days, reached for her checkbook. "The rich get richer," she sighed, tearing out the check. "Let's pray this clears. You girls can't imagine what it's like, having to live off dividends nowadays."

Three large cars rolled off into the rainy darkness. Lynn ran in, fresh from playing scales, and Miss Henderson, whose smile revealed her poorly fitting English dentures, waited to collect her charges for supper in the nursery. Caryll and Zoe went upstairs to change.

She headed across their bedroom to her boudoir.

"Zoe, I have to talk to you."

"Later," she said. "We're having dinner alone."

"This is something I'd just as soon the servants didn't hear."

She made a pretty moue. "Won't you come into my parlor said the spider to the fly."

Thick shagged white carpet showed the indentation of her high heels. At the dressing table she turned to him. Venetian-mirrored paneling reflected endless vistas of an ordinary-looking man with thinning brown hair as he faced an impatient beauty.

After a long silence she inquired, "Is it that bad, poor baby? Another battle with the lakefront phantom?"

"Uncle, yes." Caryll's gaze shifted from her reflections to his wife. "He mentioned that Justin's in Detroit."

Zoe's hand jerked. A perfume flacon toppled. The stopper had not been secured, and the sweet, libidinous scent that Guerlain made solely for Zoe Bridger filled the room. She mopped a handkerchief. Caryll watched her closely: Zoe, pitiably blanched, fingers erratic, lashes aflutter. But not in the least surprised.

"You knew," he said. "How?"

"I can't remember."

"Zoe, we're talking about your only brother."

"He must have telephoned. Yes, that's it. In January. Something about wanting to see me. The girls. You."

"And you never mentioned it."

She fretted the perfumed-soaked cobweb of linen. "I blocked it, I willed myself to forget it, do you understand, Caryll? It's traumatic for me to think about him, you know that." Tears intensified the darkness of Zoe's huge, pleading eyes. "We were so close and now it's as if I don't exist for him."

"In his letters he always asks about you." Caryll spoke gently, comfortingly. "Honey, he remembers all sorts of little things about you. He misses you like anything. Did he mention why he's here?"

Zoe shook her head.

"He's a labor organizer," Caryll said.

Zoe sat on the silk-pillowed vanity stool. "You mean she's turned him into a Bolshie?"

"Now don't you start," Caryll sighed. "I've had *that* up to here with Uncle Hugh. My God, as if Justin ever let himself be a puppet. He's the only man I ever knew who stood head to head with Dad. This is his way of putting himself on the line to improve conditions."

"But he's a radical."

"There's nothing so radical about believing in collective bargaining. Believe me, he's not the only man we know who's for a closed shop. Justin hasn't changed, Zoe. I'm positive of that. First thing tomorrow I'll call Employment for his telephone number and address."

"He's with Onyx?"

"Yes. Woodland."

"Then why haven't you seen him?"

"Maybe I have and didn't recognize him. He's in the tire shop."

"A laborer?" Zoe asked in a faded whisper.

"Honey, it's not a catastrophe," Caryll said, recollecting that an hour ago, peering at the drab throng, he, too, had been ajangle with consternation, perplexity, disbelief.

"But . . . our grandmother was a contessa. And he was a top man at Onyx."

"The workers would hardly trust him if he had offices in the Tower," Caryll said. "We're going to get together with him and his family on Sunday."

She blinked. "What?"

"We're inviting them to lunch or dinner."

"Caryll . . . I can't." The tear-drenched eyes held a look of deep hurt.

Caryll ignored this attempt at emotional blackmail. "Lunch'll be best. Then the children can be with us. It'll be fun showing off the girls. And meeting his son and daughter—and his wife."

"They're working against us," Zoe whispered.

"They're tackling the same problem but from another angle," Caryll said. "There's been too much meanness at Woodland these past years. And what's the point of it? Why do we keep Dickson Keeley's army of goons? Half of them belong in Sing Sing. Why hire an army to exclude a few labor organizers? That's the reason I'm in such a rush to get together with Justin. The sooner we start discussions, the better."

"Whatever's the matter with you, Caryll? You know Father Bridger'll never negotiate with a union."

"That's the whole point. This isn't simply a union. It's Justin. He always listened to Justin."

"And he's forever saying nobody'll tell him how to run his factories. Look at how often the President's called! It's never made a dent."

"He's always aimed at decent working conditions. Between us, Justin and me, we can convince him that a closed shop will be more efficient, fairer, and cheaper than hiring hordes of Security." Caryll had unconsciously lapsed into the businesslike determination he took on when dealing with his departments.

Zoe looked up at him, her lovely, full mouth pulling back against her teeth. "You're serious about this, aren't you, Caryll?"

"The country's on a collision course and I feel so damn helpless. The least I can do is take a stab at bettering conditions at Onyx."

"Of course I'll invite him—all of them. He's probably in the telephone book. I'll call tomorrow morning. You're right. It'll be wonderful to see him and his children." Her voice went higher. "Caryll, I'm so proud of you. I'll help all I can."

The surrender was off-key, but Caryll for once showed none of his litmus paper sensitivity to his wife's moods. Full of his plans, he kissed her forehead gratefully and went to his dressing room to get ready for dinner.

III

The next morning was sunny, and Caryll drove himself in the Swallow coupe to the Grosse Pointe Country Club—the links had just opened for the season. He preferred to spend his weekends at home playing with the girls or puttering with his watercolors; he found golf a repetitive bore and could never understand the fuss that grown men made about their scores, handicaps, and tournament standings. He had joined the club in the belief that Onyx had an obligation to participate in attempts to solve the economic foulup. Neither his hermit uncle nor his abrasive loner of a father communicated with others in the industry, so he mingled with automotive leaders along the fairways and in the clubhouse.

He did not get home until after three.

Zoe was in bed, propped by a tumble of miniature pillows. Her brilliant, uncombed hair seemed to drain all her color, and the exquisite, ashy face was slack save for one delicate furrow of pain between her brows. The curtains were drawn. The air smelled smoky and thick: next to the limp narrow hand with the carmine nails was a precariously balanced saucer filled with cigarette butts.

"You're so late," she whispered.

"I got to talking to Edsel about donating to the Relief Fund." He kissed her forehead. "Headache?"

"The usual." She pressed two fingers against her temple. "I'm sorry, honey bear. I couldn't telephone Justin."

Caryll, empathetic as a psychic when it came to his wife, realized she was not faking her migraine. He sat on the bed. "That's all right. I'll get to him on Monday and make the date."

"You aren't angry?"

"Worried about you. I better let Agnes know we won't be there tonight."

"I'll be fine."

With a seemingly casual kiss, he said, "You're not up to dancing."

"At the end of the day it wears off."

"Honey," he said as firmly as he dared. "We're staying home."

"Artie and Agnes are counting on us." She handed him the saucer. "Take these, will you?"

He watched butts whirling down plumbing, his molars grimly clenched. Though he had come to recognize that Zoe's bad times were beyond her control, he had never been able to put into manageable perspective the actions that resulted from them, the cruelties that appalled them both and left them equally heartsick.

IV

She shimmied across the waxed floor, her head tilting in a smile at her partners. Above the emerald ballgown the flesh of her arms, back, and the cleavage of her breasts were the translucent yet velvety white of the interior of a lily. She dazzled, she glowed, she vanquished every other woman, and no man could resist the near tactile pleasure of watching her. Caryll fox-trotted with his cousins' wives, friends' wives, company wives who smiled admiringly at him. His anxious desires reached out to his own wife.

She was finishing a tricky rhumba when he lost sight of her. He looked for the emerald taffeta in the crush at the buffet table, he circled the cardroom where his friends were eating the midnight supper. With a frozen little smile he continued his search through the crowded downstairs rooms of Agnes and Artie Sinclair's replica of Mount Vernon. At the last waltz Zoe reappeared in the ballroom, gliding with the top of her burnished head tucked under Dickson Keeley's squarish jaw.

Oh, God, God, Caryll thought. *Dickson Keeley!*

On the way home she sang *Body and Soul,* her breathy little voice ruffling the soft white hairs of her fox collar.

In the hall Caryll said brusquely, "I'm having a nightcap."

For a long time he sat on the den sofa, his gray eyes reflecting the glow of dying embers. He gulped his drink and reluctantly climbed the circular staircase.

Zoe, in a cherry kimono, brushed her hair with long, sharp strokes that crackled from the titian nape to the pink-gold ends. "I had supper with Dickson Keeley," she said.

"Zoe, it's after two." He sat to take off his new pumps. "I'm bushed. Let's not start."

"He said he wished that you and he could hit it off."

"How could you discuss me?" Caryll asked in a low, shaking voice.

"You're right, he's a nasty, pushy man with that Edward G. Robinson tough talk. He boasted his weight hadn't changed since he was at Princeton. He made me feel his biceps and thigh muscles—those conservative clothes are a pose. He wears black silk drawers with a dragon embroidered on the you-know."

"Shut up," Caryll growled. Beads of sweat showed on the widow's peak of his receding hairline.

"His is smaller than yours. Nothing happened. It just oozed away."

Caryll went into his dressing room. She followed, her face puffed with unshed tears. "Why did I have to tell you that, Caryll? Why do I always? I wish I were dead! Death is calm and peaceful. Dead people can't hurt or be hurt."

He unknotted his white tie. "You should have continued with Maurin," he said with enforced coldness.

"Maurin! What's the point of admitting again and again that because my father died and then Mother died and Justin left me, I'm terrified of being deserted? Where has it helped me, knowing?"

"Another analyst, then." Caryll maintained his nonjudgmental frostiness.

"Ahh, Caryll, don't act like I'm a loony who can give you rabies. I can't bear it."

"Then I suggest you beg sympathy from one of the men you seek out, my cousins, my friends, the men who work for me."

"You're right to despise me. You're so good, Caryll, so fine."

"The best and finest cuckold in Detroit."

"I never let them inside me."

"That would be more honest."

"Please, please say you love me."

"Why? Because you were unsuccessful at *soixante-neuf* with Dickson Keeley?"

"Caryll, I'm drowning."

Caryll's false remoteness dissolved: in a fury he hurled his tie to the floor. "I want to accomplish some good, manage a progressive action, and because it involves speaking to your brother—*my* friend—you punish me!"

"She owns him, that Jewish girl."

"My God."

"You're siding with him! He means more to you than I do!"

"Just listen to yourself."

"You're everything to me, Caryll. You're the one person on this earth I have."

"It won't work this time, Zoe. My mind's made up. Monday I'm contacting Justin like I said I would."

She lunged at him, clasping her hands around his neck, pressing kisses on his averted jaw, his ear, and when he did not respond, she stepped back, letting the kimono slither into a rosy pool around her bare, high-arched feet. A plastic surgeon had traveled from Rio de Janeiro to graft the scar of her three cesareans, and only the thinnest thread of a vertical line flawed the smooth flesh above her perfumed pubic triangle. Caryll had seen her nakedness since their early adolescence, yet he could never control his awe nor—when Zoe willed it—his desire. He was aware, however, even as she caressed his tumescence with skilled delicacy, that it was not merely his wife's excessive beauty or her sensuality that bound him to her. The strongest bond was her starved and frightened heart.

Embracing, they moved toward the turned-down bed.

Afterward she trailed kisses down his neck. "It drives me wild when you put anything ahead of me."

"I never have."

"You won't call Justin?"

Caryll hesitated.

"Don't let me drown!"

Caryll sighed deeply and rolled over to turn off the bedside lamp. "All right, Zoe."

"You won't see him?"

"I won't," Caryll promised, condemning himself for this starstruck, pitying love that was surely his greatest weakness.

CHAPTER 25

In the upper right-hand corner of the thick, creamy card was embossed THE WHITE HOUSE: the few lines below were scrawled in a thick, sharp slant:

> Tom,
>   *Mrs. Roosevelt and I would be delighted if you and Mrs.*
> *Bridger would join us for the weekend of May 3. We have also*
> *extended an invitation to your son and daughter-in-law.*
>   *Looking forward to renewing our friendship.*
>   *FDR*
> *P.S. There will be no discussion of the NRA.*

The postscript was a humorous one. Attempting to woo Tom into signing the code, the President, in addition to twice dispatching his secretary of labor, Madame Perkins, to Detroit, had put in many richly jocund personal calls. Tom, halfway succumbing to Rooseveltian charm, had recognized the political tiger in the man. This handwritten invitation meant that some favor, probably self-damaging, was wanted of him. Hugh and Argo MacIlvray composed his regrets.

Caryll and Zoe flew in the family Lockheed Vega to Washington.

II

Just before five on Sunday afternoon a bland-faced aide led Caryll through corridors to a small, comfortably furnished sitting room. Reddish light slanted through the western windows to touch the

President's massive, graying head. Seated behind a leather-topped desk that hid his crippled legs, wearing a nautical, gold-buttoned blazer and a navy scarf knotted around his muscular neck, he looked powerful and strong.

The aide excused himself.

Caryll had spent the weekend with the Roosevelts, he had dined several times with Harding, shown Hoover around Woodland, and Coolidge had been the honored guest at his wedding. This, though, was the first time he had been alone with a president. Sweat formed under his arms, and his boyhood stammer flourished. "G-good afternoon, M-Mr. P-President."

"Make yourself comfortable, Caryll." Roosevelt's teeth remained clenched on his cigarette holder as he smiled and gestured at the slipcovered easy chairs.

"Thank you, Mr. President." Caryll relaxed slightly.

"I looked down into the garden a while ago and saw you playing croquet with Mrs. Roosevelt, Elliott, and that pretty wife of yours."

"We've had a wonderful two days, Mr. President."

"A shame your father and mother couldn't join us."

"Dad wants a raincheck."

"He does, eh?" Behind the pince-nez the close-set eyes twinkled. "Well, Tom Bridger must have mellowed since our telephone talks. *That* Tom Bridger meant it when he said no."

Flustered again, Caryll managed a sickly smile. "You have me there, sir."

"A remarkable man, your father. The true visionary of the machine age. The world would be pretty much the same if one or the other of us politicians hadn't been born. But without Tom Bridger we'd be living in a far different place. I don't think he realizes how people look up to him."

Caryll shifted his weight uneasily. "Mr. President, he might not have signed the NRA certificate, but he complies fully with the code."

"You don't have to tell me! I listen to the Onyx hour." The smile faded. "The truth is, Caryll, I agree with him. It's far from a perfect package. We bundled too much together. Codes of competition within each industry as well as regulation of all labor practices. But there I go. I promised not to discuss *that*. I asked you here so we could talk about the main problem the country faces. It's unemployment, don't you agree?"

"Absolutely, Mr. President. Unemployment."

"Dole's not the answer. A man needs work to give him hope and pride, he needs work to give him an identity and make him feel human."

"You've made a real dent, sir, with the CCC, the WPA."

"A beginning, that's all. We need support from industry."

"Onyx has plans for a new glass factory in Nashville, and a cold sheet finishing mill at the Hamtramck."

"You do? Excellent, excellent. A step in the right direction, but the problem is enormous. Fifteen million unemployed." The President paused. "The solution we've come up with is on a grand scale."

"Solution, Mr. President?"

Letting Caryll dangle, Roosevelt fitted a fresh cigarette into his holder. Caryll jumped up, leaning across the desk with his lighter. "Thanks," Roosevelt said. "What if every employer hired two men instead of one?"

"Mr. President?"

"Don't stare at me like that. We're not asking you to double Onyx's payroll. What we have in mind is to reduce the weekly hours by half. Give one job to two men."

For the same reason that Tom had stayed put in Detroit, Caryll had traveled to Washington. He had been hoping the President *would* lay some task on him. Since Zoe's ritualized, quasi-adultery—a stab at self-destruction, Maurin, her ex-psychoanalyst, termed these episodes—had forced him to renounce his hopes of red-hot accomplishment with Justin, Caryll had sunk into deep despondency. His faith in himself, never strong, had shriveled. Salvation seemed to lay in substituting an equally meaningful task.

But this—this?

His first coherent thought was, how can any family survive on half a week's work with the minimum wage of twenty-five cents an hour? He almost blurted this out, then realized it was a foolish question to put to a politician as astute as Roosevelt. He, his Cabinet, and the brain trust, several of whom Caryll and Zoe had met at dinner on Friday, must have considered the ramifications.

The President leaned back in his chair. The gold rim of his pince-nez caught the sunlight. "Well? How will it go in Detroit?"

"The automotive industry . . ." Caryll cleared his throat. "We have a pretty good wage scale."

"So you're on our side."

"Mr. President," said Caryll, awkwardly, "we'd be asking our workers to accept a drastic cut."

"I realize that." Roosevelt looked weary and strained. "But the men who haven't had a pay envelope to take home to their families in five years, what about them? Don't we have an obligation to them?"

Caryll sighed, thinking of the men who wore no shirts under their threadbare suit jackets slogging passively from Gate Four after a turndown, the thin wraiths who leaned on lampposts cringing away when you glanced at them. His own plans had always been of bettering conditions at Onyx, but the President was forcing him to look at things on a larger scale. Unemployment, a terrible cancer, clogged the lungs and heart of the country, and there would be no health until those beaten, submissive cells were returned to society.

Roosevelt, watching him, guessed his thoughts. "If we don't find jobs for those men, and find them soon, they'll die. Maybe they'll keep on breathing, but they'll be dead. And so will their families."

"I agree with you, Mr. President," Caryll said. "How do the other manufacturers think their labor forces will react to your plan?"

"You're the first I've approached. Detroit's the obvious spot—unemployment's ferocious there—and Onyx is the place to begin. Your father has no stockholders or board of directors to contend with. Besides, he's an idealist. Oh, Tom would laugh, hearing that, but between us, what else can you call him? His seven-dollar-minimum day, his lack of discriminatory hiring are landmarks." The toothy smile flattered yet was sincere. "In a couple of weeks I'm discussing this with Henry Ford, Alfred Sloan, Chrysler. My arguments to them would have bite if Onyx were already on the bandwagon."

"It's up to my father, Mr. President. He's the boss."

"Don't I know it!" Roosevelt laughed. "Still, you're his second in command."

"Like Vice-President Garner," Caryll said, and then reddened furiously. One did not joke with presidents.

Roosevelt laughed again. *"Touché."*

"I'll explain your thoughts to Dad. I'll try to make him understand our larger obligations." He was sweating again.

"The unemployed of this country are in agony, Caryll. Relief's no answer for them. Self-respect is."

"I'll do what I can to convert Dad."

"You're with us, then?"

"All the way, Mr. President. I'll do my best."

"I'm counting on you, Caryll," said the President in the insinuatingly warm tones with which he addressed his friends during his Fireside Chats.

Deep in Caryll's being the moths of doubt flittered, but he did not let these misgivings invade his conscious mind. Desperate to absolve himself of his earlier weakness, it seemed to him that convincing his father to agree to the President's plan would be the means. He climbed the ladder of the Lockheed Vega, his shoulders squared with determination.

III

"The White House, our country's swank new booby hatch!" Tom said. "The inmates are encouraged to think up schemes that elude the normal mind."

Caryll sat back in the leather chair, breathing deeply. He had come directly to Woodland from the Municipal Airport, and though it had not been a particularly rough journey, flying nauseated and frightened him: his stomach was still queasy.

"At first I thought it was nuts too," he said. "But as I gave it more time I realized Mr. Roosevelt was right. A third of the country's out of work. Those people need a lifeline."

"A lifeline can pull the rescuer into the drink, son, remember that."

"Our wages *are* high. A lot of families *do* manage on half what we pay."

"You've never been hungry. Believe me, it's to be avoided. I refuse to starve the people who work for me."

Caryll hyperventilated again, forcing himself to continue. "There are professors and engineers living in board shacks down at the dump, there are black babies dying in Inkster. Onyx is not an island.''

''Did Mr. Roosevelt promise to deliver his humanitarian message to them?'' Tom jerked his head toward the rain-spotted windows: his tenth-story office in the Tower had a hundred and eighty degree view of Woodland. Abruptly his temper flared, not at Caryll, not at Roosevelt—that brilliant and manipulative politician—but at the reality of destitute families wintering in tarpaper shacks, of malnourished babies in Inkster. ''I say no to him!''

''Dad—''

''I knew going to Washington was a mistake! That man can sell anything to anyone! He's a goddamn hypnotist!'' Tom returned to his desk, a long-faced, prematurely white-haired man in a trim gray suit, controlling his temper. ''Since I first started hiring, Caryll, I've paid the kind of wage I'd like to get. That's not about to change. No cutting paychecks in half, not in my shop.''

IV

Lynn's birthday had fallen on the Saturday her parents were in Washington, so her party was postponed a week. Since it was a warm afternoon, they celebrated outside. Spring sunshine cast a rosy, Renoir haze on the seemingly limitless grounds, and twenty little girls (nine of them Trelinack descendants) in pale organdy frocks trailed multicolored balloons across vivid green lawns and played party games under giant, newly leafed trees while parents sat on the terrace smiling benevolently at them over cocktails. Everyone trooped into the playhouse to watch Lynn cut her cake. Tom captured the bouncing, excited children on his noisy new Bell and Howell home-movie camera, then returned to the terrace. Glancing into the library, he saw his son.

Caryll was hunched over on a chair, his arms clamped around his knees, his spine arched like a cat's.

''Caryll, what the hell is it?''

''Indigestion,'' Caryll muttered. Sweat dripped from his cheeks.

Tom ran to the telephone, summoning Fairburn, his own doctor, and Balashov, Caryll and Zoe's internist.

The guests went home before Lynn opened her presents, and it was left to Miss Henderson to soothe the disappointed child. The immediate family sat in the graciously proportioned drawing room,

Zoe breaking into unnervingly erratic sobs, Maud wiping her glasses, Tom by the windows glumly watching servants clear away the debris of the party.

Balashov came downstairs and the two women rose, Zoe pliant as a flower, Maud pillar-like—her once trim waist and fine bosom had collected postmenopausal padding.

"It's an intestinal spasm," said the doctor, his hands working in a prudent washing gesture.

"What's that?" Tom asked. "An ulcer?"

"We don't believe there's damage to the duodenal wall, no," said the doctor carefully. "The pain is this intense because it's self-perpetuating. We've given him a hypodermic. Generally these episodes pass when the cycle is broken."

"Pain doesn't jump out from walls," Tom said. "What caused it?"

"We can't be sure," Balashov replied. "We think stress."

"But he's going to be all right?" asked Zoe in a high little voice.

"We believe so," Balashov said, the American Medical Association's voice of caution speaking to the near and dear of an immensely rich, drugged patient. "We'll begin running tests on Monday."

Maud took off her glasses, wiping them again. "I don't like that waiting," she said.

"We can't disturb him until then, Mrs. Bridger," the doctor said, bowing slightly.

"But you're doing everything you can for him?" Zoe asked.

"Absolutely, Mrs. Bridger," the doctor said with another little bow.

Tom insisted the doctors spend the night in the house.

A high-legged hospital bed was installed in Caryll's upstairs study, and the older of the nurses—two were spelling each other—pinned a linen guest towel over the desk lamp. By this withered light Tom sat charting the rise and fall of the chest beneath the immaculately turned covers. Caryll's face, slackened by opiates, was worn and lined. *He's a man,* Tom thought with a ripple of shock. *A man in early middle age who looks older.* The thought was damning. *When have I ever credited him with adulthood? To me he's always been a boy.* A boy to be cherished, guided, looked after, protected from all manner of evil. Never to be respected, deferred to, listened to. Tom smoothed the taut covers. Stress, Balashov said. Stress? *Since he came back from Washington he's been pale and edgy. Caryll, I squashed you good and well on that, didn't I? When you tried to convince me about Roosevelt's idea, I shut you up with my usual sledgehammer finesse.*

The bedroom door opened and Zoe came in, tying her flimsy robe around her waist. Her third visit in an hour. She gazed down at her husband, her matchless eyes filling with tears. For years now Tom had damned back a torrential resentment toward this daughter of his beloved, this wife of his son, mother of his grandchildren, this gorgeous creature who trotted around Detroit like a sleek racing mare in heat. For the copious moisture in her dark eyes, Tom forgave her every one of those scabrously ribald remarks that were invariably choked off as he approached—Zoe, forgiven much because she loved Caryll much.

"He hasn't moved," she whispered.

"He's in deep sleep, Mrs. Bridger. The morphine." The nurse spoke normally. "Why not try a little shut-eye yourself. Take that pill Dr. Balashov gave you."

"How can I sleep?"

"I never get more than three or four hours," Tom said. "I'll stand guard."

"You'll call me right away if anything happens, Father Bridger?"

"As soon as he wakes up."

"Do you think . . ." Zoe's voice trailed away. "He looks so . . ."

Tom saw Antonia in the dark, vulnerably loving wet eyes. He put his hand gently on hers. "Caryll's going to be fine, honey," he said.

She returned to the bedroom.

Tom resumed his watch.

Caryll awoke without pain. The doctors, delighted to be off the hook, prescribed Wheatena with cream and went home. Tom breakfasted with his son.

"I've been thinking about that trick of Roosevelt's," he said. "Thin paychecks aren't the idea of the century, we need fat ones to jolt the economy in the ass, but on the other hand I haven't come up with any brilliant solutions either. So we'll be guinea pigs. See how the idea goes over in—say—the rubber shop."

Caryll's spoon clinked in the bowl. He lay back in the cranked-up bed, examining his father. "Dad, why the turnabout?"

"Patriotism, what else?"

"Because of last night?"

"Sure. Don't I structure all of my major decisions around your bellycramps?"

The testiness of his father's tone reassured Caryll. "The tire department, then, Dad," he said.

Too late Tom recalled that Justin worked in tires.

Tom's choice of the rubber shop, though unpremeditated, was not coincidental. He had spent fully half of the dimly lit, anxious night brooding about his other son. Since Justin's return how many times had he resolved to visit him, to hug his only grandson and the baby—Antonia's namesake? To meet that girl whom he persisted in visualizing as darkly, biblically statuesque? Justin's address and telephone number were scrawled in the small book whose leather was curved by the warmth of Tom's body, but as often as he opened it to *H* he never could bring himself to call. It seemed to Tom that making the first reconciliatory move would be an admission as damning as a positive blood test for paternity. He had braved a heart attack to keep mum; he could wait until Justin contacted him. Couldn't he?

Setting down his cup, he moved restlessly to the window. *I don't want Justin in the thick of it, but if I change my mind, who knows what damn questions Caryll will ask?* He said, "That's right. Rubber."

"When shall we put it into operation?"

"The month of happiness and weddings," Tom said, his voice wry, his eyes forlorn. "June."

Caryll's lab tests disclosed nothing untoward, but the doctors, wanting to be on the safe side, continued his bland ulcer diet.

CHAPTER 26

On Monday, May 27, 1935, the Supreme Court exploded its decision. The NRA was unconstitutional.

A secretary popped into Hugh's silent office to blurt out the news. Hugh, after his initial exultation, sat back lacing his fingers and asking himself how he could tie this in with the crazy new policy at the tire shop, how he could best use this to Onyx's advantage. However many twists his loyalties had taken since that freezing night when he had ridden ahead of Tom's first quadricycle, he had never ceased pouring himself into his work: it was his doing that Onyx's advertising was uncluttered and effective, his doing that Tom, Onyx, and Woodland, a troika, received more columns in the country's press than Garbo, Chaplin, Will Rogers, Lindbergh, and the Prince of Wales combined. He remained immobile, gazing up at the magnificent linenfold ceiling molding. After about fifteen minutes he nodded. He did not stir again for several minutes, then he picked up the interoffice phone. "MacIlvray, come in here," he commanded.

The rest of the day he and the obese writer polished and refined a full-page advertisement that ran in more than two hundred daily newspapers: Tom Bridger, who had refused to sign the unconstitutional NRA code, had joined forces with the President to cure unemployment. *We at Onyx call it the double work week.*

The double work week . . .

It had a prosperous ring that made men and women peer out from their bleakness. Tom Bridger, that offbeat, tinkering genius who had set the world on wheels, was rolling Old Man Depression away. Hope rippled across the United States and dealers reported a miracle that had not occurred since the Crash. Down payments were made in advance on the as yet unveiled 1936 models.

At Woodland men mumbled to one another, "Double work week, what sort of bull is that?" They turned hastily away, unwilling to show the tightwire fear that soon they, too, would be on half pay.

In the red brick tire factory, old employees and new alike hefted their weekly envelopes knowing that double work week meant no milk or new shoes for the kids, no doctor for the wife when she had the new one.

Justin was changing to his workclothes in the washroom when the gangling pit worker said from the corner of his mouth, "Prof, where's that AAW headquarters at?"

"2415 Miller Road."

"Been thinking about joining," mumbled the pit worker, hiding his lip movements by shifting his licorice-flavored tobacco to his other cheek. In the rubber shop soapstone flew, parching your throat and nostrils, yet if you drank much water you became bloated, so men chewed to kill the thirst. "Yew fellers sure was right about the union. I reckon we got to stand together."

The gangling mountain man spoke for the whole tire department.

Mitch quit his part-time WPA job. He and Elisse kept the storefront headquarters open. Tonia toddled between massive workboots while men laboriously signed their names to union cards. The acrid stench of rubber clinging to them pervaded the summer stuffiness, the sound of their worried voices filled the narrow store as they lined up in front of the painted kitchen table where Prof's wife, the treasurer, sat.

Elisse entered names in her ledger, sorting crumpled bills and coins into the black tin treasury box. Membership was fifty cents, monthly dues fifty more. Sometimes a shamefaced applicant would ask if he could put down a dime or a nickle. "I'm kind of low right now."

"Next payday, then," Elisse would say, crisply businesslike, clinking change into compartments, but her vision would swim as she made note of the debt.

Day after day men came twitching from their brief, speeded-up, stretched-out work. A feverish, reckless glint in their eyes, they walked openly through the front door. Who cared if Security spotted them? What did they have to lose?

II

"As soon as we find out, we give them the swift boot," Dickson Keeley said. "Welfare's not so easy to get, and if you do get it, it's still not enough to buy beans."

"Then how do you explain a membership of nearly twelve hundred?"

It was a hot, muggy afternoon and the two were following the gravel path to the lion run—Hugh, earlier in the year, had imported two pairs captured on the Serengeti, and the carelessly brave animals fascinated him endlessly.

"Simple," Dickson Keeley retorted. "Twice as many shifts, twice as many men who think they're being shafted. They act like they're deposed royalty or something."

"You need more Security on this."

"I have a hook on every third man in the rubber shop. What got into the boss, picking tires for his double work week? Hutchinson! Even my handpicked stoolies don't turn in full reports. They're for the big bastard."

At the word *bastard* a peculiar sneer formed on Hugh's still handsome profile. After a few paces he asked, "What about Shapiro? What do the men think of *him*?"

"He's just part of the package. Without Hutchinson we'd have pulled the plug on the whole damn local."

"That's your job."

"Then give me a shot at it." Dickson Keeley obeyed Hugh because if Hugh ever told the boss about his dirty tricks, including the sexual ones, it would mean the end of him. But he was no subservient tool. "You tie my hands and then tell me I'm not doing my job. Mr. Bridger, why not let me at Hutchinson?"

Hugh quickened his step. The path turned to show an enclosed field. A vagrant breeze off Lake St. Clair rippled across the wild oats, darkening the color from cream to amber. Hugh sat on a shaded marble bench, touching a folded handkerchief to the right side of his face—the scar tissue did not sweat. A luxuriously maned lion padded toward them. This was Aries, the larger male.

"Where's the others?" Keeley inquired.

Hugh pointed. Three recumbent lions were camouflaged by the long grasses. "Still feeding," he said. "You'll have to keep working around Hutchinson. Remember, you're dealing with my nephew's brother-in-law."

"It's not as if the two are buddy-buddy nowadays. Is it because she's a kike? Is that why nobody gives them the time of day?"

"The Bridger family's not your concern."

"The hell it isn't. What's their opinion of Hutchinson's wife and kids?"

Aries stretched out near the fencing, and Hugh stared at the redness on the whiskers. It took a far less subtle mind than his to recognize that Tom would stand for no harm to his and Antonia's grandchildren. "You certainly aren't considering any games with the children?"

"Nothing to hurt them. But why not let *him* sweat a bit?"

"Forget it."

"Listen, I'd prefer to go at him direct, you know that." Keeley sat on the bench. "How about her? He'd go back to L.A. at her say-so."

"What makes you so sure?"

"Everybody knows how nuts he is about her."

Hugh rose, moving to the fence, tapping on a thick steel strand. Aries, with a low rumble in his tawny chest, looked up, and Hugh gazed into inhuman bronze eyes. "None of us would want a public brouhaha."

"I figured that."

"Then you understand the ground rules."

"Steer clear of him and the kids, no stories in the papers, don't do anything the Boss might hear about, right?"

"Right."

"But she's . . . ." The educated drawl faded.

Hugh mentally translated the silence. *Fair game.* The swing of his overbrimming avuncular love onto its dark, lunar side was irrevocable, and as once he had planned vengeance on Major Stuart for his deformity, so now he was not averse to paying off Elisse, letting her be fair game. After all, how disastrous could a little private, nonmutilating browbeating be? Not turning from the lion, he said, "Use your own judgment."

"They're as good as on the way back to L.A."

"Nobody's to know Security convinced them."

"I understand," Dickson Keeley said.

III

The temperature that July remained in the nineties, and the thin boards of the Hutchinsons' rented house clutched the steamy heat. That Thursday evening—the last Thursday in July—the warm, gluey atmosphere resounded with Alfred Wallenstein's *Sinfonietta*, which was tuned loud enough to drown out the repetitive squeals of Ben's violin.

Ben did not question why his parents had brought him to Detroit; however, he had developed a means of making it acceptable to himself. He punished them by practicing more vigorously, by antagonizing his teacher and schoolmates, by scorning the neighborhood gang, by keeping his love for his parents a yet more flamboyant secret: this intensification of himself had become a creative thing. Justin understood what was going on. Elisse did not. Wearing a hair shirt of guilts, she spent the occasional penny she had to spare on Fleer Dubble Bubble gum that he cracked belligerently, and she ignored his misdemeanors—it was she who had tuned up the radio.

Justin rested his socked feet on one of the cartons that crowded the narrow living room. He held the *Detroit Free Press*, but he was watching his wife as she sat at the desk frowning over a ledger. In her pink cotton dress, ankle socks, saddle shoes, her intent face smudged under the eyes, she looked like a tired co-ed burning the midnight oil.

Since June, when the double work week had begun, she had been setting the alarm for four thirty so she could clean and do the ironing before dawn. The rest of her hours were consumed by AAW.

Arching her back wearily, she lifted her brown curls to cool the nape of her neck, then became aware of Justin's scrutiny.

"Hey, mister," she said. "Weren't you holding a meeting tonight?"

"I don't have to leave for a bit. What's wrong there?"

"The treasury's overdrawn. Thank God your quarterly check came today. I barely restrained myself from committing forgery and making the deposit."

Justin scratched thoughtfully at his instep. "I'm holding back two fifty for our account."

"That's the Brotherhood's money!" she cried indignantly.

"I bring home half a paycheck."

"We agreed, Justin, remember? We agreed that the entire payment'd go in. The treasury's broke, I tell you."

"What's happened to all the initiation fees and dues?"

"Rent on 2415 Miller Road. Utilities at same address. Telephone," she said, jabbing down the page. "Paper for leaflets. New roller for mimeograph machine. Two used Remington typewriters. Hot plate and radio for headquarters. Fifty used folding chairs. Coffee, donuts, milk. Assorted groceries for Ladies' Auxiliary." The three hundred and eleven members, eager and pleased to be part of the Brotherhood, saw the twice-weekly lunch as an act of solidarity and hope—besides, many of them needed the baked beans or spaghetti. Elisse rustled pages. "Here," she said. "Loan to Pete Ogoczy, loan to Armand Choix, loan to Johnny Coleman. Thirty or so dittoes. At least half made by you."

"I'll have to watch it," he said, reddening. "Union officials get paid. We pay Mitch. You work full time too."

"Two fifty a quarter is eighty-three thirty a month. Isn't that a mite plush for the secretary?"

"You've lost weight."

"Oh, for heaven's sake, Justin! On purpose, on purpose."

"You dab a bit on your plate and give us the rest."

"You want me fat as Kate Smith?"

"I'm worried about you."

Ben's violin had ceased. The radio orchestra was playing the Polonaise from *Eugene Onegin*, and she hummed a bar. "I love that opera. Daddy does too—did I ever tell you he was all set to call me Tatiana?"

"He told me," Justin said. "You're overdoing it, sweet."

"That calm persistence can be irritating as hell," she said. "Justin, I didn't come here to shut myself in a glass case. Stop worrying, you have a strong, immortal, purposeful wife."

"Sometimes I feel as if we're part of a stupid charade. Where's this getting us?"

"Eleven hundred and thirty-seven members," she said, triumphant.

"All in the tire shop."

She closed one eye, squinting at him. Justin's size and general air of solid certainty no longer fooled her; she knew he was prey to the deep, mean blues: these self-abrasive questionings of his past and present had begun around the time he discovered his illegitimacy. She bore across the hot, crowded little room.

"Oh, so you don't think the Brothers're going places, is that right?" she asked, parrying curved fingertips at his underarms. Justin was violently ticklish. Laughing and helpless, he tried to fend her off. She pushed her attack, laughing as much as he. Not until they were both gasping and wet-eyed did she desist.

Chuckling still, he pulled her into his lap, and she rested her cheek against his perspiration-moist hair. "How come," she inquired, "you're gray up here and not other places?"

"That's privileged information."

They both smiled.

"Justin, I'm fine. Hunky-dory. But if it'll make you feel better, put fifty into our account."

"Fifty's not enough for three months."

"I can't bear to cut the loans, or the Ladies' lunches."

"Elisse—"

"Oh, come on, darling. Ain't we got fun?" Her voice went husky.

Their smiles faded. The radio with its glowing emerald light spread the next selection, the cool, dreamy notes of Rachmaninoff, and she inhaled sharply, suspended in the pleasure of his touch. She loved the deliberation of his hands, loved that he never fumbled or got rough and frantic, and as he rubbed slowly on the cotton above her nipples she was strung on exquisite cords that reached deep within her vagina. They were both breathing irregularly, and she thought, *How fine it is that we're both still besotted enough to go at it here and now.*

The toilet flushed upstairs. They pulled apart.

"Later." Justin's voice was a low rumble.

"Date," she murmured, kissing his forehead.

He laced his shoes, combed his hair, reknotted his tie, and drove off to a Hamtramck boardinghouse where in a bedroom crowded with sweating, frightened men with Polish surnames, he would enumerate the reasons that automotive workers should form an industrial union.

IV

An hour or so later Elisse was holding up a pair of boy's brown knickers. With a half-pay envelope the AAW families had no cash for luxuries like clothes, so she had written letters to all the Kaplans' friends, requesting castoffs, which the Ladies' Auxiliary darned and patched. The worn flannel exuded an odor of urine, one knee was gone, and so were the buttons. Reluctantly she shoved the garment into the box red-crayoned RAGMAN.

The bell buzzed.

Elisse looked up. Both Justin and Mitch had impressed on her that she must never open the door when she was alone—batterings were one facet of Security's crusade of discouraging the Brothers: as a cautionary object lesson, Mitch had twice been jumped and knocked senseless as he returned to his boardinghouse. These warnings, however, eluded her, for on these hot nights Mrs. Milacek often carried over a pitcher of iced coffee and some harmless chatter.

"Be right there," Elisse called, running to answer.

On the dark porch stood a wide-shouldered man wearing a straw hat. His silhouette was all she could discern: Detroit, unable to pay for electricity, had discontinued lighting the streets of many suburbs, including Woodland Park.

"Mrs. Hutchinson?" he asked.

"Hutchins," she retorted, fear prickling the fine hair on the back of her neck as she pushed at the door.

He propped it open with his shoulder. "Elisse with two s's, Kaplan, Hutchinson. Mrs. Justin."

Her pupils had adjusted and she made out two shadowy specters at the bottom of the steps. "Who are you?" she asked.

"I'm with Onyx. Perhaps you've heard my name." The tone was pleasant, a patrician Eastern drawl. "Dickson Keeley."

Himself, she thought. *It's bad, very*. "Mr. Keeley, my husband is out." *Thank God*.

"It's you we want to talk to," he said. The forms ceased to be ghosts, becoming two large, sweat-odored men as they clomped up the wooden stoop. The three jarred by her into the narrow, stuffy hall. "This is Smith." Dickson Keeley indicated the tall, pudgy-hipped man in a seersucker suit

Smith took off his panama, inclining his shining pink pate.

"And meet Potter." The name fitted not at all. Swarthy and sharp-featured, displaying his muscular body in a tight double-breasted suit, Potter was most people's idea of a recently immigrated Sicilian.

"Pleased to meet you," Potter said in a liquid, unplaceable accent.

"My husband'll be back any minute," she said. How could she be lying this smoothly when her legs were cold to the knees with fear? How was she able to stand? "He's bringing back some friends."

"He's in Hamtramck haranguing three of our men and four from Chrysler's Jefferson plant." Dickson Keeley glanced at his minions, who positioned themselves as though to cut off escape routes, fat Smith lounging against the front door as he took out an emery board to file the nails of his soft-looking hands while the swarthy Potter settled on the staircase, hands on upthrust knees, taut as if on the ready for an Olympic sprint. Keeley stepped into the living room.

"What's all this? A rummage sale?" Pushing aside the RAGMAN's carton, he slung his straw hat neatly to the coffee table. "I must say you're quite a surprise. Even in those old clothes you're a knockout. Real class. Your school pictures don't do you justice."

"Is that how spend your free minutes, poring over old U of C annuals?" The pounding of her heart rang loudly in her ears, but Elisse had learned the ability to project a tart breeziness, cover-up for her treacly interior. She sounded normal.

"Spunk, too. I like spunk. Tell me something. Why does a peach like you waste time stirring up a bunch of Polacks, Hunkies, hillbillies, and dinges? What's with Justin anyway? Depression or no, a lawyer with a British accent can rake in the berries. If you were my heatless cooker, I'd wrap you in sables."

Elisse's chilled thighs were about to give way, but sensing it a tactical error to sit, she moved to the window, where leaning against the ledge would appear casual rather than necessary.

"Relax, relax, I'm here as a pal," Dickson Keeley said. "I'm giving you some advice. Pass it on to Justin. He should head back West."

"You're kidding."

"Detroit's no town for him. I'd tell him myself, but his sister's Mrs. Caryll Bridger." Keeley's lips pursed, an ambiguous curve that was halfway to a smirk. "Family matters can get complicated, know what I mean? Anyway, the message'll score harder, coming from you."

"This brightens my day."

Keeley looked sharply at her.

"You want us to quit," she said. "That can mean only one thing. The Brothers are finally getting someplace."

"Every day's sunshine in Los Angeles. Nothing but blue skies all day long. You'll be happier. And healthier."

"Is that a threat?" Her voice was breathy. "You really ought to do better. You sound like the stinker in a B movie."

Smith's emery board rasped.

"Be a good girl," Keeley said. "Stop trying to prove how brave you are, cut out the wisecracks. Have you got this straight? You're telling Justin that you're ready to pack up and go home."

"Oh no I'm not."

His pupils shrank, a momentary chaos of pure fury that reminded Elisse that two AAW members had died after Security's anonymous beatings, yet his voice retained that bantering drawl as he replied, "You're sharp. Can't you see this Brotherhood business is a laugh? You really don't figure the boss is about to deal with a local, do you? Why, he'd just as soon negotiate with a hunk of steel."

His brief metamorphosis into a raging creature had sealed Elisse's terror. She was shivering in the heat; however, she forced herself to speak levelly. "People aren't hunks of steel. They think, they feel."

"I'm paid a fortune to keep out unions, and the other auto companies spend the same amounts. Don't be a fool, Elisse. There's no point for you to live in a dump like this, or to work your tail off, no point at all. The auto companies aren't going to give any union a toehold. And Onyx! You tell me. When has the boss let anyone lay down the law to him? He didn't listen to the President or Congress, so why would he kowtow to a bunch of nobodies?"

"Because he'll have to. Or close down."

"Don't make me laugh. More than half of Detroit's out of work. Every man in every plant could quit tomorrow, and the day after, they'd be lined up waiting to fill the jobs. What do you figure this double work week's about?"

"If there were a closed shop—"

"There won't be, so stop spinning your wheels." He leaned his spatulate chin toward her. "Tonight you talk to Justin."

"Never," she said.

"What good did college do you?" he asked mildly, rising to his feet. "Guys."

Smith ceased filing his nails and Potter stood in one swift, articulated movement. Both stepped into the small, stuffy room. Teeth glinted from between lips drawn back into horrifying grimaces that masqueraded as smiles.

The dingy, mustard-colored wallpaper, the cartons, the shabby, comfortable upholstery shipped from California receded from Elisse's vision. Unable to move, she panted, a small, paralyzed little creature run to earth. Her stomach froze in a spongy way, as if crushed ice packed her viscera.

Nobody spoke.

The fat one, Smith, tugged at his seersucker jacket as he took one long stride toward where she shuddered by the window. Suddenly her hypnotized state turned to frenzy. Unconsciously her fingers curved, her thumbs tensed; she prepared to gouge at his eyes. Before she could lift her arms, he imprisoned her wrists. His speed and agility as well as the strength of those soft-looking freckled hands should have astonished her, but there was no room for surprise in her incandescent panic. To escape his grasp she kicked and twisted. The celadon-green china lamp teetered, toppling quietly onto the couch, not breaking. Smith jerked his arms behind her back, about-facing her so that her heaving rib cage arched toward the other two.

Nobody spoke.

Dickson Keeley stepped over a carton to the radio, turning it on full blast so that the crazed scuffle of her saddle shoes and her barking gasps were covered by an actor's trained voice. *You can't get away with this.*

Smith forced her into the hall, skidding her balky soles across the floorboards. A wire of rationality was strung through her panic, and she bit her lower lip, refusing to cry out lest she awaken her children.

In the narrow hall a foot chopped hard against the back of her calves. Her shoes shot out from under her. She would have fallen had not Smith been holding her. He let her down onto the gritty linoleum.

Dickson Keeley struck a match to light a cigar.

For the rest of her life whenever she thought about this interlude while Dickson Keeley smoked his Havana, it was with the absolute conviction that she had been flung into a surrealistic world running parallel to the real one; a hellish world whose chemistry was composed of elements inimical to sanity.

Her face was a few inches from Dickson Keeley's black shoes, and the smell of wax polish overpowered the dusty smell of the floor to which Smith was pinning her shoulders. Potter bent over to rip down her cotton step-ins. She lay exposed to the waist, thrashing like a landed fish, fearing to shut her eyes lest she somehow be trapped in this monstrous world, forcing herself to squint up at the red tip of Keeley's cigar. From the corner of her eye she saw Potter unbutton his pants. Dickson Keeley aimed a casual kick between her knees, and Potter punched apart her vibrating thighs.

Once Justin had told her that the Germans affixed their bayonets not with normal knives but with sharp, corkscrew-shaped ones. This travesty of the act of love was like that, inflicting hideously jagged wounds into what until now had been a spiritually dedicated private joy shared by Justin and her.

She stared up at that moving red star while her small, delicate body was rattled and ground into the worn linoleum of the narrow, dimly lit hall.

V

The Green Hornet, tuned loud, woke Ben, and he went to the top of the narrow stairs.

If the men had been hitting his mother, he would have charged down, an instinctive reaction of his belligerent bravery, but one was calmly smoking a cigar, watching while the fat guy held down her shoulders and the other sprawled between her legs, his pants around his knees, his bare, viciously bouncing butt like two stuck-together bubble gums. Ben accepted that this particular harm they were inflicting on her was that adult mystery he could not be part of, even as her protector. He stood in the dark, shivering. The fat guy who held her shoulders took the other's place.

Long before he finished, she ceased struggling.

The man with the cigar bent over where she lay, her skirt rucked up. There was a lull in the radio, and Ben heard him say, "Los Angeles is the town for you, Elisse." Noise sizzled as he pressed his cigar between her limp, spraddled legs. The music blared.

The men left, for the program changed. Neither Ben nor Elisse moved. He stood what seemed hours before she rolled over and pushed herself up on all fours. Darkness pooled on the floor where she had lain.

Ben tiptoed back to bed and lay with his arms tense across his chest.

The radio went off. He would never listen to *The Green Hornet;* never, never again. He feigned sleep when she came to lead him to the toilet so he wouldn't wet the bed. Her hands trembled wildly. He could not pee.

VI

She lay pressed to the mattress, her breath coming in mechanical gasps as though an iron lung were inhaling and exhaling for her. She was not crying. At first she could not think, could not feel anything beyond the burn. Gradually, though, an undefined determination began to radiate from the bleeding, outraged center of her. A queer, woozy determination that grew stronger.

Dickson Keeley's punitive brutality had failed in its purpose of dispatching Elisse, whimpering and sobbing, back to the safety of Los Angeles. Even granted the slow, benumbed way her mind was functioning, she knew she would not go back until her purpose was accomplished.

With the plodding repetitiveness of a child learning by rote, she thought, *I have to put a stop to this sort of thing. I must put an end. Yes. I'll force the Bridgers to put a stop to this kind of thing.* Her sense of humor hors de combat, she found nothing ludicrous or mad in one small woman's declaring war on her loathed, never met, other-side-of-the-blanket in-laws and their mammoth instrument of mass production—a single one of their factories, Woodland, employed more people than lived in the entire state of Nevada. Her mind refused emotionally freighted words like terrorize and rape, her precarious stability would shatter if she thought clearly about what had transpired against a background of loud radio melodrama. *This sort of thing must stop*, she thought. In her daze she found fortification in the eleven hundred and thirty-seven members of the AAW. With a union, this sort of thing will end.

Several hours evaporated.

Justin's secondhand Seven halted outside. She inched onto her side, stifling whimpers of agony in the pillow. When he came up, she did not speak or open her eyes. In bed he kissed her averted shoulder. Once they had promised to share desire, passion, mortal love, but since then she had visited that other world, and now his kisses were moist, slightly repellent nuzzling on bare flesh. "Elisse?" he whispered. She did not reply. He must have assumed she slept heavily, for he curled around her back, and soon his breathing lengthened into a deep, regular pattern. It was then, at last, that tears squeezed in odd shapes between her tight-shut eyelids.

CHAPTER 27

The new streamliner with its silver-grooved promise of a swift glide
into the future drew the crowd's attention. Few people on Track 14
turned to react to the loud scene Ben was making. Balking at the
steps, he hurled himself at Elisse, burying his face in her white
piqué jacket, clinging to her waist with a parasitic grasp. Bending,
she kissed his curly brown hair, concealing the pain that his scrab-
bling clutch inflicted on her pelvis and her soul, saying: "Hey, Ben.
It's called the Zephyr."

"You come," he said, muffled.

"You're the one who's taking the vacation with Grandma and
Grandpa," she said.

It was the middle of August, two weeks after Dickson Keeley's
visit, and by hook, crook, and long distance wire, she had connived
this "vacation." The children's departure wrenched her as much as
if her vital organs were being removed for safekeeping.

"I don't wanna go on a dumb train."

"You let Grandpa buy your ticket."

"So what? I wanted to see what the streamliner looks like," he
replied pugnaciously.

Mr. Kaplan put his hands on his grandson's shoulders. "How
about the duets we're going to play?"

And Mrs. Kaplan fluttered closer. "The compartments on the
Zephyr are lovely."

"*Booooooard!*"

Elisse gripped Ben, torn between crushing him yet closer and thrusting him onto the protective safety of the throbbing train.

Justin, who was holding his daughter, set her tenderly on her tiny white boots. Tonia's face crunched as if in preparation for tears, but instead of crying she trotted to her grandmother, reaching up for the kid-gloved hand, a docile, pleading gesture that mangled Elisse.

"I have a good-bye present for you, Ben," Justin said as he unclamped his son from Elisse. "Come take a look." He dragged the child a few steps.

Elisse murmured to Mr. Kaplan, "I don't know what's gotten into him. He's never been a mama's boy."

The Kaplans glanced at each other, but Elisse did not see. Kneeling by Tonia, resting her lips against the warm, silken cheek, she wondered how she could entrust her precious to that sweet, vague woman and the foolish-clever stout little man in Hollywood white flannels and navy blazer. "Love you, Antonia mine," she whispered.

"Love Mommy," Tonia replied with a strangling hug.

The other passengers already leaned from windows, waving.

"Boooooard!"

"Dad gave me an AAW badge," Ben said in a combative, unassuaged tone and, not glancing at Elisse, sprinted onto the train. One more hasty round of embraces. "Look after them, Daddy. . . . Mother, remember don't let Tonia eat strawberries. . . . Byee. . . . Byeeeee. . . ."

Whistles shrilled and the Zephyr slid from the depot. Wiping her eyes with one hand, waving with the other, Elisse found herself remembering what her mother had told her, a German second cousin had sent his two little daughters to live with her uncle and aunt in London. *Hitler,* her mother had whispered with a tremulous sigh. *It's very bad in Germany.*

As they started along the emptying track, Justin took her bare elbow. Once his touch on her skin had brought tingles of erogenous pleasure, but now it only depressed her. *I'm a dry stick,* she thought, stepping away.

Sun blazed on a sullenly hot morning, and they opened the car windows. On Fort Street they passed the large brake-drum factory, Milfrond Dome, which stood on the site of the old Stuart Furniture Company. Here, Tom Bridger had driven his first gasoline-powered quadricycle, here Hugh Bridger had lost his angelic beauty, from this place had come Justin's inheritance.

"Harris is worried about you," Justin said.

"Daddy?" It was Mrs. Kaplan who kept reiterating, *Dear, you're so pale, a little holiday home would do wonders for you.*

"He said you asked them to invite Ben and Tonia."

"We had a bad connection. I can't remember who said what."

"I don't understand you, Elisse. We've never taken a weekend without them. And now you insist on sending them two thousand miles?"

"I've given up my overprotective ways, all right? What's so terrible about grandchildren visiting their grandparents? You agreed it was a good idea. They'll be out of this muggy heat." *What excuses will I find to keep them out there in autumn?*

"Harris wondered if you're pregnant."

"Chummy little chats you two had."

"Are you, Elisse?"

"In my tenth month," she said. "Oh, honestly, Justin!"

"You haven't been yourself the last couple of weeks. And . . . well . . . you've never put me off before."

She felt the blood in her face and was grateful for the protective brim of her out-of-date mannish hat. "A little problem down there," she said.

He shot her a look of concern.

"Nothing to worry about," she said hastily. "I've seen a gynecologist."

"You never told me."

"Irving Weiner, M.D."

"What does he say?"

"Cervicitis. Sorry it's been inconveniencing you."

She heard him swallow. Shamed by her flip cruelty, she squinted through the windshield at the Guardian Building, the Penobscot's stepped tower, Tom Bridger's Michigan Bank of Commerce, the Ford (no connection to Henry) Building. The brash blue day, the layers of industrial smoke, gave the downtown skyscrapers the theatrical look of a modern cityscape on a backdrop scrim. She murmured, "What a rotten thing for me to say."

"Write to your parents," he said crisply. "Make it clear there's no baby."

"Justin, you know I didn't mean it."

His left hand touched her knee. Absolution. "Now tell me what's wrong," he said.

"Nothing. The cervicitis is clearing up, I've gained two pounds as ordered, and I swear solemnly to blunt my tongue. All's right with the world."

"You've been looking—the only word I can think of is frightened. You seem so frightened, nerved up all the time." The traffic was heavier, and he shifted into second gear. "We ought to go home to Los Angeles. Pick up where we left off."

"After what we've seen here?" she cried.

"You're what's important to me."

"Justin, stop *brooding*. It's a common female problem. It's clearing up."

"You'd tell me if anything were upsetting you?"

"I'd nag you to death with it."

II

Justin had the second half of the swing shift. As his car pulled away, Elisse left the dishes soaking and went into the living room. The dingy, finger-stained mustard wallpaper depressed her utterly, and she picked up the one-eared elephant that Tonia had dropped on the floor, cuddling the worn stuffed toy to her as she telephoned Mitch. He promised to take the trolley over as soon as he closed headquarters.

At his expected knock, she jumped. Going to the front door, she called shrilly, "Who is it?"

"Me. Mitch."

She pushed the dead bolt, turned the new lock, opening the door an inch while it was still chained. At the familiar short, broad figure, she relaxed.

She had perked fresh coffee for him and set out a ragged quarter of a fudge cake. "Leftovers from the Last Supper," she said lightly enough, but her face was wretched.

"You miss them already?"

"What do you think?" She filled his cup. "Mitch, can you borrow a car?"

"For what?"

"I need somebody to drive me to the doctor."

Thick eyebrows pulled together. "Is it what I'm thinking, Elisse?"

Her face withdrew into sharpness, and her pupils swelled. Folding her arms on the checkered oilcloth of the kitchen table, she rested her forehead in her palms. Loud sobs convulsed through her.

Mitch, behind her, kneaded her shoulders. "It's all right. It's all right."

She stood up, weeping into the shoulder of his faded blue cotton shirt, which smelled of harsh sweat and Fels Naptha soap. She had not yet been able to let Justin hold her, but Mitch's squat body held no tormenting memories of the poetic delicacy of early love, no hauntings of fulfilled passion, no sepulchral reminders that the carnal joy of marriage was dead. After a few minutes she pulled away, blowing her nose.

"Have you found a decent person?" Mitch asked. "I won't take you to a butcher."

"It's not an abortion."

"Elisse?"

"Dr. Weiner's in that gray medical building on Griswold."

"You've got me baffled. If it's on the up-and-up, why can't Justin take you?"

"It's a long story," she said, sitting again. She had not intended to tell him, but the crying jag had lowered her inhibitions. She sketched a bare outline of Dickson Keeley's visit, whispering a sentence about the double rape, the burn. Mitch's head tilted so his good ear was toward her.

"The filthy bastard, those filthy, filthy bastards," he growled in a thick, choking anger that she had never heard from him.

"The burn isn't healing. Dr. Weiner prescribed a salve, but the darned burn hasn't responded. Yesterday I phoned and he said he'd have to do a mite of surgery. Daddy slipped me some money, thank God."

"Justin'll have to know you're in the hospital."

"I wept into the mouthpiece and Dr. Weiner finally agreed to manage in his office. That's why I need you to drive me."

"Now I know why you sent the kids to your parents."

"How could I risk keeping them here?"

Mitch drank his cold coffee. "You ought to tell Justin."

"Keeley's plan exactly!" she cried. "Don't you see, Mitch?

Justin's brother to the Crown Princess, so he's afraid to touch him. He thinks he can scare Justin off through me.''

"He ought to take you home."

"What?"

"If you don't tell him, I will."

"Can this be dedicated Mitch Shapiro speaking?" Since he had confessed over a bowl of soup in the Book Cadillac that hopeless love of her had driven him into the Party, then had embarrassed her thoroughly by saying he was merely trying to cheer her up, a question had lingered: Did he love her or didn't he? Yet wasn't it the height of conceit to imagine that Mitch might nurse anything so bourgeois as an unrequited passion?

"It's one thing to rough up men, but—"

"I survived."

"I know you've worked your heart out, but—"

"Oh, cut it out, Mitch!" She clapped a fist into a palm. "How can you talk like this? Now, when we're finally getting someplace?"

Mitch stared at her. Her face, thinner, tanless, pink at the nose from crying, had a lit-up fervor that dazzled and weakened him; this face was yet more lovely to him than her previous sleekly tanned beauty. Sighing, he capitulated. "Leo Jackson, he's in the Young Communist League, has a Fiver."

"My appointment's ten tomorrow morning."

"What about Justin?"

"He won't be here. He's changing to the morning shift."

III

Elisse chewed her lower lip as Mitch drove the borrowed Fiver, a trembly old 1924 Runabout with a fouled spark plug.

Over the noisy putt-popping, he asked, "How do you feel about Zawitsky?"

Elisse snapped out of her reverie. "Are you kidding?" The bearlike widower, after twenty-five years at Onyx, had lost his job—a tap on the shoulder by a uniformed Security guard and that was it—the same day that his son had gotten word of winning a scholarship. "Zawitsky's my buddy."

"I figured he'll take Ben's room and I'll take Tonia's. Then somebody'll always be around the house with you."

"So you're not telling Justin?"

"Did you really think I would?"

"You were fuming. I haven't seen you like that since Martha called you a Trotskyite." Elisse's pretty bitch smile showed briefly. "Mitch, thank you." And then she clasped her hands and was silent again.

As Dr. Weiner came into the examining room Elisse, from her position on the stirrup table, said, "Here I am, ready for the Saturnalia." A forlorn little joke referring to the toga-like sheet that draped her.

The doctor's aquiline face did not relinquish its tight-lipped aloofness. This repair surgery ought to have been done at Detroit General, where a spinal could be administered, but these years he practiced less than perfect medicine on malnourished women, battered women, women hemorrhaging from botched abortions, burying his dismay under impenetrable professionalism. He had not asked Elisse how she had acquired her loathsome burn, for the simple reason that he no longer had the emotional capital to invest in his patients. He glanced at the stout German refugee, his nurse, and she snapped rubber gloves on him.

Elisse stared through the open sash window to the madly blue sky, trying to empty her mind so the dope pills could work. But thoughts popped up, as clear and sharply formed as cartoons. Her father in his studio playing a duet with Ben. Justin holding her hand at a Garbo movie—which one? Lying on the beach at Santa Monica, the sun hot on her back. Somewhere nearby in the tall gray medical building a radio was playing—or was this, too, imagined? A trained tenor voice was singing.

From yon far country blows . . .

The doctor murmured something to the nurse, who whispered gutturally. There was the hiss of the sterilizer, the clink of instruments.

And then it began, the agony that melted like ice through her entire body, dripping through her convulsed fingertips and toes.

What are those blue remembered hills?

The dope should have stopped her from feeling this, shouldn't it? She breathed in loud gasps but did not cry out. Instead, she listened.

What spires, what farms are those?

The eternal, never-ending icy pain had been part of her existence forever.

Oh, from yon far country blows . . .

Pain.

IV

Hugh and Caryll buried their hatchet in a joint attempt to propel Tom into using the double work week throughout Woodland. Hugh thirsted after publicity to launch the new models, and Caryll had received three telephone calls ripe with Rooseveltian charm and command. Tom, though, finding the thin paychecks more abhorrent than ever, had also come to view them as further wedges between himself and Justin. The other two argued, logically, that labor unrest at Onyx had been no greater than at any rival company: more, tire production was up—the men were driven by foremen and anxiety. So why not be patriotic? Abrasively, reluctantly, Tom threw them a sop. On September 3 the battery shop went on the double work week.

The four dangling sixty-watt bulbs shed an uncongenial light in the storefront, which despite the late hour, nearly eleven, was crowded and noisy. Elisse, her face determinedly cheerful, a cushion under her, was stationed at the rickety secretarial table, signing up the last of a long line, most of them from the battery shop. Men clustered talking union, and the three female members perched together in a corner, handbags clutched on their laps—Clara Jannings, the tall, full-bosomed ex-teacher, had convinced many of her fellow loom girls to sign union cards.

Elisse folded the final torn dollar in the tin box, glancing at Justin. He climbed on an orange crate. Voices subsided, folding chairs scraped as ragged lines formed in front of him. No Robert's Rules of Order here. Justin led old and new members in an open discussion of AAW aims. Fair working conditions. Seniority rights. The end of Security. The end of chiseling foremen. The return to a full day's work that a man might feed his family.

A thin machinist asked angrily, "So how much more of this do we gotta take? When do we show them sons of bitches?"

Someone else chimed in, "Yeah, what about a strike?"

"We have six thousand, and that's jolly damn good," Justin

417

replied. "But you know and I know that if we walk out tomorrow, all six thousand strong, there would be so many applicants for our jobs that Employment would have to corral them in the parking lots."

"If the world's full of scabs, what's the point of a union?"

"Yeah, what's the use of all this if we can't put the screws to 'em?"

"There's another kind of strike," Justin said quietly. "The men don't walk out. They stay inside. A sit-down strike."

A large pitman stood. "What about the boss? What's he doing while they sit? Why don't he throw them out?"

"Management has itself a neat little problem," Justin said. "A free-for-all would wreck their expensive machinery."

After a brief silence heads nodded. Yeah. Yeah.

"Prof, tell us about it."

Justin explained that the sit-down strike had been used in Europe before the war.

The pitman said bitterly, "So we try this Europe game, so we stay in our shops until we starve, so what? They keep on making cars and trucks around us."

"They can't," Justin retorted. "That's the beauty of it. Woodland's a finely tuned machine, every part calibrated to work with every other part. If, say, batteries and tires aren't spewing out, the machine grinds to a halt."

"That's right. Nothin' works without the flow."

"What did you call it again?"

"A sit-down," Justin said.

V

Once a week she took the trolley downtown for Dr. Weiner's swift, silent examination. On the last Friday in September, after his routine swabbing with icy antiseptic, he pronounced, "Healed."

"That's a big speech for you, Doctor."

"You can sleep with your husband again," he said.

A constant drawing pain had persisted. The area around the stitches felt thin, taut, poppable as a balloon, and heaped onto Elisse's recollections of the rape were lurid fantasies of making love . . . hemorrhages, gushes of pulpy flesh, a red swamp. . . . She needed reassurance in the worst way, but looking into the purpose-fully guarded aquiline face, she found she could ask no questions.

Dazed, she emerged into the humid, swarming streets and without conscious decision made her way to the nearby opulent peace of Hudson's toy department. A polio outbreak in Wayne County had given her the excuse to let the children remain longer in California. She missed them murderously, and to buck herself up after her doctor's appointment, she would indulge herself by selecting play-things for them that she could in no way afford and had no intention of buying.

Her knees went wobbly. She rested on an upholstered stool. The glass counter boasted one magnificent display, a large, golden-curled Shirley Temple doll jaunty in a white fur coat and fur beret. Idly she turned over the ticket. Fifty dollars!

A man wandered over to examine the doll. He was in his thirties, round-faced and balding at the temples. He looked vaguely familiar, but his tailoring was discreet and at the same time modish; she knew none of Detroit's upper crust.

Catching her eye, he explained, "I have three girls. And you?"

"One," Elisse retorted. "She's this very size."

A beaming elderly saleslady swooped down on them. "Isn't she a love, Mr. Bridger? We got her in yesterday. That's real human hair. She comes with a trunk that holds three more outfits. Would you like me to add her to your bill?"

"Mmm. Clarice is wild about Shirley Temple. Yes. Please send her out with the other things."

"Of course, Mr. Bridger."

The effusive repetition of the name identified him; however, the dry churning in Elisse's chest had nothing to do with her hatred of the Bridger family, neither was she righteously indignant at the offhanded expenditure of a sum that a tirebuilder wrenched his guts out for two and a half weeks to earn. It took her several choking breaths to realize she was jealous. A dumb, vicarious sibling jealousy. That Caryll Bridger could bestow this gift while Justin could not afford any toy here! As the saleslady bore away the doll Caryll Bridger inquired, "You weren't going to take her, were you?"

Did that polite question mean *You can't afford it?* Dead, she'd rather be dead than admit Justin the lesser in any way.

"No. This." She snatched up a floppy-eared blue dog. Her tone as belligerent as Ben's, she said, "I'm Elisse Hutchinson."

"Justin's wife! Of all people!"

"He told his sister we were in Detroit and wanted to see you."

"I know, but . . . well, you know . . . families."

"The Jewish sister-in-law in the woodpile?"

He turned crimson and his neck tendons showed. "Of course not."

He's the only one who wrote to Justin, she thought. Her anger disintegrated, although her jealousy—that absurd jealousy—vibrated as strongly. "I didn't mean to shout at you, Mr. Bridger."

"Caryll. I'm truly sorry we haven't gotten together. It's nothing to do with your religion—how awful that you should have thought that. It's . . . my wife . . . she, uh, adored Justin, and, uh, no girl would have been g-good enough f-for him." He reached for the blue dog in her arms. "Let me buy that for your little girl."

Retribution? Charity? "Don't be silly," she said. The gray-haired saleslady had returned, and Elisse thrust the toy at her. "I'm taking this."

During the transaction Caryll kept his teeth bared in a polite, conciliatory smile, and when the woman handed Elisse the paper bag with Hudson's calligraphy, he asked, "Do you have time for a cup of coffee?"

Looking into the round face, she saw a flustered, hangdog appeal that tugged at her gooey heart. "I'm dying for one," she said.

The high-ceilinged tearoom was emptying of the luncheon crowd, and the hostess led them to a quiet corner. Elisse shed her jacket to better display the pretty pink fagoted blouse that her parents had bought her during their brief stay, annoyed equally by her vanity and by her rivalrous thrust to prove Justin in tip-top financial shape. Could there be anything more pointlessly inane? What was she trying to prove? That they were in Detroit for high living?

The pastry cart was wheeled over. "Go ahead," Caryll said. "Please."

"The eclairs look wonderful," she admitted.

Sugar and caffeine in her bloodstream, she continued her attempt to prove Justin's superiority by showing he had not wed a shrew but a charmer. In her own ears her witticisms sounded stilted, awkward, yet Caryll smiled and laughed.

"My brother-in-law's a very lucky guy," he said.

"And aren't I the fink, finding I like Big Business?" *What a way to put it! Too cute.*

Caryll smiled. "Even in war there are truces."

"And this certainly is no-man's-land." She glanced oh so coyly at the well-dressed shoppers adawdle over final cups of coffee.

"True," he said. "But you've got me wrong, Elisse. I'm all for your union."

She felt a frisson through her pelvis at the memory of the cigar being smoked over her head. "I'd never have suspected. And Security's not in on it, either."

He reddened. "My father's always had two firm rules. Onyx pays the tops. And nobody tells him how to make cars."

"Somebody has to. He hasn't the foggiest how grim it is, working in a speeded up stretch-out."

"Elisse, we aren't talking about some New York banker or stockholder. Dad's early life was as poor and bleak as they come. He was born on a North Dakota farm so lonely that my grandmother killed herself. My grandfather died of appendicitis because no doctor could travel the fifty miles to their farm—I've always figured that was his motivating force, to do away with that kind of isolation. As a boy he worked thirteen, fourteen hours a day at a foundry as a puddler's helper, dangerous and backbreaking work, then came home to tinker on his invention. He built his first automobile before anyone in Detroit knew what one was. He refused to turn out expensive cars like everyone else was doing, cars only the rich could afford. He fought a trust to build the Fiver."

"I never said he wasn't a giant. But this isn't 1895, it's 1935."

"Don't blame Dad for the Depression. He's lost a fortune."

"You just don't know what goes on at Woodland. The worm's-eye view. Men shrivel, they go deaf, their nerves are shot. It's tough, hard work, God, so hard. The pace is killing. And they're forever worrying they'll lose their jobs. No matter how many years they've worked, they can be fired any minute. Security's worse than the German Gestapo."

He sighed. "It's rotten, I know that, Elisse. But tell me honestly, is life any sweeter at Ford or Hudson—or any other company?"

"You try feeding a family on a twenty-hour paycheck."

Caryll fiddled with his coffee spoon. "Blame that on me. That's my fault. Unemployment is the country's big problem. I argued Dad into giving the double work week a try."

"Then I should say thank you. You've built the AAW."

"Why didn't you pick another company? Dad's more dead set against a closed shop than the rest. He's convinced he's his workers' best friend—"

"Hah!"

"—and he'll do anything before he'll let shop stewards give orders at Onyx."

"We mean business."

"You don't stand a chance."

"Let's talk about how angry the men in tires and batteries are because they can't feed their kids or pay rent on a one-room shack. Let's talk about how everyone at Onyx is terrified they'll be in the same fix, let's talk about all our John Doe members!"

"Elisse, Dad's not an easy man to read, but take it from me. In his lifetime there'll never be a closed shop in Onyx." An assuredness welded Caryll's voice. In his richly discreet tailoring he looked powerful and invincible. The ranged forces of capitalism . . .

The energy drained abruptly from her, and she felt as weak and dazed as when she had emerged from Dr. Weiner's office. "Ahh, what's the point discussing it anyway? We're the opposition, shouting across mountaintops." She nibbled at the last of her eclair. "You never told me about Petra."

Caryll smiled—could anyone with those gentle, warm gray eyes be a bloodsucking capitalist?—and talked about his youngest. As he helped Elisse on with her jacket he said, "Zoe . . . well . . . she's Zoe. Visiting's impossible. But Justin will always be my friend. And now we're friends too, Elisse. If you need anything, ever, call me."

She nodded.

"I mean it. I'm on your side."

"Caryll, you're okay," she said, managing animation, planting a kiss on his cheek, which smelled of expensive shaving lotion.

"Uh-oh. You're forgetting your package."

As she took the light, bulky bag, she had to sit down again. Panic was dizzying her. What had she done? She had thrown away the grocery money on a three-buck toy to impress the heir to the largest privately owned empire on earth, that's what. You can eat neither pride nor plush dogs, so for four adults there would be nothing except a few pinto beans and one can of tomatoes until payday next week.

Inventing an excuse about the powder room, she waited until Caryll entered a large brown elevator, then ran over to catch the next one, traveling down to the toy department.

The elderly saleslady refused to refund her money. "That item was on sale, madam."

"How was I to know that?"

"See? Here on the bill? Sale merchandise. Not returnable."

"I don't want a damn reject for my baby!" Elisse raised her trembling hand to her forehead. Through a blur she saw her saleslady waddle to a thin woman, presumably the department manager. The two bent their heads together, looking at her, and she thought she heard the name Bridger. The saleslady returned with folded bills and some change.

Elisse ducked into the emergency stairwell.

She huddled weeping on a metal-edged step that was as cold as a gravestone. What had happened to lively, witty little Elisse Hutchinson that she made scenes in department stores, that she sent her children from her, that she feared the sweet, moist marital embrace?

CHAPTER 28

In the middle of October, Lord Montgomery Edge suffered a coronary, and Edwina ended her cable to Detroit on a chilling note: *Doctors uncertain of outcome.*

Tom booked immediate passage.

When he arrived in London the Edges' pillared town house overlooking Regent's Park was abustle.

Monty, in a plaid dressing gown, held conferences with groups involved in the building and selling of the perky little four-cylinder European Tiny Onyx. Besides being Tom's viceroy in Great Britain, he was also in charge of the factories in France, Spain, Belgium, Holland, Sweden, Norway, Austria, Italy, and Turkey as well as the dealer outlets from the Mediterranean to the Arctic Circle.

Tom did not bother to disguise his relief at his friend's vigor. After a heartfelt, shamefaced masculine bearhug, he said, "You rest. Get back on your feet. I'll take over for a while."

"Old chap, I fully intend to be in my office tomorrow."

"You and your trick heart scared the water out of me. Relax. And that's an order!"

The two men smiled at each other.

Tom worked a fog-shrouded week near St. Paul's Cathedral in the imposing old stone mansion that had been renamed Onyx House. The following Monday morning Edge showed up in the City, his rested, ruddy face determined.

There was no reason for Tom to stay in London, and later he would question why he had tarried. Yet at the time the city of his cherished years with Antonia soothed him, and he lost a mite of his relentless remorse at having turned Justin against him, he grieved a little less that he had never seen his own grandchildren. This *never* was not entirely accurate: at home he had often driven by Justin's ugly little house in Woodland Park and once had been rewarded by the sight of a wiry small boy hurling his pocketknife into yellow crabgrass—the boy had a tough, angry expression that had captivated Tom.

He hung around London, booking passage at the end of November.

When he landed, newsboys on the Hoboken docks were hawking Extras: ONYX TAKEN OVER BY WORKERS.

II

During Tom's absences Caryll stepped with diffident reluctance into his father's place: he fretted over how to handle each problem the way that Tom would. On *The Onyx Family Variety Hour* he mouthed Tom's inviolable belief in the financially curative powers of low-priced automobiles, high pay, and mass production. In the executive dining room he presided over lunch from Tom's chair at the big round table.

The week after Tom's departure Dickson Keeley remarked, "We haven't done a plant-wide time-motion study in two years."

Caryll continued to cut his pink roast lamb. His old loathing had swelled morbidly since Zoe's episode with Keeley, and he could not stand to look at the man. "What do you think, Uncle Olaf?"

"Auh. We're ready for one." Olaf's new false teeth thickened his Norwegian accent. "Tom and I were talking about it."

Caryll nodded in Dickson Keeley's direction. "Go ahead."

The same afternoon pairs of men, each twosome consisting of a pacemaker and an engineer with a stopwatch, were everyplace in Woodland. A pacemaker worked one job for three days, and his speed was accepted as the norm. Since pacemakers were young, athletic specimens intent on proving their stamina, they pressed furiously, and since they were part of Security, foremen dared not complain when they neglected to bore-drill, solder, grind, or punch a part racing by in front of them. The sight of a hefty pacemaker straining red-faced at his slapdash job drove the men wild. *That* speed was being clicked off by the engineers. *That* speed was the one at which they would be expected to work. Indefinitely, and without fouling up.

Behind the time-motion pairs trailed a sinister rumor: the double work week was a success, and the boss had decided to put all Woodland on four-hour shifts during which a man would be expected to blaze out six hours of production. Which meant, or so frightened whispers tumbled from sides of mouths, a third of the men would be out of work. The loss of pay and speedup was horrifying, but what chilled to the very bone marrow was the thought of being laid off.

Men from every department at Woodland streamed through the sheet-iron back door of headquarters. For the most part they became John Doe members, which meant they did not sign union cards though they paid dues and pledged their allegiance to AAW.

III

He lay on top of her, his heart pounding, his ears warm and tingling. He had found release but none of his old triumphant joy, for he had known she was indulging if not enduring him, known that her final gasps were caused by the orgiastic rhythm of his own body.

He snapped the lamp switch. The light showed a face nearly as white as the pillow slip.

"What is it, sweet?" he whispered. The walls were thin, and Mitch and Zawitsky might be awake. Both were working full time for the union now, and it made sense for them to be occupying the children's empty bedrooms; Justin was glad to have them, but Elisse had invited them without even discussing the matter with him, and this, to Justin, somehow fit in with her new tense way and their problems in bed. "What's wrong?"

"You tell me," she murmured back.

"Do I hurt you?"

Her lashes went down as she shook her head.

"Is it the children? Are you upset they aren't back yet?"

"I *enjoyed* it, Justin."

"I've thought of everything that could possibly be wrong. The illness. You're doing too much, working far too hard—"

She interrupted him by pulling his head down. "If this is your idea of a postcoital compliment, forget it," she said against his ear.

He wanted to tell her how isolated he felt, how much it darkened him, the absence of that electricity with which she had charged their most trivial touch, but stopped himself; wouldn't he sound accusatory? He lifted up onto his elbow again. "We have to leave this miserable town."

"Because I didn't have an orgasm?"

"Since your doctor gave the go-ahead we've made love three times."

She rolled her eyes in mock exasperation.

"Like this," he persisted. "Properly."

"We're being adventurous."

"Is there somebody else?"

"Oh, Justin," she sighed. "You make every other man look like Frankenstein's monster.

"Then tell me what it is, sweet?"

She turned her head. "Since the cervicitis it hurts a little at first." She closed her eyes. "You mustn't notice. Please stop noticing. *Please*?" Her whisper shook and her hand clenched his beseechingly.

He kissed her hair. "I love you a bit too much, that's all."

"I love you the same way."

He turned off the lamp and she cuddled around him and this comforted him, yet he was unable to repress the thought that it was a poor crippled thing now, their love.

IV

Elisse needed the car to bring women to a Ladies' Auxiliary sewing circle, so Justin, who was on the six to ten shift, took the trolley. He had not thrown off the previous night's melancholy, and as he swayed along between tight-packed men in odorous clothing he was filled with wintry desolation. It was December. Nearly a year since Mitch had shown him those letters. A year ago he had hugged his children good night, a year ago his wife had not shrunk from his touch with a nervous glint in her eyes, a year ago was the land of lost content. *Whether the Brotherhood needs me, whether she wants to leave or not,* he brooded, *I must take her home.*

There were five stops at Woodland. Justin got off at the last one, and so did the remaining passengers. Everybody tramped onto the overpass. From here one could see most of the vast, lit-up industrial complex. The tops of the foundry stacks glared red against dark, racing clouds, the endless windows shed a gaudy yellow light across the snowy yards. Justin paused, recapturing the image of Tom shifting around the table models of this same scene: *How like a god,* he had thought at sixteen, and he retained the same awe. How could a single mind conceive so vast a project?

Then, one of the Lilliputians, he trotted down the iron steps.

The man punching in ahead of him had difficulty slipping his time card into the rack. It was Coleman.

In the washroom Justin hung his jacket on the hook next to Coleman's. They were of the same height, but Coleman was far thinner, a gangling boy-man entering his twenties: when he pulled off his hunter's cap his tousled blond hair, big ears, and the pale fuzz high on his cheeks made him look yet younger. This fall his parents' farm in West Virginia had been repossessed, and now the elderly couple were crowded into the frame shack with Coleman's shy, dark-haired wife and their two babies. The infant had scarlet fever—Justin had advanced a Brotherhood loan to pay the doctor.

"How's your boy?" he asked without moving his lips. A bespectacled Security guard was leaning against a sink, noting on a clipboard the badge numbers of talkers.

"Poorly, thank you," Coleman replied from the corner of his mouth. His hands trembled as he hung up a knitted muffler.

Together they went into the roaring din of the tirebuilding room. Not a pulse could be missed in nourishing the machines, and when the whistle shrieked, men moved forward while others, sweat-drenched and drunk with fatigue, backed away.

Justin worked in a frenzy. His hands flashed about the rotating drum as he positioned rubberized fabric, winding the plies at sharp angles. A helper set more material beside his machine. When the tire was built, Justin unlocked the wide, flat cylinder from the drum, straining to slam it onto the hook that clattered by on the conveyor over his head. In the same movement he turned back to his machine. With the raucous tympany of the conveyor belt, the shrill whine of machines, the bumping drone of motors, he could not hear the footsteps of Security, but he was conscious of their eternal patrol.

Out of the corner of his eye he saw his foreman leave his desk. The short, mean little man halted behind Coleman. Coleman, thrashing like a drowning man to keep the pace, dropped a diagonal of material.

The foreman's stubby arm shot up. A relief man trotted over.

The sole support of four adults and two children was being fired for dropping rubber one time.

Justin saw Coleman's mouth jerk, the desperation of his pleas moving his gaunt collarbones. A Security duo approached, the mustached one grasping Coleman's arms behind his back while the other's left knee raised to the mountain boy's groin.

Justin felt as if every cell in his body were swelling. A red-black haze dimmed his vision. His hands ceased their weaving motion. He stood erect. Not wiping the sweat that ran down his face, he strode the few steps to the master switch.

He yanked the steel handle, pulling with his full strength.

Stillness.

Silence.

Belts no longer clanked, motors no longer whirred, drums no longer rotated.

The lines of men, sinking into the depths of this magical quiet, peered uncertainly around. They saw the frozen vignette, the mustached Security grasping Coleman, the khaki knee raised again, the red-faced foreman watching.

"*Let him go*," Justin roared. A quality more potent than fury rang in his voice, his eyes were deep blue stones set in the hollow of his skull, and his hand clenched the lever as if it were a truncheon.

The two Security, startled, moved away from Coleman. He bent over, clutching himself. His jagged groan could be heard all the way to the windows. The Brotherhood—and most of the men in this vast downstairs shop belonged to the union—straightened their backs, gripping their heavy tire tools. Their anger traveled in waves, palpable, near visible.

"Start that damn current!" screamed the foreman.

From all over the shop came cries of other foremen: "What's with that fucking switch?" "We're falling behind!" "Turn on the damn current!"

A high-pitched Southern voice called, "Sit down!"

The mean little foreman's face had contorted. "Either you switch on the current, you cocksucker, or every man here gets his dismissal slip. . . ." His threat trailed on a note of querulous fear.

A large, shirtless black worker had taken a step toward him. Other men were hefting their tire tools as if to feel the weight. The mean-faced man edged toward a fire door, his metal-tipped shoes clinking loudly on the cement. Another foreman followed. A Security fingered his holster. Justin turned his sunken, furious blue gaze on the man, and he, too, headed for the fire doors. Foremen and khaki uniforms joined the exodus.

A deep voice boomed in chanting rhythm, "When they tie the can to a union man—"

Other voices joined in, "Sit down, sit down."

The deep voice, solo again, "When they give the boot to a union man—"

"Sit down, sit down."

The spontaneously roaring voices carried through the enormous brick building and out the windows, crossing the cold, dark yards, a thin, incongruously human sound for Woodland.

V

As foremen and Security guards jostled their way out of the tirebuilding room, Justin sat at the nearest foreman's desk, picking up the phone. He knew the instant the switchboard got wind of the strike no calls would be put through.

The chanting had ceased, and now men jabbered excitedly of their actions and emotions during the past few minutes. Justin pressed his hand over his free ear, and hearing the feminine babble of the Ladies' Auxiliary in the other, envisioned Elisse making the same gesture.

"We've done it, Elisse! It's a sit-down. Get in touch with Mitch right away. He and I have this all planned." He was lying. Not to deceive her but to reassure the men crowding round the desk. Though at meeting after meeting the AAW had discussed sit-down strikes, Mitch and Justin and the other officials had not even the sketchiest of strategies.

Understandably.

This night, December 2, 1935, was the first time in North America that industrial workers had sat down at their machines. But Mitch, involved in the labor movement since birth, would improvise.

A husky tirebuilder next to Justin was shouting. Most of Elisse's response was inaudible. ". . . so sudden," she said.

"Good for us! There's no book on warfare that doesn't recommend surprise."

"What about Security?"

"Shuffled out into the night like lambs."

"There's a lot more of them, Justin. And police, too."

"Nobody's going to touch us. They're too terrified about the machinery."

"How long will you be in there?"

"Until Tom Bridger agrees to negotiate."

"Until there's good skiing in hell, then."

"Track down Mitch," he said crisply.

"I didn't mean to sound negative, darling. It's come as a big jolt. I'm worried. And so very proud—"

The line went dead.

The other departments in the tire shop had also stopped working, and the queer absence of machine noise was replaced by loudly wrought-up voices as men crowded in to report on their victories and to be regaled with differing versions of how Prof had pulled the safety switch. Justin's hand was wrung and his shoulders clapped. Coleman, center of another circle, had recovered, and his protruding, blond-downed ears were crimson.

Justin alone grasped the forces aligned against them: Dickson Keeley's Security force, the Detroit police, the National Guard, the weight of city, state, and federal governments, newspapers, public opinion, and—in his legally qualified opinion—the courts.

He looked around at the flushed, exultant men. Soon their elation would ebb away and they would be three thousand bundles of gloomy confusion ready to surrender. They must be organized. Justin's mouth set firmly, and his brows lowered thoughtfully.

He opened the foreman's drawer, finding a pencil and a stack of salmon-colored work sheets. He lined up four sheets, and without thinking reached into his work-shirt pocket for cigarettes. For economy's sake he had broken the habit that had become ingrained during those executive days when he had made out lists. Sighing, he dropped his hand.

At the top of one sheet he wrote *Committees*. Each department of the tire shop would need policing, cleaning, as well as groups to sign up those who did not yet have a union card. *It's just as well,* he thought parenthetically, *that there are no loom girls*—Onyx hired women only for the day shifts.

Food and Living Arrangements. The building had a cafeteria in the basement, and Justin knew that Security, paranoid about strikes, had been squirreling away cases of canned goods and barrels of flour to feed possible scabs. Maybe there were army cots somewhere.

Strike Leaders. Justin's cheeks flattened as he considered the different men. He shivered. *I shouldn't have sat down in sweat-drenched clothes,* he thought absently.

"Them shitheads!" shouted a livid mill-room worker. "They turned off the heat!"

"Oh, Jesus, we'll freeze. All we done here tonight is get ourselves fired."

A muscle moved in Justin's forehead. He climbed on the desk. Forming a megaphone with his hands he called, "So they think they can freeze us out, do they?" He turned so all could hear. "Well, the top brass don't want to get the sack either. The boss isn't in Detroit right now, but everybody knows he's a maniac about his machinery. We won't damage it for him, but there's no harm letting them worry we might."

Men shouted, stamped their feet, banged machine tools on the pipes. After an eruptive volcano of sound, steam hissed once again in the pipes.

As Justin had not shown his anxiety before, now he gave no sign of his jolting surge of relief. His hands steady, he realigned the pages of lists. He no longer viewed his opponents as some massive, crushing weight. He was battling Caryll, decent, gentle Caryll.

At quarter to ten three men with cold-roughened faces and collars pulled to their ears burst into the idle shop. Batteries and Axles had gone out right after Tires, they said, and the intricately meshed network of conveyors and belts had sputtered to a halt. Picket lines and police had already gathered outside the gates. The police and Security had been instructed by Caryll to let everybody out; the pickets, under Mitch's command, had been instructed to prevent scabs from getting in. The machine guns positioned atop the gate-houses had been moved to the roofs of nearby shops, and now there were Security manning them.

In less than two hours Woodland had become a besieged fortress:

CHAPTER 29

The rough flight from New York had temporarily deprived Tom of proper balance, and he gripped the aluminum rails. Caryll, at the bottom of the ladder, took his arm, and the two buffeted through the wind from the plane to the waiting Swallow.

"Woodland," Tom said to the chauffeur.

Caryll climbed in next to him. "Dad, the plant's been closed tighter than a drum for three days now. You look beat. Mother's waiting for us at the Farm. Tomorrow's time enough to take a look."

"Gate One," Tom ordered the chauffeur, who was waiting at attention.

"There's no point, Dad, none. We can't get in. They're picketing."

"Gate One," Tom repeated.

The chauffeur touched the patent leather visor of his cap. "Yes, Mr. Bridger."

The limousine glided between hangars, and Caryll took off his hat, rubbing at the frown lines on his balding forehead. When he had dispatched the Vega to await the arrival of Tom's ship, he had given the pilot a report to deliver to his father: five single-spaced typewritten pages in which Caryll accepted full responsibility for shutting down Woodland. Self-blame harrowed him, he had failed in his trust, he would never forgive himself, but a kind word from his father, pale and erect next to him, would have gone a long way toward easing the painful knot in his stomach.

Tom turned to him. "Your letter said they aren't smashing the machinery. What makes you so sure?"

433

"Justin's inside."

Tom's drained weariness grew guarded. "You didn't have a clue that those departments were about to take an in-plant vacation?"

Jerkily, Caryll unwound his cashmere muffler. "There have been problems in Tires since they went on the double work week, sure, but I hadn't heard a hint of unrest in Batteries and Axles. I would have cabled you if I'd thought anything was up. Now, of course, the fat's in the fire. They've been flooding by the thousands to join the AAW. The last three days have been a shambles. Injuries, three fatalities. The police spend their time breaking up pitched battles between the men trying to get inside to work and the pickets. The lines never leave the gates, day or night. They're disciplined and organized. Uncle Hugh swears they've imported strike leaders from party headquarters in New York. For all I know he's right. That Mitch Shapiro is one. A Communist."

"Your report never mentioned Keeley. It's not like him to sit on his duff. Where's he been in this?"

"The minute it started we met at my place—Uncle Olaf, Uncle Rogers, the cousins, Zemliner, Jackson, Falconet. And Keeley. He was all for blasting them out."

"That's Keeley, all right. One thing I can say for him is he's a consistent thug." Tom's voice was flat.

There was no way for Caryll to tell if this last remark was approval or condemnation. "I scotched the idea," he said, coughing. "Uncle Olaf wanted to call in the National Guard. I said no to that, too. I probably muffed our one chance, but I didn't want any bloodshed."

"So they're sitting inside?"

"Yes. We've got them isolated. It's checkmate. Uncle Hugh and Argo MacIlvray worked out an ad. I don't know if you've seen a newspaper." He reached for one of the stack that lay on the lambswool carpet.

WE WANT TO WORK

For two days now the illegal take-over of Onyx's Woodland plant has kept the great majority of Onyx workers away from their jobs.

We don't like it.

We want to work.

Tom glanced at the newsprint, then looked out the window.

Caryll gave a tense little cough. "Dad, there's one more thing. In the report I told you that it happened on Justin's shift. It's more than that. He was the one who pulled the safety switch."

"He *what*?" Tom's face was greenish in the gloomy light.

"There was some kind of argument between a foreman and a worker. I only heard the foreman's side, so I don't know the whole story. Justin seems to have lost his temper—I'm pretty sure he was right to. The foreman looked guilty. He had a mean squint." Caryll licked his mouth. "But I want you to know it's not a case of shutting down because their leader's my in-law. It's me, Dad. I'm afraid you have a pacifist for a son."

Tom shrugged, a wretched movement of his shoulders. It was a bitter thing that Justin should have been the one to raise the hand against him. And it was reproachfully, unbearably bitter that this should have been touched off by some mean-spirited act. To their right the multitudinous chimneys of Woodland had come into view, eerily strange without their tributaries of smoke. Tom shivered at the sight, hiding his misery under sarcasm. "Welcome to the graveyard," he said.

Caryll hunched into the leather upholstery. "Dad, I don't know what to say. I've cornered you into dealing with them."

Tom continued to frown at the vast, smokeless chimneys.

"You'll have to now, of course, Dad. But at least Justin's their president. We know he's ethical."

Tom shrugged again.

On Archibald Avenue in front of Gate One maybe five hundred men shuffled in a lockstepped oval, each man's breath steaming on the next man's collar. Some had tied bits of linoleum to the sides of their faces to protect themselves from the bitter wind that flapped against their signs.

END THE DOUBLE WORK WEEK
JOIN THE AAW

FIGHT ONYX SECURITY
JOIN THE AAW

KEEP YOUR JOB
WITH
AAW

The car turned. Tom stared back at the picketers. His paternal guilt transmuted itself into fury. These interlopers! Deal with them? Fat chance in hell! He lifted the tube. "Stop here," he barked at the chauffeur. Before the car had properly halted, he jumped out. Wind tangling glossy white hair around his erect head, he strode toward Archibald Avenue.

Caryll gaped through the rear window, unable to believe that his father intended to face down the rough, hostile picketers. Alone. He breathed with hoarse little gasps, then with a peculiar whinny, plunged from the safety of the Swallow, running after the intrepid madman who had sired him. "Dad . . . come back. . . ." Wind shredded his cries.

He caught up as Tom reached the picket line. A huge, square figure in a thick plaid jacket stepped forward.

"Where do you two gents think you're going?"

"Inside," Tom snapped.

"This ain't no welcoming committee. You're crossing a picket line."

"To my own fucking shop!"

"Dad," Caryll warned in a shrill whisper, tugging at Tom's arm.

"Hey," someone shouted. "The Boss is back in Detroit."

The news was passed around. Tom's surprise arrival, his coming accompanied only by his son, fit everybody's conception of him, the unpredictable, courageous loner. Tight-packed men smiled grudgingly, but they continued their shuffling, barring his way.

"Who's in charge?"

A rangy man with a knit cap pulled far down over his wind-scraped face eased through the line. "I'm the picket captain, Mr. Bridger," he drawled in a courteous, well-bred Georgia voice.

"Let me the hell through."

"It's not up to me, sir. The Brotherhood voted that nobody crosses the line."

"*They* voted? When I left the country in October, a man could get in his own shop. Has the law changed? If not, tell them to move their asses out of my way!"

"Dad—"

"Mr. Bridger, I reckon you'll have to settle with AAW before you get into Woodland."

436

Tom glared, then turned, the wind tugging at his dark gray topcoat as he stamped back to the Swallow.

"That was some risk you took, Dad. They're desperate men."

Tom ignored the remark, snapping through the tube, "Find a hardware store." His voice had that loud, sardonic flatness, and Caryll, with a sharp pang near his navel, accepted that his father had fallen into the demon fire of rage, and until this anger burned itself out, he could not approach reason.

After a couple of blocks they came to a dingy garage whose flaking sign announced that hardware items were sold here. Tom went in, emerging with a bulky, jangling package. He ordered the chauffeur to drive them back to Gate One. Caryll said nothing. No demurral would register.

This time Tom waited for the ashen-faced chauffeur to open the door. The long, sleek automobile attracted reporters from the open beer joint, as well as ten policemen. The cops kept glancing up at store roofs where Security watched from behind machine guns.

"Let me at the gate," Tom ordered. "I promise I won't trespass on my own damn shop!"

The pickets glanced questioningly toward their captain, and in this moment of uncertainty Tom shoved with his heavy, clanking package, barreling through the line. He tore open brown paper.

Metal rang on metal as he passed a shining length of new chain four times around the steel posts of the gates, which were already locked. He snapped a Schlage padlock through the links.

"There," Tom said loudly. "Let them camp inside until they rot!" Veins stood out in his temples.

The nearest pickets heard him: they blinked as if a sudden, confusing brilliance had blinded them.

A young reporter called, "What did you say, Mr. Bridger?"

"I've given the squatters on my property permission to camp indefinitely. I've closed my shop."

"We closed it for you!" shouted a picketer with a thin, cold-empurpled face.

"Great!" Tom snapped. "Then both sides agree. The world can get along without any more Onyxes."

"You mean this is a *permanent* decision?" asked another reporter.

"The only kind I ever make. Go back to your papers, tell your readers I've quit."

"Quit?"

"Gone out of business. Is that clear enough?"

A dismayed murmur stirred like the wind along the picket line. On the rooftops the khaki men squinted through their sights. Tom jammed his hands in his pockets, striding back to the Swallow.

They drove northward toward the Farm in silence.

Caryll's jaw was tense, and around his lips the flesh had a sickly bluish cast. His father, having lost his famed temper, to all intents had committed hara-kiri in front of him, and Caryll, in shock, was unable to sort out the multiple repercussions that would affect both sides in the struggle.

After several miles Tom rested his head in his hands, and the sight of that proud, bent neck brought scalding tears of pity to Caryll's eyes.

II

Extra!
Extra!

The cries of newsboys shrilled into the wind. Extras were rare in Detroit, and many poor people bought a paper. Wire services spread the news, and Extras were printed in every language. Terrier-sturdy Fivers were still driven by millions, and Sevens, too, had become part of the world landscape. Now there would be no more.

To most people the story was as newsworthy as a declaration of war, and to those millions around the globe who depended—directly or indirectly—on Onyx for their livelihood, infinitely more disastrous.

III

Caryll rubbed the back of his neck as he proofread the draft of his reply to Prime Minister Baldwin, editing out every trace of his mortified horror, and at the bottom of the second paragraph, printing in the margin: *Mr. Prime Minister, my father's decision was reached after years of sustaining heavy losses.*

Like almost everybody else the British leader refused to believe that Tom intended to stand by that symbolic affixing of the Schlage lock two weeks earlier. Who could believe that any man walked away from factories, rubber plantations, mines, a shipping line, railroads, stretches of timber? Tom, for his part, had holed up at the Farm, refusing to open letters that arrived in thick governmental envelopes, in gray Onyx envelopes, or in five-and-dime envelopes: refusing to read any of the inundation of mail from all over the world, some addressed merely *Tom Bridger, USA*. He would not speak on the phone, and Caryll was the only visitor admitted. Abashed gate guards had turned away Hugh's Swallow and Secretary of Labor Frances Perkins's flagged Cadillac limousine. Tom's dry, cracked lips formed a smile so bitter and forbidding that even blunt, insensitive Maud kept her silence. Caryll could not bring himself to ask how to carry this albatross, this shut-down industrial giant. His few stammered questions received no reply. There was something unhealthy about his father's undeviating silence that Caryll connected with the coronary he had suffered after Justin's departure. He knew his father's omnipresent grimace was one of mortal anguish. An unstoppable force had met an immovable object and, yes, that could mean another coronary. He saw his fear reflected in his mother's bespectacled eyes.

The two weeks of acting as deputy in what he considered a great public wrong had taken their toll on Caryll. His stomach clenched, his stammer was worse, two of his nails were taped because he had bitten them to the bleeding quick. He saw his inability to so much as raise a convincing argument to his father about reopening as a devastating personal indictment.

He jabbed the buzzer on his desk for a secretary—the guest rooms had been dismantled and furnished as offices for his Tower staff. Plump, lively Betty hurried in, the pleats of her skirt swishing. She took the pile of edited letters for retyping and set down a handful of clippings.

Caryll followed the strike news obsessively. Frostbitten men still tramped with their placards while others huddled self-incarcerated within the dead heart of Woodland; a grotesque denial of Tom's closing up shop. Yet Caryll accepted that Justin—still immured—and the other strike leaders had no choice, for the cruel reality was that in Detroit alone, the closing of Onyx had drafted 125,000 more into the army of unemployed. There were no jobs. There was not enough cash in the overburdened welfare offices to feed the families for a single week, much less furnish coal or pay the rent. So the strikers were condemned to sit or trudge—and hope for a miracle.

The phone rang.

Brewster Vance, Caryll's executive aide, put through only the urgent, top-level calls, so on the other end of the line a government dignitary, a world leader, or a relative was primed to coerce Caryll into doing what he wished, to the point of daft self-flagellation, that he were empowered to do: light up Onyx. Popping one of his antacid mints into his mouth, he picked up the phone.

In the course of the afternoon he spoke to Secretary of the Treasury Henry Morgenthau, Jr., to General Douglas MacArthur, to Mayor Murphy, to his Uncle Olaf. He received a delegation of gray-faced dealers. Edsel Ford dropped by to inquire nervously if there was any truth to the rumor that Onyx would become a General Motors subsidiary. "Dad's not selling out, he's closing down," Caryll reassured. "Edsel, you tell me. How do you go about closing an empire? I've been tearing out my remaining hair." The sons of two powerful, strong-willed geniuses exchanged commiserative glances.

The butler drew the curtains at five thirty when he brought up Caryll's glass of milk, and Caryll took time to look at the clippings.

Strikers double up to save coal was the caption of a wire-service photograph of unshaven men, thin women, and thinner children crowding around a potbellied stove.

> In Hamtramck last night three houses belonging to AAW members were burned to the ground. Police are investigating arson.
>
> CAN U.S. ECONOMY SURVIVE MINUS HALF THE AUTOMOTIVE INDUSTRY?
>
> NEW YORK CAR DEALER LEAPS FROM BROOKLYN BRIDGE
>
> STRIKER BEATEN TO DEATH BY UNKNOWN ASSAILANT
>
> A Woodland janitor was found frozen to death in his home in Inkster.

Caryll set down his empty glass carefully and hunched over, his elbows clamped to his knees. *I must have an ulcer,* he thought, *whatever the lab tests show, I must.* He was a staunch believer in the current wisdom that stomach ailments were psychosomatic: he attributed his painful gut to his adoration of his wife—he never should have let his weakness where Zoe was concerned.prevent him from contacting Justin. Together, he and Justin might have averted this evil hour, this catastrophe.

He pressed his sweating forehead to his knees.

Is it too late? he thought. *Dad had wanted to give Justin five percent of Onyx. Strange, that. Still, it proves enormous trust and respect if not affection. If Justin wrote a letter—Dad hasn't opened any of his letters. If Justin wrote a letter, I would read it to Dad. Force him to listen. Between us, maybe we could nudge him into some sort of compromise. Hah! That's a laugh. Dad's changed the world, but when has he ever changed his mind? Once. The time that Justin and I, together, convinced him to build the Seven. Who knows what goes on in Dad's head? Maybe he's waiting for a token submission from the other side, from Justin.*

Caryll tentatively straightened his spine. The spasm had eased. Massaging below his waistcoat, he thought: *There'll be hell to pay if Zoe finds out, but I have to try.*

He went through his dressing room into the bedroom where sweet scents and Zoe's breathy voice twined from the open door of her bathroom—she made her telephone calls during her marathon soaks.

"I have to go out for a bit," he called.

"Hold on, Joan." Splashing sounds. "Caryll, the Rochevilles and Artie and Agnes are coming to dinner."

"Don't worry. I'll be back in plenty of time."

From the heated ten-car garage he took one of the Sevens used by the servants, driving at his cautious thirty to Woodland Park, where he slowed at unlit corners to peer at street signs.

He braked at an ugly matchbox house. The door was opened by a short, broad man who clutched a napkin and stared questioningly at him. Voices, as of a party, burst out with the aroma of peppered cabbage.

Caryll was positive he had the wrong house. "Is this M-Mrs. Hutchinson's residence?"

The man examined him. "You're Caryll Bridger, aren't you?"

"Yes, I'm sorry to disturb—"

"Elisse! You have a visitor!" The call was triumphant.

IV

The huck toweling on which Justin curled did nothing to alleviate the hardness of the floor (there had been hundreds of cases of canned food stored away but no bedding), and he had the unpleasant sensation that his bones had sunk through his flesh to be embraced by dank cement. Yet he did not stir. To get up meant to put on a confident face as president of the sour-smelling, doomed Brotherhood.

The rubber shop supervisor had had a table model Radiola stashed in his filing cabinet, and this crackling link with the outside world informed them that they were striking a moribund company. The sit-downers, though, laughed at the thought that anyone, even Tom Bridger, could walk away from a cool billion. "Old Tom's playin' it cagey, this is his way of bustin' the strike" was the sanguine consensus. After semistarvation on their double work week pay, after the preying incubus of fear at losing their jobs, the wracking speedup, the humiliation of being a badge number not a name, Security's impersonal brutalizing, they had finally restored their manhood by hitting back. And despite two isolated weeks of worrying about their families, most of them were blessed with a light-hearted assuredness of victory.

But Justin knew Tom. Tom's motivations might be complex but he never behaved deviously. Thus he shared none of the prevalent optimism. And now, feigning sleep, he saw this barren industrial complex as a metaphor for the world, the guiding hand (Tom's? God's?) absent, life bumbling along without reason or meaning.

"Hey, Prof!"

Justin groaned, blinking.

A dark, stubbled face hung above his. "Prof, wake up! Your missus is here."

"What the devil . . . ?"

"Over by the main door."

Justin was on his feet, gaping at the small, pretty woman unwinding a long plaid scarf from her curly brown hair as she smiled animatedly at him. He ran clomping in unlaced boots, halting, and as she began to laugh he swept her into a hug that raised her from the ground. Reticent about public displays, Justin was conscious of the good-natured guffaws, yet he could not deny himself an extra second of holding her, inhaling her crisp, unique fragrances—and

442

neither could he repress a tinge of anguish that this physical yearning had somehow become unilateral.

Setting her down, he demanded, "What are you doing here? How did you get past the police at the gates?"

"Magic," she laughed. "Here, help me with my coat."

"What have you got in this? Bricks?"

Dramatically she opened the front to show two filled pillowcases. Undoing a safety pin, she extricated an envelope folded from brown packing paper. Eyes sparkling, she said, "Mail wasn't part of the deal, so I sneaked it by the law."

Men were converging, drawn by the swirl of excitement.

Seeing Coleman, she went to him, resting her hand on the gangling mountain boy's sleeve. "Johnny, the baby, he died . . . the night after the sit-down started. . . . The Brothers were at the funeral, so many . . . I . . ." Her voice tightened and she shook her head.

Justin, tying his bootlaces, was appointing committees to sort and pass out the letters. Elisse wiped her eyes, staring around the enormous hall with its bewilderment of conveyors and machinery.

Justin took her arm.

"It really dwarfs you, doesn't it," she said. "Know something, I've never been inside a factory before."

"Some confession for an organizer," he said, beaming down at her.

"Well, I didn't come to see the sights. We have matters to discuss, Hutchinson, and I gave my word to be back at seven."

"You'll have to work fast then, Prof," somebody called. There was more laughter.

Elisse's face went brick red, but she managed a pert smile.

The strikers reserved the superintendent's office for committee conferences, and Justin led her to the dingy room with its metal desk, sagging couch, and wall blackboards. Closing the glass-inset door, he gripped her hands, postponing the moment when the knife-edge of reason must separate him from visceral delight.

She touched his cheek. "How come no beard?"

"I run a tight shop. We shave every day." Razors and blades had been stacked above cartons of canned peaches.

"What an incredible place this is. The buildings go on and on forever. I'd never have tracked you down without a diagram." She held up one of the yellow maps that Employment handed out. Her expression sobered. "Are you aware," she asked, "that your dearly beloved leader has closed down permanently?"

"We found a radio."

"Those newscasters get cute, don't they?" Her voice deepened into the ripely lubricated tones of broadcast. " 'We now have a new lazy man's way of striking, sitting down in a closed factory.' Justin, it's monstrous how biased the press is! They never report that Security has a regular Maginot Line, guns and all, to keep us away from you."

"But you're here," he said. "How?"

"Thanks to Caryll."

"Caryll?"

She sighed. "Chicken Little was right, Justin. The sky *has* fallen in. It's been a doozy out there, especially for the tire shop families. After months on the double work week, a real doozy. Most of them were counting on their envelopes to pay for the food they ate a month ago. Welfare's broke and our treasury's stony. Daddy scrounged from the studio orchestra and the B'nai B'rith—with the proceeds I've been running a kind of soup kitchen with the Ladies' Auxiliary, but now that money's gone too." She sighed. "They're starving us out—what a rotten way to break a strike."

"Tom's not bluffing," Justin said. "When did you call Caryll?" She had told him about that chance meeting in Hudson's toy department, and the friendship that had sprung up over pastry and coffee.

"Are you kidding? The AAW surrender? Never! He came to the house last night. Justin, the poor man's on the brink of a nervous breakdown. He's constantly bombarded to reopen. Which he's dying to do. And which of course he cannot do."

"What did he say?"

"That his father, noble and generous employer that he is, has always kept our interests close to his heart. Acting in haste, he's repenting at leisure—and, I might add, comfort. You've heard he's doing a Garbo at the Farm?"

"On every news program."

"Well, Caryll's cooked up a little scheme. It'll give the big cheese the excuse he needs to convince himself to open up if *you* write."

444

Justin's lips tensed. "Caryll knows about Tom and Mother?" he asked hoarsely. "Caryll knows about *me*?"

"No, no, of course not," she soothed. "Darling, as far as I'm concerned, the idea's absurd. If Tom Bridger felt anything for you, he could have picked up the phone at any time in nine years."

"*I've* wanted to do that, terribly much, and couldn't."

"Sometimes you are too fair-minded."

"He has a short fuse. I lit it."

"Oh, for Pete's sake! Tom Bridger starves hundreds of thousands of people and you beat your chest and cry mea culpa!"

"What have we got to lose if I contact him?"

"Your pride."

"That's not providing many jobs, is it?"

"You're going to write, Justin, so write."

Justin went to the desk, extricating a long pad of departmental discharge forms, tearing off the top sheet, turning it over, staring intently at the blue paper before dipping his pen in gummy ink. His hand raced.

Finishing, he read then blotted and creased it twice. He handed her the folded page, watching as she stowed it carefully in her purse.

Her cheeks still glowed from the cold, early morning walk, and under his scrutiny her lashes went down to cast shadows on the rosy flush. The soft full upper lip folded in a gentle arabesque on the lower. Without her faintly challenging expression she was a myth of femininity in this dead, indifferent place where until two weeks ago men had willingly sweated out their lives, she was comfort in this desert of dread, she raised him from his abysmal loneliness. Slowly, eyes still fixed on hers, his hands traced the curve of her breasts, and when she quivered, he dropped to his knees, burrowing his bristly cheeks in the softness. He could feel the deep, irregular reverberations of her heart. "How I've missed you," he muttered into her pink sweater.

She put her hands on either side of his face. "I've missed you the same way, darling." Her voice was faintly surprised, throaty.

Lust shook through him, a spontaneous surge of uncontrollable lust such as he had experienced only once before, on that morning he had nearly drowned in the strong Pacific current. His Elisse was miraculously returned to him, the long hunger of sexual frustration was over, the surcease for his brooding fears at hand. He went to the door, glancing through the wired glass to where the mail was being sorted, a magnet for the crowd. Jamming a chair against the lockless door, he sprang to Elisse, curving and straining her to him. She feverishly caressed his neck, his hair, as he pulled up her skirt. Raising her body against the wall blackboard, he pressed kisses on her throat, lowering her onto his tumescence. She gasped aloud, either in pain or ecstasy, he could not tell.

To Elisse there had been no proper sequence of events. One minute she was triumphantly repeating Caryll's message while gazing at Justin, her joy veined with guilt—wasn't she feasting herself on the sight of her husband while other wives of the sit-downers starved? And then Justin's eyes were on her in that old, meaningfully intense way, and she felt once again that dampening, that deep, delicious ache, that fierce, chaotic tumble of urges to unite with him, to be part of him, to complete herself by joining with him. Inexplicable, this return of her dead desire, but she did not question it. She forgot the cold, destroying war that capital and labor were waging, forgot the furious, didactic arguments. For Elisse there never would be any other truth beyond the small, personal truth of love. She clutched at Justin, feverishly impatient, caressing him, shoving down her underwear, curling her legs around him when he lifted her. Though she gave a whimper, she scarcely felt the pain, passion carried her, lifted her, and his ragged breath in her ear was whispering obscene endearments and she moved with him in the great, engulfing tide of life and love.

"Sweet, sweet . . ." His whisper filled the universe.

Oh now, she thought, *now, now*.

They clung together several minutes, and when they moved apart, she gave him a shy, mischievous smile. "Fast work, Prof," she said as she retrieved her step-ins.

"I don't exist without you," he said.

She kissed him lightly, tenderly. "Don't worry. You're stuck with me."

Decorously apart, they walked on scrubbed floors to the main entry. "I'll go partway with you," he said, opening the metal door.

"It's easier to say good-bye here."

Outside, he watched her make her light, swift way, a small figure dwarfed between immensely long walls, turning at the end of the tire shop so he could no longer see her. He looked up at the wheeling gulls. Their *craa, craa, craa* was the mournful, grieving sound of loss.

V

Closing Onyx, though not the reflex of Tom's temper that he regretted most—he had the ruined desolation of his heart to prove that—was the most iniquitously far-reaching. A headache constricted his skull just above his eyes, his disjointed sleep was nightmare-wracked, he felt constant quivers of shamed disbelief at what he had done. He wanted to back down. He could not back down. He isolated himself as if he suffered from the Black Death, keeping to his rooms except at mealtime or when Caryll dropped over to visit.

Together the two of them would silently follow the pine-needle-carpeted trails through the Farm's primeval acreage. That freezing, overcast morning of December 16 they took the pond trail.

A stag burst from the undergrowth, bounding in front of them, his white tail erect, his hind legs raising up together. Caryll jumped. "Jesus," he muttered shakily as the animal crashed away.

Tom turned, seeing Caryll's white lips and twitchy eye muscles. "A deer, that's all," he said.

"I know, I know."

"We frightened him more than he frightened you." He was still examining his son. His eyebrow went up. "It's not the buck, is it? You're sweating because of me. Christ, Caryll. Me?"

Caryll exhaled sharply, his breath a visible cloud. He reached into his overcoat pocket for a folded blue paper that Tom recognized as a departmental discharge form. "If you w-won't read it, I'll read it to you."

"Some choice."

"Dad?"

Tom took the paper from his son's gloved fingers, shaking it open. Unprepared for the blow of seeing the familiar writing, his wrist went hot as if he had broken it. He leaned against a tree trunk, turning away from Caryll. Squiggles floated in front of the words and he blinked fiercely.

Dear Tom,

Too much time has elapsed and too many deeds to make this easy to write. My sincere hope is that you retain a little of the regard you once bore me, as I retain all of my admiration and affection for you.

Uppermost in my mind are the men who worked for you at Onyx. I cannot believe that you would put a final end to your life's work any more than I can believe that you would refuse to hear their honest grievances. This strike is not a weapon aimed at you.

Tom, is it unreasonable that the men should wish to discuss with their employer the ways this Depression has affected them? I am president of the Amalgamated Automobile Workers, but if that distresses you, I will gladly step down. I beg you, though, meet with a negotiator. This catastrophic situation must end.

Yours as always,
Justin

The slight formality was typical of Justin, and so was the resolute wording, only the *beg* was out of character. To n stared at the blue sheet, seeing the form printing on the other side. There were no oblique referrals to that final devastating argument, not a hint of tangled bloodlines, and this, Tom decided, relief expanding through his chest, meant that Justin no longer believed them father and son.

These long, dry years he had been parched for such a letter, the excuse to see his son without any incriminatory exposures; this letter was nearly analogous to the cherished though impossible dream, holding his Antonia again. Tom blinked away the tears. Leaning against a sycamore to regain his composure, he stared at the magnificent beige and fawn patterns of the bark. "How did you come by this?"

"Elisse Hutchinson."

"Looked at it?"

Caryll shook his head. "But I can guess what he says. He wants you to reopen. Everybody does."

"Including you?"

"If I didn't think you should," Caryll said with a pretense at humorous intonation, "would I have played postman?"

Tom gave his short, barking laugh. They were opposites, his

sons, yet they shared one trait. Decency. Once again, thank God, they had joined forces, they were pushing him where he longed to be. On the paths of righteousness.

Caryll misunderstood the laughter, hearing it as denial of the letter and of himself. "Dad, there's been enormous pressure," he said earnestly. "It's a mess out there. Monty's cabled he's coming over. He shouldn't be traveling yet. I hear from President Roosevelt nearly every day. And Mayor Murphy twice a day—the city's in a worse panic than '33 when the banks closed."

Carefully Tom refolded the paper in its creases, slipping it in his coat pocket. "Tell Justin's wife I'll talk to him."

"You will? You mean that, Dad?"

"Did I ever bullshit you?"

"You'll negotiate with the union?"

"I'll negotiate with Justin." The few sere remnants of leaves danced above his excited, shining face. "I'll talk with Justin."

VI

Contrary to the devoutly sincere beliefs within the large, oil-heated homes of Grosse Pointe and Bloomfield Hills, no trail of dynamite led from Communist headquarters in New York to the factory complex in Detroit. Elisse and Mitch had firmly refused telephone offers to send Party strike advisers, Elisse because of Justin's antipathy to what he called "the Soviet experiment," and Mitch—a lukewarm comrade at best—because he had dedicated the years of his life to building industrial unions powerful enough to protect their own membership.

The AAW ran this incendiary new form of strike on its own. Therefore, no matter what later would be said and written, it was without any political motivation whatsoever that the six men the AAW had elected as their strike board made their decision that noon.

Downstairs, the Hutchinsons' little house was crowded with strikers and their families lunching on sandwiches of thinly smeared peanut butter dribbled with Karo syrup (the stale bread was donated by the bakers' union), so the meeting was held upstairs in the slant-roofed bedroom. Elisse, the secretary, waited quietly at her maple vanity, notepad in front of her, while jubilant men perched gingerly on her chenille spread or sat crossing and recrossing their long legs on her rag rug as they talked in loud, excited voices about Tom Bridger's thunderbolt offer.

"We done it!"

"Glory hallelujah!"

"The strike's not over," Mitch pointed out. "We haven't won a single concession yet."

"Old Tom agreeing to talk to us, ain't that a victory?"

"I've seen a lot of strikes lost because our side's too eager." Mitch's broad, welterweight face was somber.

Zawitsky nodded. "We're so hot to get back to work we forget the issues."

Elisse gazed into her oval maple mirror, watching the reflection of the suddenly bleak faces. Everybody in this crowded bedroom understood too well the effect of crying, hungry children in a heatless house with an eviction notice nailed to the front door, they knew how most of the AAW's tenuously loyal membership would react to Woodland's reopening. Solidarity would shatter, and as individuals they would storm Employment at Gate Four, begging for any job at any condition and any wage. Only by holding together now could they move forward, not backward.

"We gotta do something to show we're on second base."

"Yeah, but what?"

They hashed over ideas that would encourage the desperate strikers to hang on.

"How about if when Prof comes out, old Tom's there to shake — his hand?"

One by one the men nodded their home-barbered heads.

"Yeah."

"That should prove we're getting there."

"What about making it on an overpass, so everyone can see 'em?"

It was a brilliant yet simple way of showing the strikers the power of their side in the struggle.

The AAW strike board's first resolution, voted unanimously, was that the negotiating sessions commence on the Archibald Avenue overpass with a public meeting of their president and Tom Bridger.

Elisse began to write.

VII

Caryll read the list of demands to Tom, who stared through a window at the dusk-lapped terrace. His head was bent, his hands thrust deep in his pockets. Caryll saw this as a pose of defeat, and his throat ached for his proud, intractable father. That he must obey rules laid down by his own workers!

Finishing, Caryll wet his lips nervously. "Dad, I don't think you should agree to that meeting on the overpass."

"Weren't you panting to get this settled?"

"There'll be a mob, a huge one."

Tom did not turn. "Wouldn't surprise me."

"Everybody knows there's packs of Communists in town. Their tactic is to provoke incidents."

"Pour yourself a drink."

"What?"

"A little Scotch'll calm your nerves."

"I never dreamed they'd make demands."

"An idealist," Tom said dryly. "Are they waiting for my answer?"

"I'm supposed to call Elisse."

"What's the number?"

"You shouldn't go out there. Hold firm. They'll back down, there's no other choice for them."

"Give me the number."

"Dad, you mustn't expose yourself that way. It's humiliating, it could be danger—"

"The number, Caryll."

"She's expecting *me* to call."

"To repeat my words? Who are you, Charlie McCarthy?" Tom turned.

To Caryll's amazement his father was smiling without a trace of cynicism, an oddly vulnerable eagerness lifting his upper lip; Caryll decided this must be how he had looked as a boy.

"Dad, remember that hunger march on the Rouge a couple of years ago? People were killed."

"Get that drink. It'll cheer you up." Tom held out his hand, wiggling the long fingers. "Give."

Caryll fished out his little black alligator book. To him the sound of his father dialing was preternaturally loud.

"Is this Mrs. Hutchinson? . . . Tom Bridger here. . . . Yes, I know you were expecting him, but things are rough all over. You'll have to settle for me." There was a lilt to the flat voice. "I'll be on the Archibald overpass at noon tomorrow if Ju—if your husband should be passing by. Maybe I'll talk him into introducing us. Until then, so long."

Caryll snatched the telephone. "Elisse, Dad'll have three men with him."

He did not realize that she had already hung up.

VIII

The family roundly cheered Tom's decision to reopen. Later in the day, though, when they heard of the intended meeting, they raised figurative fists. To meet with Justin—that Bolshie renegade! —was to display weakness. Why crawfish now? Who among the automotive manufacturers would not simply open their employment offices? To deal with labor was unthinkable. There was a glut. Now was the time to teach the sit-downers that these outside agitators brought only hunger and lower wages. Among themselves they denounced Tom's unpredictable behavior.

Hugh had no time for outrage. Only fear for his brother. He called the Farm but Tom continued to refuse his calls, so it was into Maud's large, flat ear that he poured his dreads.

"Maud, you can't let him go into that mob."

"I've warned him, don't think I haven't." Maud's frank voice was loud. "But you know Tom when his mind's made up."

"He's been secluded on the Farm. He doesn't know how things are. The men have turned into animals. Who can tell what will happen up there tomorrow?"

Maud sighed. "Sometimes I don't understand him. Here all along he's taken a firm hand, and now to give in? I don't understand."

"You're full of good common sense, Maud. Try to make him listen."

At the dinner table Maud catalogued her own honest qualms as well as Hugh's alarums. Tom, leaving his pecan pie untouched, escaped to his bedroom.

How strange it was that nobody recognized his happiness. What was the matter with Caryll, usually so perceptive, that he didn't see that he had snapped out of the antipodean desolation of the past years and the acute misery of the last two weeks, into joy so crazy that he wanted to dance? Shaking his head and laughing aloud, Tom did exactly that on the bedside rug, springing from side to side in a wild little jig.

IX

At this same evening hour Hugh was pacing up and down the length of his office, his breath wheezing through his lips. When he had told Maud that the strikers were animals, he had meant it quite literally: in his isolation he had formed distorted images of humanity, and he indeed visualized the strikers as dark, Neanderthal creatures with vulpine teeth. Tomorrow this subhuman horde would surround the one person on this earth whom he truly loved.

That Bolshie bastard, he thought, raging at his once equally beloved nephew as he cudgeled his brain for further means of protecting Tom. Already he had called his due bills from Mayor Murphy and Police Chief Arden so that the entire force would be out. He was paying hundreds of off-duty officers from his own pocket. He had hired Captain Nugent, owner of the Nugent Chemical Company, the Midwest's largest manufacturer of gas bombs, to keep watch on Archibald Avenue.

A loud rap sounded on the door. "It's me, Keeley."

Hugh dived for his Elizabethan desk, opening its single narrow drawer and removing his white china asthma pipe. He sucked once, hastily replaced the inhaler, then called, "You're a little early, but come on in." And as Dickson Keeley entered he said, "Well, what about tomorrow? Tell me the arrangements."

The Security chief explained his deployments, then outlined his selection of his two most trusted hirelings to accompany Tom—he himself would be the third man.

"The main thing is to avoid disturbances while my brother's on the overpass," Hugh said.

"They're an ugly crew, the strikers."

"Get enough men in the crowd to prevent trouble," Hugh said, his voice high.

"I'll have over four thousand."

"With the police and gas squad, that should do it," Hugh said uncertainly.

"If they came up with this new kind of strike, who knows what else they have up their sleeves? There are no guarantees. What's eating the Boss? There's no reason for him to throw in the towel.''

"You have one concern, to see that nothing happens to him.''

"He should stick to his guns. A couple more weeks and this lousy union'd be starved out for good.''

Hugh's sentiments exactly. "I'm counting on you tomorrow," he said, standing. A dismissal.

Dickson Keeley remained in his chair. He straightened his heavily exercised shoulders. "The strikers hate my guts. When Hutchinson hammers out the clauses, my department'll take every rap. And so will I.''

"Whatever's negotiated, you'll still have a job.''

"At Woodland?''

"I don't honestly know. Maybe not.''

"Then I'm about to be dumped?''

"We'll still need you.''

"Doing what? Nursemaiding the wives and kiddies? Listening at keyholes for you?''

Hugh, in his anxiety, was not politic. "If that's how you want to put it, yes. But your salary'll stay the same. And if my brother's safe tomorrow, there'll be a big bonus.'' Hugh went to the door, opening it. "Have your men at the Farm by ten tomorrow morning.''

Dickson Keeley, having just been informed his wide-reaching power had in all probability ended, raised his square chin. His face seemed thicker. He had never been subservient, but his exit was worthy of a deposed Nero.

Hugh was too worried about Tom to notice that his hound had slipped the traces. He went back to pacing.

CHAPTER 30

Before it was light Mitch and the bear-shaped Zawitsky emerged from the house—they were on their way to hire the sound truck. Mitch paused on the top step. "Security has its hands full today, Elisse, but take care."

"Not to worry. Nobody gets in."

"You'll be at the overpass steps before twelve, right?"

"I just might be passing by."

The laconic remark that Tom Bridger had made over the telephone to Elisse had overnight become a victorious catchphrase to the AAW. Mitch gave one of his deep, rare laughs. "See you there," he said. "Bye, now."

There seemed to be a natural conspiracy to make her late.

An operator rang to tell her that a call had been placed from Los Angeles. As Elisse vacuumed and polished for the well-wishers, strike captains, and committee chairmen who would most certainly stream by this afternoon to see Justin, she was dreaming up casually offhanded ways to inform her parents, Ben, even the baby, that soon, soon, they would be home. Her felicitous mood was a fusion of victory, Justin's homecoming and yesterday's unexpected bolt of silken joy. Of course she was delirious! Hadn't she halfmaddened herself with agonizing prognostications about the permanent loss of passion? And now her fears were ended. Yesterday the old sexy E. Hutchinson had returned. The morning fled on a high tide of happy woolgathering, and then suddenly it was fifteen after eleven. She had originally planned to leave at eleven. She dialed *O*. The long distance lines, the operator told her, were still tied up.

Impatience attacked her.

Pulling on her blue felt hat without so much as a glance at the mirror, yanking on her coat—the rayon lining was shredded by yesterday's pins—forgetting to lock the front door, she dashed the four long blocks to the trolley stop.

It was a chill, still morning with an odd white sky, high cirrus clouds sifting the sun's rays so that no shadows fell on the meanness of Woodland Park. When at last the trolley clattered along, there were no seats. Standing, Elisse drummed her fingers restlessly on the pole as they inched through heavy traffic, and as the jam-up halted the tram altogether she jumped out.

Police manned barricades at Jefferson.

The pedestrians on the broad street, empty of traffic, moved toward Woodland with a holiday effervescence. Families with skipping children, a line of YCL kids laughing arm in arm, the boys with red kerchiefs instead of ties, the girls sporting red berets, a vendor pushing a hot-dog cart, groups of Brothers proudly, openly wearing AAW badges—some waved to her. She circled three bulky women shouldering homemade placards: LADIES HATMAKERS LOCAL 168 SALUTES AAW.

Damn, damn, she thought, regretting that she hadn't allowed herself more time, that she had stood around waiting for that call.

Racing along, she charged herself with gross and consistent foolishness. Oh, sure, she was bookishly clever, she had a Phi Beta Kappa key to prove that, but when it came to making decisions, minor or major, logic deserted her and she became a morass of pure emotion. She raised her eyes. Dimensionless against the queer, uncolored sky rose the blackened spires of Tom Bridger's kingdom. Yesterday the flat voice she had heard often on the radio had been traced with wit and deviltry, and she had succumbed to a sort of comradeship. Her emotions so ruled her, her brain was so soggy that she couldn't even maintain a rational hatred of the father who had denied Justin!

A rumbling filled her ears, a sound like the Pacific surf, and at first she assumed it the result of running so hard, but then she realized she was hearing the roar of a multitude. Holding a hand to her coat over her prancing heart, she galloped faster.

II

They have taken untold millions that they never
toiled to earn.
But without our brawn and muscle, not a single
wheel would turn.

Caryll could not make out the words, but he recognized the distorted notes of "The Battle Hymn of the Republic" above the multithroated roar that seeped through the closed windows of the inching Swallow. Plainclothes Security were jammed into the two long cars behind, and a cordon of police insulated all three cars. Ahead, a squad of mounted police formed a path through the mob.

Caryll's neck tendons showed like cables. He resented his fear and could not control it.

"The gang's all here," Tom said.

His father's good humor boggled Caryll. "I never guessed it'd be this thick."

"Lieutenant Eastlake estimates over half a million." Tom craned around, looking out the windows with that childlike, innocent eagerness he exhibited at an auto show.

"Looks like more."

"Probably less," Tom retorted. "The law counts in large numbers. The bigger the mob, the more indispensable the cops prove they are."

"How did so many people hear? It wasn't in the early editions."

"Papers, hell. When you're poor, you don't take a paper. It was on the radio."

"How did they get here? Most of the poor devils look like they don't have tram fare."

Laughing, Tom slapped his calf. "Shanks' mare."

Caryll frowned fiercely. "Dad. I'm coming on the overpass with you."

"That's not according to plan."

"Justin's my brother-in-law. You'll be safer with me there."

"Hugh's got everything set. Public Relations is his department." Tom was grinning. "Ours not to reason why, ours but to do or die."

Caryll winced.

"Relax, relax. All I'm going to do is shake hands with Justin."

"Don't stay up there a second longer than you have to."

The police were wheeling back a cotton-candy wagon, and the swarm of kids peered into the car. Tom waved. "Quit stewing, Caryll. It's carnival day. How's that time?"

Caryll glanced at his gold Patek Philippe wristwatch. "Ten to."

Tom slapped his son's kneecap lightly. "Smile," he said.

III

We can break their haughty power, gain our
freedom when we learn
That the union makes us strong.

The labor hymn crested above the crowd-roar that swept through the empty yards to where Justin and Coleman waited out of sight.

"Will you listen to that singin'," Coleman said. The mountain boy's large ears were red.

"There's a sound truck," Justin said, staring at his old Bulova.

"You don't think it'll set them boilin' mad, me taggin' along?"

Last night two warmly dressed members of the National Labor Relations Board had been admitted to Woodland: they had informed the sit-downers of Tom Bridger's agreement to the preliminary demands of the AAW strike board. After the bundled Washingtonians departed and the cheering stopped, the strikers voted that another man accompany Justin to the foot of the overpass: the sit-down would continue until the negotiating ended, but Justin would remain outside to be at the sessions, so Coleman was needed to bring back the straight dope on the meeting with Tom Bridger—what union man in his right mind would trust the radio news?

"Not at all," Justin said automatically. About to be thrust into Tom's presence for the first time since that disownment, he was in turmoil. Through his distraught brain, over and over droned lines from Byron that he had memorized his last term at Eddington: *Yet in my lineaments they trace/ Some features of my father's face.*

"Sure I won't make no problems?"

"Positive. Come along. It's time."

They traversed the windowed half mile of the Main Assembly, arriving at the broad yard where the dusty new Sevens had been deserted alongside half-loaded freight cars. From this point they were visible to some of the multitude on Archibald Avenue. Heads pressed expectantly against the chain link fence, and at their appearance several boys clambered up, violently waving small American flags. Police, whistles in their mouths, tussled to pull down the boys, good-natured rather than angered.

"Prof, will you look at that mob, will you just look at it!"

Justin scanned the empty overpass, then the rooftops of gimcrack diners and beer joints. He saw the khaki forage caps of Security behind the glint of machine-gun muzzles.

"Come on," he said grimly.

The two tall men fell into step, marching in time to the deliriously shrilling voices:

> Solidarity forever,
> Solidarity forever,
> Solidarity forever,
> And the union makes us strong.

They halted at the foot of the metal steps, and Justin again stared at his watch, waiting for its two hands to be joined. *I'll be facing Tom in three minutes,* he thought. His heart pounded erratically. Closing his eyes, he calmed himself by conjuring up Elisse, her pretty and mocking smile, her small, trim body and good legs.

Precisely at noon he planted his foot on a metal step, and as he climbed he took in the magnitude of the tight-packed throng with its wildly waving hats, flags, placards. From the mighty river of people rose a near visible spume of energy. He had been on leave in Paris on Armistice Day, and the crush around the Arc de Triomphe had nothing on Archibald Avenue, Detroit, Michigan. He spotted news photographers balanced on the top of a stranded streetcar or clinging to lampposts.

Reaching the first landing, he saw Tom.

Tom, trotting up the steps closely trailed by three men. The muscular one in a navy suit and homburg was Dickson Keeley.

Justin's eyes went a little out of focus, and a rush of bewilderment dizzied him. He felt this juvenile shock each time anyone breached his code of honor. *Grow up, grow up,* he thought. Turning, he bent his head, cupping both hands to shout, "Coleman. Come on up!"

Coleman held out his earlobes to indicate that he had not heard.

Justin commanded with a sweeping incurve of his arm.

Coleman started upward. Seeing the men on the landing, he lunged up to Justin. "Them damn scalawags! And me afret about watchin' from the bottom!"

Both parties reached the top step at the same time.

With a barring gesture to his three companions, Tom continued alone across the overpass. Coleman, too, hung back, his blond-fuzzed face stern as he gazed straight ahead, a sentry on duty.

Tom saw Justin's thick-soled boots, plaid lumber jacket. Workmen's clothes. *Gray hair, premature like mine.* Then he was drinking in the arched, narrow nose, the finely delineated mouth, haunting reminders of his dead love. The years had broadened Justin and enhanced the strong, calm presence.

Justin saw Tom's lithe, lean body, the windblown white hair. The gray eyes were darker because the lids were hooded, and new lines grooved the cheeks. *He looks so much older . . .* had that heart attack taken a huge toll or was it simply the normal erosion of a decade?

Neither man could gauge how the thumb of time had modeled their resemblance.

Taking a breath, Tom called, "Justin."

Justin, having never anticipated this shambles of pity and love, was flung into a momentary vacuum. He took another step so that they were close enough to feel the warmth of each other's breath. Swallowing thickly, he said, ";Tom, how have you been? I heard you weren't well."

"The old ticker acted up years ago. But since then"—Tom patted the general area of his heart—"fit as a fiddle. And you?"

Justin nodded gravely, unwilling to trust his voice.

"You look fine," Tom said. "The rewards of a happily married life. I spoke to your wife last night."

At the mention of Elisse, Justin was drained of loving compassion. He was remembering the general rottenness of their last meeting, the barefaced lying denial, that vituperative bigotry. He said tersely, "What are *they* doing here? We were meant to be alone."

"What are you talking about, Justin? Caryll told your wife there'd be others, I heard him." He added something, from his grin a jocular aside.

Justin could not comprehend the words, partly because of the roaring, screaming crowd, and also because of the blood thundering in his ears. His legs were trembling. "Elisse doesn't lie."

"I didn't mean that. Listen, I want to meet her—"

"That's a detail she'd hardly neglect to mention."

"What the hell difference do *they* make?"

"If you'd worked on the line, you wouldn't ask. Since I came back to Woodland, Security's put a couple of hundred union men in the hospital. Four so badly roughed up that they died. Keeley's a murderer. He belongs in jail. He's the last man you should have invited along if it's goodwill you're after."

"It was your union's idea that we shake in public," Tom said dryly.

Justin drew a breath against the blackness heaving up inside him. How was it that either he was overwhelmed by that old awed love or in an ungovernable rage? Why couldn't he face Tom—particularly on this mission—with the semblance of calm that he would have displayed to any other man? "Right," he said.

"Word is you have two kids." A loud cheering drowned out the rest of Tom's remark. ". . . swell gal, your wife, Caryll says."

"Tom, you have me in a bind, but I'd prefer we keep this impersonal."

The gray eyes glinted. "You're Zoe's brother," he said. "One of the family."

Your son, your son, Justin thought, and his mental processes expanded and contracted like his frantically beating heart, yet so controlled was his expression that Tom saw only the fairness and decency of the younger man. Tom shifted his weight. If it weren't for the stranglehold promise to a dead woman, God help him, he would acknowledge his dismembering lie in plain sight of this horde of people.

He reached for Justin's hand.

The shake was in the exaggerated manner of political usage, hands clasped, biceps gripped, heads brought close. It was, to Justin's clear recollection, the only time that Tom had embraced him.

A deafening roar went up to the white sky. Cameras turned and popped. A multitude of throats cried:

For the union makes us strong. . . .

"See you at eight sharp at the Book Cadillac," Tom said. The negotiating would be on the hotel's neutral ground.

"Tomorrow morning," Justin agreed.

Tom turned, jogging briskly down the steps, Dickson Keeley and the other two keeping up. Police held the shabby, delirious crowd back from their path to the limousine.

"What was you and the boss saying?" Coleman shouted.

Justin shook his head, unable to reply because he was wondering how he would get through the sessions in the hotel without disgracing himself with shouting matches or tears. He gripped the icy metal of iron railing, looking down with bloodshot, unseeing eyes. The crowd, viewing this as a celebratory pose, shook hats, placards, flags more wildly. "Huzzah! Hooray!"

Mitch stood by the sound truck, clenched fists thrust skyward, like a winning boxer; Krug's mouth moved savagely in his enthusiastic red face, Zawitsky raised his cap repeatedly. The AAW leaders were applauding him. *Where is Elisse?* His misery, lost loyalties, fears of contention in the hotel suite faded as he conjured up an image of his wife. *I need her so.*

Shiny-roofed limousines moved toward Jefferson. Police linked arms to hold back the heaving, surging crowd. *Where is she?*

"I'd best stick with you, Prof," Coleman said near his ear.

"What?"

Coleman wet his chapped lips, shouting, "We should of brung ourselves some heavy pipe."

Trotting purposefully up the steps was Dickson Keeley, his conservative homburg tilted forward, his cheeks puffed out importantly, followed by an even dozen overcoatless men whose shoulder holsters bulged under their dark jackets.

A tremor shook in Justin's throat, and his mouth went dry with fear. *Oh, stop it,* he told himself, glancing down on the noisy mob, staunchly theirs, the reporters and photographers clinging to their vantage places. "There's nothing to worry about," he said.

"They ain't coming to congratulate us, Prof."

"Go on back inside, Coleman. Tell them everything went off well. Nobody's going to hurt me, not here."

But Coleman planted his large, worn boots next to Justin's.

IV

Since Hugh Bridger had confirmed the probability that his regime was grinding to a halt, Dickson Keeley had coiled around the impending loss, finding no solace in the assurance of financial well-being—what was mere lucre after omnipotence? His acrimony spilled over in a violent gush. To attack Justin on the overpass was wildly foolhardy, but none of Keeley's innumerable enemies had ever called him a coward.

Approaching the two AAW men, he shouted, "Not in any hot sweat to join your comrades down there, are you?"

Patches whitened the corners of Justin's mouth, and Coleman pulled at his collar as if it worried him.

"Your little woman must be waiting," Keeley said, looking at Justin.

"Let us by," Justin said.

"A swell tomato." Dickson Keeley whistled appreciatively. "Hotcha!"

A snicker escaped the swarthy young man whom Justin recognized as having earlier accompanied Tom and Keeley.

"You won't talk about my wife."

"I'm handing her bouquets," Keeley goaded.

When Justin had released his grip on the railing, flakes of skin had clung to the icy metal, yet, digging his nails into his raw palms, he did not notice the pain. "I said not to talk about her, Keeley."

"Prof," Coleman said, grabbing at his sleeve. "There ain't no point arguin'. Come on."

"Families are Security's job," Keeley said. "You'd be surprised. A big part of my job. I look out for your sister—there's one red-hot mama."

The cheers directly below turned into an angered rumbling as half of Keeley's group shifted so that they were behind Coleman and Justin.

A red mist of fury at the broken truce dimmed Justin's vision. "Get out of our way!" he said in a rumble.

"We're not about to do that. We're not about to let you go before the conversation's finished," Keeley drawled. "Now your Elisse, she's one sweet bowl of honey."

"Shut up!"

"What did she tell you about that little call we paid her?"

Unbearable suspicions pressed the breath, and all reason, from Justin. "You miserable, bleeding bugger," he shouted. Flexing his knees, his full weight behind his clenched fist, he aimed at the square jaw. The move that Keeley's crew had been awaiting. The blow never landed. One of the men behind him grabbed his jacket, pulling it over his head, immobilizing his arms, muffling and blinding him. The same swift maneuver was used on Coleman.

Security closed in on their two helpless victims with the disciplined ferocity of a wolf pack. Justin and Coleman staggered and swayed as they were punched in their bellies and kidneys with fists hardened around rolls of nickles. Justin's groin was kneed, and Coleman's genitals were kicked after he fell.

AAW Brothers fought to get up the steps but were clubbed away by police.

Police were gifted by Security, paid off by Security, hired by Security when they lost their jobs on the force. Each year the chief of police received a new Swallow limousine from Hugh.

Justin's coat was released and he could again see. Three men held him while Dickson Keeley cut at his face with short, delicately cruel blows. Coleman was crawling to avoid the kicks, and Justin staggered backward, falling on his friend.

They were lifted by hands and feet, their bodies swung. They were hurled down the steps. Then dragged by the feet the rest of the way down the metal staircase.

Solidarity forever . . .

Photographers on the roof of the stranded trolley were cranking cameras aimed on the brutality.

"Get those goddamn cameras!" a voice boomed through a bullhorn.

As police hurried to obey, Dickson Keeley and his men, service revolvers aimed, rushed to the waiting limousines.

The beating had taken less than three minutes.

In those three minutes the triumphant crowd had shattered into myriad individual fragments of fear and outrage.

The infuriated Brotherhood were shoving toward the overpass. The terrified holiday throng pressed to escape. The area around the steps had become a savage whirlpool of confusion. Placards and handbags were used to thrust. Children were raised on shoulders, for there was a sickening danger of death by trampling.

"Break it up! Break it up!" Bullhorns blared.

Arms wearing khaki and dark blue rose and fell, clouting mechanically.

V

When Security surrounded Coleman and Justin, Elisse was trapped amid a group of men who shouted in angry Polish and smelled of sweat. Too short to see over them properly, she jumped up, catching truncated glimpses of Justin, his red plaid lumber jacket pulled over his head, staggering under the blows and kicks of the encircling thugs. *Oh, God, no. No!*

Her pupils dilated, her muscles hardened, and with frenzied strength that amazed her, she shoved her way through the bucking, unyielding Poles.

A sudden brilliance exploded.

The reddish radiance traveled overhead in a great arc like a comet come to destroy the human race.

Terrified men and women, teeth bared as if in exhilaration, shoved at one another. A vast, thick murmur rose from this part of Archibald, where the crowd was compressed as though in a slaughter pen.

The Very flare was the signal.

Along rooftops the gas squad snapped on rubberized masks. Police and Security below struggled to do the same amid the push of the crowd.

Elisse blinked to regain her vision. She jumped up to see.

The overpass was empty.

With a maddened shriek she shouldered her way forward, inching through the sweat-odored, churning, squirming mob with the frustrated slowness of a nightmare, her hostility shifting from that monster, Dickson Keeley, and his boss, Tom Bridger, who had authorized the assault, to the solid mass of people separating her from the overpass. "Let me through," she yelled into red faces. *Are they still beating him?*

Captain Nugent, who had fired the Very flare pistol, lifted his arm. His men unfastened bulky bombs from their military belts, lobbing them as they might softballs down onto the crowd below.

"Watch out!" a man screamed.

Something that resembled a child's toy, a bulky blue-striped ball, dropped near Elisse. She could hear a crack like china breaking as it hit a man's shoulder.

From the ball drifted a greenish wisp that darkened to gray as it spread.

Gas billowed in clouds.

People sobbed from irritated tear ducts, and sobbing, gasped in more of the burning, nauseating fumes. Streaming-eyed mothers used their coats to shield babies, gagging fathers clapped fists over children's faces.

Someone—the voice was shrill, it could have been either a man or a woman—screamed, "Poison gas! Poison gas! We're goners!"

Those around Elisse convulsed. Vomiting, hysterically maddened people struggled to escape into the side streets.

Liquid fire poured into Elisse's throat, her eyes burned and streamed. *Tear gas,* she thought. "Tear gas! It's only tear gas!" she shouted as loud as she could in a vain hope of quelling the panic, and then dropped her purse to clutch at her mouth against the humiliation of publicly vomiting. All around her, frenzied, retching people thrust mindlessly in opposite directions. *Oh, God, God,* she thought. *I must get to Justin, I have to get him out of this.*

A Security guard, his face concealed by a black-snouted gas mask, stood like an improbable rock amid the panic, raising and lowering his billy. A frenzied woman wearing a man's hat, arms flailing, inadvertently forced Elisse into his indiscriminate range. A blow landed on her shoulder. She staggered. The thick-chested man next to her, his handkerchief tied over his face, held her erect against his sour-smelling leather jacket. "I'll get you out of here, girlie," he shouted.

"Help me!" she screamed, her fists against his hard chest.

"Give me half a chance."

"My husband's trapped over there," she yelled.

"You'll find him later."

"*Now!*"

"The overpass ain't no place to be!"

For a moment each tried to force the other in the opposite direction, a frenetic dance, then the crowd tore them apart. Elisse gagged again. A khaki arm, maybe it was the same one, descended on her head.

Her hat flew off, her feet grew heavy, their weight pulling at her thighs and buckling her knees.

"Justin," she gasped.

Mitch honked the sound truck horn constantly as he steered around the clumps of racing people. Zawitsky and a couple of others clung to the running board while on the front seat, Justin, his forehead bleeding through handkerchief bandaging, huddled against Coleman's unconscious body.

CHAPTER 31

The house became a first-aid station.

Trembling, ancient Fivers and Model T's disgorged the wounded, and a red-headed young doctor risked his surgical residency at the Ford Hospital to suture gashes, feel for broken bones, syringe out burning red eyes. Odors of blood, vomit, and disinfectant permeated the living room where men, women, and children edged the sour taste from their throats with the refreshments Elisse had heaped out, sticky, stale bearclaws, largesse from the bakers' brotherhood, as well as coffee and red Kool-Aid.

Coleman's back was broken. Howling ambulances carried him and the other severely wounded to Harper Hospital on John R. Street.

Justin hunched on the stool in the crowded kitchen. His right eye had swollen nearly shut, and the gauze taped on his forehead bulged over an apricot-sized lump. Though still very dazed, he shook hands to calm the furious Brothers and with measured coherence guaranteed anxious-eyed families of sit-downers that their men were safe and well inside Woodland.

It was Mitch who organized strike captains to hustle their pickets back to the gates, Mitch who gave the official interviews.

Newsmen, fuming at the attack on their cameras, filtered through the jammed little rooms jotting down pro-AAW human interest stories, and flashing pictures. Reporters dug into their pockets, donating whatever money they had on them to the strike fund. For the first time the members of the press were staunchly on the side of the union and filed sympathetic copy.

The few intact plates of the beating on the overpass would appear in every paper tonight, would for decades to come surface in magazines and books, shadowy scars on Tom Bridger's reputation.

A thin, buck-toothed man edged over to Justin. "Daley, New York *Evening Post*," he introduced himself. "Old son, you look in need of medication." He unscrewed a finger-marked, tarnished silver hip flask, no doubt a relic of Prohibition. "Here's what the doctor orders."

"Cheers," Justin said automatically. Sweet rum burned through him, melting the encapsulation of numbness that had protected him. He realized he was nauseated and that pain cut above his eyes and ears, as though some enormous spoon were cracking the eggshell of his skull.

"Take another belt," the buck-toothed reporter said.

Justin obeyed, returning the flask.

The reporter returned to the cluster of loudly irate AAW officials surrounding Mitch.

Justin sat more erect, his thought processes raveling.

Elisse.

Mitch had told him that she had never shown up at the sound truck and therefore was doubtless making her way home on one of the crowded trolleys. But wasn't she taking a bit long? He squinted up at the red clock above the door. Roman numerals blurred. "Five to four!" he muttered.

She should be here by now. She damn well should be here.

Mitch and the reporter were now conferring by the sink. Justin tapped Mitch's shoulder. "Come outside," he interrupted peremptorily, and not waiting for a reply, went out the back door. Icy air cleared the remnants of cobwebs from his mind. "Where the hell can she be?" Justin asked.

Mitch looked bewildered. "Who?"

"Elisse."

"What are you saying? Isn't she back?"

Justin shook his head.

Mitch's heavy brows drew together in a worried frown. He had witnessed the police herding vomiting clusters of people into the paddy wagons. "They must've taken her in," he said slowly. "They've got headquarters packed."

Their streaming breath mingled as they looked at each other in dismay.

"She would have called," Justin said.

"The line's been busy." Newsmen phoning in their *sympatico* stories.

"I'll get on downtown."

"You're in no shape. I'll go."

"I'm a lawyer."

"Not in Michigan. Besides, anyone can post bail."

"Don't argue. Have any cash?" Trapped in a wave of nausea, Justin spoke loudly.

Mitch examined him, then thrust his hand into his pocket for the wadded, crumpled bills that were donations from various reporters. Justin took thirty dollars.

He had worn his clothes for over two weeks. The shirt and heavy jacket were rusty and stiff with blood. He went up to change. The three garret bedrooms rang with coughing. Pale children coughed across the width of his double bed; the young red-headed doctor knelt on the rag rug between two relentlessly hacking women. Justin edged from the closet to his bureau, waiting impatiently with his clothes outside the locked bathroom. The hot water was long gone. He flinched under a swift, icy shower, shaving for a second time today. After he was dressed in a clean white shirt and his good suit, he stared into the mirror, seeing not his damaged features but Elisse's face glowing with love and laughter as she had said, *Fast work, Prof.*

He drove to the nine-story police building on Beaubien Street. She had not been booked there. He sped to two local stations. No arrest slip had been made out for her.

Outside the second station he halted under glass bowl lights. He winced; the freezing night air made his head ache more fiercely. Police, as a courtesy to Security, often hustled union members from one station to another, beating the solidarity out of them before finally booking them. *They'll know she's my wife*, Justin thought, his good eye narrowing to the same slit as the blackened one.

Hugh, he thought. *Hugh will know the strings to pull to find her*. Justin's cold mottled hands clenched. *If he refuses, I'll kill him*.

II

He drove past the high-hedged private lane that led to Hugh's gatehouse—he would never be admitted through the magnificent eighteenth-century English ironwork gates. Justin, as a lonely boy, had often trespassed on the grounds of the neighboring estate.

The bricks of the lakeside path had sunk or buckled. Stepping cautiously through the darkness, holding up his hands to ward off branches of overgrown shrubbery, Justin was confronted by a ghostly counterpart. Two individuals moved along this path, one the man filled with outrage and fears for his wife, the other that teen-ager with his admiration for Tom Bridger—how he had admired and resented the heroic racer who had put the world on wheels! That boy's naïvely honorable vision saw only Hugh Bridger's kindnesses and generosities . . . how strange to coexist in a mnemonic duality with his schoolboy self. Justin reached the ice-covered inlet where canvasbacks halted on their spring and fall migrations. The southern boundary of this cove was cut off by Hugh's ten-foot wall. As Justin scrabbled around the end of it, clinging to the stones, he could hear the grumbling of water, the occasional sharp crack of shifting ice below him. He planted a foot on the slushy soil of Hugh's property.

At a faraway, muted roar he jumped. Then recalled Elisse reading him an article about Hugh's lions: she had made several sarcastic comments about the fact that the cost of their daily beef would feed a family of four a whole month. As Justin moved along the well-remembered paths of his uncle's exquisite self-imposed prison, his adult angers and anxieties faded and that boy—Hugh's wholehearted disciple—took over. He found himself thinking from Hugh's viewpoint. Hugh had taken him in, had endowed him with a palatial home, devotion, had schemed for his career. How had he been repaid? *I eloped with a girl he disapproved of, I returned to challenge the Bridgers.*

Shivering violently, Justin let himself into the servants' cloakroom. Sudden warmth dizzied him and he sat on a bench, resting his aching head between his knees a minute before he looked around for a clothes brush. Sprucing himself up, he hoped disjointedly that Hugh would not be evasive.

III

They awaited dinner in the downstairs library.

Tom still wore the gray suit from the noon meeting, but Caryll and Hugh had dressed. Zoe perched on the arm of her husband's chair, her head bent low to his so that a red-gold strand rested on his neatly combed, thinning brown hair. The years had succeeded in obliterating neither her passion for Hugh nor the dark, shaming blotch of his rejection, so she always intensified her normally affectionate manner to her husband in Hugh's house. *Let him never forget that one offer,* her strange little heart said. *Prove to him what he missed.*

Maud sat opposite the young couple, her ample lap covered with fine pink batiste that she was smocking into a dress for Petra—she, for one, refused to pay the outrageous prices for handmade children's clothes! The sofa table was strewn with evening editions, each with a front-page photograph of Dickson Keeley's pack attacking Johnny Coleman and Justin Hutchinson.

The grainy reproductions had activated a host of shames in Tom, and his sickened self-repugnance emerged, typically, as rage. He had barked questions at Hugh, who finally retreated to a silver cart to spoon inky black caviar onto Melba toast. His fingers shook, and he did not attempt a sprinkle of hard eggs and raw onion.

"I've told you and told you," Hugh said, his voice rising. "I do not for the life of me know why Keeley went back up on the overpass. But every report says that Hutchinson attacked *him.*" He gulped down his caviar, not only agitated by Tom's anger but hurt by it. "I tried to protect you, that's all."

"Some opinion of me you have," Tom said. "You really believe that I can't appear on a public street without a goon squad, an army of gas experts, and every cop in the state of Michigan?"

Maud's needle ceased to flash. "Tom, Hugh explained. He was worried for you. We all were. Since Onyx shut down, Detroit's been in an uproar. All the auto companies have increased their guards. Hugh did what he thought was necessary. What's gotten into you? I've never seen you take on like this."

Tom scowled to keep his composure. Justin must view Hugh's protective efforts, Keeley's thugs, and Nugent's skilled gassing of a holiday crowd as orchestrated by him. "From now on I'll smile when there's trench warfare outside Woodland."

"Oh, you and your sarcasm," his wife said, her voice without condemnation.

"The men were happy," Hugh said. "Then those reds came and stirred them up."

"Happy?" Caryll gnawed at the tape over one of his nails. "Why did we need five thousand men on the Security force?"

"Caryll, Caryll, you're blessed with an idealistic nature." Hugh returned to his chair, crossing his legs and shifting the conversation from himself. "Every automotive factory needs to police itself, you know that. Otherwise the Polacks are forever at the Irish, the hillbillies are thwacking the Negroes, the Italians kill one another, and the Jews take away everybody's pay. How would we get a single day's work done without Security?"

"Dad used to manage."

"That was before this infernal Depression. You heard Captain Nugent's report, you heard what he said." Hugh's diamond cuff link caught the light as he waved a hand. "The rioters would be burning Detroit by now if we hadn't contained them. Let me tell you something else, Caryll. If you'd followed my advice, if you hadn't been so squeamish when the Bolshies occupied the tire shop, none of this would have happened."

"I know you think I behaved spinelessly, Uncle Hugh," Caryll said. "Maybe I did. But it goes against my grain to run Onyx like a slave camp."

"What's so wrong with a firm hand?" Hugh asked.

"So that's what you call it," Tom put in sourly. "A mere hundred or so at Harper, only seventeen on the critical list."

"That miserable gas!" Caryll exclaimed. "No wonder they stampeded."

Zoe rested her narrow, shapely hand on her husband's kneecap. "Can't we talk about something else?" she asked with a pleading smile.

"Zoe's right," Maud said. "There's no unscrambling eggs. The riot's over."

"A sweet opening to the negotiations," Tom said.

"*Toujours l'audace*," Hugh said. "I cannot for the life of me understand why you're against showing strength."

473

"Oh, Jesus," Tom said.

"Listen to me. This can be turned to our account."

"You really play Machiavelli to the hilt, don't you, Hugh," Tom said. "I went into this on the level."

"MacIlvray and his boys are working on releases," Hugh said.

"Releases?" Tom asked. "What kind of releases?"

Hugh gestured to the strew of newspapers. "That's the other side. We have to tell ours."

"I'm ashamed enough as it is," Tom said coldly.

"This is vital, Tom. The press has never cracked down on you personally before. At the worst they've grudged you admiration. The news tonight is a direct attack on you. Maybe you can take it on the chin. But rotten publicity like this can kill sales for years. Trust me."

"And you trust me." Tom went to the marble fireplace where Yule greenery draped the Neville crest. Though he spoke in restrained tones because of the others, his eyes were the same gray granite as when, an adolescent forced to stand *in loco parentis*, he had been driven too far by his angelic-faced sibling's hypochondria or laziness. "No releases from Onyx."

"Tom—"

"No releases. And that adder, Dickson Keeley, doesn't work in my shop anymore. From here on he doesn't work for any member of my family. Is that clear? Do you understand—"

He stopped as the door opened. There was a moment of silence before he grunted, an obscene, belchlike sound as though a fist had hit him above the stomach. He reeled back a step, resting an arm on the mantel, leaning heavily on the broad ledge of marble as he continued to stare at the door.

Hugh gasped and his chair creaked as he rose.

Caryll's head turned, his eyes widening as his mouth opened in a stupefied *o*, then he, too, stood.

Maud's sewing rustled to cover her short, wide satin shoes.

The Tudor beamed library was drained of sound and motion, save for the fire's crackling flames.

IV

Justin stood gripping the antique brass door handle. Eerie lighting from the chandeliers of the Great Hall darkened his bruises to black.

The four men were standing. In this moment of tension a familiar esemblance connected them, weaving around them so that it was mpossible to miss. Despite Hugh's scars, his whippet leanness, and dyed yellow hair (an odd vanity in a recluse), despite Caryll's ponderous Trelinack build and balding temples, the likeness was here.

Between Tom and Justin it was so absolute as to be electrifying.

The beating had smudged Justin's face in the way an impressionist artist might blur the features of his subject in order to show character and bone structure. The ultimate effect was to make the shape of Justin's head more distinct. Though it had not been apparent before, he and Tom had the same long skull, the same curve of jaw.

The pewter hair and the white shone with identical lambency. Both men were tall, both bodies showed the vigor that carried them tirelessly through days of heavy, damaging labor. There was a force, a power in their carriage.

Hugh looked from one to the other, and though his shock at seeing his loved and hated nephew was so immoderate to be a stranglehold around his neck, a secret smile curved his hard mouth. The long-delayed emergence of genetic configurations fit his cherished belief in ties of the blood. The mysteries of heredity cannot remain forever hidden.

Caryll's gaze, too, moved from his father to Justin and back again, his hand involuntarily clenching on his stomach as he viscerally experienced the shattering recognition of the long, well-guarded secret.

Maud peered through her glasses at Justin, not looking at Tom. Her cheeks, high-colored without benefit of rouge, went sallow, and the small, harsh sound that emerged from her throat seemed to rise from deep within her bosom.

Zoe, who had continued to look at Caryll, turned to the entry. She saw Justin.

For her there was only the djinn-like materialization of her brother: in her emotional ferment there was nothing else. Her fingers loosened on the stemmed crystal, and splashes of martini darkened the exquisitely draped azure silk jersey of her dinner gown. She set down the cocktail glass, and the clink rang through the pall of unnatural silence.

Justin closed the door.

Zoe and Justin stared at each other with a hunger that swept aside animosities as well as the harsh victories of time. Their innocent selves returned, the strong, incorruptibly fair older brother, the willful, turbulent little beauty, who had dwelled together in the tall early Victorian house with a joyous, vibrant black-haired woman.

Justin held out his arms, and Zoe plunged across priceless antique Aubusson rugs. Each clasped the other's waist, hugging.

"Oh, your poor face," she said in a rushed whisper. "Your poor, poor face."

"Zozo, how I've missed you."

"You've gone all gray." She pressed her warm, perfumed cheek to his. When they pulled apart, he clasped both her hands.

Tom had kept his eyes on Justin, and Maud's owl gaze, too, remained on the embracing brother and sister.

But Caryll continued to stare from his father to Justin, his expression of painful recognition usurped by one of horror. *Zoe?* his lips moved silently. *Zoe, too?*

Hugh ran a fingernail down the arm of his chair, an irritating rasp that he did not realize he was causing. Surprised by the blundering of delight at Justin's presence, amazed by the resurrection of his old avuncular love, horrified by Justin's bruises, he said the first thing that flashed into his head. "I didn't hear any car."

"I took the Guelin place's lakeshore path, climbed over your wall. Then the servants' cloakroom."

"Yes, that door's always-open."

Justin leaned against the doorjamb, his urgency about Elisse muted by a wave of vertigo only in part attributable to his bashing. Expecting Hugh alone, he had not calculated on the psychic cost of seeing his sister and the gathered Bridgers. He inhaled deeply to regain his equilibrium.

"Dad?" Caryll muttered, stretching his hand with a child's gesture of dependence toward Tom. "My God, Dad?"

Tom's normal sardonic expression had deserted him: the lower half of his long, angular face had fallen, giving him the appearance of toothless age. He turned away from Justin's accusatory bruises and Caryll's burning, horrified eyes, resting his elbows on the end of the mantel.

Maud's topaz beads were rising and falling on the rich, gloomy brown satin over her bosom. With a loud, incongruous burst of laughter, she said, "Now I see why you pushed to marry *her*."

Tom did not shift. The fire flickered ruddy patterns on his white hair.

"Mother, then it's true?" Caryll asked.

"Everyone said she was a whore."

Zoe asked shrilly, "What is all this?"

"Mother?" Caryll repeated.

"You have eyes," Maud said loudly. "See for yourself."

Caryll looked neither at his father nor at Justin. Touching the tip of his tongue to his lips, he said, "Yes."

Zoe returned across the room to her husband. "Please, Caryll. What's going on?"

Caryll reached to hold his wife, then his arm jerked to his side as though the gorgeously sensual body were corseted in molten metal.

"*She's* not your father's, Caryll." Maud's laugh was mirthless. "He didn't start going to England until after she was born. If he had, the story would have been quite different. But he didn't. So he's not his child."

"What *is* everybody talking about?" Zoe cried, tossing her vivid, burnished head, a gesture left over from childhood tantrums. "I can't bear it!"

"Justin and Caryll are brothers," Maud said with clogged vindictiveness.

"Brothers-in-law," Zoe denied.

"Half brothers," Maud said in that same thick intonation.

Zoe flopped into the sofa, limp. After a moment her beautiful, stricken eyes sought Justin. "Is it true?"

Yet in my lineaments they trace/ Some features of my father's face. "Afraid so. Yes."

"Father Bridger and Mother?"

Justin nodded.

"But that's hideous. . . . There was Uncle Andrew, too. Creepy . . horrible . . ." Zoe's murmur was barely audible. "Why didn't you ever tell me?"

"When I found out, I left Detroit. I felt . . . ashamed. Zozo, you can understand that, can't you? Ashamed."

Tom's shoulders twitched under the finely tailored gray worsted, but he gave no other sign. His inner anguish at the disintegration of his long-kept vow to Antonia far outbalanced the hysteria that ripped the air in Hugh's library.

"So you're Hugh's nephew. That's why he brought us here." A blush stained Zoe's flawlessly rounded throat. "Who told you?"

Hugh caught his breath. Somewhere in the office wing a phone jangled, then was silent.

"I found out, that's all," Justin said.

"How?" Zoe persisted.

"Einstein." Justin managed a battered grin. "I proved the theory of relativity."

No one smiled. But Zoe nodded and rested her head back.

Hugh exhaled raggedly. Tom's love letters would remain a heap of blackened ashes. Justin never betrayed a confidence, and had he, Hugh, accepted this, he could have avoided nearly a decade of treading on eggshells with his brother as well as general wretchedness. That old tribal affection for his nephew was reasserting itself in stronger and stronger waves.

"Zoe . . . ?" Caryll muttered raggedly.

"Your mother's right, Caryll," Justin said. "No need to worry. This has nothing to do with Zoe. I'm the only bastard." He forced another bruised grin.

"You look rotten, Justin," Hugh said. "How about a drink? It used to be Scotch."

"Nothing, thanks."

"You need bucking up," Hugh said.

"You do look woozy, Justin," Zoe said.

"I'm fine."

"Why are you here?" asked Maud bluntly.

Justin planted his muddy shoes apart. His bruised face suddenly wary, vaguely hostile, as though he had been thrust into enemy territory, he looked directly at Hugh. "My wife is missing."

"Your wife?" Hugh asked, the warmth retreating from his voice. "I want her."

"She's not here." Hugh was overly polite. "I do assure you she's not."

Caryll asked, "Was Elisse in that mess today?"

"Yes. She was supposed to meet me at the sound truck after I came down from the overpass. She never showed up. I don't know where she is, but the police took a lot of people in."

"If she's been arrested," Hugh said, "you can post bail."

"I tried to." Justin's eyes showed intensely blue between slitted, bruised lids. "She hasn't been booked."

"Then she hasn't been arrested."

"Find her."

"I'm afraid there's no way I can."

"The department's in your pocket."

"Hardly. Might I suggest you telephone some of her union friends. Maybe she stopped off to visit."

Tom took a step away from the fireplace. His left hand clenching and unclenching, he spoke to Hugh, his first words since Justin had opened the door. "Call Arden."

"Say she *has* been taken downtown, Tom," Hugh replied. "How would he know? The police chief? One woman? On a day like this?"

"Call," Tom ordered.

"There's no point."

Tom strode to the shadowy ell where a spindle-legged Tudor cabinet housed the telephone. "What's his home number, Arden?" he snapped.

Hugh recited from memory.

Tom asked the operator for the number, then identified himself, asking for Chief Arden. Waiting, he switched on the floor lamp. Without a greeting he said that he was looking for Mrs. Elisse Hutchinson, yes, that's right, she was the AAW president's wife, and the last anyone had seen her was in that crappy deal on Archibald. At the inaudible reply his expression briefly wavered, the vulnerable upper lip curling back to reveal his uneven white teeth. "I see," he said in a flat, inflectionless tone, listening another half minute before he replaced the earpiece as delicately as if it were a precision tool.

Justin had come to stand near him. "Where is she?"

"Quite a few women are in the Fifth Precinct Station."

"So she's there?" Justin asked.

"Probably. I'll run you over."

"That's quite unnecessary," Hugh said. "I'll have Gallagher take him in his car."

"Yes," Maud said. Concentric circles formed around her mouth so that her face seemed like an illustration of the angered, puffing wind god. "You stay put, Tom."

"Come on, Justin."

"You're not to go!" Maud cried.

"Maud," Tom said, a plea undershadowed by warning.

"She had your bastard—"

"That's enough!" Tom snapped.

"I've been square with you. But every single day of our marriage you lived a lie!"

"We'll go over this when we're alone."

"Hah! As if you could ever explain! You're beyond me. First you push him ahead for all he's worth, then there's years without a word to him, and now suddenly you're taking up with him again. Who could understand what goes on in your head besides automobiles? All right, I can't figure *you* out. But you can understand *me*. Tom, you aren't leaving this house."

"Let's go, Justin."

"Tom—" Justin started.

"Don't you dare, Tom!" Maud was screaming.

"Let's get a move on," Tom said to Justin.

"Leave this room and we're through!" Maud had never intended a challenge, but she could repress neither her fury at always playing second fiddle to her dead rival nor her own inviolable honesty: it was the same as that long ago day in their stateroom with the foghorns wailing. She opened her mouth and her anguish burst out. "Go with him and as far as I'm concerned it's like you're on top of that skinny, black-haired whore again!"

Tom gripped Justin's arm, propelling him from the library.

V

For a minute there was silence in the room, yet the large, warm library seemed to ring with the sound of furious voices.

Hugh pulled back a curtain, staring after the moving red lights, his thoughts focused on his nephew and brother on the front seat of that Onyx. Shivers reverberated along his skin. It took him a while to pinpoint what he felt. *Left out. Cast away. Abandoned. Forsaken. I should be with them. They're my people. Not Caryll. But what am I to them? A cipher puffed with grandiose dreams of past and future king-making, a scarred, marred gargoyle. Alone,* Hugh thought, *forlorn, forlorn.*

The taillights disappeared around the curve. He went to pour himself a stiff drink. *At least I'm forlorn in style: Russian caviar and Polish vodka.* The thought garnered him no comfort.

Maud's hands were clasped on her lap. Her seated figure had a granitic heaviness as though she had suddenly gained thirty pounds. Why had she hurled down that gauntlet? Though the revelation of Justin's identity had shocked and horrified her, she accepted that men were men and the past was the past, so why had it seemed so monstrous a betrayal that Tom would drive his natural son to the police station? Why was she caught up in this irrational cyclone of jealousy? Antonia was dead, and by her own sensible lights Maud had always been realistic even about *that*, as she mentally referred to Tom's major adultery.

He lied to me, he deceived me all along, he lived a lie, that's why I'm in this state, she told herself, but her honesty balked at this. If she were outraged solely by the deception, why did she have these sharp, feverish visions of stabbing the dead woman, shooting her with a pearl-handled revolver, of tightening her hands around that long, slender neck? Why this mosaic of murderous urges? Bending stiffly, she fumbled for her sewing. Unconscious of what she was doing, she pulled at the pink batiste, ripping her fine stitchery.

"Mother Bridger," Zoe murmured. "You're ruining Petra's dress."

Maud's fingers continued to rip apart the smocking.

Zoe's tears oozed silently without marring her loveliness. Her weeping had nothing to do with her mother-in-law. Though the revelation about her brother's disparate blood had jarred her to her roots, it was the apparition of Justin himself—battered, still so very dear—that shocked her psyche from its self-centered locus. She had been lashed with pity for his poor bruises and for that awful, humiliated smile. Justin, whom she had always considered as invincibly strong, was vulnerable, as vulnerable as she. Maybe more vulnerable because the good have fewer defenses. Dabbing at her tears, she glanced at Caryll.

His neat brown hair was stringy with sweat. Catching her gaze, he sighed. "I hope she's there," he said.

"She?"

"Elisse. She has to be." Caryll shook his head and returned to his painful reverie.

From earliest memory he had attempted with woeful lack of success to pour his soft, artistic self into the outsize mold of that iron genius who had drawn the earth together and had hammered out the machinery of mass production. Though in his adulthood Caryll had come to question the benefits of assembly lines, he had never doubted the heroic image of his father. Tom Bridger was a giant of a man. A billionaire altruist who had given the world its first seven-dollar day, a brilliant offbeat from the top of his intuitive, uncultured head to his narrow (sometimes worn down) heels. Even Tom's rages to Caryll were protean and therefore admirable.

For the first time Caryll was noting the dark crevices that defaced his idol.

In a moment of complicated clarity he accepted that Tom's siring of a bastard did not offend him. Indeed, Caryll, loving and respecting Justin, derived a slender security from sharing with him the responsibility of being the giant's son. No. It was Tom's treatment of Justin that shook him with a grief surely akin to what he would register at his father's graveside. Caryll reviewed the sordid, disgraceful way that Tom had kept aloof from Justin—even after that mess at school, when to show a touch of friendship would have been natural. His own semirepressed questions about Tom's abrupt yet oddly generous treatment of his friend were answered. His father obviously felt a good deal for Justin, yet did not care to accept paternity. Caryll, himself a tenderly devoted parent, was unutterably horrified.

A tap on the door. "Dinner is served," announced a tall footman.

"We aren't staying," Caryll said with unaccustomed curtness. "Have my car brought around."

"Immediately, Mr. Bridger, sir." The sound of the footman's step was cut off by the closing of the metal fire door that led to the kitchen wing.

"I'll come with you," Maud said. The color had returned to her cheeks in red, splotchy marks.

"We'll be glad to drop you off," Caryll replied.

"I'm not going back to the Farm."

Caryll gave his mother a penetrating look, asking quietly, "Would it help, then, to stay with us awhile?"

"Yes." Maud crushed the small, ruined dress into her sewing bag. "Until I find out how to file for a divorce."

They all stared at her.

Hugh's nostrils flared, then he forced his expression into a show of earnestness as he reverted to his self-determined role: his brother's keeper. It all came down to this. Tom would be happier and better off with his wife than without her. "Come on, Maud, you've got too much common sense for that."

"I've had it up to here," she cried.

"This must come as an awful shock, I realize that, Maud, but you can't walk out on a whole life together, a good marriage—"

"He always wanted *her*."

"You're his wife, the one who helped him get started. You gave him his home, his heir. He's always relied on you and your honesty."

"All along she's had her claws in Tom through Justin." Maud's voice had sunk to a loud, unhappy whisper.

"I'm the one you should blame, Maud," Hugh said. "I put my nose in and brought him to Detroit."

"You've always done Tom's dirty work for him!"

Hugh winced, but he said smoothly, "At least stay and have dinner."

"You aren't going to change my mind, Hugh!" she cried. "Why couldn't he have been honest with me? I've always been with him. Was he trying to protect her reputation, or what? Why did he have to skulk? That's what hurts. All the lying and pretending. As if I cared where he poked his peter!"

The vulgarity burst out with a look of twisted misery. Hugh looked into Maud's flushed, sweating face and fleetingly empathized with his sister-in-law. Like him, she lived by the light of Tom's sun, and, again like him, she yearned to feel the warmth of her devotion reflected back.

"Masquerades and lies," she cried. "The pair of you! Always lying about everything to do with that whore—"

Zoe covered her ears and ran from the library. Caryll hurried after her, trotting behind the sensually swaying, rounded hips to the vast, high vestibule where Maud's shouts were no longer audible.

"I couldn't take any more," she murmured, her enormous wet eyes fixed pleadingly on him. "Ahh, Caryll, let's get home?"

"We have to wait for Mother," Caryll said, tears in his own eyes. Ducking into the brocade-lined coatroom to get their things and regain his composure, he said, "Zoe, remember how we used to badger Justin about those photographs and memorabilia of his father? *Your* father?" He returned to settle the cape around her shoulders, and his nostrils were tickled by the drifts of specially compounded perfume rising from tawny stone martens. "Can you imagine what it must have done to him when he found out?"

"I felt so sorry for him. . . . I'd never seen him ashamed."

"I couldn't look at him. God, the way Dad's treated him, it's really pathological. Never inviting him—either of you—to the Farm, not even when it would have been perfectly natural. And those summers we worked at the Hamtramck, me and the Sinclairs and him! The four of us always ate in the executive dining room. Justin was never asked—well, I invited him a few times. Can you imagine Dad doing that, always leaving him out? He always handed him the tough assignments, and very few bouquets for doing well."

"Later on, though, he gave him important jobs."

"Justin earned his promotions. But you've hit on the paradox."

"Paradox?"

"From the day Justin started at Onyx, Dad went out of the way to teach him everything. Automobiles, engines, industrial planning, things he's a genius at." Caryll's voice was musing. "Now I think of it, he must have been trying to compress their relationship within the limits of business. But why? He could have told at least the family. Mother's a thousand times more hurt, finding out this way. And God knows it's crushed me." With distraught movements Caryll pulled on his overcoat. "Remember about the wedding present? I told you he was set to give Justin the same number of shares. When I asked why, he came up with some rigmarole about wanting to keep Justin at Onyx, but looking back, I'm pretty sure he had in mind that both of us would inherit equally."

"That proves something, doesn't it?"

"But what?"

"Don't you think he cares a lot?"

"I always sensed he did, far more than he let on. But after Justin left, he never contacted him, never saw him until noon today. Could you imagine going nearly ten years without seeing Clarice or Petra or Lynn?"

Zoe, devoted to her pretty little daughters, said, "Never. The whole thing's beyond me. . . . Do you think . . . maybe it's because she's Jewish?"

"Hugh's the family bigot, not Dad." Caryll's voice caught, and he said gruffly, "Listen to me, talking so authoritatively. What do I know about Dad? That he's been a model father to me, and he's treated his other son abominably."

"Caryll . . ."

"Yes."

"Do you still feel the same about me?"

"What a question."

"If it turns out I'm like Justin . . . ?"

"My sister?"

"Yes."

"I was a champion fool about that. One thing I am positive of. Hugh's too stuck on our noble line to permit incest." Caryll's voice shook with the atypical irony. He fumbled with the knot of his scarf.

"But say if . . ." Her thick dark lashes lowered. "Then would you still love me?"

"Ahh, Zoe, if it were possible for me to stop, I would have years ago."

Her sigh shivered on her furs. "It gives me the willies, your father fooling around with Mother."

"I only met her once, at the Southwark opening, but she was so vivid, I can still remember feeling happy at being with her. She certainly wasn't another floozy to him."

"How are you so positive? Didn't you just say he's a big, dark mystery to you?"

Caryll's sigh was wrung from him. "Feet of clay," he muttered.

Zoe in her silver-strapped evening sandals was taller than he. Looking into her husband's troubled, bleak gray eyes, she straightened his white silk muffler, a sincerely tender gesture. "This isn't your problem, Caryll."

"Who says? To discover that all along he's abdicated his most basic responsibility!"

"Mother Bridger says she's leaving. Are you thinking of it?" asked Zoe.

"I'm too confused to think."

"Poor honey bear."

"Dad needs me," Caryll said in spite of himself, then added angrily, "The job's hell."

"Yes, your poor stomach."

"I waste half my time trying to figure how he'd handle any given situation."

"Caryll, I know sometimes I'm . . . bad. . . . But that doesn't mean I'm not on your side. I care, care a lot. Whatever you decide, it's all right with me."

He clasped the warm, slim hand, grateful that for all his beautiful wife's frailties she had never been grasping or meretricious. Then into his mind came Tom's expression as he had listened on the phone, a peculiar baring of teeth, a glint of eyes centered with fear. What had he heard that had impelled him to accompany Justin? A shiver went down Caryll's spine. *I hope Elisse is okay,* he thought, and though this was one of the times he and Zoe were perfectly attuned, he knew enough not to voice this particular alarm.

Maud's heavy step was sounding in the Great Hall: he hurried for her thick sable coat.

CHAPTER 32

Silence clamped on the cold dark streets of Detroit. Curtains or blinds were drawn in mansions and shabby houses alike, store windows were barred, a few cars made their way through the night, but no pedestrians. After the riot the city crouched licking its wounds.

The station was on the eastern edge of Highland Park, a long way from Hugh's house. Tom, spine curved, fingers tensed lightly on the wheel, handled the little Seven coupe as though it were a racer.

They sped along Lake Shore Drive in silence.

Justin, despite his clogging apprehensions about Elisse, could not dispel the awkwardness—no, it was more an unmanning edginess—that he felt in Tom's presence. Between them on the leatherette seat rose the specter of the lifelong deception. Though the truth had burst out a few minutes earlier in Hugh's library, not until Tom admitted paternity would the ghostly barrier be swept away and a lost and devalued part of Justin's self be restored. It was an old story, this reprehensibly childish need to hear fatherhood stated in Tom's flat, laconic tones, yet that did not make it any less powerful. Justin glanced at Tom. In the dim light the long-familiar profile appeared relaxed. Yet how could Tom ignore the catastrophic scene, the mass recognition? How could he behave as though nothing worth mentioning had transpired amid Hugh's resplendently bound first editions? Why wasn't he admitting the truth? *Why this purposeful silence?*

Justin, atwitch with unanswerable questions, clammy with fears about his wife, tried to take his mind off his own problems by listing the major points in the negotiation that would commence tomorrow morning.

Tom braked for the stop sign at an empty intersection. When the signal changed, he continued along Jefferson.

Justin said, "You should have turned, Tom."

"Don't worry. I'll get you there."

"This is out of the way."

"A minor detour."

"We don't have time for detours."

"We'll take five extra minutes. There's no traffic."

Scarcely a car moved in the normally congested downtown, no lines waited by the ticket booths of effulgently lit movie palaces, not even at the Hindu splendor of the Fox on Woodward.

"Tom," Justin said edgily. "Let's go straight to the station house."

"No more than five minutes extra, I promise you."

Justin, by now grasping that they were headed to the mansion built by his great-uncle and inhabited by his mother, breathed deeply in an attempt to relax. Soon it began to seem predetermined, this drive through a deserted city, destiny that Tom should choose that old house as the place to tell him.

Woodward Avenue had fallen on hard times. Its arboreal arch of great trees was long gone. Commercial buildings, hock shops, shabby Coney Islands, mom 'n' pop groceries interspersed the once proud residences—many of which, having diminished into boardinghouses or kitchenette apartments, were defaced by the metallic gleam of fire escapes.

Between the limestone towers of the Major's chateau glowed a white neon sign: NALLEY'S FUNERAL CHAPEL. The lovingly tended gardens had given way to blacktop for mourners' parking.

Tom braked at the curb. Shifting to neutral, nursing the idling motor, he gazed musingly at the house. "A Versailles in old Detroit."

"The architect had Chenonceaux in mind—or so Mother told me." Justin's throat went taut as he mentioned Antonia.

Tom made an uncertain gesture, a reaching out toward Justin, a hapless attempt at physical contact that was more poignant for its failure. His hand cupped the gearshift.

"It's been one long time without you, Justin."

Euphoric gratitude roiled through Justin, and he stirred in the car seat. "I wrote often."

"You did? I never got any letters."

"Never mailed them."

"I swiped photographs of your kids from Caryll," he confessed.

"You did?" Justin was conscious of a vibrato in his voice, a sound Verdi might have used in an aria to show desperate hope. *Say it now,* he thought. *Now!*

"It used to kill the best part of an hour to get out this far," Tom said. "That is, for those of us who couldn't afford a bicycle. Even for the carriage class it took five times as long as it does now. Distances, kid, in case word hasn't reached you, have changed."

The shift from unprecedented, rumble-voiced closeness to jaunty banter sank Justin's anticipations. "That's pretty much your doing, Tom," he said levelly.

Tom touched the horn. "Not to toot my own," he said, "but next to you sits pretty much the cause of low morality in youth and the reason for weakened leg muscles and lower-back pain. Yeah, and meager church attendance, too. Robbery—felons now have speedy getaway. I've handed a lethal weapon to drunks and imbeciles. Disfigured the countryside with billboards and ratty tourist courts. Caused parking problems and a dearth of lonely farms for forward-thinking youths to abandon."

Tom seldom made so lengthy a speech, and he never catalogued his accomplishments, even in this backhanded manner. Justin's hopes teetered higher again as he decided that Tom needed to buck himself up before the denouement. "I never think of you as a farmboy."

"I was, I was. The question is, should I have stuck it out in North Dakota?"

"The world's better off by a long shot that you left."

Tom turned, the whiteness of teeth and hair showing in the dark car. "You wouldn't bullshit me?"

"Life's certainly more democratic. And God knows healthier. I can remember flies hovering over the carpet of horse manure on every street."

"Then you're saying I haven't turned in too rotten a performance?"

"Why ask me, why does *my* opinion matter?" *Get on with it, get on with it!* God, he was as impatient as Ben—and even more vulnerable! He yearned for some of the calm that others attributed to him. For a moment there was only the sound of the idling engine.

"The way I look at it, Justin, a man's life works in cycles like an engine. The first stroke you're a kid, taking in your air and gas—your ideas. The second stroke you're growing up, compressing your charge. That means deciding your goals, what you want to do or be. Then you ignite and explode. The third stroke you're full-grown, delivering your full power. Doing your main work." Tom shrugged. "Then suddenly you're old and look into your exhaust gases and try to see what you've done. Maybe if you're lucky you've accomplished some good you can pass on to your next generation."

Justin held his breath.

Tom stared at the curved neon letters. "Jesus, what's happened to this place! A funeral home!" He shook his head and fell silent.

The freezing, quiet night wrapped Justin in an unendurable expectancy. He spoke first. "Tom, why did you bring me here?" His voice strove to be casual, but some vital part of him cringed. *Begging*, he thought. *I'm begging*.

"The first time I was invited here, I met your mother. . . ."

The flat voice faded on a dreamy, tender note that Justin would not have believed in Tom's range had he not read those yellowed love letters.

A mindless euphoria buoyed him, and he recalled standing at the Rutland Gate front door, determined to "look after Mother," shivering in the draft as the pale, clear gray eyes of the tall stranger gazed down at him with a pinpoint intensity. That moment was strung to this by inexorable wires. "Tell me about her," he said hoarsely. "Tell me about Mother."

"She came down . . . it was as if she were flying . . . she didn't seem to touch the steps. . . ."

After a silence Justin prodded, "So Uncle Andrew introduced you?"

"Yes. She was beautiful. . . ." Tom shook his head. "I didn't really know if she was beautiful or not. She glowed and shone . . . it was impossible to tell. . . ."

Tom's long, narrow fingers jumped to the ignition key, plunging them into silence with a jerk that seemed unconscious, involuntary. An approaching car threw beams of light, and Justin saw Tom's baffled, agonized expression, the sweat running down his forehead and cheeks. He appeared in the clutch of some violent struggle that his mind had little control over. His muscles clenched in a spasm, as though a pair of inhuman foxes were battling within the terrain of the lean, strong body. His face twitched and he bent forward.

Justin, remembering the earlier heart attack, inquired, "Tom? Are you all right?"

The Seven rocked in the air current of the passing car, and Tom's expression altered jerkily, as if one of those ravenous foxes, having demolished the other, had taken over. His lips took on a set, sardonic grin.

"What is it, Tom?"

"Coming here makes me feel old, that's all. Brings back the days of my youth."

"Yes," Justin heard himself say hoarsely. "You were telling me about Mother."

"The Major had invited me to breakfast. You can bet I was quaking; still, I managed to blab out a request to use his showroom as a shop. That was the beginning."

"And Mother?"

"She didn't eat with us. She came down after—I told you, as if she were flying."

"Tom, *for Christ's sake, the family knows about us!* You saw their reactions tonight. You heard them!"

Tom peered ahead and the profile was implacable. "Listen, you want fiction stories, then go back to Hugh's. He'll tell them to you."

Rejection once again. He hadn't thought it possible. A groan escaped Justin, and he set his teeth into his lower lip to silence it. And then he was buried in a crushing avalanche of emotion—anger, hurt, shame, perplexity, loss, embarrassment for his evaporated pipe dreams. Yet in his misery he could not repress a twinge of pity for Tom, for his desperate attempt to maintain such a lie. Why? For what? Justin clenched his fist against his forehead, and a sharp jab of pain brought him back to reality.

Elisse. The circumstances of his birth seemed a ridiculous trifle in comparison to this ultimate exigency. *Elisse. The police have her, and God knows what they're doing to her. And here I sit: Why aren't I at the station, bailing her out?*

"Tom, let's get a move on," he said curtly.

"Right." Tom started the car. "Sorry about the detour."

After a mile or so they passed a brightly lighted delicatessen.

"Stop!" Justin ordered.

The coupe squealed to a halt. "What's up?"

"That place was open. Back up. I need to get some sandwiches."

"Food! *Now?*"

"For the women. It's something we always try to do when people are taken in. Most of them have never been inside a jail and they need a bit of cheering." His voice was brusque with anger that the deli sandwiches for the imprisoned women had won over his nerve-strung personal terrors about Elisse.

Tom shifted into reverse. "There's such a thing as having principles that are too high, Justin, God help you."

At the old three-story fortress-like police station, Justin flung open the car door.

"I'll tag along," Tom said.

"No need." Justin, one foot on the running board, hefted out two cartons redolent with spicy odors.

"The voice of a substantial taxpayer greases the gears of the law."

"You better get back to Hugh's." Justin could not help venting some of his shame at Tom's ultimate rejection. He added tonelessly, "Mrs. Bridger seemed upset about something or other."

"The hell with you!"

"Thanks for the lift," Justin said in the same colorless tone.

"I'll hang around for—"

"Somebody will pick us up. We don't need you!" Justin burst out, and the Onyx rocked as he kicked shut the door.

II

The crowded cells resembled animal cages with their barred roofs below the ceiling. The place smelled of vomit, nervous bodies, and lidless toilets.

A turnkey shouted above the shrill feminine hubbub, "Here's your pimp, girlies."

Sixty or so blushing women rose from bare-springed cots, straightening shapeless coats with embarrassed tugs. To most of them, being here, for whatever reason, was a scarring disgrace.

Justin peered around.

Elisse was not here!

The dizziness returned, full force, and gripping the lower carton harder, he said in a loud, clear voice, "To those of you who don't know me, or can't recognize me behind these shiners, I'm president of the Amalgamated Automobile Workers. I'm proud of you, proud that you were arrested standing up for the right of every American worker to organize. Tomorrow morning we'll have lawyers down here to bail you out. In the meantime, here's an evening snack from the Brotherhood."

As he passed thick corned beef or ham sandwiches between bars, he repeated, "Has anyone in here seen Elisse? My wife? She's yea high." He held his hand to his shoulder. "Brown hair."

"Oh, men," shrugged one jovial loom girl whom he recognized as an AAW member. Swallowing a mouthful of sandwich, she said, "Elisse isn't just 'yea high' with brown hair. She's kinda stunning. A lot like Janet Gaynor, as a matter of fact."

"I think so, too, Gertie." Justin smiled. "Was she with you today?"

Gertie shook her head. "Not today, Prof. I never seen her today."

"I did." A thickset woman spoke up from a nearby cell.

Justin strode to her. "Where?"

"Near the overpass."

"When was that?"

"A minute or so before the creeps gassed us." The fat woman wore a frayed man's hat, which gave her a Tugboat Annie raffishness. "She was crazy. She didn't see nothing except the way they was working on your face."

"Was she arrested?"

"They packed me into a Black Maria."

"You're sure she wasn't brought in?"

"She wasn't with us, I never seen her after that, so let's hope she wasn't."

Justin hurried to hand out the last few sandwiches.

III

The pudgy-faced desk sergeant continued his telephone conversation, idly picking his ear with the eraser end of his pencil, ignoring Justin.

When he hung up, Justin demanded, "Where's Elisse Hutchinson?"

The sergeant yawned mightily. "Didn't you find her in the south cellblock?"

"You know all the women in there have been booked."

"So? Since when do you union comrades give your real names?"

"It's illegal to hold her without booking her."

"You Bolshies and your rights."

"Where have you got her?" Justin's palm slammed on the desk, rattling the pencil holder. "Where is she?"

The full cheeks quivered. "You're sucking for more of that medicine you got on the overpass!"

A flat voice behind Justin said, "Chief Arden figured Mrs. Hutchinson was here."

The sergeant goggled at Tom. "Mr. Bridger," he mumbled respectfully. "What . . . why are *you* here, sir?"

"We're together." Tom indicated Justin. "What about that other woman?"

"There aren't any, Mr. Bridger."

Tom's mouth twitched. "Arden mentioned one." His voice was low and frightened.

Steady, steady, Justin told himself. He felt as though every drop of his blood had halted in the terrible necessity that he not move or scream out questions. He must wait, he must listen. The wall clock ticked noisily against his ears. In this big, shabby place that smelled of stale tobacco smoke, everything was in abeyance. The little cluster of blue-uniformed cops beyond the scarred oak barrier formed a tableau. The crown of pain encircled his head.

The desk sergeant's full face was composing itself into jowled gravity. "The chief told you about *that?*"

"He did."

"Everything, sir?"

"How should I know? He's home. Give him a ring and find out."

"That's not necessary, Mr. Bridger." The sergeant turned. "Mushski, take the union man down to 117."

"Me?" asked a young cop, nervously fingering back his profuse, wavy blond hair.

"You, Mushski." The sergeant added with a veiled vindictiveness, "It ain't up to us to deny anyone their rights."

Tom followed the young cop and Justin to the freight elevator: none of the three spoke as they jerked down to the basement with its dank labyrinth of corridors. The torn muscles in Justin's groin had stiffened, and he spraddled as he limped swiftly after Mushski. They turned at a hallway. The one door was at the end. Above the scarred woodwork was painted *117*.

Mushski gripped the doorknob, blurting, "Here we are."

Justin blinked rapidly, and Tom gripped his arm.

The profound chill with its reek of carbolic and undertones of thicker, meatlike odors told them where they were even before Mushski pressed the switch. Four dangling bulbs glared on unplastered brick walls and a gray cement floor with moisture darkening around the drain hole to prove a recent hosing down.

Along the windowless walls ranged waist-high tables. Four were occupied by sheet-draped bodies. The feet protruded, bare and pitiful for their veined whiteness, their bunions and corns, their manila-tagged right big toes.

"They haven't made any announcement yet, or contacted the families," Mushski said apologetically. "There was four deaths on Archibald today. Three men and a woman. The woman got no identification on her."

Tom, having secured this information on the telephone in Hugh's library, had been hoping against hope that it would have nothing to do with Justin's wife.

Justin limped to the table where the policeman was drawing back the sheet from the head of the smallest corpse.

VI

A khaki arm descended and the billy club hit her head. Her hat flew off. Her feet grew heavy, their weight pulling at her thighs and buckling her knees.

"Justin," she gasped.

The heaviness of her feet drew her inexorably downward.

Again she thought trampled to death, *this time in conjunction with herself.* If I fall under this herd, I'll be trampled to death. *Yet she was not afraid. Death was an abstraction inextricably mingled with old people, death was not possible, that was all. How could she die? She was young, Justin needed her, her children needed her.* I can't duck out on Ben and Tonia, *she thought,* not permanently, not until they're grown. They need me. *To halt her fall she grasped at the lapels of a man's coat.*

495

The blow to her head had dulled neural connections between her brain and her hands. Vomit-soaked fabric slipped through her fingers. She sank to her knees, making weak, swimming movements at the trousers and skirts struggling and pressing around her. You have to pull yourself up, she thought, her brain desperately alert, her hands sliding sluggishly along a coarse-haired fur coat. She continued to fall into the squirming, shoving darkness, the enveloping darkness, the inevitable darkness. She struggled with her enfeebled resources to rise, and a tormented, screaming wail gathered loudness until it filled the universe.

A heavy workboot caught her just above the nape, a coup de grace. She fell under the feet of coughing, gas-panicked stampeders.

Boots and shoes trampled her, puncturing her intestines and organs, pulping her flesh. There was no merciful lulling, no numbness. Her maddened scream was cut off when a woman's narrow heel destroyed her larynx.

In agony, Elisse's life was, quite literally, stamped out. In the last instants that she would wear the raiment of mortal flesh, however, she was vouchsafed comfort. A sense of failure had always dogged her. To her mind she was a rotten daughter, an apostate mother, of late a sadly tepid wife, a Jew in name only, a zero in her dedication to the causes to which she adhered. Her decisions inevitably had been governed by her emotions. She was, or so she had believed until now, betrayed at every turn by that spongy will of hers. She had never possessed the fixed compass point of logic or the eternal truth of ethics. Now, though, she perceived her life differently. On this little ball of spinning mud, she, a finite atom, had made the minuscule decisions permitted her from the only place she could trust. Her own soft and very mortal heart.

A body stumbled athwart her head, smothering the last breath from her.

And then she was remembering from earliest childhood. She and her parents stood around a table set with the good red Haviland china, the bone-handled English sterling silver, and a dish arrayed with a sprig of parsley, a lamb shank, a hard egg, a broken matzo, all the Passover symbols. Her father, with a foolishly happy smile, held up a sacramental ruby imprisoned within a wine glass. Behind him glowed a large form. The angel Elijah, *she thought,* he's come to drink his wine. How wondrous that the angel should have Justin's *face. Nobody in this world would ever know that Elisse Kaplan Hutchinson's final comprehensive thought before the last revelation engulfed her was the one with which for five thousand years Jews have greeted Death. Elisse's piping voice joined with Daddy's and Mother's in the only Hebrew words she knew:* Adonai elohenu, Adonai echod.

The Lord our God, the Lord is One.

V

"Oh my sweet, my poor sweet," Justin whispered. Bending to kiss what had been his wife's forehead, he was transfixed by the same desire that had overcome him years earlier. To elope with Elisse, to carry her to some enchanted green land where he could cherish and protect her, to live the rest of his days with her in that place where she would make him smile with her sharp, witty tongue, where she would share his life and love, where the warmth of her heart would melt the bitter curse of his loneliness.

Unless he could take her to that land his tormented, breaking heart was doomed to a death as irrevocably final and absolute as hers.

Shuddering with vehement, uncontrollable sobs, he stooped to lift the martyred remnants of her.

Tom and the young policeman took his arms, propelling him from the icy morgue.

VI

It was nearly three in the morning.

Tom hunched shivering in his car. A freezing wind had come up, whirling occasional scraps of old newspapers in a dance past the feeble bulb on Justin's front porch.

Justin, after that maddened, wrenching outburst in the morgue, had leaned his head against the basement corridor wall for what had seemed an eternity. He had gasped aloud in a harrowing struggle to control the physical manifestations of his grief, then had returned upstairs, paying no attention to Tom or the police other than to avert his head from them as he spoke into the telephone. He spoke quietly and without inflection, first to his home, then to Nalley's, the mortuary in the Major's chateau.

Soon after, the man whose name Tom had so often heard—Mitch

497

Shapiro—had arrived. It was the stocky labor organizer who had wept when he and Justin shared a mourners' embrace, Mitch who had given Tom such a bloodshot glance of contempt that Tom had retreated to wait in his Seven outside the fortress-like station until the two emerged. Tom had been incapable of leaving Justin. That demented sobbing outburst over the poor, mutilated corpse had wracked Tom; he had never witnessed grief so engulfing, so raw, and the eruption was doubly devastating, coming from a man as self-contained as Justin. Though he knew his help was not wanted, he had followed the old car here.

A furious gust buffeted the Seven, and the draft penetrated Tom's overcoat, which was open so he could massage his left shoulder and upper arm.

His promise to Antonia, kept at such great cost, had been broken by the fixed and immutable laws of heredity. In Hugh's library, drenched with benumbed horror, Tom had accepted that he must unload his heart to Justin and accordingly had driven him to the Major's old place for the purpose of confessing; yet, gazing up at the limestone walls, fumbling for the right words to explain his lie-buttressed lie, he had experienced a prickling numbness on his left side, a numbness that had quickly sharpened to minor though ineffaceable twists of pain. To confess would cut his last tie with Antonia, and that he was not strong enough to do. The twinging persisted, a reminder of his old heart trouble.

Justin's was the only house with electricity on, and this outlined the cracker boxes on either side—once, far back in his own youth, Tom would have considered these nice homes. He lifted his gaze to the moonless, wintry sky . . . stars bright, stars remote, dusty trails of stars . . . a wave of weariness after this interminable day overcame him, and he closed his eyes.

Antonia stood on the sidewalk, the dim porch light picking out the slender, white-stockinged ankles as well as the pale face with its malevolently whipping strands of black hair. The apparition terrified him to the point of breathlessness, for he fully comprehended that Antonia had lain more than twenty years in damp London soil, he had seen the marble canopy over her bones.

It's a nightmare, he told himself, and with tremendous effort opened his eyes.

She was still there, substantial, three-dimensional, wind-tousled, but now she was bending her face to the window to show her glinting anger.

"I've kept my word, darling," he said. "Don't haunt me like this. I kept my promise."

"Promise? What promise? There was nothing good or human in what you did."

"But . . . his not catching on was so important to you."

"*Justin* was important to me. My son. Had you no emotions of your own? Why have you acted like some ugly, brainless machine? Years ago when he came to Detroit, lonely and proud, you should have told him, helped him. Certainly that night at Woodland when he begged you, you should have embraced him." When had Antonia ever used this loud, hectoring tone? "And now you've killed him."

"He's alive."

"He's dead."

"No! I swear to you. He's inside."

Her accusation shrilled through the closed window. "You saw him in the morgue. Dead. Dead. You killed him. You killed my son."

"For God's sake, he's alive!"

"*Without his wife he's dead.*"

Tom's head jerked forward. He awoke.

His heart was rampaging. How could a heart pump so violently and painfully without propelling blood through fragile capillaries? His mind was sharply logical. Instantly he perceived that Antonia's nightmare dialogue came direct from his own inflamed conscience. To him the promise was the wafer and wine, the external symbol that gave substance to the holy invisible. And as far as Justin being alive—having suffered a similar loss, he knew the sophistry of *that* argument. Antonia was right. Justin's body still moved, but his spirit was as crushed as his wife's body.

It was a minute or so before he realized that Justin had come outside. The heavy lumber jacket he had worn on the overpass tossed over his shoulders, his hands gripping the porch rail, his head bent, he shuddered with sobs. There was a terminal loneliness about the figure venting its grief in frozen privacy on the narrow porch. Justin might have been washed up on some desolate, uninhabited island, the last shipwrecked survivor that a more merciful fate would have allowed to perish: his loneliness was so absolute that Tom shivered. Moving stiffly, he buttoned up his coat.

At the slam of the car door Justin looked up. By the time he reached the shelter of the porch, Justin was blowing his nose.

"Justin," Tom said quietly. "I didn't have a chance back at the station to say this. But I'm sorry, so damn sorry about your wife . . . about Elisse."

Justin made a low, snorting sound, and the veranda creaked as he moved to the opposite end.

Tom waited before he said, "All right?"

Justin nodded.

"I've been waiting to talk to you," Tom said. "I dozed off and had a nightmare . . ."

He had thus intended to launch another explanation of the stages of his love affair with Antonia, to tell about that half-assed posthumous loyalty. But the icy wind and the twinging of his left arm and shoulder gave him the oddest sense of dislocation. *I can't say it, even now. I'm an intractable monster, not a man.*

The dim wattage showed the miserable little twitch of Justin's mouth as he fought for control. Tom told himself he should not be here like a sleepless predator prowling the night of Justin's grief, yet he remained on the icy, windswept porch.

"Remember what I said about a man's life being like the strokes of an engine?" Tom asked. "Well, part of me has misfired completely. I never intended conditions at Onyx to be such a disgrace, but things went out of control. Power's like that. A fulcrum. You remain an ordinary human being with the usual quirks and faults, but as you become more powerful your actions become more exaggerated. The principle of the lever, understand? When I lower my pinky, a thousand Sevens rise. When I hire Dickson Keeley, one bad man, I crush entire factories."

There was no reply except the wind.

Tom clasped his palms together, the tips of his long, icy fingers touching. "What happened to Elisse, I feel guilty as hell about it."

"So do I." Justin's breath clouded.

"You? Why you? *I* hired Keeley, Hugh paid that fucking gas squad. How are you to blame for what happened today?"

"Elisse shouldn't have been here. I never should have brought her to Detroit."

"Come off it, Justin," Tom said gently.

"I'm taking her home tomorrow."

"Train?"

"Yes. It doesn't leave till noon, so I'll be at the opening."

"What?" Tom asked, bewildered.

"The negotiation."

"That's postponed, damn it, Justin."

"The strike's starving people."

"Onyx can open. Do what has to be done in Los Angeles, then come back. We can settle the grievances then."

"The AAW strike committee will be at the Book Cadillac at eight."

"For now, just call off your pickets and bring out the sit-downers."

"And have them believe they've been sold down the river?" Justin asked in a clipped voice. "It's all been settled. I'll lay down our terms, then the committee'll take over."

The pains in Tom's shoulder and chest had lessened, but an intolerable arthritic malaise remained deep in the bones. He crossed the porch to rest a hand on the plaid lumber jacket.

Justin flinched from his touch. "What a hideous death," he said, blowing his nose again. "She was such a little thing. It always surprised me how small . . . she had so much spirit and heart, she seemed big." Justin rested his forehead on the post.

"Anything I can do to help you through the meeting?"

"Send Caryll for your side."

"You mean I should stay clear?"

"Yes." Justin straightened. A crumb of peeling paint stuck to his bruised cheek. "Being with you is impossible," he said. "It shouldn't matter anymore, but it does. I despise myself for being your bastard."

"Justin—"

"There's nothing more for either of us to say, Tom." He opened the door and went inside. Tom heard a chain being fastened. The iron sound of finality.

He stood on the porch another minute, then went slowly down the rickety steps and through the wind to the car whose metals, rubber, fabrics, had come from mines, plantations, and factories that he owned.

He gripped the steering wheel and closed his eyes, thinking of Justin's last words: *I despise myself for being your bastard*. That his offspring, so fine a man, should despise himself seemed the worst of the numerous sins that Tom attributed to himself.

The Onyx coupe reverberated with the gasping sound of bitter, irreconcilable loss.

VII

For five days the AAW strike committee, dressed in shabby, carefully brushed suits, conferred with Onyx representatives in a seventh-floor suite with a view of the Aztec-tiled Michigan Bank of Commerce, the Bridger-owned skyscraper. Tom Bridger attended none of the sessions, and Justin Hutchinson only an hour of the first before he climbed on the streamliner with his wife's coffin. Thus it was Caryll Bridger and Mitch Shapiro who faced each other from either end of the long walnut bargaining table. The settlement that they announced on January 13, 1936, jolted the country—the most commonly used heavy black headline:

AUTO UNION WINS ALL!

For days the country talked of little else. The contract granted the union more than it had asked. Some decided that the public outrage over the deaths and the open beating of the two union officials had shamed the company into capitulation, others said it was Caryll Bridger's earnest generosity that had prevailed, but the consensus was that the automotive pioneer, Tom Bridger, a puzzling oddball, never did anything halfway.

At Woodland's reopening the first shift swung in singing and waving small blue and white union flags. The double work week was ended, the few remaining Security wore uniforms, a seniority system from now on would govern layoffs and rehiring, and shop stewards were to be elected that week. Those fired for union activity were already lined up outside Employment for their back wages— they would be rehired according to the new seniority system.

To the other auto manufacturers' consternation Onyx announced that all their plants would from now on be operated as closed shops, and the company would automatically check off dues from pay- checks, transferring them to the AAW treasury.

"Tom Bridger," pronounced the aging Henry Ford, "has made a gift of the automotive industry to Moscow." This same angry sentiment resounded more blasphemously in every thick-carpeted executive suite of every motorcar factory.

In later years the settlement would be hailed as the greatest about-face in industrial history, the major landmark in American labor relations, the first contract ever wrested from an automotive company—and the most generous. Walter Reuther would say in 1946, when the AAW merged with the United Auto Workers, "Labor of America saw in the AAW victory a brilliant glow that lit the darkness of the Depression."

Each time Tom glimpsed a blue and white union button on the lapel of one of the multitude of workers, he would think of Justin and again experience that irreconcilable, guilt-ridden grief—yet he never regretted those buttons. They meant that the spirit of his older son lived within his factories.

EPILOGUE

The display spots were off in the new Onyx Museum, and the tall, angular white-haired man and the somewhat shorter, wiry young staff sergeant cast uneven, slow-moving shadows as they traversed the stillness of the three cavernous halls of automobiles.

Tom's ironic, occasionally grieving voice had finished what he knew of his life's story, and the two were silent as they reached the last car, the 1947, the postwar model. Her sapphire-blue paint glowed with the iridescent depths once seen only on the forty-times-painted, lovingly hand-buffed automobiles of aristocracy. Her hood was long, sleekly long, she was built without a running board to mar her distinctive lines, her white sidewalls shone like ivory around silver-chromed hubcaps; she drew both pairs of eyes from the vista behind her, lumbering tanks, drab khaki trucks, jeeps, ambulances. Her design conjured up the happy highways of peace.

Tom turned away, unable to look upon Caryll's legacy to the company that had destroyed him.

Ben, in his quick, nervous stride, circled the model once, then read from the lectern: " 'Hundred horsepower hydraulic brakes.' Etcetera, etcetera." He formed a circle with thumb and forefinger. "Perfecto," he said. "Quite a museum you have here altogether, sir. How dare anyone challenge that you're the colossus of the low-price field?"

"A couple or three companies do," Tom replied. "Well?"

"Comment you want on your cautionary tale?" Ben asked. "The history of the automotive industry is a picture of human crime and misfortune."

"Is that what you think?"

"Why else would I misquote Voltaire?"

"Are you always so damn itchy?"

"I'm allergic. Believe it or not I invariably break out in hives when I learn I'm grandson to the legend of our machine age."

"A sharp tongue won't cut me, Ben. At twenty I lacked your education but spoke the same language."

"As a matter of fact, this afternoon's restored my faith in Mendel. I've always wondered with Sir Galahad for a dad how I turned out to be such a turd."

Tom smiled. So did Ben; then, clearly deciding this was an act of treachery, he frowned. "I don't know the legalities for turning down a bequest, but count me out."

"You've lost me."

"That stock Uncle Caryll left me in his will, I won't take it."

"Why the hell not?"

"I despise reparations. Is that clear enough?"

"All I know is there's only five percent of Onyx that doesn't belong to me. Caryll and Zoe's wedding gift. Caryll's left you his ownership. Those two hundred and fifty shares are two and a half percent of the shop."

"The whole Onyx shooting match?"

"Yes."

Ben whistled. "A cool fortune."

"Quite a few million," Tom agreed.

"Good. Excellent. Double insurance. I'll turn it down. And Aunt Zoe's bound to contest."

"She won't."

"Well, you know the beautiful lady and I don't, so I'll have to take your word that she lacks the mercenary instincts of your wife."

The vast sums involved in Tom and Maud's divorce had captivated a Depression-sunk populace hungry to learn that the incalculably wealthy had their problems, too. On the other hand, their quiet remarriage a year later was buried on back pages.

"What was that crack about reparations?" Tom asked.

"I'll tell you." Ben's voice slid up a half octave. "At Onyx good and decent people were barbarically savaged. My parents. That's what I mean by reparations. There's no way your millions can make it up."

"Your uncle wanted you to have his holdings." Tom's sigh wa
grievingly deep. "He was a fine man. Ask your father."

"I was at Buchenwald at the liberation. I've always connected i
with Onyx in my mind."

"What an ugly thing to say!"

"You think so?" Momentarily the edgy tension left Ben's fine-
featured face. Above the ill-fitting uniform he looked a wrung out
deserted child. "I have a missing piece of your story. About Mother.'

"I've always felt I'm guilty of her death."

"A regrettable accident. I blame you for it, too. But this inciden
probes deeper into the true heart of evil. One night she was visitec
by certain of your dignitaries—"

"What?"

"You didn't know?"

"I swear not. Who were they?"

"Later I recognized one from photographs, your former big man
Dickson Keeley." Ben stared at the center of the gleaming new
windshield as he described shivering on the dark stairtop, the broadcast melodrama of *The Green Hornet* assaulting him as he saw his
mother violated.

Tom's hands trembled, and he sank down on cold marble, his
back curved against a tire. "Oh, Jesus Christ. Jesus Christ."

"Mother and I are Jewish, sir. He didn't come to help us."

"Your father, did he know about it?"

"Mother sent me and Tonia away right after," Ben said with a
wan smile. "But I'm positive Dad never knew. Mr. Keeley diec
intact."

In 1942 the Lincoln that Dickson Keeley was driving blew up, ar
inferno death reputedly caused by Keeley's underworld chums. Hugh,
from his lonely lakeside hermitage that was visited only by Tom,
claimed to have certain knowledge of the underworld connection.

"Thanks for the tour, sir." Ben gave a mocking salute. "Interesting exhibits, fascinating tales."

He walked to the empty rotunda.

Halted.

His hands were at his sides, bending and contorting as though
fingering his violin. The anger around his eyes and mouth softened
He gazed back into the hall where Tom sat, white-haired Lear on the

506

floor, dwarfed, surrounded, overwhelmed by vehicles of his own making.

Ben returned slowly.

Tom didn't look up. "Museum's closed," he said.

Not smiling, Ben rested a strong, long-fingered hand on blue metal. "I don't blame you for what happened to Mother, not anymore."

"You should."

"Know something? Since that night I've visualized you as Lucifer. The evil one. The lord of darkness. You had all the horror and glamour of absolute evil. You gave us cars to speed and lust in. You were a hundred times larger than the devil, and a thousand times more vengeful. You sent your werewolves to destroy Mother. I must've read everything written about you. Biographies, articles, doctoral dissertations, newspaper fluff. A lot of them put you down out of envy. Because you're a monumental success."

"Screw the pity, Sergeant Hutchinson. You don't have to flatter me."

"You think I'm saying this because you're old? Because one of your sons just died and the other won't come near you? Not me. Never. Not Ben Hutchinson. Not that kind of crap. No." Ben rapped sharply on the new Onyx. "I believe you. You never meant harm to Mother. And as for not being able to tell Dad what you feel for him, well, I can't tell him how much I love him, either." The words clicked out, staccato.

Tom looked down at the creases of his black trousers. "How is he, Justin?"

"Dad? He's living. But he's lonely, lonely, and more lonely. By now he should have gotten over Mother, wouldn't you think? But he hasn't. Did you know he's been running illegal immigrants into Palestine? Well, the last trip, the *Elisse* was sunk."

"I heard he was wounded."

"If you know, why ask?"

"Hugh keeps tabs. Is Justin's leg mended?"

"Not properly. The bullet smashed the kneecap. But the instant he heard about Uncle Caryll, he had himself sprung from Hadassah Hospital, that's in Jerusalem, to sail to New York. I'm stationed in New Jersey. With me in tow he's come to offer our manly aid to the most ravishing widow in the world, I am quoting the Hearst chain."

Tom said, "This marble's damn cold." He pushed to his feet. "Is that a definite no, then, on the shares, Ben?"

"Let me give it some cool-headed consideration."

Uneven footsteps sounded in the rotunda, and they both turned.

"Ben?" Justin's voice called.

"In here, Dad. We're in here."

Justin limped toward them, leaning heavily on his stick, a large, strong-looking man in a Harris tweed topcoat, his silver hair wind-blown around his tanned face. He met Tom and Ben at the archway to the rotunda, and here, at the apex of the long-halled vistas of automobiles, the three men halted awkwardly.

Justin lifted his right arm, a curious wavelike gesture that seemed an irritable dismissal yet in reality was an effort to make the first move at shaking hands. The cold hostility in his deep-set blue eyes was also misleading. Long ago he had released his confused accusations, resentments, ambivalences toward this man who was his father, and now he was experiencing that old loving admiration as well as primitive shock at temporal erosion. *Tom's an old man*, he thought. *Old . . . how is that possible? Where have the years vanished?*

"So, Dad," Ben said.

"Hello, Ben."

"Mr. Bridger's been telling me about a promise he made to the first Antonia Hutchinson. He'd very much like to get together with you and explain about it. For a continuation of these tripartite armistice talks, I vote we go someplace without a single Onyx."

Tom's eyebrow arched, but he found he lacked the strength to look at Justin, so he waited.

After an endless moment Justin said, "That sounds very good to me. What about that idea, Tom?"

"Sure," Tom answered, shaken. A translucent film stung in his eyes.

"Let's go, then," Ben said, draping his arms around his father and grandfather. For a few moments the three were joined in a loose embrace, then slowly, at Justin's pace, they circled the original gasoline-powered vehicle, that frail dragonfly contraption, moving slowly toward the hazed, wintry light.

THE SEEDS OF SINGING

by Kay McGrath

To the primitive tribes of New Guinea, the seeds of singing are the essence of courage. To Michael Stanford and Catherine Morgan, two young explorers on a lost expedition, they symbolize a passion that defies war, separation, and time itself. In the unmapped highlands beyond the jungle, in a world untouched since the dawn of time, Michael and Catherine discover a passion men and women everywhere only dream about, a love that will outlast everything.

A DELL BOOK   19120-3 $3.95

DAVID NIVEN